Don Coldsmith
three complete novels

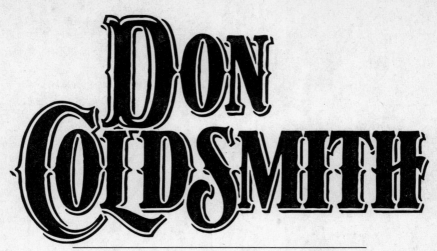

Don Coldsmith

THREE COMPLETE NOVELS

The Changing Wind

The Traveler

World of Silence

WINGS BOOKS

NEW YORK • AVENEL, NEW JERSEY

This omnibus was originally published in separate volumes under the
titles:

The Changing Wind, copyright © 1990 by Don Coldsmith
The Traveler, copyright © 1991 by Don Coldsmith
World of Silence, copyright © 1992 by Don Coldsmith

This 1995 edition is published by Wings Books,
distributed by Random House Value Publishing, Inc.,
40 Engelhard Avenue, Avenel, New Jersey 07001,
by arrangement with Bantam Books, a division of
Bantam Doubleday Dell Publishing Group, Inc.

Random House
New York • Toronto • London • Sydney • Auckland

Printed and bound in the United States of America

Library of Congress Cataloging-in-Publication Data

Coldsmith, Don, 1926–
[Selections. 1995]
Three complete novels/Don Coldsmith.
p.   cm.
Reprint of novels from the Spanish bit saga.
Contents: The changing wind—The traveler—World of silence.
ISBN 0-517-12333-9
1. Indians of North America—First contact with Europeans—Fiction.
2. Indians of North America—Great Plains—Fiction.   3. Historical
fiction, American.   I. Title.
PS3553.O445A6   1995
813'.54—dc20   94-43893
                                                                      CIP

8 7 6 5 4 3 2 1

CONTENTS

THE CHANGING WIND
1

THE TRAVELER
253

WORLD OF SILENCE
499

THE
CHANGING
WIND

INTRODUCTION

A year or two after the release of *Trail of the Spanish Bit,* one of my students approached me with a suggestion. Why not, she asked, write in more depth about the life and career of White Buffalo, the medicine man? This character appears only briefly in the first few books of the Spanish Bit Saga.

I considered at some length. In many ways, this man represents a pivotal character in one of the greatest cultural changes in the human race. His life spans the entire time period of this cultural change. The Stone Age hunter of the plains and mountains evolved, in a single generation, into the finest light cavalry the world has ever seen. The factor that made the difference was the acquisition of the horse. This must have been not only a profound change, but a major threat, to one in the priestly function of White Buffalo, holy man of the People. I tried to imagine his feelings, his thoughts and fears. I wrote a few chapters and a brief outline but then became preoccupied with other projects and shelved the idea.

In 1987, Greg Tobin, a senior editor at Bantam, suggested a spin-off novel to supplement the Spanish Bit Saga. Would it be possible, he asked, to select minor characters from the early series for an original novel, a "superedition," connected to but not a part of the series? I mailed a proposal the following day, with the material I had outlined.

So this is the story of one man's lifetime. We see him at first resist, then accept, and finally take part in the cultural shift. It will alter his civilization forever as the winds of change sweep across the prairie and the People advance into the centuries that mark the Golden Age of the Horse.

—Don Coldsmith
1989

PART I

THE VISION

1

There was little about the childhood of Small Elk that foretold his place in the story of the People. Perhaps his mother, Dove Woman, anticipated that her son was destined for greatness, but such expectations are regarded as a mother's privilege. However, his father also suspected that here was a child with an unusual mission.

The two older children of Dove Woman and White Buffalo had grown, married, and had their own lodges before the coming of Small Elk to the lodge of the medicine man. That alone set him apart, but there were other things that his father noticed. There was his curiosity. The child would sit for long spaces of time, watching a column of ants going in and out of their underground lodge. There were those in the tribe, White Buffalo knew, who would regard this as useless activity. And, he had to admit, for some it may have been. But not for Small Elk. There was something about the *way* the child watched the creatures. His father was certain that Small Elk *understood* the apparently aimless scurrying around the anthill. He did not say so, but there was a look of wonder on the small face, the wonder of learning. White Buffalo saw in the shining dark eyes an understanding of the spirit of the ants.

It was, in a way, like the understanding that had been in the eyes of the infant the day of his birth. White Buffalo had seen many infants. Most were squalling in protest at the indignity of having been thrust from the warm and protective lodge which had been theirs for the past nine moons. True, it was a rude shock to enter a world that included cold and hunger. But occasionally there would be an infant whose approach to life seemed different. And this was such an infant. After the preliminary protest, and the cough to clear newly expanded lungs, this child was quiet.

The woman who had assisted Dove Woman with the birth had lifted the lodgeflap to allow the father to enter and see his son. White Buffalo paused a moment, allowing his eyes to become accustomed to the dim interior of the lodge. He smiled at his wife.

"Our son is here," Dove Woman said softly.

"It is well with you?" he asked.

"Of course. Come, look at him."

She lifted the corner of the robe that covered her. White Buffalo knelt and looked into the small red face. It was only then that he felt the impact of the tiny newcomer. The eyes, which in most infants are squinted tightly shut against the new experience of light and air, were wide open. They looked around the lodge and then directly into his own with a shocking intensity that startled White Buffalo.

It must be remembered that White Buffalo was no ordinary man. His medicine was considered strong, his vision accurate. His contact with things of the spirit was an ongoing vibrant thing. Even so, it was with something of a shock that he looked into the dark eyes of this newborn child. There was knowledge there, and an interest, a curiosity, that burned brightly in those eyes. Unaccountably, White Buffalo felt for an instant that he was the one under scrutiny, not the child. This small one seemed to already possess an understanding of the nature of the world and a desire to learn more about it.

"This is a strong spirit," he told his wife.

"Of course"—Dove Woman smiled. "He is ours, yours and mine."

White Buffalo nodded, still entranced by the strange feeling of communication he had had for a moment. The moment had passed now.

"Let us call him Small Elk," Dove Woman suggested.

White Buffalo knew that this was because of their experience the evening before. It was exceptionally fine weather, early in the Moon of Roses, and they had walked a little way from the lodges to be alone and enjoy the setting of the sun. Dove Woman had grown large and was impatient to bring forth her child. It was pleasant to walk with her husband and to admire the lavish colors of the western sky.

"Sun Boy chooses his paints well this evening," she observed.

"Yes," her husband agreed.

After all their years together, there was little need for talk. They communicated without it, each understanding what the other felt. This evening they were comfortable with each other and with the world. It was a time of waiting, of wondering about the new life in Dove Woman's belly.

"Oh, look," she exclaimed suddenly, pointing to an area near the stream.

A cow elk had come down to the water to drink. She raised her head and sniffed the breeze, catching the scent of the couple who watched. They were near enough to see the droplets of water that dribbled down the animal's lower lip. The cow fidgeted, uneasy but undecided.

It was unusual for elk to approach the village this closely. The cow was in no danger at this time, but she could hardly know that. The People had hunted well, with the greening of the prairie. White Buffalo had selected the time for the annual burning of the prairie to remove the winter's dead grass. The buffalo had appeared as expected, in the Moon of Greening. The spring hunt had been successful enough to add prestige to White Buffalo's reputation and respect for the power of his medicine, successful enough that there would be no interest in killing a thin cow elk during the calving season.

The cow turned nervously, sensing something wrong, and finally sprang away, clattering across the white gravel of the riffle toward the other bank. Only then, as she turned and made a quiet lowing sound over her shoulder, did they see the calf. It came scrambling up out of the tall grass beside the stream, a confused scramble of long legs, knobby knees, and floppy ears.

The mother paused to wait while the calf stumbled after her through the shallows. They quickly disappeared in the willows across the creek, and Dove Woman laughed softly.

"It is a sign, my husband."

"Your time is near?"

"Maybe so."

She smiled and leaned against him.

Looking into the face of his son the following day, White Buffalo realized that the incident by the stream *had* been significant. Dove Woman had felt it too and had chosen his name. He nodded in agreement.

" 'Small Elk.' It is good."

As the child grew, White Buffalo wondered sometimes if he had been mistaken. Small Elk seemed much like other children, no better or worse, no more or less mischievous. He participated in the games, dances, and instruction of the Rabbit Society with the other children. But no, there was that other quality, the desire of this child to be alone sometimes, to watch ants or silvery minnows in the stream, or the red-tailed hawk's lazy circles in the summer sky.

When Small Elk was in his fourth summer, he came to his father one afternoon with a small object in his closed hand, his face shining with excitement. White Buffalo was reclining on his willow backrest, enjoying a smoke during a moment of leisure.

"What do you have there, little one?"

"It is a stone," the child confided in hushed excitement. "Its spirit is good."

White Buffalo became more attentive. This was not the usual play of a three-year-old.

"May I hold it?"

Small Elk proudly placed the stone in his father's palm. It was white and rounded, polished by many lifetimes of tumbling in the rolling waters of the stream. White Buffalo closed his fingers around the smooth sphere, thinking as he did that it was much like an egg. The egg, perhaps, of one of the small ducks that sometimes nested in the reeds along the stream. It was warm, and the feeling was good.

"Yes," he told the child, "its spirit is good."

"Father, do all things have a spirit?"

"Yes. Some are stronger spirits than others."

"But this is a good spirit?"

White Buffalo felt the smooth surface in his palm, the warm, comforting sensation that was unmistakable.

"Yes," he said seriously, "this is good."

"I will keep it," Small Elk announced happily.

White Buffalo was still a little surprised that he was carrying on this conversation with a child of three. However, his expertise with things of the spirit told him not to ignore it. Small Elk was showing signs of spiritual awakening quite early. It might be that this child would be offered the power of a strong medicine when he was ready—if, of course, he chose to accept the responsibility of such a gift. The idea pleased the holy man, that a son of his might follow in his steps. But for now . . .

"Come," he said to Small Elk, "let us make for you a medicine bag. Your stone will be its first spirit."

It would not do to try to influence the boy. However, it would do no harm to make the means available to him if and when he was offered the gift. After all, he could still refuse the responsibility if he wished.

S mall Elk sat on the grassy slope with the other children of the Rabbit Society. One of the women was demonstrating the use of the throwing-stick. She was holding a stick not quite as long as her arm, the thickness of her wrist. A few steps away, slender willow twigs had been stuck in the mud to form a miniature fence as a target.

"Now, see!"

Bluebird suddenly whirled her arm and released the stick in a hard overhand throw. The missile whirled, end-over-end, at the willow target, knocking one of the slim twigs flat as it bounced beyond. The children laughed happily. One of the boys ran to retrieve her stick.

"Now, see again!" she called as she readied the stick for another throw.

This time the throw was a sidearm swing. The clublike stick spun horizontally, whirring toward the row of twigs. When it struck, the damage was apparent. Because of the flat spin, not one but several of the willow twigs were broken or knocked flat, in a path two handspans wide.

"So," Bluebird announced, "you will kill more rabbits with a sidethrow. Now, try it. Don't hit each other!"

"When can we try the bow?" asked Red Fox.

"Later. Soon, maybe, if you have one. But it is good to know the throw-ing-sticks."

"But I would rather eat buffalo than rabbit," one of the girls protested.

"So would everyone," Bluebird agreed. "But when meat is scarce, in the Moon of Hunger, it is good to know how to hunt with the stick. Or, when the hunters are unsuccessful. Then what?"

The children took their small throwing-sticks and began to play at hunt-ing rabbits. Bluebird walked over to speak to her friend Dove Woman, who sat watching.

"I will stand clear now," she laughed. "They are reckless sometimes."

Dove Woman smiled.

"At least, the dance is not so dangerous."

Hers was the teaching of the first dance-steps to the smaller children of the Rabbit Society. From others they would learn the skills of hunting and the use of weapons, and compete in running, wrestling, and swimming. Both boys and girls learned all of these skills. It was not until later that their diversity of interests would sharpen the fine skills of the hunter-warriors and the domestic skills of the young women planning for their own lodges.

There was a yelp from one of the dogs, hit by an accidental bounce of a thrown stick.

"Be careful there!" called Bluebird.

Then she spoke aside to Dove Woman.

"Better a dog than each other. Now they will be more careful."

"Yes. There is no way to keep dogs away from throwing-sticks, I think."

"Your Small Elk seems good with the sticks."

"Thank you. Your daughter, also."

Dove Woman was pleased. These two children, Small Elk and Crow, were nearly the same age. Their mothers were friends and usually chose to set up their lodges near each other.

"They play well together," Bluebird observed.

"Yes, for children of five summers, they quarrel very little."

Both women laughed.

"Will your Small Elk become a medicine man?" Bluebird asked seriously.

"Who knows?" Dove Woman shrugged. "White Buffalo says he may. We will see if he has the gift."

The children were becoming tired of playing with the sticks now and were straying off to other pursuits. Small Elk and Crow were near the stream, sitting on a level rock. Between them were a number of miniature green lodges, made by rolling cottonwood leaves into cones and pinning the edges together with a grass stem.

"Let us make a whole village!" Crow suggested.

"Why? We need only one lodge, you and I."

Then they both giggled.

"Elk, do you know how to make a moccasin from a cottonwood leaf?"

"No. I have seen them. It is harder than making the little lodges."

"You could ask your father. He knows all things."

"Yes, but . . ."

Small Elk was a little uncertain whether a holy man's area of skills included the making of toy cottonwood-leaf moccasins.

"I will ask, sometime," he agreed cautiously.

The conversation was interrupted by the approach of one of the other boys.

"Want to go swimming?" asked Bull Roarer.

He stood there, whirling a noisemaker on a thong around and around his head in a wide circle. With each revolution, the flutter of the flattened stick at the thong's end made a deep whirring noise, like the distant bellow of a buffalo bull. It was a common toy, but this boy's affinity for the pastime had led to his being called by the name of the device, "bull roarer."

"Who is going?" Crow asked.

Bull Roarer continued to swing his noise maker.

"We three, Fox, Otter, Cattail, my sister Redwing."

"We will ask," Crow announced.

She jumped up and ran to her mother with the explanation and request. Bull Roarer's sister was a few summers older, a reliable supervisor, and both Bluebird and Dove Woman quickly agreed.

Most children of the People were strong swimmers. The bands must always camp near a water supply, and summer camp was frequently selected with an eye to its recreational possibilities. Of course, this went hand in hand with the more serious purpose of the selection, availability of game. Grass and water, essential to the buffalo, also make a campsite esthetically pleasing. In turn, the presence of a clear, cool stream in the heat of a prairie summer invites swimmers.

The summer camp this season was in a favorite area of the People. Sycamore River, trickling over white gravel bars and long level shelves of gray slate, was a favorite stream. Its deep pools were spaced at intervals along its course like beads on a thong.

The pool the children preferred was perhaps two long bowshots below the camp. It was ringed with willows on the near side, except for a level strip of white gravelly sand, a perfect place to lie in the sun to dry after a swim. Across the pool, a stone's throw away, cattails formed a backdrop for the scene, as well as a site where ducks and smaller water-dwelling birds might build their lodges.

The memorable event of the day for Small Elk, however, was not the swimming party. It happened on the way back to the camp. He and Crow had lagged behind the others to watch a shiny green dung beetle roll an impossibly big ball of dung, larger than itself.

"What do they do with it?" asked Crow. "Where is he taking it?"

"To his lodge, maybe," Small Elk suggested.

He hated to admit that he had no idea what a dung beetle does with balls of dung. He would ask his father later. White Buffalo, who knew all things, could surely tell him about dung beetles.

The children rose to move on. It was just at that time that the rabbit sprang from a clump of grass beside the path and loped away ahead of them. Small Elk was startled for a moment but then reacted almost without thinking. He was still carrying his throwing-stick from the earlier lessons of the day. The missile leaped from his hand, whirling toward the retreating animal. His throw was wide and should have missed completely except for unforeseen circumstances. The whirling tip of the stick struck a sapling beside the path and was deflected, bouncing crazily end-over-end. Even so, the rabbit would have escaped harm if it had continued in a straight line. But rabbits do not run in straight lines as a custom. They sometimes zig and zag, taught to do so at the time of creation to escape the strike of the hawk or the lunge of the coyote. In this case, the escape trick proved the rabbit's undoing. It bobbed to the left just as the whirling stick bounced to the right. There was an audible crack as the hard wood met the skull of the animal.

"Aiee!" exclaimed Crow softly.

Small Elk rushed forward to grab the kicking creature, wriggling in its death throes. He picked it up and watched the large brown eye lose its luster and become dull with the mist of death. It was his first kill, and he should have felt good. It should have been a glad and proud moment, but that was not what he felt. There was a letdown, a disappointment. The rabbit had been more pleasing to look at in life than it was now, its eyes glazing and a single drop of blood at the tip of its nose. He was confused. Why had he wanted to kill the rabbit? For meat. Yes, for its flesh, he thought. That is the way of things. The rabbit eats grass and in turn is eaten by the hawk, the coyote, or man. That is the purpose of a rabbit. He watched as a flea crept into sight from the thick fur of the rabbit's cheek and burrowed into another tuft.

Then he remembered watching his father at a buffalo kill early in the spring. The medicine man had stood before the head of a massive bull . . . yes, of course. He would perform such a ceremony. He placed the rabbit on the ground, arranging it in a natural position. Then he stepped back, faced the head of the dead creature, and addressed it solemnly.

"I am sorry to kill you, my brother," he stated, trying to remember his father's words of apology, "but I am in need of your flesh to live."

He felt a little guilty for such a statement, because he was not hungry or in need at the moment. What had White Buffalo said next?

"Your flesh feeds us as the grass gives your life to you."

Yes, that was it. Small Elk felt better now, and forged ahead. How was it? . . .

"May your people be fat and happy, and be plentiful," he told the rabbit.

Feeling considerably better about the incident, he picked up his kill and moved on toward camp. In his preoccupation, he did not notice the expression in the eyes of the girl beside him. It was an intense look of surprise mixed with admiration and approval.

A similar expression might have been noted on the face of the man who had watched the whole scene from behind a thin screen of willows. White

Buffalo waited, perfectly still, until the children had moved out of sight. Then he rose, a satisfied smile on his face. He must share this with Dove Woman.

"It is good," he said quietly to himself. "And Small Elk performed the apology well."

3

It was in their seventh summer that the Head Splitters came. Among the People, youngsters were warned against this threat from the time they were small.

"Don't go too far from the lodges. The Head Splitters will get you."

Sometimes, even, it became a tool for discipline.

"If you don't behave, the Head Splitters will get you!"

Usually that sort of threat was not used because it was not necessary. The loosely organized instruction of the Rabbit Society was carried on by nearly all adults. The shared parenting made all adults responsible for the welfare of all children, and after all, the future of any group lies in its children. On the other hand, such a system makes all children responsible to any adult, and misbehavior is difficult. So the threat of the Head Splitters was rarely used for discipline, except perhaps in a joking way.

Actually, the danger was quite real. For many lifetimes, past the memories of the oldest of the band, these enemies had staged sporadic raids against the People. Both tribes hunted buffalo, and both were partial to the Tallgrass Hills, so their paths occasionally crossed.

Small Elk had seen them, as the People moved from one camping area to another. They would encounter a similar band of travelers moving across the prairie, carrying their lodgecovers and baggage or dragging it on poledrags behind the dogs. There was a time-honored ritual for such a meeting. The two columns of travelers would halt, perhaps a long bowshot apart, and wait while two or three chiefs from each band approached one another in the no-man's-land between.

It was understood that there would be no fighting. It was too dangerous. Both groups were vulnerable, with women and children and all possessions exposed to the enemy. So the principal chiefs of the two groups would make small talk, using the universal handsigns of the prairie. They would discuss the weather, the quality of the summer's grass, and the success of the hunt. Sometimes there would be veiled threats and insults, but it was only talk. No chief would risk his family's safety by initiating a skirmish.

Even knowing this, the heart of Small Elk always beat fast when such a meeting occurred. He watched the confrontation from his mother's side, seeing the prominently displayed stone war clubs that were the trademark of the Head Splitters. Even at a distance, the suggestiveness of these weapons was a chilling thing.

"What do they talk about?" he whispered to his mother.

Dove Woman placed a hand on his shoulder reassuringly.

"Small things. The weather, the hunting, where we will camp this season."

Small Elk was alarmed.

"Broken Horn will tell them where to find us?"

Dove Woman smiled.

"Yes, and they will tell us. You see, if they mean us harm, they can find us anyway. And hunting will be better if we are not too close together. So, the chiefs exchange that knowledge."

The conversation was finished now, and the chiefs parted. The two columns resumed travel. It was a relief to have the meeting over. Looking back later, it had been an exciting diversion on the long trip to meet the other bands of the tribe for the annual Big Council.

A raid by the Head Splitters was a different matter. It would be carried out by a surprise attack, a ruthless strike by a force of strong, heavily armed warriors. They would quickly kill and plunder, taking supplies and robes, perhaps weapons, anything easy to carry.

And children. The threat of abduction by the Head Splitters was not an idle one.

"But what happens to the children?" Small Elk asked in wonder as he and his playmates discussed the situation.

"Maybe the Head Splitters *eat* them," Bull Roarer suggested with a horrible grimace.

"No, that's not true!" scolded Crow. "They just keep them forever. Besides, they want mostly girls."

"We will ask someone," suggested Small Elk. "There is Short Bow."

The children approached the subchief, who was reclining on his backrest nearby.

"Uncle," began Bull Roarer, using the customary term of respect for any adult male, "could you tell us of the Head Splitters?"

Short Bow puffed his pipe a moment.

"What of the Head Splitters?"

"Why do they steal children?"

"Don't they want mostly girls?" asked Crow.

Short Bow nodded seriously.

"Yes, that is true. Our women are prettier than theirs. They want them for wives."

"*Aiee!*" exclaimed Crow. "To be the wife of a Head Splitter!"

"You are safe," teased Bull Roarer. "They want only the pretty ones."

Crow made an obscene gesture, and the boys laughed. The girl had not yet started the spurt of adolescent growth that would make her long-legged and shapely like other women of the People. It had been known for generations that Head Splitters coveted these girls as wives. Their own racial stock was slightly different in bone structure, and the lanky athletic build of the women of the People was greatly admired.

On the day that the Head Splitters came, the three friends had been playing along the stream. It was a warm, sunny afternoon in the Moon of Growing. The children had been watching minnows and trying to catch the small spotted frogs that hid in the grass along the shore. They watched a muskrat pull himself out of the water and shuffle along the opposite shore. It was a narrow path that the creature followed, because a rocky bluff rose almost from the water's edge.

"Let's try to climb the bluff!" Bull Roarer suggested.

They made their way upstream to a point where they could cross and started back along the bluff's base.

"Look! A path!" Crow pointed.

It was a narrow ledge, rising from the water's edge and angling upward against the face of the bluff. It was far from being a path, but it did appear to have been used by small animals. The three crept upward, clinging closely to the rock. They were nearly back to the point where they had seen the muskrat when there was a sudden flash of motion ahead.

"A fox!" Small Elk pointed. "Look, there is his lodge!"

The fox had disappeared, but they found that the shelf widened to perhaps a pace across and several paces long. The opening to the fox's den showed evidence of recent use.

"Maybe there are pups inside!" Bull Roarer said excitedly.

The boys were trying to peer into the dark hole when there was a sudden gasp from Crow.

"*Aiee!* Head Splitters!"

The others whirled to look. They were about a long bowshot from the camp and high enough on the bluff to see over the tops of the newly leaved trees. A dozen warriors, painted for combat, slipped quickly among the lodges.

"They have not been seen!" Small Elk exclaimed. "Should we? . . ."

His question was interrupted by a scream of terror from the village, immediately answered by a chorus of yipping, falsetto war cries from the attackers. It was the first time any of the three had heard the terrifying war cry of the Head Splitters. Small Elk felt a chill up his spine, and the hairs on the back of his neck stood erect in his terror.

"Get down!" he mumbled.

The three crouched on the narrow ledge, watching in fascinated horror. There were few men in the camp; most of them were gone for the day on a spring buffalo hunt. It was decided later that the Head Splitters must have watched and waited for such an opportunity.

They saw Sits-in-the-Rain, who often told tales to the children around the story-fires, start up from his backrest in front of his lodge. The old man reached for his bow, but age had slowed his reflexes. The Head Splitter who struck him down hardly bothered to break stride as he moved on.

A lodge toppled, and greasy smoke began to billow out from under the collapsed lodgecover as its own cooking fire began to devour it. The invaders seemed everywhere. People were running in all directions, a few standing to fight and being clubbed down where they stood.

Bull Roarer was crying as he saw his mother's lodge fall. They could not see whether she was trapped inside as it began to burn. His sister scrambled out under the edge of the lodgeskin and ran for the bushes, pursued by a yipping Head Splitter. This was too much for Bull Roarer. He jumped to his feet, the others trying to pull him back out of sight. The boy jerked away, lost his balance, and fell over the edge. His scream was unheard in the village because of all the noise, death, and destruction there, but it was heard by his friends on the ledge.

"We must help him!" Crow gasped.

They peered cautiously over the edge. Bull Roarer lay below, partly in the water, his left leg crumpled under him, jutting out at an unnatural angle. His big dark eyes, full of agony, looked up at them helplessly.

"Lie still; make no noise!" Small Elk used the handsign talk.

Bull Roarer nodded.

"We will help you as soon as we can," Small Elk continued.

There was another gasp from Crow. Directly across the stream, looking up at them, stood a Head Splitter. He moved a little to see what occupied their attention and discovered the injured Bull Roarer. Chuckling, the man took an arrow from his quiver and fitted it to his bowstring. Then he seemed to consider and lowered the weapon. Apparently he thought the crippled boy not worth an arrow; he would have to cross the creek to recover it. He looked up again at the two on the ledge and smiled as he pointed to them.

"I will get you next time!" the man signed.

He turned and trotted to join the others, who were withdrawing, laden with loot. Small Elk and Crow were already scrambling down the narrow path to help Bull Roarer. From the direction of the camp there now rose a mournful wail as the women began the Song of Mourning.

4

The children scrambled quickly down and along the ledge to where Bull Roarer lay, partly in the water.

"We will help you!" cried Crow. "Does it hurt much?"

"A little," said Bull Roarer between clenched teeth.

His face was pale and sweaty, his eyes wide and bordering on panic. Small Elk knelt in the water beside the injured boy. He had seen his father examine such injuries.

"Do not try to move yet," he advised. "Now where does it hurt? Only your leg?"

"Y—yes, I think so. Elk, it hurts a lot."

"Does it hurt in your belly?"

"No. I don't think so. My leg . . ."

Small Elk was looking at the twisted leg. Something was definitely wrong with it. There appeared to be an extra joint, like an extra knee, between the real knee and the hip. This gave an odd zig-zag appearance to the leg and accounted for the awkward position of the foot, which could never be used if it pointed in the present direction.

"Your leg is broken," Small Elk said professionally.

"I know that," snapped Bull Roarer irritably. "Help me!"

"It must be pulled straight," Small Elk stated, "and I do not know how."

The crying and the wailing sounds continued from the camp. There was an occasional scream as a new casualty was discovered. People called out names of missing loved ones.

"Bring your father," Bull Roarer demanded. "He can fix my leg."

"He is not here!" Small Elk reminded. "He went with the men."

"Maybe we can pull him out of the water," Crow suggested. "There is enough space here for him to lie more comfortably."

The two took Bull Roarer by the arms to drag him ashore. The injured boy screamed as the broken leg moved and bone grated on splintered bone.

"It looks straighter now," Elk observed.

He picked up a small stick and handed it to Bull Roarer.

"Here. Bite on this. We nearly have you out."

One more sustained pull, and they were able to drag the victim ashore to lie full length on the damp grass. Tears streamed down his face, but as the pain subsided, he removed the stick from his mouth, crushed and broken from the pressure of his teeth.

"*Aiee!*" he whispered, his face still pale. "It hurts less when you do not move it."

"This leg is shorter than the other," observed Crow.

"Yes, and the toe points backward," Small Elk noted. "Should we not turn it to the front?"

"No, no," Bull Roarer protested, "you will turn it the wrong way! Go and get help!"

"I will go," Crow suggested. "You can stay with him."

She jumped to her feet and ran nimbly along the bank to the point where they had crossed. Small Elk sat down near their suffering friend.

"Elk, I think I am going to die," said Bull Roarer weakly.

"No, you are not," Small Elk snapped. "I will not let you."

"All right. But can you stop the leg from moving?"

The damaged muscles, protesting this injury to their form and function, were twitching spasmodically. With each spasm, the uncontrolled motion created new waves of pain.

"I don't know," Small Elk admitted. "I will try."

He attempted to hold the foot still against the paroxysm of muscles. It seemed to help some, but his own muscles quickly tired.

"I am going to let go for a little while," he told Bull Roarer. "I will get some rocks to prop around your foot."

This appeared to be the best answer yet and seemed to comfort the injured leg. Crow came splashing back across the shallow riffle, carrying a small buffalo robe.

"No one can come yet," she announced as she spread the warm cover over Bull Roarer. "Dove Woman says keep him warm. Someone will come soon."

"How bad is it for the others?" Small Elk asked.

"Bad. Some are dead. Several lodges burning."

"I saw mine burning," Bull Roarer said. "Is my mother alive?"

"Yes. She is looking for your sister. Elk, your lodge still stands. Mine is gone, but my mother is safe."

"But I saw my mother's lodge fall on her," Bull Roarer said.

"Yes," Crow explained. "She hid under it, hoping the Head Splitters would leave before the fire reached her."

"How did your mother and mine escape?" Small Elk asked.

"They were both in your lodge. The Head Splitters spared it because of its medicine, Dove Woman said."

The lodge of Dove Woman and White Buffalo was painted with designs and symbols that marked it as the dwelling of a holy man. To confront an unknown medicine could easily be hazardous, just as walking into a dark cave could be, without knowing what dangers lay inside. The attackers had simply chosen to avoid the risk.

"Who all was killed?" Bull Roarer asked.

"I did not ask about everyone," Crow said. "Sits-in-the-Rain is dead. I saw Otter's mother mourning, but I do not know for whom. Cattail's lodge is burned, but I saw her. Her family is safe."

"Is my mother coming over here?" asked Bull Roarer.

"Yes, she said she will, after she finds what happened to Redwing. Dove Woman will come, but she is helping some who are wounded first."

Before long, Dove Woman and Bluebird came across the stream. Dove Woman, who often helped her husband with his healing ceremonies, understood his work quite well.

"*Aiee!*" she exclaimed. "This is a bad injury, Bull Roarer, but we will fix it. White Buffalo will soon return. He will want to bind the leg here, before we carry you across the river."

Dove Woman had brought some strips of hide from an old robe and now began to cut splints from the willows along the shore. She was still occupied with this when the men returned, attracted by the plume of greasy black smoke from the burning village. Songs of mourning rose again.

"Elk, go and bring your father," Dove Woman instructed. "Tell him I have bandages and splints."

Small Elk darted away and soon found his father near their lodge. White Buffalo, concerned for his family, had already learned that their daughter was alive, though her lodge had been destroyed. The family of their older son was unscathed.

"Is your mother safe?" he asked.

"Yes. She wants you to come and help Bull Roarer."

"Where?"

"Across the river. He fell from the cliff."

They crossed, and White Buffalo knelt to examine the injury.

"Bull Roarer, I am going to move your leg," he warned. "Here, bite the stick."

With one quick motion, he twisted the injured leg into a more normal position. The grating of the bone was quite audible as it snapped into place, and the boy's scream was muffled by the stick in his teeth.

"There," the medicine man said. "It will feel better now."

He began to bind the strips of buffalo hide around the leg, incorporating the willow splints as he did so. Finally he rose.

"Now, I will carry you," he announced.

He picked up the boy, whose pain in motion was not nearly so great with the splints in place. As they stepped out of the water, Bull Roarer's mother met them.

"Is he all right?" she asked anxiously.

"A bad break, but it will heal," White Buffalo assured her. "Where will you stay, Pretty Robe?"

"My mother's lodge. Here, this way."

Those whose lodges were destroyed were salvaging what they could and moving in with relatives for the present. It appeared that there were only four fatalities, though several more people were wounded or had suffered burns from fighting the fires.

Three children were missing. One small girl escaped and made her way home a few days later, but Redwing, sister of Bull Roarer, was never seen again.

5

It had been seven winters now since the attack by the Head Splitters, and there had been no further trouble. As usual, they had encountered traveling bands of the enemy each season. There was no direct reference to the incident, beyond the smug demeanor of the Head Splitters.

Of course, the band they encountered that next summer may not have been the same band that carried out the attack. One Head Splitter looks much like another. Still, both Small Elk and Crow felt that they recognized one of the subchiefs who came forward to talk.

"That is the one!" Crow whispered. "The one who was about to shoot Bull Roarer."

"I think so too," Small Elk agreed, "but they all look alike. What do you think, Bull?"

"How would I know?" Bull Roarer asked, a trifle peevishly. "I was lying in the water below."

If the man recognized them, he gave no sign, but it was hard to forget the threat that day at the cliff. The Head Splitter had promised to return.

The stolen children were not seen, at this or any later encounter. It was assumed that they would be hidden, silent under threat of death if they made their presence known. Or, someone suggested, maybe they had been traded to some other band. Even some other tribe. Bull Roarer's mother had mourned the loss of her daughter, as if Redwing had died in the attack, and then resumed her usual activities. Life was hard, and losses were to be expected. The period of mourning allowed relief from the pressure of grief, and life went on.

Those events seemed long ago now. The seasons had passed, and the children grew. Bull Roarer's leg had healed, and in a few moons, he could walk again. But he would never walk properly. The leg was too short by nearly a hand's width. The boy walked with an odd rolling gait.

"Will it grow like the other?" he had asked White Buffalo.

"No," the medicine man answered. "It will always be different. But you are alive, and you can walk. Does it hurt?"

"No," Bull Roarer admitted, "but I am very slow."

"It was a very bad break."

It was difficult for the active youngster. Formerly one of the best, he could no longer compete in many of the games and contests. In such things as swimming he could still excel, but out of the water, his ability was limited. In time, even his swimming skills began to suffer. There was no way to keep his muscles in condition. He tried to remain cheerful, but it was difficult.

His problem had become even more apparent since the other boys had begun to hunt. Bull Roarer had participated in a few hunts, short forays near camp, carefully supervised by an older warrior. No one said anything, but it was not necessary. All could see that Bull Roarer could not keep up with the group. It was equally apparent that they could not wait for him while their quarry escaped. No, Bull Roarer would be unable to participate in the hunt.

It was even more frustrating for him because he was an excellent shot with the bow. But what good was that if he could not place himself in a spot from which to shoot? Often, he cried privately. He could hunt small game, of course, but one does not support a family on rabbits and squirrels. Neither can a lodge be made from rabbitskins. Bull Roarer feared that he was doomed to a life of poverty, unable to find a wife who would consent to share such a fate. He would always be dependent on the charity of those more fortunate, and when times were hard . . . He shuddered to think that in lean years, when the hunt had been less than successful, the Moon of Hunger took on an even more ominous meaning.

Supplies always ran low in the time just before the Moon of Awakening, when the earth began to green again. In the best of years, it was a time of hunger. In the worst, it became, instead, the Moon of Starvation. Some would not survive. Bull Roarer was aware that sometimes older members of the tribe walked off into the night at such times, to die in the silence of the prairie snows. It was a heroic gesture, one designed to save desperately needed food for the children, who represented the People's future. Regardless, those who would starve would be the poor and needy. Who could give them food when his own family was hungry?

Increasingly now, Bull Roarer felt that this would be his fate in life—existing on handouts from his friends or those who took pity on him. Eventually, he would come to the point where a hard winter or a scarcity of game would bring about his own starvation. Sometimes the young man had considered walking into the prairie as the old ones did, so as not to prolong the tragedy of his thwarted life.

It is probable that on these occasions, seldom though they had been, he had postponed the act because of his friends Small Elk and Crow. These three were almost inseparable as they grew. The others seemed to feel almost a responsibility for the accident that had made Bull Roarer a cripple. When he was dejected, one of the others was always near, to distract him and bring a smile to his face.

Now they had seen fourteen winters, and subtle changes were taking place in all their lives. As the other young men became more proficient at the hunt, Bull Roarer became more morose. Today, for instance. There had been a hunt, hastily organized, when someone reported a band of elk grazing a short distance north of the camp. The other young men, and some of the girls, seized their bows and ran to join the hunt.

Bull Roarer watched them go, lonely and dejected. It was not unusual for young unmarried women to participate in the hunt; after all, that was where the young unmarried men would be. Except, of course, for the lame and crippled, he reflected bitterly. He wandered along the creek, skipping stones and longing for the company of his friends. How useless I am, he thought. Small Elk and Crow were the only close friends he had left. The others had gradually drifted away as it became increasingly apparent that Bull Roarer could not keep up.

Now he felt completely abandoned. Even Crow had left him for the hunt. He resented this. Crow could have stayed behind with him. Probably, he decided, even she and Elk had remained loyal only out of pity. He could not blame her for preferring the company of one who was able-bodied. He wondered how the hunt was going.

Small Elk gripped his bow with sweating hands, an arrow ready on the string. He glanced to his left, where Crow returned his glance, her face alive with excitement. Their good fortune was incredible. The animals had moved into a small box canyon and were still inside. Short Bow, the organizer of the hunt, had quickly deployed the youngsters across the entrance. More experienced hunters were posted between them at intervals. Short Bow himself was beyond Crow. Now he motioned them forward, cautioning quiet. They moved into the canyon, crouching to stay in the concealment of clumps of sumac, dogwood, and bunches of real-grass.

Small Elk was aware that the animals were up ahead of them in the canyon. It was not that he heard or smelled them, as sometimes happened. It was more like a feeling, a knowing without the use of his other senses. He should soon be able to smell or hear them. By sheer good fortune, the hunters were downwind of the herd.

Then he heard a muffled snort and froze in his tracks like a rabbit.

Between the tall stems of the real-grass ahead, he could see the shapes of large animals. Most were still grazing, but one old cow stood, alert and staring. Her ears flared wide, and Small Elk was sure she was looking straight at him. The cow snorted again, and the others raised their heads to look. Then everything seemed to happen at once. The wary old cow leaped aside and struck the ground, driving forward.

Short Bow had explained to the young hunters how it would happen. The elk, trapped in the box canyon, would rush to escape and in doing so, would run past the hunters into open prairie. There would be a moment, the space of a few heartbeats, when they must pass between two of the hunters, and someone, perhaps everyone, would have the opportunity for a shot.

"Try not to hit each other!" Short Bow had cautioned.

It was a joke, repeated since they were small, but this time there was no laughter.

Now, as the herd came charging down at him, Small Elk was sure that he would be lucky to survive, much less shoot. A great bull, his antlers as wide as a man's outstretched arms, thundered down on him. Small Elk stepped quickly aside. There was nothing graceful about it, he simply jumped to safety while the bull rushed past, its mind too only on escape. The animal brushed so close to him that Small Elk could see the thin strips of furry skin hanging and fluttering from the antlers. The bull would soon be polishing those antlers in preparation for the rutting season. Small Elk felt the patter of bits of dirt and grass thrown up by flying hooves, and the bull lunged on past him. He stood there in wonder, completely forgetting to shoot. There was another rush of hooves, and a young cow raced past, her eyes rolling wildly. Small Elk raised his bow and loosed an arrow as the animal passed. He thought that the shaft struck the cow's flank but could not be sure. In the space of another heartbeat, the animals had dashed through the brushy mouth of the canyon and into the open plain.

Now there were shouts and yells of triumph and disappointment as the hunters turned to pursue the retreating herd. Small Elk ran, dodging among the bushes toward the open where the animals were rapidly outdistancing their pursuers.

"Enough!" called Short Bow. "Now look for the wounded."

Small Elk now remembered to fit another arrow to his bow.

"Elk! Over here!" Crow shouted.

He turned and trotted toward the sound of her voice. There, her eyes shining, stood the girl, bow in hand, her smile wide in triumph. In front of her lay the carcass of a fat cow elk, an arrow protruding from just behind the ribs. The animal was still kicking feebly.

"Our kill!" Crow called. "That is your arrow. Mine is in the other flank."

"Are you sure? This is my arrow?"

"Of course! Look at it. I saw you shoot, and the cow turned away toward me. I shot too, and she went down."

"Good!" Short Bow observed as he passed. "You two have done well."

Crow was practically jumping up and down with excitement.

"I can hardly wait to tell Bull Roarer!" she exclaimed. "He will be so pleased."

6

Crow and Small Elk had excitedly described the hunt, repeatedly and in detail. It was only after the first flush of success had begun to fade that they noticed that their friend was not altogether pleased with their success. Actually, it was Crow who noticed. Bull Roarer listened politely, quietly congratulated them, and lapsed again into silence.

"*Aiee,* what a hunt!" Small Elk was still chortling. "My friend, this cow came rushing past; I shot, but could not see where the arrow struck. Then Crow placed her arrow too. You—"

He started to say, "You should have been there," but suddenly realized the problem. It was an uncomfortable moment, and there had been few such moments in the lifelong friendship of these three.

"Come, Elk," Crow interrupted the awkward silence. "We must help with the butchering."

Bull Roarer sat and watched them go. Normally he would have helped too. Normally, of course, the others would have good-naturedly demanded it.

Crow was silent and depressed. They had, in their excitement, failed to realize that their success would only hurt their friend, who could never accomplish such things. He could have helped with such chores as skinning and butchering, but that would only call attention again to his handicap. She could understand Bull Roarer's fears, and her heart went out to him. He would feel that he was good for nothing but menial tasks.

She could see that Small Elk felt it too, but neither of them spoke. It was an unpleasant thing, this obstacle that had come between them. She felt that they must find a way to help their friend, not from pity, but from friendship. They had had so many good times during their childhood that it must not be spoiled now. She thought of speaking to Small Elk about it but rejected the idea. She would think of something.

It was only a few days later that another hunt was planned. This would not be an urgent situation, as when the band of elk had suddenly become available. This was a carefully planned foray into the prairie, where a fragment of one of the migrating buffalo herds had wandered close. Small Elk's father, caped in the sacred white robe that gave the holy man his name, performed the buffalo-dance ceremony at the fire the night before. Hunters sat, meticulously putting finishing touches on their weapons, readying everything for the hunt. It was an important hunt, the first in which the youngsters would take part as fully eligible hunters, ready to prove themselves. There were still a few who had not yet made a kill of large game. Small Elk and Crow, of course, with their success in the elk hunt, carried some degree of prestige.

The morning dawned with a slight chill in the air, mist rising from the stream like a thin white veil of smoke. The hunters were already stirring.

"Come on, Crow," Small Elk called. "It is time to go. We must not keep Short Bow and the others waiting."

The girl stood in front of her parents' lodge, watching the hunters' preparations.

"You go ahead," she said. "I will stay here with Bull Roarer."

Small Elk stared at her for a moment, a mixture of emotions struggling within him. Then he turned on his heel.

"It is good," he snapped over his shoulder.

Crow knew that it was not. It was bad, all of it. She had been forced into a situation where she appeared to choose between her friends. She was not rejecting Small Elk, her lifelong friend and more recently her hunting companion, but Elk obviously felt her decision as a rejection. In his eyes, she supposed, her staying behind appeared to be a choice of the company of Bull Roarer. *It is not that way,* she wanted to shout at him. *Bull Roarer needs me more, needs us both. We cannot leave him now, in the time of his greatest need.*

The girl watched Small Elk stride away, the hurt and anger reflected in every motion of his body. She had never realized before that one can *walk* angrily. Tears came to her eyes as she realized that his hurt had come between them. It would never be the same again, the easy, happy friendship they had shared. She hurried to a secret place behind the lodges and dried her tears, then ran to the stream to wash her face. She rose, combed out her hair and replaited it, and then went looking for Bull Roarer. She walked along the stream, knowing that he often sought solitude there, away from the camp.

He was seated on the trunk of a fallen cottonwood, idly tossing pebbles into the pool. He looked up irritably.

"You should go," he said sharply. "The hunters will be leaving."

"They are gone," Crow said.

"You are not going?"

"No. What shall we do today?"

Bull Roarer stared at her, first with a puzzled look, then with hurt and anger. She had not been prepared for this.

"Go away!" Bull Roarer almost shouted. "I do not need your pity!"

Crow was silent, fighting back the tears. Now both of the young men were angry at her. She had tried only to help, and was completely misunderstood by her two best friends.

"Bull Roarer, I—"

"Do not deny it. You are here only because you feel sorrow for me." He struck the crippled leg with his hand. "I can do nothing, with this useless stick. I wish the Head Splitter had killed me that day."

Crow was angry.

"Of course I feel sorrow," she snapped at him, seating herself on the log, "because you are my friend. But mostly, you feel sorrow for yourself!"

He looked at her, fighting back the tears.

"Crow, you do not understand. My spirit wishes to do things that my body cannot."

She sat silent, unable to comment. *Everyone,* she thought, *experiences that sometimes.* But that would be little consolation to Bull Roarer. His limitation was more pronounced, more permanent.

There was a sound of someone approaching, and Crow turned to see one of the older men of the band, following the path along the stream. She recognized Stone Breaker, who now noticed the two young people on the log. Ordinarily, unless he had something to tell them, he would simply nod and leave them alone. Privacy was always prized and respected. But Stone Breaker came over to sit near them, putting down the bundle he carried. Crow quickly brushed at her eyes, hoping there were no remaining tears. She resented the man's intrusion.

"*Ah-koh!*" he greeted. "May I join you?"

"*Ah-koh,* Uncle. Of course," Crow said politely.

She used the traditional term of address for any adult male older than one's self, even though she knew Stone Breaker only slightly. Bull Roarer said nothing.

"It is a pleasant day," the man observed. "Let me see . . . you are Crow Woman?"

Crow blushed, but the man seemed not to notice. She felt much less resentful now. It was the first time she had been called Crow *Woman,* and the attention was quite flattering. She had begun to notice changes in her body—a swelling and sensitivity in her breasts and the sprouting of hair in places that hinted at her coming womanhood. She was experiencing new emotions, new and strange urges. But she had thought no one noticed except herself. Her parents, maybe, but they had said nothing. Now it was an honor to have her maturity and coming womanhood acknowledged in this way. She sat up straighter, quite aware of the slight pressure of her enlarging breasts against the soft buckskin of her dress.

"Yes, Uncle," she said self-consciously.

"And Bull Roarer?" the old man asked.

Bull Roarer nodded. Crow wondered if the next question would be why the young man had not gone on the hunt, but it did not come. Stone Breaker seemed not to think of that obvious question but still seemed not to notice the crippled leg. Crow would have thought the man quite dull and nonobservant, except for his obvious powers of perception about her womanhood. He must have some purpose here, but what could it be?

Stone Breaker opened his little pack and took out some flakes of flint, a piece of heavy leather, and a tool made from the tip of an antler. It was fitted with a handle made by wrapping the shaft of the horn with rawhide. He spread the leather pad over his thighs and studied the flints. Finally, he selected one, a smooth blue-gray flake as wide as two fingers and twice as long. It seemed already partly shaped.

"This is a good place to work," Stone Breaker said conversationally. "The light is good, and my eyes are not what they once were. My legs, either"— he chuckled.

Crow glanced in concern at Bull Roarer, wondering if the remark had hurt him, but he was busily tossing pebbles into the stream. The girl was still a little surprised at Stone Breaker's disregard for their privacy. She was now willing to overlook it because of his flattering observation of her womanhood.

Stone Breaker placed the flint on the leather pad across his knee and held it tightly with his left hand. He pressed the antler-tip tool on the flint's surface, near the edge, and a tiny flake snapped off the stone. He moved the tool a little and repeated the chipping.

Crow was aware that this man had a reputation as a skillful worker of flint. This, of course, was the reason for his name. Some men made their own arrowheads and spear points, but one made by Stone Breaker was highly prized. Her mother used a skinning knife of his workmanship.

He worked rapidly, and an arrowpoint began to take shape. This would be a fairly large and heavy point, it appeared, a hunting tool, made from the blue native stone that appeared in veins in the softer white stone of the hills.

Now, Bull Roarer too was watching as the shape of the point continued to emerge. Stone Breaker paused to hold it up and examine it for balance and symmetry. He nodded to himself and continued to work. Finally he laid aside his leather pad and tools to stand and stretch.

"Aiee," he said, "I become stiff from sitting."

"May I see the stone, Uncle?" Crow asked.

"Yes, of course," he said casually. "Would you like to see others?"

Without waiting for an answer, he reached into a small pouch at his waist and drew out a pair of buckskin-wrapped objects, which he unrolled and displayed on his palm. Both were of a stone that was plainly not native to the area, used as a display of Stone Breaker's craft. Crow knew that this man, like others of the tribe, traded extensively with anyone they contacted. Meat and robes to the Growers in exchange for corn, beans, and pumpkins. Sometimes people traded even with the Head Splitters during the occasional chance meetings. This trade, Small Elk had said, was the source of such things as the pipestone of his father's ceremonial red pipe, found far to the north somewhere, in only one place.

Now she saw the two objects in Stone Breaker's palm. Neither, she suspected, was intended for use, but only to demonstrate the skill of the maker. One was a miniature arrowhead, precise in every detail but so small that it was no bigger than Stone Breaker's thumbnail, of stone of a dark, lustrous red color, warm in character. The other was an amulet, slightly larger, of rosy pink stone. It was more intricate in shape and seemed to represent a bird in flight.

"They are beautiful!" exclaimed the girl.

Now even Bull Roarer was looking over her shoulder at the objects.

"These are my best work," Stone Breaker was saying proudly, as he began to rewrap them carefully. *"Aiee,* it is bad that I have no son to teach these skills!"

Crow glanced at Bull Roarer. It appeared that he had not yet figured out the reason for the old man's unorthodox behavior. She said nothing but resolved to let her friend think this out for himself. What good fortune, that this respected weaponsmaker of such great skill had practically invited Bull Roarer . . . She felt better than she had in many days, and her heart was not nearly so heavy.

7

Bull Roarer quickly became proficient in the skills being taught to him by Stone Breaker. At first, his arrowheads were rough and imperfect, though usable. His work was slow, painfully slow, and his right hand had become sore from the unaccustomed pressure of the flaking tool.

"Let it rest a few days," Stone Breaker advised. "Your hands will become hardened like mine, but slowly."

He showed the young man his own hands, strong and callused from many seasons of such work. Bull Roarer impatiently waited until his blisters had partially healed and the tenderness was receding. Then he resumed the practice of patiently chipping the flints. He could tell that his work was improving and was frustrated again when his hand became sore.

"*Aiee,* you still work too long at a sitting!" Stone Breaker reprimanded gently. "Now you will have to rest again."

"But my fingers will never be as skilled as yours, Uncle!" Bull Roarer protested.

"They will, my son, but you are too impatient. Someday, when you have worked the stone as long as I have, you will be even more skillful."

Bull Roarer, not convinced, sat depressed and frustrated, watching the work of his tutor.

"You could pick out some stones and examine them," Stone Breaker suggested. "Decide what you will do with them."

He pointed to a rawhide storage bag against the inside wall of the lodge. Bull Roarer dumped the contents on a level spot outside and spent an afternoon sorting stones while the old artisan worked nearby.

"Will this make a spear head, Uncle?"

"Yes," Stone Breaker decided, after examining the large shard of flint, "but not a good one. See, the thin vein of another color? It will be a weak spot, and the spear will break easily. It would make two very good arrowpoints."

"Should I break it now?"

"If you wish. But if you leave it in one piece, it is easier to hold. You can rough out both ends, and then break it in the middle before you start the fine work."

The Moon of Ripening was at hand, and the hunters were pushing to harvest meat for the winter. This increased the demand for the skills of Stone Breaker, and his supply of flints was growing low.

"We need more stone," he told his apprentice one morning. "We will visit the quarry."

Bull Roarer knew that Stone Breaker occasionally went out into the prairie to obtain more material, but he had never wondered where.

"How far is it, Uncle?"

"Half a day's travel, maybe. We will sleep there. It is good that this summer camp is close."

"Are there other quarries?"

"Of course, but this is the best. See, this smooth blue-gray stone comes from there."

He held up the piece he was working. Stone Breaker seemed to have a preference for this type of material, though maybe it was just more available, Bull Roarer thought.

They set out the next day, traveling slowly because of Stone Breaker's age and his companion's disability. Bull Roarer carried his bow; Stone Breaker, no weapons except a knife. His dog, a massively built wolfish creature, pulled a pole-drag on which Stone Breaker tied their sleeping robes, a few supplies, and empty rawhide storage bags.

"We will carry our robes on the way back," he explained. "We can bring more stones that way."

The Blue Stone Quarry was very unimpressive to Bull Roarer. Stone Breaker led the way along a gametrail into the upper end of a small canyon. A clear spring came bubbling out from under a limestone ledge, and Stone Breaker knelt to drink.

"The quarry is just above," he said, pointing as he rose and wiped water from his lips. "There, behind that bush."

Bull Roarer saw nothing but knelt to drink, then followed the older man. Only a few steps away, Stone Breaker stopped and pointed again to the shelf of stone opposite the spring.

"There," he said simply.

Bull Roarer looked. It looked exactly like a hundred other rocky ledges in the Tallgrass Hills. Many of them possessed a layer of blue-gray flint, and this one seemed no different at first. There was the horizontal blue stripe, but this one appeared darker and more uniform. It took a few more moments to realize that there was a marked indentation here in the rocky wall. Bull Roarer stepped forward for a closer look. Yes, this little cleft had certainly been formed by many generations of people who had come to obtain the finest of stone. Now he realized that around and below him on the slope lay discarded or useless fragments of stone. He was walking on shards of flint which had been rejected by centuries of workmen.

Here was one, he thought as he picked it up from beneath his feet. A fine flake of flint, clean and blue, just the size for a large arrowhead or small scraper. He turned it over and began to understand. The other side of the flat stone was white—the soft limestone unsuitable for their purpose. He tossed it aside, wondering even as he did so how many through the years had picked it up as he had, only to reject it as he had, and for the same reason.

"Do not bother with those," Stone Breaker was saying. "If they were usable, someone would have taken them before this."

Bull Roarer saw other flakes that had been partially worked and then discarded because of a hidden flaw or accidental fracture.

Stone Breaker was kneeling in the narrow cleft, his skilled fingers examining the face of the flint vein. He grunted to himself and finally spoke.

"Yes, others have been here since I was. Bull Roarer, bring one of the poles from the drag."

For the rest of the day, until it became too dark to see, they worked. The old man would select a protruding bulge of flint. By prying with the pole and striking with a heavy boulder, they would break loose a block of the fine blue stone. It would be set aside and a new chunk selected.

"That will be enough," Stone Breaker announced as the last pumpkin-sized chunk fell away. "We cannot carry more."

Bull Roarer was exhausted from the hard physical labor and fell asleep quickly. Stone Breaker smiled knowingly as he finished his pipe, knocked out the dottle, and rolled in his own sleeping robe. Yes, the boy would be good at this, he thought to himself. He had seen how Bull Roarer's hands touched the stone, with reverence for its spirit. He was glad for this opportunity for his apprentice to experience the spirit of the quarry. It was always an uplifting thing, to sleep here and commune with those who had come to this canyon for the same purpose, maybe since the time of creation. He thought his apprentice felt it too.

Stone Breaker's heart was full of satisfaction as he drifted off to sleep.

Though Bull Roarer was now showing more interest in life, the same influences were driving the three childhood friends apart. Crow continued to spend time with Bull Roarer, and he continued to tolerate her presence. It was, after all, pleasant to be able to share each small success with someone. Crow, in turn, was increasingly shut out by Small Elk. He had not been the same since the day she stayed behind while he went on the hunt. Crow's heart was heavy for this, but she did not know what to do. If she tried to rekindle her friendship with Elk, Bull Roarer might become depressed again. He was still a bit moody sometimes, especially when his fingers were sore.

It was some time before Crow, with her feminine instincts coming strongly to the fore, realized that it had become a matter of jealousy between the two young men. Bull Roarer had begun to call her Crow Woman, teasing at first, after Stone Breaker used the flattering term. Now, not only he but most of the band were using the name, and it had begun to fit her. Fit her, in fact, as well as her new buckskin dress, with the chest cut somewhat roomier to accommodate the changes in her body. It would have been an exciting time, a time of pride in her newfound maturity. It was unfortunate that it was happening at the same time as the rift between her two friends. It made things so much more complicated. *Aiee,* she thought, *things were so much simpler when we were children.*

As for Small Elk, he felt completely alone, abandoned by his friends. Bull Roarer resented his ability to run, walk, and hunt. Crow, now calling herself Crow Woman, had also abandoned him, preferring the company of Bull Roarer. It made his heart heavy, though he understood. Bull Roarer, people said, was rapidly becoming skilled in the craft he was learning from Stone Breaker. How could he, Small Elk, compete with such success? Of course, any woman would prefer the security that such a skilled artisan could provide. Why *should* Crow choose him, a young hunter with no special skill?

His heart was very heavy.

8

As Bull Roarer's prestige increased in the band and even as widely as the other bands of the People, the schism widened. Small Elk seemed intent on proving his worth as a hunter and doggedly pursued that elusive goal. Maybe he tried too hard, but ill fortune surely followed his efforts. Stubbornly, he continued.

Crow Woman, irked at his stubborn narrow-mindedness, spent more and more time with Bull Roarer, which seemed to push Small Elk more firmly into his self-defeating pattern.

By the time of their seventeenth summer, some were seeking the flintpoints of Bull Roarer, even in preference to those of Stone Breaker. There was much talk at the Sun Dance that year. Young Bull Roarer was surely destined for greatness as a weaponsmaker. People told one another this as the various bands gathered for the annual religious ceremonies in celebration of the return of Sun Boy, the grass, and the buffalo. Such skill was rarely found in one so young. Flintpoints and tools made by Bull Roarer were traded as objects of great value. It was no wonder that there were young men in all the bands who envied his success.

Yet another reason for envy was the beauty of his almost constant companion, Crow Woman. How fortunate can one man be? men asked each other, with much envious clucking of tongues.

All this did not go unnoticed by their former friend, Small Elk. As he became more embittered, his skills deteriorated. Before he realized what was happening, their roles had reversed. Bull Roarer, once avoided because of his handicap, now carried himself proudly, admired by others, while the embittered Small Elk sought solitude. His heart became heavy over the loss of the girl who had been the best friend of his childhood, the girl who had never really been his at all.

It was an evening late that summer when the southern band was beginning the fall hunt, that Stone Breaker called his apprentice to him. Bull Roarer crossed the open space from his parents' lodge, wondering what the older man might want at this time of day.

Stone Breaker watched him and the odd rolling gait that had resulted from the old injury as a child. It had prevented the youngster from participating in normal activities but was no handicap now. Stone Breaker was pleased that he had chosen to help the boy. There was no way that he could have foreseen the rapid progress his apprentice had made, and he was pleased to take some of the credit for Bull Roarer's success.

And how the boy had changed! The swing to his rolling stride, which had once appeared labored and difficult, now looked proud as the young man approached. Stone Breaker sat leaning on his backrest, smoking comfortably. He had come to an important decision.

"*Ah-koh,* Uncle," Bull Roarer said in greeting.

The old man nodded to acknowledge the greeting and pointed for him to sit. Bull Roarer settled himself on the ground before his tutor. After a suitable pause to satisfy custom, Stone Breaker began to speak. It was apparent from his tone that this was a matter of some importance.

"My son," he began, a dreamy look of nostalgia in his expression, "do you remember the day, there by the river, when you first watched me work flint?"

"Of course, Uncle." Bull Roarer smiled. "That seems long ago."

The old man nodded, and took a puff on his pipe.

"Yes. I hoped you would find an interest in such work. You have."

"Your instruction, Uncle," the young man began, "it has—"

Stone Breaker waved a hand to silence him.

"Hear me, Bull Roarer. I told you once that you would be as skillful as I."

"No, Uncle, I—"

"Be still," Stone Breaker admonished gently. "You are as skilled as I am now. Maybe better. You will gain skill, while I will lose mine."

"No, you are still the best," Bull Roarer insisted.

"My eyes are failing," stated the old man. "You have not seen that I do not try the smaller, finer pieces that I once loved?"

"I . . . I had not noticed, Uncle."

"Yes, it is true. I can still get by, feeling the edges on the larger things. Spear points, scrapers, but . . ."

40

He spread his palms in frustration, then continued.

"Well, I have many winters. I will continue to work, but I have something to give you."

"Give me?" Bull Roarer was puzzled.

"Yes. I will give you my name. I will announce it at the next council."

Now the young man's head whirled. He had not expected such an honor, perhaps the greatest that could be given to a young person.

Since it was forbidden among the People to speak the name of the dead, it had become common to give away one's name. Usually it was passed to a grandson or other close relative. There had once been a problem over this, it was said. A popular young subchief had been killed, gored by a wounded buffalo. Since he was young and had never given his name, it could not be spoken. It was an unusual name, worn by no one else, but contained common words, that, now forbidden, were lost to the language. The People had devised new words to replace the old, and in a generation, the original words were forgotten.

This story ran through the mind of Bull Roarer as he sat dumbfounded before this respected man who had so changed his life. It made good sense, this gift of Stone Breaker's; in all the tribe, there was no other who carried this name. This gift would prevent the loss of the words *stone* and *breaker* at the old man's death.

But more important, of course, was the honor. Few men of the tribe were so respected. Besides the skill that had earned the name, Stone Breaker was respected for his kindness and charity. He had always had a reputation as a teacher in the Rabbit Society, freely giving advice to the young in the use of weapons and tools. It was overwhelming to Bull Roarer that he should be the one chosen to carry on the honor of so respected a name. He swallowed twice to clear the lump in his throat before he could speak.

"I am honored, Uncle. I will wear it with pride."

"And you will bring honor to it, my son," said the old man.

There was no public announcement until the next council, but that was not far off. With the fall hunts beginning, frequent councils were held, and it was not half a moon when herds were sighted and the hunters met to prepare strategy.

It was then that Stone Breaker made his announcement, and young Bull Roarer stood to receive the approval of the band. It was given freely, because both Stone Breaker the Elder and the young man who now assumed the name and the prestige were quite popular and well respected. Several people made short speeches about the fine qualities of both men or complimented their workmanship. One suggested that now Stone Breaker the Younger would probably want to take a wife and establish his own lodge. Everyone laughed at the young man's embarrassment. Crow Woman blushed becomingly, her face shining in the firelight, glowing with excitement and pride.

The discussion quickly turned to the practical matters of the next day's hunt. It was a time of happiness and expectation, and everyone in the band felt that times were good. The buffalo were moving, it was said, into an area where they could easily be maneuvered and trapped. White Buffalo performed the Dance of the Buffalo in his ceremonial cape, and the council began to break up.

There would be little sleep tonight; excitement ran too high. Men would be talking and planning, checking bowstrings and the fletching on their arrows or the lashings of their spear heads if that was their preference in hunting buffalo.

It was a time of expectation for the entire band, and there was much happiness. Everyone looked forward to the coming day.

Everyone, that is, except one young hunter who had sat on the far periphery of the council circle. The firelight could barely push the shadows back that far, so no one noticed his glum countenance or that he slipped away early, before the council adjourned.

Small Elk wanted to be alone. His heart was very heavy, and he could not find it in himself to appear pleased and excited over the events at the council. He had been especially hurt by the jokes about the taking of a wife by Bull Roarer, now Stone Breaker the Younger.

9

"Father," said Small Elk, "I wish to go on my vision quest."

White Buffalo took time to think very carefully before he answered. The young man had weathered many disappointments in recent moons. His father had seen how the lack of success in the hunt had affected him. And in truth, there had seldom been such a persistent run of bad luck for anyone in the medicine man's memory. Small Elk had not made a kill worthy of the term for two seasons. That was odd, too. On their first hunt, Small Elk and Crow had achieved such success that their prestige had been high. Then, abruptly, there was no more success. It had crossed White Buffalo's mind that the strength of his son's personal medicine was helped by the presence of the girl, Crow Woman. This was not uncommon. However, it was also a matter that could not be helped. One could not interfere in such things.

He also suspected that part of his son's problem now related to the same matter. He noticed Small Elk's glum looks over the jokes about Stone Breaker's probable marriage. White Buffalo was probably the only one who saw Small Elk slip away into the darkness, alone and dejected. He wished that he could bear some of the young man's hurt.

Now Small Elk had come with talk of a vision quest. He must be very cautious in his counsel now. This was a turning point in the young man's life and must be handled carefully. It was unwise, of course, to enter the vision quest when one's heart was heavy. The dark thoughts of personal disappointment might easily interfere. One's mind and spirit must be free and open to receive the visions properly. Yet he had seen Small Elk's anger flare over disappointments. It was unlike the boy's basic nature, quiet and easygoing, but must be reckoned with at a time such as this.

"Why do you wish a vision quest now?" White Buffalo asked cautiously.

"It is time," Small Elk answered vaguely. "I am grown now."

It was difficult. White Buffalo wanted to answer something like "then why not behave like it?" but knew that the matter was more complex than that. Such a remark would only drive the young man away. That would not be good, because at this time, Small Elk needed all the help and kindness possible.

It was also difficult for White Buffalo, as holy man, to advise Small Elk in matters of the spirit. There was a certain conflict with his own feelings. Maybe, if he could maintain the purely detached approach of his office . . .

"My son," he began, "this is good, but there are things to consider."

He saw anger flare slightly in the eyes of his son, then come under control again.

"What do you mean?"

"Well, the season . . . that is probably all right. But you must be ready in your heart."

Small Elk said nothing, but at least he appeared to be thinking.

"You see, it is not just the fast and the visions that are important, but also the preparation for them."

He paused, trying to think of a way . . . ah, yes!

"Remember, now," he continued, "each spring, in the Moon of Greening, we burn the grass. This makes it come back greener, better for the buffalo. It makes the herds come back."

"But what has this to do with me?" Small Elk demanded.

"It is much the same, my son. The buffalo will not return without the greening of the grass. A vision quest is not a success unless the heart is ready."

"But my heart is ready, Father."

It would not have been nearly so difficult, the medicine man thought, if this were someone else's son. He could merely state "you are not ready," and his judgment would be accepted.

"Yes, your heart is ready," he acknowledged cautiously, "but for what? No, wait . . . hear me out, my son. You have had bad luck in the hunt. *Again.* Your bowstring broke with the first shot today, I am told."

Small Elk nodded glumly.

"And you feel that you must escape this season of misfortune?"

"Yes. A vision quest . . ."

White Buffalo nodded.

"I can understand this need, Elk, but there are two needs here. One is the need to get away from the misfortune that follows you. The other is your quest. Now, what if the misfortune follows you, and your quest is spoiled?"

He paused and saw that Small Elk was beginning to understand. No one would wish to risk his vision quest.

"Maybe," he suggested carefully, "you could get away somewhere first, leave the bad luck behind, and then, when that has been overcome, it would be a better quest."

The young man nodded thoughtfully.

"Yes, maybe so," he agreed. "But where?"

"One of the other bands?" suggested White Buffalo innocently.

This was the important moment. Small Elk must think it his own idea.

"My mother's people!" Small Elk proclaimed triumphantly. "The Northern band!"

White Buffalo managed a look of surprise.

"Yes!" he exclaimed. "It is good, Elk. Your grandmother would welcome you!"

Now the young man was warming to the idea, showing more excitement for this than for anything since, *aiee,* how many moons!

"Their band is near the Big River this season?" Small Elk asked.

"Maybe so. But they said they will move to winter camp on the Salt River. You could meet them there, winter with them, and we will see you at the Sun Dance next summer. Then, that might be the time for your vision quest."

"Yes. It is good, Father!"

His mother's reaction was somewhat different.

"Of course not!" Dove Woman sputtered at her husband. "Have you gone mad, to think of letting him do this?"

"Be calm, Dove," he said soothingly. "Look at him. This is the first interest he has shown. His spirit has been slowly dying."

"But how can he find them?"

"Ask the Growers, if he must. But we know they will camp on the Salt River this winter. He has visited your parents there before."

"He traveled with them, after the Sun Dance! This is different. He must not travel alone."

White Buffalo took her hand and looked seriously into her eyes.

"Dove," he said, "that is the important part. He *must* travel alone. He needs to find himself."

Dove Woman shook her head.

"It is too dangerous."

"I know, he is your youngest," he said gently. "But he is grown. That is part of his trouble. He wanted to go on a vision quest. This is no more dangerous."

"Aiee, a vision quest!" wailed Dove Woman.

"He can do this easily," White Buffalo assured her. "He needs to regain his spirit. We will see him again in a few moons."

Reluctantly, Dove Woman finally consented. Now Small Elk became eager, restless to be off. The change in his spirit did not go unnoticed among the People. Several remarked to his parents that Small Elk appeared heavier, or seemed to be growing nicely. They replied that yes, he was preparing to winter with his grandparents in the Northern band.

It was several days before his supplies were prepared and extra moccasins readied for the journey. By that time, everyone in the band was aware of his plan. Many of his peers stopped by to wish him a good journey, and many seemed a little envious. One even offered to accompany him, an old friend who had drifted away.

"No, Otter, I must go alone. My father has said so."

"Ah, it is a medicine thing, then?"

"Yes. A thing of the spirit. Like a vision quest, almost. But different."

White Buffalo, who happened to overhear, felt that he would be greatly pleased when his son actually departed. Small Elk was trying to gain too much prestige out of this.

On the evening before his departure, Small Elk was surprised when Bull Roarer, now Stone Breaker the Younger, approached. The two stood, not speaking for a moment, both embarrassed.

"I wanted to wish you well," Stone Breaker mumbled.

"And you," agreed Small Elk, "though it seems you have already done well."

"Stone Breaker has been good to teach me," the young man said modestly.

He hesitated a moment.

"Elk, we should not have drifted apart."

"That is true," Elk agreed.

It was difficult to remain jealous of the success of a friend who was trying to make amends. They stood, both awkwardly silent, for a little longer, and Bull Roarer–Stone Breaker finally broke the quiet.

"May you have a good journey, Elk," he said, extending a hand.

Small Elk clasped the offered hand, still uncomfortable, and the other turned away. Elk watched him go with the rolling gait that now identified him. Now it seemed like a proud walk, this swing to the step of a successful young man. Elk found that he could not begrudge his former friend's success. Their differences were like ashes in his mouth, and he left the camp to wander in the deepening dusk, alone with his confused thoughts.

"Elk?" someone spoke from beside the dim trail.

It was Crow Woman, standing in partial concealment behind some dogwoods.

"I have seen you come here sometimes," she said. "I hoped you would come tonight."

A mixture of emotions now flooded over him. He was angry at her. Why did she want to seek him out tonight, to confuse further his already confused thoughts? He was also angry at himself. Crow Woman stood there in the dimness of the fading twilight, her large dark eyes looking straight into his. He had never seen a woman half so beautiful. Her long body had ripened into the fullness of womanhood. The gangly frame of adolescence had now been filled out, angles replaced by soft and graceful curves. He had not been this near her for many moons. They had avoided each other, and now all the old hurt came rushing back.

"Why?" he blurted roughly.

"I wanted to see you."

"You could have done that at any time."

She chose to ignore the accusation.

"I wish you a good journey."

Why would she do this? She had avoided him these past many moons; then, when finally he had nearly worked out a way to escape the hurt, she had gone out of her way to seek him out and hurt him again. Carefully, he held in his anger.

"I am sorry, Elk," she said softly. "I would not have hurt you."

It appeared for a moment that she would have come into his arms, but he turned away. It was partly from the darkness that he did not see the tears in the girl's dark eyes. Partly, too, because of the tears in his own.

10

↔

I t was early in the Moon of Greening when the traveler stopped at the winter camp of the Northern band. He inquired as to the location of the lodge of the chief, so that he might pay his respects according to proper protocol. There he visited, exchanging small talk about the weather, the mild winter just past, and the season to come.

He was traveling somewhat earlier than usual, the stranger said, to join the Eastern band before they broke winter camp. There was a girl there whom he had met at last year's Sun Dance. He had been unable to dismiss his constant thoughts of her and with favorable weather, had left his own Red Rocks band far to the southwest to go to her.

The old chief smiled. Ah, young romance! This young man had undertaken a dangerous journey in winter. But he had survived, and such a romantic effort would certainly impress the young woman of the Eastern band. Actually, the foolhardy journey would probably seem quite appropriate to the Eastern band. They had always had a reputation for foolish ways.

"And where did you winter?" the chief asked.

"I traveled some. I spent part of the Moon of Snows and the Moon of Hunger with the Southern band. Of course, I supplied my own food."

The chief nodded.

"And now you travel on?"

"Yes, my chief. I bear greetings from Broken Horn. He says they will meet you at the Sun Dance. Oh, yes . . . is there a young man, Small Elk, staying with your band? His parents wished me to bring him greetings. He stays here in the lodge of White Antelope?"

"Yes, of course. He is with his grandparents. He wintered with us, you know. Is there any other news of the Southern band?"

"No, I . . . yes! Their weaponsmaker is dead. Stone Breaker. He gave his name away. He was very old, I heard."

"Yes. A good man."

The traveler left the chief's lodge to seek the lodge of Small Elk's grandparents. There he was welcomed as a long-lost relative since he brought greetings and news from White Buffalo and Dove Woman.

"*Aiee,* come inside, young man," Fox Woman invited. "Tell us everything."

"Thank you, Grandmother."

He sat and carefully related all the details he could recall while Fox Woman prepared food.

"That is all I remember," he said finally. "They and their other children are well. They sent special greetings to their son."

He nodded across the fire to Small Elk, who had said little.

"Is there other news of the band?" asked Small Elk.

"Yes, I just told the chief, your weaponsmaker is dead. Stone Breaker."

"The old man?" asked Small Elk, his voice tight.

"Yes. He had given his name to his apprentice. I heard he is quite skilled, too. A young man with a limp."

"Yes, I know him."

"Ah! And did you know he had married? Yes, a beautiful woman. She is with child, someone said. I cannot remember her name."

"Yes, I know her, too," Small Elk said, trying to choke back emotion.

"It is good!" their talkative guest chortled. "I am glad I remembered to tell you."

Small Elk was not quite so pleased but gradually decided that it was just as well. He began to realize that he had spent the winter without really coming to grips with his loss. Now it had been forced on him, and though it was a shock, maybe this was the only way to recover his sense of reality. Before, there had been the possibility that things could change. Now there was little hope. Crow Woman was not only married but pregnant and beyond reach for him.

He had made some progress during the winter, had done some growing up. It was possible, now, for him to think more calmly, almost objectively. He wished that he could rejoice in the happiness of his two friends. Maybe someday he could do so. For now, he would continue to try. It would not be easy.

* * *

The Sun Dance that year was to be held at Turkey Creek. It was customary to choose a central location for ease of travel. It was never satisfactory for all but was usually most difficult for the bands to the far west. Occasionally, the Red Rocks, or the Mountain band, farther north, would decide not to attend. Those seasons were rare, however, usually restricted to years when the location for the Sun Dance was too far east to allow for the journey to be practical. Of course, if the Big Council chose a site too far *west,* the Eastern band was sure to protest loudly.

It had been a tradition of the People to scatter widely each season. But likewise, their tradition of oneness, though they might be scattered, was strong. This and the strong sense of the sacred nature of the ceremony had made the Sun Dance their most important annual event.

That, of course, was not to deny its importance as a social event. It might take many sleeps to travel to the prearranged site. Upon arrival there, people were ready for celebration, so there would be feasting and dancing, renewing of friendships, the greeting of relatives, gambling, gaming, and smoking—all leading to the seven days of the Sun Dance.

The northern band would be the first to arrive. It was their responsibility to begin to prepare the open-sided arbor in which the Sun Dance would be held. It had been their task since the election of their popular young chief, Many Robes, as Real-chief of the entire tribe. With honor goes responsibility.

One facet of their preparation fell to the family of the chief—the selection and securing of a large buffalo bull for the ceremony. A magnificent animal was found, and the hunters—relatives and friends of Many Robes—were able to stalk and kill it successfully. It was good. The ease with which this preceremonial was carried out seemed a good omen for the year. The skin, with the head still attached, was stretched over a framework of poles at one end of the dance arbor to form an effigy in honor of the return of the buffalo.

Small Elk had never seen these early preparations before, since the office of Real-chief had not been in the Southern band for a number of years. He was fascinated by the size of the bull that the hunters had selected. He would have gladly taken part in the hunt if he had been invited. He was beginning to recover his confidence in his ability. But he was young and an outsider, and he knew that the chances for such an invitation were remote. It, the ceremonial hunt, was too important to risk the participation of amateurs.

Still, it was easy to become excited over these goings-on. Enthusiasm began to return, and Small Elk felt a thrill in the air over the coming festivities. This excitement and anticipation, of course, was an important part of the purpose of the celebration, the rejuvenation of the traditional urges that had led the People onto the plains for centuries.

The Red Rocks band was next to arrive at the site of the Sun Dance. This was unusual, in that they had the farthest to travel. But maybe not. This band held fiercely to tradition. Their very name told of their devoted preference for a specific place, a place long important to them. Sometimes they wintered elsewhere, but their favorite locale was in the Red Rocks.

Their other fierce loyalty, however, was to the rest of the tribe. It was very seldom, in the memory of anyone, that the Red Rocks missed a Sun Dance.

The helpers of Many Robes showed the Red Rocks the area assigned for their camp. This was only a matter of traditional welcome; they could have located their camping area themselves. It was always the same. The circle of the camp was open directly to the east, and all lodgedoors faced that direction to welcome Sun Boy's appearance each morning. The Northern and Southern bands would camp in their respective segments of the circle, and the Mountain band in the northwest. The Eastern band would erect their lodges just north of the symbolic gap left for Sun Boy.

For now, the Red Rocks proceeded to the southwest segment of the camp circle and began to establish their camp. It had always been so, from before the time of memory. Probably since Creation, it was said. The same arrangement was always carried out in seating of the bands around the council fire. That too went back into antiquity. There was even an empty space in the circle, reserved for a band that had occupied a southeast position. They had been exterminated long ago, killed by a warlike tribe who lived in the woodlands to the east. The empty spot in the camp and the empty seats in the Big Council had served as a grim reminder for many generations.

In another day or two the scouts reported the approach of the Mountain band, and again there were happy family reunions, the greetings of old friends, and the hustle and bustle of establishing camp. Excitement increased, and the festive atmosphere became stronger. It was a time of joyous celebration.

Small Elk, though he had mixed feelings, looked forward eagerly to the arrival of the Southern band. It would be good to see his parents, his brother and sister, and their families. His slightly uneasy feeling of apprehension revolved around greeting Stone Breaker and Crow Woman, now his wife. That would be difficult, at best. He would be expected to congratulate his friends and be happy with them in the happiness of their marriage. He was not certain that he could handle that in a convincing manner but knew that he must try. Eventually, he must overcome his jealousy and learn to live with the disappointment—either that or concede that he could not live with it and join a different band permanently.

There were eligible young women in the Northern band. Some had cast sidelong glances at him and smiled invitingly. He was certain that his grandparents would welcome a permanent move to their band. It was not uncommon. There was a constant shifting in the bands. Some families, in fact, seemed to change loyalties every two or three seasons, to follow the band whose chief seemed at the moment to carry the greatest prestige. He seriously considered such a move for a time.

No, he finally decided, he could not do it. His father had always looked with scorn upon those who instead of facing their problems, tried to avoid them by moving to a different band. Besides, he was not ready to become romantically involved with any of the beautiful daughters of the Northern band.

He was ready, he thought, to talk seriously with his father about his future. He believed that White Buffalo would approve a vision quest this season. That would certainly help to show him the right way. It had been a stupid thing, he realized, to consider a vision quest out of anger and disappointment. Those were the wrong reasons. Yes, he looked forward to the arrival of his parents and the expected talk with his father.

Even so, he was caught totally off guard when the day finally came. The scout who had been watching to the south came trotting into the camp.

"The Southern band comes!" he announced as he made the circuit of the area. "The Southern band has arrived!"

11

Small Elk found himself avoiding contact with anyone except his parents. He realized what he was doing. Everyone else was hurrying around, greeting friends or family, exchanging jokes, stories, and small talk. Although he had assured himself that he too must do so, he found it difficult to mix with the others. He stayed away from the gregarious happiness, only belatedly joining his parents to help set up their lodge. He studiously avoided even looking around at other families, as they too began to establish their campsites.

This was going to be more difficult than he had thought. He kept imagining Crow Woman in the arms of his friend Stone Breaker, now her husband. Despite his resolve, he now wondered if it would be possible for him to accept it. Maybe he should consider again the possibility of joining another band.

He was somewhat distracted for a time by the reunion with his parents and the tasks of setting up camp. He knew it would be a day or two before he could find an opportunity to talk to his father, and that too was worrisome. It was midafternoon when the Southern band arrived, so there was much to do before dark. That was both good and frustrating—good, because it postponed the inevitable meeting with Stone Breaker and

Crow Woman; bad, because it also postponed his chance to talk with his father.

Without actually realizing that he was doing it, he spent the evening finding ways to keep busy and avoiding prolonged conversation with anyone. He did not want to spend the evening hearing about the marriage of Crow Woman or her pregnancy. Also, he was not ready for his mother's questions about the girls of the Northern band. He rather suspected that a romance with a young woman of her own band would not be entirely unwelcome to Dove Woman.

Small Elk also found himself reluctant to go out and mix with the other young people, as would be the usual custom. There would be the risk of encountering Crow Woman, Stone Breaker, or both.

Never was a lodge so meticulously aligned, so carefully set, or the thongs which held the cover to the poles tied and retied so many times. At first Dove Woman attributed her son's overattentiveness to his happiness at the reunion. Gradually she began to see his preoccupation but was puzzled by it.

"Let him alone," advised White Buffalo. "He will work it out."

Reluctantly, Dove Woman did so. She tried to ignore the repetition of tasks, the meticulous tying and retying of the lashings, the readjusting of the laces over the door, and the interminable fussing with the smoke flaps.

Finally, it was apparent even to Small Elk that there was nothing more that he could do to help his parents establish the camp. He must settle down to make small talk, and the the subject of Crow Woman's marriage would surely come up. Another idea struck him.

"I will bring some fuel," he said, and was off like an arrow from the bow.

His mother shook her head.

"What is the matter with him?" his mother asked. "Why is he behaving so?"

"I am not sure," White Buffalo said slowly. "He will tell us, when he is ready."

"Is it about Stone Breaker's marriage?" Dove Woman wondered. "He should be happy about that."

"Maybe," his father answered. "He knows of it, because he told us that the traveler stopped with them."

Puzzled, they settled down in their new campsite to wait for Small Elk's return.

Shadows were lengthening, and Small Elk had gone far upstream to gather wood and buffalo chips. He had felt a need to escape the social pressures of the day. He wished there was some way he could leave the entire tribe for a few days—until after the Big Council and Sun Dance, maybe. A vision quest still seemed like a good idea, but he really wished to discuss that with his father. *Aiee,* growing up, assuming the duties of a man, was difficult.

He picked up a dead cottonwood limb and added it to the stack in the crook of his left arm. Already, he had almost more than he could carry. But it would soon be dusk, and if he waited a little longer, he could unobtrusively slip back to his parents' lodge. Now the sleepy sounds of the creatures of the day were becoming fewer as they settled for the night. A great blue heron beat his way overhead, hurrying to his lodge before darkness fell. There were sounds of some of the night-creatures, coming alive with the departure of Sun Boy and his torch.

Small Elk turned to start back and noticed a figure on the path ahead of him.

"*Ah-koh,* Elk," said Crow Woman.

For a moment, he felt that he had lived this before. The girl carried an armful of sticks, but somehow he doubted that an accident had brought them together. He remembered well their last, emotional meeting. He had a moment of anger. Why would she repeatedly torture him this way, seeking him out to imply things that never were and never could be? He could not stay angry, however. The look in her eyes would melt any but the coldest heart.

At their last meeting, he had thought that he had never seen her more beautiful. Even that was eclipsed now. She stood there, straight and tall, not moving, looking directly into his face, and her spirit reached out to touch his.

"I followed you," she admitted.

"I know. Crow, you should not have—"

Now anger flared in her face. He was distressed by it, but *aiee,* how it accentuated her dark beauty. Her eyes flashed, and she stamped her foot impatiently.

"Elk, what is the matter with you?" she demanded.

As she moved, the fringes at the bottom of her buckskin dress swayed, and the motion caught his attention. He looked at the attractive exposure of long tan legs, from above the knees downward. He should not be appreciating this, but he had always admired Crow's appearance, even before the advent of her womanhood. Now she was another man's wife, and it was wrong to look at her with the thoughts he was thinking. Forcibly, he tried to raise his eyes, trying not to stare at the womanly curves that he found so appealing. The willowy shape of her hips, the flat belly . . . wait! Even in the dim light . . . The traveler had told him, three moons ago, of her pregnancy. This was not . . .

"I heard you were pregnant!" he blurted.

Immediately he felt like an idiot, but it was too late. If she was angry before, now her face showed a rage that was frightening. For a moment, he thought she would hit him with her firewood. Instead, she threw it to the ground and stepped toward him.

"*What?*" she demanded. "Elk, I should walk away and never speak to you again!"

Now his anger rose. How could a woman for whom he had such high regard be acting so shamelessly?

"Yes, you should!" he snapped. "You shame your husband."

"My *husband?* Elk, you have gone mad!" she shouted at him. "You know I *have* no husband! I would not come here—"

She turned and started away.

"Wait!" he called.

He dropped his own firewood and ran to catch her.

"Crow! You and Bull . . . Stone Breaker. I was told . . . the Falling-Leaves Moon? You were not married?"

Slowly, a light began to dawn in her face.

"No!" she said flatly. "Stone Breaker and Cattail. You remember her? *She* is pregnant."

They stood, staring at each other in disbelief for a moment, and then both burst out laughing. In another moment, they were in each other's arms, both trying to talk at once, interrupting, and dissolving into laughter again.

"Elk," she whispered in his ear, "there has never been anyone but you in my heart."

"Or you, in mine!"

Now both were laughing and crying at once, holding tightly.

"I did not know what was wrong!" she murmured.

"Nothing is wrong, now!"

"We must tell Stone Breaker," she said, laughing. "He will be pleased for us."

"Our parents too," Elk agreed. "I am sure my mother thinks something is wrong with me."

"Mine too," she said. "We will go and tell them. But first, let us stay here a little while."

She snuggled closer in his arms, shivering a little, only partly against the chill of the prairie night.

12

↔

The world was bright, happy, and exciting after the reunion of the two childhood sweethearts. They threw themselves wholeheartedly into the celebration of the Sun Dance and all that it stood for.

For Small Elk, the prayers of thanksgiving for the return of the sun and the renewing of the prairie would carry a broader meaning. His ritual prayers would also hold the gratitude for the return of Crow Woman. At first, he could hardly understand what had happened. How could he have been so wrong, have misinterpreted events for so long? Gradually, he came to understand. His jealousy had been one of the major obstacles. He had been unable to see objectively, to realize that the relationship between Crow and Bull Roarer had been one of friendship, not romance. Bull Roarer had badly needed a friend, and Crow had seen that need. Small Elk was now feeling a guilt that he had not been there to help. He had nearly destroyed himself with jealousy. First he had been jealous of Crow's attention to their friend, then jealous of Bull Roarer's success. *Aiee,* it was not pretty.

In his jealousy, he had completely overlooked the fact that Cattail, the quiet, sweet child who was their childhood playmate, had also matured. Now, with the clarity of hindsight, he realized that she had been around all along. Probably she too had been jealous, jealous of Crow's attention to the rising career of Stone Breaker. But Cattail had been persistent, patiently waiting. Small Elk would never know whether Stone Breaker had first asked Crow Woman to join him as his wife and been refused. He knew that Crow Woman would respect such a confidence, and for this he loved her even more.

Regardless, Stone Breaker, now the respected weaponsmaker of the Southern band, had now taken a wife. Small Elk had gone to visit their lodge early in the morning after his meeting with Crow Woman. His reception was cool. Cattail, her belly large with the expectation of the child, apologized for the disarray of the lodge.

"We only arrived yesterday," she explained.

"Yes, I know. And only last night I heard of your marriage. I wanted to wish you well, both of you."

Gradually, the atmosphere warmed as they began to recall incidents from their childhood. Then Crow Woman stopped by, and soon they were laughing together. The intervening years were stripped away, and they were children again, giggling and reveling in the joy of one another's successes.

"You wintered with your grandparents?" Stone Breaker asked.

"Yes."

Small Elk was reluctant to reveal the bitterness and jealously with which he had left the band last autumn.

"I needed some time away," he explained.

The others nodded in understanding. It was apparent that for Small Elk, life had not been as kind. Privately, he was just beginning to realize how his jealousy had nearly devoured him from within. Much of his bad luck, it seemed, had been self-inflicted.

The moment seemed good now, and he related the story of the traveler's visit, when he learned of Stone Breaker's marriage.

"He did not know the name of your wife," he finished, "and I thought it was Crow Woman. I was very jealous."

"You thought . . . *aiee,* Elk, it is no wonder you avoided me yesterday!" Stone Breaker collapsed into laughter.

"When did you learn?" Cattail asked.

"Only last night. I encountered Crow Woman while we were gathering wood. She did not seem very pregnant, so . . . well, then she told me."

Now all four were laughing. Finally, Stone Breaker paused, wiping the tears of laughter from his eyes.

"Ah, my friends, we have been apart too long. Now, when will you two be married?"

There was a moment of embarrassed confusion. Crow Woman blushed becomingly, but did nothing to help Small Elk answer.

"I . . . we . . . ah . . . there has not been time to talk of it," he mumbled.

"Of course!" Stone Breaker broke into laughter again. "Last night!"

Maybe a trifle too much laughter, Small Elk thought. Maybe he *had* been rejected by Crow Woman. No matter, now. Stone Breaker and Cattail obviously had a good marriage and were pleased and proud about the pregnancy.

"We will talk of these things," said Crow Woman, relieving some of the pressure that Small Elk was feeling.

The others nodded.

"I will speak with my father, also," Small Elk explained. "I have not seen him since last season."

"About your marriage?" Stone Breaker asked, puzzled.

"No, no. I may take a vision quest."

"Yes, you should do that first," advised Stone Breaker.

The women laughed.

"No, I—"

"We understand, Stone Breaker," Crow Woman said, teasing. "You have hardly been out of your lodge since last fall!"

"Will you follow your father's medicine?" asked Stone Breaker, attempting to change the subject.

"I do not know," Small Elk answered slowly. "I am not sure I have the gift."

He had been so preoccupied with his jealousies, he realized now, that he had given little thought to such things. He should be making these decisions. It was quite usual for the son of a holy man to follow his father as an apprentice. However, he must first have the gift, the visionary second sight, to make such a choice. Even then, some who were endowed with the gift refused it, unwilling to accept the responsibility and sacrifice required for such a career. Small Elk's older brother, Blue Owl, had not chosen such a path. Small Elk was not sure whether it was due to a refusal or whether Blue Owl had not received the gift. One did not ask such things. While it was permissible to ask whether such an apprenticeship was upcoming, the reasons for the decision were quite personal.

When he was younger, Small Elk had often imagined himself following his father's footsteps. In recent moons, the past two years, such thoughts had rarely occurred to him. He now regretted the wasted time.

"It is one of the things that my father can help me with, to find the answers," he explained to the others.

The next afternoon, Small Elk went to talk to his father. White Buffalo was pleased with the change in his son. He and Dove Woman were not certain what had caused the change, but it was certainly for the better— something that had happened that first night, it seemed, when the Southern band arrived at the camp on Turkey Creek. Elk had spent the morning with his friends, and it was apparent that the reunion had been a happy one. Probably joy over the marriage of Stone Breaker and Cattail, they decided.

"Father, I would speak with you," Small Elk began.

White Buffalo remained silent, waiting.

"I asked of a vision quest, before," the young man went on.

His father only nodded.

"I was not ready, then. You told me, but I did not believe. Now I know I was not ready, but maybe I am now."

"Maybe," answered the medicine man cautiously. "Tell me more."

"Well, I . . . after the Sun Dance, of course . . . Crow Woman and I have spoken of marriage. But would it not be better to take the vision quest first?"

"Probably." White Buffalo's eyes twinkled. This was going well. "But, I am made to feel there is more?" he asked.

"Maybe so," Small Elk said cautiously. "I have wondered, Father. Do you suppose I might have the gift of medicine?"

Aiee, thought White Buffalo, *of course you have, my son, but you must discover it for yourself.*

"Why do you ask this?" he said aloud, trying to control his elation.

"No reason, but I wondered how one finds out such things."

"Oh. Well, no one can tell you that, my son. You must seek it."

"How?"

"There are many ways. Start to mention it in your Sun-Dance prayers. *Ask* for the gift, if you wish. That could do no harm. But, only if you wish it."

"I . . . I am not sure, Father."

White Buffalo nodded in understanding.

"Then what *do* you wish, that you are sure about?"

"I wish to marry Crow Woman, and to go on a vision quest."

"Ah, you are answering your own questions. Your vision quest may answer your doubts about the gift. But it might be difficult to think in the right spirit of the quest with a new wife at home." It would be hard enough, he added to himself, to concentrate on *anything,* with a new wife like young Crow Woman waiting for one's return. No, it would be better to postpone that distraction.

"Your quest should be first," he suggested. "It may provide some other answers. When you return, then you will be better able to plan."

"And the marriage?" Small Elk asked.

"It is good, Elk. But, you should wait. Wait until your vision quest is behind you. Who knows? Maybe the quest will help you decide when it should take place."

Small Elk nodded, looking a trifle disappointed.

"But before that, even," his father was saying, "comes the Sun Dance."

13

The Eastern band straggled in, almost on the appropriate day, in their usual state of disorder and disarray. The time-honored jokes were exchanged about the ineptness of the Eastern band. This opportunity for wry humor at the expense of one group was never overlooked. If anyone of another band made a mistake or suffered any accident or misfortune, someone was sure to comment on it.

"It is to be expected. His grandmother was of the Eastern band."

The origin of this good-natured ridicule was lost in antiquity but seemed to be self-perpetuating. Some of the members of that band even seemed to revel in the reputation and to behave foolishly just to produce laughs. And people with a more serious approach to life may have transferred their loyalties and their families to other bands through the generations, leaving the reputation of the Eastern band more accurate each season.

With the arrival of the last band, it was time to begin the announcement of the Sun Dance. For three days, the keeper of the Sun Doll danced ceremonially around the entire encampment, chanting his announcement to the People. Three circuits each morning he traveled, ending each time in the Sun-Dance lodge. Meanwhile, the medicine men from each band had tied their respective medicine bundles in place around the sides of the lodge. Excitement was building.

The Sun Dance proper would continue day and night for seven days. Exhausted dancers would drop out, and others would take their places. Those who beat the drums also traded off for a half-day's sleep, to return later. The throb of the drums and the chanting were continuous.

Dancers placed carefully planned sacrifices before the buffalo effigy—a well-tanned robe, a choice otter skin, or a perfectly fletched and painted arrow; medicine sticks, carved, painted, and decorated with fur and feathers. One man sacrificed a favorite bow with which he had found spectacular success at the hunt in an effusion of thanksgiving.

There were also prayers of thanksgiving for the return of the sun after the long, dark nights of winter, when Sun Boy's torch had nearly gone out. There were also prayers that involved pledges and promises of patriotism, sometimes mixed with supplication. One might publicly pledge a specific sacrifice at the next Sun Dance in return for good health or good hunting this season. The aged and infirm attempted to dance and sing the chants of supplication for healing. As the excitement of the dance stirred their blood, arthritic old limbs actually seemed to take on a new and youthful vigor.

Small Elk participated, of course, with prayerful chants of thanks for his good fortune. He had nothing to sacrifice but pledged to do so when he was able. His supplication was that he be helped with his vision quest and with the decisions ahead. He also mentioned good health for himself, his family, and his intended wife.

It was not before the third day of the dance that Elk found occasion to talk with his father again. White Buffalo, occupied with his ceremonial responsibilities, finally decided that things were going well enough for him to take an interval of rest. He slept for part of an afternoon, ate sparingly, and drank deeply. When the medicine man stepped out to return to the Sun-Dance lodge, he encountered his son.

"*Ah-koh,* Father."

"*Ah-koh,* my son. You did well at the dance lodge. It brought me pride."

"Thank you, Father. But I must talk with you. When the Dance is over maybe?"

White Buffalo shrugged and spread his palms, secretly delighted at this overture.

"Of course, Elk. Why not now?"

They walked together, a little way from the camp, away from the clamor of drums and chanting.

"Yes, my son?"

"Father, you know that I . . . Crow Woman and I . . . we wish to marry!" he finally blurted.

"Yes . . . you have talked with her parents?"

"No, but I think they will agree."

"Probably," White Buffalo observed. He was actually quite certain. He and Dove Woman had already discussed the matter, and the two mothers of the couple had long hoped for this.

"But I also wish to take my vision quest, as we spoke before."

White Buffalo nodded understandingly. "It is good. Do that first."

"There is more. Do you think I might have the gift of spirit, to follow you?"

White Buffalo's heart leapt for joy. He managed to control his delight, for such a decision must not be based on the wishes of others.

"Maybe," he said calmly. "Your vision quest should tell."

Then he saw the young man's dilemma. Elk was afraid that his thoughts of the coming marriage would interfere with the spiritual nature of his quest. It was something to consider. It would be possible to marry now and seek his vision next year. But no, that would postpone the decision about his career. Not only that, but by that time there might be the distractions of a family. And the longer the quest was postponed, the more difficult it would be. He took a long breath.

"My son," he said slowly, "my heart tells me that the sooner you seek the visions, the better. I will cast the bones, but I am already sure."

"As soon as the Sun Dance is over?" Small Elk asked.

"Yes! Have you thought where you will go?"

"Some. There is a hill above Sycamore Creek, above the place we camp sometimes."

"Yes, I know the place. You knew we are to camp there this year?"

"No! I had not heard. It is good!"

Elk paused a few moments, then spoke again. "Father, I could leave tomorrow, to go and begin my fast. When you arrive there for the summer camp, I will already have my quest behind me."

White Buffalo considered that proposal. Yes, that would give the boy time alone to think. It would be dangerous . . . *aiee,* a vision quest always held a certain amount of danger. Alone on the prairie . . . but that was the purpose, to be alone, to experience the things of the spirit. Elk would arrive in the selected area a few sleeps before the rest of the band and would be undisturbed. He had proved himself able to travel alone last season.

"Yes," the medicine man agreed. "Yes, Elk, I think maybe this is good. Then, when we arrive, you will be ready to begin whatever your heart tells you. When will you start?"

Small Elk shrugged. "Tomorrow?"

"Good! Now go, make your preparations. I must go back to the Dance now."

"Your vision quest? Now?" Crow Woman's eyes were wide with wonder. "We have just found each other again," she protested.

"This is one reason why," he told her. "It will help me know what I must do, and we can be together sooner."

"Yes," she agreed reluctantly, "but I wish I could go with you."

"But then it would not be a vision quest," he reminded her playfully.

"I know."

She snuggled against him, her body warm in the cool prairie twilight. "Elk, when you return, I will be waiting."

"Good," he agreed. "Then we will start another quest, we two, together."

She smiled at him in the gathering dusk. "You start tomorrow?"

"Yes. At daylight. Have you told your parents? About us, I mean?"

"A little. Only that you thought I was married to Stone Breaker."

They laughed together quietly.

"Not that I was pleased to be wrong?" he teased.

"Well, yes, that too."

"Good! Then they will not be surprised!"

"You will talk with them now?"

"No, not until after my quest. I must keep my spirit free to receive the visions."

She nodded, understanding.

"My heart will be with you," she said.

Dove Woman again protested a lone journey of this type, but not so long or so strongly. He had proved his ability already, and she knew she could not keep him a child forever.

"Take care, my son," she told him as she wrapped a small pack of dried meat and a little pemmican for his journey. "If the weather is hot, eat the pemmican first, before it becomes bitter. Save something to eat when your fast is over."

"Yes, Mother," he answered her, smiling. "I know this."

"I know you do, but mothers say such things. It is our privilege."

She hugged him and smiled, pretending that the tears were not welling up. *Aiee,* her youngest, on his vision quest! It seemed only yesterday he was a babe at her breast.

She watched him until his long strides carried him to the crest of the little rise. The rays of the rising sun struck his face as he turned to wave, then crossed over.

Dove Woman turned back toward her lodge. *I have never noticed before,* she thought, *how much Small Elk walks like his father.* From beyond the lodges, the rhythmic cadence of the drums and the chanting went on.

14

Small Elk sat by his fire, uncertain what to expect. From time to time, he felt the sharp spasm of a hunger pang. Sometimes his belly rumbled loudly in protest against the indignity of emptiness. This was a disappointment. He did not know how a fast was supposed to proceed, but surely there must be more to it than this.

He had reached the hilltop on a pleasant evening a little before dark. There had been time to gather fuel and to establish his camp. He broke a stick of dried meat in half and chewed one portion while he gathered wood. He would begin his fast immediately after lighting his fire. That was always an important step, the symbolic lighting of the fire. He used rubbing sticks, the yucca spindle whirling in the little depression of the fireboard as he drew the bow back and forth. Smoke began to pour forth, and a black powdery ash gathered below the notch in the flat board. Soon smoke seemed to be issuing from the little pile of powder itself. Elk laid aside the sticks and the firebow, and picked up the precious spark on its tuft of shredded cedar bark. Carefully, he breathed on the spark, watching it glow and recede with each breath. Smoke became more dense, pouring from the tinder. He blew a trifle harder. He was ready when the cedar bark burst into flame, and he thrust the blazing tuft into a little opening in the pile of sticks he had prepared. The smallest sticks began to ignite, and the yellow tongues licked upward, the fire growing rapidly. He added a few larger sticks and sat back to chant the Song of Fire.

It was a time-honored ceremony, this song, performed as a ritual whenever a new fire was kindled. It was in two parts, the first a prayer of thanks for the gift of fire. The second, perhaps more pertinent to each new fire, was a statement. "Here," it said, "I intend to camp. The fire indicates my intention to live here a little while." The fire was a public gesture to whatever spirits might live in this place, a request for permission to stay here, and a marker of the site. Ceremoniously, he placed the other half of his stick of dried meat on the fire to appease the spirits of the place.

Small Elk finished the ritual and spread his robe to prepare for the night. There would be little sleep; he was too excited. He was actually beginning his vision quest, that most important of lifetime experiences. How could one sleep?

That had been a day ago. Nothing had happened, except that he was hungry, and his belly was growling aloud in protest. He was bored. Since his Song for Morning, there had been very little to do. He had watched a circling hawk for a while, and observed a band of antelope on a distant hilltop. He assembled a supply of firewood and a stack of chips of buffalo dung, which would burn slowly and long, with little flame.

Beyond that, there was nothing to do but wait. He took a sip from his water skin and settled himself to watch the setting of the sun. Sun Boy had chosen his paints well tonight. The reds and purples, made more brilliant by the presence of a few clouds to the west, had never been more intense. He watched the bright disk slide beyond earth's rim, and twilight began to settle across the prairie. Far below him, in the giant oaks along the stream, *Kookooskoos,* the great hunting owl, sounded his hollow rendition of his own name. A cautious doe and her fawn made their way out of a thicket of dogwood on the slope below him and ventured into the open to browse. Far to the north, across the river, a coyote called, and another answered. Stars began to appear, one by one, and Small Elk tried to guess the location of the next one he would see. He abandoned that pastime when suddenly it seemed the sky was full of the tiny points of light, and the background had faded from gray to the deepest blue-black.

Something at the edge of his vision made him turn to see the fiery circle of the rising moon sliding into sight in the east. *How odd,* he wondered, *the size and color is so different when it first rises.* He had always noticed this, but tonight it seemed especially so—the glowing red, with the markings in purple on its surface. So plain tonight . . . a face, a rabbit, or a woman combing out her long hair, depending on how one chose to perceive it. He watched with fascination while the disk became smaller and brighter. Soon its light was silvering all of the prairie in a ghostly splendor. He was no longer bored. He felt that he dared not sleep because he might miss something on this night of beauty and enchantment. Surely it was a night of strong medicine.

Even so, the moon, now tiny and white, was directly overhead before Small Elk began to realize that perhaps this was a part of his fast. The sharpness of the senses, the intensity of color, the distances that he could see across the silvery prairie . . . were these the early effects of the fast?

He was a little startled when he suddenly awoke with the sun shining in his face. It was morning, and he had not expected to sleep. There was no mistaking it now. He felt a sense of exhilaration and well-being that he had never known before. The hunger pangs had ceased, replaced by a calm confidence, a clarity of understanding. That made such things as an empty belly completely unimportant. The joy of this new sense of perception made the day pass rapidly. He observed the world with new insight, from the hugeness of the clouds in the distance to the smallness of the tiny creatures in the grass at his feet. All seemed to have their place in the world.

That night he began to dream, but the dreams were not materially different from the things he had observed while awake. This in turn led to a strange trancelike state when he woke in which he could no longer decide what was dream and what reality. He felt that there was nothing that he could not do. He could fly from the top of his hill if he wished, to soar high among the clouds with the eagles. He could burrow into the earth with the lesser creatures if he wished.

From that point on, it became impossible for him to distinguish . . . no, not impossible, but *unnecessary* to distinguish even night and day. His existence seemed above and beyond such mundane things as days, or even moons, so he was never certain afterward when the visions began.

They were not actually visions—in the sense he had expected, anyway. He had thought of them as . . . well, maybe bizarre night-dreams of exceptional clarity. If he actually had an expectation that could be defined, that was it. So he was confused, even in his dream-state, when it began. It was, at first, merely an understanding. He was looking at a distant antelope (or at a vision of one, he was never certain) when he suddenly realized that he was thinking the creature's thoughts. They were shy, timid thoughts, yet curious. He knew that the creature could see far greater distances then he and that the ability to do so was part of the fear that the antelope felt. Fear of some distant, as yet unseen predator. The animal now raised its head, flashed white rump-patches, and disappeared over the hill.

He lifted his attention to the red-tailed hawk that soared above. Its attention was focused on a tuft of grass as it hovered, watching for any suggestion of motion. Small Elk's spirit now seemed to enter that grassy clump, to feel the terror of the white-footed mouse which crouched there, afraid to run, yet afraid of the terrible strike of the hunter's talons.

The hawk decided that the clump held no food and lifted a wing to catch a rising air current and soar away. Small Elk diverted his attention closer, where a bird sat on a stem of sumac and scolded. It was an urgent tone, and his searching spirit entered the head of the bird to experience its alarm at the approach of a great blue snake. He transferred his thoughts there and found that the snake was hunting, looking for a nest. It had actually been attracted by the bird's protest. It could not find the bird's lodge, however, and moved on. So did Small Elk, or at least his spirit. He experienced the dull awareness of a large fish that lay under the roots of a sycamore, waiting for prey to drift past.

He enjoyed a mud slide with the spirits of a family of playful otters as they plummeted down a steep bank into the pool below.

The process of getting "inside the head" of these creatures was becoming easier, more rational. He spent a little while with the thoughts of a coyote as she hunted. There was not an urgency to the hunt as there had once been. Her pups were grown and were hunting for themselves now.

He moved among a herd of buffalo and felt the calm reliance on the herd for protection, a group spirit. A large bull grazed quietly, and for some reason, the spirit of Small Elk moved toward it.

Welcome, my son. I have expected you.

It was not a spoken statement, only a thought, but it came to him with shocking clarity.

You are my medicine animal? My spirit guide? he asked.

There was no direct answer, but he felt that it was true. There was a feel, somehow, of humor, as if his surprise had been mildly amusing.

What am I to do now? Small Elk thought to himself.

Continue your visions, the thought came.

He was not certain whether it was an answer to his question or merely a coincidence. The buffalo grazed on, and now he felt a sort of oneness with them a part of the herd-feeling.

It was then that the visions began which were to prove so puzzling. He was traveling, in spirit, over great bodies of water and large areas of land. There were plains and forests and great areas of snow and ice, but he did not feel the cold. He saw wondrous things, the stuff of dreams and unreality. There was a real-bear, which prowled across endless snow when it should have been hibernating. It was not the color of a real-bear either as it stood on its hind legs to see farther across the snowpack. It was pure white.

He moved on, and saw great cats like the long-tailed cougar, but with heavy manes like the buffalo. There were strange, ugly creatures like large deer with a deformity, a hump on the back, that did not seem to bother them at all. A huge creature with great flapping ears appeared to have a tail at both ends, but one proved to be an extension of the nose with which it pulled down trees to browse. There were little men with tails who appeared to live in the tops of trees. All of these things were seen in rapid sequence. They seemed quite believable in the dream-state, as even ridiculous dreams will. Most of them were quickly forgotten, as dreams usually are when confronted with reality in the clear light of day.

One of his visions, however, persisted. In later days, even years later, it would somehow recur unexpectedly. It was as nonsensical as the other visions but was certainly more persistent. In this vision or dream, he watched from a hilltop over a vast expanse of grassland. Below him grazed a scattered herd of animals, moving slowly across the prairie, like buffalo. But they were not buffalo. They were long and lean like elk, but they had no antlers or horns. They were all colors—black, white, gray, red, and spotted. Yet all were formed alike and appeared to be the same species.

One came running, fast as the wind, across the plain and up the slope toward him. He was frozen with fear, but the creature may not even have seen him because it paused nearby and rose on its hind legs to give a long wavering call. In its eye was a proud, confident look, like the look of eagles. It gave the cry again, a sort of challenge like the bellow of a bull elk at rutting season. But different . . . there was no question that this creature was different from any others he had ever seen. And his heart was made to feel that it was real. The other fanciful creatures of his vision might be purely dreams, but this one was significant in some way.

After he woke, he tried to remember all he could about the creature. An elk without horns, but . . . *aiee,* it made no sense at all! When it had stood on its hind feet to thunder its challenge across the plain, it had pawed the air with its front feet, directly in front of him. He had seen the feet plainly. That was the thing that assured him that it was either a bit of madness or a creature of the supernatural. Still, he was certain what he had seen, as clearly as if he were awake: The creature had worn a turtle on each foot!

15

"*turtle*? On each foot?" White Buffalo was incredulous.

"Yes, Father, it seemed so. Can this be?"

The medicine man pondered a moment. "Who knows what can be?" he answered thoughtfully. "And this seemed to be your medicine-guide?"

"What? No, no, Father, I think not. It—"

White Buffalo held up a hand to stop him. "Wait. You need not reveal your guide to me . . . to anyone."

"But I may?"

"Of course."

"It seemed to be a buffalo."

White Buffalo was pleased. That would seem to say that Small Elk's medicine inclined him toward the buffalo medicine of his father. He nodded.

"We will talk more of that, but now, tell me of the strange creatures."

"It is as I have said, Father. There were many strange creatures. Some I have forgotten. The visions did not last. But this one is still quite clear in my head. It was as big as an elk . . . bigger, maybe. They were of different colors, but the one I saw closely was gray."

"And it wore a turtle on each foot?"

"Yes, Father? What does this mean?"

"It could mean many things, my son. But I did not see it. Tell me, what did *you* see as its meaning?"

Small Elk shook his head. "I do not understand it all. I saw many things, but this one . . . I am made to think it is more important than all the other visions."

"Yet this is not your spirit-guide, your medicine animal?"

"No. That is the buffalo. But this one . . . with the turtles . . . is of great importance, somehow. *Aiee,* I do not know!" He shook his head in despair.

"Do not be concerned, my son," the holy man advised. "Some things we understand now, some later. Some, never, maybe, because they are not *meant* to be understood. But now, about the buffalo. You think that is your medicine?"

"Yes, Father, I am sure of it now. And I am made to think that I should follow you. Can it be so?"

White Buffalo nodded, pleased and proud. "Of course, my son, it is good that you wish to learn the duties of the medicine man. But it is hard. You must accept much responsibility."

"Yes, I know. I am ready."

"Good. What about your marriage?"

"I cannot do both?"

"It would not be best. Either would demand your complete attention for a while. But why not start your instruction and plan for the marriage later?"

Disappointed as he was, Small Elk managed to control his feelings, at least in part. After so long a time, when he felt he had lost Crow Woman forever, it had been such a thrilling discovery to find her again. Their reunion had been partly marred by the necessity to part again, even for a little while. Now he had the vision quest behind him and was looking forward to planning their own lodge.

But he could see the difficulties in a marriage at this time. It would be very hard to turn aside from the company of Crow Woman in their own lodge to devote time away from her to learning. *Aiee,* there should not be such a thing, the necessity to make such a choice. But it must be. He should not postpone his apprenticeship now that the trail lay plainly before him with his quest behind. And now that he and Crow Woman had resolved their misunderstandings, they would be able to share each other's company. What little time he was able to spend away from his duties as the medicine man's apprentice they could share.

He dreaded telling Crow Woman of his decision. He was certain that she had her heart set on an immediate marriage, as he had. Now he must explain. . . .

"It does not matter," she assured him. "We were apart for a long time. Now we can be together when we can, when your duties allow. And later, together always."

She snuggled next to him in a suggestive way that implied that the rewards would be worth whatever delay was necessary. *Aiee,* this could become more and more frustrating!

He also told her of his vision quest, omitting the part in which he identified his spirit-animal, the buffalo. Later, perhaps, it would be good for her to know that too; he felt a closeness in their spirits that said so. But he wished to share now the visions of the strange creatures, especially that of the hornless elk with the turtles on its feet.

"You are joking," she accused, eyes wide with wonder. "You are teasing me."

"No, no, it is as I told you. It came close to me, rose on its hind legs, and pawed the air!"

"Like the real-bear?" she asked. "The bear-that-walks-like-a-man?"

"No, not like that. It is hard to tell, but it was different."

"And it seemed something special? Your spirit-guide?"

"No. White Buffalo asked me that. That was another . . . I will tell you some day. But this . . . Crow, you know my spirit well. What could it mean?"

"Aiee, I know nothing of vision quests, Elk. It must be something of meaning. If it is for you to know, someday it will be shown to you. You have dreamed of it since?"

"Yes, twice. It was the same both times. The strange animal came and stopped on a hill near me, to stand and cry out. Its cry was frightening and loud, a roar almost, but there seemed little danger."

"Then it must be a good sign. I do not know, Elk."

There was little time to wonder. Now that the decision had been made, White Buffalo was anxious to proceed with his son's education. Elk was only too willing. The sooner he began, the sooner he and Crow Woman could establish their own lodge. However, he had not counted on the immense quantity of information that his father was eager to give him.

It was nearing the Moon of Ripening, when all things that grow are completing the year's cycle and preparing for the winter's sleep. It would be a while before that process would be completed. But already, the bluish stems of the big grasses were pushing upward, sometimes taller than a large man before the seedheads opened.

In the giant oaks along the streams and in the canyons, busy squirrels hurried to gather and store acorns. Sometime soon, the restless herds of buffalo would be migrating, drifting south for the winter. It would be a time for the People to hunt, to store as much food as possible for the winter. It was the responsibility of White Buffalo, possessor of the buffalo medicine, to predict their arrival. He would also assist with the plans for the hunt, sometimes using his calfskin cape to mingle with the herd and gently maneuver them to an area favorable to the hunters.

"But how do you tell when the buffalo will come?" asked Small Elk.

"Patience!" White Buffalo said impatiently. "You have much to learn before that."

They walked the prairie together. White Buffalo sniffed the air, seeming to study the maturing grasses, the stage of development of the nuts and acorns along the timbered streams, the profusion of golden flowers of different types.

"At this moon, most of the flowers are yellow or purple," he pointed out.

"Why, Father?"

"To tell that it is the Moon of Ripening!" White Buffalo said.

Small Elk wanted to ask about the buffalo but sensed that it would not be advisable.

"Now, at about this season," his father was saying, "there will come a change in the weather. Rain Maker has been resting, and the land becomes hot and dry. Then comes the change, and that tells the buffalo to move. One day we notice that the prairie smells different, *feels* different. We must be able to tell, just a little while before it happens."

Elk started to ask why, but realized his own answer. The holy man must be ready to tell the others, so that they could be ready for the hunt.

"There are many things to watch for," White Buffalo explained. "Hear how the insects in the trees sing at evening? It is their time."

Small Elk remained quiet, sensing that more was coming.

"The change sometimes comes with rain, sometimes not. The summer wind is from the south. When it begins to change—but look! There is a sign!"

He pointed across a little meadow. Elk saw nothing except some swallows, apparently from nests in a nearby cliff. The birds were swooping low, crisscrossing the meadow, darting after an occasional insect.

"But, I—" Elk began, but his father held up a hand.

"When birds fly low, the weather is about to change. Rain, maybe."

"Why, Father?"

"*Aiee,* Elk, you have asked such things since you were small! Maybe they are hunting insects, and *they* fly low. Yes, *'why?'* I suppose. There is a difference in the air . . . do you not feel it?"

Elk nodded. It was something that could not be described, but it was there. A different *spirit.* The wind, which had been blowing steadily from the south for many days, was now quiet. The air was still and heavy.

"The South Wind," said White Buffalo. "It is resting. A change is coming."

Strange, thought Small Elk. This had been happening each autumn since he was born. No, since Creation maybe. He had never noticed before—well, that the wind usually came from the south. That was a recognized fact and gave the area one of its names. There was even a tribe who called themselves South Wind People. Small Elk had noticed that the wind sometimes changed and that the change often meant rain, but he had not even begun to realize the intricate connection here, the thing his father was teaching him. This change, this time in the late summer, was a signal. At least, it seemed so.

There was a stirring in the air now, a breathlike movement that seemed to come from nowhere and everywhere, and to have no direction. White Buffalo pointed to a distant line of timber to the north. The trees were writhing in the grip of the changing wind, like a great green snake, their tops twisting to show the silvery undersides of the leaves.

"It comes," he said softly. "The changing wind."

He turned back down the ridge toward the camp.

"Come," he said over his shoulder. "I will make the announcement."

Small Elk was puzzled.

"That it will rain?"

"No. They can tell that, and it is coming soon. I will tell them of the buffalo."

"But Father! We saw no buffalo!"

"No. But things are right. All the signs. This is the season. I will dance the Buffalo Dance and bring them."

"But . . . what if they do not come?"

"Ah!" said White Buffalo. "Sometimes they do not, and the dance does not work. Then the People will say someone broke a taboo, or the buffalo are displeased with where we camped—or maybe, even, White Buffalo is getting old, and his medicine is weak."

He paused a moment to catch his breath and continued. "But most of the time, Elk, they will come this way. Then, the People say, 'Aiee! White Buffalo's medicine is strong. He has brought the herds back again!' "

Small Elk was astonished at this revelation.

"Then your medicine does not really? . . ."

"Ah, did I say that? Who knows, my son, why they come. When I see that everything is right, I say, 'the herds may come.' It would be foolish to say that when things are *not* ready. The medicine is strong, but I must help it, by knowing when to use it. Now, I am made to think, is the time to do the Buffalo Dance. Maybe they come, maybe not."

"But more likely than not?" Small Elk persisted.

"Of course. If the herds were more likely *not* to come, I would not try the dance."

"And in the springtime?"

"Ah, you will learn that later. That is a matter of firing the grass at the right time. You have much to learn before then. Come, we must hurry."

They approached the medicine man's lodge, and he called to Dove Woman. She unrolled the bundle and shook out the white buffalo cape with horns attached, the symbol of office. White Buffalo swung it across his shoulders and tied the thongs under his chin and across the chest. He settled the horned headdress portion on his head and nodded to Dove Woman. She began a rhythmic beat on the small dance-drum as White Buffalo picked up his rattles and eagle-fan and began to dance.

Small Elk had watched this ceremony all his life, but now he seemed to see it for the first time.

"Watch the cadence," Dove Woman whispered. "Next time maybe he will let you try it."

People were coming to watch the ceremony, and in the distance came the mutter of Rain Maker's drum in answer to the one held by Dove Woman.

16

The buffalo did come, and the People were loud in praise of the medicine man's skill. Small Elk was mildly confused. He was not certain whether the skills included *causing* the herds to return or skillfully *predicting* the event.

"Does it matter?" his father asked with a quiet smile. "They are here. Either way, it was successful. Maybe both are true."

On one point White Buffalo was absolutely correct. Either way, it was a successful season. After a day of rain, which freshened the prairie and brightened the green of the grasses, the sky cleared to a bright autumn blue. Days were warm, nights cool. On the third day, the scouts spotted the first of a large herd, grazing as they came and moving slowly southward. It was soon enough after the ceremony for White Buffalo to take credit for the herd's appearance. He modestly accepted the praise and the attention that fell to his office and his buffalo medicine. He conducted a ceremony for the hunt, and it too was an outstanding success. White Buffalo was riding high on a crest of prestige.

"Will you use the calfskin to move the herd, Father?" Small Elk asked.

"No, it is not necessary. The buffalo already come where we want them. Anyway, that works better in the spring hunt."

White Buffalo and his apprentice watched this hunt from a low ridge overlooking an isolated meadow. A few animals, some twenty in number, had detached themselves from the main herd and grazed into this meadow. It was formed by a loop of the stream which meandered past, partly enclosing this level spot of choice grass. It was a long bowshot in diameter, making it ideal for the hunters, hidden in the brush, trees, and rocks around the perimeter. Short Bow would loose the first arrow.

This was the first time that Small Elk had had the opportunity to watch a hunt as an observer. He could see the entire sequence unfold. The animals moved, unhurried, into the loop of the stream, past the narrowest part of the opening. Short Bow waited until they were well into the meadow and chose a fat yearling as his quarry. The animal jumped as the arrow struck, staggered a few steps, and stopped, sagging slowly to the ground. The others milled around nervously, now catching the scent of the hunters. Another animal stumbled and fell.

This could go on only a few moments before the herd began to panic and run, but now there were at least three kills. A fourth animal was struggling along, probably with a fatal wound. A hunter, unable to restrain himself further, let out a yell of triumph, and the buffalo started to run. They were deterred on three sides by the creek and its screen of timber; it was by no means a barrier, but by nature the buffalo saw the open plain as their path to safety. They turned to rush back to the plain, where they had come from.

Now came a crucial and dangerous part of the hunt. A few men, the bravest and most daring, would jump out from concealment among the trees to try to turn at least some of the animals back toward the other hunters. Small Elk saw Short Bow leap from behind a clump of willows, flapping a robe and yelling at the top of his lungs. This signaled the others, who seemed to appear like magic to confront the running herd. The leading buffalo paused and shied away from the noise and the threat of danger. Some tried to turn back uncertainly; others dashed ahead toward the blockers, who leapt nimbly out of the way. One man, Elk thought it was Bluejay, was tossed high in the air by a large bull as it thundered to safety. That unusual sight itself seemed to turn back some of the herd.

Now those remaining in the meadow seemed to feel trapped. In a panic, they crashed through the brush and small trees to reach the streambed. There they were met by another rain of arrows from the hidden bowmen as they clattered and splashed across the stream to safety. In a short while it was all over. Dead or dying buffalo were scattered across the meadow. Men poured out of concealment to identify their kills and congratulate each other.

"Come, White Buffalo, make the apology for us," someone called.

The medicine man and his assistant made their way down the hillside. The hunters had already selected the largest bull of the day, and one was busily chopping off the head. Then two men carried the massive trophy aside, placing it in the spot indicated by White Buffalo.

"There," he said, pointing. "The nose to the east."

The head was propped in a more lifelike position with stones, and White Buffalo took a pinch of some powdered plant material from a pouch to sprinkle over it. He sang:

> *We are sorry to kill you, my brother*
> *but your flesh is our life, as the grass is yours.*
> *May your people be numerous and prosper.*

The women were now beginning to straggle over the hill, preparing to start the butchering. They were chattering over the success of the hunt. *"Aiee,* the medicine of White Buffalo is powerful!" Elk heard one say.

As the butchering began, Bluejay came hobbling up. His left arm hung limp, and pain lined his face.

"Ah, Bluejay!" one of the other hunters exclaimed. "You will do anything to avoid the butchering!"

There was general laughter, even as several helped the injured man to lie down and White Buffalo came to help with the broken arm, a mixture of concern and relief that the injury was no worse. The man could have been killed, and fatal injuries were not unusual in such a hunt. That Bluejay's was the only injury and not a life-threatening one was a cause for joy and laughter. An arm would heal. In the importance of things, anyone would prefer a broken arm to being gored in the belly, would he not?

The band moved into winter quarters, choosing a favorite area in the southern portion of their range. There were thickets of scrubby oaks, which would hold their dead leaves for most of the winter, to provide an effective windbreak. The campsite itself was bordered by such a thicket on the north and west, leaving the east ceremonially open to the sun. This location also had a major advantage in that there were no trees to the south for perhaps a hundred paces or more. The rays of Sun Boy's dying winter torch would strike the camp unimpeded. Beyond that open space was the river, clear and swift over white gravel. Their water supply would be convenient and reliable.

Another advantage to this location was the presence of numerous squirrels. In a hard winter, a few of these could make the difference between survival and death. There were also signs of deer in the thickets, drawn by the same acorns that sustained the large population of squirrels. In the dark moons of winter, a change to fresh meat might prove a refreshing diversion. Not that there was any threat of starvation this year; the fall hunt had gone well. *Aiee,* how well! Every lodge had a store of dried meat and pemmican, stored in rawhide packs behind the lodge-linings. Even the arm of Bluejay, the only casualty of the fall hunt, was healing well.

The People utilized the long still days of the Moon of Falling Leaves to prepare their lodges against the onslaught of Cold Maker. Some, whose locations gave more exposure, carried brush and sticks to build a small snow fence directly northwest of their own lodges. Everyone cut and carried armfuls of dry grasses to stuff in the space around the bottom of the lodge. Between the outside cover and the lodge-lining, which hung like a vertical curtain of skins, was a dead space for storage. Supplies would keep well, away from the heated inside of the lodge. But in winter, stuffed with dried grasses, any remaining space became an important part of the winter preparation; it was insulation against Cold Maker's howling winds.

By the first frosts, late in the Moon of Falling Leaves, most of the lodges were ready. Even then, there would be a period of perhaps half a moon of fine open weather, cool at night and pleasantly warm by day, the Second Summer. Some called it Spirit Summer. It was a happy time, a time of excitement but no urgency, a time to enjoy the pungent smells of autumn and rejoice in the beauty of Earth.

Long lines of geese trumpeted their way south, and in the distance, the challenge of the young bull elk resounded across the prairie. It was the rutting time for the deer in the thickets, and the clash and rattle of their antlers in the battle for a harem of does was frequently heard. It was a good time to hunt, the bucks more concerned with rutting than with caution, but few men bothered to hunt. There was enough stored already.

It was discovered that a half-day's travel downstream, there was a village of Growers. This led to an increase in hunting for a short while. Surplus meat and hides could be traded for corn, beans, and dried pumpkins. There was brisk trade for half a moon before Cold Maker put a virtual stop to travel.

During the pleasant time of Spirit Summer, Small Elk worked and studied as never before. It seemed that his father would never finish with the gathering of plants, seeds, and flowers. Bunches and bundles of herbs hung from the lodgepoles to dry, bringing the pungent smells that Elk's memory always associated with autumn. As they gathered the plants, Elk received instruction in identification and habitat.

Once, they spent an entire day lying on the ground, painstakingly scraping and brushing dirt from the roots of a gourd vine. The root was branched and convoluted, and when it was exposed, it was apparent that it could be interpreted as the likeness of a human figure. This, said White Buffalo, was especially good, but even more dangerous.

He explained as he scraped and brushed. This gourd, whose dried fruits were used for rattles and whose root was powerful medicine, was different from many plants. It would die each autumn but come to life again in the spring and so live forever. The silvery blue color of its vine and leaves identified it. The danger in digging the root was accidentally breaking it. That would be very bad medicine. No one but a medicine man would ordinarily even attempt this dig, and even he was in jeopardy. White Buffalo told as he worked of a medicine man who broke such a root and returned to his lodge to find that his son had been bitten by a real-snake. Another had broken a root such as this human-shaped one, destroying one of the legs.

On the way home, he had fallen among the rocks, badly shattering his own leg, which never healed properly.

By this time, Small Elk was having second thoughts about his apprenticeship. His father read his face and chuckled.

"Is the responsibility too heavy?" he asked teasingly.

Small Elk was more serious. "I think not, Father. Are there many who are offered the gift but refuse it?"

White Buffalo wanted to laugh aloud, but saw that his son was serious. "There is no way to know," he answered. "I am made to think that in some generations there are many who are offered the gifts of the spirit, and sometimes only a few."

He scraped a few moments in silence.

"Elk," he said seriously, "if you have doubts, if you want to refuse, it is no disgrace."

Small Elk took a deep breath. "No, Father, it is not that," he said slowly. "I was only wondering if I am worthy of such responsibility."

Ah, thought White Buffalo, pleased beyond measure. What better evidence that this boy *is* worthy? Again, he felt the strong suggestion that Small Elk would somehow become very important to the People. Just how, he was unsure. But there was much to suggest it. Those strange visions at the time of his quest . . .

"Here, Elk," he said, handing him the slender digging tool, "you scrape a little while. But be very careful."

The shadows were growing long when they returned to the lodge, but Small Elk proudly carried the root of the gourd-that-lives-forever. More importantly, the root was unscathed. Small Elk's pride was well justified but was no greater than that of his father. It had been a day well spent.

17

"We have hardly seen you this fall!" Stone Breaker protested.

It was the Moon of Long Nights, when Sun Boy's torch nearly goes out. There had been no extreme weather yet. Cold Maker had blustered and bluffed occasionally, and several times the grasses had been powdered with frost when the sun rose. Once there had been a light dusting of snow, which soon disappeared.

"I have been busy with White Buffalo," Elk explained.

"Yes, we know," Stone Breaker said. "But now, you are here, and welcome to our lodge! Both of you."

It was a chilly overcast day, and White Buffalo had decided that it was a poor day for instruction. Elk was quite willing to take a day's respite from his learning to be with his friends. Such a day was good for socializing. Many of the people were visiting in one another's lodges, smoking, visiting, or gambling with the plum-stones or the stick game. Crow and Small Elk had decided to call on their friends, and were warmly welcomed to Stone Breaker's lodge. Crow Woman was holding the baby, a fat, happy child that Cattail called Little Bear. The name seemed to fit quite well. Crow Woman was thoroughly enjoying cuddling and rocking the infant.

"How motherly she looks!" Cattail teased. "Elk, could you not do something about this?"

Everyone but Small Elk was amused; he knew there was no answer for the present. At that moment the infant, rousing, turned his head and attempted to nurse at the buckskin-covered breast of Crow Woman. Disappointed, he wrinkled his small face and stuck out his tongue in disgust.

"*Aiee!*" shouted Stone Breaker with glee. "He is used to better food than leather!"

"Here, you take him!" Crow Woman handed the child to his mother. "I cannot help him."

Cattail loosened the front of her dress to uncover a breast, and Little Bear began to nuzzle hungrily.

"Your learning goes well, Elk?" asked Stone Breaker.

"Yes, but there is much to learn. Sometimes I think my head cannot hold it all."

Stone Breaker nodded understandingly.

"I think it would be very hard."

Small Elk shrugged. "Maybe. But, I could not do your work."

"Oh, you could." Stone Breaker held up his work-hard hands. "But it takes a long time to grow such calluses. *Aiee,* my blisters were so sore when I started!"

"But now, my friend, I hear people speak very highly of your work."

"Thank you, Elk. What are you working on this winter?"

"Many things. Plants, preparing them for use; also the rituals and dances. When the Moon of Greening comes, I suspect that White Buffalo will have much to show me about the grasses."

"Is that not when the burning takes place?" Stone Breaker asked.

"Yes, but I have not yet learned how to tell when the time is right."

"What if you choose the wrong time?" Cattail asked.

"Maybe the buffalo would not come back."

"Then everyone would starve," suggested Stone Breaker. "What a responsibility!"

"Except for Little Bear," said Crow Woman, pointing at the noisily feeding infant.

Everyone laughed.

"But seriously, Elk," Stone Breaker said, "you are learning the dances and chants?"

"Yes, but what—"

"And your mother beats the cadence, as she does for White Buffalo?"

"Yes. Sometimes I do, for my father."

"Ah, yes! I have a thought. Would it not be well to have your own assistant, to beat your cadence? Someday, Elk, it will be so. Would it not be better to have her learn as you do?"

He pointed to Crow Woman. There was a long silence.

"I . . . I do not think it is done, Stone Breaker. I do not know of a medicine man whose cadence is set by other than his wife or assistant."

"That should be no problem!" insisted Stone Breaker. "She would be a better wife *and* assistant later if she learns now, while you do."

"It sounds good to me," laughed Cattail. "You could be together more!"

It sounded so sensible, so reasonable, that surely there was something wrong with the idea. Finally, the other three teased and cajoled until Small Elk's temper flared.

"All right," he snapped. "I will ask, now!"

He rose and left the lodge. The wind was cold as he crossed the camp to the lodge of his parents. White Buffalo was sitting against his willow backrest, enjoying a smoke.

"*Ah-koh,* my son," he said. "Back so soon?"

Elk nodded, speechless.

"Does it look like snow?" Dove Woman asked.

"Maybe tonight," Elk guessed. "It grows colder."

Cold, however, was hardly the word for the reception that his question brought. White Buffalo stared at his son with an expression of righteous indignation that left a chill hanging in the air.

"Of course not!" he sputtered. "Elk, have I not taught you better?"

"But, Father, if Crow could learn while I do—"

"No," White Buffalo stated positively. "It is not good. Elk, you are not taking this seriously."

There was no use arguing, and Small Elk left the lodge, angry and frustrated. It was not easy to return to his friends' lodge and face the others. He told them very tersely that White Buffalo would not consider such a thing and sat again by the fire. In a little while, the antics of the baby and the bright conversation had lifted his spirits a little.

When Crow Woman rose a little later and left the lodge, no one attached any particular importance to it. She threaded her way among the lodges and slapped on the lodgecover of the medicine man.

"It is Crow Woman," she called. "May I come in?"

Dove Woman lifted the doorskin, and the girl stooped to enter.

"*Ah-koh,* Uncle, Mother," she said. "I wished to tell you, do not be angry with Small Elk. We urged him to ask you about the drum."

Crow Woman was in no way provocative, but she was an exceedingly attractive and straightforward young woman. White Buffalo had to admire her bold approach.

"It is nothing," he smiled. "It is forgotten."

"It is good," Crow Woman said. "Uncle, may I ask a question?"

"Of course, my child. What is it?"

"How did Dove Woman learn the cadence and the beat to accompany the dances?"

If White Buffalo had chanced to look, he might have seen that there was a twinkle in the eye of his wife.

"Why, I taught her," he said proudly.

"Ah, yes, then Elk can teach me."

"No, no, child. This was after our marriage. It is not proper for a woman to be the helper of a medicine man unless they are married."

He appeared suspicious, realizing that something was happening that he did not quite understand.

"It is good!" exclaimed Crow Woman. "He can teach me later."

She paused to think for a moment.

"But, Uncle, I will keep the drum cadence for him for many years. I would hope to be the best help that I am able. Would it not be best for me to learn it directly from you?"

Few men can resist flattery from a beautiful young woman. White Buffalo looked at his prospective daughter-in-law sympathetically.

"Possibly," he agreed, "but that cannot be until you and Elk are married."

Crow Woman gave him a quick hug and jumped to her feet.

"Oh, thank you, Uncle," she said brightly. "We will talk of when."

She vanished through the doorway, and the skin swung back into place. White Buffalo looked at his wife, bewildered.

"What? What was that . . ."

Dove Woman was laughing, her eyes squinting closed until the tears of laughter could scarcely escape from beneath the lids.

"My husband," she was finally able to say, "I think you just gave permission for your apprentice to marry! *Aiee,* she will make a good wife for a holy man!"

She collapsed into laughter again.

Crow Woman and Small Elk, the medicine man's apprentice, were married soon after. They sat together by the fire in the lodge of the girl's parents, and their fathers united them in marriage by placing a robe around the shoulders of the two, making them one. It would have been usual for them to live in the lodge of Crow Woman's parents until they had their own. In this case, however, one of the reasons for marriage at this time was that they could be instructed together in the duties that would be theirs. Crow Woman moved into the lodge of Small Elk's parents, to observe and learn from White Buffalo and Dove Woman. It was not the best arrangement, but it would be temporary.

People immediately began to contribute skins toward the lodge of the newlyweds. There would be no honeymoon, because Cold Maker had descended with a vengeance; it was a hard winter, and it was well that the People had supplies. Even so, they were together. There would be other disadvantages to marriage at this time. Even after they had established their lodge, there would be little time together. When warm weather came, there would still be no honeymoon, for that would be the time for the most demanding part of Small Elk's instruction.

But at least they were together.

Stone Breaker and Cattail were delighted, of course, for the happiness of their friends. The two girls had long conversations about establishing a lodge, the feeding of babies, and the care of husbands. Crow Woman's time was necessarily limited by the fact that she must live up to her part of the instructions. There were times when it seemed to her that White Buffalo was intent on punishing her for her part in contriving the early marriage. But probably, she decided, it was only that the life she had chosen *was* difficult and demanding, one of responsibility. She watched her husband's parents, how Dove Woman was an important part of the medicine man's skills, and reveled in her own learning. There was much of importance in the way a wife could help a medicine man.

By the time they had worked together through the Moon of Snows and the Moon of Hunger, which was not especially hungry this year, even White Buffalo agreed that the marriage had been an excellent idea. By the Moon of Awakening, the medicine man half believed it had been his idea all along. He could never have hoped for a finer assistant for Small Elk than this delightful young woman. She intuitively perceived many things of the spirit and seemed to put them into practice without thinking. In her hands, the dance-drum spoke with authority and meaning. *Aiee,* the world was good. White Buffalo had an apt pupil to carry on his work, and Elk had a wife-assistant second to none.

Now winter was nearly over. Long lines of geese honked their way back north. Here and there, as a snowbank began to melt, small sprigs of green appeared. The upper twigs on the willows began to show a bright yellow color as their buds swelled. Little rivulets of snowmelt trickled and joined together to swell the prairie streams.

It would soon be the Moon of Greening and another great step in the instruction of Small Elk. White Buffalo called his son to him.

"Elk, you have done well so far."

"Thank you, Father."

"No, no, it is nothing. But you are now ready to begin *serious* instruction. So far, it is all just preparation."

Elk did not answer.

"Now, my son, this is where we begin to talk of the medicine of the buffalo. It is like a vision quest, and no one can help you, not even your wife. What you start now is far more dangerous. Not at first, but soon. Are you ready?"

Small Elk paused only a moment.

"Of course, Father."

"Good. Then let us go out on the prairie. The greening has begun, and you have much to learn before the buffalo come."

18

⟷

"There are seven or more kinds of grasses here," White Buffalo said, pointing to the tiny green sprigs among last year's growth. "All are different, though they look much alike now. This one," he knelt to touch the new growth, "is the tall real-grass. At the time of awakening it looks much like the other tall one, the plume-grass, but it does not matter. They, together, give the sign that it is time to burn."

"Is it time, Father?" Elk asked.

"No. Another few days. It should be about this tall." He indicated with thumb and forefinger. "Then we must have a day when the wind is right, both in direction and strength. If we send smoke through the camp, we lose some respect."

"And then the buffalo will come?"

"It is to be hoped for. Usually, it happens. This is all very much intertwined, Elk. The herds are now far to the south, who knows where? Something happens to start them moving north. Maybe nothing but a few warm days, Sun Boy's torch warming again. Probably, they are already moving. Now, we burn the old grass to prepare a good feeding-ground. The new, tender grasses entice them into this area, instead of somewhere else."

"This always brings them?"

"Almost. If the season is bad somewhere else—or good, maybe—they take a different trail. A few always come. But now, let us talk of the calfskin."

Elk had never seen his father actually work a herd with the calfskin. He knew it was one of the most important parts of the medicine man's art, and also one of the most dangerous.

"I have not used this often in the past few seasons," White Buffalo admitted. "It takes agility and quickness, and my bones are old and slow. You have that now. Sometimes it is almost necessary to work the herd in this way. Now, first, you must begin to practice the movements of a calf."

He watched critically while Small Elk, feeling somewhat foolish, stooped to mimic the motion of a buffalo calf.

"You can observe them, and do better, when the herds come," White Buffalo said. "No, a little more stiff-legged. That is better. We will let you wear the skin, and that will help."

The calfskin was a soft-tanned hide, with the wooly, yellowish hair of the young animal still intact. It held none of the sacred medicine of the white cape, but was merely a tool. A very useful tool, it was true.

"I once would wear out a calfskin in a season or two," the medicine man recalled. "It is a good method to handle the herds."

Small Elk continued to practice, away from the camp and under the watchful eye of his father. Never, it seemed, could he do quite well enough to please White Buffalo. He began to resent the discipline. His muscles were sore, his legs aching, from the unnatural position.

"I do not see the importance," he complained to Crow Woman one evening under the stars. "White Buffalo has not even used the calfskin for two or three seasons."

"But he is very wise," the girl reminded him. "There is surely a reason."

At the next instruction session, White Buffalo attempted further explanation. It was as if he had sensed the unrest in his apprentice.

"You do well, Elk," he stated, "but I am made to think that your heart is not in it."

Small Elk started to speak, but his father waved him to silence.

"No matter. More important," White Buffalo continued, "is that the ceremony of the calf helps you to understand the buffalo. You must feel their feelings, get inside their heads. Only then can you move the herds and put the buffalo where you want them."

Small Elk was still in doubt. It seemed to make little sense that it was possible to do without the calfskin ritual, but that his father insisted on it. It seemed unfair that he was required to develop this uncomfortable, tedious, and dangerous skill. He made the mistake of mentioning this one evening after a grueling day. White Buffalo flared in anger.

"When you have been a medicine man for forty winters," he said hotly, "then you will know enough to question this!"

"But Father, I—"

"Enough! There may come a time when your ability with the calfskin ceremony makes the difference whether the whole band lives or starves. Now, we will speak no more of it!"

The day came when White Buffalo declared that it was time for the burning ceremony. There was great excitement. He chose several young men as helpers and stationed them along the edge of a wide expanse of open prairie. A gentle breeze rustled the dried grasses of the winter. In some areas the tough seedstems of the real-grass and plume-grass still stood taller than a man's head. The burn would remove these tough, dry stems to expose succulent new growth.

White Buffalo chanted a prayer of thanks for return of the grass, while Dove Woman kept the cadence on the drum. Then he stooped to place a few carefully protected coals in a clump of curly, pink-colored little-grass. Flames licked upward, and the puff of smoke signaled the waiting helpers to begin. The fires grew like living things, expanding and merging. Soon the appearance was that of a fiery snake, crawling across the low hills, with blackened prairie on one side and the ragged remnants of last season's growth on the other. It was always fascinating to watch, to smell, and to listen to the sounds of the fire. The People did little else that day. In some areas, the breeze fanned flames into a roaring inferno, racing ahead of the advancing line only to die down and fall behind when it encountered an area with less fuel to sustain its advance. In the places where the taller grasses stood in abundance, the crack of the exploding stems was like the popping of corn. Then the flames swept on, leaving blackened prairie that would be lush and green again in a few days.

Night fell, and from any slight rise, the crawling line of flames could still be seen snaking over hills a day's journey away. They would burn out when they encountered a stream too wide to jump or when the next of the frequent spring showers occurred.

"It is good!" declared White Buffalo.

Now, there was only the waiting for the arrival of the herds.

White Buffalo was confident, but when the scouts reported that the first animals had been sighted, it came as a great relief to Small Elk. This season, he had a more personal affinity for the event. However, all things seemed timed perfectly. The grass was lush and green, the buffalo calm and unexcited.

This would not be a big, heavily organized hunt. There was no need to store a large quantity of meat until preparation for the next winter. Besides, the hot season was ahead, and meat does not keep well in hot weather. This was a season to procure some fresh meat, to revel in the life-giving juices of the raw liver, a delicacy enjoyed a bite at a time during the butchering. After the nutritional deprivation of the winter, even with good supplies, there was a craving. There are some things that dried meat and pemmican simply cannot supply.

White Buffalo, after the appropriate ceremonies for the first kill of the season, turned his attention again to Small Elk's instruction. They spent an entire day on a rise near a calmly grazing herd. There were many calves, their yellowish color quite obvious among the darker coats of the older animals.

"It is a good season!" White Buffalo spoke with approval. "A good season for you to learn the calfskin. Now, watch the calves. See, a calf is never far from its mother. But sometimes several will lie down together. One cow watches over them. See, to the left there? The others graze, and then return."

Small Elk nodded.

"Now, watch when they play," White Buffalo continued. "You must make your motions look like theirs. And *think!* Your thoughts must be theirs. Here, put on the skin. Tie it well. Now, practice a little before you go down. Ah, that is good! That little kick, yes!"

Small Elk's heart was beating fast. This was a climactic day, one he had long been preparing for. White Buffalo seemed every bit as tense.

"Remember," he cautioned, "do not place yourself between a cow and her calf. And do not panic. They can smell the fear. Above all, do not try to run."

With his palms sweating, Small Elk made his way toward the herd. He was certain that they would run, but none of the buffalo seemed to notice him. He moved among the first animals, trying to mimic the stiff-legged walk of the young calves. He must think like the buffalo, now, react as they would. He passed near a grazing cow, and she lifted her head to threaten him. For a moment, he felt the grip of fear. The horns—so black and shiny and sharp, the broad forehead so big—*no*, he told himself, *she is not threatening Small Elk. She threatens a calf that is not hers, lest it try to suckle.* In that way, he slipped "inside the head" of the cow. As he had seen the calves do, he made a move toward the cow's flank, pretending to try to nurse. She swung her head again, and he dodged playfully aside to trot on a few steps.

A large bull grazed peacefully, and Elk approached it. Bulls, he had noticed, paid almost no attention to a small calf. Their minds were on other things. Boldly, he approached the huge animal, who continued to crop grass. As he had expected, there was no reaction. As he had seen calves do, he nosed curiously, and actually brushed against the massive shoulder. Then he moved on.

He felt, rather than saw, a calf approach him to play. The creature loped around him, playfully made a make-believe charge at him, and then approached to try the head-pushing game. Trying to behave like a normal calf, he pushed back, but the calf was persistent. Besides, it was stronger than he and had a weight advantage; he was handicapped by his stooped-over stance. He could not stand without revealing his true identity. Finally, in desperation, he slapped the calf boldly across the nose. The startled youngster retreated, and Elk glanced around to look for reactions from other animals. There were none. Apparently the adults had ignored the episode as the play of the young. In retrospect, he realized that it would have been more in character if he had retreated to end the game. But no matter . . . he moved among the herd, with growing confidence now. A cow swung a threatening horn his way, and he stepped aside without a thought.

White Buffalo had advised that the first time or two in the herd, he should merely get the feel. The skill of moving them would come later. For now, he found that despite the uncomfortable position, he was actually beginning to enjoy this experience. It was a spiritual uplift, a feeling of power, to be able to move through a herd of the great animals at will. If he was perceived as a human, he could be in great danger instantly. But the smell of the calfskin, as well as the scent-killing herbs that White Buffalo had rubbed on him, seemed to prevent identification.

He skirted around the edges of the herd, pleased at his success and looking forward to the time when he could advance to the next step, trying to manipulate the herd's movement.

A flash of motion caught his eye on the side *away* from the herd, and he turned curiously. *Aiee!* Here was a thing he had not foreseen. A wolf, one of the gray ghosts that follow the herds, was creeping through the short grass. Always ready to pull down a sick or crippled animal, a straggler or a stray calf, the great wolves were always circling and ready. It took a moment to realize that while the calfskin might fool the buffalo with their poor eyesight, the wolf would perceive it quite differently. Here was a calf which was not quite right, which appeared misshapen, which moved oddly—*aiee,* he had suddenly become the quarry!

It was tempting simply to stand up, jerk the calfskin aside, and flap it at the wolf to drive it away. Surely, it would not attack a man standing upright. But there were some doubts. What effect would this action have on the buffalo? He must do something quickly. The hunter was so close that he could see the glitter of the yellow eyes as it crept forward on its belly. At any moment now, it would make its rush.

Then the idea came. He was pretending to be a calf . . . what would a calf do? There was no time to stop and consider. He raised his head toward the herd and let out a bleat of terror as he began to scramble away.

The effect was, to say the least, startling. At least six or seven cows answered his bleat with a protective motherly call, even as they charged forward. For a moment, Elk was sure he had made a fatal error. Even if he escaped the wolf's rush, he seemed in danger of being trampled by the defensive action. He turned toward the wolf, who now seemed confused. It appeared about to rush at him but seemed to reconsider, then turned to retreat. The cows thundered past Elk on each side, brushing close and kicking up dirt in his face but avoiding injury to him.

The confused wolf barely made its escape, turning on an extra burst of speed to elude the horns of the leading cow. Elk watched it retreat over the hill, tail between its legs. He in turn retreated, before the return of the cows, to rejoin his father on the rise.

"Aiee!" greeted White Buffalo, his eyes bright with excitement. "Elk, you have done well. You will be a great medicine man!"

Small Elk untied the thongs, removed the calfskin, and stood erect, working the stiffness out of his back.

"Thank you, Father!"

It was the greatest compliment his father had ever given him.

"Of course," White Buffalo added as they turned toward home, "you take too many chances."

PART II

THE WINDS
OF CHANGE

19

In later years, it would be referred to as the Year-of-No-Rain. There was no apparent reason, though there were many theories. The older members of the band were only too ready with accusatory explanations, with much clucking of tongues and wagging of heads. No one was certain exactly what taboo had been broken. As far as could be determined, no one had committed such a blatant transgression as eating bear meat. Surely the breaking of personal, private vows would not bring misfortune on the entire band, though that was a possibility.

The greening was not satisfactory. White Buffalo studied the sparse growth day after day, shaking his head and muttering to himself. The People grew restless and complained against the holy man. The prairie burned, though White Buffalo warned that it was not good. It was never determined how the fire started. It may have been from natural causes. It was possible, some pointed out, for sparks from the stones in the grass to ignite the grass. However, that usually occurred only under the trampling hooves of running animals, and there had been few. More commonly, spears of real-fire would ignite the dry prairie grasses, but again, Rain Maker had not come, with or without his spears of real-fire.

There was one frightening theory that Rain Maker was dead and would never come again. This was discussed only in whispers because it was apparent that without rain, the grass would not grow, and the buffalo would have nothing to eat, would disappear. Then the People would die.

Regarding the fires, most people suspected that someone, tired of waiting for the holy man's proclamation, had fired the dead grass on his own. That too was seldom discussed publicly. It was a serious infraction, if true, and the council must decide punishment. It would be far preferable if the rains would come, greening the prairie and restoring the season to normal. That would remove the problem and the council's need to act.

But the rains did not come. Neither did the buffalo. The People were reduced to hunting rabbits and squirrels. They had already made great inroads on the dogs, having eaten far more than would have normally been consumed by the Moon of Growing. There were barely enough dogs left to carry or drag the baggage when the time arrived to move the camp.

There was an increasing mutter of discontent against the medicine men for their inaction. It was tempting to perform the rain ceremony, but White Buffalo was quite definite in his stand: It was not the time to do so.

"Tell me, Elk," he asked his assistant privately, "have you seen any of the signs of rain?"

"No, Father, but maybe . . ."

"Ah, this is one of the hardest things," White Buffalo said sadly, "to wait until the right time. Look, Elk, we burn only when the signs are right?"

"That is true, Father."

"You would not dance the ceremony for the buffalo when there is snow on the ground?"

"Of course not."

"Ah, and we do not dance for rain when there is no chance at all. Our ceremonies must be within possibility, or we fail and lose our respect."

"But, Father, we are losing it now."

"Yes, my son, but when the rains do come, it is restored. If we say now, 'It will not rain,' the People will be angry, but they will know we are right. Then, when times are good again, they will say '*Aiee,* the medicine of White Buffalo is good! He was right about the rain!' "

Small Elk nodded, not totally convinced.

"Our visions," White Buffalo continued, "must tell things as they *are,* not as we wish them to be."

Early in the Moon of Roses, the council decided not to attend the Sun Dance and the Big Council. The Southern band was tired, frustrated, and weak from lack of supplies. It was doubtful that they could make the journey. A runner was sent to take the message to the other bands, and returned in due course, tired and thin. There would be no Sun Dance, he reported. All the bands were in trouble because the drought was widespread. The Mountain band had not been heard from, but it was assumed that they too were experiencing problems. It seemed likely that their solution would be to pull back farther into the mountains instead of coming onto the plain as usual.

Later, many of the People tried to blame the problems of the Year-of-No-Rain on the fact that there was no Sun Dance. That, of course, confused cause and effect. There was no Sun Dance *because* the People were already suffering from the worst season in the memory of the oldest of the band. Still, in later years, the story became confused with the retelling.

There was one puzzling question that was never really resolved. Where had the buffalo gone? If they were not here or in the areas of the other bands, then *where?* Again, fanciful explanations suggested that they had gone back down the hole in the earth, from where they came at the time of Creation.

The Southern band did move, in the Moon of Thunder, though in truth there was no thunder. There was no rain, and the water dried up in the stream on which they were camped. Despite the fact that the People were really too weak to make the move, they must find water or die.

There were several favorite springs in the Sacred Hills, but it was unsure whether they would remain productive in a year that was worse then any other in memory. White Buffalo studied the yearly paintings on the old Story Skins, and found no record of a worse year. He recommended that rather than risk the reliability of the springs, it would be safer to travel in the other direction, a bit farther, to reach one of the larger rivers. Though he said nothing at the time, he confided later to Small Elk that in part, he had considered the possibility that the People could eat fish.

"*Aiee! Fish?*" Small Elk exclaimed.

It was known that some of the tribes who lived along the streams ate fish regularly, but it was not an acceptable thing for the People.

"We may not have to," White Buffalo explained, "but it would be good to be where they can be found. People can eat many strange things if they are starving."

Even the river ran low before the end of the summer. There was much sickness, especially of the stomach and bowels. Thick green scum formed around the edges of stagnant pools as the stream's flow slowed to a trickle. There were many who despaired that times would ever return to normal. For the first time, Small Elk saw the beginning of a change in his father.

The holy man had always been vigorous and cheerful, kind and gentle, though a strict teacher. He had always been noted for his intelligent, quiet good humor and his optimism. When times were hard, White Buffalo could always be counted on to furnish calm reassurance. "Of course things will be better," he always advised. "Has it ever been otherwise?" He was the solid footing on which the Southern band relied for reassurance. That help, and the traditional habit of taking one day's problems at a time, had served the People well for many seasons.

"Of course it will rain again," White Buffalo assured the first serious questioners in the Moon of Thunder, which held no thunder. "It always has."

The Red Moon, always parched and dry, was even more so this year. The muttering and rumor increased, and there were whispers. Even though

Rain Maker might not be dead but only sulking, there was certainly something wrong with the medicine man. Maybe his power was weakening.
White Buffalo seemed tired, discouraged, and unconvincing when he gave
his predictions that Rain Maker would return. Something seemed to be
drawing the strength from his body, and this too became a topic for rumor
and whispered suspicion.

There was a great sense of dread. Already, the People were hungry.
Seldom was there hunger in summer. That was bad enough, but the implications that it carried were terrifying. It was time for the coming of the herds,
time to be preparing and drying the supplies for the winter. Yet there were
none to prepare. The Growers had few crops and none to barter, even if the
People had had meat and skins to offer.

"The Moon of Starvation will come early," someone observed.

"Hush! Do not talk so," an older woman warned.

Small Elk sought out his father to discuss the possibilities.

"Of course it will rain," White Buffalo repeated his long-standing advice.
Now it seemed that he only half believed it himself.

"It will rain," he went on, "but it may be too late."

"What do you mean, Father?"

"Elk, we must say nothing of this. It would cause great alarm. But look at
the lateness of the season. The wind has not changed yet. There is no sign
of rain, and it is late. Soon, Cold Maker brings frost, and there will be no
growth."

Small Elk began to understand. There was presently nothing for the
buffalo to eat, and that was why they had gone elsewhere. The People
longed for the rain that would make the grass grow and bring back the
buffalo, but now . . . The time for growing was becoming short. If there
was no growth, there would still be no grazing for the herds, and they would
not come.

As alarming to Small Elk as this threat was, it was no worse than the
change in his father. In his dejected state, White Buffalo seemed to shrink,
to lose stature, and to become indecisive. His posture, his walk, and his
attitude became hesitant.

Some of the People began to seek out Small Elk for advice and counsel.
Elk was unprepared for this; he was not yet skilled enough in the ways of the
holy man.

"But you *are* skilled," insisted Crow Woman as they talked one night.
"You have studied with White Buffalo for four winters now. Did you not
make the decision when to burn last season?"

Their baby girl stirred restlessly, and Crow Woman rose to pick up the
child and put her to breast.

"I made the decision, that is true," Elk answered. "But, Crow, it was with
his approval."

"Of course. But your choice was right. You always choose as your father
would."

Small Elk was still uneasy. Even after the years of instruction, with Crow Woman by his side, he relied on the thinking, the experience, of the older man. Sometimes he wondered when his status as apprentice would change. Maybe this was how it would happen. The People would gradually come more to Small Elk for their spiritual counsel and less to White Buffalo as the strength of his medicine ebbed with the strength of his body. Elk was not ready to see this happen. He wondered if his father had ever suffered from this sort of insecurity about his medicine.

Elk had gained confidence through the years of instruction, but there was always the knowledge of White Buffalo to sustain him in indecision.

"But you never rely on it," Crow Woman reminded.

"True, but I could if I needed it."

Crow smiled and touched his arm, showing her confidence.

"Ask your spirit-guide," she suggested.

Small Elk was embarrassed. He should have thought to do so before, should have been trying to make that contact. He had been preoccupied with the troubles of the People and with a new baby in the lodge. Three years they had tried without success, while Stone Breaker and Cattail had produced two more children, now three in all.

Elk looked at the sleeping infant, now cuddled in Crow's arms. White Moon they called her, after the full moon which shone at the time of her birth. It had been the Moon of Awakening, just before the onset of the Never-rain season. It had been a happy time, a time of beginnings. The child began to grow and thrive. She was doing so even now, though it was proving a drain on the strength of Crow to nurture the child.

"It is nothing," Crow had said as she adjusted her dress over hip-bones that had become more prominent. "I will be fat when the buffalo come."

His preoccupation with all these things had prevented Elk from seeing the obvious: He should be in touch with his spirit-guide in this season of emergency. Now that Crow had brought the matter to his attention, he wondered why White Buffalo had not mentioned it. Could it be that his father was failing more rapidly than he realized?

The next morning he declined to eat, informing Crow Woman that he would fast for a few days while he attempted to make contact with his guide.

"I will be back," he assured her. "Three, four sleeps, maybe."

He kissed her, cuddled White Moon for a moment, and left the lodge. This would not be as intense a search as his vision quest. He need not remove himself as far from the camp. He carried only a water skin and stopped to fill it at a clear spot in the stream above the camp. There were a couple of women gathering nuts among the trees, and they nodded to him. Normally, the People gathered few nuts, and those only for variety and flavor. This year, every possible source of food was being utilized, even the acorns from the giant oaks along the river. Though they were bitter and inedible, they could be leached in water to remove part of the bitter taste. He waved at the gatherers and moved on up the slope and away from the village.

By noon he had reached the hilltop that he sought and settled down by the symbolic fire that marked his camp. His belly was beginning to protest, and he took a sip of water. The pangs would pass. Now there was nothing to do but wait.

20

The fasting experience was difficult to describe, as always. There were the initial pangs of hunger, but that was a familiar sensation this year. After the first day, his discomfort was forgotten as the brilliant clarity of all the senses began to dominate. It seemed to happen rapidly this time, and Elk wondered about the effect. The People had been virtually fasting from time to time all summer. Did that make it quicker?

One feature of the clarification process that Small Elk now noted was that his thinking became clear. He sat on his hilltop and watched the sun rise over the parched tallgrass prairie with a new understanding. It was almost as if he were a disinterested party, an outside observer with no real contact with the situation. What did it matter, he was now able to wonder. The People lived or died, and if they lived, their descendants would live in the Tallgrass Hills. If they died, someone else would live here. It did not matter. He thought of the Death Song:

The grass and the sky go on forever . . .

He considered chanting the song to himself to indicate his understanding but decided against it. After all, the next line carries a different connotation:

. . . but today is a good day to die . . .

That was a thought he was not prepared to approach. Not yet, at any rate. His purpose was to try to find a way to help his people. Besides, he reminded himself, the Death Song was used only when it had become certain that death was imminent.

He retreated from thoughts of death. He had an increased clarity of understanding about death's place in the scheme of things but must not dwell on it. It was not appropriate now, and he moved his thoughts away from thoughts of death, almost reluctantly.

Little else happened that day. Elk's distant vision seemed improved, and he watched a doe and her fawn in the far distance, so far that he could barely have seen them at all without the clarity of the fasting. They tiptoed along a distant stream, searching for pools which still held water. Another doe joined them. The deer were better off in such a season, he noted, than buffalo. Deer were normally browsers, preferring brushy areas to grass. The buffalo were more dependent on the grasses.

Even so, he noted, the deer he watched now had only one fawn between them. In a good growing year, each of these does might easily have two fawns. How useful is their medicine, he thought, to tell them these things. This year you should have only one, for it is a poor season, or this is a year of plenty, so all deer should have twins. His clarity of thought seemed to make him understand all these things. It was a thrill, an excitement beyond description, to know of these things, part of the plan of Creation, if even for a short time.

He watched the smooth circle of a buzzard, riding on fixed wings high above him—searching, searching. *Ah, my brother,* he thought, *your hunting must be good this year. But do not look at me; it is not my time yet.* As if the bird understood, it suddenly lifted a wing and shot away to the northwest on a puff of air known only to itself. Elk watched it go. Ah, to have such vision and such power to fly high above and see the distances. He recalled his vision quest, its sensation of flight, and all the strange creatures he had seen a few seasons before. That had been odd. He had seen the strange creatures, had dreamed of the turtle-footed one twice more over the ensuing moons, and had then forgotten them. *Aiee,* much had happened. With a sort of surprise, he recalled how vigorous and domineering his father had seemed then. Now the medicine man seemed old and tired. When had it happened? How had he failed to notice?

Small Elk slept that night and dreamed—not the mystical, exotic dreams of his vision quest but real and believable nonetheless. He found himself walking through a herd of buffalo, not in his calfskin disguise, but upright, as a man, and the animals did not react to his presence. He recognized the visionary nature of the dream, because he was inside the heads of the animals, feeling the collective thoughts of the herd. It came to him as a low, comfortable hum, like distant conversation, without individual words. Yet the thoughts were clear, comfortable and comforting. They grazed calmly, and it was good, the way of things as they should be. A calf approached to butt playfully at him, and Small Elk laughed and patted its head.

"Run and play, Little Brother," he murmured quietly. He was aware even as he did so that the youngster perceived his thoughts, though not his words.

Ahead of him loomed a giant bull, and it took Elk only a moment to recognize it.

Ah-koh, Grandfather, he thought at the creature, wordlessly.

The bull raised its head, fixed understanding eyes on him, and stood quietly.

Ah-koh, my son, the thought came quietly back at him.

The large dark eyes shone with intelligence and understanding. And calm . . . Elk had never experienced such a feeling of calm confidence.

Grandfather, he began in the strange, wordless conversation that seemed perfectly reasonable. *We have seen none of your people. It is a season of no rain.*

Yes, that is true, his spirit-guide acknowledged.

Small Elk waited a moment, but there was no further message.

We . . . we will die, unless . . .

Yes, came the answer, before Elk had even finished, *some of you. Some of my people too. But some will live. It is the way of things.*

But . . . but how? What can I do?

The great shaggy head now turned and lowered to crop grass again.

You will know, the thought came as a parting farewell. *Watch for the signs that you know.*

The dream vanished, and Small Elk was awake, standing alone on the top of his hill. He was sweating profusely, and his body was cold in the chill of the night breeze. He picked up his robe and drew it around him. The black of the sky was dotted with an endless number of tiny points of light, like the campfires of a mighty tribe. There was beauty in it, and a calm reassurance. *But what am I supposed to do?* he asked silently. *I have no answer. The children are hungry.*

From somewhere out in the vastness of the dark prairie came a thought, wordless, a mere awareness of an idea.

You will know.

Small Elk was still at a loss, but more confident now. *You will know.* He had received the same thought in two ways, both in the dream and in reality, though he was not always certain which was which.

Now he watched the sun rise and realized that his present mission was finished. He had contacted his spirit-guide and had received a most frustrating answer to his question regarding what he should do: nothing. Nothing but wait. At least he had been assured that he would know when the time came. He picked up his water skin, tossed the robe over his shoulder, and set out for the camp of the Southern band.

* * *

Though it had been chilly when he started, by midmorning the sun's rays were causing sweat to run in rivulets from his face and body. He paused to rest on the top of a low ridge, hoping to catch a stirring of air. The prevailing breeze from the south should be present. Its breath had been hot this season, blistering the skin and sucking moisture from the lips as it dried the whole world of the prairie. But, Elk reasoned, he was wet with sweat, and in the drying, he would cool a little. He faced south, and lifted his sweating face to catch any stirring of the air. But, it was still.

Too still. It took him a little while to realize that. There was a heavy, muggy stillness. What . . . were the signs present? He looked to see how the insect-hunting birds were behaving. No, that was no good. The swallows were gone, having moved south for the winter already, so their flight could not be observed. He looked around again. It was nothing he could identify specifically, but something . . . in the stillness there was expectation. The sky was a brilliant clear blue, beyond all reality. It appeared that he could reach his hand upward and thrust it into the blue of the sky, as one could thrust it into water. He reached but could not touch the brilliance that was there. Still, there was something . . . an air of expectancy. There must be . . . yes, there *was* a change of some sort in the air. And with the expectation of change, should he not dance the ceremonial dances for rain, and . . .

Elk was already tossing the robe aside and reaching for his fire-sticks. He had no drum, but the cadence of the chant would suffice to set the tempo of the dance. He had prepared his tinder and readied the fire-sticks when a thought came to him. White Buffalo had often said that much of the effect of a ceremonial was through the spirits of the observers. Elk had sometimes suspected that part of the task was to impress those observers and increase the prestige of the medicine man. But no matter—there was no question that there was more excitement, more suspense, and emotional uplift where people were gathered together to participate. Was that not the purpose of the gathering of all bands to celebrate the Sun Dance?

Quickly, Elk put away the fire-sticks and picked up his robe and water skin. He glanced at the sky. There was nothing apparent yet, other than the feel of impending change. Yes, he should be able to reach the camp before anything remarkable occurred. He started off at an easy trot, pausing frequently to walk, to rest and conserve his strength. By midday, he jogged into the village and paused at his own lodge to speak to Crow Woman before continuing to the lodge of his parents.

"Father," he called, "it is time. The change is coming, and the buffalo will return."

His mother lifted the doorskin and held it aside for White Buffalo. Elk was startled at his father's appearance. The old medicine man was stooped and bent, and appeared to have aged in the few days they had been apart.

His spirit is dying, thought Elk. *He has given up.*

"Father!" Small Elk began excitedly. "The change is coming! I feel it. We must dance the Rain Dance, and the Dance of the Buffalo!"

"No, my son, it is not time. Look, do you see clouds? Has the wind changed?"

It seemed that White Buffalo considered the conversation at an end. He started to turn away.

"Father!" Small Elk spoke sharply. "You must listen to me. I have fasted, have seen visions, and I am made to feel that it is time!"

There was not the least spark of interest in the old man's eyes.

"No," he said wearily. "It will happen, sometime, maybe. Not now. Go back to your lodge."

Small Elk took a deep breath. He had never defied his father before, but White Buffalo was refusing to listen to his own medicine.

"Father," he said with a voice tight with emotion. "I am going to dance the Rain Dance."

The old man stood, his mouth open in astonishment for a moment. Elk stood transfixed, afraid that his father would challenge his right to do so. A few curious onlookers waited expectantly. Was this to be a clash of the medicines of the two? A contest, to see whose gift had greater strength?

Finally, White Buffalo threw up his hands in resignation. He turned and shuffled feebly into his lodge, jerking the doorskin closed behind him. Small Elk turned to speak to his wife.

"Crow, this is our most important ceremony. Are you ready?"

She nodded. "I have your paints ready. Come, we will prepare you for the dance."

It was quickly done, the face-paint that would honor Rain Maker and draw him closer. The two proceeded to the center of the village, the council area, and Crow Woman began to tap softly on the drum. Elk danced a few tentative steps, and Crow steadied the cadence. The voice of the drum began to speak with authority, and the People began to assemble.

"Small Elk does the Rain Dance!" The excited murmur ran through the crowd. "The Dance for Rain!"

21

When Small Elk began his ceremony, there were many doubters—this despite the fact that there had been grumblings all summer because the medicine men would *not* perform the Dance for Rain. Now there were grumblings that the young apprentice did not know what he was doing.

Word had spread quickly that the two medicine men had quarreled. Or at the very least, there had been a disagreement. It had been a public thing, right in front of the lodge of White Buffalo, and a number of people had seen and heard it. As the story spread, it grew, and the seriousness of the quarrel was exaggerated.

"I thought White Buffalo would strike him," reported one witness.

There was a gasp of disbelief, but before long, the rapidly moving tale related that Small Elk *had* been slapped across the face by his father. This was a very serious breach of custom. To strike another was practically unknown among the People. Such an act would be reserved for, perhaps, a captured enemy. A Head Splitter, for instance, might be subjected to such an act as part of the ridicule and demeaning treatment that he must suffer before he was killed. But to strike one's own son . . . *aiee!* There were those who suggested this as evidence that White Buffalo's mind was gone, that he was insane. Others insisted he could do nothing else in the face of open revolt by his apprentice.

But, countered the other faction, Small Elk has studied the skills of their craft for four, maybe five seasons now. He has the knowledge, the *right* to disagree. The argument became partly a generation- or age-related split, but not entirely. There were young people who supported the authority of White Buffalo and oldsters who supported Small Elk's right to challenge.

There were a substantial number who took neither side but took great glee in observing the clash of power and prestige. There were bets within this group on whose medicine would prove the stronger.

Small Elk was largely unaware of all this as he began the ceremony. He concentrated only on the drum cadence and the song. The sun's rays beat down, and soon sweat was pouring from his body. He was still in his fasting state, not having taken time to eat. Consequently, he was still experiencing a bright clarity of the senses and of the mind. This was a great advantage in the spiritual part of the ceremony. However, it led to a disregard of reality. Elk was largely unaware of the gathering tension in the crowd that quickly assembled to watch the ceremony.

"He does do the steps well," admitted an old woman who had watched a lifetime of Rain Songs.

"Yes, but he has no authority to do so!" snapped her friend who sat beside her.

The ceremony continued. From time to time, Small Elk looked to the heavens. Clear bright blue still pervaded the entire expanse. He would have been discouraged, except that the very brightness held excitement and promise. His energy continued to flow. He finished the cycle of the ceremony once, then repeated it. Crow Woman appeared tired. The physical strain of maintaining the cadence as the afternoon dragged on was wearing at her strength. Additionally, the excitement of the ceremony itself lent added stress, he knew. Cattail was caring for Crow's baby, but . . . he hated to put her through this, but it might mean survival for the desperate band, now heading into winter unprepared. He nodded to her, and the drum cadence began again.

A mutter went through the crowd, a quiet ripple. It was apparent that there was a restlessness. There was a look of triumph beginning to show on the faces of those who had wagered against the success of Small Elk. Some of those not wagering were beginning to change loyalties. After all, had not White Buffalo been a wise leader in things of the spirit? Maybe it was unwise to side with the apprentice in this test of strength.

Small Elk danced on. He was tiring now, beginning to be discouraged. Had he been wrong? Was it only the exhilaration of his fast that had led him mistakenly to expect the wind's change? He began to doubt, to wonder. What would be his father's reaction? Would he now abandon his son? When this was over and Elk had failed, would his father refuse to teach him more, deny the validity of Small Elk's gift?

It was the first that he had thought of failure. Now he realized that success too could drive them apart. White Buffalo might easily hold anger against the son who had shown his medicine to be stronger than his own. But that seemed unlikely now. He was nearing the end of the third repeated cycle of the chant, and nothing had changed. Surely his spirit-guide would not mislead him. There was only one explanation: He had misread the signs. In doing so, he had failed. He had failed his guide, his father's teaching—yes, even his calling.

Elk finished the cadence, and the drum ceased to speak. He stood, swaying, defeated, his defeat like ashes in his mouth. He was exhausted, ready to drop. Three times he had completed the ceremony and . . . nothing.

His paint was dissolving in sweat, running down his face. The crowd shifted a little in embarrassment, and a few people, their eyes averted, began to move away from the scene of failure.

Small Elk's older brother, who had had his own lodge before Elk was born, now approached angrily. They had never been close because of the difference in their ages.

"Let it go, Elk!" the older man hissed. "You dishonor your father."

Elk looked around him for support. No one seemed willing to look at him. Across the circle he encountered the gaze of Stone Breaker. It was a look of friendship, of understanding, and he held and treasured it for a moment. But it was not right. It was a look not of confidence but pity. It promised friendship despite failure, and that was not what Small Elk needed. He needed the support that would come with the belief that he was *right*, faith in his skill and knowledge. He looked to Crow Woman. She sat, tired and discouraged, her hands limp on the skin of the silent drum. But in her eyes shone love and confidence. At least Crow was still with him in spirit.

"Come on, Elk," his brother urged angrily.

Small Elk drew himself up proudly. He looked at the sky, the parched hills, and the trees on the opposite bend of the river a few hundred paces away. Their leaves hung limply in the afternoon heat. He must keep confidence in himself, in his ability to interpret the signs. He focused his eyes on those distant trees, and the wilted leaves seemed to shimmer in the heat. He wiped the sweat away to clear his vision, and looked again. Yes! There—the tired leaves in the tops of the giant sycamores were stirring. A stray puff of wind had put them into shimmering motion. Now it increased, bending the tops of the branches. Small Elk smiled and turned to his brother.

"You must get out of my way, Antelope," he said gently. "I have work to do."

"Look!" someone cried. "The wind changes!"

The cool breeze swept across the open meadow, stirring the seedheads of the grasses. The People watched it come like a flood of water sweeping across the level space toward them.

"The wind has changed!"

"Look! It comes from the northeast!"

There was no hint of rain, but as the breeze swept through the village, there was a feel, a smell, a *spirit* of change. An old woman gave a joyful shout.

Small Elk turned to Crow Woman. She sat, smiling her approval.

"Now is the time," he said softly to her. "Can you beat one more cadence?"

"Of course!"

She did not look so tired now. Elk's blood was racing as Crow began her measured strokes and the drum began to sing with authority. People cheered and danced, and those who had departed began to drift back.

Then there was a sudden silence. Someone pointed with a gasp of amazement. White Buffalo had emerged from his lodge and was standing there, observing the dance. His face was stern, but even the most unobservant among them could not fail to notice one fact. The holy man was wearing his ceremonial paint. A gasp ran through the crowd. Was White Buffalo going to challenge the authority of his son?

He strode over to the council ring, and it seemed to the onlookers that he had grown taller, more sturdy. There was a confidence, a strength, that no one had seen in a long time. He nodded to Crow Woman, whose beat never faltered as she nodded back. Now the old medicine man strode forward and fell into step with his son, dancing the cadences of the Rain Dance.

For a moment Small Elk seemed not to notice. Then he turned and came face-to-face with White Buffalo. Neither broke step, but Small Elk smiled and shook his gourd-rattle high for a moment. His father was more dignified, merely nodding a greeting as they passed.

"All bets are no good!" cried one of the wagerers.

The crowd roared with laughter.

It was during the night that the rain came. Small Elk heard the dull plop of the first fat drops as they struck the lodgeskin. He was already awake, waiting. He had been sleeping the well-earned sleep of exhaustion when the distant mutter of Rain Maker's drum roused him.

"Listen!" said Crow Woman softly. "Do you hear it?"

"Yes," Elk whispered. "My vision . . . it was true!"

"Your heart was good," Crow stated simply, "and you made a good decision."

"I am glad that my father is not still angry."

"Your father is proud, Elk. Did you see how tall he stood as he danced?"

"Maybe so. Crow, it hurt my heart to go against him."

"I know. But you were right, and he knows it too now."

"About the change in the wind," he agreed, "some rain, maybe. But Crow, I do not know if the buffalo will come."

"One thing at a time," said Crow Woman soothingly. "Listen. The rain comes."

At first there was only an occasional drop, plunking on the taut, dry lodgecover, but soon there were more, and then a constant drumming as Rain Maker seemed intent on making up for his summer absence. Real-fire flashed, illuminating the doorway and the smokehole. Then, a few counts later, the boom of the thunder-drum would shake the earth. Elk and Crow Woman snuggled together, reveling in the smell of rain and the storm's cooling effect.

The height of the booming thunderstorm moved on, leaving behind only the rain, a steady quiet patter that lulled the senses, soaking into the thirsty ground. In some seasons a storm of this kind in early autumn would bring the threat of a flash flood, sending the People scrambling to move the camp to higher ground. Not this time. The water would be quickly swallowed up by the great cracks in the earth. They had opened through the hot moons of the summer, widening as the hot winds dried and cracked the prairie. In some areas the yawning fissures were large enough to thrust an arm into or to present a hazard to walking. Now, with the moistening effect of the rain, soon there would be no wounds in Earth's skin to remind them of the dreadful Year-of-No-Rain.

By morning, the main part of the storm had passed. For a little while after daylight, the thinning patter continued. Then there was only the occasional drip of water from the trees. Children ran, shouting and splashing happily in the puddles, while adults spread their belongings to dry. The river was beginning to stir, the small rivulets between stagnant pools widening in a promise of normal flow to come.

As the sun broke through clouds to the east, the medicine men stood on the hill behind the camp, evaluating the scene.

"It is good," pronounced White Buffalo.

At no time did he ever mention their quarrel.

In the glorious feel of this moist autumn morning, it was possible to see the change in the prairie—mostly a change in color. From the stark, sun-baked yellow-brown that had become so familiar, the general tone was now of green. Not the lush green of spring, but a mature green that would soon ripen into the yellows, pinks, and muted reds of autumn grasses. Here and there were autumn flowers, already striving for blooms to re-create before the dying of winter. Their golds and purples had seemed wilted and pointless. Now they blazed in all their glory, heralding the season.

"It is good," White Buffalo repeated.

"Yes," Small Elk agreed.

"Now," White Buffalo continued, "comes the greatest question. Will the buffalo come?"

22

When the scouts reported the approach of buffalo, the People accepted it almost as a foregone conclusion. There was very little surprise, only delight, at the good fortune that had come their way. It was seven days since the rain and the weather change that had broken the drought. Small Elk, in the minds of the Southern band, was responsible. He knew that his major part in the event had been to announce the change, not to cause it. In truth, the People might realize this too. But there was much of the spirit about the medicine man, secrets not revealed to ordinary mortals. This gave him the ability to foresee the future. This time, the young medicine man had boldly announced the coming of rain when there seemed no signs. He had even challenged his teacher. More importantly, he had been right. Small Elk's prestige soared. Quiet discussions among the lodges suggested that possibly White Buffalo was past his prime, that he would soon step aside in favor of the young holy man. Had Small Elk not performed the ceremonies to bring rain? *Aiee,* the Southern band was fortunate to have reared such a man!

By the time the buffalo came, morale was high. There was no longer any question whether the herds would come, only *when.* From hopeless despair to open optimism had been a matter of only a night's rain, a few cool days, and a hint of green on the hills.

There would be no individual hunting, at least at first. In a time when the survival of the entire band would depend on success, no individual had the right to threaten the success of the others. No one would disturb the herd until the council decided that the time was right, based on the advice and counsel of the medicine men. The kill must include enough animals for the entire band.

Small Elk and White Buffalo went out together to view the approaching herd. Since the rain, the older man had undergone a great change. He no longer appeared so weak and frail. Much of his strength had returned with the life-giving moisture that had given a new strength to the world. With White Buffalo's returning confidence, however, was a new respect for his apprentice. He now treated Elk almost as an equal. It may have been, in part, an effort to convince the People that there had been no real quarrel between them, only a professional disagreement. Regardless, the People saw their two medicine men as seers of great skill whose medicine was strong, and it was good.

The two men crouched in a sumac thicket and surveyed the herd. It was half a day's travel away, and at the slow rate at which the grazing animals usually moved, they would not approach for a day or two. One thing was immediately obvious. This was not a great seasonal herd of many thousands.

"There are only a few hundred animals," Small Elk observed.

"Yes, but we had none before," his father reminded him.

They watched for a little while the excruciatingly slow movement of the leading edge of the herd. It was like pouring honey from a gourd on a cold morning, a motion barely perceptible.

"They move in the valleys," Small Elk observed.

"Yes. It will be wetter there, and the grass will be better."

They studied the direction of the buffalo's progress. It would be necessary to surround the herd partially, so that the hunters, all shooting at once, could bring down several animals. Small Elk studied the roll of the land and the herd's movement. This herd, a group which had split off from the main herd during the migration, would move steadily southward. It would reach a suitable place to winter and stop there, much as the People did to establish winter camp.

A long line of geese went honking past high overhead, sounding much like barking dogs in the distance. Elk wondered if they too made a kind of winter camp somewhere far to the south. He turned his attention again to the buffalo, trying to estimate their direction of movement. It would be basically south, with some variation, depending on the gently rolling hills. Tomorrow they would be on an open flat, there to the northwest. It was wide and level, with no places to hide a hunter. Certainly, the grass was not tall enough this season to be a practical concealment. Another day south would bring the herd to rougher country, approaching the river west of the camp.

At that point was an abrupt bluff, a cliff that dropped away from the flat grassland to jumbled rocks below. It was too steep to descend, so the herd would move in one direction or the other to find an easier slope.

They would probably not move in the direction of the village. The scent of man was there. The herd would shift to the west to avoid the precipice. In that direction was rocky broken ground with many hiding-places. Even better, the slight breeze, if it held, was from the northeast, carrying the scent of the hidden hunters away from the herd. It was good, except for a problem or two. The hunters could easily be in position by that time, but the first animals to enter the rocky ravine would be alarmed by the man-scent. They would retreat back into the open prairie and be lost. There should be a way to put the herd where it would be easy to approach and yet ensure that there would be no flight. How to use the man-scent, and yet not cause a stampede . . . or maybe stampede into the ravine, where they would be slowed in their flight, long enough to shoot, and shoot again.

He studied the distant terrain with this in mind. Yes, if the herd was gently moved, by careful use of men showing themselves upwind . . . if they could be made to approach the cliff at about the gray boulder near the rim, and then turned west into the ravine . . . How, he wondered, could they be made to approach the right spot to turn?

"Father," he said suddenly, "do you think the calfskin will work now?"

"Maybe," answered the old man cautiously. "It is better in spring, when there are calves. Why?"

Quickly, Small Elk outlined his idea. His father's eyes widened.

"Aiee! It is very dangerous, Elk."

"Not really, Father. And if it is successful, our kill will be great."

"But if they run in the wrong direction?"

"A few will still have a chance at a shot. Will you help me? Dance the Buffalo Dance?"

White Buffalo paused only a little while.

"Yes," he said simply. "But we must hurry. Come, we will talk to Short Bow and Broken Horn."

It was a busy night. Men, women, and children were kept from sleep to accomplish the tasks that must be ready by daylight. When the sun rose, all was ready, the hunters in position in the ravine. A few men had spent most of the night circling far to the north, to approach the herd from that side. They would show themselves from time to time at a distance, just to remind the buffalo of their presence and keep the animals moving in their generally southern direction.

The day dawned crisp and clear, bright golden sunlight streaking the prairie. Dense plumes of mist rose from the surface of the river below to hang like a furry white robe over the water. The creatures of the day were beginning to stir. An owl, who had stayed out too long, made his way across the grassy flat, pursued by a trio of noisy crows. A great blue heron sailed majestically toward the river and glided out of sight below the bluff. Small Elk had always marveled that a creature so ungainly and awkward-appearing on land could be full of grace and beauty on the wing.

He turned to watch the approaching herd from behind the boulder where he crouched. He carried no weapon but wore the calfskin, firmly tied in place with its thongs. The skin of the animal's head covered his own, and the legs were fastened to his wrists and ankles. Now, as the herd approached, he must concentrate. It was time to get inside the heads of the herd.

He focused his attention on one old cow in the forefront of the advancing animals. She appeared to be the leader, picking out the path. She was nervous, probably from the knowledge of something behind. Yes, now he began to feel the cow's concern. The hunters who had circled behind had shown themselves, and the entire herd was aware and alert, moving a little faster, but not yet alarmed. The leading animals were now approaching the critical point, where the plan would depend on Small Elk's ability to feel their thoughts. At any moment, they should smell the smoke and man-scent from the village. Yes . . . *now!* The wary old lead cow stopped suddenly and raised her head for an instant. Elk knew that she had caught the scent—also that it was not an immediate threat but a matter for caution. Nervously, the cow shifted direction, moving a trifle toward the west and the ravine.

To keep the main body of the herd moving in that direction, the People had spent a good part of the night carrying and placing objects from their lodges in a long line. Several hundred paces the line stretched, from open prairie, angling toward the bluff. It consisted of old robes, rawhide packs, worn-out buckskin garments too useful to discard. Anything long-used that would carry the scent. This assortment of items would not, of course, stop the buffalo. That was not the intent. When they became excited, there would be no stopping the rush. The immediate goal was to shift their direction ever so slightly, to place the herd's leaders precisely at the right point when the moment came.

Now the lead cow and her companions felt better, having angled away from the man-smell. They moved on, into the ever-narrowing trap, even pausing to graze a little. A long bowshot from the cliff's edge, Elk felt a sense of unrest among the leaders. Something was not quite right. They stared southward and sniffed the air, trying to make up for limited eyesight with their keen sense of smell. But the breeze continued to favor Elk's undertaking. What little stirring there was had continued to move from the northeast, pushing the herd almost unconsciously to the southwest, toward the angle where the ravine met the cliff's edge. His main concern was whether they would come close enough.

The lead cow now decided that something was wrong. She circled, snorting nervously, turning back toward the prairie. *No,* Elk thought, *she must not do that!* Tense and sweating, even in the chill autumn air, Elk stepped from behind his boulder and assumed the position of the calf whose skin he now wore. A few steps into the open . . . *now!* He voiced the bleat of a calf in trouble, the tremulous scream for help that would strike to the heart of every mother in the herd. In an instant, a dozen alarmed cows came thundering toward him. It was an alarming thing, seeing that charge and knowing that the edge of the cliff was only a step or two behind him. He bleated in terror again, and the rush came on. He hoped that the hunters in the north end of the ravine understood their part in this scheme.

At the last possible moment, Small Elk dodged out of the path of the thundering animals and took refuge behind his boulder. The confused animals slid to a stop, almost at the rim, and milled uncertainly, unsure at the calf's sudden disappearance. Elk crouched there, wondering what they would do if they discovered him. But the great shaggy heads turned this way and that in confusion. The notoriously poor eyesight of the buffalo was helping him. In addition, his scent was obscured, not only by the herbs he had used to anoint himself but by the cloud of dust raised by pounding hooves.

What was wrong? The moments dragged past. The hunters to the north should have acted by now.

Then he heard it. A chorus of yells in the distance, followed by a low rumble as the herd began to run. Ah, finally! He could visualize the men, jumping from concealment to startle the herd. Shouting, flapping robes, swinging their arms, and rushing forward as if in attack. The buffalo, if they behaved as he expected, would come crowding down upon the ones near the rim. Their course as they ran would be somewhat limited by the man-smell of the carefully placed objects on the east and on the west, by the ravine where bowmen lay hidden. The crushing force of the herd would push down the narrowing course. . . .

The thunder was louder now. The animals that he could see were milling in panic. A few broke away toward the east, but the smells from the camp would soon deter them. Others tried to escape into the broken rocks of the ravine to the west. Elk could see that direction quite clearly. Hunters rose up, yelling and shooting. The animals tried to turn back toward the open prairie but were met by the oncoming rush. There was a crash as the main portion of the herd smashed into those near the cliff's rim. Animals fell, to be trampled into the dust by those coming on. The herd was pushing, thrusting, running in panic. Elk saw the first cow, helplessly struggling, go over the edge. Another balanced for a moment, scrambling to survive, then toppled and fell. Yet another, and then the full force of the rush came, dozens of them, realizing their doom at the last moment but pushed by the relentless thrust from behind. It was like a gigantic brown waterfall, with death waiting at the bottom.

Then, suddenly, it was over. The survivors split into smaller groups and broke away, east or west, it did not matter now. People were rushing forward, laughing and cheering the success of the hunt. From the direction of the village, women and children began to straggle out to begin butchering and preparing the meat.

Small Elk stood up and began to untie the thongs of the calfskin. It was over. Finally, the drought and the threat of famine were at an end.

23

The thunder died, to be replaced by shouts of joy and cheers of triumph. But there was to be mourning too.

"Where is Antelope? I cannot find him!"

"He was in the ravine. Otter, did you see him?"

"There he is! What about those on the north end?"

"They are safe."

Confusing reports and rumors flew back and forth as relatives searched for missing hunters in the aftermath of the carnage. The men from the north end came straggling in. The scattered survivors of the herd, they reported, had fled out into the prairie where they were grouping together again. Barking Fox was dead, tossed and gored by an aggressive cow in her escape. The family of Fox began the Song of Mourning as they started out to retrieve the body. Short Bow went with the mourners to show them the way.

The task of skinning had already begun when Cat Woman, wife of the Southern band's leader, began to inquire as to his whereabouts. She had at first supposed him to be assisting others who might be in need of help.

"Small Elk, have you seen Broken Horn?" she inquired.

"Of course, Mother, he was directly opposite me, where the ravine meets the cliff, there."

"I mean now, since the rush of the herd."

"I . . . I am not sure. Maybe . . . come, we will ask Black Bear. He was on that side."

". . . not since the herd went over," Bear admitted. "He was on my left, and I saw him stand to shoot."

"*Aiee,* Broken Horn is too old to do these things," his worried spouse fretted. "He thinks he has to show the young men."

"He has shown us much, Mother," Black Bear said. "He gives us of his strength."

"He is a good leader," added Small Elk.

The two young men were still with Cat Woman when a wail of anguish came from below the cliff. The first of the People had made their way down to evaluate the extent of the kill.

Small Elk stepped to the edge and peered cautiously below. He could see a jumble of brown bodies. A few animals that had survived the fall were crippling away, and a few hunters pursued to finish them. Elk could not see the area from which the wailing came. There were trees that obscured the view of that sector, where the ravine opened below.

"What is it?" he called, dreading the answer.

"Broken Horn!" came the reply. "He is dead. He went over the edge with the buffalo!"

At Small Elk's elbow, Cat Woman gave a long shriek of grief and began to chant the mournful cadence of the Song of Mourning. She had feared the worst, and her fears had proved true.

The immediate family of Broken Horn quickly received the ill tidings, and began to chant the Mourning Song. Others joined in, for Broken Horn had been a good leader for a long time and would be missed. Close friends assisted in the retrieval of the body, and the traditional mourning continued.

But life goes on. Even as the mourners paused for their sad tasks, others began to skin and butcher the buffalo kill. The immensity of the food supply that had come to the People was beyond imagination. It was apparent that some of the meat would be wasted, even with the cooperation of every pair of hands, down to those of the smallest child. However, it was important to salvage as much as possible. Any dried meat, pemmican, and robes not immediately needed for the winter could be traded to the Growers for corn, beans, and pumpkins.

The work was beginning. Those most adept at skinning assisted others by slitting the hides up the belly and down the inside of each leg. Then the removal progressed, and the fresh skins were spread, flesh-side-up, on the ground. As meat was removed from the carcass it was piled on a skin to be transported, as time permitted, back to the village. In anticipation of a feast, some of the men hacked out chunks from the humps of some of the choicest animals. Fresh, crisply broiled hump-ribs, with their extra layer of flavorful suet, would be a treat that the People had not enjoyed for many moons.

"Small Elk!" someone called. "Over here. We need you to make the apology!"

Three men stood waiting with the severed head of the largest bull. This would be an important ceremony, the most important for generations, for this hunt had provided the kill that would enable the Southern band to survive. Small Elk walked over to the three.

"White Buffalo should do this," he explained. "I am only his assistant."

"We asked him," said Black Bear. "He said to find you, that your skill made the big kill possible."

"Is this true?" Elk asked the others. "White Buffalo said this?"

"Yes, of course, Elk. We would not say untruth about such a thing."

Elk stood for a moment in stunned astonishment. It was the greatest honor his father had ever granted him. He would have gone to White Buffalo to talk to him, but time was passing. The ceremony must be completed, and the hard work of preparing the meat must go on.

"It is good," said Small Elk. "Bring it over here."

There were those who said that this was the beginning of a new era in the history of the People, when Small Elk made the apology for this hunt. Others said no, it was at the dance ceremony later, and still others recalled the election of the new chief. But all agreed that this occasion, the most successful hunt at the end of the worst season in memory, was an important time. Small Elk faced the buffalo head, while those nearby watched reverently.

> *We are sorry, my brother, to take your*
> *lives, but upon yours, ours depend. . . .*

Even as the People worked, the smell of roasting hump-ribs began to drift across the area. Several fires were kept burning downwind of the butchering. Someone would pause in his or her task, step to a fire, and cut a piece of meat to chew, even while the work continued.

Necessarily, much of the heavier skinning and rolling of the carcasses was done by the men. Some of the men withdrew and stationed themselves as lookouts as soon as possible. There was every possibility that any Head Splitters in the area would also be aware of the presence of buffalo. This was no time to be attacked, when the winter's food supply depended on the tasks at hand.

As meat became available, women began the jerking of strips of muscle, to strip them away from the larger joints. These were sliced thinly and draped over willow racks to dry. Children were stationed with leafy branches to shoo away flies and an occasional enterprising bird.

The festoons of drying meat grew as the carcasses shrank to piles of stripped bones, but it was apparent that the hard work of salvaging the meat would go on. Before midday, most of the better-quality animals had been selected, bled, and gutted. Even the pile at the bottom of the cliff had, for the most part, been pulled apart and sorted for quality. A few animals had fallen into inaccessible places, in crevices or among the rocks. Some were in the water, in places too shallow to float but too deep to work in. These were abandoned as unsalvageable, at least for the present. One yearling cow hung grotesquely in the crotch of a tree above the stream. The unnatural posture suggested that it had died in the fall, probably from a broken neck or back.

Some of the People worked on by the light of the fires. Others slept for a little while, to rise and begin again. Out in the darkness, beyond the circle of the firelight, coyotes quarreled over the leavings of some of the butchered carcasses.

"Little Brother wants his share," a woman joked as she worked.

"Maybe he would come and help us," her friend suggested, laughing.

"Not likely. He is good at sharing the kills of others."

"Are not we all in time of hunger? *Aiee,* whose kill *is* this?"

She pointed to the fat cow they were butchering. Both laughed.

"You are right," the other agreed, turning to call into the darkness. "You are welcome, Little Brother. Take all you need, for we have plenty. We are fortunate this night."

She paused, and there was a chuckling chorus from the unseen guests in the darkness.

"Their cries sound like laughter," observed one of the women, who was heavy with child. "It is pleasant to hear. Maybe I will call my child that."

"What? 'One-Who-Laughs'?"

"No! 'The Coyote.' He is clever and cunning. Already, he runs a lot."

She pointed ruefully to her swollen belly, and the others laughed.

"Aiee, he will be hard to catch when he comes outside!" one suggested.

"No, I think not," said the expectant mother seriously. "He moves much, but quietly. He would rather not run if he can walk. So, I think he knows much, and saves his strength. Like the coyote."

"Does he also laugh, like the voices out there?"

The others laughed.

"I have not heard him yet," admitted the swollen one, "but I think he will!"

The work continued. There was good reason to hurry the preparation of their winter supplies. In only a few days, all the meat not processed would spoil. It was dangerous to eat tainted meat. Only two winters ago, a young hunter of the People had eaten a few bites from a dead elk that he found and had died before Sun Boy's appearance the next day.

Aside from that easily avoided danger, there were other problems. The buffalo killed in the fall from the cliff were upstream from the village. Their water supply would soon be fouled by the rotting carcasses, and a move would be necessary.

In addition to that, the nuisance of flies and the odor of rotting flesh would soon become intolerable. Already the sickly-sweet odor of blood and death was beginning to be noted. It was good that the nights were cool now, to retard the decay.

By the third day of hard work, it was decided to hold a celebration. The event that had been the turning point in the survival or death of the Southern band must be commemorated. The period of mourning for the dead would be past. There had indeed been mourning, despite the other demands. The songs had been sung, the bodies carefully wrapped in fresh buffalo-skins and placed in tree scaffolds. Cat Woman had mourned her husband by slashing her forearms and tossing handfuls of ashes on her head. Broken Horn had been a good leader.

Along with the ceremonial festivities, at some point the council would meet to select the new chief. There was, of course, much speculation. Some scurried around, promoting favorite candidates, but no clear choice had yet emerged. It should be one who had exhibited leadership qualities. Some men who had achieved a high degree of respect in the band were still not eligible for consideration. Small Elk was riding high on a swell of popularity because of the success of the buffalo hunt. But his area of expertise and knowledge, his priestly function, held a place of its own. The situation was much the same with Stone Breaker. Popular and successful, still his skills were not those of leadership, even without the handicap of his crippled leg.

A strong swell of opinion favored Short Bow, and this movement seemed to grow. He was renowned as a leader of the hunt. Short Bow was quiet and reliable, and had helped many youngsters perfect their skills through his teaching in the Rabbit Society. That alone would carry the weight of many votes.

Soon it appeared a foregone conclusion. Short Bow had few detractors. However, no one had consulted Short Bow. When someone finally mentioned the possibility to the candidate, he was astonished.

"No!" he said firmly.

"But you are a respected leader," his friend pleaded.

"In the hunt, yes. But not in politics. Besides, I am too old. There are many young men."

"But who? None stands above the others."

"*Aiee,* I cannot choose one. That is the task of the Warrior Society."

His gaze fell on a popular young man who sat a little distance away, avidly devouring a slab of broiled ribs. His ability to eat was legendary. It seemed to require huge quantities to fill this young hunter's large frame. It had earned him a nickname which by this time had become permanent.

"What about Hump Ribs, there?" asked Short Bow. "None other is more capable at the hunt. He is respected by all. He would be a good leader."

"*Aiee,* maybe so," commented another, chuckling. "None is more skilled at eating, either."

In this way, almost by accident, the ground swell of opinion began to settle on this candidate. Mention of his name brought a smile, and there were none who had a bad thing to say. By the time of the meeting, most of the People were convinced that there was very little doubt. The new chief of the Southern band would quite likely be the likable young man with the voracious appetite, Hump Ribs.

24

As expected, the selection of a new leader for the Southern band was quickly accomplished. There was simply no opposition to the elevation of young Hump Ribs to the position. It was one of those fortuitous situations which seems so obvious once it has been accomplished. Everyone realized how appropriate the new leader was in this position and wondered that it had not been recognized earlier. Of course, there were those who claimed to have said so all along.

The new chief, quiet and mild-mannered, could be criticized by no one. He had simply never aroused any animosity in anyone. One possible danger, that he would not lend firm leadership, was quickly dispelled. The first public act of Chief Hump Ribs was to announce the day of departure, three days hence. Wise heads nodded. It was a good decision and met with the approval of the council. Some would grumble, feeling that there was not enough time to finish preparation of the bountiful provisions that had fallen to them. Most, however, realized that the move was urgent. There were an increasing number of flies, invading the lodges and clinging sleepily to the inside of the lodgecovers in the chill of the autumn nights.

The odor of rotting flesh was also becoming objectionable. Yes, it was time to move to winter camp, and the first pronouncement of the new leader was a good one.

Small Elk was pleased. Hump Ribs was a year or two younger than he but of the same generation. It was a bit startling to realize that the power and prestige of leadership was passing to this generation, but it was good. Elk resolved to seek out the new chief and offer him congratulation and support, but the evening was too busy and exciting at the moment. Fires were lighted, and the drums began to sound in preparation for the dance.

There is something in the beat of the drum that stirs a primeval spirit in the heart of mankind. It may be a racial memory of the pounding of the surf on beaches where life-forms that became our ancestors first crawled onto the land and breathed air. Or perhaps the echo of the beating mother-heart that sustained us in the womb. Maybe, even, the reassurance of the pulsing throb of the living planet that sustains all life. In answer to its rhythms, our feet become restless, our bodies begin to respond to the cadence of the drum. The pulse quickens. We find ourselves answering to the urge to join in the magnificent celebration of Creation, of Life.

In this case, the occasion was one of thanksgiving for the events that had provided survival. First, young men draped in buffalo robes enacted the role of the herd, moving slowly, swaying, mimicking the grazing motion of the animals. Then other dancers joined, reenacting their own parts in the drama, reliving deeds of valor. The dancers who represented the herd were crowded to one side of the arena and finally began to collapse. The front ranks first, simulating the spectacular rush of the buffalo over the rim of the cliff. Excitement reached a fever pitch, the drum cadence quickened, and more dancers joined in. The buffalo dancers cast aside their costumes and rejoined the others, now no longer buffalo but participants in the joyful thanksgiving.

The dance continued until everyone was near exhaustion. But there was yet one more event to occur, one unique not only to the People but to this band. The Southern band, more specifically its medicine man, was custodian of the White Robe. It had been handed down for generations. The exact story of its acquisition was by now indistinct with antiquity. It was known that a young medicine man of long ago had returned from a special fast carrying a magnificent buffalo-skin of pure white. He had tanned and prepared it as a ceremonial robe, complete with the horned headress that was part of the cape. The medicine man had, at the same time, taken the name White Buffalo. This name had been handed down through the generations, the cape with it.

There was thought to be something supernatural about the cape. Around the story-fires, its origin had been told and retold, and had grown with the telling. It was popularly believed that the original White Buffalo had received it as a direct gift from heaven. Small Elk had once studied the story-skins to find out, but without success. The first record was a pictograph of many winters past. A man stood holding a white robe up to heaven. Nothing more, except this consecration.

Through the other pictographs, there was an occasional indication of someone with the White Buffalo name. That was handled differently. The figure of a man or woman would be depicted in whatever action was worthy of entry into the story-skin. The name was indicated by a small picture in a circle above, connected to the figure by a line. It was difficult to tell one generation from another in the story-skins. The White Buffalo name appeared, but there was no way to tell when it had been handed down. Small Elk had been frustrated, and his father had chuckled to himself in amusement.

The big dance-drum was quiet now, after the reenactment. Dove Woman began a slow, solemn cadence on the smaller medicine-drum, and the crowd quieted. Small Elk, who had been dancing with the others, now seated himself to watch the medicine dance of White Buffalo.

As the old man danced into the circle of firelight, the crowd parted to admit him to the arena. The change in the holy man was apparent immediately. A moon ago he had appeared old, feeble, and small. He was beaten, by the years and the Never-Rain summer. This did not appear to be the same man. He looked taller, confident, radiating his priestly authority. The white cape was as impressive as always as it swung and fluttered in the motion of White Buffalo's medicine dance. Onlookers were spellbound with the beauty of the ceremony.

Three times, White Buffalo circled the arena, his steps quick and precise, while the People watched in fascination. At the finale, he stopped, facing the fire, while the drum fluttered to a climactic rumble. White Buffalo lifted his arms to heaven and chanted thanks for the bountiful hunt.

Then the old medicine man did a thing which had never been seen before by anyone present. As the medicine-drum fell silent, White Buffalo called to his apprentice.

"Small Elk, come!"

Surprised, Elk scrambled to his feet and approached his father.

"Let it be known," the old man announced to the assembly, "that the success of this hunt was due to the medicine of Small Elk."

There was a murmur of approval.

"He has learned well," White Buffalo continued. "His medicine, that of the buffalo, has become strong and sure. His time has come."

There was a gasp as White Buffalo loosened the thongs at his throat and removed the headdress. With a dramatic flourish, he swung the cape and headdress and allowed it to fall across Small Elk's head and shoulders.

"My son, I give you my name," he intoned solemnly. "You are no longer Small Elk, but White Buffalo, medicine man to the People."

Elk stood numbly, caught completely by surprise. In his ears echoed the shouts of approval from the crowd. He was dimly aware that his mother's medicine-drum was beginning the cadence again. He turned to look, and Crow Woman was seated beside her, joining with her own drum in the celebration of the rite of passing the authority. Crow smiled at him, and he wondered if she had known.

"Let us begin the dance," his father said. The weathered old face was serious, but there was a gleam of pride and triumph in the medicine man's eyes.

Small Elk, now White Buffalo the Younger, moved out in the steps of the White Buffalo ceremony. It was a time of mixed feelings. For years, he had worked and studied toward this night, and it had come as a surprise. Now, with the handing down of the name and the office, he was perhaps the most influential medicine man in the entire tribe. It was the greatest triumph of his life, and it was a bittersweet accomplishment. For to achieve this honor, it was necessary that his father step down. It was a little frightening. Always before, he could refer to the older man's knowledge and skill with any question or problem. It would still be possible, of course, but now, he, Small . . . no, White Buffalo, would be the final authority. There was a moment of panic as he wondered whether he really wanted this responsibility.

On around the circle he danced, now followed by his father. Past the two most important women in his life, as they kept his cadence on the medicine-drums. The faces of Dove Woman and Crow beamed with pride.

He spotted his boyhood friend, Stone Breaker, who waved proudly. They had come a long way since the day of the Head Splitter attack, when the boy fell from the cliff. And Hump Ribs, the new chief of the band. The young leader nodded as he passed, and Elk nodded in return. He would go tomorrow to pay his respects. The two young men would be working together for many years, it was to be hoped, and they must understand each other.

Slowly, he began to realize that this was a turning point in the future of the Southern band, a changing of the generations. Stone Breaker had already assumed his place in the new way of things. Now, in one night, the People had not only accepted a new band chief but a new holy man.

It was a time of triumph and looking to the future, but a time of sadness also. Things would never again be the same for the Southern band. Tears of emotion formed in the eyes of the young White Buffalo. He felt one trickle down his cheek and hoped that it would not be too apparent a streak in his facepaint.

25

$\longleftrightarrow$

With the great success of the buffalo kill that fall came a change in the fortunes of the Southern band. Hump Ribs proved an able leader. By the time the band was ready to strike the lodges and move to winter camp, he had announced their destination. They would move almost directly south through the Tallgrass Hills, to camp on one of the clear streams in the region where the grassland meets the oaks. There the climate would be milder through the moons of winter. They could also camp among the scrub-oak thickets, which would cut the bite of Cold Maker's icy breath.

The new chief's confidence was a thing of wonder to some. It was as if he had been planning for most of his life what he would do if he ever became the band's leader. The transition was accomplished far more smoothly than anyone could have foreseen, and without offense to any as far as could be seen. Of course, it is difficult to find fault when one is comfortable, well provisioned, and full-bellied, as the Southern band was.

Hump Ribs guided his band by a route past a village of Growers. They had traded there before. It was a great pleasure to have plenty of meat, pemmican, and robes to trade. Though the Growers had suffered from the poor season, they had an adequate crop of pumpkins and some corn. The

People spent a few days there and moved on toward the oaks country. Weather continued to favor them. This was considered a good omen, and the new leader's prestige increased.

Small Elk, now White Buffalo, had paid a courtesy call on the morning after the celebration. He offered his help to Hump Ribs and congratulations on his selection as chief. Hump Ribs modestly stated that he would welcome the help of the new holy man.

"I am pleased for you, too, Elk . . . or White Buffalo. It was a good plan, yours of the hunt. The Moon of Hunger will not be so bad this year."

"I was fortunate," the other answered. "It could have gone badly."

"Ah, but it did not, my friend. Your medicine is good, and you are skillful with it. I welcome your help. You will tell me, if you have things I should know?"

"Of course."

They had not known each other well before but were already developing a mutual respect that would stand them in good stead in the years ahead.

The band did winter well. There were few problems and very little of the winter sickness that usually came with Cold Maker's onslaught. One exception was White Buffalo the Elder. After giving his name away, it seemed that he also gave away his ambition. He was not as he had been earlier, during the deadly drought. Then he had seemed to shrink from lack of hope. Now it was as if he had completed a task. He was pleased and satisfied, and ready to relax with the pleasantries of a nap in the sun, a smoke with friends, and play with his granddaughter. He gave his son advice when asked but offered very little otherwise.

"I fear for him," White Buffalo the Younger told his wife. "He has decided that his life is over."

"Maybe," Crow agreed, "but he seems happy. His thoughts are good."

The old man continued to seem at peace with his world and pleased to give his responsibilities to others. They did not notice further deterioration as they had in the summer, but in the Moon of Long Nights, White Buffalo the Elder died quietly in his sleep. His passing was mourned by the entire band, for his medicine had been good. His burial scaffold was placed in a thicket of scrub oak, his head to the east, and his feet toward the grassland to the west, where the buffalo would pass in their spring migration.

"His work was finished," Dove Woman said simply, after the period of mourning. "He knew it was time to cross over."

There were many who admired the old medicine man's ability to do so. Not everyone is so fortunate as to choose the time of one's crossing.

When White Buffalo unrolled the story-skin to record the events of the year, he was surprised to find new pictographs already there. In his father's familiar style, hordes of buffalo poured over the cliff like a waterfall. Standing over them was the figure of a man clad in a calfskin, his arms raised to heaven. It was with something of a shock that he saw the identity mark, a white buffalo in a circle, connected to the figure. Tears came to his eyes. His father had realized the reluctance that young White Buffalo would have to depict himself in this, the first pictograph of his new office. The old man had done it for him, and in a very flattering way.

"What is it, my husband?" Crow Woman asked.

Wordlessly, he turned the skin to show her the picture. She smiled, then came to sit by him and leaned her shoulder against his.

"His gift to you," she said. "Your father knew that you would not paint such a picture of yourself."

Slowly, White Buffalo rerolled the skin, wrapped it, and tied the bundle. Once more, he realized how deeply perceptive his father had been. It was, somehow, like a message of comfort from the Other Side.

Dove Woman moved into the lodge of White Buffalo and Crow.

"I do not wish to be a burden," she told her son's wife. "This is your lodge."

"Remember, Mother, I lived in your lodge at first, and you helped me much. I am proud to have you here."

It was noted that Dove Woman and her husband had always been extremely devoted and close. She had been like a partner in her husband's medicine. From time to time, he had seemed to confer part of his gift on Dove Woman, and she had performed many of the routine ceremonials. She was held in high regard in her own right. Now she seemed to have no direction. She was quiet and smiling, at peace with the world though obviously lonely. Early in the Moon of Awakening, she crossed over to rejoin her husband.

All of these events served to mark the beginning of a new era for the Southern band of the People. Supplies had been more than sufficient for the winter, but the taste for dried meat, even pemmican, becomes jaded. There comes a craving for fresh meat, the flow of the life-giving juices that will nourish both body and soul.

There was another urge, less well defined. The wild geese still feel it today, the restless call that stirs in the subconscious, an instinct that tells them, "Go north . . . *now!*" The quiet echo of this primitive migration urge still sounds in the souls of men and women today. We may stand on a hill in the pale sun of late March or early April, and watch the long lines of geese high overhead. Their distant call seems to reach out in harmony with the human instinct, calling, tempting us to come, follow the trail of the geese to the north, to the unknown adventure and excitement of the new season.

It was so that year, in the Moon of Greening, when Hump Ribs and White Buffalo stood on the hilltop and watched the sky, dotted with the graceful figures of the great birds—moving, shifting in ever-changing patterns against the blue but always moving north.

"Are the signs good?" Hump Ribs asked.

"For the move? Any time now," the medicine man answered.

"Then we move. We are a people of the grasslands. We should greet the return of the sun and the grass in the prairie, not here in the brushland."

There was a sense of excitement in the air, a spirit of expectation, as the band broke winter camp to start north. The start was early, but Hump Ribs wished to leave the scrub-oak country and range out into the grassland in expectation of the buffalo herds. The move would also allow them to cover part of the distance to the site of the Sun Dance.

The Real-chief, Spotted Elk of the Northern band, had sent word that the Sun Dance would be held at Walnut Creek. That site had been selected but not used last season, in that terrible Year-of-No-Rain. The runner also said that the other bands had survived. Hardest hit was the Red Rocks band, which had suffered heavy losses from starvation in the Moon of Hunger. A number of the old members of that band had walked out into the teeth of a blizzard during the Moon of Snows. They had gone, singing the Death Song, as warriors into a hopeless battle. They fought Cold Maker to the death for the lives of the children. In this way, there had been enough food, though just barely, to keep the Red Rocks alive until spring.

In the autumn, the Southern band had reported their good fortune in the hunt and the loss of their chief. Now, they sent word by Spotted Elk's runner that they had wintered well and were en route to the Sun Dance and Big Council.

"We will stop to hunt, of course," Hump Ribs explained, "but we will be partway there."

The messenger laughed.

"You like the shelter of the scrub oak, but you miss the tallgrass prairie."

"Of course," Hump Ribs agreed. "That is why we wintered there."

Their leisurely migration continued. Each day, White Buffalo went out to read the progress of the greening. Small sprigs of grass were beginning to sprout among the dead stems of last year's disastrously short growth. He realized that as they traveled, the greening was moving north with them and at almost the same rate. There was little difference in the height of the sprigs of real-grass now, compared to that at the start of their journey. They would be able to choose the area of the spring hunt, *then* burn the grass and await the herds.

One bright spring morning as the band traveled, White Buffalo went out with one of the "wolves" to look for his signs of the season. It was an area of rolling hills, and they were out of sight of the moving column. The medicine man was kneeling to examine more closely a plant that was unfamiliar to him when he heard a startled exclamation from Woodpecker. He straightened to see three well-armed strangers only a short bowshot away. Their dress, hairstyle, and weapons marked them as Head Splitters.

White Buffalo had no weapon except for a knife, and the scout, though appropriately armed, was badly outnumbered. Nervously, he fitted an arrow to his bowstring. The enemy warriors seemed suspicious but approached in a circling fashion that gave a hint where their main party might be.

"Shall we fight or run?" young Woodpecker asked.

"Neither," suggested White Buffalo. "These are their wolves. They do not know where our party is, either. Let us talk to them."

He made the sign of peace, right hand upraised with palm forward. The strangers seemed to relax a trifle, and one made the same signal in answer. They came a few steps closer, weapons still ready.

"Who are you?" the one who seemed to be the leader signed.

"I am White Buffalo, medicine man of the People."

There was a hurried conversation among the Head Splitters. The power of a strange holy man was not to be trusted and might be dangerous, but the strangers apparently wondered if White Buffalo spoke truth.

"We do not believe you," one signaled. "A medicine man would not be so stupid to be alone and unarmed, with only that one for protection."

He pointed derisively at the sweating Woodpecker.

White Buffalo was thinking rapidly. Why not take advantage of the other's doubt? He laughed aloud.

"You are the stupid one," he signed, while Woodpecker gave a little gasp of despair. "My medicine is strong enough to protect us. Would I dare be here otherwise?"

There was another discussion.

"You lie!" the Head Splitter accused.

White Buffalo laughed again, hoping he did not sound as nervous as he felt. Slowly, he reached a hand into the medicine pouch at his waist.

"Shall I show you?" he asked.

"No! It will not be necessary," the other replied quickly.

White Buffalo withdrew his hand from the pouch, empty. Now there was a slight exclamation of surprise from Woodpecker. Over the rise behind the Head Splitters strode a determined-looking warrior, then another. A couple of dogs ranged around them, sniffing curiously at new smells. Then came two women, leading a large dog that was harnessed to a poledrag. Immediately behind them straggled other people, dogs, and children. It was the main party of a traveling Head Splitter band.

For some reason, the three enemy scouts seemed not to notice. They were staring, absorbed by something behind White Buffalo and Woodpecker. The medicine man glanced over his shoulder. There, over the other ridge, came the People.

Both groups stopped and waited, discussing the situation among themselves. White Buffalo was greatly relieved, and it was obviously even more so with Woodpecker. Now two men detached themselves from the People's group and made their way down the hill. White Buffalo recognized Hump Ribs and Short Bow, who had participated in many such meetings.

From the other hill came a large, heavy-set man with an equally large ax in his hand. His demeanor plainly marked him as the leader of this band. With him was a young man of wiry athletic build whose dark and shifty eyes caused more anxiety than the size of his leader. Here was an unpredictable, hence dangerous man.

Each of the approaching groups joined their own wolves and paused for formal conversation. The People's representatives were still outnumbered, but it was no matter now; there would be no fight. Both groups on the opposing hilltops included women and children, the families of the envoys below. It would be too dangerous to fight.

"Greetings," the big man signed. "How are you called?"

This would be a formal discussion, carried out under strict protocol.

"I am Hump Ribs, of the People," the young man answered. "And you?"

"Bull's Tail. How is it that I do not talk to your chief?"

The young man drew himself up proudly.

"You do so," he signed. "Broken Horn is dead, killed in our most successful hunt, last autumn."

Bull's Tail laughed derisively.

"You lie. No one hunted well last season. I should not talk to you. I know that one, though."

He pointed to Short Bow.

"Our chief speaks truth," Short Bow signed. "The buffalo kill was great."

The astonishment in the eyes of the Head Splitters was apparent. They must believe Short Bow who was known to them, but it was obvious that their own winter had not been good. White Buffalo now began to notice that their buckskins were tattered, dark with the smoke of many lodgefires. They had had a difficult year.

Apparently, Hump Ribs was noticing the same thing.

"We have plenty of supplies," he signed. "May we give you some?"

White Buffalo nearly laughed aloud. Of course the Head Splitters would refuse rather than admit their poverty. More importantly, however, it allowed Hump Ribs to establish himself as a successful leader in the minds of the enemy. It was a triumph of diplomacy. The enemy had been faced down.

"No, we have plenty," Bull's Tail signed, though the lie was obvious.

"It is good," agreed Hump Ribs calmly, apparently not noticing the discrepancy.

He will make a great leader, White Buffalo thought to himself with amusement. The young chief had not only handled himself well but had embarrassed an older, experienced adversary.

There was one, however, who was obviously displeased. The dark wiry young man with the shifty look glared in anger. That would be one to watch for in the future.

"How are you called?" White Buffalo signed to him.

The young man stared angrily for a moment. White Buffalo realized that the man was very young, younger than he by several seasons. He must be well respected to be chosen to accompany the chief. This in turn implied again that this was a dangerous man.

"I am Gray Wolf. Remember it. You will hear it again!"

26

At the Sun Dance that year, the entire tribe buzzed with excitement over the doings of the Southern band. Even before the Big Council, where each chief related the events of the year to the assembly, the rumors made their rounds. The story flickered through the big encampment with the speed of real-fire in a thunderstorm, and the excitement rose. There was a new young chief in the Southern band, a nobody who had risen after the death of Broken Horn. Under his leadership the band had prospered. His decisions had been good. In a confrontation with the Head Splitters on the trail to this very gathering, he had publicly humiliated old Bull's Tail, one of the enemy's capable leaders. That story had grown, of course. In some versions, young Hump Ribs had heaped supplies on the ground before the hungry Head Splitters, forcing Bull's Tail to refuse the gift to save face.

Most of this, it was said, was due to the powerful medicine of a new holy man of the Southern band. In a time of starvation and drought, he had caused rain to fall and an immense herd of buffalo to appear from a hole in the ground.

"But is White Buffalo not their holy man?" someone asked.

"Yes, of course. White Buffalo gave away his name to this, his son, and then crossed over. His wife too, the medicine woman Dove, also crossed over. *Aiee,* my friends, this man is good! He has the medicine of both parents. Did you hear of the event with the calfskin, when he drew the buffalo over the cliff's edge?"

"Only a little part. How did he escape, himself?"

The teller of the story paused a moment, unsure. His listeners were so intent . . . it would be a shame to admit that he did not know.

"I have heard," he half whispered, "that he leapt into the air and *flew,* while the herd passed under him."

"Aiee! The holy man can *fly?"*

"Well, maybe not. But the calfskin cape . . . it would let him float a little while, you know, with the help of his medicine."

"But I have heard that the death of their chief, Broken Horn, was caused by the buffalo. Is this a doing of the new holy man?"

That was an obvious suspicion which caused ugly rumors for a day or two. Could the young chief and the holy man have plotted to kill Broken Horn and take control of the band?

This was quickly proved untrue by the members of the Southern band themselves. First, the death of Broken Horn had occurred *before* the young medicine man had taken his father's name and prestige. White Buffalo the Elder was still powerful at the time. Next, young Hump Ribs did not seize the leadership. He was persuaded, after older and more experienced men had refused. He had been nominated, in fact, by the respected subchief Short Bow, after refusing the honor for himself. The final argument: Cat Woman, widow of the greatly respected Broken Horn, strongly supported the young chief and the holy man.

All in all, the members of the Southern band, when such questions were raised, became quite indignant. It was apparent that they would tolerate no suspicion over the events of the season. The rumors dissolved like wisps of fog on a sunny morning and were gone. They were rapidly replaced by admiration and even envy for the band that had most successfully weathered the Year-of-No-Rain. The Southern band had never been a great political power in the tribal council. Now, however, even the Real-chief spoke with respect. The Big Council sought the opinion of Hump Ribs when the time came to choose the site for next year's Sun Dance. Suddenly it was a matter of prestige to belong to the Southern band.

When the tribes separated after the events of the annual festival, the Southern band had grown by perhaps ten families. Of course, some of these were not the most desirable of members. Some people were constantly changing loyalties, looking for the reflected glory belonging to the most affluent band. However, it was still of some advantage to the Southern band. Sheer weight of numbers tips the balance of prestige, and the other bands noticed the swing of loyalty and were envious.

* * *

It was a good season. The grass grew lush and tall; the children were fat and the women happy. There were no more encounters with the Head Splitters. Hunting was good, and the Southern band settled in for the winter, quite comfortable and secure.

In fact, when White Buffalo unrolled the story-skin to record the year's events, there were few worthy of mention. It was somewhat frustrating to consider that in this season, his first of recording the pictographs, there was little to record. He decided on a successful hunting scene in tall grass, depicting several hunters of note killing buffalo. Above these, and slightly larger, was a figure identified as Hump Ribs, presiding over the scene. He was not pleased with it, but Crow assured him that he had done well.

"It is a good problem to have," she joked, "a season so successful that there is no event unusual enough to note."

Good omens continued, and the Southern band prospered. It was a mild winter, with little illness and practically no hunger. It seemed that the existence of the band was charmed, governed by the powerful medicine of White Buffalo and led by the skill and diplomacy of Hump Ribs.

White Buffalo knew that it was false. Things were going too well, and someday it must end. He was concerned that when it happened, there would be much dissatisfaction, and the people would begin to blame Hump Ribs.

This also put White Buffalo in an untenable position. It would be difficult to overcome the complacency of the People, whose existence was basically day-to-day, hand-to-mouth, anyway. In his position as a prophet and seer, he should warn that change would come. The problem was, when? If he issued warnings of dire misfortune and nothing happened, he would lose face, the People would chuckle behind his back, and his effectiveness would be impaired. On the other hand, if he did not voice a warning, when trouble came, he would be blamed for lack of vision. He wished that his father were here, so that they could consult. He tried casting the bones, but that was little help. The patterns that had seemed so clear when his father was the holy man never quite materialized.

Crow Woman sensed his unrest.

"What is it, my husband?"

There was little that he could keep from her or would wish to. He shared his concerns, and she nodded understandingly.

"The question is, when?" he finished. *"When* shall I try to tell them?"

"How do you know when to announce the coming of the rains or the buffalo?" Crow asked.

"That is simple. A change in the wind, the other signs. But in this, there are no signs!"

"There must be signs, sometimes."

"Yes, Crow, but I do not know what to look for because there is no way to know what form the changing omens will take."

"Could you warn that there will be misfortune someday?"

"Maybe. But I should be able to support that with a sign, and I have none. The casting of the bones . . . *aiee,* maybe their power is gone, with my father's passing."

"No, surely not," Crow said. "Have you asked Grandfather Buffalo?"

"No. That would be wise," he agreed.

He fasted, went out alone, and achieved contact with his spirit-guide, but he felt that it was little help. There were more questions than answers.

You will know, he was advised, *when the time comes, how to proceed. You cannot foresee everything. It is a gamble.*

How odd, White Buffalo thought, waking from the vision. His guide had seemed almost flippant about it. The comment about gambling . . . that seemed completely inappropriate. He tried to reason it through. It was true, of course. When the medicine man observed the signs and predicted rain or announced the time to burn, he was sometimes wrong. It was a matter of close observation, an attempt to be right more often than wrong. The holy man's skill and the power of his medicine were judged not by whether he was correct *every* time but *most* of the time. But in this case, he should have something to go on. This time it was important that he be right. There had been no major pronouncement since the Great Hunt. None had been necessary. His prestige still depended on the memory of that event. Prestige had a habit of fading, like the daylight when Sun Boy slips beyond the edge of the earth. White Buffalo needed something to reinforce his position, to solidify prestige.

And he must predict correctly. *Aiee,* if there were only some way, when he cast the bones, that he could know how they would fall. A gamble . . .

He was walking through the village one day, late in the Red Moon. Plums were ripening along the streams, and the People were gathering the fruit to dry or to eat. This always resulted in a seasonal gambling fever, with the plum-stone game. He paused to watch a group of young men, rolling the plum-stones on the smooth flesh-side of a robe spread on the ground.

The man who held the stones shook them between his cupped palms and with a triumphant flourish, cast them on the flat surface. The seeds skittered and bounced, and came to rest. There was a shout of glee from the man who had cast them. Of the five plum-stones, three displayed a red dot. The player swept them up to cast again. Three more times he tossed before the stones betrayed him, and he passed to the next player.

White Buffalo stood, deep in thought. The plum-stone game was an old one, highly favored among the gamblers. Any odd number of stones would be used, usually five or seven. All would be painted with a red dot on the side. The gambler's win or loss depended on whether there were more of the red dots exposed when the stones came to rest or the plain yellow of the natural stone.

What had caught White Buffalo's attention as he watched the game was one particular plum-stone. He could identify it at each throw because it was slightly larger than the others. It was considered best to have complete uniformity, of course, but sometimes a little variation occurred. The peculiar thing about this plum-stone was not its size but that it almost never came to rest with the red dot facing upward. He watched, fascinated. Apparently this plum-stone was flattened slightly on the one side, which affected its tumbling motion. The players seemed not to notice. They would probably lose these stones or throw them away before the next game anyway. White Buffalo watched a little longer to verify his impression, then slipped away. His heart was good because he might have found an answer.

For several days, well away from the camp, he studied hundreds of plum-stones. Thousands of times he tossed his selected specimens across a skin —choosing, discarding, selecting again. The stones must have an asymmetry, flattened on one side but not enough to be noticeable. Yet he must be certain that they would behave in a predictable way most of the time. Finally, he selected nine plum-stones which fit the requirements. It remained only to paint them. Not red . . . that was too familiar to the gamblers. Black. Yes, that would do. And for this purpose, black should be the favored side. Carefully he painted not just a dot but one entire side of each plum-stone. He could hardly wait for the pigment to dry, so that he could test his theory.

Finally, he was able to toss the stones. On the first throw, seven were black, two yellow. The second resulted in six and three; the third, eight and one. White Buffalo was delighted. Many times he cast the black stones, and only once did they show more yellow than black, five to four. That was no problem. The ceremony of Black Stones which he intended could be based upon three throws. Now he had his predictable ceremony. A thought occurred to him. Could it be that the assortment of sticks and bones he had inherited from his father was such a thing? No, surely not. His father would have told him. But this new ceremony . . . it must be used very seldom and very cautiously. It would be easy to misuse. Maybe, when the time came to pass on his medicine to another, he would destroy the black stones instead. He wondered for a moment who that successor might be.

Now his task was to decide when to use his new skill, and how. When the time came to move, perhaps. He conferred with Hump Ribs, though he did not mention the black stones.

When the chief announced the day of the move, White Buffalo also announced his ceremony of prediction. It would be held that evening, after dark. The flicker of firelight would make it more difficult to see the skittering plum-stones and determine how the thing was accomplished.

There was much interest. The ceremony began with a dance. Crow Woman, who knew only that it was a new ceremony, beat the cadence while her husband established the mystic mood with the dance. When the time came to cast the Black Stones, White Buffalo explained that three tosses were required. The stones would tell of good or ill, depending on the showing of dark or sunny sides of the plum-stones. Palms sweating, he rolled the first toss from a painted rawhide box that he had crafted for the purpose. There on the skin, plain for the onlookers to see, were seven black and two yellow stones. There was a gasp from the crowd. The next throw resulted in a score of eight and one; the third, in nine black stones.

Even White Buffalo was startled. He made a very formal ritual of gathering the plum-stones and storing them away in the little box. Then he spoke.

"There is danger on our trail," he predicted. "I cannot say what form it will take, but we must be ready when it comes. We have been blessed with good omens for many moons, but sometime it must end."

"When, holy man?" an old woman asked.

"Ah, Mother, I cannot tell that," White Buffalo answered seriously. "Even the Black Stones do not say."

27

Stone Breaker bent over the vein of blue-gray flint, pounding and prying at the block of material he wanted. It was loose, shifting a little with each pry of the stick but still not breaking free. It was much like picking the nut meat from a cracked shell, he thought to himself. Yes, the fragrant oily meat of the walnut was equally reluctant to come free. It must be teased out painstakingly with a sharp wooden awl. Some of the old women were highly skilled at such things. It had been good, in the time of No-Rain, to have such skills for survival.

The young man sitting near him gave a long sigh. Stone Breaker had taken a journey ahead of the band as they traveled, to secure some flint blocks. By moving a day ahead of the slower column, he would have an extra day to quarry the stone. The rest of the band would overtake him sometime today. One of the young warriors had agreed to accompany him for protection. He could also undertake any of the tasks that were difficult because of Stone Breaker's handicap. The young man, Turtle-Swims, had no particular interest in Stone Breaker's craft. This was only an opportunity to escape the boredom of the slow-moving band. Turtle had found the quarrying operation equally boring. He sat near the skin carriers on which were piled chunks and flakes of flint while Stone Breaker continued to work.

Stone Breaker was aware of his companion's disinterest, of course. His purpose was not to create an interest in the craft. Idly, he wondered if someday he should select a likely successor, as Stone Breaker the Elder had done. Ah, that should be a long time off. Maybe their child, now six winters old, would develop an interest. If not, so be it!

He was aroused from his thoughts by an exclamation of surprise from Turtle-Swims. Stone Breaker looked up to see three men standing on the canyon's opposite rim. They were scarcely twenty steps away, had the ground been level. But between them was a rough and rocky cleft of the little canyon's upper end. A man could, with no problem, walk down one rocky slope and up the other to the spot where Stone Breaker now worked in the quarry.

The situation looked desperate. These men were obviously Head Splitters, obviously confident. Their main force must be just behind the ridge.

Turtle had been negligent, Stone Breaker realized. It was his function to protect. Turtle should have been acting as a lookout instead of sitting in the canyon, bored with inactivity. He had depended too much on the approach of the rest of the band.

Now, as if to compensate for the mistake, Turtle-Swims leaped to his feet and started to fit an arrow to his bow. He was still looking down at the bowstring, fumbling to adjust the arrow, when he was struck from above. Stone Breaker heard the soft thud and turned his eyes from the Head Splitters back to his companion. Turtle looked upward for a moment toward the warriors above, a startled expression on his face. Then his knees bent, and his body collapsed limply, his hands still clutching the bow as he fell. Stone Breaker saw the feathered end of an arrowshaft sticking from Turtle's shoulder, near the neck. Horrified, Stone Breaker followed the estimated course of the shaft with his eyes and saw the head protruding half a handspan through Turtle's back on the other side.

He looked up in terror. The Head Splitters were chuckling. One was fitting a new arrow to his bow. Now the man raised his head to voice the yipping falsetto war cry that had struck such terror in the children so long ago. Stone Breaker felt for a moment that he was once again a helpless child, waiting for the death-dealing blow of the Head Splitter's arrow. He held up a hand in the sign for peace, and the others laughed.

"You, Lame One, what are you doing?" one signed.

"Digging flint," Stone Breaker signed back. "I do no harm!"

The Head Splitter, whom Stone Breaker now recognized as the evil-looking warrior they had seen last season, now laughed. What was he called? Ah, yes, Gray Wolf.

"*That* one does no harm!" announced Gray Wolf, pointing to the still body of Turtle-Swims. "*I* will decide who does harm."

Stone Breaker had given himself up for dead. The three men started across the gully, picking their way among the rocks. They paid little attention to Stone Breaker. What harm could he do? With a twist of the old hurt, he realized that he could not even run or try to escape. The enemy regarded him as harmless, a nothing. It was a long time since Stone Breaker had experienced bitterness over becoming a cripple, but now it returned. Along with it came the helpless feeling that he remembered from childhood, when he lay in the mud with the crippled leg under him, waiting for the Head Splitter to shoot.

Then his brain began to work again. These men were not a war party. There would be more of them. They must be wolves of a larger group of Head Splitters. Wolves of a war party? No, he thought not. Such scouts would not travel in threes, but singly, not openly like this. The other possibility that occurred to him was that these men were the advance unit, the wolves, of an entire band, traveling as the People were. If so, their families were vulnerable. Maybe he could plant that seed of anxiety, play for time. Possibly, he could even postpone the inevitable until the People arrived.

The Head Splitters approached now. Gray Wolf, who assumed the role of leader, walked up and slapped Stone Breaker across the face. Stone Breaker attempted not to show a reaction. This was a ritual, a counting of honors. It was a greater show of bravery to strike and thus insult a live enemy than to kill one. An idea struck Stone Breaker.

"You are a brave man," he signed, "to count honors on an unarmed cripple." He turned to the others. "Is he as brave with women and children?"

The other warriors laughed, and Gray Wolf's face was livid with rage. Stone Breaker thought for a moment that he had gone too far. However, his bold insult might have saved him. Now, if Gray Wolf harmed the prisoner, he would face the ridicule of his companions, who would also carry the story back to the tribe. In these few moments, Stone Breaker realized, he had achieved the upper hand. Gray Wolf was now on the defensive. He must save face with his companions. The danger would be that the Head Splitter's fiery temper would flare into a destructive act. Stone Breaker must continue conversation, keep the man distracted.

"How are you called?" he asked. "Gray Wolf?"

"Yes," the other signed. "Remember it."

"You are the chief?" Stone Breaker signed innocently.

"The war chief," Gray Wolf answered.

"Ah, yes. Your chief, what is his name . . . Bull's Tail?"

He had managed to remember.

"Bull's Tail was killed last season," signed one of the others. "He gave his name to his son, but that one is a child. White Bear is chief."

Stone Breaker had been thinking quickly; ". . . killed last season . . ." It must have been an accident in the fall hunt. He could take a guess, and . . .

"Bull's Tail was killed by a buffalo?" he inquired casually.

"How did you know?" came the astonished rejoinder.

Stone Breaker shrugged.

"Our buffalo medicine is strong," he signed. "Our new holy man has great skill."

An expression of wonder and doubt came over the faces of the Head Splitters. Then Gray Wolf reacted suddenly.

"Enough of this! That is nothing to me. Now, Lame One, is there any reason I should not kill you?"

Stone Breaker swallowed hard and tried to maintain his dignity. He hoped his captors would not notice his sweating palms and his near-panic.

"You wish to take the risk?" he asked in signtalk.

Gray Wolf reached for the stone war club at his waist. His swing had actually started when one of the others stepped in to seize his arm and stop the blow.

An argument broke out among the Head Splitters. Stone Breaker could not understand a word of their language, but the content was obvious. The others objected to killing the prisoner because of his boast about the People's medicine man. It was too great a risk. Gray Wolf was angry and destructive, and was arguing his right to kill the prisoner.

Stone Breaker edged away, out of the reach of the wildly swinging weapon. As he turned, he caught a glimpse of motion above him. He looked up and was astonished to see, on the rocky ledge overhead, the figures of Hump Ribs, White Buffalo, Short Bow, and several others. The warriors were looking down on the squabbling Head Splitters, and Short Bow appeared ready to shoot if there was danger to Stone Breaker.

"Ah-koh, my friends! It is good to see you!" Stone Breaker said as calmly as he could.

His captors stopped squabbling and looked up. They had no way to escape, no place to run.

"Go ahead, kill us!" one of the Head Splitters signed arrogantly.

Another began to chant a mournful wail that was apparently their tribe's version of the Death Song.

Short Bow readied an arrow.

"Wait!" said Stone Breaker. "It is better to let them go."

"Let them go?" Short Bow was indignant.

Quickly, Stone Breaker explained his dialogue with the enemy. He had, without much thought, planted the seeds of doubt in the Head Splitters' minds. He had boasted of the medicine of White Buffalo, its strength and help to the People.

"If we let them go, they will carry this story to their tribe, and they will fear us," he explained. "Besides, I think their band is near."

"Yes," agreed White Buffalo. "We see them, over there. The People are near too."

"But they have killed Turtle, here," Short Bow protested. "Let us kill two and let one escape with the story."

"No, let them live," Hump Ribs interrupted. "But let us count honors first. There is time."

The young chief walked around and down into the gully. Solemnly and with dignity, he slapped Gray Wolf across the cheek, then repeated the gesture with each of the others. Gray Wolf looked as if, at any moment, he might burst into a mad suicidal rage, but he managed to keep his dignity.

One by one, the other warriors walked past and counted honors as the Head Splitters stood stoically.

"Go now," Hump Ribs signed. "No, leave your weapons."

The other warriors started up the canyon slope, but Gray Wolf held back a moment. He looked from one to the other of his captors with a dark, malevolent stare. It was as if he wished to fix in his mind the men who had shamed him, for future vengeance. The approach of the People could be heard now, the busy hum of conversation, the yipping of a dog, and the cries of children at play as they traveled.

Gray Wolf climbed the rocky slope and stood on the gully's rim to look back.

"You have made a great mistake," he signed insolently.

"You made the mistake," Hump Ribs answered. "You should not have killed our brother here."

He pointed to the still form of Turtle-Swims.

"No," Gray Wolf answered. "You should have killed *me*. You will mourn over that mistake."

With one final obscene gesture, he turned and was gone.

There were those who said that the medicine of the People was still strong. In an encounter with the Head Splitters, only one man had been lost. In addition, they had counted honors on the enemy and shamed him.

But some were uneasy. Among them at first was Short Bow, who favored genocide for Head Splitters when possible. Hump Ribs, White Buffalo, and Stone Breaker were uncomfortable with the results of the encounter but could not decide what would have been a better path of action.

Much later, it was agreed that this marked the turning point toward a period when good things did not happen to the People. Many times White Buffalo would remember the bitter remark of Short Bow at the camp that evening.

"That Head Splitter Gray Wolf was right."

"How do you mean, Uncle?" Hump Ribs asked.

The old warrior shrugged simply, as if the answer were apparent.

"We should have killed him."

28

It was not that there was so very much *bad* luck. The hunting was adequate. The winter was, if not mild, at least tolerable. But there seemed an absence of anything especially good. Maybe, after the extremes of the Year-of-No-Rain, followed by the great buffalo kill, an average year or two, either moderately good or bad, seemed uneventful.

But no, that was not the case. Beginning with the death of Turtle-Swims, things did seem to change. There were those who said that perhaps Turtle had caused it, that he had done something to displease the spirits. Stone Breaker, the only one of the People present at the young man's death, was certain that that was not it. Turtle-Swims had been careless and had lost his life as a result.

There were other things, however. A young couple, meeting outside the camp that summer for a romantic interlude, were standing under a giant cottonwood when it was struck by a spear of real-fire, the boom of Rain Maker's thunder-drum, and a spatter of rain. Then the storm was gone, leaving the two dead and their families to mourn.

An old woman was bitten by her own dog, which had been acting irrationally for a day or two. The dog was killed by her husband, but not before the woman became ill did the event take on ominous proportions. Then it was remembered that a smell-cat had walked boldly into the village about half a moon ago. It had been a source of much amusement, and the dogs had killed the animal. This dog, it was now remembered, had been scratched or bitten.

White Buffalo did his best with chants, ceremonies, and herbs, but he knew that it was useless. The old woman went mad, as her dog had done, and died in agony, convulsing and frothing at the mouth. There was no recovery from the Fears-Water Madness.

Hump Ribs announced a move, which was good. The madness might be restricted to this area. Meanwhile, children were instructed to avoid any animals, dogs or wild animals, which seemed to behave strangely. There were no more cases of the madness.

All of these things seemed to increase the prestige of the young medicine man. Had not White Buffalo foreseen these evils? He was, the People said, probably the most skillful of all holy men; his medicine was strong and his visions accurate.

White Buffalo saw all of this with misgivings. True, he had predicted evil things with the black stones, but now a gnawing doubt assailed him. He would dream at night of the skittering plum-stones, dancing on the surface of the spread skin and coming up black, relentlessly, time after time. He would wake with a start and find it difficult to fall asleep again. The doubts grew larger. Could it be that his manipulation of the answer he sought in the stones was improper? Was it evil to try to *cause* a certain result as he had done? He considered burning the black stones, but could not bring himself to do so. He was afraid to use them again, so they remained in his medicine pouch. He confided in Crow Woman.

"You mean, you *caused* the plum-stones to behave that way?"

Her eyes were wide with amazement.

"Well, yes, in a way," he admitted. "I chose stones that would do that."

"That would all come up black?"

"Yes, they will most of the time. I painted them that way."

Crow Woman rocked with laughter.

"*Aiee*, my husband, you are clever. May I see them do it?"

"I . . . I think not, Crow. I have thought of burning them. Maybe they are evil. I am a little bit afraid of them."

"Afraid? I do not understand."

He was not certain that he could explain it, this question in his mind that he might be abusing his gift. He sighed deeply.

"Do you think, Crow, that I have *caused* these misfortunes with the Black Stones?"

"I think not, my husband," Crow answered thoughtfully. "They would only predict."

"Maybe I should have painted them the other way," he mused. "Make the yellow sides come up more often."

Crow thought a little while.

"No, that would not work. It would predict only good things, and bad things *do* happen. You wanted to tell the People that, and you did. They trust you more than ever."

"But if I had not cast the black stones, would the lovers have been struck by real-fire? Or old Bird Woman have gone mad?"

Crow put her arm around him.

"What did you wish to tell them, my husband?" She went on, without waiting for an answer. "That there will always be evil times ahead, that the good times we were having must not be expected to last. You have done that, done it well. They understand. Do you see bitterness? No. Mourning for the dead, but respect for your skill."

"Then you think I should not burn the plum-stones?"

Crow Woman laughed.

"Of course not! *Aiee,* it was clever, Elk."

She called him that, sometimes, when they were alone. It was a pet name, the name from their childhood.

"But it may not be wise, to try to control such things," he protested.

"You said you do not control them," she observed. "It is only that you know more about what they will do. Is that not also true of the grass, the storms, the buffalo? You do not question that knowledge."

"That is true," he agreed reluctantly.

"Then, your use of such things is not wrong. It is one part of your knowledge, your skill as a holy man."

Somehow, he always felt better after he had talked to Crow Woman.

It was that fall when a young hunter came running into camp, bleeding from a dozen minor wounds. His left ear was gone, and blood still gushed from the side of his head. He was almost hysterical as he related a horrifying story.

He and three others had been hunting, some distance from the village, when they were attacked by Head Splitters, some nine or ten in number. White Owl had been killed instantly in the first onslaught, struck down by an arrow. Red Dog had watched while the others, one at a time, were tortured, mutilated, and finally killed after many honors were counted. Then the skull of each had been crushed with a stone club, *after* their deaths. It appeared that this blow was symbolic, solely to identify this as the work of the Head Splitters.

Red Dog had cringed in terror when they approached him. He had expected the same torture and ignoble death, emasculated and mutilated. Instead, they had all counted honors, slapping him and pricking his skin with knifepoints. Then they freed his hands. As an afterthought, the Head Splitter who appeared to be the leader suddenly stepped forward and with a single sweeping motion, had slashed Red Dog's left ear from his head.

"The rest of your carcass belongs to me," the Head Splitter signed, as he waved the severed ear before his quaking prisoner's face. "Now, go!"

He struck the youth across the face again and pushed him to the ground. As Red Dog rose to his feet to run, his captor signed once more.

"Tell your people that Gray Wolf does not forget."

Red Dog finished his story and cried unashamedly, comforted by his family and friends.

Hump Ribs called an immediate council. There was much anger and not a little fear. It was apparent that this had been a war party, specifically for this purpose. The general area of the Head Splitter camp was known; it was three sleeps away. Thus, this could not be a hunting party, far from home. It appeared to be a vengeance raid by the young subchief Gray Wolf. They had marked him as a dangerous man before.

"He seeks vengeance for his loss of dignity at the flint quarry," White Buffalo suggested.

"But what of their principal chief, the one they called White Bear?" asked Stone Breaker. "Does he not keep the young men from such things? This is not usual, even for Head Splitters."

"*Aiee,* but sometimes the young do not listen," said an old man on the other side of the fire. "This is a bad one."

"We should have killed him when we had the chance," Short Bow offered.

There were murmurs and nods of agreement.

"That is behind us," Hump Ribs reminded them. "We cannot go back and do it now. But we must decide. What *will* we do?"

Some in the council favored immediate pursuit and reprisal. Calmer heads suggested that it was too risky. It was not known how many were actually involved in the enemy raiding party. Red Dog had seen nine, "maybe ten," but were there others nearby? Maybe this was only a small portion of the party, and the whole event a trap to entice the People out onto the prairie for ambush. It was a sobering thought. The few hotheads who argued for immediate retribution were quickly argued down. Besides, it was pointed out, to go out with a large war party would leave the village poorly defended. Maybe *that* was the Head Splitter plan, to attack undefended women and children while the men were gone.

"It is enough!" Hump Ribs announced finally. "We need to find a winter camp anyway. We move, in three days. We will go southeast, away from Head Splitter country."

There were a few voices of dissent, but not many. Hump Ribs's decision could be rejected by a vote, but it was apparent to most that the plan was a good one. Preparations began for departure.

The weather was uncommonly fine, with bright warm days and cool nights. It was the time of the Second Summer. They traveled into territory that was somewhat unfamiliar. There were fewer large expanses of grass and more trees. In some places, great groves of nut trees were prominent and oaks unfamiliar to the People. The world seemed brilliant as they traveled. The familiar clumps of scarlet sumac shone against the muted yellow-orange of the grasses. Large trees not familiar to the People produced a blaze of flaming red. It seemed that the whole world was aflame with beauty. Some became uneasy at the unfamiliarity of the terrain.

"We are people of the prairie," White Buffalo heard someone say. "We must not forget our beginnings."

"But the Eastern band camps in wooded areas," another responded. "It is good for them."

"*Aiee,* the Eastern band!" the first man responded. "Are we to become as *they* are?"

Everyone laughed.

"I wonder," observed a young woman, "if there might be worse enemies in the woodlands than Head Splitters."

"There *are* no worse enemies than Head Splitters," an older woman answered. She had just finished the mourning period for a favorite grandson.

That evening Hump Ribs sought out White Buffalo.

"Tell me," he asked, "what you can of this matter, my friend. Is there danger here?"

"There is danger anywhere," White Buffalo observed. "But here, I do not know. I have never been this far south and east."

"It is beautiful country," the chief observed. "I have never seen such colors in the trees. Yet I am made to feel that it is not for us. Can you seek a vision?"

"You know that some are uneasy over this?" White Buffalo asked.

"Yes. That is why I seek the help of a holy man."

"I could cast the bones."

"Good. A public ceremony?"

"No, I think not. Come to my lodge."

Shortly after dark, Hump Ribs came to the lodge of White Buffalo and Crow Woman. Even such a private ceremony was very formal, and White Buffalo began with a chanted prayer. He burned a handful of powdered plant material on the fire, filling the lodge with aromatic smoke. Then he drew out the container of small bones, wooden fetishes, and stones, and tossed them across the surface of the spread skin with a dramatic flourish.

"You do not use the black stones?" asked Hump Ribs.

"No, they are for another purpose," answered the medicine man.

Not even the chief, who was also his close friend, would share the full story of the Black Stones. He was absorbed in studying the scatter of small objects, and the position in which they had come to rest.

"There are good signs and bad," White Buffalo announced. "Nothing unusual. It is like all other things—light and dark, hot and cold."

"But what does it mean to us? Is it safe here for the winter camp?"

"No place is ever free of some danger, my friend. But I am made to think that we should seek a place to winter where there is some grassland, some woodland, some open prairie, and some woods, much like last season. And, as I said, I see both some good and some bad for the People."

Hump Ribs nodded, understandingly.

"It has always been so. Then tomorrow we stay here while the wolves search for a winter camp. So be it."

29

$\longleftrightarrow$

Despite the misgivings of some, the winter proved uneventful. There were some indications that other tribes shared the area, and this caused a certain uneasiness. A trace of smoke on the distant horizon, a footprint in the damp earth at a spring or stream, gave constant cause for concern. Constant vigil was maintained, except for the hardest part of the Moon of Snows. Then everyone huddled over the fires in the lodges and seldom went out. It was a mild winter, however. White Buffalo was unsure whether it was due to the different locale or simply a milder season than most. Maybe both.

Overall, though, it was apparent that the People were uneasy here. There was an unrest, a sense of not belonging. White Buffalo pondered at length about this feeling. Once again, the idea that the People are people of the open plain, the grassland, was a constant thought—in simplest form, *this is not our home.* He wondered how long it would take to become one with the land. The People considered the rolling Tallgrass Hills, the Sacred Hills, the source of their strength, the nourishment of their spirits. Yet they had not always lived there. The old legends told of their migration from the northeast, long ago. How long no one knew, but many generations. Surely, the People who first came to the Tallgrass Hills did not feel that land to be their source of life. How long had it taken? A generation? Two? Even three or more, maybe.

There was another possibility, of course, that came to White Buffalo as he considered. He knew the feel of strength, power, and spiritual uplift that came to him sometimes when he greeted the rising sun over the hills. Or when the moon was full, covering the grassland with its soft silver-blue light. At such times there was a feel of spiritual power, a Something, mystical and wonderful. It seemed to come from the earth and the sky, to be everywhere.

Maybe, White Buffalo thought, the People had been wandering since Creation, searching for this place of the spirit. When they found it, they stopped, realizing that their search was ended. From that time on, they had wandered only within the grassland areas that they had made their own. The spirit of the prairie had nourished the People ever since, and would forever. At least, he felt, if he had been with the first of the People to set foot in the Sacred Hills, *he* would have known.

As the Moon of Awakening came, everyone became more restless. White Buffalo recognized the symptom and approached Hump Ribs.

"Ah-koh," said the chief. "Sun Boy renews his torch!"

"Yes. Its warmth is good," agreed White Buffalo.

They sat down to smoke in front of the chief's lodge. It was the first time that a social smoke outside the dwellings had been possible that season. White Buffalo looked at the swelling buds on a tree nearby.

"You wish to speak of moving?" asked Hump Ribs.

White Buffalo was a bit startled. Maybe he should not have been, he realized. Hump Ribs had shown remarkable perceptiveness as a leader. From a quiet, likable young man, in a very short time he had become a quiet, thoughtful leader. He anticipated well, and his judgement was good. The chief had already realized the concern of the holy man.

"Yes," White Buffalo said simply.

Hump Ribs nodded.

"The prairie will soon be greening," he noted. "We should be where our roots are. It has been a good winter, here in a strange land, but I am made to think it is time to go home."

It was a long speech for the soft-spoken Hump Ribs, but there remained little to be said. The announcement was made that day.

There were some, of course, who complained. It was always so, the wailing that there was no way that the People could be ready to move on three days' notice. As usual, the complaints were ignored, and those who complained were busy like everyone else, preparing to strike the lodges at the appointed time. It was merely part of the adjustment to the change. Maybe there was even less complaint this time, because there was a strong feeling that the People did not belong here, among wooded hills and strange plants —strange spirits, even. The feeling was even stronger when the wolves reported that they were being observed. Yes, the timing was good.

The travelers were observed from a distance for several sleeps, and a constant watch was maintained against possible attack, but none came. One morning the scouts reported no trace of those who had followed them. This resulted in one more day of extra caution. It might be a trick, to catch the travelers off-guard. Still nothing happened, and everyone began to relax.

The mood was cheerful and optimistic. The People were going home to an area they understood, one which gave them life. It was ironic, then, that the sickness began to appear. At first, it seemed only the usual cough and congestion of the springtime, though more severe. An old woman succumbed first, after coughing greenish phlegm flecked with blood for a few days. Then it was noticed that many children were ill and that they were recovering very slowly. Usually the illness of the small ones was rapid in onset but with equally rapid recovery. This time it was more prolonged.

"We must stop here," White Buffalo advised.

Hump Ribs agreed. During the days of travel, it was not usual to set up the lodges for each night's stay. Families slept in the open, and only in inclement weather did they build a temporary shelter. This was different. The lodges were needed for treatment. By closing the door and smokeflaps and sprinkling water on heated cooking stones, a sweatlodge was created. The steam filled the interior and soothed the tortured lungs of the afflicted.

White Buffalo was active day and night, performing his chants and prayers, moving from one dwelling to another, sprinkling his powdered plant materials over the heated stones in the lodges. This produced aromatic steam to liquefy the cloying congestion of sodden lungs.

It was a demanding, exhausting torture. There was even a time when White Buffalo wondered why he had ever consented to the responsibility of being a holy man. He had not eaten or slept for two days, except in short snatches. Finally, a time came when no one was pleading for his immediate attention, and he made his way to his own lodge, almost staggering from exhaustion.

As he approached, he noted that the doorskin was tightly closed, the smoke flaps too. *Aiee!* He hurried forward, calling out to Crow Woman. Her face was drawn with worry and lack of sleep as she held the skin aside for him to enter. She did not need to tell him.

"It is White Moon."

The child lay on a pallet of robes near the firepit, breathing heavily. A quick glance at the labored respiration, the sucking in of the small belly in a frantic effort to breathe, the anxious look of distress on the little face, made his heart sink. He had seen no child as sick as this, their own.

"I have kept the steam," Crow said, "and used the plants as you have taught me."

Mechanically, White Buffalo reached for his rattles and began the prayer-chant. Moon's eyes opened and focused in silent recognition. She smiled a wan little smile and closed her eyes again. All through the night they huddled together over her, hoping that the combined strength of their spirits would reach out to hers. For a time she seemed to improve a little, rousing enough to sip a mouthful of soup from a horn spoon. But this seemed to exhaust her. She sank back, unresponsive. Dawn was just breaking when she gave one last little sigh and was gone.

"She has crossed over," said Crow Woman simply, tears streaming down her face.

She gave a final caress to the now peaceful face, and began the wailing chant of the Song of Mourning.

When the People moved on, there were seven burial scaffolds in the trees where the sick-camp had been. Four were small scaffolds to accommodate the small bodies of children. The other three victims had been elderly, people of many winters whose bodies were simply tired of fighting.

Very few families had escaped the sickness entirely. The wife of Hump Ribs himself had been quite ill, having contracted the fever after caring for her own children. Slowly, she recovered. All of the children of Stone Breaker and Cattail had been ill, but they too had finally overcome the malady. Some of the People suffered for nearly a moon, and many had still not regained full strength when they moved on.

Everyone was loud in praise of White Buffalo's expertise in the emergency. His medicine had been strong, people reminded each other. He had predicted something of this sort, the bad luck. When it happened, he had been tireless in his efforts. Many gave his medicine credit for the recovery of their children, and his popularity and prestige soared. It was too bad, people told each other, about the holy man's own child. Her survival was not meant to be.

White Buffalo entered a period of deep depression. To him, it made little difference that he was held in high regard by the People. He felt that he was a failure. He had been unable to help his small daughter, their only child, who had been the joy of their lives, his and Crow's.

After the period of mourning, Crow Woman had seemed to recover and return to some sense of normality. She tried to comfort her husband, but his grief seemed unreachable. At one point, she tried to console him and was met with angry accusations that *she* did not feel the loss as he did. Wisely, she withdrew.

White Buffalo was nearly destroyed by his grief but also by guilt. He should have been able to do *something,* he thought. If not, what was the use of anything, of his entire profession and skill? He tried, through long and sleepless nights, to discover his exact source of error. Surely, he was being punished for some oversight or some misdeed. Could it be his neglect of some part of the ceremonial ritual? Or was it wrong that he had helped Hump Ribs with the decision to go to the new area? No, the family of Hump Ribs had survived. Yet . . . once more, the doubt over his creation of the Black Stones ceremony gnawed at his guilt-tormented mind. He felt useless and wondered if he might even be going mad. Usually he consulted Crow

Woman with his problems, but with this he could not. Part of his guilt involved her. He had betrayed her, he felt, by not having the skill to save their only child. He was unable to approach her to share their grief together.

He must do something or go mad. He approached Crow Woman one evening after a period of absence when he had left the other travelers for an afternoon.

"Crow, I need to go away for a little while."

There was hurt in her eyes.

"I am sorry, my husband. How long?"

"A few days. I will catch up with the band, but I must be alone a little while."

"It is good. I will pack you some food."

"Good?" he blurted.

"Yes, my husband. Your heart is troubled. This will help you find peace."

She was already busy gathering dried meat and berry pemmican and placing it in a small rawhide pack.

"I may fast," he said.

"Then you will need this when your fast is over."

When White Buffalo rejoined the band a few days later, he said little about his quest. One does not ask about such private things, but it was apparent that whatever had happened, he had found himself. The People rejoiced for him.

With his wife, he was attentive, almost apologetic. Crow Woman assumed that he had talked to his spirit-guide, though he never said. There was a renewed interest, an inquiring quality about him, and he seemed older, more mature, with even more dignity than before. He was kinder, more thoughtful.

There was one other thing. From that time on, for the rest of his life, White Buffalo's hair was nearly as white as the sacred cape.

30

Suddenly, it seemed, they were old. White Buffalo, after the loss of their only child, had gone through a long period of mourning. For a while Crow had feared for his sanity, but finally he seemed to recover.

For many years they continued to hope for another child, but there was none. It was difficult to share the joy of Stone Breaker and Cattail at the progress of *their* children. Crow Woman never conceived again, and it was only gradually that she and White Buffalo began to realize that it was not to be. Nothing was said between them, but there was an understanding. Each knew that the other knew also, that the chances were ever more remote through the years. Finally, the hope was gone, and both settled in the knowledge that they would never again know the joy of a small child in their lodge.

The seasons passed, and the pictographs on the story-skins, painted each winter by White Buffalo, kept the record of the People. White Buffalo threw himself into the duties of his priestly calling, and his reputation grew. His influence and that of Hump Ribs, an able chief, gave the Southern band prestige among the people, and the band grew also. They migrated with the geese and more importantly, with the buffalo. Hump Ribs chose their wintering places well, and each summer they met the rest of the tribe for the Sun Dance and the Big Council.

There were losses in the band. One by one, the parents of the new generation crossed over. The parents of Crow Woman were gone and others of their contemporaries. Short Bow, who had seemed stolid and immortal to White Buffalo and Crow as children, grew bent and crippled by the aching-bones ailment, and finally he could no longer hunt. He lost the will to live and crossed over that winter, leaving two wives and a child of ten winters, a boy belonging to the younger wife.

This began a time when there was no clear warrior leadership in the band. The skill of Hump Ribs was in the area of diplomacy and in planning the seasonal moves. But no warrior rose up to lead the hunts or to lead the defense against the Head Splitters as Short Bow had done. The Southern band receded in numbers again.

They continued to encounter that dreaded enemy. There were few episodes of open warfare, but the enemy subchief Gray Wolf was a constant threat. At their chance meetings, he was boastful, insulting, and obscene. It was apparent that there could be no hostilities in such encounters, and secure in this knowledge, he had made open threats at each opportunity. This harangue was expected. It was irritating, sometimes infuriating, but no one ever made the mistake of starting open warfare, which would risk the lives of women and children.

Hump Ribs developed the knack of avoiding confrontation where possible. This brought scorn from the Head Splitters and a reputation for timidity on the part of the Southern band. There seemed little doubt, however, that it prevented bloodshed.

It did not, of course, prevent the sporadic raids which struck terror in the hearts of the People. At any opportunity, it seemed, Gray Wolf would swoop down on unsuspecting hunters or unsupervised children. He and his followers delighted in the opportunity to terrorize and kill and kidnap. Always, if possible, a mutilated survivor was left to tell the tale. The constant threat of kidnapped children revolved around the beauty of the women of the People. Small girls would soon be beautiful young women, to become slave-wives of their captors or sold to others. Boys were more trouble than gain to their captors, and their usual fate was a single blow with a war ax.

To avoid this danger to the children, Hump Ribs led his Southern band in new directions on unpredictable migrations. Some seasons they managed to avoid the depradations of the Head Splitters entirely. At other times, they blundered into frequent contact for a season. It was a dangerous game, this run-and-hide.

White Buffalo thought about it often. Short Bow, he knew, would disapprove. He had always been one to stand and fight. But Short Bow was dead, and there were few warriors who demonstrated his type of leadership. It was not that Hump Ribs was a bad leader. On the contrary, he was very good. But sometimes White Buffalo thought that it would be good to have someone like Short Bow as a leader in the hunt and against the Head Splitters. Such a man could work well with Hump Ribs. But none came up through the Rabbit Society.

In truth, Gray Wolf and his followers killed so many young men over a few seasons that there were not enough husbands. Multiple marriages had always been known among the People, but were not common. Usually, a wife might take in a widowed relative as a second wife for her husband and to help in the lodge. More wives than two were rare. Now, however, several lodges had three or four wives. Something must be done for the women without husbands, and this had always been the way of the People.

"Maybe you should take another wife," suggested Crow Woman to her husband.

White Buffalo was astonished.

"Wh-what?" he blurted.

"A second wife. Maybe she could bear you a child. There is Gray Fox, who has lost her husband. She is pretty."

"No!" White Buffalo was firm. "No, I will not think of it. *Aiee,* woman, she would not know the chants and the drum cadence. What good would she be?"

Crow Woman smiled to herself. That was the answer she had sought. If he had wished it, she could have tolerated such an arrangement, but she was pleased with her husband's response.

As for White Buffalo, there was only one choice. What Crow suggested was unthinkable. Not the living arrangement—that could be made tolerable, except for the fact that a newcomer would be an outsider. She would be unskilled in the knowledge of the medicine that he and Crow shared. That was not the main obstacle. He could not tolerate the idea of what another child in the lodge would do to Crow. If it were their own, his and Crow Woman's, it might possibly take the place of the happy child that they had had for a few short seasons. But to watch Crow as she tried to accept the child of another woman, yet from the loins of her husband? He knew that he could never do that to her.

Meanwhile, as these things occurred among the People, the years fell behind, marked only by pictographs on the story-skins, lines in the faces, and graying hair. It had happened so quickly. One day, it seemed to White Buffalo, they were young, and their lives were ahead, the years full of expectation. Then one day he realized with some surprise that they were growing old, and their lives were no longer ahead, but behind. He could not say when it happened. There had been no middle years, it seemed. Even more puzzling was the discovery that there had been no dividing summit. Somehow, he thought, there should have been a sort of recognition of having crossed the hilltop and started down the slope. He was not ready for the Other Side, the crossing over of the spirit; even this life was such a mystery. There were young and old, and surely there had been a day when the change had happened. When had it been, and how had he missed it?

He knew that it was past because the aching of his joints on cold mornings reminded him. His step was not as quick and sure, though he could still perform the ceremonial dances. It was frustrating to have a young mind in a body that was beset by the ravages of time. Crow Woman, who was now past her child-bearing years, was still beautiful to him. The woman who had warmed his bed in their youth still did so. The sensation of shared warmth under the robes was still thrilling and exciting. For a little while they were young again, their blood racing faster and making them forget the tragedy and disappointment that life had brought.

White Buffalo thought sometimes about passing on the heritage of the buffalo medicine. The knowledge, the skills, the cape itself, as his father had done before him. It was easy to postpone such things. In the early years, he had expected to pass the calling to his son. Or, perhaps, to his daughter. There were respected holy women among the People. White Moon had shown promise . . . but that was gone now. White Buffalo wiped a tear from the corner of his eye. He was sitting alone on a hill near the camp, where he loved to go and meditate. He thought again of the years when he and Crow had thought, *Surely this year there will be another child.*

In that way, year after year, he had postponed the decision about his medicine and who would be the next holy man of the Southern band. Now it was time to face the question. There was no single event which had brought him to this way of thinking but a series of things. He had finally accepted that Crow could not bear another child. He refused to consider a child by a new wife. And now, while he still had some good years, he must find a successor. There was time to do so, but the seasons flew past much more swiftly now than in his youth. Yes, he must begin his search.

He told Crow Woman of his decision that night as they settled in, snuggled under the robes against the crisp autumn chill.

"I am made to think," he observed casually, "that I should find someone to learn my medicine."

She looked at him seriously in the flickering light from the fire.

"Are you not feeling well?"

"What? Oh, yes . . . I am well. But we are no longer young."

"We are not old, either." She cuddled against him suggestively. "I will show you."

He smiled at her.

"Sometimes my bones tell me otherwise."

Both chuckled.

"But, Crow," he went on, "it takes time to learn the dances, the ceremonies, the medicine of the plants."

"Yes, I well remember," she mused.

"So," he continued, "I must find an apprentice."

"What will you do?" she asked.

"I do not know. What do you think?"

"You could watch the Rabbit Society."

"Yes, that is good. You watch too. First, the child must have the gift of the spirit. But it is also necessary to have the interest. Also, most important, he must be willing to make the sacrifice . . . take the responsibility for the demands of such a life."

"He . . . or *she?*" Crow Woman asked mischieviously.

"Well, yes. But a young woman would have even more sacrifices to make. She would have to take a vow of chastity or wait until her years of child bearing are over."

This was a delicate area, and he hated to go into it. Crow's fertile years were barely past, and he thought the subject might be painful to her. Then he saw the mischief in her eyes. He seized her and tickled her in places that he knew would provoke a response.

"Stop!" She giggled. "I only meant that—"

"Of course," he said more seriously as they settled back down. "I should look for women also who would make good apprentices."

"There is a girl I have seen," Crow said thoughtfully. "She seems wise beyond her years. She reminds me . . ." She paused a moment. "No! I know! Do you remember a young man called Mouse? I think he is a nephew of Stone Breaker, on Cattail's side."

"Maybe," White Buffalo answered. "A thin, muscular boy, big ears and a sharp nose."

"Yes," laughed Crow. "Mouse!"

"I remember him. A quiet young man. It is good, Crow. We will watch him."

"Could I ask Cattail about him?"

"Of course. But do not say why. No one must know what we are seeking."

"Not even Cattail? Stone Breaker?" Crow asked in wonder.

"No. It must not be. Would I try to choose an apprentice for Stone Breaker?"

"No, my husband. But, he already has one. Their oldest son."

"Oh? I did not know. Well, it is good. Stone Breaker too sees the need to choose an apprentice."

"Yes, I suppose so. But he is no older than you, and you can still warm my bed," Crow said seductively.

She cuddled against him, and White Buffalo forgot the urgency to select an apprentice. They were young again, and in love.

31

←→

Mouse seemed a likely prospect. White Buffalo observed the youngster in the activities of the Rabbit Society. It was easy to do. There were always a few adults watching the instruction, cheering the children on. As they learned the skills of the hunt, the use of weapons, and the simple athletic skills of survival, it was possible to observe and estimate the potential of each.

And the potential of the one called Mouse did seem great. He was calm and mature in his approach, well liked but not an obvious leader. His range of skills was impressive, from his use of the bow to his well-coordinated speed in swimming. Yes, thought White Buffalo, this one will do to watch. Whenever opportunity offered, the holy man made his way to the activities of the day and sat to observe. Sometimes he chuckled to himself at a particularly clever triumph of someone, especially Mouse. Each day he was more certain.

There were also indications that the young man might have the gift of the spirit; at least, he seemed to have wisdom and insight beyond his years. It was something that could be nurtured, encouraged as it grew. If, of course, Mouse wished to do so. The youth appeared to be about fourteen or fifteen summers. There were few things that were notable about his appearance. He was neither tall nor burly in build but rather short and slender. His muscles were well defined, however, and his strength was deceptive. The large ears and pointed features made him appear rather comical, and the name he bore was quite descriptive. However, White Buffalo soon saw that here was a young man who would some day be taken quite seriously. There were leadership qualities behind that seriocomic face. While the appellation Mouse fit his description quite well, it had no correlation at all with the youth's spirit. Some day, thought White Buffalo, this one would outgrow that name and shed it as the snake does its skin. Little did the holy man realize that he would witness the event that caused such a change.

It was a warm day, early in the Moon of Falling Leaves. The word had been passed that soon the band would move to a wintering area, but a specific day had not been chosen. There was still good hunting, the weather was uncommonly fine, and the temptation to stay a little longer was great. There had been no contact with the Head Splitters this season, so it was a great surprise when the enemy came.

White Buffalo was sitting on the slope outside the camp, watching several young people practicing with the bow. Primarily, he was watching the quiet demeanor of the one he had begun to think of as his successor. The one called Mouse was active and skilled in this game. His arrows were usually in or near the white spot at the center of the grass-filled target-skin. Still he was quiet and unassuming, though confident. Of the six or eight others, two were young women. Naturally, there was some flirtatious courting going on, and White Buffalo smiled in amusement. He leaned back against a massive sycamore and closed his eyes, soaking in the comforting warmth of the sunlight. It seemed to help the stiffness in his joints to warm them in this way. He dozed off for a moment.

"You are next, Mouse!" someone called. "See if you can beat Red Hawk's shot!"

White Buffalo stirred and opened his eyes. He wanted to see this shot and to take a vicarious pride in the skill of his pupil. Of course, Mouse was hardly his pupil yet. He had not even approached the boy about such an apprenticeship. He must do so soon, maybe during the journey to winter camp. That would give Mouse a chance to consider as they traveled. Yes, he would speak to the young man soon.

Mouse loosed his arrow, and the cries of approval indicated another successful shot. Several ran toward the target to retrieve arrows while Mouse followed, pausing to fit another arrow to his bow.

At first, White Buffalo thought, in his sleepy state, that his eyes were deceiving him. But, no! There were shadowy figures flitting among the dogwood behind the target. He sat upright, wide awake now, ready to sound the alarm. Maybe it was only some of the dogs from the camp. Then he noticed the figure of a man crouching behind a bush only a few steps beyond the target. Even as his mind tried to interpret the message from his eyes, the man rose, part of a concerted rush. One of the girls screamed as a painted warrior sprinted toward her. Two other enemies were equally close, swinging the dreaded stone axes. More were visible among the bushes.

There was complete confusion. Some of the young men of the People had actually left their weapons behind when they ran to the target. One of the most arrogant braggarts, a popular youth called Red Hawk, turned with a squeal of terror and ran like a rabbit. An arrow came searching after him but missed.

Amid all of the terror and danger there was one who seemed to remain calm. Mouse dropped to one knee, took aim, and calmly drove an arrow into the chest of a charging Head Splitter. Surprise was evident on the man's face as he fell forward from his own momentum, driving the arrow on through, to jut upward from his lifeless back. Mouse roared a slightly high-pitched version of the gutteral war cry of the People and reached for another arrow. The Head Splitters paused. They had not expected resistance from these mere children.

"Fight!" yelled Mouse to his companions. "Shoot!"

He released another arrow, wounding a warrior who turned to cripple away, clutching at a bleeding arm.

A slim girl stepped forward to pick up the ax dropped by Mouse's first victim and turned to defend herself. The man who had almost reached to seize her now stopped, confused. His hesitation was his undoing. An arrow from the bow of one of the other youths struck him in the side. As he turned, trying to pluck away the offending shaft, the girl stepped forward and swung her captured ax.

"After them!" cried Mouse.

The fleeing youths turned to join the pursuit. Mouse sounded the war cry again. Now there were answering war cries from the camp, and warriors came pouring out to assist. The Head Splitters were in full retreat, leaving three dead and others carrying arrows in wounds of varying severity.

"Enough!" shouted Hump Ribs as he and the others caught up with the fight. "Do not go farther. It is too dangerous."

The young men began to withdraw, talking excitedly.

"We did it! We drove off the Head Splitters!"

"Is anyone hurt?" asked Hump Ribs.

Quickly, they looked from one to the other.

"No, we are all here," Red Hawk announced.

"Good," Hump Ribs answered. "What happened?"

"They came out of the bushes!"

"That one nearly grabbed Oak Leaf!"

Everyone was talking at once. White Buffalo had made his way down the slope in time to hear his impressions verified.

"Mouse killed that one," Oak Leaf said admiringly. "He turned the attack on them."

The others nodded.

"Who sounded the war cry?" asked Hump Ribs.

"Mouse," said several at once.

Hump Ribs looked over at White Buffalo, who nodded agreement.

"I was on the slope there," he told Hump Ribs later. *"Aiee,* that one is a fighter! He saved us from losses today. Our Mouse, it seems, speaks with a loud voice."

There was a celebration that evening in honor of the victory. The dances reenacted the events of the day—the first arrow from Mouse's bow, the turning of the fight, and the defeat of the Head Splitters. There was no immediate danger of counterattack. It was well known that Head Splitters avoided fighting at night. Their fear was that a spirit crossing over as it left a dying body would become lost in the darkness to wander forever. Thus there would be no attack tonight. Probably not at all. The attackers had been severely punished.

The hero of the day, of course, was Mouse, who was rather embarrassed by all the attention, though proud. Partway through the celebration, Hump Ribs stood by the fire to make a proclamation.

"We will move camp in two days. But for now, we celebrate."

He beckoned Mouse forward, and everyone shouted approval.

"Our young Mouse," Hump Ribs announced, "has done well. He has shown bravery and gathered honors. Ours is not a timid mouse, but a Mouse That Roars!"

The crowd shouted with approving laughter.

"Mouse Roars!" someone cried.

The young man had acquired a new name, one that honored his bravery and would commemorate his deeds forever.

"It is good!" stated Hump Ribs. "You shall be Mouse Roars!"

The celebration continued, but White Buffalo and Crow Woman made their way back to their lodge.

"You were right about this young man," Crow said as they prepared for sleep. "He is a leader."

"That is true," acknowledged White Buffalo.

"Then why do you not seem more pleased, my husband?"

White Buffalo did not respond at once.

"Is something wrong?" Crow finally asked.

"No, not really," he answered wearily.

He was tired from the excitement of the day and the celebration. The throb of the dance-drums still sounded across the camp, and the chant of happy, triumphant songs echoed the cadence. He had been excited, but now in the aftermath he felt old and tired again. There was a disappointment that he did not quite understand in the thrill of victory.

Crow Woman snuggled close to him under the robes.

"Elk, is there something that the others do not know?"

"Maybe. Gray Wolf was one of those I saw. He tried to get his warriors to turn and fight."

"But that is nothing new."

"Yes, I know. But, today was not the end, only another fight."

"Yes, my husband. It has always been so."

"That is a bad one, that Gray Wolf," he said, almost to himself.

"But what . . ."

"I do not know, Crow. I am made to think he will become more of a problem than ever, and for a long time."

"Is there something we must do?"

"I think not. This is ours to live with."

"But what of Mouse? Mouse Roars." She chuckled in the flickering firelight. *"Aiee,* he has proved himself!"

Suddenly, White Buffalo realized what it was that was bothering him, causing his depression.

"Yes," he said slowly. "He has proved himself. But now I cannot ask him to be my apprentice."

"Why not?" asked the astonished Crow Woman.

"I saw him today, when he 'roared.' *Aiee,* that was something to see! The others were running in fear, and he turned it into victory."

"But then—" Crow interrupted, but he waved her to silence.

"That is it, Crow. He is a leader. But that sort of leader. He might make a great medicine man, but the People need him as a warrior, a chief who can stand and fight the Head Splitters. Mouse Roars can do that."

He fell silent, and Crow was silent too for a little while. Finally she spoke.

"Then we look some more."

"Yes."

Mouse Roars never knew that he had been considered, and the dejected White Buffalo continued to search in the Rabbit Society for the next holy man.

32

The girl was tall and well formed, and moved with a confident grace. Her walk reminded White Buffalo of the gentle sway of willows in a summer breeze or perhaps the nodding of heavy seedheads on the real-grass in the Moon of Ripening. It was not a seductive walk. At least, not intentionally, he thought, as he watched her at the games and contests. But it would be difficult for any man to watch her and not see the beauty of her body. Part of that beauty was that she appeared unaware of its effect on men. She used her long legs well in the contests of running, jumping, and swimming. She handled the bow with equal skill.

White Buffalo found it necessary to overlook her grace and beauty, and concentrate on her spirit. That, after all, was the thing which had caused Crow to notice the girl and to suggest that she would be one to observe.

Crow seemed determined to see that a woman would at least be considered. Certainly White Buffalo had no objection. His only reservation was that it would be a greater sacrifice for a woman.

He was impressed immediately with this young woman. Big-Footed Woman, she was called. Not that her feet were exceptionally large. True, they were ample, but a tall woman must have long feet to carry her longer frame. The reason for such a name, it appeared, was her skill in the athletic contests. Her strides, her accomplishments, were great, bigger than most. Her feet carried her well. As a thinker might be said to have large thoughts, so were this young woman's feet in deeds of speed and skill. Yet her deeds were also those of spirit and thought, White Buffalo noted. He recalled that it had been Big-Footed Woman who had grasped the fallen Head Splitter's ax and helped to repulse the invaders. A cool head. And confidence. Not *over* confident but secure in the knowledge of her own skills. *Mature,* that was it. The girl seemed to have wisdom beyond her years.

"She reminds me of you at that age," he told Crow Woman.

"Aiee!" Crow laughed. "I was not so pretty or so athletic. Besides, that was when you did not like me, so how would you know?"

"I was talking of her spirit," he began.

Then he saw that she was teasing him. There was no way that he could win this discussion.

"Woman," he snarled with a terrible grimace, "you test my patience!"

He threatened to tickle her, and she retreated, still laughing. Finally they tired of the game, and she turned to the fire where a stew of corn, beans, and dried meat bubbled in the pit. Crow removed a cooking stone with her willow tongs and deposited it in the coals, replacing it with a freshly heated one. The stew hissed and subsided to quiet bubbling again.

"Elk," she said thoughtfully as she came to sit beside him, "it is good that you see good things in this girl's spirit. I think she has the gift."

"This may be," he agreed. "Let us observe her a little longer, and then I will talk to her. Your feel for the spirit is good, Crow. You could have done this."

She leaned her head on his shoulder.

"Yes," she said thoughtfully, "I think so. I knew it then, but I would rather have borne your children."

A tear formed at the corner of her eye, and she brushed it away.

"You knew," White Buffalo said sadly, "and you rejected the gift, for me. Now you have neither."

"No, no, Elk. I have you. I have helped with *your* gift. I would do so again, to be with you."

They sat, leaning together, enjoying the warm comfort of touching, until suddenly Crow sat upright.

"Aiee!" she said, "I am neglecting my cooking. The stew will be cold."

She began bustling around, busily attending the cooking pit which needed little attention.

The Southern band had settled into winter camp now. Crow and White Buffalo had continued to observe Big-Footed Woman and continued to be pleased. The girl was quick and observant, thoughtful of others. Already she was assisting with teaching the first dance-steps to the tiny beginners in the Rabbit Society. She was popular, but in a different way. Friends seemed to come to her for advice and counsel. There were others who appeared destined for leadership, but this one's role seemed different. Perhaps her maturity lent itself well to helpful friendship, and her warm wisdom was appreciated by her peers.

"It is good," White Buffalo observed to Crow. "This one will learn well and has the spirit to use her gifts wisely."

Still, it was a long time before they approached her. White Buffalo must be very sure, certain that his choice was a good one. Eventually, Crow Woman issued the invitation.

"The holy man, my husband, wishes to talk to you. Will you come to our lodge?"

The girl seemed surprised but quickly regained her composure.

"Of course, Mother. But what could he want of me?"

"He will tell you."

"When? Now?"

"As you wish, child. There is nothing urgent in this."

The sunny smile that they had noticed lighted the girl's face.

"Then let us go now," Big-Footed Woman suggested. "I would not keep the holy man waiting."

Pleased, Crow led the way to their lodge.

The girl's eyes were wide with wonder as White Buffalo questioned her about her thoughts and feelings about the matter at hand.

"You mean, Uncle," she finally blurted in astonishment, "that *I* might have such a gift, a gift of the spirit?"

"Why not, my child? You are wise beyond your years, and you know many things. I am made to think that you *do* have the gift of vision, of the spirit."

"*Aiee!* What must I do, Uncle?"

"That is your choice," he said simply. "One may refuse the gift. Some do, for the trail is hard. There is much to learn, much responsibility. It is quite permissible to say no."

"Must I say, now?"

"No, no. Think on these things. Then come back and tell me."

The girl nodded.

"Uncle, another question. I . . . you see, I know no holy woman. Are there some among the People?"

"Oh, yes, my child. Only one now, I think. She is of the Mountain band. But, there have always been medicine women of the People as well as men."

"Their position is much the same?"

"Yes. There are always differences from one holy one to another, men or women. But much the same. You would develop your own medicine and follow where it takes you."

"I see . . . maybe . . . might I start to learn and *then* see where it leads?"

"Of course. But do not think too hard about it now. Go, think carefully; you will be guided in the right way."

Big-Footed Woman left the lodge of the holy man, still full of wonder.

White Buffalo was pleased with her reaction. The girl had shown humility yet was pleased to think that she might be chosen for so special a vocation. Her every reaction was good.

"Yes," White Buffalo told his wife, "this one has the gift. I am made to think that she will be back quickly."

It was only two days when young Big-Footed Woman returned, humbly and in earnest.

"I am ready, Uncle," she announced. "I am ready to learn."

Her instruction started that very day. White Buffalo was delighted with her quickness of thought, her eagerness to learn. Crow Woman too welcomed the young woman's presence and helped with her instruction. Very quickly, Big-Footed Woman was learning the drum cadences of the ritual chants, and White Buffalo acknowledged that her drumstrokes spoke with much authority. Very quickly, she also became a part of their lodge. Both Crow and White Buffalo felt pleased and happy in her presence. Crow said nothing but did not fail to notice that her husband was showing more interest in life. She had not heard him chuckle so much since . . . well, not since the loss of their own White Moon. This young woman, it seemed, was taking the place of the daughter they had lost. The surprising thing was that it seemed right. Through all the years, both the holy man and his wife had assumed that no one could possibly take their daughter's place. Now it appeared that they need not have been concerned. The years that White Moon had been with them were still fresh in their memory, they found, now that there was someone to help them forget the sadness. It was a pleasant thing to have the bright cheeriness of the young woman in their lodge. It was a winter of happiness that had not been theirs since their loss.

Big-Footed Woman continued to learn rapidly, and White Buffalo was ever more pleased with her progress. In the Moon of Awakening, he suggested to Crow that they ask the girl to move into their lodge.

"It is good," agreed Crow Woman. "The time is at hand when you will have much to show her, many lessons. I will ask her tomorrow."

When Big-Footed Woman arrived the next morning, cheeks flushed from the wind, Crow was ready to make the offer. It was exciting—the thought of a daughter in her lodge again. The girl had become so much a part of their lives that this seemed a completely natural step.

"I have something to speak of with you," Crow began.

Big-Footed Woman's eyes were sparkling with excitement.

"I too, Mother! Let me tell you first. I am going to marry!"

"What?" White Buffalo exclaimed. "Child, you cannot . . . I mean, you must think on this. You would cast aside your gift?"

Crow sat dumbly, unbelieving.

"Not cast it aside, Uncle! I would only postpone it. You have said some women do so, until after their child-bearing years."

"Yes, but girl, that is a long time from now. I need—"

He had started to say that he must have someone *now* to whom he could impart his skills. But that would be unfair. Frustrated, he lapsed into silence.

Crow Woman regained her composure.

"Who is your young man, child?" she asked pleasantly, trying to keep her voice from trembling.

"His name is Coyote. May I bring him in?"

"Of course! Bring him!" Crow said.

Big-Footed Woman gave Crow a quick hug and slipped through the door-skin.

"Aiee!" exclaimed White Buffalo. *"Coyote?* How can she do this?"

Coyote, who had been a child at the time of his father's death, was often a source of amusement to the band. The youngster was adept at practically nothing. He was a bit fat, a bit lazy, and seemed to take nothing seriously. From the time he was small, he had been a buffoon, more interested in jokes, pranks, and laughter than in learning.

"I will not allow it!" White Buffalo sputtered.

"It is not yours to say," said Crow. "You must accept her choice."

"But I do not have to approve!" he snapped.

"No. You must respect it, though."

"Do *you* approve?"

"I did not say that, my husband. Only that the choice is hers. My heart is heavy too!"

By the time Big-Footed Woman returned with her self-conscious young man, White Buffalo had at least recovered his composure.

"Coyote," the girl said proudly, "my almost-parents, Crow and White Buffalo."

The young man nodded, embarrassed, and giggled nervously. White Buffalo recalled now that this chuckling little laugh, like the chortling cry of the coyote in the night, was the origin of the boy's name. He took a deep breath and determined not to show his repugnance if he could help it.

"I knew your father well," he ventured. "Short Bow . . . a man to admire."

"Yes, Uncle. He was such a man. It is good that you speak well of him. Thank you."

Well, thought White Buffalo, the boy is polite at least.

"He gave his name away, did he not?" White Buffalo asked.

He knew that to be true, or the words *short* and *bow* would not be in use. It was actually a cruel thing to say, a reminder to Coyote that *he* was not the recipient. But the youth only smiled, unperturbed.

"Yes, Uncle. To my oldest brother, before I was born."

Somehow, White Buffalo felt that he was losing control of this conversation. At every turn, the young man spoke quickly and appropriately, even with what seemed a degree of wisdom and maturity. This was disconcerting to White Buffalo, who was prepared to be critical.

"Mother," the girl was saying to Crow, "you wanted to speak of something before?"

"What? Oh, yes, I have forgotten now, in the excitement. It was nothing," Crow said.

The conversation continued a little while, and then Big-Footed Woman rose.

"We must go," she apologized. "I will bring him again."

The two young people ducked out the door, and then the girl turned to poke her head back inside for a moment.

"I am so glad you like him!" she whispered, eyes glowing with excitement. Then she was gone.

"Like him?" sputtered White Buffalo. "I cannot tolerate him!"

"Now, Elk—" his wife warned.

"Yes, I know. I will try. But Crow, he has spoiled it all!"

His heart was very heavy.

33

White Buffalo did not know which he resented most. Young Coyote was preventing Big-Footed Woman from carrying out her calling, and that was bad enough. But to make matters worse, the medicine man found that he resented the girl's choice. This Coyote was a buffoon, a lazy nobody without a serious thought in his head. Why, why would a beautiful, intelligent young woman choose to burden herself with such a man? He recalled that this was not uncommon. Such a young woman, with such potential, would sometimes choose such a nobody. It was a thing of wonder, of resentment and envy to all other men.

There was another odd thing here, however. White Buffalo felt a sense of rejection. It irritated him, embarrassed him a little, and it was something that he did not feel free to discuss with Crow. It was actually much like the feeling of rejection that had obsessed him long ago when he thought that Crow had married their friend Stone Breaker. It was ridiculous, of course. He had never wanted this young woman in that way. She was more like a daughter to him. To them both. Yet it bothered him, the thought of this beautiful girl and the short, fat little Coyote in bed together. The girl's long, graceful legs . . . *aiee!* In a completely illogical way, he was jealous. He would not have been so, he told himself, had Big-Footed Woman chosen one of the handsome, capable young men of the band. But *Coyote? Aiee,* life is strange.

Crow Woman, wise in the ways of such things and even wiser in the ways of her husband, had some idea of his frustration. She felt much the same, as a mother does who feels that her daughter has not chosen well. She brought up the subject one evening as White Buffalo sat silent and sullen.

"You are thinking of Big-Footed Woman."

It was a statement, not a question.

"What? Oh, yes. Maybe. My heart is heavy for her, Crow."

She came and sat beside him.

"Elk, we know this young woman well, do we not?"

He gave a deep sigh.

"I thought so, but . . ."

"Now, think, my husband. Has not she shown good judgement?"

"Yes, always. That is why—"

Crow held up a hand to silence him.

"Yes," she agreed, "she has. So, my husband, let us see it this way: Either she sees something fine in this young man that we do not see, or . . . ," she paused a moment for effect, "or she will soon see her mistake."

Crow was always so logical. She could make things seem astonishingly simple. White Buffalo could not argue with her reasoning. He was still frustrated, but the course of action that Crow's statement suggested was the only one available to them—waiting.

Probably the most difficult thing was that Big-Footed Woman continued to spend much time at their lodge. They were glad for her presence, of course. She had become closer than family in many respects. Only the instruction had ceased. The problem, an irritation that grated on the already stressed emotions of White Buffalo, was that the girl usually brought Coyote along. The young man was jovial and pleasant, and his chuckling giggle was not so obnoxious as his nervousness began to decrease. He was even helpful sometimes, bringing firewood for Crow Woman or assisting in some minor way around the lodge.

Gradually, Crow began to appreciate the quiet helper—the gentle understanding, the hidden maturity of Coyote. He still made jokes and soon began to tease Crow in a mischievous, flattering way. By the end of a moon, Crow was completely won over.

"She is right, my husband. This is a kind, gentle, and very intelligent young man."

"But he has no ambition!" White Buffalo snapped irritably. "And he does not do well at the hunt."

"Maybe that is not his skill," Crow suggested. "For some, another way is better. Stonebreaker does not hunt, nor do you."

"That is not the same, Crow. He does *nothing.* He is lazy."

"He has many friends," Crow observed. "Big-Footed Woman says his counsel is sought after."

"And I do not understand that, either," White Buffalo sputtered. "Everything is a joke to him."

"But his jokes *teach,* Elk. They are wise."

Even though these two women, most important in the life of White Buffalo, understood and admired Coyote, the holy man was slow to accept it. Coyote seemed not to notice, casually coming and going, apparently taking nothing seriously. Sometimes he asked questions, which irritated White Buffalo at first.

"Uncle, it is said that the Head Splitters do not fight at night."

The holy man nodded but said nothing.

"Why is this? I have heard they are afraid that spirits of the dying, crossing over, will become lost in the darkness."

"So it is said."

"But, Uncle, *our* spirits sometimes cross over during darkness."

"Yes, that is true."

"Yet they do not become lost?"

"That is our belief."

"Then, Uncle, if we have to fight Head Splitters, we should do so at night? It would give us advantage."

White Buffalo sat silent a moment. No one had suggested this before.

"Maybe," he admitted. "Of course, one does not fight Head Splitters by choice."

Coyote chuckled.

"Of course. Uncle, do you believe the thing about spirits crossing over in the dark?"

"It does not matter what I think but what Head Splitters think."

Coyote chuckled again.

"That is *their* problem then, Uncle?"

White Buffalo smiled, a little reluctantly. This young man had far deeper insight than he had imagined. Maybe, as Crow Woman had suggested, there were qualities in the young man seen only by Big-Footed Woman.

Gradually, White Buffalo was convinced. The fact that Coyote could carry his own end of an interesting conversation helped greatly. So did his thirst for knowledge. The young man asked about everything, from uses of the herbs and plants to how the geese know when it is time to fly south.

"The buffalo see that the grass is drying, I suppose," he said one day, "but how do the geese know? They start before it is cold."

There were other questions, about things of the spirit. Over a period of time, White Buffalo came to look forward to Coyote's visits. Then came a day when the holy man reached a startling conclusion. He was actually covering information in these sessions that he had taught before. These were the things he had been teaching to Big-Footed Woman. Ah, he thought, of course! Here is a young couple who can work together, as Crow and I do. The spirit-force is strong in both. *Aiee,* what a wonder that he had not seen it before! This Coyote, who was already beginning to learn, could be his apprentice. Yes, of course! He, White Buffalo, would begin at once to teach them. The only thing that still stood in the way was Coyote's agreement. He could be asked at his next visit.

Crow Woman was not so certain.

"He may not wish to do so," she warned.

"Of course he will," White Buffalo scoffed. "Look at him, the questions he asks. Already, he understands many things. Things of the spirit. Crow, this is the one! Big-Footed Woman came to bring him to us. It is meant to be!"

When the two young people next came to the lodge, White Buffalo could scarcely contain his enthusiasm. As soon as possible, he contrived to draw Coyote aside.

"Let us walk," he suggested.

The two men strolled out of the camp toward the crest of a low rise a little distance away. Coyote asked his usual questions, his casual manner concealing his depth of thought and the solemn character of the inquiries.

"Uncle, the People do not eat bears, but some others do. Why?"

"Because . . . well, that is our way."

"Yes, Uncle. But *why* is it our way?"

"It has always been so, since Creation."

Coyote walked in silence a little way. He appeared to realize that questions like this could irritate the holy man.

"Some were told to eat bears at Creation, but we were told *not* to do so?" he asked cautiously.

"Yes," White Buffalo stated crisply. "It is the way of things."

"What would happen if one of the People *did* eat bear meat, Uncle?"

"That would bring very bad happenings."

"On the eater, or on the People?"

"Both, maybe. *Aiee,* Coyote, you ask questions that are too serious. Only after much instruction—"

White Buffalo paused, aware that he was about to imply too much. He tried to relax and remain calm.

"But let us not speak of bears, my son," he said in a kindly voice. "Your questions do, however, remind me of why I asked you to walk with me."

Coyote interrupted briefly to point to a pair of young foxes a bowshot away, rolling and playing like puppies in the sun.

"Yes," White Buffalo nodded, smiling in spite of himself. He was slightly irritated by the distraction. But, this very character of young Coyote, the inquisitive observation, was the very thing that made him a likely apprentice.

"Coyote, let me speak with you of a serious matter. Here, sit."

He pointed to a ledge of white stone near the rim of the hill, and the two men sat down. White Buffalo hurried into his subject, before some other sight or sound could distract young Coyote.

"I am made to think," he began cautiously, "that you have the gift of the spirit. I could teach you my medicine, you and Big-Footed Woman, to use for the People, after me."

Coyote was silent for a little while and looked unusually serious.

"You would allow *me* to learn your medicine, Uncle?"

"Of course. That is what I am suggesting."

"I thought you did not even like me."

White Buffalo brushed this aside.

"I was offended when you stole my apprentice. But now you bring me another. Yourself. You have the gift. Now, when do you plan your marriage?"

"I . . . I do not know, Uncle."

"Well, no matter. We will continue instruction, and when that happens, so be it!"

Coyote appeared troubled.

"Uncle . . . I am pleased that you think well of me and would take me as apprentice, but . . ."

"Wait!" White Buffalo said quickly. "You do not need to give an answer now. Think about it; talk with your wife-to-be."

"I have thought already, Uncle. I cannot do this."

"But . . ." the holy man sputtered, "you have the gift; you love the learning . . . you could be a great holy man."

"That is true," Coyote stated, with no modesty whatever, "but the task is too hard. No, I do not want to take the responsibility. I must refuse the gift."

White Buffalo stared at him in amazement. Slowly, the realization dawned.

"You *knew*," he said in astonishment.

"Of course. I have known for a long time," Coyote said calmly. "And I knew that I must refuse. My way is not to work that hard. Maybe it is like bearmeat, Uncle. Some eat it, some do not. And I am made to think that I should not do this."

White Buffalo stared at the younger man. He felt a strange mixture of emotions. Surprise, anger, disappointment. He argued, cajoled, almost pleaded, but Coyote was firm.

How ironic, thought White Buffalo. He had searched for years, almost but never quite finding an apprentice worthy to become his successor. Now he had found one who seemed already to have the gift of the spirit and to recognize it. How tragic to have him then reject it.

Coyote rose and stretched.

"No, Uncle," he said. "I am honored, but it is not to be. I am not a White Buffalo. I am only Coyote, the laugher on the hills and the teller of small jokes."

PART III

TWO
MEDICINES

34

W hite Buffalo sat in the sun in front of his lodge and leaned
against the willow backrest. The years had continued to
pass more swiftly, and he had still found no successor to
whom he could teach his medicine. It was still a worry to him, but he had
nearly decided that this was meant to be. Through the passing of the seasons, year after year, he had searched, but no suitable apprentice had been
found. The likeliest would have been Coyote, although his wife, Big-Footed
Woman, could easily have been the one. But both had rejected the gift, and
they had married.

Aiee, that seemed only a short while ago, but it was many years. Their
lodge had several children, and the eldest were now of fifteen or sixteen
winters. That seemed hardly possible. How could it be, when he, White
Buffalo felt no different? He had sometimes felt old then, and he did now,
sometimes. At these times he worried more about a successor, but the years
had numbed his anxiety about it. Maybe the Southern band was simply
destined not to have a holy man . . . or woman. That would be unfortunate,
but in the long view, it probably made no difference. If the Southern band
died out entirely, time would go on. One band had been destroyed many

generations ago and was now remembered only by the empty space in the council circle.

At first, when Coyote had rejected the gift of the spirit, White Buffalo had been furious, then hurt. It was some time before the holy man had been able to converse with Coyote without becoming angry all over again. Slowly, however, he had been able to realize that the decision had been Coyote's to make. He was helped greatly in this by the wisdom of Crow and Big-Footed Woman.

Slowly, he came to tolerate, even appreciate, the presence of Coyote. In a year or so, the two men had become close friends. There was a great difference in their ages, but this was more than overcome by the communication of their spirits. Coyote continued to have a vast respect for the knowledge and skill of the holy man. White Buffalo, in turn, increasingly appreciated the whimsical wisdom of Coyote. The young man had an uncanny knack of cutting cleanly through to the heart of any matter. But it was done in an unassuming, jocular way. No one could take offense.

White Buffalo noticed this especially when Coyote would speak in council. These occasions were rare, because the young man was not inclined to venture opinions. Usually, his comments were phrased in the form of questions, allowing others to think that they had thought of the solution themselves. It was a strange but quite effective form of leadership.

One incident was fixed in White Buffalo's memory. There had been a heated discussion over the move to winter camp. The weather had remained warm and pleasant, and the hunting was good. There was much reluctance to move yet, though it should have been time to go. Hump Ribs, unwilling to risk an unpopular decision, had called a council. The discussion was going poorly, popular opinion leaning against the wisdom of an immediate move. Finally Hump Ribs, frustrated by the opposition, had looked around the circle.

"Coyote," he said, "you have not spoken."

Coyote looked startled, as if he had been roused from half-sleep.

"What?" he stammered. "Oh, I was listening to the geese."

He pointed overhead, and in the sudden silence could be heard the honking cries of southbound flocks.

"How do they know," Coyote asked, as if to himself, "when Cold Maker is coming?"

There was a murmur, and the discussion was resumed, but the tone was different. Coyote's simple question, actually a diversion, had put the problem into its proper place. White Buffalo chuckled to himself. Soon the vote had turned, and the question was not whether to move but how soon. No one seemed to realize that the tide of opinion had been turned by Coyote's simple ploy. *But Hump Ribs knows,* thought the holy man. *He did this intentionally.* This observation pleased White Buffalo greatly. It showed the skill and wisdom of the chief, and of young Coyote.

Through the years, this odd combination of leadership and wisdom had worked well. Probably, few people were aware of the process. Coyote was content *not* to be a leader but to help quietly to bring about that which was for the good of the band. People laughed at his droll remarks but valued his counsel and appreciated it. Their appreciation was shown by gifts of meager value. A shared haunch of meat, an extra skin. The lodge of Coyote and Big-Footed Woman was never hungry, and the mention of the name of Coyote always brought a smile.

Under the leadership of Hump Ribs, the Southern band had remained stable, neither gaining nor losing lodges. It was respected by the other bands, though others were larger and carried more prestige.

The Southern band, however, continued to be a favorite target of Head Splitter raids. The run-and-hide tactics of Hump Rib's chieftainship had been only moderately effective. Gray Wolf had mellowed not at all and led an attack whenever opportunity offered. The enemy chief, it seemed, still held a grudge, a bitterness from long ago, when he had been shamed by Hump Ribs and the other warriors of the People.

When White Buffalo saw Coyote approaching on this pleasant summer afternoon, he perceived immediately that something was wrong. The usually placid face of Coyote was drawn with care. He approached the seated holy man and sat down, puffing just a bit from his exertion.

"*Ah-koh,* Uncle," he said.

"*Ah-koh,* Coyote," the holy man answered.

He assumed that there was a matter of some concern—probably the Head Splitters, though no one else seemed to know of it.

"There is some difficulty, my friend?" he asked.

Coyote looked at him sharply.

"Do you know of something, Uncle?"

"No. You seem concerned."

"Oh. I do not know, Uncle. It is something to talk of. You may know some meaning."

"Coyote, what are you talking about?"

"Strangers, Uncle. From the south. A man from one of the Caddo tribes stopped with us this morning. I talked with him at length."

"Are these strangers Caddo?"

"No. They are like gods, it is said. They come from far away, no one knows where. Their skins are bright and shiny, and they are many. Too many to count."

"*Aiee!* What is their purpose?"

"No one knows that either. But this Caddo said that some of his people were tortured and killed. That is why he came north."

"To escape?"

"Yes, and to warn."

"But why should Caddo warn people of the Tallgrass country?"

Coyote shrugged.

"They felt it important. There is more, Uncle."

"More?"

"Yes. It is said that these strangers have with them many dogs of great size."

"Dogs?"

"Yes, Uncle. They carry burdens, and some of the gods ride on their backs."

"Nonsense! The Caddo tells tales."

"Yes, that was my thought. But he seems sincere. He says that some of those who first saw this thought that they were all one—a large body like a dog's, but with the upper part of a man on the front."

"Surely that cannot be," White Buffalo pondered. But his resolve was weakening. He was remembering some of the strange things he had seen on his vision quest long ago.

"Probably that was only talk," Coyote said, "and this man agrees. It is now known that it is a dog, ridden by these gods with shiny skins."

"Where were they seen?" asked White Buffalo.

"They come from the southwest. Now they travel nearly straight north."

"And they still come? *This* way?"

He had not quite understood the immediacy of the problem.

"Yes, Uncle. They are maybe only six or seven sleeps away."

"Aiee! Does Hump Ribs know?"

"I sent the Caddo to him."

Somehow, it seemed that Coyote always knew what was happening more quickly than anyone else. Of all the men in the band, how appropriate that the visitor had encountered Coyote.

"It is good," White Buffalo stated. "Now, my friend, there are things we must do."

He rose quickly, almost forgetting the little jab of pain that went through his knees when he moved quickly.

"Come, I will go to Hump Ribs. You wait for me by the stream, there."

The Caddo visitor had already departed when White Buffalo tapped on the lodgeskin of the chief. He was beckoned inside, and for a little while talked earnestly with Hump Ribs. The story was much the same, that of the advancing party of gods. Hump Ribs was inclined to doubt the story of the traveler, but there was much that seemed convincing. Unless the Caddo was completely crazy, he must have a story of much importance. And the man had not in any way seemed crazy, Hump Ribs admitted.

"So Coyote says also," White Buffalo commented.

"He talked to Coyote?"

"Yes, Coyote sent him here."

"Ah, I see. That makes sense."

"What will you do?"

"Nothing, for now. Send wolves, of course."

The holy man pondered a moment.

"Yes," he said slowly. "That is good. But my friend, I am made to think that this is a very unusual occurrence."

"You have had visions?"

"No, I have not tried yet. I will, of course, but meanwhile, our wolves should leave to begin their journey."

"Yes, that is true."

"Now, we must have their discoveries quickly. We may have to move the camp out of the gods' path."

"Yes. I will have wolves waiting at places a sleep or two apart, to carry the word."

"Ah, that is good," White Buffalo agreed. "One more thing . . . I would have Coyote go with the wolves."

"*Coyote?*" asked Hump Ribs in astonishment. "He is . . . well, my friend, he is not one of our ablest warriors."

"True," agreed the holy man, "but he *is* one of our ablest *thinkers.*"

Hump Ribs considered a moment.

"Yes," he said. "That is true."

"Just as you need warrior information, I need things of the spirit, and Coyote can observe those."

"Yes, it is good," replied the chief. "Coyote does have that ability. Did you not once consider him as an assistant?"

"Once, long ago," White Buffalo said sadly. "He refused."

Hump Ribs laughed.

"He is lazy," he commented.

"A little, maybe. But he is useful as he is. He does not want to lead but is a keen observer. We both use that to our advantage, my friend."

Both men chuckled.

"Do you think this mission is too dangerous to send such a man as Coyote?" Hump Ribs asked.

"I do not know. Maybe I will have more thoughts on this later. But for now, my chief, I am made to think that this event of the gods' advance into our territory is too dangerous *not* to have a man like Coyote with the observers. Now I must go."

He rose and made his way to the river where Coyote waited. Quickly, he outlined the plan.

"Anything you see, or even *think,* I want to know," he said. "If it is important enough, you come back yourself. If it is only about their location and direction, Hump Ribs's wolves will tell us."

White Buffalo felt that he was not expressing well what he wished to say, but Coyote nodded in apparent understanding.

"I will do so, Uncle."

Coyote moved toward his lodge to gather a few supplies, and White Buffalo watched him go. The little man's casual gait belied the importance of his mission. The holy man could not have explained it, but he somehow felt that these events were a most important turning point in the history of the People. Whether for good or bad, he did not know.

35

It was much as the Caddo had told it, Coyote reflected, watching the moving column in the distance. There was a very large number of the big dogs the man had described. Some were indeed ridden. Not only that, they could be ridden at great speed, much faster than a man could run. For this reason, the wolves of the People had elected to stay some distance away and watch only the column as a whole.

The gods were very dangerous according to a group of wolves whom they had encountered from another tribe. These warriors told, in sign talk, of capture and torture. None survived capture, it seemed. And the gods moved on, northward, relentlessly, day after day. Their purpose was still not known.

Coyote viewed this entire venture with a confusion of emotion. His curiosity told him to get closer, to learn of these strange beings. His natural reluctance to expose himself to danger, or even much exertion, told him to stay away. He wondered sometimes what he would do if suddenly confronted by one of the gods astride his great dog and carrying the long spear that the wolves had noted. Coyote would prefer to run in such a situation, but he was not very good at running. The thought crossed his mind that he could leave the wolves to return to the band and report his impressions to

White Buffalo. He was only two sleeps away. But his natural curiosity won out, and Coyote stayed.

It had been decided not to move the camp. The path of the gods would bypass the area if they continued on their present course. That was the situation as told to the Southern band by word of mouth. Coyote, however, hearing the news from the messengers who shuttled back and forth, read a deeper meaning into such a decision. He knew that White Buffalo and Hump Ribs would be in constant communication. They would know from the messengers that an attempt to move would be useless. The Southern band, with lodges and baggage, would be more conspicuous, and more vulnerable, on the move. With the speed of travel that the gods possessed, the People could not escape anyway. Coyote knew this, but it was reassuring to most of the People if their leaders merely announced that they would not move. It would be a narrow miss at best, Coyote realized, if the column continued as it was, and he was concerned for the safety of his wife and family. Well, another day, and he could go to them. And, of course, to the holy man, to tell him of the amazing things he had seen.

White Buffalo waited, restless and impatient. He had not heard from Coyote. The chief's messengers had reported daily on the progress of the gods, and the holy man had talked in turn with Hump Ribs about their observations. The approaching column of gods was traveling rapidly, now only two days away. It had become apparent that it would be futile to break camp and run. The People would be even more vulnerable while traveling. Besides, they might remain unnoticed if they remained quietly where they were now camped. Hump Ribs and White Buffalo discussed the situation, and the chief announced that they would stay, remain alert, and avoid all contact if possible.

"Could your medicine be used to stop them?" asked Hump Ribs.

"I do not know," White Buffalo answered thoughtfully. "Maybe. I must think on this."

It was a truly important decision that White Buffalo found thrust upon him. At first he had been startled that Hump Ribs would even suggest such a thing. Then he realized that the chief did not fully understand what he was asking. In the scheme of things, a holy man was given powers of the spirit to use as he saw fit. Sometimes his ceremonies and visions were successful, sometimes not. But one basic premise remained true. The medicine of the holy man must be used only to help, not harm. Medicine used for evil, even against an enemy, was very dangerous, possibly fatal, to the holy man who invoked it.

In the present situation, if White Buffalo attempted spells to harm the invading column, even to save the People . . . *aiee,* he had no desire to die, unless that seemed the only way. To complicate his narrowing choices further, the nature of the invading gods was quite unclear. They tortured and killed, it was said, so maybe they were bad gods. Still, the torture was, so far, merely rumor. If these were indeed gods and *not* evil, any attempt to injure them would surely be fatal.

If only he had more information! Why did Coyote not return? Coyote's keen insight might easily provide the information he needed.

Meanwhile, White Buffalo sought solitude to commune with his spirit-guide. In anticipation of such a need, he had begun his fast earlier. Now he prayed and chanted, and waited for his guide to join him. He had great difficulty falling asleep, and even then, he woke several times, having had no visions.

It was nearly morning before he reached the strange mystical state between sleep and awakening and found himself approaching his spirit-guide.

Ah-koh, *Grandfather,* he greeted.

The great bull rolled an inquisitive eye at him, but there was no answering thought.

Grandfather, I have come for help. I am in great need.

Yes?

Ah, at least there was an acknowledgement of his presence.

There is a large number of godlike persons approaching my people. It seems that they mean us harm.

This may be true, came the answer.

Ah, so the gods *are* dangerous, White Buffalo thought.

It has been suggested that I use my medicine to try to stop them.

There was no response for a little while, and White Buffalo began to be afraid that he would get no answer. Finally the bull rolled an eye at him, and the mind-talk continued.

That is yours to decide.

The vision started to fade, and White Buffalo felt the grip of panic.

Wait! Don't go . . . Grandfather, I need you!

The bull was moving away now, but paused to look back.

It is yours to decide, came the spirit-message. *Maybe they will turn back.*

White Buffalo awoke, shaking and in a cold sweat. He had never before totally lost his composure in the presence of his spirit-guide. And he felt that he had never received less help in time of need. This was probably the greatest danger to the People in White Buffalo's lifetime. He had been able to serve them well, but now he had grave doubts. He was angry that he had received little help. Yes, angry at his spirit-guide.

In desperation, he was ready to use his gift to do harm to the approaching gods. If, of course, it was possible. But what else could he do? There was so little time. Tomorrow might be too late. He hurried back to the village, already planning his ceremony to invoke harm to the gods.

Crow's face was anxious and drawn.

"How is it, my husband?" she asked.

"Not good, Crow," he said as he began to search among his herbs and medicine things.

"You did not find your spirit-guide?" she asked in astonishment.

"Yes, but it was no help."

"No help? How can this be?"

"Crow, I have no time to explain. I will perform a ceremony to try to stop these strange god-beings."

Crow's eyes were wide with wonder.

"But, Elk, is that not dangerous?"

He hesitated, wondering if his wife knew how dangerous this could become.

"Elk," she persisted, "is this good use of your gift? You have said that if a holy man uses his power for evil, it will kill him."

"That is true," White Buffalo agreed, "but is this evil, to try to save the People? Maybe these gods are bad gods."

"And maybe not," retorted Crow. "My husband, you could be in great danger. I wish you to think carefully about this."

"I know. I have thought, Crow. I must try to use my medicine to stop them."

"As you must," Crow Woman said sadly. "I do not understand, though, why your spirit-guide would not help."

"Nor do I. The only message was that maybe the gods will turn back."

They looked at each other, and a great light began to dawn on both.

"Elk!" gasped Crow Woman excitedly, "that is it! They do not *have* to be defeated!"

"Only to turn aside, to pass our camp, without discovering it. I can use my medicine for such a purpose, Crow, because it would not be evil!"

"How can I help?" she asked.

"The drum cadence. Let me prepare my ceremony, and we will begin. Bring my facepaint."

"Will it work against gods?" Crow asked.

"I do not know, but it is all we have. Anyway"—he paused long enough to smile at her—"we do not know that these are gods. That is only the word of the Caddo."

Inwardly, he wished that he knew more about these strange beings with shiny skins and dogs that could carry a man. He wished that he was younger, so that he could have gone with the wolves instead of sending Coyote. *Aiee,* what had happened to that one? Why did he not return or send word?

White Buffalo busied himself with preparations for his ceremony, now with greater confidence. He still might offend the gods with his attempts to turn them aside, but at least he would not run the risk of death from his own medicine.

The drumbeat began just after sunset. The dances, prayers, and chants, with intermittent ceremonial incense burning, continued throughout the night. It was a private ceremony, carried out within or just in front of the holy man's lodge. The People knew that something was going on, possibly something important. It was assumed that it had to do with the advancing column that was being observed by the wolves of the People. Consequently, there was a curious scatter of onlookers who came and went during the night, discussing quietly these events.

Sun Boy was lifting his torch above earth's rim when White Buffalo finished the last chanted prayer of supplication, and the drum fell silent. Half-stumbling, he made his way to the lodge and almost fell into his sleeping-robes. Crow Woman covered him with a robe and lay down near him, watching with concern as the holy man fell into the deep sleep of complete exhaustion.

It was nearly evening when White Buffalo awoke. He lay there a moment, becoming oriented to the day. Crow Woman lay sleeping. He knew that she too must have been exhausted. Quietly he rose and slipped outside.

He was just relieving his bladder behind the lodge when he heard a shout. One of the wolves was returning. White Buffalo hurried to the lodge of Hump Ribs, arriving at almost the same time as the messenger.

"Come in," the chief beckoned to the holy man, as he held the doorskin aside for the messenger.

It was apparent that the scout had news of great importance. He had the appearance of one who had been running, striving to reach the village before dark. But was his news good or bad?

"My chief," the runner panted, "the gods have turned back. This morning, they broke camp and moved away to the west, or southwest."

A broad smile broke the stern countenance of Hump Ribs. The crisis, the threat to the Southern band, appeared to be over. He nodded approvingly.

White Buffalo sat numbly, listening to the more detailed description of the messenger. His prayers and ceremonial chants had been successful, but he found that he had mixed feelings about it. It was over, and he had not had the opportunity to see the gods, to try to fathom their secret powers. And it was too late. He had been born at the wrong time. If only this had happened when he was young, so that he could have been with the wolves, could have seen for himself the wondrous god-beings. His mind wandered for a moment and then was sharply jerked back to reality by the words of the scout.

"One god was left behind," the man was saying. "He appears to be lost. He rides one of the elk-dogs."

"Elk-dogs?" asked Hump Ribs.

"Yes, my chief," the messenger chuckled. "Coyote calls them that. These dogs are as big as an elk. We have not seen one closely. Oh, yes, holy man, I have a message for you. Coyote says to tell you he will watch this lost god today and come to you tonight."

"They are that close?" asked White Buffalo in amazement.

"Oh, yes. The lost one has continued this way. I do not know, since I left, but they should be very close tonight."

"It is good," said Hump Ribs. "I will go back out with you."

36

"Uncle, I am made to feel that this is very important," Coyote said wearily.

His fat round body was not well suited to hurried travel.

"Yes, yes, go on!" White Buffalo urged impatiently.

"Well, they told you that the gods have turned back?"

White Buffalo nodded.

"But there was this one who appeared lost," Coyote continued. "We followed him. Uncle, the shiny skins that we have heard of . . . I do not think they are skins. A garment, maybe . . ."

White Buffalo exhaled a sigh audibly and impatiently.

"Forgive me, Uncle." Coyote hurried on. "There is so much. . . .This lost one is apparently abandoned by the others. Maybe they expected him to rejoin them, but he is injured."

"Injured? How?"

"He fell from his elk-dog."

"Wait. It is true, then, that they ride on the backs of these animals?"

"Yes, Uncle, and some carry burdens. But this one was startled by a real-snake. When it rattled, the elk-dog jumped, and the shiny god fell. We thought he was dead and came near to see. A long time he was dead, but then he rolled over and woke up."

Ah, thought White Buffalo. A god is immortal. He cannot die.

"But then," Coyote continued, "the god vomited. Uncle, would a god crawl on all fours, and grovel in his own puke?"

Before the holy man could answer, Coyote hurried on.

"Forgive me, Uncle, there is so much . . . the god then sat and seemed to remove his head."

"His head?"

Coyote giggled at his little joke and continued.

"So it seemed to some. There was a headdress, round and shiny. He removed it and appeared to take his head off. Some of us had seen that it appeared to be fastened with a leather strap or thong, so it was not really his head, but . . ."

"Go on, Coyote," White Buffalo urged.

"Yes . . . well, he is called Heads Off because of this and how it appeared. Hump Ribs called a council to decide what to do."

"Hump Ribs is still out there?"

"Yes, Uncle."

Coyote paused, seeming reluctant to relate his own part in these events.

"There were those," he said slowly, "who wished to kill the god and his elk-dog to remove the danger. But Uncle, I am made to think we must know more of this."

"What do you mean, Coyote?"

"Well, there are many things. Could a god be injured in this way? His head is bloody, and the shiny headdress probably saved it from being burst when he struck. Then he was sick. Several times. I do not think . . . Uncle, I do not believe these are gods at all. They are *men,* from a far tribe, much different than ours."

White Buffalo had begun to suspect something of the sort.

"How, different?" he asked.

"He has fur," Coyote said.

"Fur?"

"Yes. Black fur, which grows from his face. Not like ours, which we pluck with the clam-shells. This is black and curly, like that of the buffalo."

"Could it be a mask or a garment?"

"No, Uncle. It grows directly from his face."

"Aiee, that is strange."

"Yes, and the shiny skins—as I said, I do not think it is their skin. It is of the same material as the headdress."

"You think the fur covers his whole body, like the bear?"

"Maybe. I do not think so. His hands are not hairy."

"Did he speak?"

"Nothing we understood. He moaned a lot and said words strange to us. Oh, and he does not know handsigns. They meant nothing to him."

"You have been close to him. It did not seem dangerous?"

"Not really. He is sick and weak. My fear was that somebody would kill him before we could learn of his tribe. But they are not thinking so much of that now."

"Why?"

"Well, he seems harmless. And I . . ."—Coyote paused to chuckle at his own cleverness—"I gave him a name."

"A name?"

"Yes, Heads Off, as I said." He giggled again. "It is harder to kill someone if you know his name."

Yes, that is true, thought White Buffalo. *Coyote is clever, as always.*

"What is happening now?" the holy man asked.

"Nothing. He has bedded for the night. We are watching him. The elk-dog stays near."

"The elk-dog? It did not run away?" White Buffalo asked in amazement.

"What? Oh, no. It stays with him and eats grass."

"This 'elk-dog' eats *grass*?"

Coyote giggled.

"Yes, Uncle. Now it seems more elk than dog. But it has no horns."

"Tell me more of this elk-dog."

"Well, some wanted to kill it. It looks good to eat. But I thought it must, for some reason, be better to ride it than eat it. Otherwise, Heads Off would have eaten it already!"

Coyote sat back, smiling, pleased with his reasoning.

"So they will *not* kill it, you think?"

"No. I talked to Hump Ribs, and he told them not to. We could kill it later if we really need the meat."

"Tell me more of this elk-dog."

"Well, it has a beautiful skin. Gray in color, like a gray wolf, but shorthaired, like an antelope. It eats grass, and its eyes look at us without fear. It is proud . . . a look of eagles is in the eyes . . . oh, yes, I nearly forgot—its hooves are not split like other animals'."

"What?"

Coyote held up a hand, fingers apart, to demonstrate.

"There is no cleft. The foot is solid, Uncle." He paused to chuckle. "When we first saw it, it seemed to wear a turtle on each foot."

White Buffalo's head whirled. He had been so preoccupied with the invading god-beings and his ceremony . . . but now . . . he had completely forgotten his vision of so long ago. A lifetime ago, it seemed. The strange creature of his vision, the one that had seemed so important but was never seen again. Was he now to learn of it, in this strange way? His heart was pounding, and his palms were sweating.

"A turtle?" he asked in a hoarse whisper.

"Yes," laughed Coyote. "Of course it only looked that way. The hoof was solid, not split."

"Yes," said White Buffalo absently. "Coyote, I must see this animal. I will go back with you."

"There is no need, Uncle. It is just over the hill. You can see it in the morning."

"It is *here?* That close?"

"Yes. Heads Off, too. Hump Ribs said we will watch him but not bother him, until we see what he will do."

"But, he is sick with a broken head?"

"Yes, but it seems he will recover. We will see."

Coyote wandered off. White Buffalo was not certain whether he meant to return to the watch or to spend the rest of the night at home. The holy man turned back to his own bed.

"Elk," Crow Woman whispered, "did I hear right? Coyote spoke of the creature of your visions, the turtle-footed elk?"

"Yes," White Buffalo said thoughtfully. "Crow, I have never told anyone but you, and my father before his death. No one knew of this creature, that I had *seen* it long ago. *Aiee,* what can this mean?"

Crow shook her head.

"I do not know, but it must be very important."

"Coyote said that, too. *Why* is it important?"

"Do you not feel that?" asked Crow.

"Of course. But I do not understand it."

"Maybe it is not *meant* to be understood, my husband."

"That is true. We will go and look at this creature, the elk-dog, in the morning."

There was to be more than one startling development that next day. The People awoke to find that buffalo had come. For most, this news of immediate importance overshadowed any speculation about elk-dogs and gods who remove their heads. Here was food for the coming winter. Times had not been hard, and there was food, but at the Moon of Falling Leaves it is wise to make preparations. There may be very little hunting for the next few moons, and every lodge should have a season's supply of dried meat and pemmican stored in the space behind the lodge-lining. Therefore, the arrival of the buffalo was an important marker in the trail of the seasons.

It was immediately apparent that this was not the main fall migration. Only a few hundred animals, the forefront of the great herds to come. They were sleek and fat from grazing on lush grasses in the Sacred Hills and farther north. Now, like the People, they were moving south for the winter season. The move was early, even before the seasonal change in the wind. White Buffalo wondered if this was an omen, a sign of a coming hard winter. He would cast the bones later.

But for now, his greatest desire was to go and see the elk-dog and its strange rider. With Crow Woman, he started in the direction indicated by Coyote.

He was interrupted by a group of hunters who asked him for a prediction for the coming hunt. Impatiently, he performed the ceremony and sent them on their way. Of course they would have a good hunt, he thought to himself. The season, the fat herd—everything was right.

Again, he and Crow started for the hill from which they could see the god and his elk-dog. As they topped the rise, it was like a dream in which one can see everything at once. The gently rolling valley spread before them, the buffalo just moving into the northern end. And there, scarcely a long bowshot away, was the elk-dog. It was calmly grazing. White Buffalo gasped in wonder. He had already known but still it was a shock to see the creature, warm and alive, in all its graceful beauty. It raised its head and seemed to look at him. Even at such a distance, he caught a hint of the intelligence in the dark, wideset eyes.

"Aiee," he said softly.

"It is beautiful," Crow Woman whispered at his side. "This is the turtle-footed creature of your vision?"

"Yes," he answered simply. What more was there to say?

Now their attention turned to the figure near the elk-dog. Yes, thought White Buffalo, it was as Coyote suspected. This was a man, not a god. The man moved stiffly, as if from injury, even limping a little. He picked up something from the ground, something not seen well at this distance, and approached the elk-dog. It was difficult to see, but the man appeared to wrap some thongs around the creature's head and place something in its mouth. *Ah,* he thought. *This is his secret, the way he controls the elk-dog, his elk-dog medicine.* White Buffalo longed for a closer look, to determine the nature of this powerful spell over so large and strong a creature. He could see a shining sparkle, a reflection of sunlight, around the elk-dog's nose and mouth. It reminded him of the flash of silvery minnows in the stream, when they turn as one, and their sides glint in the sun. This must be part of the powerful medicine.

Even though he was beginning to understand, he did not quite know how —ah, now the man picked up a small robe or pad with thongs and straps attached and carelessly tossed it on the animal's back. He tightened the straps, placed his foot in a dangling loop of some sort, and stepped up, to sit astride the creature's back.

They saw now that the man carried a long spear. Its point, too, sparkled like the medicine around the mouth of the elk-dog.

"Should we run?" whispered Crow.

"I think not," White Buffalo answered, his voice hushed in awe. "He does not even see us. Look, he rides toward the buffalo."

Fascinated, they watched while the elk-dog trotted calmly toward the grazing animals. The man seemed to select one, and moved toward it, a fat cow. It was over in a moment—a sudden rush, a thrust of the long spear. The elk-dog slid to a stop, withdrawing the weapon, and the running cow took a few more frantic leaps, stumbled, and fell to lie kicking in the grass. White Buffalo was astounded at the efficiency of the procedure.

"Ah, so *this* is the real value of the elk-dog! To hunt!"

It was the voice of Coyote, who had joined them, unnoticed.

White Buffalo nodded, still entranced by the scene below.

"Maybe," he said slowly. "Maybe there are even more things that this elk-dog can do. But do you see how his medicine controls the animal? *Aiee,* he is powerful, Coyote."

The man had dismounted now and was rather clumsily hacking a chunk of meat from the hind quarter of the cow with a knife. He succeeded and withdrew to some distance away, to build a cooking fire, using sticks from a packrat's nest in a scrubby tree on the hillside. He appeared to have no use for the rest of the carcass.

It was not long before some of the hunters had sent word back to camp. A butchering party approached, cautiously at first. When it appeared that the elk-dog's rider, who owned the kill, did not object, they fell to the work of butchering with enthusiasm. In a short while, only stripped bones remained.

By evening, the word had been passed from Hump Ribs and the council. Heads Off, the outsider, and his elk-dog, were not to be bothered in any way. There was a strong feeling that it would be good to have him in the area. It was apparent that he could easily kill more buffalo than he could use, and someone might as well benefit from his kills.

White Buffalo had grave doubts, however. He saw too ready an acceptance of this strange foreign medicine. He would remain cautious until he knew more. Of one thing he was certain—things would never be the same again. It was a time of change, and in his declining years, he had come to dread change.

37

There was change in the wind. It had been some time since Heads Off's first kill when White Buffalo saw the signs of the seasonal shift. From the gentle breezes that blew from the south all summer came the change to a new direction. A cutting northwest wind whipped across the prairie, chilling the bones of the elderly and nipping the noses and ears of the young. Cold Maker was coming.

That was not the only change observed by White Buffalo. The People had developed a new attitude toward Heads Off, the outsider. With the help of his elk-dog, the newcomer could kill a buffalo, almost at will, whenever he was hungry. The People watched closely because Heads Off never used more than enough meat for a day or two. The remainder of the kill was always utilized by the women. Winter stores were filling with much more ease than ever before. Increasingly, there seemed to be a dependency developing. The People were relying on the skills of Heads Off and the elk-dog. This worried the holy man. The People, he feared, would be unprepared when the visitor moved on, leaving them to fend for themselves in the old ways.

He wished that the man would do so and went so far as to carry out, quite in secret, a ceremony with prayers that Heads Off would go, to rejoin his own tribe. Of course, at first the head injury prevented it. It was apparent that any activity caused much head pain. Heads Off would lie on the ground for some time after a kill, holding his injured skull in his hands.

White Buffalo was somewhat offended by the attitude of Coyote. Coyote seemed fascinated by the stranger and had assumed the role of protector. He had given Heads Off a buffalo robe to protect him from the weather and was teaching him the hand-sign talk. Coyote reported faithfully to the holy man, however, so there was a certain advantage to the tenuous arrangement. White Buffalo could remain well informed without seeming to do so.

It was some time before the holy man realized what he found so worrisome. Everyone in the band was talking about Heads Off, his activities, his skills. White Buffalo was threatened with a loss of prestige. Yes, that was it. He could hardly admit to jealousy, but it must come to that. In final form, the outsider presented a threat to the professional skill of the holy man. His elk-dog medicine was becoming more important daily, eclipsing the traditional buffalo medicine of the People. Again and again, White Buffalo found himself wishing that the man would go and take the cursed elk-dog with him. He wondered if his own position in the tribe would become obsolete. No one seemed to need him anymore. He performed small ceremonies designed to move the intruder on his way, though he was careful not to use his medicine for harm. It was more of an attempt to persuade, he told himself.

The young men, too, were fascinated by the novelty of the outsider and his elk-dog. There were two especially, youths not quite grown, who followed him and pulled grass to feed the elk-dog. *Aiee,* that was a bad sign, White Buffalo thought. It was unlikely that any gifted youth would be interested in apprenticing to the medicine man when they had the elk-dog to follow. To make matters worse, one of the favorites of the outsider was Coyote's son, Long Elk. The other was Standing Bird, son of Mouse Roars.

Meanwhile, Heads Off had been invited to live in the lodge of Coyote. It was now understood that "Heads Off hunts for the lodge of Coyote." Of course, Big-Footed Woman was generous with the kills, and the arrangement continued to benefit all.

All except White Buffalo, of course. He was increasingly frustrated. It was becoming extremely irritating to have Coyote popping in, every day or two, to relate the wonderful events that had occurred. Coyote seemed as completely charmed by Heads Off as the boys.

Something must happen soon, White Buffalo reflected as he strolled through the camp. They had made the move to winter camp shortly after Heads Off joined them, and he had accompanied them. According to Coyote, the stranger was staying with them to find water, since the People knew its location. Their southward migration was the proper direction for Heads Off too, so it seemed logical. Except, of course, that White Buffalo did not like it. Heads Off had stayed so long now that with the change in the weather, it would soon be too late to travel. He was looking for Coyote, to ask him about it.

His eye caught a group of children at play. One boy rode on the back of another and struck a third with a long stick. Even without an explanation, it was easy to tell what the game represented, but he stopped to ask.

"We are playing Heads Off, Uncle," a child replied. "He strikes the buffalo with the real-spear, and the buffalo falls down."

"Yes, I see," the holy man said, half to himself.

He saw only too well. The young of the People were being corrupted by the influence of the stranger. Something must be done to stop the spread of this evil. But what? He was certain that Heads Off was using his medicine to invade the minds of the children, but what to do? It must be done quickly, for when even the children's play was affected, how long before they would lose their time-honored heritage?

Reluctantly, he began to think that to remove the threat, the stranger must be destroyed. The most powerful medicine of the People must be their own, the medicine of the buffalo. He told himself that this was not just a threat to his own prestige but to the People's way of life. A test of power between the two medicines. He was uneasy, because in a clash of power, he was not certain that his own medicine was strong enough to triumph. Maybe, if he could not use his medicine against the intruder for fear of defeat or the risks of misuse . . . maybe he could kill Heads Off himself. No, that would not be good. That would surely sacrifice all his prestige. Maybe someone would be willing to assassinate him. . . .

"*Ah-koh,* holy man, are you looking for something?" asked Mouse Roars.

Mouse Roars was seated in front of his lodge, smoking comfortably against his backrest.

"I . . . ah . . . yes, have you seen Coyote?" White Buffalo stammered.

"Yes, Uncle, Coyote and Heads Off are in the lodge of Hump Ribs." He pointed at the chief's dwelling. "Shall I tell him when he comes out?"

"No . . . no, Mouse. It is nothing. I will see him later."

He turned and stalked off toward his own lodge, angry and even more frustrated. *Aiee,* for Coyote to take Heads Off to visit the chief . . . were they all in a plot to discredit him?

It was later that day when Coyote appeared at the lodge of the holy man.

"*Ah-koh,* Uncle," he began pleasantly.

White Buffalo merely grunted a greeting. He was still angry.

"I have come this time at the bidding of Hump Ribs," Coyote said formally. "He wishes me to bring Heads Off to see you."

Ah, then the test of medicines was to be at the request of the chief. The thought was like ashes in his mouth. After all his years of faithful service, of selflessness and sacrifice for the People, such ingratitude was beyond belief. Yet to refuse the contest would admit weakness. All his prestige would be gone and his medicine weakened.

"I think his medicine is very powerful," Coyote was saying, "but Heads Off has used it only to help with the hunt. Maybe I can persuade him to bring his medicine, so that you can examine it."

"This is not a contest?" White Buffalo asked.

"What? Oh, no, Uncle. Hump Ribs wishes you both to use your medicine to help the People."

That was not quite Hump Ribs's interpretation but Coyote's. He was carefully manipulating the shifting power structure as skillfully as any diplomat of other cultures.

White Buffalo set the scene carefully—his paints, fragrant-scented herbs and powders to toss on the fire, ready for use. He shook out the white cape and brushed it with a hawk's wing, smoothing and grooming the thick white fur.

"*Ah-koh,* Uncle, we are here," called Coyote, outside.

Crow Woman welcomed the visitors into the lodge. White Buffalo noticed at once that Heads Off was wearing the strange shiny garment once thought to be his skin. It was also apparent, however, that the young outsider had adopted the garment of the People to some extent. His feet were now covered by soft moccasins, which showed the unmistakable patterns and craftsmanship of Big-Footed Woman. He also wore new leggings and breechclout, undoubtedly from the same source. White Buffalo found himself somewhat irritated by this easy acceptance of the interloper. Big-Footed Woman was treating him like family.

The customary small talk ensued, and the holy man was surprised at how rapidly the newcomer had learned to communicate. There was some hesitancy, but between his knowledge of some words and some hand signs, a conversation was possible. White Buffalo did not fail to notice, however, that it was constantly assisted by Coyote. At times he was not certain whether the ideas being expressed were those of the visitor or of Coyote.

The holy man found, however, that he was powerfully intrigued. Rarely, once in a lifetime, perhaps never, would this opportunity happen to understand the medicine of another. Especially a medicine so powerful and so different from his own.

As he began his dance, imitating the dance of the buffalo, his mind was occupied with these thoughts. He concentrated on perfection of the ritual, giving meaning to each shake of the head, each pawing motion of a hoof. As he began to feel each swaying motion, once again to get "inside the head" of the great animal he represented, he felt at home, confident. This was a medicine that the stranger did not have, *could* not have.

There remained the doubt, however, the silent fear of being displaced. If the stranger and his medicine remained with the People, there would be no need for the medicine of the buffalo. White Buffalo's usefulness was over. So he must do something. He could wait a little while. Maybe for the winter, even. But then, if the stranger did not leave . . . how should it be done? By use of his medicine? Simply kill him? Or maybe someone could be found who would act as an assassin. Kill the elk-dog, maybe? That was a possibility that had not previously occurred to him. With no elk-dog, could there be elk-dog medicine?

White Buffalo finished the ceremony, and the drum fell silent.

"Now," said Coyote. "Come, we will show you the elk-dog medicine."

Coyote led the way outside to the place where the elk-dog waited. The shiny medicine-thing was in the creature's mouth, and the pad was strapped to its back. White Buffalo had not seen the creature up close before and was impressed by its size. It did not appear too threatening, however. It turned its head to gaze curiously at him with large gentle eyes. There was little that was frightening. And this was plainly the creature of his vision quest.

Now Coyote was talking.

". . . this circle, I think, Uncle, the ring around the jaw. That is the medicine that lets him control it."

Maybe, White Buffalo thought to himself. *That is not too complicated.*

"What is the purpose of the elk-dog?" he asked. "Besides hunting buffalo?"

"Heads Off says, to ride long distances, for war, or to hunt."

"Do his people eat elk-dogs?"

"No. Hump Ribs asked that. Sometimes if they are starving, but not usually, Heads Off says."

The little man cleared his throat, a trifle embarrassed, and went on.

"I am made to think, Uncle, that the medicine of Heads Off is greatly different from yours."

"Of course!" snapped the holy man.

"No, no," Coyote said quickly, "I meant no harm, Uncle. It is only that the medicines seem to work well together."

"What do you mean?"

"Well, Uncle, your medicine makes for easier kills. One medicine helps the other!"

Of course. Coyote, the thinker, had found the answer to the dilemma. It was only necessary to acknowledge the new medicine to remove its threat— to point out its differences.

"Yes," White Buffalo said slowly, "they are quite different, these medicines. Mine brings the buffalo, to be killed with the aid of the elk-dog. It is good. They will help each other."

White Buffalo was quite pleased with the outcome of the meeting. This was a situation that he could now manage. But he was no more pleased than Coyote, who smiled to himself as he turned away. It had gone quite well.

38

⬌

Once he had decided in his own heart and mind that the two medicines were not in conflict, White Buffalo settled into a more comfortable existence. He still did not feel, somehow, that his position allowed him to associate closely with the stranger and his medicine. He was content to observe, to let Coyote relate to the new elk-dog medicine.

He sometimes felt pangs of jealousy that Coyote's interest lay there, instead of in his own, the medicine of the buffalo. It was different, however. It became apparent that the medicine of the elk-dog was a very physical thing. Agility and active use of the body were required, while Coyote was a bit clumsy and at best, lazy. Coyote's relationship to the medicine of the elk-dog was that of a thoughtful observer rather than a participant. That pleased White Buffalo. It also kept him informed, as Coyote continued to share his observations. But the stranger seemed less threatening now. No longer semisupernatural, he could be observed as a man. A strange complicated man from a far tribe, it was true, but that was only a matter of interest now. It was discovered that the black fur did not cover the entire body of Heads Off. Coyote had seen him remove his garment to empty his bowels.

"His butt is as shiny as mine," Coyote reported with glee.

Heads Off proved quick to learn. By the time Cold Maker arrived in earnest, the hair-faced outsider could use sign-talk well and converse in the tongue of the People. He still spoke with an accent but was understandable. Coyote continued to instruct and inform the visitor.

It was known that Heads Off wished to return to his own tribe. It was simply too foolhardy to attempt in the winter moons, noted on the plains for unpredictable weather. So Heads Off waited, a little impatiently at times. When the band moved north in the Moon of Roses, White Buffalo supposed, Heads Off would move south, the direction from which he had come. That would be a time of mixed feelings. The People would regret the loss of easy procurement of meat when Heads Off was no longer there to kill buffalo. To White Buffalo's way of thinking, however, that would be an opportunity to return to the traditional ways. He would no longer need to be concerned by any possible threat to his own prestige. Yes, it would be good to see the visitor go when the time came.

Meanwhile, the moons passed in winter camp, with gambling and smokes and storytelling. Heads Off participated, and his communication skills continued to improve. Coyote related that they had exchanged Creation stories and that Heads Off had reacted much as anyone else would in the telling.

"Is the Creation story of his tribe a good one?" asked White Buffalo.

"I have heard worse," Coyote observed. "Their Great Father made First Man out of mud and breathed life into him. Then he gave the man a woman to live with."

White Buffalo nodded.

"I must listen to it sometime."

"He liked our story also," Coyote went on. "I told him how we crawled out of the earth through the log."

That had always been a favorite story of the People. They had lived in darkness, it was said, until they were summoned by a deity who seated himself astride a hollow cottonwood log. With a drumstick, he tapped on the log, and with each tap, another of the People crawled out into the sunshine. There was a joke involved in the telling. It was customary when a stranger was present to stop at that point in the story, hoping that the listener would ask the obvious question: Are they *still* coming out? No, said the standard reply. Alas, a fat woman got stuck in the log, and none has come through since. That is why we are a small tribe.

"Did you tell him about the Fat Woman?" asked White Buffalo.

"Yes," chuckled Coyote, "but he did not understand it. Uncle, I am made to think that the tribe of Heads Off does not enjoy its religion very much."

"Perhaps that is their way," suggested the holy man.

"Maybe so," Coyote pondered. "Maybe he would like to hear the Creation stories of the Growers. Did some of them not come up out of a great river?"

"I think so. Someone to the north of us . . . Mandans, maybe, crawled out much as we did, by climbing the roots of a large grapevine."

"Ah, yes, I remember that one. A good story."

* * *

It was still assumed that in the spring, when the People moved north to the Sun Dance, Heads Off would return to his own tribe. Despite the interesting contact for a few moons, White Buffalo continued to look forward to that event. It would be the time of returning to the old ways. The confusion of the strange medicine from outside would be finished, and it would be good.

There was still a question in White Buffalo's mind, however, that refused to go away. *Why?* Why had he been given the vision of the elk-dog so long ago? When he first saw the animal in the flesh, he had known that it was the creature of his vision, and it seemed that all was complete. Yet there was something missing, something not quite right. Soon the hair-faced outsider would leave, and the great episode would be at an end. The holy man had already painted the event on the story skin. It was a figure of Heads Off, removing his headdress in the incident which had provided his name.

Still, something was missing, and White Buffalo could not think what it might be. There seemed, in the events of the past year, not enough importance to give meaning to the vision of his youth. Ah well, maybe he was only showing his age, the holy man pondered. The visions of youth are always bright with the promise of the future and become less important with the reality of the passing years. But he did not believe it. There *was* something, a purpose of some sort, he was sure. He had simply not seen it yet. Maybe he never would . . . Heads Off and the elk-dog would be gone soon, and he, White Buffalo, would have missed the entire significance of this important event in the lives of the People.

He worried, prayed, and even discussed the matter with Crow. That was unsatisfactory because even with her keen insight and intuition, Crow had not seen the *vision* of the elk-dog. She could not understand.

It was now common knowledge, as the Moon of Greening changed the prairie almost before one's eyes, that soon the People would start their move. Not everyone realized, probably, that Heads Off would be traveling in the other direction, but it was foremost in the mind of White Buffalo. He was wondering when Hump Ribs would announce . . . maybe he should go and talk to the chief.

These thoughts were interrupted by the approach of Coyote. The little man was laughing.

"Heads Off cannot leave us!" he announced with glee. "His elk-dog is pregnant!"

A mixture of emotion washed over the holy man. Regret that the incident of Heads Off's stay would *not* be over. Relief that he might have the opportunity to solve the mystery. And many questions came to mind about elk-dog reproduction.

"What . . . how? . . ." he mumbled in surprise.

Coyote laughed again, the high-pitched animal chuckle of his namesake.

"I do not know all, Uncle," he admitted. "Heads Off was very angry. I think the elk-dog may not travel well when it is near to birthing."

More confusion whirled in the thoughts of White Buffalo. The elk-dog at first had been an almost supernatural creature in his mind. Now it was almost commonplace. Even the earthy process of reproduction marked it as a quite ordinary creature, though one with special talents. Why, then, *why* had he been subjected to the startling vision of the elk-dog so many summers ago? It must be something to do with the *medicine* of the elk-dog. Yet he had satisfied himself that the elk-dog medicine was not *his* medicine but that of Heads Off.

Aiee, every time he thought he had solved the mystery, there was a new twist to the path he was following. And such a ridiculous twist. *Aiee!* A pregnant elk-dog!

It was only half a moon later when the elk-dog gave birth to a black, furry creature with knobby legs and large curious eyes. Long Elk and Standing Bird were enthralled and in a short while were handling and stroking the small elk-dog. It was a source of much amazement to all. In a remarkably short time, the foal could lope alongside the mother.

According to Coyote, this event led to much indecision. Heads Off was undecided whether he could travel with the small elk-dog. Apparently there was some thought of killing or abandoning the foal to spare the mother the stress of nursing. In the end, Heads Off decided that such a thing would be unwise. This pleased Coyote greatly.

The visitor had still not chosen his path of action when the word came that the time to move was at hand. White Buffalo waited, with the old confusion of mixed feelings, to see what Heads Off would decide. In the end, with apparent reluctance, Heads Off mounted the elk-dog and followed the People, the small elk-dog scampering playfully alongside.

"Why does he do this?" the holy man asked Coyote as they walked.

"I am not certain. Maybe the elk-dog would not travel well with her young. It is a far journey that Heads Off must go."

"But he goes with us?"

Coyote spread his palms, perplexed.

"We travel more slowly . . . *aiee,* Uncle, I do not know. Who knows what a Hairface is thinking?"

So the confusion continued for the holy man. He still felt, somehow, that he was overlooking something. He would have been more comfortable if Heads Off had gone home to wherever his own tribe lived. But again, that would not solve the question that still burned below the surface like hot coals deep in the ashes of an almost-dead campfire. *Why* was the elk-dog so important to the life of White Buffalo? He was a holy man of a small band of hunters belonging to a tribe that was not a great power on the plains.

A hundred times he almost convinced himself that the coming of the stranger, riding on an elk-dog, was an isolated incident. Heads Off would be gone as soon as the small elk-dog was able to travel well. The entire season of the elk-dog would be only a memory and a picture on the story-skin. Then why, he asked himself, was he given the vision, and the sense of the elk-dog's importance? Once more, he would arrive at the same point with no apparent answer.

One further incident occurred which confused White Buffalo even more. The band was traveling without incident when one of the wolves trotted in to report that there were Head Splitters over the next ridge.

"They are traveling too," he told Hump Ribs. "Women and children . . . it is as usual."

Still, there was a thrill of excitement and potential danger that swept through the band like a chill wind. Children clung closely to their mothers, and men checked their weapons, all the while hoping they would not be used. Hump Ribs, Mouse Roars, and another warrior moved forward to the low ridge to meet the delegation from the enemy column. Coyote and White Buffalo followed closely, and the rest of the People grouped closely together some distance behind, protected by the rest of the warriors.

There were the usual greetings, small talk, and comments on the weather, carried on in hand-signs between the chiefs. Then an apparently meaningless observation by the enemy leader seized the holy man's attention.

"I see," signed the Head Splitter, "that you have an elk-dog."

There was a moment of confusion, there being no standard hand-sign for "elk-dog," but there was little doubt of meaning as the Head Splitter pointed to the animal. The mare was grazing calmly while Heads Off had dismounted to hold the rein.

"Yes," Hump Ribs replied calmly, as if elk-dogs were an everyday sight, "it belongs to an ally who is spending the season with us."

White Buffalo smiled to himself. Hump Ribs was certainly handling the situation well. Then a slight doubt arose in the back of the holy man's mind. It concerned the Head Splitter's attitude. The enemy chief had also tried to act as if elk-dogs were commonplace. This implied that the animal was not unfamiliar to him. As far as could be observed, this band of Head Splitters had no elk-dog, but they had *seen* them. This indicated, in turn, that there were more elk-dogs on the plains. The implications of this idea made the holy man's thoughts whirl. What if the Head Splitters too could hunt as easily as the hair-faced outsider? They would become wealthy and powerful. And dangerous, more dangerous than before. The People might easily be driven from the Tallgrass Hills that had been their home for many generations.

Now White Buffalo was more confused than ever. This, perhaps, was the importance of the elk-dog vision. But how did the office of the holy man fit into this? He still did not understand.

39

The Sun Dance that year was memorable. The Southern band had much news to report at the Big Council, and Hump Ribs was equal to the task. He told the council in glowing terms of the elk-dog and of the powers of Heads Off with the lance. It was obvious that the Southern band was well fed and well dressed, and that the reason was the outsider and his hunting skill. Of course, each member of that band took pride in telling of their collective good fortune.

White Buffalo was quick to note the difference in the condition of the Southern band from the others'. The Red Rocks band, for instance, looked thin and ragged by comparison. They had eaten many of their dogs. The Eastern band had also seen better winters. Maybe, thought the holy man, the elk-dog was even more important than he had thought.

All of the People were fascinated by the elk-dog and her foal. All the bands had heard of these creatures, but none had seen them except the Red Rocks. They sometimes ranged far to the southwest and had encountered a band of strangers, they said, who possessed such an animal. It was used as a dog to carry packs, but they had not seen it ridden.

Because of the great interest, Hump Ribs, through Coyote, arranged for a demonstration of the hunt as carried out by the outsider. Heads Off was willing, and the wolves began to scout for buffalo. A small herd was located and arrangements made for an appropriate site where the spectacle could be well seen. White Buffalo took an active part in the preparation. How could he do otherwise? He must strengthen his own position by pointing out the effectiveness of his medicine in attracting the buffalo. Heads Off also seemed to take an interest in the preparations, as one should who wishes to show his medicine well, thought the holy man.

The meadow which had been selected was relatively long and narrow, bordered along one side by the stream, and on the other by the ridge where the People sat. From generations of hunting buffalo, the People understood the importance of quiet and concealment. Even so, there was a tension in the air as the first of the herd entered the meadow from the far end. White Buffalo found his palms sweating. The wary old cow in the lead paused, sniffed the air, and finally seemed to decide that the meadow was safe. She led the way, the other animals scattering to feed in the grassy flat.

Now Heads Off nudged his elk-dog forward from behind the shoulder of the hill. He chose a fat yearling bull and carefully moved toward it. A good choice, thought White Buffalo. That one will be excellent eating. It was a distinctive animal also, an odd mouse-colored hue, different enough to attract attention. Yes, a good choice.

The demonstration went extremely well. Heads Off pursued, and managed to drop his quarry directly in front of the party of warriors who sat on the ridge with the real-chief. A cheer of victory went up, a yell of triumph, led by the voices of the proud Southern band. Heads Off turned the elk-dog and rode slowly up the slope to face the assembled council. He lifted his lance.

"I give this kill," he shouted, "to Many Robes, chief of the People!"

Aiee, what a clever thing, White Buffalo thought. This outsider understands the use of medicine. Possibly Coyote had suggested such a dedication, but no matter—it was good. That distinctive skin . . . no matter where Many Robes chose to use it, the robe would always recall Heads Off and the strength of his elk-dog medicine.

The rest of the annual celebration—the Sun Dance, with its prayers, sacrifices, and ceremonies—seemed almost an anticlimax now. The days were completed, and the People began to disperse to their separate areas for the season.

None could fail to note, however, as they went their separate ways, that the Southern band had grown. Seven lodges, with possibly ten hunters, counting young men still in their parents' homes. Of course, White Buffalo observed, some were the opportunists, always ready to switch allegiance for some gain in social status. Everyone knew who these were.

But there were others whose reputations were above reproach. He noted Two Pines, of the Red Rocks, with his family. Another lodge appeared to be that of Two Pines's daughter and her husband. Well, the Red Rocks had suffered. Not from lack of leadership, perhaps, but from the whims of fortune. They would be in a time of change, some seeking a band with a stronger chief. Such was the shifting of political prestige. These changes did take place, and White Buffalo was pleased that it was to the Southern band that the discontented were shifting. Sheer numbers would strengthen the band's reputation.

Of course, he knew that it was largely the novelty of the stranger and the elk-dog that created the attraction. No matter. Once the newcomers became members of the band, even for a season, they would see the leadership of Hump Ribs. At least, the more desirable individuals would. It was a good feeling to see others wishing to join the Southern band. It had long been one of the weaker bands of the People. Now the prestige was moving their way, and it was good. Possibly, when Heads Off went to rejoin his own tribe, the numbers would shift away again. That was to be expected. Meanwhile, let the Southern band enjoy the honor.

The hunting was good that season. Every lodge was able to store an adequate supply of food for the winter with the help of Heads Off. The young outsider seemed to enjoy using his skills for this purpose. But the time came when Heads Off announced that he must leave. The small elk-dog was growing rapidly, and Heads Off thought that it should travel well now.

There were many who were sad to see Heads Off go. Especially disappointed were the two young men who had spent so much time learning of the elk-dog. Strangely, though, the holy man found himself reluctant too. After the threat to his authority had been set aside, he had rather enjoyed the novelty of the elk-dog, as well as its efficiency. White Buffalo actually found himself wishing for Heads Off to stay. There would be great benefits from the elk-dog's continued presence, not only to the Southern band but to the whole tribe. It was apparent that if Heads Off remained, there were now not one, but *two* elk-dogs. That would make the hunt even easier as the younger animal grew to maturity. Possibly Long Elk or Standing Bird could learn to ride and use the long spear. Already, Heads Off had allowed them to sit on the larger animal.

White Buffalo did not share these thoughts, even with Crow. A few moons ago he had actually considered killing the stranger, and now—*aiee!* It was a good joke on himself; unfortunately, one he could not share. Now he wondered if there might be some way he could prevent Heads Off's departure.

As the season drew to a close, the preparations of Heads Off to depart neared completion. Finally, the actual day was decided. There were many who regretted this loss. Life had been much easier when the difficult part of the hunt had been carried out by the hair-faced newcomer.

"One more hunt, Heads Off," some of the young men requested. "Let us go into the winter with plenty."

"It is good," Heads Off agreed. "Tomorrow, a last hunt, and then I must go."

White Buffalo rose early and watched the hunters go out. He wished them well and performed the ceremony for success in the hunt. But then, after their departure, the holy man performed a private ceremony outside the camp, unknown even to Crow. He burned fragrant herbs, chanted, and prayed that the stranger who had become one of them *not* depart. He wondered if this complete reversal of position might displease the spirits but decided that he must risk it.

It was later in the day that White Buffalo saw Heads Off ride in, jerking the elk-dog savagely to a stop. He was puzzled. Word had been sent back that the kill had been made, and the butchering parties had already gone out. Why, then, was Heads Off so furious? The young man stripped saddle and bridle from the horse, released it to graze, and stalked away to be alone. In his present mood, no one dared speak to him. Curious, White Buffalo waited.

Sun Boy had passed the top of his run before people started to trickle back to the camp, laden with meat. Impatiently, White Buffalo waited, wondering what event had provoked the rage he had seen in Heads Off. Finally, Coyote approached and came straight to the lodge of the holy man.

"What is it?" White Buffalo demanded. "Heads Off came back, and—"

"*Aiee,* Uncle, he was mad with rage! He broke his spearpoint."

"*Broke* it? But it is made of the shiny metal . . . it can be broken?"

"Yes! It struck a bone and snapped. It was maybe this long, you know, and broke near the middle." Coyote indicated with his hands. "My wife found the broken point as she butchered and gave it to him, but it appears that it is useless."

"But spearpoints do break," White Buffalo observed.

"Yes, but he has no other."

White Buffalo began to understand. The weapon had been part of the medicine of the elk-dog. It was different from any other weapon and essential to the hunt as Heads Off performed it. Without it, he could not hunt, and . . . *aiee,* without it, Heads Off was virtually unarmed!

"I will talk to Stone Breaker," Coyote said. "Maybe he can make a new point."

During the next days, it was quite unpleasant to be around Heads Off. It was a little while before the others realized the gravity of the loss. Stone Breaker did indeed craft a magnificent spearpoint of the finest blue-gray stone. Some said that it may have been his finest work yet. However, when Stone Breaker and Coyote took the point to give to Heads Off, the young man's reaction was quite irrational. He shouted angrily at them in his own tongue and seized the carefully crafted spearpoint in a rage. He threw it into the river, accidently cutting his finger on its sharp edge as he did so. This, of course, further angered him, and they felt it best to let him alone.

In a few days, when his rage quieted, Heads Off did seem apologetic. Stone Breaker managed to recover the spear point from the crystal-clear stream, but he and Coyote decided to wait awhile before approaching the subject again.

Heads Off made several attempts to repair the broken point. Coyote faithfully reported to White Buffalo on these occasions. The metal could be heated in a fire until it glowed red, like hot coals in the ashes. Heads Off then tried to make the broken parts stick together by pounding them with a rock. Coyote had assisted him in this, but each effort was a failure.

"Once, I thought it would work," Coyote related. "It did stick together until he tapped it on the ground, and then it snapped again."

Finally, Heads Off gave up the effort at repair. He remained withdrawn and depressed, and no one had summoned courage to suggest the stone point again.

"Has he said what he will do?" asked White Buffalo.

"No," Coyote answered, "but what can he do? He cannot travel without a weapon, so he must stay another winter with us."

White Buffalo said nothing. He was a bit apprehensive as he thought of his secret ceremony. He had attempted to cause Heads Off to remain with the People and had succeeded. At least, it appeared so; yet something had gone wrong. The thing that had made Heads Off stay was the loss of his spearpoint, part of his elk-dog medicine.

White Buffalo's heart was heavy because the possibility that he had caused this dilemma nagged him. His prayer had been granted, that Heads Off remain with them. But there was this cruel twist. The medicine, the reason they desired Heads Off to stay, was gone. Now he could not leave, but there was no longer a purpose for wishing him to do so. The secret ceremony had been too risky, White Buffalo decided. He had overstepped his authority, had misused his medicine.

40

Ⅰt was spring before Coyote managed to coax Heads Off into testing a
spear with the stone point. Stone Breaker flatly refused to offer *anything*
to Heads Off again but agreed to cooperate with Coyote. With the skill of
a weapons expert, he assembled a spear, using the broken weapon as a
pattern. Coyote had quietly borrowed it for the purpose. The new weapon
was tipped with the recovered stone point, carefully scraped and smoothed
for balance.

"Its heft is as good as his own," insisted Stone Breaker, still somewhat
disgruntled by the rejection of the past autumn. "He should appreciate this,
but *I* will not offer it to him.

"No, no," Coyote agreed. "I will do that. You have done your part well."

So it was that Heads Off, convinced by Coyote that he had nothing to
lose, agreed to try the new lance. He made his kill flawlessly and seemed a
new man. He was almost jovial and made a great show of thanking Stone
Breaker for his efforts.

But now, White Buffalo observed, the same dilemma had returned. Now,
with a weapon, the rearmed Heads Off was ready to depart. The solution
came about in a very frightening and unexpected way.

The holy man was relaxing in the warm sun of the Growing Moon when it happened. He heard a cry of alarm and looked up to see a dozen Head Splitters mounted on elk-dogs, charging into the village. It was terrifying, happening so rapidly that no one had time to think. The total surprise and the unfamiliar appearance of attackers on elk-dogs caused complete and utter confusion. Very few even tried to resist as the enemy swept through, clubbing and spearing, riding boldly through the camp, yelling their blood-curdling falsetto war cry.

There were some exceptions. He saw one aged warrior, Black Dog, step calmly into the path of the charging horsemen, singing the death song:

> The grass and the sky go on forever,
> But today is a good day to die.

Black Dog loosed his first arrow, which knocked one of the leading warriors from his horse as if swatted by a giant hand. The old man managed to shoot again, but White Buffalo could not see whether the arrow struck. Black Dog was overrun and trampled beneath drumming hooves.

The People were running in terror, fleeing for the questionable safety of the river and its fringe of timber. Resistance was still thin. He saw Heads Off running toward the fight, pausing to grab the lance. Mouse Roars emerged from his lodge and began shooting calmly at the invaders. A warrior came swooping down on Heads Off, club swinging, and an arrow from the bow of Mouse Roars struck the rider down. Heads Off turned.

Both he and White Buffalo saw the young chief on the spotted horse at the same moment. Horsemen were riding among the lodges, striking or thrusting at targets of opportunity. As Mouse Roars readied his arrow for another shot, the horse came stepping quietly from behind his lodge. It was a beautiful creature, white with reddish rosettes over the entire body, spots no larger than a man's palm. The rider urged the animal toward the unsuspecting back of Mouse Roars. White Buffalo tried to yell a warning but could not make himself heard amid the screams and war cries. Heads Off was running forward, but too late. The Head Splitter's club swung, and Mouse Roars slumped forward, his weapon under him.

The attacker turned, and as the wife of Mouse Roars rushed from the lodge to kneel beside him, the horseman circled, looking at the mourning wife. He seemed to consider, to decide that the woman was not young enough, or perhaps not pretty enough, to be worth abducting. The great stone club swung again, and she fell across the body of her husband.

Now Heads Off rushed forward and charged at the horseman, screaming a challenge. The young chief reined toward him and kicked the horse into a run, his club whirling for a death blow. In the space of a heartbeat, it was over. White Buffalo had expected to see the form of Heads Off fall to join those of the others, but it was not so. Heads Off had dodged the swing of the club and had thrust his buffalo lance up over the elk-dog's shoulders into the belly of the attacker. He had grabbed the elk-dog's rein, and was hanging on as the animal reared and plunged, bucking frantically to dislodge the flopping corpse on its back.

The horse quieted, and now Heads Off was shouting to the others to catch the loose elk-dogs. A few warriors were still shooting, but the battle was over. The Head Splitters were retreating after the death of their leader but leaving a village strewn with the dead. White Buffalo saw a small girl, thrown across the shoulders of a Head Splitter's elk-dog, screaming and struggling as she was carried off. A riderless horse thundered past and clattered across the gravel bar at the river.

People were returning or emerging from lodges where they had hidden, and the wailing dirge of the Song of Mourning began to rise here and there. Standing Bird stood, numbly staring at the bodies of his parents. Others were frantically calling names of missing loved ones.

A hastily called count indicated that there were three Head Splitters dead but seven of the People. In addition, it appeared that four were missing and presumed abducted. One was a boy of about ten summers; two were small girls. The fourth was Tall One, the oldest daughter of Coyote. She had run forward to stop the abduction of one of the younger children, and the abductor, probably pleased with his good fortune, had taken her instead.

Tall One had recently developed into a strikingly beautiful young woman with the intelligence and poise of her mother. It had seemed only natural to those who observed that Heads Off had been attracted to her, living in the same lodge. Still, nothing had come of it. Perhaps Heads Off himself had not realized it until now, when the girl was taken. But it did explain his active participation in the hastily held council.

The discussion was loud and argumentative, largely about what should be done, which direction to flee. Into this argument, head-on, came the hair-faced outsider. At first he shouted in his own tongue. Then, in the moment of calm that resulted from the shocked surprise, he seemed to realize his mistake and calmed somewhat. He proposed pursuit of the Head Splitters, pointing out that there were no more than ten and that their leader was dead. Instantly, several youths volunteered to go with him, led by Standing Bird and Long Elk. It was a touchy moment, but Hump Ribs rose to the challenge.

"Wait," said the chief firmly. "If there is to be a war party, *I* will lead it, with the help of Heads Off."

Clever, thought White Buffalo. Hump Ribs enlists the help of Heads Off without giving up his own authority.

It was quickly decided. A war party of fifteen would proceed on foot and would probably overtake the Head Splitters in the darkness. That in itself would give the People an advantage. White Buffalo performed a ceremony for success, and they were gone, following the trail left by the horses.

They were back shortly after daylight, and Coyote came to relate the events of the night.

"Hump Ribs let Heads Off direct part of the attack," he explained. "Part of the plan was to steal elk-dogs. That would create a diversion, and when the Head Splitters stood up against the sky, Hump Ribs' bowmen . . . *aiee,* my friend, it was a great victory."

The little man chuckled, still excited.

"You recovered the children then? Your daughter?"

"Yes, yes. And elk-dogs too!"

"Elk-dogs? How many?" asked the astonished holy man.

"I do not know, Uncle. We caught two or three after the battle. Maybe six more. All they had."

"You captured *all* their elk-dogs, Coyote?"

"Of course! Well, not I, but those who were with Heads Off."

"But how?"

"Long Elk said they took thongs, like those they had been using on the small elk-dog, and tied them around the lower jaw . . . you remember, the medicine-circle, the ring?"

White Buffalo nodded, still amazed.

"Well, they rode on some of the elk-dogs and led the others."

"Were the Head Splitters all killed?"

"No, a few got away. Some wanted to chase them, but Hump Ribs said to spare them. They could tell their tribe that the People are to be reckoned with!"

Coyote danced a joyful little step or two, then stopped suddenly.

"Uncle," he said seriously, "something else! He asked me for Tall One!"

"What . . . *who* did?"

"Heads Off! She rode on the elk-dog with him on the way back. You have not seen how they look at each other?"

"I . . . ah . . . well, yes. Will you let her marry him?"

"Why not, Uncle, if she and her mother agree? Which they will. We will be proud to have him in the family. And it may prevent him from leaving."

White Buffalo looked at him sharply. Was Coyote aware of the holy man's changing feeling about this? Did he even suspect the part White Buffalo had played, or attempted to play, in keeping Heads Off with the People? There was just a hint of a cunning smile on the little man's face. Maybe . . .

"Well, I must go and rest, Uncle," Coyote continued. "It has been a long night. But I wanted you to know."

He turned and started away, then turned back.

"Uncle," he said seriously, "I am made to think that this man brings important things to the People. Beyond what we have talked of before. It is good, this feeling, to beat the Head Splitters."

This was a far more serious conversation than one could usually have with Coyote.

"You think this is because of Heads Off, Coyote?"

"Yes. Or, because of his medicine. Maybe . . . did you see, yesterday, Uncle, how great an advantage they had when they attacked on elk-dogs? But now *we* have elk-dogs."

"What are you saying?"

"I am not sure, Uncle. But, all my life, the People have feared the Head Splitters. We always run and hide. Now . . . this feels different. Uncle, you and I have talked of the two medicines, yours of the buffalo and his of the elk-dog."

"Yes."

"But we have thought more of the elk-dog for use in the hunt. Maybe this other use, to defend ourselves, is more important even. And, when we move, think of all an elk-dog can carry. Uncle, there is a change in the wind."

There were, it turned out, eleven elk-dogs in all, not counting Heads Off's gray "First Elk-dog" and her foal. Within a day or two, several of the young men had asked for the help of Heads Off in learning to use the animals. The Rabbit Society gave way, among the older boys, to instruction by Heads Off. Long Elk and Standing Bird, already well along in the skills of handling, progressed rapidly. One of the other boys inquired about the use of the real-spear. Wooden lances were contrived for practice until Stone Breaker could produce the special spearpoints necessary. Day after day they practiced, charging a willow hoop tied loosely to a bush until they could thread it neatly on the spear shaft most of the time.

Meanwhile, some of the young men had begun to experiment with the use of a bow from horseback. This was foreign to the experience of Heads Off but appeared useful.

"Look, Heads Off," one called. "To use the real-spear, you approach the target from the left. For the bow, it is better from the right."

It was true, and in a combat situation or in a buffalo hunt, this could be significant. In addition, it was soon noted that some horses preferred to approach the target from the left, some from the right. Quickly the bowmen capitalized on this fact, trading for horses with the tendency to run to the right side. Heads Off was pleased and proud over their progress. He could hardly wait to let them try their skills at the hunt before they started north to meet the rest of the People at the Big Council.

In a very short while, the group of young men were being called the Elk-dog Society, at first as a joke suggested by Coyote. But they wore it with pride.

41

I t was with great pride that the Southern band arrived at the Big Council that season. A dozen warriors rode elk-dogs, and made a great show of doing so. By day's end the others were referring to the Southern as the Elk-dog band. It was in a joking, tongue-in-cheek way, but their envy was plain.

The Elk-dog Society had progressed rapidly. Already they had staged a buffalo hunt, killing nearly a dozen animals at a single sweep. Hump Ribs, a natural storyteller anyway, managed to extract every bit of attention with his report to the Big Council on the night after their arrival. By custom, the chiefs, seated around the circle in their assigned places, told in turn of their band's doings during the year just past.

On this occasion, though most of the bands had little news, it was obvious that there had been much change in the Southern band. The news had spread like a prairie fire in a high wind when the Elk-dog Society arrived. But still it remained for Hump Ribs to relate the tale formally in the Council. And Hump Ribs, aware that this occasion was coming, had rehearsed carefully. The listeners were spellbound as the deep voice of the Southern band's chief related the details of the attack by Head Splitters, the bravery of Black Dog, of Mouse Roars, and of Heads Off. And the pursuit and capture of the elk-dogs, the rescue of the prisoners, all lent suspense and interest to the story.

By the end of the seven days of the Sun Dance, there was much talk of the rising prominence of the Southern band. This band's unique characteristic, of course, was the possession of elk-dogs. That much was plain, and there was surely prestige and honor involved. But there was more, a vaguely defined something, an attitude. There was a change in the Southern band's approach to the world. Of all the bands, perhaps this one had traditionally been the most conservative. Maybe *timid* would be a better term. It was, in the end, a run-and-hide mentality, resulting from generations of persecution by the Head Splitters.

But now the winds of change had swept across the prairie. It was strange that fate had chosen this band, which seemed least likely of all the People to lead the change. But whether it was by chance or that the gods of the grassland had so decreed, it was happening. There was a difference in the posture of the young men, a straight-backed pride that had not been evident before. The others of the People saw the change, and although they may not have realized what they were seeing, they spoke with respect.

Possibly no one was more affected by this than Hump Ribs. When he had become chief, he was unassuming and quiet, not a well-known warrior. Circumstances had beckoned to Hump Ribs as they had to the Southern band. This had provided the opportunity for his leadership qualities to emerge and grow. In the years since his election, Hump Ribs had changed. Formerly the reluctant leader of a small band, almost embarrassed when he spoke to the Council, he had risen in confidence and in prestige. He was considered a statesman, one of the finest leaders to emerge from the warrior ranks of the People in many generations. There was talk of his fitness for real-chief when the time came to elect. After all, old Many Robes had weathered many winters. Someday, death would end his tenure, and the People would elect a new leader. For several generations the real-chief had been selected from the Northern band, but it was not a requirement. It might easily be that with the rising respect accorded the Southern band, this would be a manner of recognizing an existing shift in political power.

Of course the reflected glory fell on others of the band also. White Buffalo found that there was greater respect for the strength of *his* medicine. Heads Off, who had been regarded largely with curiosity last season, received a measure of respect, acceptance, and even honor now. He was regarded as one of the subchiefs of the Southern band. Coyote, the amusing buffoon, pretended to be unaffected by all this but secretly reveled in the greater attention to his droll stories and antics. These were exciting times.

The term "Elk-dog Society" seemed to catch on rapidly, and the handful of young warriors who were fortunate enough to ride elk-dogs considered themselves an elite guard. The name, started in jest, was worn proudly by the Elk-dog Society. Quickly it became apparent that there were now two societies in the Southern band, the old Warrior Society and the youthful Elk-dog warriors.

Of course, there was some shaking of heads and clucking of tongues among the elders. Could there be two warrior societies? No one seemed to know. There was an uneasiness in some of the older warriors, yet so far, the elk-dogs had brought only benefits. It was already apparent that elk-dog medicine and buffalo medicine worked well together in the hunt. That had been proven and was already well accepted. But this was a new and different question. In armed conflict, how would elk-dog medicine combine with the old ways? There were many misgivings, yet the effectiveness of the charge into the village by mounted Head Splitters had been awesome.

"But they could have been stopped," stated Two Pines. "We were caught by surprise. Black Dog and Mouse Roars killed two of them!"

"Ah, but where is Black Dog? Mouse Roars? Dead!" argued another. "Men on foot cannot stop men on elk-dogs!"

"If they had had help," Two Pines insisted, "it could be done. We were taken by surprise, and that must not happen. Our wolves must be alert."

"But the elk-dogs move too rapidly!"

"Ah, but *we* have elk-dogs too!"

The arguments raged on, hindered not at all by the inexperience of the participants. Coyote watched and listened quietly and without comment. Finally, when the opportunity offered, he approached Heads Off.

"Heads Off, your warriors use elk-dogs in battle?"

"Yes. We have talked of this, Uncle. What is it?"

"Yes, I know. What I wish to know, is this . . . not *all* your warriors ride elk-dogs and carry spears?"

"Oh, no. We talked of the bowmen, who fight on foot. Then there are those who use"—he paused, searching for a word—"a . . . sort of long knife."

"On an elk-dog?"

"Well, sometimes. Sometimes on foot. Others use a very long spear, on foot."

"I see . . . then there are several warrior societies?"

"I . . . I guess so. Yes, warrior societies. Why?"

"Ah, the men talk. About the Elk-dog Society, you know. It seems like a new warrior society. But there is still the old one. So, can there be *two?*" He chuckled.

Heads Off laughed.

"Why not? My tribe calls them lancers, bowmen, pikemen, swordsmen."

"It is good," decided Coyote. "We have Warrior Society and Elk-dog Society."

Coyote giggled again, and Heads Off nodded.

"Yes, they are already called that," he agreed.

The entire concept of elk-dogs for the hunt and for battle was so broad, so far-reaching, that it was hard for the mind to grasp. White Buffalo was only now beginning to understand the importance, the *why* of his elk-dog vision so long ago. The use of the elk-dog, he now realized, was to be the greatest change in the ways of the People in his entire lifetime. Maybe even, the holy man was beginning to see, the greatest change since the People came through the log. It had been difficult for him to accept at first, and it was still a thing of wonder. White Buffalo had thought that he had reached the height of his powers, his medicine-gift. He had even thought himself on the way down, but now, *aiee,* this might be only the beginning. These were exciting times as the winds of change swept the grassland, opening a new way of life—and perhaps of death.

When the Sun Dance finished this season, the Southern or Elk-dog band, had grown again, by ten more lodges.

The marriage of Tall One to Heads Off took place in the autumn of that year, in the Moon of Falling Leaves. The holy man noticed that since the Sun Dance—no, even before that—there had been no talk of Heads Off's departure.

"He speaks no more of it," Coyote explained. *"I* will not ask him. He talks only of marriage."

It was apparent to everyone that this was a devoted couple. They spent much time together, walking beside a clear stream or sitting on a hilltop. They watched the hawks circling high above on fixed wings, riding the invisible currents of the wind. This special courtship was a source of pride and pleasure to the band. It was romantic, the manner in which Heads Off had helped to rescue his intended bride from the Head Splitters. The story grew with the telling, becoming even more romantic. In an odd way, this courtship increased the prestige of the outsider. Heads Off, largely due to circumstances, was following custom. By example, then, he was becoming one of the group, the People—even more specifically, a respected member of the Southern band.

Normally, when a young couple decided to marry, they would first live in the lodge of the bride's mother until they could set up their own lodge. However, the women had decided, possibly at the suggestion of Coyote, that an honored warrior such as Heads Off should have a lodge. After all, it was due to his elk-dog medicine that materials were available. The summer was spent in dressing and sewing skins for a lodge cover befitting the dwelling of an important couple.

It was also in this season that the People realized that a lodge could be much larger than before. Prior to the elk-dog, the size of a dwelling was limited to how many skins could be handled and moved by three or four people. Transportation of a lodge on a pole-drag was likewise limited to the strength of people and dogs.

Now the limiting factor was the strength of the elk-dog. Many skins were available, and with materials and the ability to transport . . . *aiee!* How large could a lodge be? There was a joke that the limit would be found in the availability of lodge poles. Long poles were at a premium and were traded as a precious commodity. The size of one's lodge, of course, reflected the hunting skill of the owner, his ability to obtain larger numbers of skins.

All of this influenced the construction of the lodge of Heads Off and Tall One. Possibly he was unaware of it to some extent. Finally, in time for the ceremonial nuptials, the lodge was finished and was set up for the first time. The band was already in winter camp, in one of their favorite areas where the grassland meets the scrub oak.

The ceremony was carried out in front of the lodge of Tall One's parents, with many friends, relatives, and well-wishers in attendance. Coyote, trying his best to retain his dignity, performed the ceremonial prayers for the happiness of the couple. The two knelt side-by-side before the symbolic fire of their union, and Coyote dramatically drew a robe around the shoulders of the two.

They rose, the robe still covering the new couple as they made their way past smiling faces to their own lodge. Inside, the first fire of their new home was burning; there was food and the bed of soft robes opposite the doorway. The doorskin fell silently into place behind them, and the People dispersed to their own lodges. Their hearts were good, for the happiness of these two.

42

It was no surprise to the Southern band when the news spread that Tall One, daughter of Coyote and wife of Heads Off, was pregnant. In fact, it had become something of a joke, the preoccupation of this young couple with each other and with their privacy.

The young elk-dog men, during the warm days of late fall and early winter, would have some question about the elk-dogs but could not find Heads Off to ask.

"Let him alone," advised Long Elk. "They are in their lodge."

"Aiee," one answered, "he has not been *out* of that lodge since the Moon of Falling Leaves!"

"Think about it," suggested Standing Bird. "Would *you* have left that lodge?"

There was general laughter, the ribald amusement that reflected a certain envy. Tall One was certainly one of the most beautiful women. Her lithe grace and shapely form could be expected to arouse the imagination of young men. Fantasies could not even begin to approach the reality of a winter in the warm and loving lodge of Tall One.

"It is true," agreed the questioner. "Let him alone."

There was laughter again.

By the Moon of Greening, Tall One was showing her enlarging belly. Her buckskin dress now appeared smooth and taut around the waist. There was much speculation among the People. What would be the appearance of the child? Would it bear fur upon the face, like that of Heads Off?

The newcomer had by this time settled into the ways of the People quite comfortably for the most part. His dress, the trim and plait of his hair—everything indicated that he belonged, except for the facial fur. That remained the mark of an outsider. The men of the People, of course, possessed some facial hair. It was thin and scanty, and at the onset of puberty, the emerging hairs were plucked as a part of increased interest in one's appearance. Heads Off had actually considered such grooming and with Coyote's help had experimented. However, one session with the clam-shell tweezers proved adequate to dissuade the continuance of such a project. In half an afternoon, only a patchy bare spot resulted on one cheek.

"This is not good, my friend," Heads Off had protested. "I know now why this custom is not found among my people."

Coyote giggled.

"It would be a great test of manhood," he teased.

"There are other ways to test manhood, Uncle," Heads Off protested again. "Follow your customs in most things I will, but *aiee,* my face is sore!"

"It is true," Coyote had concluded. "The face-plucking is not for those with heavy fur."

So it was decided. The hair-faced outsider did not attempt to pluck his face, and this was easily accepted. He was respected for his willingness to follow the customs of the People in most other ways. The current situation provided an amusing diversion with many jokes and questions. Some of the inveterate gamblers were already quietly betting on whether the upcoming offspring would bear facial fur.

However, first things must come first. The birth was expected no sooner than the Moon of Ripening. First the band must travel to the Sun Dance, which would be held on the Walnut River this season. But even before that, an odd incident occurred which cast a suspicious shadow over events to come.

The spring hunt was excellent, and every lodge was well supplied. Perhaps the outstanding successes of the year for the Southern band influenced the chief's decision about the day of the move. Surely, any leader would anticipate the honor and prestige that would go with such a year. Therefore, it may have been that Hump Ribs called for the move a bit early.

The usual protest arose from the women. They couldn't possibly be ready in three days. The meat from the recent kill was not yet prepared. Even while they protested, they started preparations for the move.

Big-Footed Woman was among the most vocal of the protesters. It was foolish, she scolded, to think that all the fat from the recent kills could possibly be cooked down properly in so short a time. Mere men, even chiefs, could not understand such a problem. Just because times were now improved was no cause to become wasteful. Good food had never been wasted by the People, even in times of plenty. She, for one, would never leave meat on the prairie to rot. She had no intention, she continued, of leaving this campsite until her work was done. The men wisely refrained from argument.

In fact, it was noted that both Coyote and Heads Off scrupulously avoided their wives after the striking and packing of the lodges. It seemed advisable to avoid contact, where possible, with the sharp tongue of the irate Big-Footed Woman. Let her vent her wrath, and perhaps by day's end her temper would be cooled somewhat.

By noon, the column was on the move, but it was time to stop for the evening camp before Coyote and Heads Off noticed anything amiss.

"Where is your mother?" Coyote asked Long Elk.

"She stayed behind to finish cooking the fat," Long Elk answered. "You did not know? She said they would catch up later. Tall One is with her."

It was immediately apparent that Heads Off was quite upset at this turn of events. He seemed to blame himself, fidgeted and paced, and finally spoke to his father-in-law.

"I go to look for them," he explained, as he swung up onto the gray mare.

"I go with you," Long Elk said quickly.

Shadows were growing long over the abandoned campsite, but one fire still burned.

"Mother, we *must* leave! Please forget the rest of the fat," Tall One entreated. She had stayed behind to help finish the cooking and to help with the carrying. She had had no idea that her mother would stay this long over her silly grudge.

Actually, Big-Footed Woman hadn't intended it this way. She would, she thought, let them leave without her. She was certain that the men would come back as soon as their absence was discovered. She would then grudgingly consent to leave, having proved her argument.

But the men had not come. Her anger was rekindled, and her stubborn streak began to manifest itself even more strongly. She would stay here until they did come, she decided.

But that was while the sun still shone. Now the darkness was falling, and the whole thing began to seem a little foolish. Maybe they should pack up and travel, she thought. They could follow the trail of the entire band, even in complete darkness. She was about to capitulate and in fact had drawn in her breath to speak when Tall One held up a hand to listen.

Unmistakably, there was a sound of hoofbeats. Three or four elk-dogs were approaching at a walk. Both women brightened considerably, and Big-Footed Woman began to plan her scathing remarks for the men. She turned her back and began paying utmost attention to skimming melted grease and spooning it out to cool.

"Here they come," she murmured, savoring her moment. The horses came closer, to the very edge of the firelight, and stopped. She heard a chuckle, but not until a gasp of surprise and fear came from Tall One did she turn.

There were four men, each sitting on his horse in a relaxed, amused posture. They made no immediate move, merely sat smiling and chuckling. It took a long moment for the significance of the situation to make itself felt to Big-Footed Woman. Somehow her mind was slow to grasp so unexpected a scene. She had been certain that when she turned, she would see her husband and Heads Off.

But these men were complete strangers. And by their ornaments and weapons, Big-Footed Woman could see that her bull-headed escapade had backfired. These men were not even of the People.

They were Head Splitters.

"Hello, Mother," signed the oldest of the Head Splitters, apparently the leader. "Is our supper ready?"

Foolishly though she had acted that day, Big-Footed Woman was wise enough not to do anything foolish at that moment. If either of the women rocked the delicately balanced situation, the result might be instant tragedy. As it was, the Head Splitters seemed to be enjoying the game. Their only chance, both women realized, was to play along and stall for time.

"Get down and sit," signed Big-Footed Woman. "You are early. My husband will be back soon."

Laughter from the Head Splitters. They could see that the camp was abandoned. They slid from the horses and wandered around the fire, poking at the strips of fat.

"Get away from my cooking," the woman said irritably, reinforcing her demand with sign language and a gentle shove. "I will say when it is ready!"

More laughter.

It's working, she thought. We will be safe as long as I can keep them laughing. Maybe the men will come.

Of course, both women knew that their cause was hopeless. They could feed the strangers and for some time possibly dissuade them. Eventually, the Head Splitters would tire of the game and would kill them, probably after raping them. Already the small one with teeth like those of a squirrel was letting his glances rove over the long body of Tall One. The best that might happen would be that they would take her with them instead of killing her outright. Too bad, thought Big-Footed Woman. I did want her to bear the child of Heads Off.

Even while her mind was busy with such morose thoughts, her hands were busy with the cooking fire. She chattered on in a combination of talk and sign.

"Stay back, you'll kick dirt in my cooking!" she ordered.

The Head Splitters were enjoying this scene immensely. One of them made an exaggerated move to escape her scolding, and the others rocked with laughter. Big-Footed Woman began to cook some small strips of meat and hand the morsels to the men. She wondered how long she could continue this process. She cooked small portions, only a few at a time, assisted by Tall One, who had thus far been silent.

Full darkness fell, and the process of cooking and feeding the strangers continued. Tall One kindled a torch and propped it nearby for light. Once the older man impatiently demanded that they cook bigger portions.

"Mother," said Tall One finally, "don't you think that little one looks like a squirrel?"

Tall One glanced at the little man. Complete absence of any understanding shone on all four faces as they chewed pieces of meat or joked among themselves.

Her mother nodded. "And the big one is the ugliest I ever saw."

The big one in question smiled and nodded.

"I thought so," concluded Tall One. "None of them understands a word of the talk of the People. Now I will tell you my idea. I do not intend to go to bed with Squirrel Tooth over there."

She smiled at the man again, and he responded with a toothy grin.

Rapidly, Tall One sketched her plan.

Her mother nodded. "It is good. Even if it does not work, we may escape in the darkness."

Finally it seemed that the nearly insatiable appetites were becoming satisfied. Squirrel Tooth was looking hungrily at Tall One. It was time to make a move. Tall One strolled over to replace the sputtering torch with a fresh one. Instead of propping it for light, she suddenly lifted it high and dashed off into the darkness, the flame bobbing and dancing over her head.

The Head Splitters leapt to their feet and ran after her, shouting to each other as they ran. Big-Footed Woman quickly picked up a heavy stone war club and slipped into the darkness.

Tall One ran down the familiar path, counting on her pursuers' unfamiliarity with the terrain. She looked back, slowing her pace slightly. It was important that the pursuit be as close as possible. The line of flight led straight across a level area with no obstructions, and her long legs kept her barely ahead of the running warriors. She wondered if they thought her stupid to be carrying the torch.

A hundred paces behind the abandoned lodge site, the level meadow dropped off sharply to the river. The edge was a shelf of stone, jutting out of the earth and ending abruptly. Below lay a tangled pile of jagged pieces broken from the shelf through the centuries and dropped into the stream's bed.

Straight for the edge ran Tall One. As she neared the drop, she sprinted faster, pulling slightly away from the runners behind. She waved the torch high, then suddenly flung it ahead of her and dodged quickly to the left, slipping quietly into a clump of bushes. The plan worked perfectly. The men, in full stride, continued to pursue the bobbing, flashing torch as it bounced over the rocks. The two in the lead did not even break stride as they plunged over the edge. It seemed a long time before the dull sounds of their bodies striking rock was heard. The third man, Squirrel Tooth, realized something was wrong just as he reached the ledge. He attempted to save himself but overbalanced and fell, a short exclamation of surprise choked off by the dull thud.

The fourth man was warned and managed to stop at the edge. He called into the dark, but there was only a low moan in answer. The torch lay far below, flickering in a crevice near the water. He turned to look for the girl, shouting angrily. Tall One hugged the earth and tried not to breathe too heavily.

"Tall One!" a voice called from the darkness. "Bring the big ugly one back to the fire and let him catch you, almost!"

The big man turned toward the voice, but the girl jumped up with a frightened squeal and ran back toward the fire, the warrior in hot pursuit. She dodged around, barely staying out of his reach, until she saw from the corner of her vision where her mother was located. Twisting, turning, the agile young woman maneuvered her pursuer into proper position and finally stumbled, sprawling with a little scream.

The man loomed over her in rage, and his hands reached for the girl. She was glad that he had no weapon. At the last moment, there was a dull *thunk,* and the Head Splitter slumped forward, falling almost on top of her. Big-Footed Woman brushed the hair back from her face as she hefted the borrowed war club in case another blow was needed. It was not.

The exhausted women made their way back to the fire. As they built up the blaze, they suddenly heard hoofbeats again, and both slipped warily into the darkness.

Heads Off and Long Elk rode into the circle of the firelight and paused, calling their names. Big-Footed Woman stepped quickly from hiding.

"Heads Off! Long Elk! Over here," she called.

They returned to the fire.

"Mother!" shouted Long Elk. "We were very worried!"

"Oh, we are all right," she managed to say calmly. "We traded meat to some travelers for four elk-dogs."

She pointed to the animals, tied in the shadows.

Heads Off was irritated. He had been nearly frantic with worry and did not appreciate the light treatment of a near-tragedy.

"Come on," he snapped gruffly. "Let us join the rest."

"Of course, Heads Off," answered his wife meekly, "as soon as we finish skimming out the fat."

43

What had shown every promise of being a triumphant, prestigious Sun Dance full of celebration was almost a disaster. It became quickly apparent that with the exception of the Southern band, no one had fared well.

The Eastern band, of course, rarely fared well. That was assumed to be due to their own foolishness. But the others had suffered too. The Red Rocks, especially, were at a low point in their entire history. They had been attacked more than once by the Head Splitters. The enemy now appeared to be usually mounted, and the frightening impact of an attack by well-armed horsemen was demoralizing.

Additionally, there had been encounters during travel. These noncombative confrontations, where protocol prevented open hostilities because of danger to families, were quite useful sometimes. It was possible to see whether the enemy had fared well and to observe changes in customs and attitudes. The reports were all the same. The Head Splitters, who were probably of several different bands, had all behaved similarly. They were arrogant, even more than usual. They had many elk-dogs, and they were insolent and threatening.

One fact stood out above all others, however. At each contact, the Head

Splitters had mentioned the same theme. Gray Wolf, who now appeared to be their principal war chief, was looking for blood. The young chief killed by Heads Off in the skirmish the previous year had been the son of Gray Wolf, who had now declared an oath of vengeance against "Hair Face."

"I will decorate my shield with that fur," Gray Wolf had vowed.

Repeatedly, this message had been relayed to the bands of the People at any encounter. It was causing much consternation and fear. Coyote attempted to put the threat in proper perspective.

"I have heard it said," he observed whimsically, "that to use a cat's fur, it is first necessary to skin the cat."

This attempt to lighten the burden of worry fell largely on deaf ears. There was, in fact, some animosity, both toward elk-dogs and toward Heads Off, bringer of the elk-dog.

"It was not so before the strange beasts," one old woman babbled. "We should drive them away!"

"Yes, and the hair-face too," a man of the Mountain band said quietly. "It is against this outsider that the Head Splitters vow revenge."

"Stupid ones!" Big-Footed Woman replied indignantly, "Look for yourselves. Which band among us is strong? Whose children are fat, and their women happy? The Southern band, who have elk-dogs!"

"But the Head Splitters . . ." the old woman insisted.

"Mother," said Big Footed Woman gently but firmly, "All your life the People have feared the Head Splitters. That has nothing to do with elk-dogs!"

It appeared that a complete rift in the tribal structure was a distinct possibility. White Buffalo was alarmed and was pleased when Many Robes called the Big Council at the earliest possible opportunity. This friction must be resolved.

The Council opened in a confused jumble of misunderstanding and resentment. The smug attitude of some of the Southern band was creating much friction.

"Even our women can defeat Head Splitters!" boasted one man.

The episode of the capture and clever escape of the two women had been told and retold, but some had begun to resent even that.

"It is not for you to boast!" snapped an old warrior of the Red Rocks. "Wait until you are attacked again!"

"The Head Splitters have elk-dogs, many of them!" another burst out. "They move fast, strike, and are gone!"

Several suggestions were introduced. Some favored merging two or more bands, to gain strength in numbers. To others, the answer was to move out of the traditional territory of the People, away from the Head Splitters. The wrangling continued.

Finally, Many Robes held up his hands for silence, and the noisy argument quieted. The real-chief looked around the circle for a moment as if searching, and his eyes lighted on Coyote.

"Coyote, my brother," he said, "you have not spoken. Tell us, what do you think?"

Coyote paused a moment, and once again White Buffalo marveled at the man's skill. He could recall no one who could manipulate a group of people as Coyote could, achieving what he wished but able to make others think it had been their own idea. White Buffalo had long been aware of this, but now he wondered . . . yes, surely, the Real-chief must realize it too. That was why he had waited until the proper moment to ask Coyote's opinion.

The crowd was quiet, waiting to hear Coyote's remarks. This might be quite humorous, and the interest mounted, a relief from the heat and anger that had held the Council in its grip. Coyote waited, like a performer skilled in the use of the long pause, waiting for the right moment. He giggled nervously, and the crowd smiled and relaxed.

"My chief," Coyote began, "there is much that I do not understand. But it is a question to me . . . I hear the People say *'aiee,* the Head Splitters have elk-dogs.' Why do the Head Splitters not say *'aiee,* the *People* have elk-dogs'?"

There was a moment of silence, and argument broke out again.

"But they have more!"

"We have *none!"* shouted a man from the Mountain band.

Many Robes held up a hand, and the crowd quieted.

"Hump Ribs, your Elk-dog band has not been attacked?"

"No, my chief, except for the women."

The crowd chuckled.

"Then they are attacking only those of us who have no elk-dogs," observed the real-chief.

"This is true, my chief," spoke Black Beaver of the Red Rocks. "But it seems their quarrel is with Heads Off and the Southern band, who now have elk-dogs."

There was a murmur of assent.

"But they do not attack that band yet," Coyote said whimsically. "Maybe they fear *our* elk-dog soldiers."

Again, there was a moment of silence as the crowd reflected on the truth of Coyote's remark.

"Yes!" exclaimed Two Pines. "If *all* bands had elk-dog warriors—"

"We need more elk-dogs!" stated young Standing Bird, who was already gaining recognition as a skilled rider and hunter.

"But where can we get elk-dogs?" one of the dissenters asked scornfully.

"Where did *ours* come from?" Coyote asked with a bland smile.

"The Head Splitters?" someone asked in astonishment.

"Maybe we could . . ."

"Aiee! I don't know . . ."

"We *could!"*

"No, it is too dangerous!"

Many Robes gestured for silence again.

"Black Beaver," he addressed, "your band is in closest contact with the Head Splitters. Where do *they* get elk-dogs?"

The chief of the Red Rocks shrugged.

"We do not know. But they have many. They seem to bring them from the south or southwest. It is said that there are tribes of hairfaces living there."

Glances turned toward Heads Off, who seemed embarrassed by the attention. Coyote intervened. "My brothers," he began jovially, "let us ask my daughter's husband. Heads Off, is your tribe living in that area?"

Heads Off, still embarrassed by this turn of events, hesitated for a moment and then managed to speak.

"I do not know, Uncle. They have villages farther south. Has anyone seen other hairfaces?"

There was silence.

"No, only stories," said Black Beaver finally.

White Buffalo wondered if the outsider still longed to return to his people. But now Many Robes was speaking again.

"Then more elk-dogs . . . for the People . . . must come from the Head Splitters, it seems."

"Can we trade with them?" asked someone.

It was not unheard-of to trade with the enemy, and such commerce was often useful. Any tribe might easily have more robes or meat than they needed, and, enemy or not, one must be practical.

"Our women traded with them this season," Coyote observed with a chuckle.

There was general laughter. Big-Footed Woman's exchange of bits of meat for the weapons and horses of her captors was the joke of the year.

"Maybe," Coyote went on, "we could trade for more in this way."

"What do you mean?" someone demanded.

"Wait!" Many Robes held up a hand. "What Coyote suggests is this: If we are to have elk-dogs, we must get them from the Head Splitters. They will not wish to trade, so we must take them."

"*Aiee!* Did I say that?" Coyote asked softly. Everyone laughed again.

"Could this be done?" Many Robes asked.

Again, there was the murmur of discussion. Though there was some dissent, the general tone was now *how* to effect the proposed course of action. Gradually, a plan emerged. The Southern band would accompany the Red Rocks for the season, along with warriors from any of the other bands whose interest leaned toward elk-dogs. Raids would be attempted to acquire more horses from the enemy, and the Southern band would teach the others the use of the medicine of the elk-dog.

Quickly the excitement grew. Each band could see itself becoming as successful and wealthy as the Southern band after the coming of the elk-dog. Young men rushed to state their wish to participate.

In the aftermath of this council, the excitement of the Sun Dance was almost anticlimactic. Yet there were many prayers, sacrifices, and vows made in the ensuing days. When the People struck the lodges to move out in separate columns for the season, it was with greater excitement than ever before. There were many good-byes that held greater importance than before. Relatives who were separated each year now realized that this season would be different. There would be different dangers, but also adventure and the promise of reward if the proposed scheme proved successful.

Hump Ribs sought out Heads Off after the council.

"Can this thing be done, Heads Off?"

"The elk-dogs? I think so, Uncle. If they are there, we can get some. And our young men are becoming skilled."

Hump Ribs nodded, pleased—not only at the prediction of success but at another thing that Heads Off had not even noticed. "Our young men," he had said. Yes, the chief thought, Heads Off is really becoming one of the People.

Meanwhile, White Buffalo was doing much thinking of his own. This entire concept, the idea of absorbing and using the medicine of the elk-dog, was so large, so far-reaching. He could see it working, helping the People. Yet it was happening so quickly. He found doubts forming again. Could it really be done, this grand plan for the season? He must go and think—and pray, and cast the bones. . . .

These were exciting times. The People seemed ready for this major change, but sometimes White Buffalo wondered if *he* could still handle the excitement.

44

The two men cautiously worked their way up the slope toward the crest of the ridge. Both were aware that today was the culmination of the season's effort, but for the moment, that was forgotten. More important now was the danger of their position. Sees Far carefully crept alongside a large rock, hoping that its broken outline against the sky would make his own silhouette less conspicuous. The rising sun was behind them. This too was calculated to make observation more difficult for the enemy.

The raiding party had worked its way deep into enemy territory, carefully avoiding all contact. Now it had become apparent that a large band of Head Splitters was camped ahead. Tracks had suggested that they had many horses. This appeared to be a summer camp, much like that of the People, though in somewhat different terrain. Now they were scouting to plan the attack.

Sees Far peered over the rim and suppressed a gasp of amazement. He motioned to his companion, and Heads Off wriggled forward to join him. Below lay a large camp of scattered lodges, possibly as many as those of the Southern band and the Red Rocks combined. There was little activity at this sunrise hour. Here and there among the lodges were tied horses—only a few, probably favorite mounts of warriors who would rather not risk pasturing them with the herd.

And the herd! *Aiee!* Heads Off immediately saw the reason for the gasp from his companion. Quickly they estimated. There must be at least a hundred animals. The two remained a little while, studying the terrain and the best route of approach and retreat. Then they quietly withdrew.

"Aiee, so many elk-dogs!" Sees Far exclaimed when they were at a safe distance. "Where did they all come from?"

"I do not know," Heads Off admitted, "but they have young, as ours do. It would not take long to have many elk-dogs."

"How old must a cow elk-dog be to have young?"

"Three years, maybe. It would not be called a cow elk-dog . . . *aiee,* Sees Far, I do not know! We can talk of this later. Now let us plan."

They returned to the rest of the party and related what they had seen. Hump Ribs was willing to relinquish the planning to Heads Off.

"There is a small stream," Heads Off explained. "We can cross there, in the dark, and move them across, to come this way. Those who are riders will take ropes and catch an elk-dog to ride. Others can stop any pursuit."

It was decided that if any problem arose, a long yell would signal everyone to escape as best he could.

The day seemed long, the waiting interminable. Men slept, talked, gambled, or checked their weapons. The attempt would be made just before dawn, to take advantage of the Head Splitters' well-known reluctance to fight at night. But by moving out just before dawn, they would have good light for traveling rapidly. Pursuit was likely, but if most of the enemy's elk-dogs could be stolen, the numbers of mounted pursuers would be few.

It was a bold and risky plan, but expectations were high. White Buffalo had promised to strive to the utmost of his ability and the power of his medicine for the success of the raid. His signs, it was said, had been good. Every man knew that at this very time, back at the summer camp several sleeps away, the holy man would be actively helping. There would be chants, fasting, ceremonial dances, and prayers. Probably White Buffalo would not even sleep during the night or two of importance to the raid.

By the time of the late rise of the half-moon, men were beginning to stir in the camp. One by one, they began to rise. They wakened the few sound sleepers and quietly moved out, led by Sees Far and Heads Off.

The yellow smudge of false dawn was barely showing in the east when the young men of the Elk-dog Society began to move among the grazing animals, knotting thongs around lower jaws and choosing animals to ride. So far, there had been no evidence of any sentry or wolf. Apparently the Head Splitters, deep in their own country, felt completely secure. The word was passed quietly, and the horsemen began to urge the herd toward the creek. Still there was no alarm. It was not until the splash and clatter of many hooves stirred the gravel of the ford that some early riser in the enemy camp noticed anything amiss.

A warrior, awakening, rose to attend to the urge of his aging bladder. It was no longer efficient enough to maintain capacity completely through the night. He yawned and stretched and stumbled sleepily out of the lodge and around to the rear to urinate. It was only then that he heard the rattle of gravel at the stream. He paused a moment and realized that the herd was crossing at the shallow ford. What a nuisance, he thought. The creatures wander. A bear, maybe, like the last time. Or possibly one of the great long-tailed cats that sometimes came down from the foothills. He raised his voice in a long yell to rouse the others. He noted even as he did so that this seemed to startle the herd. Startled the stalking bear probably, he thought, and that in turn had panicked the elk-dogs. Now, from the sound, the entire herd was in full flight. It would take some of the young men most of the day to round them up. Well, it was no concern of his. This whole elk-dog thing was for younger men. Having done his duty by raising the alarm, he turned to a more important matter, loosening his breechclout to relieve the now urgent pressure of his swollen bladder.

The Elk-dog men of the People, meanwhile, assumed that the long yell was a signal that they were discovered. Quietly, they swung up to the backs of their horses and quickened the pace, urging slower animals across the ford. As the herd began to move as a unit, the men rode back and forth, circling, keeping the animals together, continuously pushing ahead. They passed half-hidden bowmen, stationed to delay pursuit, but so far there was none.

It was well past daylight when Heads Off suggested a stop to evaluate the success of the raid.

"*Aiee!*" someone cried, "this must be every elk-dog the Head Splitters had!"

"There were a few more in their camp," Sees Far said, "but most of those we saw are here."

"They may have others somewhere else," warned Heads Off. "But is there no pursuit?"

The bowmen were now rejoining the main party.

"We saw no one," Two Pines said, puzzled. "We left wolves to watch."

Sometime later, the wolves reported that they were indeed followed.

"Only two riders. They ride slowly and do not seem alarmed."

"Could it be," asked Sees Far, "that they do not *know* their elk-dogs are stolen? That they believe the herd only wandered off?"

That seemed the likeliest explanation. Perhaps this had happened before.

"Or," suggested someone, "the medicine of White Buffalo is very powerful, to close the enemy's eyes."

"They will not stay closed," warned Hump Ribs. "Soon they will see our tracks."

"Those who follow must be stopped," Standing Bird said firmly. "I will go."

"Wait!" called Heads Off, "you—"

"Let him go," advised Hump Ribs. "He is thinking of his parents."

Standing Bird had picked up his bow and now started back on foot, jogging.

"Let us move on," Hump Ribs decided. "He will catch up."

It was much later, when they had paused for a rest stop, that someone pointed to moving figures in the far distance.

"We are still followed!"

"But by only one," Sees Far noted.

They watched as the rider made his way down the opposite slope and crossed the valley toward them. He was riding one horse and leading another, it appeared. And there was something familiar about the way he sat—his posture and balance.

"It is Standing Bird!" exclaimed Sees Far.

Standing Bird rode toward them, unhurried, and finally swung down. He removed the rawhide war bridle from one of the animals, and released it.

"We are no longer followed," he said simply.

B ack at the camp of the People, the days passed slowly. White Buffalo was certain that the raid was over. He had *felt* the time of decision and was optimistic that the raid had gone well but was hesitant to say so. After all, he could be wrong. It was possible that his urgent wish for success could make him misinterpret his feelings and the signs that he now saw.

Aiee, he would be glad when this was over! It was not unpleasant, this slightly different country of the Red Rocks band. Different, with a variety of plants not found in his own Tallgrass region, or in the Sacred Hills. But not unpleasant. However, he would be glad to move back to a more traditional locale. The season was still fairly early, and White Buffalo hoped that they could survive winter in a more familiar site. He would urge such a move, perhaps.

But his feeling for the season was good. Elk-dogs had made the Southern band strong and prosperous, and could do the same for all the People. His signs had been good for this raid, and he was sure of the success of the raiders. Well, almost sure. There were always factors which might interfere with all the good signs that might be present. Some unknown things even, of which he might be completely unaware in a strange country.

He tried to maintain his composure, to radiate confidence that he only partly felt. That was important in his position, not to reveal any doubts. Not that he had any real doubts, of course, but . . .

Crow was hurrying toward him from across the camp. He half rose from the backrest, a little flare of alarm rising in his throat. Then he saw the smile on her face.

"It is her time," Crow said happily. "Tall One! She is ready for birthing!"

White Buffalo sank back on his rest, relieved that there was no emergency.

"It will go well, I know," Crow Woman was saying. "Her family has always had easy birthing. *Aiee,* Elk, I can hardly wait to see this child! A child of Heads Off!"

She entered the lodge, and he could hear her singing happily to herself as she went about her work. *Aiee,* she should have had a child.

A man trotted into the camp from the west, and his voice rose in a long hail.

"Ah-koh!" he shouted. "Hear me, my brothers! The raiders return! More than a hundred elk-dogs, and we have lost no one!"

White Buffalo smiled to himself as he settled back once more to lean on the willow rest. It was good. Yes, his medicine was strong, even in this strange country, and his instincts were still good.

45

As it happened, the son of Tall One and Heads Off did not have fur upon his face. Tall One and Big-Footed Woman were quite disappointed at first. They had hoped that the child would show the mark of his heritage. Heads Off, startled initially by their disappointment, assumed that there was something wrong with the child. He was almost frantic with worry.

"But what is it? The child is deformed?" he asked anxiously.

"He has no fur," Tall One said sadly, stroking the ruddy cheek.

"Aiee," Heads Off cried, laughing. "Newborn babes do not have facehair!"

Gently, he unwrapped the infant.

"Look, there is no hair on the private parts either. That comes later."

"Will he have facehair later, Heads Off?" Big-Footed Woman asked.

"Maybe. Probably some. He will have to decide whether to pluck it."

Now it became a matter for joking and laughter, that Tall One had anticipated a fully furred infant. The entire band laughed about the hairless babe for most of the winter with new jokes constantly. Tall One named the child Many Elk-dogs, in commemoration of the day the raiding party returned in triumph. But the name did not stick. The People immediately began calling the infant Bald Eagle. After all, were his head and face not bare and white like those of the eagle?

Both names, of course, were nicknames. They would be used only until his second year, at the time of the youngster's First Dance. Then he would receive his name from the oldest male relative, in this case, Coyote. While it was customary for this ceremonial Uncle to bestow his own name, it was not always so. Somehow, White Buffalo had the idea that when the time came, Coyote would surprise everyone with a name other than his own.

But that was in the future. For now, the most important thing before the People was to learn the use of the newly acquired elk-dogs. Heads Off had thrown himself wholeheartedly into the teaching of his skills. It was little short of amazing how rapidly the young men learned. Standing Bird and Long Elk, already experts, assisted in the instruction. The young men were learning the use of the long spear and the bow on horseback as well as care and feeding of the animals.

In addition, Heads Off seemed obsessed with trying to get the elk-dog men to ride in unison, working together. He took a dozen or more willow hoops and fastened them to bushes a hundred paces or so away. Then the fledgling lancers were formed into a line and led into a full charge by Standing Bird. Each man would attempt to thread a willow hoop, a handspan across, on the shaft of his lance as he swept past. Accuracy was rare at first, but soon nearly every target dangled on someone's lance after the charge.

Heads Off came over to where White Buffalo and Coyote sat on the slope to watch.

"*Ah-koh,*" he said as he sat down to join them.

"Your young men do well," observed White Buffalo.

"Thank you, Uncle. They learn quickly."

"Heads Off," Coyote asked, "why do they learn this . . . the running at targets all at once?"

"Uncle," Heads Off said seriously, "these warriors will have to fight Head Splitters on elk-dogs. It is done so in my tribe, the learning to strike at the same time. This brings fear to the heart of an enemy, all charging at once."

"I see. But what protects them from arrows of men on foot?"

"Well, I . . . they move quickly. Our warriors wear a metal shirt."

Coyote nodded. "We have no metal shirts. Could they carry a shield?"

"A shield? Like a man with a war ax would use?"

"Yes, maybe. One a little smaller, but of good rawhide, from the back of a bull."

"It might work, Uncle. Would it turn an arrow?"

"Unless it strikes straight on. A spear too, unless it is a direct blow. Will you try it?"

A shield was brought, of the heaviest of bull's backskin, stretched and dried to rocklike hardness. Coyote fastened it to one of the dogwood bushes, and the young riders galloped past in turn, loosing an arrow or thrusting with a lance. Incredibly, only one arrow caught the shield just right and penetrated to half its length. All others were turned aside, glancing from the flint-hard surface of the rawhide, like a flat pebble skipped on the surface of a still pool.

"It is good!" shouted Heads Off in delight. "Let each warrior carry a shield. A little smaller maybe."

White Buffalo, too, was impressed. *Aiee,* there was much to learn about this elk-dog medicine. He and Crow had been given an elk-dog by the returning raiders. They would not ride it but used its great strength to drag the lodge poles and cover during a move. It was good, and it made him and Crow happy to use this method of transport.

"Oh, yes," Crow explained to an acquaintance, "we have an elk-dog. The raiders gave it to us in thanks for my husband's help."

On every fair day during that winter, the elk-dog warriors practiced. On inclement days, they repaired weapons or worked on their new shields.

There were no Head Splitter attacks on anyone that spring. At first, this was difficult to understand. Finally, after much discussion, it was decided that the loss of elk-dogs the previous fall had been an even harder blow to the enemy than they had realized. The stolen horses must have been the major concentration of all elk-dogs held by the Head Splitters.

"But they are angry," reported Black Beaver as the People gathered for the Sun Dance. "We encountered a traveling band only a moon ago. They blame Heads Off . . . Hair Face, they call him. Ah, that Gray Wolf is a bad one! He threatens again to use the face hair on his shield."

Heads Off approached Coyote about these repeated threats.

"Tell me, Uncle, what do you know of this man? He has long threatened my life. What do you know of him?"

Coyote giggled, a little nervously perhaps.

"Who knows anything about a Head Splitter? But this one . . . well, you have seen him. You might not remember . . . your first season with us. A big man, one of their subchiefs then. Probably a little crazy."

"What will happen, Coyote? How will this thing come about?"

Coyote shrugged.

"They will attack us sometime."

"This season?"

"Probably. We must be ready."

The first inkling that hostilities were being resumed came shortly after the Sun Dance. Four youths, confident in the glory of their manhood and the strength of their elk-dog medicine, had boldly left the Sun Dance before the others.

As the Southern band traveled the next day, White Buffalo had been watching a pair of buzzards circling high on fixed wings above the prairie. Suddenly, first one and then the other broke the perfect symmetry of the circles to drop away to the plain below. Another and yet another of the creatures appeared in the distance, each dropping as it neared the same spot.

The four bodies had been placed side by side, almost ceremonially, where the travelers would be sure to find them. The skull of each was split by a blow from a war ax. There was no sign of their elk-dogs.

Two of the four had apparently been already dead from arrow wounds when they had been placed here. The shattering of their heads was purely symbolic, a message to the People. Travel was delayed for a day to allow for mourning and for scaffold burial of the corpses. Then Hump Ribs called a council.

"We must be very careful, my brothers. We must have wolves out at all times."

There was some discussion but basic agreement. This season, it seemed, would be a time of decision. A summer campsite was selected largely on the basis of defensibility.

And the attractive stream with its tree-lined banks and clear pools over white gravel received a new name. No longer would it be known as Sycamore Creek, but as Head-Split Creek.

Despite the expectations of conflict, there was none that summer. Impatient, the young men suggested a campaign against the enemy, but Hump Ribs objected, and the council firmly backed him. There must be no unauthorized forays. Mention of the fate of the four who had met the enemy at Head Split Creek quieted the discussion.

White Buffalo was pleased with Hump Ribs's handling of the matter. Quiet, firm, and sensible, the band chief seemed to grow in stature as he held the office. Again White Buffalo recalled that some men seem to grow when a position of leadership is thrust upon them. It had been so with Hump Ribs. Part of his leadership was a matter of circumstance, of course. The Southern band had been the one to acquire the First Elk-dog and had the advantage of Heads Off to teach the young Elk-dog men. But even that might not have been, had not the insight and quiet leadership of Hump Ribs allowed for it.

Now the Southern band, increasingly called the Elk-dog band, was easily the most prestigious band of the People. Its leader, in turn, was respected above any other of the band chiefs. It seemed certain that when the time came, Hump Ribs would be the new real-chief.

At the appropriate season the band moved into winter camp. Again, the chosen site was for the best defense against attack by mounted warriors. It was an excellent site, a long narrow meadow several hundred paces in width, protected on the south by the river. On the north was a rocky slope, gradually curving down to meet the river at the east end. The only access to a mounted attack was from the west.

No winter attack was anticipated, but a close watch was kept. With the

Moon of Awakening the wolves began to range farther across the prairie. The reason was twofold. This was the time of year favored for forays by Head Splitters. In addition, the buffalo herds would be migrating northward, following the lead of the restless geese.

Long Elk and Standing Bird, ranging to the west by two days' journey, first observed the Head Splitters. At least fifty mounted warriors, well armed, traveling eastward with their wolves well deployed. This was no hunting party. Long Elk stayed to observe their progress, while Standing Bird hurried to report the approach of the enemy.

It must be assumed that the Head Splitters knew their location, so it also followed that the camp might be under observation. A carefully contrived charade was carried out to make everything appear normal. Women scraped skins and chattered to each other at their work. Men lounged against their backrests and visited, and children played happily among the lodges. To the enemy they must appear totally unsuspecting.

The horse herd had been carefully divided. Mares, foals, and immature animals were herded into the meadow behind the lodges, openly watched over by youths too young for combat. The best of the hunting horses, meanwhile, were kept hidden in the heavy timber along the creek, each under the care of its owner. White Buffalo's vision promised success in the venture.

Part of the strategy involved enticing the enemy to attack at the proper moment. A decoy hunting party set out next morning in an innocent manner. Four young men, mounted on the fastest and most surefooted of horses, set out casually, wandering as if looking for game. They were sure to be observed and avoided any opportunity for surprise or ambush by using the terrain. Finally, at the proper location, they showed themselves at the top of the hill, and pretended panic at the discovery of the enemy.

They turned and urged their horses in frantic escape. The Head Splitters, scenting blood, raced in hot pursuit. The four youths pounded across the valley, down the long strip of meadow, and in among the lodges, screaming the warning.

Behind them came the rolling thunder of dozens of hooves. Women screamed, children scurried, and there was a general exodus from the village as the People fled in panic before the charge. Echoing down the valley and reechoing from the rocky hillside, came the chilling war cry of the Head Splitters.

46

To the charging Head Splitters, this must have seemed an ideal raid. To be able to pursue four terrified youths directly into the unprotected camp of the enemy was beyond all expectations. People were screaming and running frantically away from the attack, toward the timber beyond the horse meadow.

White Buffalo and Crow ran with them, but stopped in a rocky outcrop and settled down to watch. Nervously, the holy man began to chant, while his wife beat the cadence on the drum.

The first of the riders had almost reached the nearest of the lodges when the unexpected happened. From behind and within the front row of scattered lodges, suddenly appeared well-armed warriors. The seasoned bowmen of the band, led by Hump Ribs himself, loosed a flight of arrows at almost point-blank range. The effect was devastating. Several riders were swept from their mounts, and horses in the front ranks went down before the withering fire. The charge faltered, then reformed for another approach, just in time to be met with another barrage of arrows. Casualties were heavy again.

The horsemen milled in confusion, attempting to reorganize under the shouted commands of their chief. Just at that moment came a long yell from the timber. Dozens of young warriors of the Elk-dog Society poured out of the trees with lances ready, cutting off the avenue of retreat. A few of the Head Splitters fled in panic into the broken rocks of the hillside. Others turned to meet the new attack, and in the space of a few heartbeats, the two groups of horsemen were mixed in a dusty, bloody melee.

The Head Splitters were traditionally fierce fighters, skilled in the use of weapons. In addition, they were fighting for survival, trapped between the foot soldiers of Hump Ribs and the mounted lancers of Heads Off. There was no retreat, and the invading force fought with the ferocity of a trapped cougar at bay.

The men of the People, although backed by a tradition of defensive combat only, had readied for this day. The pent-up resentment of years, perhaps centuries of abuse by the Head Splitters was reaching its climax today. Lances found human torsos as vulnerable as the rib cages of buffalo, and warriors tumbled into the dust.

Heads Off kneed his mare through the milling, fighting crowd, searching for the Head Splitter chief. He made a run with the lance at a youth scarcely older than Long Elk. The young warrior initially made a firm stand, readying his shield and club. At the last moment, his resolve faltered, and he threw himself backward from his horse to avoid the lance thrust. Heads Off swept past, unable to stop his charge, and as he glanced down, saw the young Head Splitter's face contort in agony. His own horse, stepping backward to avoid the impact, had crushed the boy's chest.

Heads Off dodged the swing of a club and thrust out in answer with his lance. The point drew blood, but he knew that it was only a flesh wound. The next moment the tide of battle had swept the two apart, and he lost sight of his adversary in the dust and confusion.

Still, he must find and challenge the Head Splitter chief, Gray Wolf. The other would be looking for him also. The reports of personal revenge had continued. Now was the time to resolve this conflict once and for all.

Across the meadow, White Buffalo saw two of the elk-dog soldiers charge at a tall, burly Head Splitter on one of the largest horses he had ever seen. The two made an excellent run. One or the other would certainly strike home. To his amazement, the Head Splitter was as quick as he was large. He parried the lance of one attacker with his rawhide shield and almost simultaneously swung his war club at the other lancer. The club was longer and heavier than most, and even the glancing blow to the shoulder bowled the young rider from his horse. The youth rolled, regained his feet, and ran, his left arm hanging useless as he dodged the pursuing Head Splitter.

Heads Off reined his horse around and kneed her in that direction. The boys were clearly outclassed by a veteran combatant. As he moved closer, the young man gained the shelter of the broken rimrock. The pursuer abandoned the chase and reined his huge bay around to rejoin the battle. As he turned, the symbol on his painted shield became visible to Heads Off for the first time. A geometrically styled design of an animal, with erect ears and a drooping tail—a wolf! This must be Gray Wolf, the mighty warrior, real-chief of the Head Splitters.

At almost the same instant, the other seemed to recognize his sworn enemy. He roared a challenging war cry that was more of a bellow and kneed the bay forward in a charge. The heavy war club whistled in a deadly circle as the two horses approached each other at full speed. Heads Off directed the lance point at the soft midriff just below the ribs and confidently braced himself for the shock of contact.

To White Buffalo's complete surprise, at the last instant the other swung his shield into position. The parried lance-thrust slid on past, and the shoulder of the larger horse crashed into the gray mare's. The little mare rolled, but her rider had kicked free and managed to get out of her way. He was dazed and somewhat disoriented as he floundered around in the dust, trying to avoid the finishing blow that must be coming.

Momentum had carried the Head Splitter's horse beyond the fallen Heads Off, and now they whirled for another run. Heads Off was on hands and knees in the dust. The whirling war club began to gain momentum in circles designed to finish the fight at the end of the charge. Dimly through the dusty haze, White Buffalo saw the big horse thundering down and saw the deadly swinging club.

The next action of Heads Off was more instinct than reason. He dove directly under the front feet of the galloping bay. His reasoning, if he had any at all, was simply to put something between himself and the deadly club. The Head Splitter would be unable to strike directly beneath his own horse. The horse unwittingly assisted too. A horse instinctively jumps to avoid obstacles under its feet, and the big bay tucked up his forefeet neatly and cleared the rolling body. Momentum carried the charge beyond, while Heads Off floundered around looking for his weapon.

White Buffalo gasped as the pounding hooves thundered down on the unhorsed Heads Off, who was at a definite disadvantage. He was on foot. The other's mobility and the length of the club made the lance less effective. He could throw the weapon, but if he missed, he would be unarmed.

The great horse approached, the rider swinging his ax. Then, to White Buffalo's astonishment, Heads Off leaped aside and turned to thrust his lance deep into the soft flank of the elk-dog. Instantly the holy man understood. Now they must fight on foot.

The bay screamed and reared, nearly falling backward, then bucking convulsively until it fell headlong. Heads Off was already running forward. The impact had torn the lance from his grasp, and he snatched the knife from his belt. Gray Wolf was rising from his knees when Heads Off dived headlong over the dying horse to prevent his finding the war club.

The two rolled in the dirt—kicking, biting, gouging. Gray Wolf kneed at the other's groin, grasped his knife wrist, and rolled on top, striving to turn the blade toward its owner.

In desperation, Heads Off swung a long sweeping blow with his left fist. It collided with Gray Wolf's ear, startling and confusing him. The use of fists in combat was entirely unfamiliar to the Head Splitter. Heads Off struck again, and the grip loosened on his wrist. Another blow and he wrenched the knife free and thrust upward with all his strength in a last desperate effort of survival. The point entered the other's throat between the jawbones and sank deep. Blood spurted over Heads Off's face, as the massive weight of the warrior's body sank heavily on his chest. He lay his head back, unable to move.

The sounds of battle were farther away now. Someone pulled the dead Head Splitter's body away, and Heads Off rolled over and filled his lungs. Weakly he crawled over and sat on the dead horse, still breathing heavily.

The Head Splitters were on the run, leaving their dead behind them. A number of warriors of the People rode in hot pursuit or loosed arrows after the fleeing remnants of the attacking force.

Coyote came over, leading Heads Off's gray mare. He handed Heads Off a heavy, blood-spattered club.

"Here, Heads Off. You will want to keep this."

Heads Off looked at the dead chief and shook his head, still unable to speak.

"No matter, I will keep it for you. You may want it later."

Coyote stood quietly, his presence comforting. A loose horse clopped past, reins trailing, nickering in bewilderment. Women were returning from the timber, looking for loved ones. Here and there a sudden cry, a wail of grief, and the rising notes of the Mourning Song.

The heaviest fighting had been in the meadow, where the horsemen had clashed, and the heaviest casualties were there. The wounded were being assisted by their friends and relatives.

Tall One glided gracefully through the carnage and embraced Heads Off.

"I am proud, my husband."

"I want to go home," he gasped. "To lie down."

They moved in that direction.

Near the first of the lodges, a cluster of people, both men and women, crowded together in a knot. There was a sense of urgency, of extra tragedy, in the keening wails arising from this group. Some simply stood, numbly staring. Attracted by the dread fascination of the unknown, Heads Off motioned, and the three altered their course. They elbowed their way into the crowd toward the motionless figure in the center of the circle. White Buffalo, too, hurried over.

The dead warrior was Hump Ribs. The People of the Southern band were without a leader.

47

I n the aftermath of the Great Battle, a feeling a numbness settled over the Southern band, like the heavy pall of a gray cloudbank. There was mourning and the duties attendant upon those who cared for the dead. The People went about their daily tasks of living like sleepwalkers, numb from all the death and destruction. The weather was warm, and very quickly the stench of rotting horseflesh became overbearing. The level meadow along the stream was no longer pleasant, but a place of death. There were still bodies of Head Splitters rotting among those of their elk-dogs. It was time to move.

It would have been time anyway, because the gathering of the People for the Sun Dance and Big Council was imminent. The travel time would be no more than sufficient to reach the appointed place. But, there was no one to say the day, to announce that now or three days from now we will move. There was no leader. Despite this, the need to move quickly became apparent, and the People seemed to move by instinct. The packing, preparation, and striking of the lodges happened. One family began to take down its lodge, and someone else, seeing it, followed suit. A great deal of organization was not needed. The purpose and direction were plain. It remained only to do it, and the People did.

They straggled out of the campsite, still numb, bedraggled, and mourning. Behind them, the trees along the river held burial scaffolds, stark against the sky. They were easily visible, even at last view, amid the budding twigs of new spring growth. Death gives way to new life, thought White Buffalo. He stood a moment, looking back, thinking that the scene looked very much like a heron rookery, with its dozens, sometimes hundreds, of heron lodges. Scaffolds of sticks, built by the herons to hold new life, as these scaffolds held death. He sighed and turned to follow the procession, wending its way to join the rest of the People. The Southern band was confused. They had won a great victory over the traditional enemy. Yet there was still death and mourning, destroying the taste of that victory.

Coyote waited beside the trail and fell in beside White Buffalo. The two walked in silence for a time, and it was Coyote who finally spoke.

"The People need a leader."

Yes, thought White Buffalo. A leader. Someone to inspire, to point a direction. Just now, the People were floundering. They were moving toward the Sun Dance because there was nothing else that was solid and lasting. They would seek that celebration because its time and place had already been set. But beyond that, the future was indefinite. There should be a council within the band to select a new chief. None had been called in the numb confusion that had followed the battle. Why? White Buffalo wondered for a moment. Who should have called such a council? The Southern band had enjoyed good leadership for many summers, but now, who?

Mouse Roars had been a leader and teacher, respected and followed by the young men. But Mouse Roars was dead. His son Standing Bird had shown leadership talents but was still too young. Two Pines? No, he still bore the stigma of having changed loyalties when he left the Red Rocks. Sees Far? His skills lay in other directions, as a scout and tracker.

White Buffalo himself could, and probably should, call a council to make the selection. He had been avoiding it, he decided, because he saw no clear candidate for leadership. *Aiee,* nothing was ever simple, even in victory. He studied Coyote as they walked along. Why had the little man brought up the subject? He thought about Coyote's ways, how Coyote had no desire to lead but managed to manipulate situations without seeming to do so.

"Yes, we should call a council," White Buffalo said tentatively.

"A good thought," Coyote answered and walked on in silence.

Ah, the holy man thought, I am right. He *does* have an idea.

"Who will they select?" White Buffalo wondered aloud.

"Who knows?" Coyote shrugged. "Who is a leader?"

"Two Pines is well thought of," ventured the holy man.

"Yes, that is true. But will the young men follow an outsider?" Coyote asked.

"My thoughts also. *Aiee,* we need someone like Mouse Roars."

"Or Hump Ribs," said Coyote. "That is the problem."

"Coyote, who do the young men follow?"

The little man giggled.

"Heads Off, of course."

"No, I mean . . ."

Suddenly, Coyote's purpose became clear. White Buffalo had been racking his brain to think of a leader but had found none. He had been thinking, however, of the traditional warrior-hunter, the bowman, fighting on foot and teaching others to do so. The interests of the young men did not lie in that direction but in the skills of the elk-dog. They were following the one who could teach *those* skills, those of the elk-dog medicine. The idea of two warrior societies came back again. It was a fact of life now. What was more, the Elk-dog Society was assuming the stronger position.

And that, the holy man now realized at last, was the basis of the present problem. There was no clear leader emerging because he would be expected to come from the old traditional warrior-hunter society, now called the Bowstrings. There was no leader there, because the young men were following the call of the elk-dog and of another leader.

White Buffalo doubted that Heads Off was even aware of the political implications here. There would probably be young men who would choose the more traditional ways, but just now . . . *aiee,* the chief *must* be an elk-dog leader, and there was none except . . . It was unthinkable, the thing that kept repeatedly intruding itself into his mind. If Two Pines was unacceptable because of changed loyalty, then how could a complete outsider hope to lead? The answer came back to him: Heads Off leads because of his special medicine, which Two Pines does not have. Which *no one else* has.

White Buffalo stopped in his tracks and stared at Coyote in amazement.

"Heads Off?"

Coyote giggled nervously.

"Why not, Uncle? The young men follow him already. They followed him into battle. He is respected by the elders, even though they do not understand him."

"But, he . . . I . . . Coyote, this is not done."

"It has not been, Uncle," said Coyote almost gently, "because until now there has been no elk-dog medicine. But there is change in the wind."

Yes, change, thought the holy man. Once again, he wondered if he was ready. But he must. It was not possible to go back.

"Would he do this, Coyote?"

Coyote shrugged.

"Who knows? Let us ask him."

It was late in the day before they contrived to walk with Heads Off while he led his horse for a little while. White Buffalo, after some small talk, came straight to the point.

"Heads Off, the men want you to become the new chief."

"What? Oh, no, Uncle, I could never do that."

"But the young men follow you already," Coyote pointed out.

"No! I only teach them. No, Uncle, both of you . . . I could not do this. I do not know the customs of the People . . . I . . ."

"But you have learned much, my son," White Buffalo reminded him. "You speak the tongue. You have married here, sired a son. No one knows *all* of the customs, and we will help you, Coyote and I. Your wife too."

The three argued for a long time, Heads Off resisting.

"Could this really be done? You would advise me closely?" he asked finally.

They nodded eagerly.

"How is this done, the choosing of the chief?"

"We call a council."

"When?"

"Tonight."

"Aiee!"

"No, wait!" Coyote suggested. "Talk to Tall One. Ask what she thinks."

Yes, of course, thought White Buffalo. *An excellent plan!* The girl could present the situation in a proper light.

"Of course! Speak to her," he urged. "We will talk later."

When the council of the Southern band was held two days later, there was little discussion and no argument. The journey continued, but now there was a sense of direction, of pride in belonging. The People began to look forward to the Big Council, to the telling and retelling of the story of their victory in the Great Battle. Their entire mood had changed. They had a new leader. He might be a good leader or not—only time would tell. But he was a leader, and the band responded with purpose.

Meanwhile, White Buffalo, Coyote, and the women worked to prepare Heads Off for his appearance at the Big Council. Tall One and Big-Footed Woman worked tirelessly to create new buckskin garments with embroidered quillwork. Heads Off's hair was trimmed and replaited.

"He needs something around his neck," Coyote observed.

"His medicine?" White Buffalo asked.

Without a word, Tall One took down the bit, the marvelous artistry in metal, whose medicine controlled the elk-dog. She hung it on a thong around the neck of the confused Heads Off, where it dangled and bumped gently against the white buckskin of his shirt.

It was worn so a few days later when the Southern band proudly followed Heads Off to his seat in the circle of the Big Council. There was pride in their eyes when he in his turn rose to address the Council.

"I am Heads Off," he announced in a ringing voice, "chief of the Elk-dog band of the People. My brothers, this has been a very big year for us."

48

White Buffalo shifted comfortably, scratching his shoulder
against the backrest as he lounged in the sun. Life had
been good the past few summers. Fourteen in all, he
counted, since Heads Off had become band chief, and much had happened.

The entire tribe had prospered with the expansion of the use of the elk-
dog. In these few years, the People had become a major power on the plains.
Other tribes, even, sometimes referred to this tribe as the Elk-dog People.
There had almost been a split in the tribe as everyone became more affluent
through greater ease in hunting. A small, militant splinter group of young
elk-dog men who called themselves the Blood Society had withdrawn from
the tribe entirely. At least for a time. They had returned to assist in another
battle with the Head Splitters and were now welcome again. This had resulted in not two but three Warrior Societies with slightly differing interests
and motives but mutual respect.

The People, able to kill and skin more buffalo and to transport heavier
lodge covers, now made their dwellings larger and finer. Some were con-
structed of thirty skins. Wealth was expressed in this way and in horses.
Children learned to ride before they could walk. It was common to see a
toddler, tied to the back of a trustworthy old mare while she was turned

loose to graze. The sons of Heads Off and Tall One had been raised so and were fine riders. Especially Eagle, the older boy. Coyote, in a surprise move at the First Dance, had given the child the nickname he had borne all along. It had seemed to fit, as the boy matured and soft fur appeared on his upper lip only a few seasons ago. The young man remained Eagle, and as Coyote said, the youth's eye carried such a look, the look of eagles. This one would earn fame.

The other child was called Owl. Two years younger, he had never seemed quite as aggressive or as popular a child as his brother Eagle. But his name fit well. This child had arrived in the world wide-eyed, as some infants do, eager to see and to learn. His large dark eyes, much like his mother's, seemed to glow with an inner curiosity as well as wisdom. Yes, Owl was well named.

There had been other changes as the People adapted to the new affluence that the elk-dog provided. Time formerly spent in the quest of food for survival could now be devoted to things of the spirit. More elaborate decoration of simple garments and household things, more songs and ceremonies. There was a surge of interest in the throaty melodies of the courting flute, which in turn led to seasons of romance.

And, all in all, it was good. White Buffalo could hardly believe that at one time he had resisted such change, had even considered destroying Heads Off to stop it. Heads Off had been a good leader. He had made mistakes, as all leaders do. But people forgive their leaders for honest mistakes. Only one thing people find unforgivable in a leader, White Buffalo observed— indecisiveness. A wrong decision is forgiven more easily than no decision. And Heads Off had never been guilty of that. True, he could never, as an outsider, be more than a band chief, a subchief in the structure of tribal politics. But, the Elk-dog band was still the strongest and most prestigious of the bands of the People. That had been the function of Heads Off.

White Buffalo filled his nose and mouth with the fragrant smoke from his pipe and blew it out gently, savoring the mixture of tastes. Tobacco, sumac, the roasted bark of the red willow, and other favorite substances lent their fragrance. Everything, he now believed, had its function, its place in the world. As Heads Off did. As every person does, maybe. His own position, that of interpreter of the change for the People. Only after the fact had he known. His entire career as holy man had been shaped by forces of the spirit-world, to help the People take this great leap forward as they changed to accept the medicine of the elk-dog.

He thought of Coyote, who had changed not one bit in the past seasons. A little grayer, a little fatter, maybe, but the same likable buffoon. White Buffalo had been irritated, angry even, when Coyote had refused the gift of the spirit and had taken another path. Now he realized that that too had been part of the entire plan. Coyote had been used as a go-between, to help bring together the medicines of the buffalo and the elk-dog. As he looked back, White Buffalo could see many things that had not been apparent. All the events that had taken place in his lifetime had come to rest in proper perspective. From his earliest feelings of the spirit, his strange visions on his vision quest, the dreams of the elk-dog as a youth . . . Now it all was seen as a part of his mission, his life's work.

It was satisfying, this feeling that he had been permitted to be a part of so great a change. But there seemed to be one thing that still did *not* fit. It had begun to bother him many years ago that no young person had come forth to become his apprentice, to learn the medicine of the buffalo. He had realized, in light of the sweeping changes brought about by the elk-dog, that there had been a reason. The lives of Coyote, Big-Footed Woman, the other possible holy ones, had all held other purposes. Parts of the pattern, which had been fitted together like the multicolored quills of decorative embroidery on a ceremonial shirt. But there was still a flaw. Somehow, the purpose of his own life seemed incomplete. So far, it was full, satisfying, overwhelming almost in its scope, but what now? There was an emptiness, a regret, in this, the autumn of his career. It was not difficult to identify, of course. It was a feeling of concern, of failure almost. Disappointment. There had still never been a young person to accept the gift of the spirit, one to whom he could teach his skills, his medicine.

He had tried to put it away, to crowd it back in his thoughts, but it was difficult. It was much like the disappointment that he and Crow had never had another child. That had been pushed aside, accepted, but was still a deep hurt sometimes. He did not understand it, any more than he understood the lack of someone to carry on the medicine of the buffalo. Was he to die with no successor? Was that too part of the plan?

His reverie was interrupted by the approach of Coyote, who had with him his grandson Owl.

"*Ah-koh,* Uncle," Coyote greeted him, "we would speak with you."

Coyote's tone was serious. This then was no idle visit. What was it? The holy man motioned for them to sit.

The youngster, of maybe twelve summers it seemed, appeared uneasy and a little frightened. Coyote was quick to assist, explaining that Owl had questions about his background and why his father, the band chief, was considered an outsider. The boy had been teased and bullied, it seemed, by a couple of ne'er-do-wells.

White Buffalo thought it over. He could see the young man's dilemma. At twelve summers, one does not wish to be different. He had seen the older boy, Eagle, successfully adjust to the fact, but this child seemed to have more misgivings.

Well, why not start at the beginning? A trifle bored by the entire thing, the holy man nevertheless wished to help the grandson of his friend Coyote. He brought out the story-skins, and spent some time showing the pictographs of Heads Off on First Elk-dog, the buffalo hunts on horseback, the Great Battle with Heads Off defeating the Head Splitter Gray Wolf. The boy had heard the story before, but now seemed to be searching for new meaning.

"Your father is now one of us," the holy man concluded. "Heads Off is well honored by the People."

"But what of his own tribe, Uncle?" the boy asked. "Their medicine?"

An odd question, White Buffalo thought.

"His medicine is very powerful," the holy man said. "As strong as my own, in a different way."

He warmed to this, a favorite topic.

"Mine is the medicine of the buffalo. My visions tell the People where to hunt, how to find the herds. Your father's medicine is that of the elk-dog. With this medicine, he controls the elk-dogs, so that men ride upon them to hunt or fight."

He pointed to some of the pictures with the metal bit worn as an ornament on the chest of Heads Off. The boy nodded. He knew that talisman well. All his life it had hung in the place of honor over his parents' bed.

"Tell me, Uncle," said the boy suddenly. "How do you know where to find the buffalo?"

White Buffalo almost gasped. This was a much more complicated question than it appeared. It involved the very heart of the holy man's expertise and was not a question to be taken lightly. It implied deep soul-searching questions by the young man. White Buffalo shrugged.

"The visions, of course."

He could tell that the youngster was deep in thought, but he was completely unprepared for the next question.

"Uncle, how does one become a holy man?"

Like a wave of water moving down a dry wash in the time of flash flooding, the answers came flowing over White Buffalo. Of course! Why had he not seen this before? A sensitive young man who carried the blood of two gifted ones, Coyote and Big-Footed Woman, besides that of Heads Off himself. Of course this one might receive the gift of the spirits.

The holy man looked across, over the boy's head, and his glance met that of Coyote. The little man's face was squinted in his good-natured half-smile, but his eyes reflected more. Coyote understood what was happening. How long had he known?

The pieces were falling together too rapidly, though they seemed to fit so well . . . he must have time . . . to pray and think, and seek visions.

White Buffalo tried to assume an expression of serious dignity, though he wanted to leap and sing for joy.

At last he was finding the answer he had sought so long. He turned back to the boy, trying not to speak too gruffly.

"Come back tomorrow. We will talk."

There was satisfaction in the boy's face, and in Coyote's. And White Buffalo's heart was very good.

THE
TRAVELER

PART I

THE
STORYTELLER

1

Woodpecker lay on his belly in the sunlit meadow and watched the rabbit as it came toward him. Surely now, at any time, it would sense his presence and flee. But it came closer, nibbling eagerly at the succulent grass of springtime. Never in his nine summers had he seen such a thing.

He flattened his body to the ground and held his breath—waiting, waiting. It seemed a long time as the rabbit nibbled, hopped a step or two, nibbled again. Twice he emptied his lungs, slowly, not to disturb the long-ears. Then, just as carefully, he refilled his chest with a long, slow inhalation. Finally, against all reason, the creature hopped, unafraid, within an arm's length of his face. Then it seemed to notice him for the first time, and froze, motionless. He was looking directly into the eye—large and brown and shining. It reminded him of the shiny seeds of the bur chestnut. They were not good to eat like other nuts, but marvelous to play with. The rabbit's eye was like that . . . shiny and glistening as it stared into his. It had one other characteristic that the shiny nut-seed did not have—life, recognition, and awareness of the world. And, of course, fear. He was not certain whether he *saw* the fear in the unblinking eye of the rabbit or *felt* it in the animal's spirit.

It made him think, somehow, of the tales around the story-fires, of long-ago times when the animals could talk. He wondered when they had lost that ability. It was always there in the Creation stories. *Maybe,* he thought, looking into the depths of the rabbit's eye, *maybe they never lost it at all. What if, for instance,* men *had lost the ability, or the wish, to listen?*

Softly, he began to whisper. "It is well, Little Brother," he said. "Talk to me . . . I will listen . . . I mean no harm to you."

There was no sign that the rabbit heard unless the slight twitch of its whiskers indicated it. Woodpecker took this motion seriously, however. The creature was so close that he could count every hair on its nose. He watched the nervous quiver of the whiskers, and for a moment, *there,* it seemed that the rabbit *was* ready to speak. Woodpecker waited, and finally, when nothing happened, he whispered again. "Go on, Little Brother . . . speak! I will tell no one."

The rabbit jumped convulsively, startling the watching boy as it fled. It had been so close. The dirt and dry grass kicked up by the rabbit's long hind feet struck him across the face, and he jumped uncontrollably. Then he laughed at himself for his response and sat up to watch the bobbing fluff of white tail bounce out of sight in the bushes along the stream.

He was pleased with the day. This was closer to the rabbit than he had ever been. More important, his medicine had been good. He would long remember this as the day he had *almost* persuaded the rabbit to speak, as it had done in long-ago times. Maybe next time . . .

Woodpecker rose and started along the stream toward the village. Then he remembered his original mission and retraced his steps to the meadow. He picked up the sticks he had laid aside when he first saw the rabbit and hurried on, gathering sticks for the cooking fire as he went. In his excitement over the rabbit, he had almost forgotten. Today he wished to finish quickly because it was an exciting time. The Storyteller was here.

Of course, there were always stories. In the moons of winter or in bad weather, the elders of the tribe gathered in the longhouse and told and retold the stories. Stories of the People, of long-ago times. The boy thrilled at these tales, stories of how the Redbird became red, how Bobcat lost his tail, and why the moon is red when it rises.

There were stories of Creation, and Woodpecker loved these most of all. There were tales of the Trickster, who had been present at Creation and could speak all languages—not only all human tongues but those of all animals and birds. Even the song of the stream murmuring over the rocks was language to the Trickster, it was said. When the wind sighed among the tall treetops, it was talking to the Trickster.

"Good day to you, Uncle," it said.

At least, that was according to the Storyteller. The one that had created the greatest impression on young Woodpecker was not of the People but an outsider. Once or twice each season, a Trader would come to their village on the river. Travelers came oftener than that, of course, but the ones who entranced the imagination of Woodpecker were those who told stories well.

Some people could not tell a story at all. And the Trader could tell one to perfection. He and two or three of the old storytellers of the tribe would sit and trade stories as long as anyone would listen. Longer, probably. More than once, Woodpecker had fallen asleep while the stories still flowed freely and had been carried home in his father's arms.

Of course, that was when he was merely a child. Now he could probably stay up all night if necessary. He was prepared to do so tonight, for a number of reasons.

One was the Storyteller, of course. Some knew him as "the Trader," but to Woodpecker, he was the Storyteller and a master at his craft. If anyone knew where the man came from originally, they had forgotten. Even his tribe was a question. For the past ten, maybe twenty seasons, he had traded up and down the rivers of the region. He traded with all and seemed to have no enemies. He was welcomed for his stories as well as for the fascinating assortment of items he carried.

The Trader would enter a village or camp, attract attention with the stories, and spend the next day in trading from his packs. There was some limit to what could be exchanged because items taken in trade must be small enough to transport on the back of the Trader. All of the reasons for this were not well understood by Woodpecker. He only knew that when this man came to the village, a wonderful evening was in store.

Also, it was the Moon of Roses, and the weather was exceptionally fine. The story-fires would not be confined to the longhouse but outside in the night. All stories, of course, were best when told by firelight. For some stories, it was a requirement. Stories of the Trickster must never be told until after dark. He had decreed it himself long ago, shortly after Creation.

There was always more excitement to stories after dark. One could see strange little movements in the dusky corners of the longhouse. During the more frightening stories, children would edge quietly closer to a parent or older friend, casting fearful glances behind. The circle of firelight seemed safer somehow; some racial memory suggested that it was so. The flicker and crackle of the flames pushed back the demons of darkness and made the world seem a safer place.

While this was evident in the longhouse, it was much more so outside. It was deliciously fearsome to hear the scare-stories of long-ago times retold in the darkness under the starry black dome of night. There was a fire, of course. Any story, properly told, must have a fire. But in the longhouse, fearsome story-creatures were confined to the dark corners and along poorly lit walls away from the fire. Outdoors, with the whispered night-sounds out beyond the fire's reach, the whole world might be filled with such terrors. Woodpecker found it a delicious fright, fearful yet relatively safe. At least, it had never been known for a story-creature to come out of the dark to assault cringing children. Still, they cowered and squealed and giggled, and the story was a success.

Woodpecker arrived at the lodge and deposited his firewood where it would be convenient to the cooking fire. His mother glanced up and smiled at him. It had been hard for her, he knew, since his father's death two winters past. He had all but forgotten what his father looked like now, but he remembered the incident.

One of the other men had come to report that Red Squirrel was dead. A freak accident: He had climbed upon a fallen tree to watch a band of deer some distance away. He had slipped and tumbled into the tangle of brush below. That might not have been serious, but unknown to any of the hunters, the brush pile was the winter lodge of a bear. A sleeping bear was slow to waken in the Moon of Snows but quick to anger. The end for Red Squirrel was quick but unpleasant. It was some time before the others could recover the mangled remains.

There was the traditional period of mourning, and soon after that, Owl Woman and her son moved into the lodge of her mother. Woodpecker wondered sometimes if his mother might marry again. There were men who looked upon her with favor, but she did not seem interested. It seemed quite satisfactory to her to remain in the lodge of her parents.

The boy had mixed feelings. It would be good to have a father again, like other children. Bent Arrow, perhaps, or Lame Fox. Fox had demonstrated some interest. He had only one wife and was considered a good provider.

Meanwhile, Woodpecker felt uneasy and out of place because his family was different. He had withdrawn into the story-world of long-ago tales. These, at least, seemed predictable, unchanging, and timeless. Woodpecker could imagine himself as a skilled and respected storyteller, his calling above and beyond that of most of the People.

With this in mind, he would build a tiny fire of sticks—a pretend fire, not lighted of course—in some hidden retreat. A circle of stones and sticks would represent his audience, and he would spend long times telling stories aloud. Not stories of the Trickster. Those could only be told after dark. Woodpecker could not easily be alone in his secret places after Sun had gone over to the other side of Earth's rim.

The boy was not completely isolated of course. He took part in instruction with the other children. He had long ago mastered and enjoyed the simple hopping steps of the Rabbit Dance. Now, he was relatively proficient with the bow and could *almost* make fire with the firesticks; at least he could make much smoke. With a little more coordination—well, maybe someday.

He had helped plant the corn this season, and the beans and pumpkins. There was a great sense of satisfaction that he could do this work, but it was tiresome. His mind would wander, and he would tell himself the stories, silently. Then one of the adults would notice and speak to him harshly.

"Not so deep, boy!"

And he would return to the present, carefully placing the seeds in the furrow, covering them and pressing the dirt down firmly.

Today, he could hardly wait for dark, and the story-fire. His mother, who had some idea of Woodpecker's restlessness, smiled to herself.

"Come, eat," she called to him. "You will want to be there early, at the stories."

"Are you coming too?"

"Maybe." Owl Woman smiled. "I will be along later. You eat and go ahead. You will want a good place in the circle."

"Yes, Mother," Woodpecker agreed breathlessly.

He had not been aware that she understood him so deeply. He finished his stewed corn and beans, and rose. "I will meet you later, Mother," he called as he trotted away.

His grandmother watched him go, somewhat disapprovingly. "He is a little bit lazy, that one," she suggested.

Owl Woman smiled sadly. "No, Mother. He is busy thinking of other things. He is much like his father."

The older woman's face softened, and she patted her daughter's shoulder. "Maybe so," she said gently. "He is a good boy."

"Yes. He will make us proud."

Maybe, admitted the grandmother to herself. *In a different way. This is an unusual child. He spends much time in thought, but he also talks well. We will see.*

2

The shadows were growing long as the Storyteller prepared for an evening of entertainment. He remembered this village as a good one. For stories, at least. There were a couple of old men here, he recalled, who could match story for story until far into the night. A tale would remind one of the other storytellers of another, and that tale in turn of yet more as the stories went on and on.

Maybe, he thought, he could use some of the Creation stories tonight. Stories from various tribes, their own stories of their origins. The tribe he visited last season—how did that tale begin? Four brothers, who came up out of a lake to create the four bands of the tribe. Or the tribe to the southeast. Their first people, it was said, came from the sky. Slid down the dome to reach Earth. Yes, a good story.

This tribe had already heard the tale of the grapevine, and the people who climbed out of Earth on its roots. Their own story was similar, was it not? Ah, well, no matter. A good story was always worth retelling.

He rose and walked from the place he would sleep to see where the fire would be. Yes, near the longhouse at the center of the village. A couple of young men were bringing sticks for the fire. Then he noticed a much younger boy, enthusiastically engaged in fuelgathering. The youngster looked familiar. Yes, he remembered now, from last season. This was the boy who had become so entranced by the stories. When other children had become distracted or bored and wandered off, this boy was still listening, fascinated. It was good to see young people who understood the importance of the story-fire and the Storyteller.

"Good day, young man," he said to the child.

The boy smiled a little shyly and nodded a wordless answer.

"You will come for the stories?"

"Yes, Uncle."

"I remember you from last year. You liked the storytelling."

The boy nodded. It was plain, the excitement in this child at the prospect of the story-fire. It was to be hoped that someone would encourage the boy in this interest.

"Is your father a storyteller?" he asked.

"No, my father is dead," the boy answered. "A bear . . ."

"Aiee, too bad. Your mother?"

"We live in her mother's lodge. How is it you speak my tongue, Uncle?"

The Storyteller smiled. "Ah, a trader must speak many tongues. And hand-signs, of course. Some tongues are easier than others. Do you know any others?"

"No, only a little sign-talk."

It was apparent that the boy was interested and intelligent, and could communicate well. The Trader suspected that the boy was overly modest in his mention of "a little" sign-talk. An idea began to form in his mind. The boy's mother was a widow, living in her parents' lodge. She might welcome an opportunity such as he had in mind. A season's travel for the boy, then home for the winter. An extra pair of hands would be useful on the trail or the river.

It had been a lonely trail since the loss of his wife a few seasons ago. The two had approached the world with happiness in all Earth's glory and in each other. They had only a few seasons together, wandering the trails, trading with distant tribes for exotic foods, furs, and other objects of value, such as stone for making pipes, implements, and weapons. Lark had succumbed to an illness of a strange sort during a visit to a tribe that had the illness. Their holy men had been of no help, going through the ceremonies but privately shaking their heads in despair. Their medicine was ineffective, one explained to the distraught husband, because the spirit of the disease was foreign.

"Foreign?" asked the Trader through his tears.

"Yes. Our people first fell sick with it from the *French.*"

"I know little of them."

"Of course. They are one of the tribes from beyond the Big Water."

"Mishi-ghan?"

"No, no, the Big Salt Water. They have pale skins and sometimes grow fur upon their faces. Their eyes are light-colored, sometimes."

"*Aiee!* They are blind?"

"No, they can see, even with light eyes. But no matter. They bring good things—blankets, knives—but also some bad spirits sometimes. Like that which oppresses your wife. Many die."

It was painful, watching Lark weaken and suffer. When the end finally came, with the sores covering her once beautiful body, he had welcomed the relief for her.

That had been a lost season for the Trader. He had very little memory of it. The period of mourning helped, but he still felt lost, abandoned. In the seasons since, he had immersed himself in the storytelling, using the ever-lasting stories as a sign of permanence that seemed to escape him otherwise. He missed Lark deeply and had found no one who could take her place. Maybe he never would.

However, the conversation with the boy was bringing a new idea to his mind. It was not possible to replace Lark, but companionship—that could be quite pleasant on the trail. If the boy's widowed mother would consent to the season's apprenticeship . . .

"How are you called?" he asked.

"I am Woodpecker, Uncle."

"It is good. Will your mother come for the story-fire, Woodpecker?"

"Maybe so. Why do you ask?"

"I only wondered. We will see."

It was nearly full dark now, and people were gathering. It was time to light the fire. Someone brought a brand from one of the cooking fires, and orange tongues of flame licked at the tinder and crept upward, flickering through the jumbled pile of fuel. Firelight pushed back the circle of darkness, enlarging the lighted area. There was something about a fire, a declaration of human existence, that was exciting and thrilling. It prepared the scene, stimulated the imagination, and readied the spirit for the coming entertainment.

The elders of the village were ceremoniously making their way to the front rows now. Yes, the Storyteller remembered these men. That one-eyed man; he had been a good storyteller last season. A dry sense of humor. Well, young Woodpecker had had an advantage in his childhood. He had listened to this man and, yes, the portly man next to him. The visitor remembered that one as a powerful orator.

One of the chiefs spoke a few words of welcome and sat down again, relinquishing the council to the visiting trader. The Storyteller stood, having carefully positioned himself against a background of dark trees for maximum effect. The crowd was still waiting expectantly. The only sounds were those of the crackling fire and the cries of the distant night-creatures beyond the reach of its light. It was warm, but in such a setting, there was always a chill of excitement that sent icy fingers up one's spine and caused the hairs to prickle on the back of the neck.

The Storyteller was about to speak when he caught a glimpse of a face in the back rows of the listeners. It was such a striking face, one of the most beautiful women he had ever seen. The large dark eyes were well spaced and the other features exquisite. It was a face that showed, even at this distance and by firelight, intelligence, humor, and a hint of sadness, all at once. So striking—the thought crossed his mind that it was an apparition, a trick of the flickering light and shadows. Maybe the woman was not real at all and existed only as an ideal in his own mind.

He tore his attention away, and began his story a little shakily. "In the long-ago times, when Earth was young, Bobcat had a long, long tail. . . ."

That was always a good starter. There were many versions of it. He would tell one, giving one of the local storytellers the opportunity to counter with his own, always a good way to ensure popularity with the host village, make their own storyteller look good.

It was hard work tonight, resisting the temptation to stare again at the beautiful face in the back row. A time or two he risked a quick glance while other storytellers were talking. She was still there, smiling in absorbed amusement.

As the crowd began to tire and thin out, the pretty woman disappeared, and he was sad. The stories ceased earlier than they sometimes did because his heart was not in it. He was distracted. This was the first time since the loss of Lark that any woman had impressed him, beyond the bounds of a temporary diversion to relieve the call of nature, of course. This feeling was different.

Ridiculous, he told himself. A woman like that has a husband. Probably a jealous one. He would put her out of his mind.

He slept poorly and awoke with his senses dulled. It was not good to trade when he was not at his best. But there was no help for it. He must finish here and move on. Maybe that would help to rid his mind of the face in the firelight and its sad-sweet smile.

He spread his goods on a robe and began the day's trading. Some things he kept hidden, to bring forth as a dramatic surprise those items he considered best. He was engrossed in haggling over a trade involving an exceptionally fine otter skin and a black obsidian knife when he noticed the approach of the boy. Ah, yes, Woodpecker. He had suggested that the boy bring his mother. He had almost forgotten.

"In a moment," he said aside to Woodpecker.

"Yes, Uncle."

Finally the deal was completed, and the customer turned to leave, pleased with his new knife. The Trader looked up. "Now, my young friend!"

He almost choked on the last words. He had not really looked at the boy's companion until now. "*You* are his mother?" he blurted, feeling completely stupid.

"Yes, of course." Owl Woman smiled, looking a trifle confused. "Woodpecker said you wished to talk with me."

She was even more beautiful in daylight, he thought. The dim light of the fire could not do justice to her fine features and the texture of her skin. He could now see that she was tall and willowy, and the soft curves of her body pressed suggestively against the restraining buckskin of her dress.

"How are you called?" the woman asked, bringing him back to reality.

"Ah . . . I am c-called many things," he stammered. "Mostly good, I think. My first name was Turtle. Now, I am the Storyteller, or the Trader." *Or whatever you would like to call me,* he thought. *Anything.* Then he made an attempt to recover his composure. "And how are *you* called, Mother of Woodpecker?"

She laughed, and he was pleased at the little wrinkles at the corners of her eyes. It was far better than the hint of sadness he had seen earlier.

"I am Owl Woman," she said. "As you have mentioned, the mother of this one."

She paused, waiting. Now was the time, the Trader thought, to ask about the apprenticeship for the season. He could not bring himself to do so. What if she said no? Or, worse, became angry? It would destroy any possibility of seeing her again, and he was not willing to take that chance. As things now stood, Woodpecker did not know of the plan, so talk of it could be postponed. He could perhaps stay here an extra day or two, become better acquainted.

Owl Woman's look of puzzlement was changing to one of impatience. He must do something very quickly. "I wished to tell you," he blurted clumsily, "you have a fine boy. He understands the stories well. I can tell that he has a talent."

He felt like an idiot. What a stupid thing, to ask the woman to come here, but of course he had not known who she was. *Aiee,* he felt like a child. But Owl Woman was smiling.

"Thank you!" she said. "He is much like his father, who was killed . . ." The sadness returned for a moment.

"Yes, Woodpecker told me."

She smiled again. "You two have become friends," she observed. "Will you be here long?"

He had planned to depart no later than the next morning, but he now experienced a sudden change in plans. "A few days, maybe," he answered, trying to sound casual. "Maybe I will see you again."

"Maybe so," she said with a smile that was almost an invitation. She turned away.

"Mother, may I stay and watch the trading?" Woodpecker asked.

Owl Woman paused for a moment and looked questioningly at the Trader. "Maybe so," she agreed, "but do not be a bother."

"It is good," the Trader said quickly. "He will be no trouble."

3

Owl Woman sat bolt upright in her sleeping robes. It must be nearly dawn, she thought. Yes, the doorway opening was clearly showing the gray light of coming day. Her parents were stirring in their pallet of robes.

"What is that noise?" she asked.

A plaintive hollow call, like the *coo* of a dove, wavered outside, rising and falling, continuing on and on. It was not unpleasant but was unlike anything she had heard before.

Suddenly her mother chuckled somewhat nervously. "Someone is playing a flute."

"What?"

"A sort of whistle, but with holes. They are used by some of the prairie people."

"For what purpose?" Owl Woman asked.

Suddenly Yellow Bowl gasped in realization, then laughed aloud. "For *courting!*" She chortled. "Owl Woman, maybe someone is courting you!"

"Nonsense!" Owl Woman snapped irritably. "I know no one who—" She paused. The Trader! Could it be? He had acted very strangely when they met.

"Ah, you *do* know!" teased her mother. "The Trader? Of course! He travels everywhere. He would know of the flute; maybe his tribe uses it. What *is* his tribe?"

"I do not know, Mother. Why would he . . ." Owl Woman was confused but excited. She had been quite impressed by this young man, even in his embarrassment. She had been at a loss to explain that, but now . . . She had wondered whether he had a wife and finally mustered courage to ask whether Woodpecker knew. No, the boy said, he believed that the Trader had no one.

"I will go and see about this," Yellow Bowl was saying as she shrugged into her dress.

"But, Mother, I—"

The older woman waved her objections aside and stooped to pass out the doorway. Owl Woman waited nervously.

The song of the flute stopped, and there was a long pause before it resumed. It was rapidly growing light when Yellow Bowl returned, chuckling to herself. She stooped to reenter the lodge and straightened inside.

"Well?" asked Owl Woman expectantly.

"It is as we thought," stated Yellow Bowl. "He plays a courting song. And he has no wife."

"This is his tribe's way?" asked Owl Woman.

"No," answered her mother. "This is a custom that he learned from a plains tribe where he visited. It is nice, no?"

"But why does he play it for me?"

"That is the best part! He says that you are a special woman who deserves a special courtship!"

Owl Woman frowned. "No, he has traded for this whistle thing somewhere and wants to play it."

But though her words were sarcastic, her heart was very good. It was exciting to have a man like this interested in her. "What does he expect to happen now?" she asked her mother.

"I do not know. Maybe you should ask him."

Owl Woman was slipping her dress over her head. She did not want to take time to replait her hair but attempted to pat it into shape as quickly as possible. *This is silly,* she told herself. But her heart beat rapidly, and her palms were damp. A bit angry at herself, she ducked through the doorway and straightened to full height outside.

She did not see him at first and followed the hollow flute tones until she located his position. He was seated, his back leaning against the trunk of a giant old sycamore. His eyes were half closed, and the warbling notes from the flute rose and fell, rhythmic and clear, in the still morning air.

Embarrassed a little at what their neighbors might think, Owl Woman paused before the seated musician. "What are you doing?" she demanded in a half-whisper. "You will wake the whole village!"

He lowered the flute and looked at her with a placid smile. Even in her state of tension and embarrassment, she did not fail to notice that it was a nice smile. It showed even white teeth and crinkled the corners of his eyes in a way that suggested a sense of humor.

"Then they will know that I feel much for you," he said calmly.

"Is this the way of your people?" she asked, trying to regain her composure.

"No, no. I learned it from others. People of the plains, to the west. It is a pleasant custom, no?"

She did not answer but stood fighting a mixture of emotions. It was pleasing, flattering, to have such a man courting her—at the same time, embarrassing. She could see that people were sleepily looking out of lodge doors to see what was going on. She saw Bent Arrow, who had shown considerable interest in her, poke his head out, then quickly withdraw it. Ah, how the other women would tease her over this! Her mother had already started.

Her greatest concern was that she was far from certain that she was ready to be courted at all. The loss of her husband, even though it was a constant threat to young wives, had been a crushing blow. Such things always happen to someone else, she had told herself repeatedly, not to us, not to Red Squirrel. And such an ignoble way to cross over. No chance to fight for life or even to die heroically.

Her heart still hurt for her husband. She hoped that on the Other Side, he knew that she would always consider him brave and noble. She was not ready to let go of his memory. Yet here she stood, more excited over the interest of a man than she had been for years. Her heart quickened. She was amused at herself, and a bit irritated. She wanted to turn and walk away but was afraid that such an action would start the song of the courting flute again, drawing more attention to her predicament. She must know more. "What do you expect to happen now?" Owl Woman demanded.

He shrugged. "Whatever you wish."

His expression was questioning. She realized that whatever the customs of this strange courtship, he was waiting for her to make the next move. The flutesong, it seemed, was his question, and he had now asked it. He expected her to answer.

The entire scene suddenly struck her as outrageously funny. Here was a courtship in progress. It involved two people of two entirely different cultures, and neither of them knew whether it was progressing properly. She wondered whether the Trader knew what was supposed to happen next.

Well, she must do *something*. What if she rejected his courtship? Would he sit forever outside her lodge, playing the flute? The thought caused a moment of panic. She knew of no way to silence this obvious act of his. On the other hand, she was certainly not ready to give him any encouragement, and for that matter, such encouragement might renew the flutesong.

"Look," she began, "I do not understand what is happening." She was distressed at the look on the face of her suitor, a look of pleasure. "No, no," she insisted, *"nothing* is happening."

He moved his arm a little, and she thought he was preparing to play the flute again. "We must talk," she said quickly. "Later?"

He seemed to think for a moment, and then nodded. "When?"

"Are you not leaving today?"

"Not yet. I must know—"

"Of course," Owl Woman interrupted, unwilling to let him finish that question. "Let us meet . . . just before dark?"

He nodded. It was obvious that he would have preferred it sooner, and for a moment the possibility that he would play the flute all day occurred to her. But she forged ahead. "There is a clearing upstream, near the river . . . an old cottonwood log."

"Yes, I know the place. It is good."

With a sense of relief, she saw him place the flute in a handsome beaded case and tie its thongs. At least that threat was over for the present. He rose with the quick smile that she was beginning to expect and, yes, enjoy.

"Until sunset, then." He turned and was gone.

Owl Woman stood, looking after him. What had she done? She was to meet a man who was practically a stranger to talk of romance. And neither knew the courtship customs of the other. The whole thing was sheer idiocy. How had she become entangled in such a situation?

She turned away, disturbed at her behavior, at the same time beginning to plan her tasks for the day. She must wash her hair, see that her buckskin dress was presentable. Maybe her new moccasins . . .

Shadows were growing long when she stepped into the clearing. The Trader was seated on the big trunk of the fallen cottonwood. She had thought that he might be playing his flute when she arrived and was somewhat relieved that he was not. Still, it would have been nice. . . .

She shook her head to free it of such thoughts. This must be a calm conversation. She must find out from the man what he expected and how seriously *he* considered this courtship.

He rose as she approached with his quick gentle smile. "I am pleased that you came," he said.

"Only to talk."

"Of course. I made you uncomfortable this morning. I am sorry for that."

"It is nothing."

There was a clumsy pause. Then both started to speak at once, and both stopped again. They laughed.

"You first," he said.

"How many wives have you?" she asked. Instantly, she was sorry. She had intended to ask that as a challenge, to put him off guard. She had not expected the hurt that she now saw in his face. He looked so vulnerable that she not only regretted the rude question but wished for a moment that she could comfort him in her arms. *What an odd thought!*

"I have no wife," he was saying sadly. "She died, from the pox, two seasons ago." The enormity of the loss he had suffered was apparent.

"I too," she blurted. "My husband was killed . . . but you know of that."

"Yes."

It was quiet for a moment. *We have much in common,* she thought. *I can see it in his face.* "Do you have children?"

"No. We never had . . . you have only Woodpecker?"

"Yes."

"He is a fine boy."

This was not going well. A clumsy silence, punctuated by small talk. But maybe there was progress after all. She did know much more about him now. They had both suffered a great loss. He had no children, while she had had young Woodpecker, so like his father, to comfort her. But . . .

"I do not know if I am ready to think of courtship," she said shyly, amazed at herself.

He looked at her in the twilight, serious yet pleased at her statement. "I am not sure of myself either," he said. "But I am ready to try if you are."

"I may need some time. How long will you stay?"

"Who knows? Tomorrow is tomorrow. We will see."

4

"**W**hat is your tribe, Uncle?" Woodpecker asked respectfully.

Things had happened so quickly that the boy was still somewhat confused. His mother and the Storyteller had quickly become interested in each other. To the amusement of the People, they started almost immediately to make plans for marriage. Owl Woman's other suitors were disappointed, of course, and suffered the friendly jibes and ribald jokes of the villagers.

The marriage ceremony was a strange mixture of customs. The ceremony of Owl Woman's tribe was included but also bits and pieces of other tribal ways. The Trader, now known to her as "Turtle," had picked up interesting and meaningful ideas from many tribes in his travels. It was like the song of the courting flute in a way. That had been embarrassing at first, but as Owl Woman quickly accepted her own feelings, she became almost defiant about it. She was proud to be pointed out as the woman who was to become the wife of the traveling Storyteller, the most exciting man she had ever known.

So on the day of their marriage, the happy couple had come to the point where it did not matter to them. The good-natured jokes and jibes were accepted as they were intended, as expressions of well-wishing. There were, of course, those oldsters who shook their heads, clucked their tongues, and predicted that no good could come of this.

"Does the jay nest with the robin?" someone asked.

But all in all, the People were happy for their daughter to find a husband. There was certainly precedent. Many among the People traced their heritage to outsiders who had married into the tribe. It was the usual thing for the husband to join his wife's people, but this was a special circumstance. The whole thing was viewed as an amusing diversion as the new couple prepared to move on down the river, following the call of the Trader's vocation.

Woodpecker had hardly had time to catch his breath. It had been so sudden for him, the acquaintance with the Storyteller. He had held the man in awe, had admired and respected him more than any other person in his young life, anyone since the loss of Woodpecker's father, of course. He had not quite understood why the Traveler had wished to meet his mother, except that somehow it involved Woodpecker.

Then suddenly everything seemed to change. The boy felt almost forgotten in the swift progress of the whirlwind romance. His mother and the Storyteller had seemed oblivious to the whole world, their attention absorbed in each other. He felt a small pang of jealousy at first. That quickly abated when they included him in their planning. When he finally realized that this magnificent person, the Storyteller, was to be his new father, Woodpecker was overwhelmed. He would be the envy of all the boys his age. It was like the best of dreams, the preparation to depart on an exciting adventure with his mother and his new father.

There was a question of how he should address this important new person in his life. Woodpecker had considered him the Storyteller, though others called him the Trader, depending upon the man's importance in their lives.

"Whatever you wish," was the answer when Woodpecker ventured to inquire of his mother. "Why not ask him?"

Woodpecker went to the little fire where the Storyteller still camped, pending the marriage.

"What would you have me call you, Uncle?" he asked. "Uncle," of course, was a customary term of address for any adult male older than oneself in many tribes.

The Storyteller spread his palms in the gesture of not-knowing that was now becoming familiar. It was a thing of habit, and Woodpecker had already noticed its usefulness in trading. "What would *you* call me, Woodpecker?" The Storyteller skillfully turned the answer into another question.

"I do not know, Uncle. My heart would not be good, to call you Father. Not yet, maybe."

"That is true," observed the other seriously. "What have you called me until now? To others, I mean."

"I have thought of you as the Storyteller."

"Yes, I am called that."

"But it seems distant, Uncle. You will be my mother's husband."

"Yes . . . well, as I told your mother, I was first called Turtle."

Woodpecker thought for a little while. "No," he decided, "it is a good name, but would it show respect to call you that?"

Turtle smiled, inwardly pleased. Many boys would not feel this. "It would depend *how* you used it," he noted. "But as you wish."

Woodpecker pondered a little longer. "Maybe . . . Uncle, maybe I could call you that!"

"What? Turtle?"

"No, 'Uncle'!"

"Why not? It is good! Now, how shall I call *you*?"

" 'Woodpecker,' I suppose. That is my name. Until I earn another, anyway."

Woodpecker did not realize the depth of the question. His new father was asking tentatively to call the boy his son, the child he had never had. But, since Woodpecker had not realized, it was best to drop the subject for now.

"It is good! Woodpecker!" said Turtle proudly.

The three had traveled several sleeps now and were beginning to fall into a pattern. They had stopped at one village to trade, a village much like their own. Woodpecker was proud to be a part of the Storyteller's family. He could see the envy in the eyes of the children, became just a trifle haughty, and behaved as if he considered himself better than they. His mother quickly stopped that trend.

"You must be friendly to everyone," she advised gently. "If we are not well liked, no one will wish to trade!"

It was so obvious that Woodpecker was ashamed. Of course! That was his new father's entire approach. One trades freely with those whom he trusts, and one trusts his friends. Thus, in the first three days on the trail, Woodpecker learned his first lesson in trading.

He brought out his bull-roarer, a toy Turtle had given him. It was a device from the far prairie tribes, Turtle had told him. A flat stick, scraped thin and fastened to a slender thong, it could be whirled rapidly around one's head by the thong to create a roaring noise like the distant bellow of a bull. Woodpecker whirled the noisemaker, which attracted some boys of his own age. He allowed them to try it, then showed the construction so they could make similar devices themselves. The game caught on quickly, and the prestige of the Trader and his family increased. Turtle nodded, pleased.

"He is a good boy," he told Owl Woman. "He can be a great help to us."

She too was pleased.

They traveled on foot, following an ancient trail along the river. Turtle took the lead, followed by young Woodpecker, and Owl Woman brought up the rear. Each carried a pack. Woodpecker was pleased to be allowed to carry some of the important trading goods. Turtle had been careful not to start with too heavy a burden.

At a village a few sleeps downriver, Turtle assured them, he had left a canoe. When they reached there, travel would be easier. Paddling was easier than walking with heavy packs.

It was the second night after they left the first trading stop that the question occurred to Woodpecker: What was the tribe to which Turtle had been born? Everyone had always considered the Trader to be without a tribe. Yet he must have been born somewhere. The boy thought long and hard about this. Finally, after their little camp was established and they had eaten, he ventured to ask.

"What is your tribe, Uncle?"

Turtle did not answer immediately. The fire flickered hazily, sending shimmering patches of light dancing in the leafy cover overhead. "We call ourselves the People," he said finally.

"But that is the same as ours," the boy protested.

"Yes."

"But . . . you are not of *our* People."

"No, no, of course not. But does it matter?"

"Yes! It matters!" gasped the astonished Woodpecker.

"Why?"

"Well . . . well, because . . ."

"Because your tribe is *better*?"

Woodpecker was embarrassed. He had not foreseen that question. But now that he was faced with it, it was hurtful to admit, and he was sorry that he had hurt the feelings of the man he had come to admire so much. He did not notice the twinkle of amusement in the eyes of Turtle or the smile on his mother's face.

"Woodpecker, it is good to take pride in one's tribe," Turtle observed, saving the boy from having to make an embarrassing answer. "But why do we like to hear stories?"

Woodpecker was confused. What did stories have to do with which tribe was better? "I . . . I do not know," he stammered.

Turtle seemed not to notice. "Because," he went on, "they are *different*. You know how Bobcat lost his tail?"

"Which . . . ?" He began to see the point as Turtle continued.

"Yes. In one story, it was frozen in the ice. In another, an eagle swooped down and snatched it off. All are good stories." He picked up a stick and poked a couple of burned ends into the fire. "Now," he went on, "if I think I am better than anyone, they will say, 'I do not wish to trade with him.' Then the trade would stop."

Woodpecker was still confused. "Then, *no* tribe is best?"

"Well, each must think his own is best. That is why he calls his the People. But even if we think this, we have better trading if we do not *act* like it. It is like the bull-roarer."

"But what . . . ?"

"You were proud to show it to the other boys. It is a good noisemaker, yes?"

"Yes, very good, Uncle."

"But it is not of *your* tribe."

Woodpecker was a little ashamed. He had been proud of the toy, proud to flaunt it at first.

"You did well," Turtle went on. "You showed it, shared it. Every tribe has *something* that can be used by others. That is how there can be traders. The trader sees . . . this tribe can use that which the other has . . . he helps them to get it by trading what *they* have. He does better by not showing his pride in his own tribe. He *has* it, but does not let it interfere."

Woodpecker thought about it a little longer. "Then, this is why you say little of your tribe, Uncle?"

"Yes. I do not wish to boast. It might cause bad feelings."

"How is your tribe called by others, then?"

"Some call us Traders, and use the hand-sign for *trade*. We are allies of the Finger-cutters."

He made the hand-sign for *mourning,* a sawing motion across the left forefinger.

"Why is their sign the one for mourning, Uncle?"

"That is how they mourn . . . cut the finger."

"Ah! Uncle, will you tell me more of hand-signs?"

Turtle laughed. "All in time, Woodpecker. You will learn much as we travel."

Another thought occurred to the boy. "What is your tribe's sign for *itself*?"

Turtle solemnly made the sign for *tribe,* rubbing the back of his left hand with the right forefinger. Then he doubled his right fist and gently thumped his chest over the heart three times.

"Mother?" asked the puzzled boy. *"Mother-Tribe?"*

"Yes. We say, 'Mother-of-All-Tribes.' "

They looked at each other and laughed together.

"But you do not say that to other tribes!" Woodpecker accused.

"No. Not when I am trading!"

They laughed again, and Owl Woman, watching the two, smiled to herself. Her heart was good.

5

The bond between the two continued to grow stronger. To Turtle, this was the child he had never had. To the boy, it was, in a way, the restoration of his lost father. It was not quite the same, but a good feeling to be a family again. He could see the light in the eyes of his mother, who now laughed again and appeared younger than at any time he could remember.

In some ways, this was even better than before his father's death. He felt guilty about feeling so, but even his father had not been able to make the stories come alive as Turtle could. Woodpecker felt that this life, with its new sights, sounds, and experiences, was the best of all possible worlds. His new father seemed willing to answer his questions—eager almost. He knew much about many things and seemed pleased to have an interested intelligent pupil to share them with.

"Woodpecker is a fine boy," Turtle told his wife after an especially exhaustive conversation. "He has a feel for language . . . the tongues of different tribes."

That was true. There are some, it has always been noted, who never master more than one or two tongues, and even then, with halting and a heavy accent. Others slip easily from one language to another, learning a working use of a new one as easily as changing garments. It is not a learned skill but one a person is born with. If he does not possess it, he will never have it, but if he is born with the gift, it will be his always.

Turtle had always had the gift. Possibly his tribe's status as traders was a help. Because of their location in the Great Plains and their mobility within this area, they came in contact with many cultures and traded with all. The Grower tribes along the streams and fertile valleys, the fishermen of the great rivers, and the hunting nomads of the prairie—all had commodities for potential trade. Turtle had grown up in this atmosphere, exposed to many languages. This had enabled him to perfect the skills that allowed him to become the Storyteller and the Trader.

It was pleasing to him, then, to find that his new son was quick to learn and interested in learning. In no time at all, it seemed, Woodpecker and his new father were chattering in various tongues, to the confused amusement of Owl Woman.

She too was pleased with the relationship that she saw growing between her son and her husband. The rapid use of other tongues, however, was beyond her. Laughing over the impossible task, she threw up her hands in despair and returned to her cooking fire. She did not feel excluded from their shared activity. It was simply a thing in which she had little interest. So she watched with pleasure as the instruction proceeded.

"Show me more of the signtalk, Uncle," Woodpecker pleaded.

Turtle chuckled. It amused him that even though the bonds between them grew stronger each day, Woodpecker still used the term "Uncle." Whatever was comfortable for the boy, of course. Turtle had decided that this usage was out of respect for the lost father. He doubted that under similar circumstances, he could call anyone else Father either. Probably, Woodpecker would never do so. Yet, the use of "Uncle" was a mark of respect, and Turtle understood.

"Hand-signs are of little use here," Turtle observed.

Camped on the middle Ohio River between two villages, they were traveling by canoe now. Turtle seemed to have contacts everywhere, friends and acquaintances from whom they could borrow needed transportation or would keep Turtle's possessions until his return.

"But, I would be ready for later," Woodpecker argued.

"Yes, that is true. In the western areas it is necessary," he agreed.

"In the region of your home?"

"Yes. Our people trade with many tribes, and most use the hand-signs. Mostly, those west of the Big River, the Mississippi. This side, there is little use."

Woodpecker nodded eagerly. "So, teach me more, Uncle."

"Well, you know some already. Let us start with signs for different tribes."

He made the sign for *people,* then one with both hands, like the flapping of wings.

"What do you think this tribe is called?"

"Bird . . . Bird People?"

"Yes, almost. These are the Crows."

"Crows? I do not know them, Uncle."

"Of course not. They live to the west. They were Growers until the horse came."

"Then they became hunters?"

"Only part of them. Some stayed with farming. Others hunt buffalo."

"Ah! Their tribe split in two?"

"Yes, but they meet together each summer."

"And the sign . . . for both halves is the same? The birdsign?"

"Yes. They also are called sometimes by another sign, Like this." He doubled a fist and placed it on his forehead, fingers outward. "That is like a Crow warrior's hair-knot," he explained. "Now, they have enemies, the Lakota. Here is their sign." With a forefinger, Turtle made a slicing motion across his throat.

"The Cut-throats?" Woodpecker gasped.

"Yes. Some call them the Enemies."

"*Your* enemies, Uncle?"

"No, no." Turtle laughed. "I have no enemies. But these are very jealous of their hunting grounds. When the Growers began to hunt, you see . . ."

"Yes . . . but the Cut-throat sign?"

"That is their mark . . . to tell who did the kill. Even a kill with an arrow might be marked that way, to claim credit."

"It is a boast?"

"Yes, maybe."

"What are other signs for tribes, Uncle?"

"*Aiee,* boy, you never tire of learning. Well, so be it. Now here is a tribe to the south of my home. Oh, you remember Finger-cutters, my tribe's allies?"

"Yes."

"They have a southern tribe. They are still one, but yet two."

"So, one could sign South Finger-cutters?"

"Yes, maybe so. Now, in their area is another, with a sign like this." He made a wavy line.

"A snake?"

"Good! Yes, the sign of a snake! Now, there are others, many of them. Their tongues are different, but all use some of the sign-talk. Here is one . . . what is their name?" He made the sign for a man on a horse, the right forefinger and middle finger straddling the edge of the left hand.

"The Horse People?" guessed Woodpecker.

"Yes! A small tribe, in the Tallgrass country. Here is another." He made a sign with two fingers upright, near his face.

"I do not know that sign, Uncle."

"That is *wolf.*"

"Wolf People?"

"Yes . . . Pawnee. Now, one more . . . too many will confuse you." With both hands, he pushed his hair backward over the top of his head, from the forehead.

"I do not understand."

"This means *haircutting* . . . they cut the hair short. Osage is their name."

"Where are they, Uncle?"

"Across the Big River. They are more woods dwellers than some of the others. And farther south. Now, enough! Let us sleep. Tomorrow, we must travel."

Woodpecker lay in his sleeping robe, still excited over all he was learning. Too excited to fall asleep quickly, he listened to the sounds of the night-creatures. Deep in the trees sounded the hunting cry of the great cat-owl. Nearer at hand, a small green heron gave his raucous squall, and on the ridge, a fox barked. Farther away, the chuckling call of a coyote rippled across the distance. A fish splashed in the river. The boy listened to these sounds as a comforting nightsong. He would dream of faraway places, new people, new creatures, new stories to tell.

The world is full of stories, his stepfather had once said. From time to time, they allow themselves to be told. Turtle was surely a master at story-telling. Woodpecker had already heard most of them many times, sometimes in different tongues. Still, each time was exciting.

Sometimes, when he used a tongue not quite familiar to him, Turtle also used hand-signs. This, Woodpecker saw, would be a valuable thing, hence his interest in the sign-talk. Even when a storyteller knew well the tongue of his listeners, would it not be effective to insert a hand-sign here and there for dramatic effect?

He fell asleep, thinking of how one could use the signs. When Bobcat, for instance, froze his long tail in the ice, and lost it as he leaped . . .

6

"**A**nd when Bobcat leaped, he was jerked up short by his long tail, frozen in the ice, and Rabbit jumped away to escape. . . ."

The children around the story-fire squealed with delight, and Owl Woman smiled proudly. She turned to look at her husband and to enjoy the light in his eyes. Both were proud of young Woodpecker. In the five years since they had been together, he had grown almost to a young man.

In their second season of travel, Turtle had suggested that the boy start to tell stories to the children before the serious storytelling began. Woodpecker had jumped at the chance. Turtle's motives were not completely charitable. He was well aware that the stories he told were to engender trust for the coming day of trading. Not entirely, of course. It was a pleasure to himself and the other participants as well as the listeners. But it did establish credibility and friendship, fostering better trade. Likewise, with Woodpecker telling stories to the children—how could anyone distrust people whose son tells stories to little children?

And the boy was good at it. He had taken to the storytelling with even more success than Turtle had imagined. He made clever modifications and jokes, and dramatized with hand-signs. He was mastering several languages and dialects, and when they were in contact with those who used hand-signs, he increased his proficiency in those also.

This season, when they had approached a village a moon ago, children had run out to greet them, shouting happily. "Look! The Storyteller comes!"

It was with some chagrin that Turtle realized that the youngsters were crowding around Woodpecker, not himself. In the eyes of these children at least, Woodpecker was "the Storyteller."

Turtle looked at his wife and smiled.

"I have been replaced!"

Owl Woman shifted the baby on her back and began to loosen the straps of the carrying board. "Not really. To the adults, there is no storyteller like yourself."

"But he is good, Owl. Next season I will ask him to take part in the serious stories."

She smiled. "He helps the trading," she observed.

"Yes, greatly. He is taking more interest. For a while, I thought he only liked the storytelling."

Owl Woman nodded. She unwrapped the baby, loosened her tunic, and put it to the breast. "Turtle, next season can we go home?"

He looked at her sympathetically. He had had some trouble retracing the trading routes he had first explored with Lark. It was uncomfortable challenging the ghost of his first love. They had talked of it. Owl Woman was having no problem. This was all new territory for her, with nothing to remind her of her first marriage, but she could understand.

They had decided, by common consent, to explore territory new to him also. They had pushed farther south and westward along the rivers, finding new people to trade with, and established new contacts, new friendships. It was successful. They had avoided his people and hers, to avoid their ghosts of the past. But now the situation had changed somewhat. A baby girl had been born to them a few moons ago as they wintered with friends among the Sacs. She was a beautiful child, and Owl Woman felt that now her life was complete—except that she would like to show their success to her parents and her friends at home.

"Home?" he asked. "Your village?"

"Yes. I would show my mother." She glanced at the infant.

"Of course. I thought . . . you did not seem . . ."

"I know. But now it is different, somehow. Do you not feel it?"

"Yes. I would like for my people to see our family too. I had hesitated to speak of it."

She laughed happily. "It is good! How shall we plan?"

Turtle thought awhile. "If we start in that direction now," he suggested, "we could winter in your village."

Owl Woman's eyes lighted. "Could we do that?"

"Of course! That is a good thing about trading. We can go wherever we want!"

So it was decided in a few moments. Woodpecker, completely unaware, was laughing and talking with children who looked forward to the story-fires that evening.

"Will you tell us of Bobcat?"

"No, Rabbit's long ears!"

"Wait, wait," he cried in mock alarm. "I will tell them all!"

It was not until they had set up their temporary camp at the edge of the village that his parents told Woodpecker of their decision.

". . . so we will winter at home," his mother explained, "and start to make our way west to Turtle's people next spring. The Moon of Greening, maybe."

Woodpecker sat in stunned silence for a moment.

"What is wrong?" asked Owl Woman. "Do you not *want* to go?"

"Yes, yes, of course!"

"Then what is it, my son?"

"I . . . well, when I left, I was 'Woodpecker.' Some of the others are probably warriors now, with proud names."

"You do not like 'Woodpecker'?"

"Of course, Mother. It is fine for a child, but . . ."

"What?"

"But . . . well, I would like to feel that I have *done* something, some-thing important enough to . . . to change my name . . . take a man's name."

"But, my son, surely there are men called Woodpecker. It is a good name. You only think of it that way because it is *your* childhood name!"

"Wait!" interrupted Turtle. "Owl, if he has outgrown the name, he should have a new one."

"But he has not outgrown it . . . ," began Owl Woman.

"That is for him, to say what he feels," admonished Turtle. "If he thinks it is outgrown, it is so."

"What name would you take?" demanded Owl Woman.

"Well, I do not—"

"See?" she interrupted. "You do not know!"

"Wait, wait, now," Turtle said soothingly. "The children already call him the Storyteller."

"But *you* are the Storyteller," Owl Woman protested.

"I am not the only Storyteller," Turtle pointed out. "Also, I am called the Trader much of the time. He could be 'the Young Storyteller.' Or he 'the Storyteller' and I 'the Trader.'"

Owl Woman looked from one to the other, realizing her defeat. She seemed to see her son for the first time, his face almost on a level with her own. How sudden and unsuspected it had been! She smiled, blinking back a few tears. Her son was grown, almost a man.

"It is good," she said tightly, "but you will always be Woodpecker to me."

"Of course, Mother."

"Just as I am always Small Turtle to *my* mother!" said Turtle.

"Yes," agreed Owl Woman. *"Just* like that. Turtle, I want to meet your mother. Next season!"

"It is good! Next season."

So Woodpecker became "Storyteller," except for his mother. The children in the villages where they traded already called him that. Usage solidified the designation, and they settled comfortably into the shifting pattern.

The infant sister, as she grew, did not remember her brother by any other name. Her earliest memories were of listening to his stories. The child was called Lark, after Turtle's lost first love. He had protested, but Owl Woman was firm. "I owe much to a sister called Lark whom I never met," she explained, cuddling close to her husband in the robes. "I know I would have loved her."

Turtle could not speak because of the lump in his throat, but he managed to nod. Their marriage became even stronger.

There was one other change that occurred that summer before they reached the home village of Owl Woman. It was less than a moon after the decision to go home, and the name changing. They had entered a village to trade, and were preparing their camp when Turtle drew Storyteller aside. "Tonight," he suggested, "I will start the Creation stories, and then we will both answer their storytellers."

"But the children . . ."

"Yes, go ahead with those. But this town has two or three good storytellers. We will answer. I will tell one, then they will answer, then you . . . and so on. But you start with the children. When it is dark and the elders come to the fire, I will start with a Creation story."

"You would let me tell stories with the elders, Uncle?"

"Of course. Why are you called Storyteller?"

It was a glorious evening. Turtle began the formal part of the stories with a Creation story from the plains. This tribe, he related, crawled into the open world from below, First Man and First Woman, through a hollow cottonwood log. One of the locals countered with a similar story of their own, and then Turtle nodded to his assistant.

Young Storyteller rose, a nervously tight tone in his voice and his palms moist. "I have heard," he began carefully, "of a tribe to the south and east, whose world was water. They lived above, on a great blue dome, the sky. But they wished to live on the earth, so tiny Beetle was sent to the bottom of the water, to bring mud and spread it to dry on the surface. Buzzard flew over it, fanning with his wings to dry the mud . . ."

His listeners were enthralled, and by the time the humans slid down the dome to dry ground, Storyteller had earned his new name. He sat down amid a murmur of approval.

"Well told," whispered Turtle proudly.

Storyteller was still intoxicated with the excitement of the moment and his coming of age, but he did not overlook the pride in Turtle's words. "Thank you, Father," he whispered.

It came easily and seemed no disrespect to his first father.

7

Storyteller the Younger had noticed the girl at the story-fire but did not recognize her. She was tall and slim, with shapely legs and womanly bulges beneath her buckskins that suggested further beauty. Her eager smile at the story-fire had been mildly disconcerting to him. Twice their eyes had met, and his line of thought was interrupted, to the extent that he had to look away, gather himself, and resume the story. He hoped that the listeners would perceive this as only a dramatic pause in his narration. Thereafter, he avoided eye contact with the girl.

In fact, probably no one had noticed except Turtle, who had heard the young storyteller relate this tale many times. Never before had the youngster placed a pause at that point in the story. Curious, Turtle watched closely, and when it happened again, looked quickly in the direction of Storyteller's gaze.

There was no longer any question. Well, some questions, perhaps. Turtle did not know who this girl might be and what she might mean to Storyteller. Had the boy known her before, or was this their first meeting? But the main question had been answered: Yes, this was the cause of the awkward pause in the flow of the story.

Now Turtle watched the girl instead of Storyteller. She was remarkably pretty and seemed unaware of her beauty, with the innocent charm of youth. He could understand how this creature, on the verge of flowering into the fullness of womanhood, could distract Woodpecker . . . no, Storyteller. It was amusing now to watch the two. It was plain that the young woman was entranced with Storyteller's art, just as he was with her beauty.

To Turtle's amusement, the young man dared not look at her again, for fear of interrupting the flow of his story. It would be enjoyable later to discuss this with Owl Woman. He looked around to see if his wife noticed this interplay. Owl was seated some distance away. Turtle felt it necessary to be near the story-fire so that he could rise to speak. Owl Woman usually sat well back to see how the stories were coming across to the other listeners.

He tried to catch her eye for some time. Finally she looked around, and their eyes met. Owl nodded and smiled. So the scene had been so subtle that even the young man's mother had missed it. It had taken the expertise of another storyteller to pick up the slight hesitancy, the break in the smooth rhythmic flow of the narrative. Turtle chuckled to himself and waited for the coming of darkness and the transition to stories that would please not only the children but everyone.

They had been welcomed here before and had planned to return here for the winter two seasons later. Young Storyteller was welcomed enthusiastically. He was now an important part of the routine. There were, of course, a few boys his own age who had a tendency to jeer or sulk in jealousy, but that was to be expected. The girls seemed enthralled, especially the one whose eager smile and bright gaze had so disconcerted the young man.

The story-fires burned far into the night, the local storytellers trading tales with the visitors to the enjoyment of the crowd. Finally, it was Turtle who brought the festivities to an end. "Ah," he exclaimed, "I must seek my bed. We will be trading in the morning, and I will be an easy mark unless I have some sleep!"

The crowd laughed and began to disperse, greatly pleased at the evening's entertainment.

Storyteller looked for the girl as the people separated to go their own ways, but she had disappeared in the darkness. He spent a restless night dreaming of that smiling face in the crowd, so alluring yet so unattainable. Then he would wake and lie staring at the leafy vault overhead. The whisper of the river and the soft sigh of the breeze in the treetops made a background for the voices of the night-creatures. It was a night of great medicine, frustrated by the one question that dominated his thoughts: Who was the exciting girl at the story-fire?

He rose early to walk along the stream, absently gathering sticks for the morning fire, still preoccupied with the excitement of the previous evening. Ahead was a little clearing, much like that where he had played as a child, the place of mystical charm where the rabbit once came close and almost spoke to him. He smiled to himself. That was another world and seemed long ago now.

The clearing that had seemed so remote, he now realized, had been no more than a bow shot from the village. The clearing had probably shrunk appreciably since his early years. He wondered if any other child ever felt that way about this place, that it was a place of enchantment. Lost in thought, he sat on a log at the edge of the glade, watching a rabbit. The creature came cautiously into the open, pausing to nibble, sitting erect to stare around for any danger. In his mind, it was the same rabbit. This was a place of exceptions where anything might happen, and probably would if he could allow his mind to accept the strong medicine of the mystic.

His eyes were half closed as he watched the daylight brighten, the warm rays of the rising sun probing into the clearing. He could imagine that this was the first morning of Creation and that the magic was still strong. "Speak to me, Little Brother," he said softly to the rabbit. "I will do you no harm."

Someone giggled, and he was jolted rudely back to reality. He was somewhat embarrassed, resentful of the intrusion. He glanced around, ready to react defensively, but when he saw the intruder, his mood softened instantly. It was the girl from the story-fire, she of the bright eyes and eager smile. She was even more alluring in the morning sunlight.

"I am sorry," she said, stepping into the open. "I did not mean to intrude."

"It is nothing," he blurted clumsily. "I was . . ." He looked around for the rabbit, but it was gone. "I was just enjoying the morning," he mumbled, hoping that he would not appear too foolish.

"I too." She smiled. "It will be a beautiful day, yes?"

"Yes . . ." There was a long and clumsy pause. "I . . . do I know you?" he asked. "You were at the fire last night."

She laughed, a rippling musical sound like none he had heard before, yet familiar somehow. "I am Plum Leaf," she said. "We played together as children."

Of course! Two, three seasons ago, when they stopped here, they had played—yes, in this very clearing. Both were a trifle shy, and when the other children began more boisterous games, these two drew aside to play more quietly. How could he have forgotten? But then, he had left immediately and had not seen her since.

"Forgive me," he said clumsily. "You have changed!"

She laughed again, the little musical trickle that he found so delightful. She turned slowly, a complete turn to face him again. "You like the changes?" she asked provocatively. "You have changed much yourself, Woodpecker."

He was dumbfounded. This was not the shy, retiring child he had known, but a capable-looking young woman, confident in her womanhood and her beauty.

Then he realized how much he had changed. From a shy and retiring boy, he had become the confident Storyteller, proud of his expertise. "We have both changed," he laughed.

"Yes. I liked your stories last night. I was proud." Then she became embarrassed. Her statement of pride implied a relationship that was not there. It might have been once, but no longer. There was a clumsy moment as both pondered that implication.

"Has it been well with you?" he asked, seeking safer ground.

"Yes . . . my brother, Tall Pine, . . . you remember? He is married. Big-Eared Man—he was older than we—he drowned last year."

"But what of you?" he asked.

Her eyes dropped shyly. "There is nothing to tell. I grew up, like you. Is it exciting, to travel and trade?"

"Yes, mostly. Sometimes hard work."

"Dangerous?"

"Maybe, a little." He could not resist a little boasting.

"I think that would be an exciting life," Plum Leaf said, her eyes dancing. "Your mother seems very happy."

"Yes. She and my—her husband—are well suited to each other."

"You told me that he courted her with the flute." Plum Leaf chuckled happily. "I thought it was very romantic. He is an exciting man."

There was a strange pang for a moment as the young man wished silently that Plum Leaf might feel that way about *him*. Maybe she did. After all, she was here with him, at this odd hour and place. Did that signify something?

"When will you travel on?" she asked.

"Soon . . . no more than a day or two. My grandfather is old. My mother wishes to be with them. We will winter there."

"Yes, that is good." Her tone was a bit sad, befitting the conversation about the ailing grandfather, but her face was radiant. "Then, we will have no chance to become reacquainted," she suggested cautiously.

"No . . ." This was moving almost too rapidly for Young Storyteller, yet the excitement drew him like a moth to the flame. "I . . . I should go back to the camp," he said. "They will wonder where . . ."

"Yes, of course!" she agreed. She turned and led the way back toward the village, her stride long and confident. He liked the way she moved and hurried to walk with her. She matched stride for stride, and it occurred to him that they walked well together. For a moment he wondered what others would think when the two returned together.

An old woman peered sleepily out of her doorway and smiled at the two. They waved self-consciously and hurried on.

Young Storyteller's heart was very good.

8

"Things are very bad here," said Yellow Bowl, shaking her head and clucking her tongue.

"How so, Mother?" asked Owl Woman. "My father's health?"

She had been startled at how feeble her father appeared. Once a proud warrior, Bear Sits now shuffled weakly, his aging joints stiffened by the years and old injuries. It hurt Owl Woman to see him so. She remembered his active years when she was a child growing into womanhood.

"No, no, not that. It is the way of things that one grows old. Bear is well respected and proud. He is older than I, you remember," said Yellow Bowl.

"Yes, but he has changed so . . ."

"Of course, Owl. The years have passed. But oh, they are good to you! You have never looked prettier! And how Woodpecker has grown, and this lovely child . . . Lark, you call her?"

"Yes, Mother. But, you said things are bad? How so?"

"Ah, yes! I am sorry . . . there is much to tell. You remember the stories of tribes from beyond the Big Salt Water, men whose eyes are bluish, yet they still see?"

"Yes, Mother, but there have been such stories for a long time."

"No, it is real! They are here."

"Ah! *Here,* in the village?"

"No . . . well, yes sometimes. They have built a town downriver, only a sleep away."

"You have seen them, Mother?"

"Of course. Everyone has seen them."

"But what do they do?"

The older woman shrugged. "Hunt a little. Trade for some furs. Mostly, they fight. They are warriors."

"Fight who, Mother? Our people?"

"No, no. Not now, anyway. One wonders, of course. But they fight each other."

"I do not understand."

"Nor do I," Yellow Bowl stated, shaking her head sadly. "There are two kinds of them."

"Two *tribes* of these outsiders?"

"Yes . . . maybe so. They speak different tongues, anyway."

"How are they called?"

"Well, the nearest town is of *Yen-glees.* The others are farther north. They are *Fran-cois.*"

"And they fight?"

"Yes. To see who will stay here."

"But why?"

"To trade! For furs, robes."

"What do they offer?"

"Oh, knives, beads, cloth." Yellow Bowl was preparing food and turned to hold up a small knife. "See?"

Owl Woman examined the knife closely. Its blade was smooth and shiny, and its edge straight rather than chipped in serrations. "What sort of stone . . ."

Her mother laughed. "Not stone . . . it is called metal. Very useful! It can be resharpened."

"Mother, this is strong medicine! I must tell Turtle. Knives such as this would be good for trading."

"Yes, that is true. They have axes too, made of this."

"Axes?"

"Yes. They can be thrown, as a weapon. A small ax."

"Mother, these are useful things. Why do you say that times are bad?"

Yellow Bowl's face fell, losing the cheerful good humor that it had shown a moment ago. "Ah, my child, that is the bad part. Each of the outsider tribes has tribes here for friends."

Now Owl Woman was completely puzzled. "But how is this bad?"

Yellow Bowl clucked her tongue. "Well, you know how tribes have others who are enemies? Some have always fought. Now, if your enemy joins the Yen-glees, then you join the Fran-cois."

"But why? For what purpose?"

"To kill the other. One tribe is paid to kill Yen-glees, another to kill Francois."

Owl Woman was beginning to understand. It was horrible, this thing of hiring to kill. It was one thing to kill in a battle over territory or political unrest, quite another to kill for payment, to kill someone with whom you have no quarrel.

"How . . . how are they paid?"

"In trade goods."

"No, Mother. Paid for each kill?"

"Oh. Yes, proof is required. A scalp. They skin the top of the head."

"Skin? . . ."

"Yes. Some have become quite wealthy."

For Owl Woman, the enormity of this situation was just starting to sink in. "And our people kill for the Yen-glees?"

"We have tried to be for neither. This is what the chiefs say. But some of the men hunt scalps on their own."

"For which side?"

Yellow Bowl shrugged. "Who knows? Who pays the best?"

"Mother!" Owl gasped in horror. "The hair of men is sold like that of a beaver?"

"Not quite. It is usually worth more."

Owl Woman was silent. Even Yellow Bowl, without realizing it, was thinking of the hair of the slain as an item for trade like a beaver pelt. Times were worse, it seemed, than her mother was aware.

It was difficult to tell how much of all this her father understood. Bear Sits spent most of his time merely staring blankly. He smiled and spoke when spoken to, then lapsed back into his detached haze. It seemed too much effort to concentrate, even to think about the situation that had developed. The old warrior appeared to have simply lost the will to question, perhaps even the will to live. Owl Woman wondered if he could last another winter.

Worst of all, the thing that permeated the village was something that could not be seen or heard. It was an uneasiness, a feeling. At first, when the travelers had arrived, it was not quite so apparent. In the excitement of the homecoming, more subtle things were overlooked. Only gradually it had become apparent, a vague unrest that kept everyone tense and suspicious. Even after learning its source, Owl Woman could hardly believe the change. It was a moody brooding thing that oppressed the very spirit of the place. She was saddened by it and a little fearful. She was glad that Woodpecker had not grown up and come of age in these surroundings. But that saddened her again. How different from the mood of the People in her own childhood.

Childhood—ah, Woodpecker was no longer a child. Even as the two women visited, he and Turtle had gone to make their courtesy calls on the chiefs and prepare for the storytelling. She would be proud tonight, at the fire, when both her husband and her son took prominent places in the festivities.

Yes, it could be a good stay here, she tried to convince herself. Despite the strange mood, it *was* home. Trading could be very good. She must tell Turtle of the medicine-knives made of a new sort of stone. Yes, here was opportunity. They carried a good variety of items for trade. Red medicine-stone for pipes, from west of the Big Lakes, heavy to carry but valuable since there was only one known source. Turtle had also acquired several shards of shiny black stone from the far western mountains. It was unexcelled, he said, for knives and arrowpoints, flaking cleanly when worked and leaving a very sharp edge. Probably only a skilled stonebreaker would wish to trade for that.

Turtle was fascinated by the odd and unusual, and loved to trade for new and unknown items. Only last season he had obtained a small flat cake of a substance from the far South, "choko-latl." It was used as food, or for flavor, in the region where it was grown, at least so said the trader from whom Turtle obtained it. There were medicinal properties to the choko-latl too, they had been told. A small piece, broken from the slab and stirred in hot water, made a pleasing drink.

They had sampled the choko-latl out of curiosity.

"Its taste is strange," Owl Woman said as she sipped the dark fluid from a horn cup.

"But good," added Storyteller. "What does it do?"

"Everything, the man from the South said." Turtle chuckled. "More strength, bravery. It makes one a better lover."

Owl Woman smiled smugly. "Then you need none," she stated flatly.

Storyteller, in the self-consciousness of newfound puberty, said nothing.

"They use it to flavor meats too," Turtle said. "I cannot think how that would taste."

He had not traded any of the choko-latl, but now, Owl Woman thought, he might wish to do so for some of the new things brought by the outsiders. Yes, it should be good trading.

She had no chance to speak to him of the things she had learned, good and bad, before the time came for storytelling. Turtle, true to his word, boasted of his son's ability and promised the children extra storytime just before dark. It was exciting to come home to such recognition. Storyteller had developed his skills and showed great promise. Owl Woman was eager for her friends and relatives to see how well the boy had grown and matured.

As the crowd gathered, Owl Woman and Yellow Bowl arrived early to choose good places. Bear Sits had stayed at the lodge.

"I will come later," he said vaguely.

"Will he come?" Owl asked her mother.

"Probably, if he remembers." Yellow Bowl sighed. "His spirit wanders."

They settled down in an open space and watched the crowd gather. It was pleasing to hear the remarks about the new Storyteller.

"They say he is very good for one so young."

"Is he not one of the People?"

"Yes! You remember Owl Woman, whose husband was killed? He is her son."

"Son? Ah, yes, there was a child. She married the Trader, no?"

"Yes, that is the one. . . ."

The two woman laughed softly together.

"Is he really good with the stories, Owl?" her mother asked.

"Of course! But, you will soon see."

Shadows were long now, and the assembling crowd was growing. Turtle threaded his way among them, carrying a firebrand toward the stack of fuel. There must be a fire for stories. Even when it was not needed for heat and not yet for light, there must be a fire. The rising of smoke to mingle with the spirits of the place was necessary for the mood, for the stories to come alive. Excitement was in the air as cheery little tongues of orange licked at the dry tinder and began to grow. In a short while, the heavier sticks began to ignite, and the fire assumed a life of its own.

Storyteller stepped forward and selected a place to stand. Turtle had taught him well the showmanship of the storyteller. He must avoid the possibility of a chance shift in the breeze, blowing smoke or sparks in his direction to interrupt the story. He chose a spot where the background would be good, a solid mass of dark foliage that would stir the imagination and improve the imagery of the story. He was especially nervous tonight. Many of his childhood friends would be there, and he must do well.

The young man's palms were damp as he held his hands to the darkening sky in a silent invocation. The murmur of the crowd died, and silence descended.

"In the long-ago times," he began, "animals could speak as we do, and all tribes spoke the same tongue. . . ."

9

I t was late in the autumn of that year that Owl Woman saw the restlessness in her man. Not a restlessness to be free from her, simply the longing to be on the trail again.

The trading season had been cut short by their arrival at her home village. Turtle had cheerfully accepted it and had carried out a brisk trade for a few days. Then it settled down to a sporadic, one-at-a-time trickle that Owl Woman knew was a frustration.

The Moon of Ripening had passed and the Moon of Falling Leaves, and it was now the Moon of Madness. Maybe that was part of Turtle's restlessness. The coming of the Mad Moon always affected people to some extent. Maybe it was a frustrated migration urge, a primordial wish to join the great geese in their long lines of flight across the clear blue of autumn skies.

The deer were rutting, the bucks polishing their new antlers on trees, preparing to establish their right to the strongest and most alluring does. Bull elk were bugling. Many of the birds had gone south already, but of those who would stay, the madness seemed to hold sway. Grouse and quail flew wildly, blindly, and irrationally through the woods, sometimes crashing into trees or rocks in their frantic celebration of the Moon of Madness.

Squirrels scampered fearlessly where they would not have risked going earlier, gathering and burying nuts, more nuts than they could ever use. The forgotten nuts in the ground would sprout in the Moon of Awakening to begin new trees. This, at least, lent some purpose to the activity of the Moon of Madness. It was part of the way of things.

But Turtle fretted over his own inactivity, and Owl Woman was concerned. "There is a village of our people only one sleep upriver," she observed casually one morning. "Maybe you could take Woodpecker, and the two of you could spend some time trading."

Turtle was silent for a moment. "Are you trying to get rid of me, woman?"

There was a moment of concern, but then she saw that he was teasing her. "Maybe." She giggled. "Old Lame Badger, there, once wanted to marry me."

They discussed the possibility seriously then, and it was decided.

"You are sure you do not want to go with us?"

"No, go ahead. It will be good for me to visit with my mother. She will enjoy her granddaughter, too. You and Woodpecker need some time together. But I will miss you both."

So it happened that the two storytellers traveled upstream to trade. Yellow Bowl had grave doubts about the wisdom of such a trip. "You do not understand the danger," she protested.

"It will be all right, Mother," Owl assured. "He has traveled and traded everywhere, with strange and unknown tribes. He can get along with anyone."

Yellow Bowl, unwilling to prolong the argument, shook her head in despair, clucked her tongue, then closed her lips in a tight determined line. She would not discuss it again.

The first night away from the village the two men spent at a pleasant glade where a spring trickled from the rocks. There were indications that this was a common stopping place; there were ashes of burned-out fires and several spots where travelers had spread their sleeping robes. The spring, they noticed, had been cleaned out and flat stones placed around the rim to form a clear pool of sparkling water.

They saw no other travelers and arrived at their destination the following afternoon. It was a good evening of stories, and the trading was brisk the next day. It was undoubtedly helpful that Storyteller was one of their own and many remembered his father.

Turtle was able to barter for a very fine steel knife, an object he had been unable to acquire so far. Everyone who possessed one wished to keep it, he decided, and the trade value was very dear. The specimen he was able to buy cost him dearly—a medicine pipe, a shard of the finest black obsidian, and half his cake of choko-latl. He hated to part with the choko-latl; there was no telling when he might acquire more. But first and foremost, he was a trader, and the function of a trader is to trade.

The knife was certainly an incentive. It was apparent that its medicine was important, its spirit strong. In the right light, it sparkled like the reflection of sunlight on water, and at times it seemed that blue fire licked along its cutting edge. Turtle spent much time staring at the knife, trying to fathom its spirit. But as with many things of the spirit, its mystery continued to elude him. Meanwhile, it was surely a useful item. Storyteller too was greatly impressed by its mystery. He would never ask to use the knife; it was too important a thing. It was much like the personal quality of one's medicine, which was inappropriate for another to covet. In the back of Storyteller's mind, however, an embryonic idea was forming. *Someday,* he thought, *someday I will have such a medicine-knife.*

They spent another night at the host village and set off for home with plenty of invitations to return for more stories and trades. It was that evening that their world was rudely shaken apart.

Until now, they had rather discounted Yellow Bowl's dire predictions of doom. It is the privilege of the older ones to voice warnings and caution the younger generation. Such warnings are partly taken to heart and partly observed, but after all, the older ones are cautious. Their advice must be tempered with reason.

Shadows were growing long when the travelers approached the camping spot by the spring. They would stay here and travel on to the village tomorrow. Through the trees ahead, they could see a campfire burning and smell its smoke.

"Good!" said Turtle. "We will have company tonight."

They walked in boldly, unthinking of danger, to confront three well-armed men. The strangers were obviously surprised and drew weapons threateningly.

"Greetings, my friends. We come in peace," announced Turtle in his wife's tongue. Simultaneously he extended his right hand, palm forward, in the hand-sign for peace.

"Who are you?" one of the strangers demanded. "You speak our tongue. Why?"

"Wait!" exclaimed another. "Are these not the storytellers?"

"They carry heavy packs," said the third greedily. "We can—"

"Stop!" the second insisted. "You cannot harm them. They are our people."

"Not this one," argued the man who had spoken first. "Look at his hair, his moccasins!"

"But his shirt and leggings," the other man replied. "They are ours."

It was a fearful, chilling thing to realize that the strangers were debating their fate—even worse, as if they did not exist and the ultimate decision did not matter much.

"One scalp is hard to tell from another," said the hard-looking warrior who had looked greedily at their packs. "Who is to know?"

"*We* are to know. These are the storytellers. This younger one is a relative of mine. His mother was married to an uncle . . ."

Reluctantly, the others lowered their weapons.

Turtle laughed nervously. He had occasionally been robbed in his travels but never threatened this way. "Look, my friends," he ventured, striding boldly past them, "we would like to make camp before dark. We—"

He stopped short. Beyond the fire were two sleeping places with rumpled robes tossed aside. Near each lay the body of a man, sprawled grotesquely in death. The brightness of the blood that still flowed from their wounds told that they had been killed only a short while ago.

"Who . . . who are they?" he mumbled.

"Enemies," one man said.

The other strangers laughed.

"They are nobody, now."

The one who seemed to be their leader sighed impatiently. "Let us get rid of them," he urged. He drew his knife and stepped forward, gripping the hair of one of the prostrate forms.

"Wait!" said one of the others. "That one has good hair. We can get two, maybe three scalps."

"I know how to take a scalp," snapped the other, slashing a circular cut around the top of the head.

"But there are three of us and only two scalps. We can make another. Look, if you cut this way—"

"Where will we take them? Yen-glees?"

"It does not matter. Who pays the best now?"

"I am not sure."

"Well, we can ask. No hurry. Scalps keep well when dried."

They laughed again, finished their ghoulish work, and stripped the bodies of anything useful. Then they dragged them into the darkening woods and returned to the fire.

"Well," said one to Turtle, "where are you heading?"

The casual conversational tone was so bizarre under the circumstances that Turtle could hardly answer. "My wife's village," Turtle mumbled. "It is as you said. We are storytellers and traders, returning home."

"Good! Let us do some trading! What do you have?"

Mildly protesting, Turtle opened the packs and still under duress, tried to carry on trade. The goods offered by the strangers were largely the possessions of the dead men, for which Turtle had no desire at all. However, he felt obliged to keep the others in good humor. They accomplished a few trades, but when one of them offered a still-oozing scalp, it was too much.

"We do not deal in scalps!" he snapped.

The three men laughed.

"You wear one!"

"But it is not for sale," insisted Turtle.

They laughed again.

It was a long, sleepless night, but Turtle and Storyteller were not harmed. At daylight, the strangers left, heading upstream. Turtle urged haste as they broke camp to head downstream. They made one stop, to dispose of the belongings of the dead they had been forced to take in trade. The items were bundled together, weighted with stones, and dropped into a deep hole in the river.

"We will say nothing of this, Storyteller," Turtle advised.

"Not to my mother?"

"Maybe to her, later. Not now. My son, these are bad times."

10

↔

n most respects, it was an uneventful winter. The two Storytellers, Elder and Younger, would not have believed it could be so after the chilling experience at the camp beside the spring. It was a day or two before they fully realized the narrow margin of their escape. If one of the warriors had not been a distant relative of Owl Woman's, their bones would even now be moldering in the forest with those of the other victims. Their scalps, no doubt, would by this time have become merely a commodity, to be traded for a knife, a mirror, or with other scalps or furs, maybe a blanket.

They decided after much discussion that neither would say anything to Owl Woman about the incident. She would only worry. They would agree that they had been well received and that the trading was good but not great. Some of their trades were ill-advised probably, they would admit. Turtle, who usually shared everything with his wife, would go so far as to say that the People there were quite preoccupied with the rewards of scalping. This, he stated flatly, could do great harm to the trade. Turtle even mentioned that someone had offered them a scalp in trade. He had refused, he related, by implying that among his own people there was a religious taboo.

In this way, everything the returning traders reported was literally true. They did not relate the entire story yet managed to share their fears and the reasons for them. The women were quite upset with even this superficial description of the events upriver. Yellow Bowl shook her head and clucked her tongue.

"It is as I told you," she said almost triumphantly.

Owl Woman demonstrated a deeper concern. "This is worse than I thought, Turtle," she said as soon as they were alone. "I am worried about Woodpecker."

"You need not worry for him," Turtle stated positively. But he could not tell her why or how he was so certain. "He understands the danger," he finished lamely.

"I do not like it!" Owl insisted. "Turtle, let us go on. Let us winter with your people."

Turtle shook his head. "That would be my choice too," he admitted. "I did not expect this problem. But we are here now, and the days grow shorter. My people are many sleeps away. No one travels the prairie at this season."

"But the good weather holds!" she insisted. "Look, the day is warm, though nights are cool."

"Yes, for now. But, Owl, this is Second Summer, when everyone uses good weather to prepare for winter. Any day now it will be over, and Cold Maker will waken."

She said nothing, and Turtle tried almost desperately to explain. "It is different here, Owl. When it snows, your people go inside by the fire. Even travelers in the woods can make a shelter. A traveler caught in the open prairie is dead!"

"Then how do your people live there?" she demanded.

"You will see, when we go there. They move to a sheltered area . . . before Second Summer . . . and stuff the lower part of the lodges with dry grass, a line of brush, maybe, to break the wind. Right now, they have done these things, and they are ready. We . . . if we left now, we would be in the open, searching for them, in the worst of the Moon of Snows!"

Finally, he managed to convince her. To stay here was the lesser of two dangers. Here, there might be danger. On the open prairie in winter it was certain. For a time, Turtle was afraid he would have to argue the merits of a quiet sleep by freezing to death versus the violence of being killed for one's pelt. It did not quite come to that, however, for which Turtle was thankful.

They settled in for the winter. There was little travel, even in the more sheltered woodlands, as the Moon of Long Nights descended. It was too dangerous because of Cold Maker's unpredictability. In the open country of his home, a storm could be seen approaching for half a day. Here, with trees and hills obstructing one's view, it could descend suddenly and unexpectedly.

Turtle had had to deal with that when he left the wide skies of the open plains to trade in the woodlands. For a season or two, he had experienced a sort of trapped, panicky feeling, like the one a caged bird must feel. He would find himself wanting to run, to escape to some place where he could at least see the horizon. He had never entirely overcome the feeling but had managed to control it. Some of his brothers of the prairie, he knew, could never have wintered in the close confines of such areas.

So while he did not relish the prospect of wintering here, he was prepared to tolerate it. It helped greatly that his bed was shared by Owl Woman. She always tried to understand, usually quite successfully. She did not fully understand his occasional need for the open spaces and the spiritual feel of the big sky, but she was willing to try. And that in itself was important.

'The warm days of Second Summer continued that year well into the Moon of Madness before Cold Maker awoke in his ice cave somewhere in the northern mountains to sweep down across the land. In only a few days, people were adapting well. Through the Moon of Long Nights there came a succession of snows, blanketing the woods and freezing the edges of the river. On days when the sun was seen at all, its watery yellow rays seemed barely to warm the day before it began to sink again.

Turtle's stories from the plains perhaps expressed it best. It was the annual struggle since Creation between Cold Maker's onslaught and the waning torch of Sun Boy. Cold Maker pushed his adversary far to the south in the Moon of Long Nights. But each year, Sun Boy managed to renew his torch in time, slowly to battle his way north, driving Cold Maker back to his icy lair in the mountains. At least, it had always been so. Turtle always managed to leave just a little bit of doubt, the slight twinge of fear that *this* season . . . It left a delicious hint of danger hanging in the air.

One of the storytellers of the village who was also a holy man performed a ceremony to assist the sun's return. He chanted and danced, and made symbolic sacrifices over a fire in a clearing near the village. This ceremony was carried out annually, it was said. It was performed late in the Moon of Long Nights and was sure to prevent the dying of the sun. The ceremony was successful once more, and by the middle of the Moon of Snows, it could be seen that the days were growing longer. There was still much winter ahead, of course, but the turning point had been successfully passed.

Turtle congratulated the holy man, agreeing that the ceremony had been impressive as well as effective. "Sun Boy," he stated seriously, "needs the help of all of us to banish Cold Maker again each winter."

The old priest's eyes twinkled in friendship. This was a skill for which Turtle was well known, the ability to see events in terms of the customs of others. It had made him successful both as a storyteller and a trader.

There was much need for storytelling during the Moon of Snows. It was impossible to travel much, not at all without snowshoes. It was better to stay inside, smoking with friends and acquaintances, sometimes gambling, and exchanging stories.

Turtle did not gamble and advised his apprentice against it. "It is a bad habit for a trader," he explained. "Everything can be lost very quickly."

Both men, however, were in demand at the social "smokes" in the longhouse where stories went on and on. Paths in the snow were beaten down by the pressure of many footsteps—from each lodge to the others, to the woods for fuel, to the river for water, and to the longhouse.

It was a fairly heavy winter, said the people of the village. At a time near the end of the Moon of Snows there came a storm that seemed to be the most furious of Cold Maker's attacks yet. For two days, he howled around the lodges and piled snow among the trees. The river froze completely, so that a man could walk to the other side. Those who ventured out suffered frostbite on their faces and fingers. Lame Dog lost part of an ear from not wearing a head covering when he went out for firewood. Even the gatherings at the longhouse were discontinued.

Everyone relaxed when Sun Boy reappeared, but it was apparent that the winter was not over. Still ahead was the Moon of Hunger. There might not be many more of the prolonged severe storms this season. What attacks by Cold Maker did come would be short-lived. His dreaded power was weakening, and he only struck back in retreat.

But the Moon of Hunger was aptly named. Provisions for the winter, no matter how many or how well stored, would run short by the Moon of Awakening when it became possible to hunt again. There could be hunger in the village and even starvation. This year, despite the severity of the winter, supplies had been good, and there was little actual suffering.

There was one tragedy. During one of the brief but furious late snows, Bear Sits had stepped outside to relieve his bladder and had not returned. By the time the others had realized the danger, it was snowing harder and growing dark. They tramped the nearby woods and inquired in other lodges, but the old man could not be found. It was assumed, even when his body was not discovered after the storm, that he was dead. No one could have survived the night in the open. In his senility, he might have wandered off in the wrong direction, into the storm.

The crossing over of Bear Sits was observed with the ritual Songs of Mourning.

Yellow Bowl did not take the loss well. She was convinced that her husband had not merely wandered off, but that it had been a deliberate act. Bear Sits had sacrificed himself, she insisted, to be sure that there was enough food for the children. "But there *was* enough," she cried repeatedly. "There *was!*"

Turtle had a slightly different theory. During Bear Sits's more lucid moments, he thought, the old warrior was depressed at what he had become. He was now virtually helpless, his eyesight fading, his memory for all but his youth nearly gone. The journey through the storm to the Other Side was a last defiant gesture of courage. If it provided more food for the living, so be it. But the gesture itself was for Bear Sits, his last decision as a warrior—to die on his feet, fighting.

After the three days' mourning was ended, there was some concern that Yellow Bowl would not be able to return to the activities of the living. She continued to mourn. Owl Woman and Turtle took her aside. "Mother, it does not matter," Owl insisted. "Of course there was food, but it does not matter now."

"It does!" Yellow Bowl argued. "He knew what he was doing, but he was wrong! We had plenty."

Turtle finally tried a new approach. "Mother," he said, "Bear Sits was a great warrior. For whatever reason, he did this as he wished. He crossed over when he chose to do so."

That idea seemed to help. Gradually, the mourning of Yellow Bowl became more appropriate, and she resumed the life of the village as they looked forward to the coming of spring.

The body of Bear Sits was never found. In body and in spirit, he had crossed over.

11

The Moon of Awakening brought mixed feelings to Storyteller. The major feature of the previous year had been the renewal of his acquaintance with Plum Leaf. The conversations had been halting at first, but quickly grew more comfortable as the relationship solidified. Storyteller had managed to prolong the trading for several days. At every spare moment, the two young people shared hopes and dreams. He told her of the time when he was a child and felt that the rabbit almost spoke to him. He had never told that to anyone but unashamedly shared it with her, knowing that she would understand. She did, of course, and smiled her knowing smile as she placed a hand on his arm.

They had found that as children, both had loved the little clearing where their reunion had taken place. Both had considered it a special place of enchantment where wonderful things might take place.

"Maybe they still do," he had suggested. "That is where we found each other."

She smiled and snuggled closer.

"Ah, but soon I must leave," he reminded her.

He could hardly bear to part with the beautiful girl who had become a part of his life. They had talked of it. They had talked of many things—of marriage, even, though both wondered if they were too young. If their lives were a little different . . . If their world was a bit more stable . . . If Storyteller was not committed to travel and trade . . .

"But you *must* do that," Plum Leaf insisted. "That is your life."

It was true. At one time, he could have envisioned himself as a resident of this village, a hunter like his grandfather Bear Sits, and a mighty warrior. That had been his aim in life as a very young child. His father too had helped this image. It was after the loss of his father, maybe, that the boy had turned to things of the spirit. Then, the coming of Turtle, who had changed his life and that of his mother so greatly. Now he could think of nothing except to follow this line of endeavor.

The coming of spring would make travel possible, and Turtle would wish to leave. Storyteller too wished to leave the area that had become so threatening. It had been his home as a child, protecting and sheltering. But now its spirit had changed. The dark threat of mercenary violence hovered over the entire region. He could not erase from his mind the memory of the two dead men in the glade by the spring, their sightless eyes staring unseeing at the darkening sky while someone ripped the skin from their heads. Sometimes he dreamed about it, waking in a cold sweat of fear. Yes, it would be good to leave this region of bad medicine.

But travel toward Turtle's people would be to the west, while to the south lay the village of Plum Leaf. They would be moving *away* from her. This was the cause of his mixed feelings.

There came a day, finally, when the village awoke to a new sound. The wind had changed in the night and blew softly with a warm breath. The new sound was the drip of melting snow, forming in crystal drops along the edges of the thatched roofs, to fall to the snow below.

The rising sun sped the process on its way. Soon little rivulets sliced their crooked paths toward lower levels, merging into tinkling streams that rushed toward the river. Cold Maker's power was broken, and he was in full retreat. They would leave soon, and he thought of the parting last season as they had prepared to travel.

He and Plum Leaf had met at the clearing for one last time. They had made small talk for a while to avoid more serious conversation. Finally, Plum Leaf had approached what was on their minds. "When will you leave?"

"I do not know . . . It depends much on the weather."

"I do not wish to see you go."

"I know. My heart is the same, Plum Leaf."

"When will you come back?"

He shrugged. "Who knows? Maybe next year."

"Does your father know about us?"

"Yes. My mother too. I do not know whether they know how serious we are."

"Can you ask them?"

"Yes, maybe."

It was so frustrating—to talk of this but to be unable to make plans.

"I *will* come back for you," he promised.

"I know. And I will wait for you."

"Promise?"

"Of course!"

"I will speak to Turtle," he said. "I know he wishes to visit his people next season. Maybe winter there."

"Then it would be more than a year. . . ."

"Yes. Plum Leaf, I must talk to him. And to my mother, of course . . . see what they plan."

The proper occasion had not seemed to arise, and nothing definite had been asked or promised. But now Storyteller felt that he must know. He approached Turtle about his plans for the coming season.

Turtle was rather noncommittal. His was a day-at-a-time, see-what-happens approach to life.

"Who knows what may happen, Storyteller? The season is young. First, let us leave this area, for reasons you understand well."

"Yes, Uncle. But . . . there is this girl . . ."

"Ah! That is it! Yes, I remember her. Your choice is good." He chuckled.

"But, Uncle, I need to know . . . when will I be able to see her again? I . . . I do not like to think of her so far away!"

"You *are* serious!" Turtle observed. "Well, it could be many moons before we come back. Maybe she should go with us!"

Storyteller gasped. "Father . . . I . . . we . . . I have not courted!"

"But you are sure?"

"Of course."

"And she is, also?"

"Yes, but I . . ."

"Then where is the problem?" It would never be said that Turtle's approach to anything would be commonplace.

"But, Uncle, there must be *some* courting!"

"Yes, of course. We will go south for her, then go on."

"Is there time? Before we go west to your people?"

Turtle laughed. "Who knows how long such things will take? But you said she is ready. We will leave when your courting is finished!"

"Uncle . . . one more thing. Can you teach me to play the courting flute?"

"*Aiee!*" shouted Turtle happily. "Yes! It worked with your mother!"

"Yes. Plum Leaf spoke of that. She was greatly pleased to hear of when you did that."

"Ah, so was your mother! Yes, it was good. I will teach you. But this may take longer!"

"Or shorter, if I learn quickly!"

Both men laughed.

So it happened that when the storytelling traders moved on to the west, their number was increased by one. Plum Leaf was now the wife of Story-teller the Younger.

Her mother had at first resisted. "She is so young!"

"That is true," admitted Owl Woman. "I had doubts when they came to me. But think of this: They have decided, and it will be good."

"That is true. But . . ."

"Look! How old were you and I when we married?"

The two women giggled like children.

"Yes. But she . . . my oldest, you know. I am not ready to be a grand-mother!"

"Nor am I!" Owl Woman laughed. "But I will look after them. She will not forget the ways of your people. My husband is not of *my* people, you know."

Finally, Acorn, mother of Plum Leaf, consented, and the two were married, to start out into the world together. Owl Woman was pleased, both for her son and for the chance to have another adult woman in the party. Lark, just approaching womanhood, was delighted at the prospect.

"If we travel well," Turtle noted as they loaded the two canoes to start upriver, "we will be in the prairie by the Moon of Roses. That is a beautiful time."

It would be good, he thought, to see again the country of the big sky, the open plain, and the far-off edge of Earth. He had not realized until now how much he missed the prairie, how closed-in he had felt by the winter among the forest trees.

12

*"*It is so big!" said Owl Woman in awe.

The five stood gazing over a vast expanse of grass. For several days they had seen larger areas of grassland and smaller areas of forest. Now there was almost entirely grass. It was nearly a moon now since they had left the village to travel southwest toward Turtle's home country.

They went by canoe at first, stopping to tell stories and trade as they traveled down the small river to progressively larger streams, as other streams joined the one they rode on. They came to a great river, which Turtle said was the *Missi-ssippi,* the Father of Waters, and floated southward on it for several days. They camped at night or stopped at one of the villages along the shores.

Turtle seemed to be watching for something on the west bank of the Big River. Finally one day he pointed ahead with his paddle. "There!" he said. "The *Miss-ouree!*"

They stopped to trade for a day with the people of a town at the place where the great rivers joined, then moved upstream on the Missouri. It was apparent that the country was changing. While there were trees along the river everywhere, they could see vast open areas from time to time. Storyteller was enthralled by his first sight of a large herd of buffalo; hundreds and hundreds of the animals grazed calmly on open grassland.

It was obvious from Turtle's increasing excitement that, experienced traveler though he might be, coming home was important to him. He spent increasing amounts of time in discussion with the natives at each stop. Usually he seemed familiar with their tongue, but sometimes he resorted to hand-signs. Storyteller noticed increased use of the signs as they moved westward. Turtle was asking, he realized, for information regarding the summer camp of the "Trader People." Usually, he received a negative shrug.

Then came an evening when they stopped as usual, and Turtle's usual question brought a new answer. "Yes! They were here, in the Moon of Falling Leaves, traveling southwest. Our hunters saw them following the herds."

"But you do not know where they are this summer?"

"No, no. We have not seen them this year."

Turtle explained how the great buffalo herds would migrate south in winter and each spring move north again, following the greening of the prairie. "My people sometimes burn the grass to make them come into an area."

"How is that, Uncle?"

"When the old dry grass is burned, it makes tender new grass. Then the buffalo come."

"Do your people follow the buffalo?"

"Sometimes, if we need meat. Usually not. It is easier to let buffalo come to you."

"But, Uncle, why did they go south?"

"Who knows?" Turtle shrugged. "The chiefs did not like the thought of a coming winter, maybe. This is not unusual, Storyteller. A hard winter or two makes people think of warmer places, no?"

After another day or two, and questions at another village, Turtle elected to leave the river and turn southward. He made arrangements to leave the two canoes, trading for horses for each of the adults, and one pack horse. Little Lark would ride the pack horse or ride behind one of the others.

"How will he know where to go?" asked the bewildered Plum Leaf.

"I do not know," answered Storyteller, equally puzzled. "The spirit of this prairie is strange . . . different. Maybe it takes special medicine to understand it."

"The sky is so wide." Owl Woman pointed. "Look, you can see farther than you could travel in a whole day!"

"Maybe that helps to find his people."

Turtle had led the party away from the river with seeming confidence. It took a few days for the inexperienced riders to become accustomed to the swaying rhythm of the horses' gaits. They were stiff and sore after a day's travel. Even Turtle admitted that he was feeling the protest of unused muscles. Before long, however, they became accustomed to the new activity. In his eagerness, Turtle continued to set a demanding pace.

On the third day after they left the river, the travelers came to a smaller stream. A haze of smoke hung over a fringe of trees far upstream, and Turtle pointed. "That is a village of Growers," he stated flatly.

"You know where we are, Father?" asked Storyteller in astonishment.

"No, but that is where they would be." He nudged his horse in that direction.

It was late afternoon before they approached the town. It was as Turtle had said, a collection of lodges made of logs and mud. Surrounding the village were carefully tended fields of corn, beans, and pumpkins.

"How did you know, Father?"

"Know what?"

"That these were Growers?"

"Ah . . . well, hunters' lodges are different . . . skin tents, you know."

"But you could not see the lodges from a half day's travel away!"

"That is true. Well, maybe. You can see a skin lodge much farther. See, these are dug partly into the ground. The lodges of my people are tall . . . maybe two, three times the height of a man."

"So they can be seen farther?"

"Yes, of course. But there are other things. These lodges are close together and close to the river. Our lodges are more scattered."

"Why, Uncle?" asked Plum Leaf.

"Well . . . you children ask many questions!" he complained mildly. "Well, my people have many horses. They need more room to ride among their lodges. And the door must face east, of course."

"East? Why?"

"To greet Sun. But come now; we must pay our respects to their chief."

Storyteller and Plum Leaf were still puzzled about Turtle's preoccupation with the doorways' facing east. They only saw that he was excited, eager to be back in his own country. They spoke of it to Owl Woman, who smiled affectionately.

"Yes! He is like a child coming home, is he not? I think . . . maybe . . . there is something about this farseeing land that makes him that way. He has spoken sometimes of how he feels closed in, trapped, if he cannot see far enough. I have never known what he meant, until now. The far distance is beautiful, no?"

They watched the sunset, a blaze of color across the vastness of the rolling hills in the distance.

"See how the nearer hills are green, those beyond bluish?" observed Owl Woman. "Then in the shadows they are purple."

"But the sky!" Plum Leaf pointed. "So many colors."

Turtle returned from his courtesy call to rejoin the others. "Yes, it is good tonight," he agreed, seeing their wonder at the brilliance of the spectacle. "Some tribes say Sun Boy paints himself before he goes to his lodge on the other side of Earth. Tonight, he chooses good colors for his paint. Well, come, we must camp."

"We are welcome, then?" Owl asked.

"Of course. Growers always have crops to trade. They trade with everyone."

"Have they seen your people?"

"Yes! They know where they wintered, south of here."

"And now?"

"This summer, they are not sure, but he told me of a camp of Cut-Fingers, maybe two sleeps, he said. They will know."

"We trade tomorrow?" asked Storyteller.

"Not much. They have only crops to trade, and we cannot carry enough. We will trade a little, to show that our hearts are good. But they will like stories tonight, Storyteller."

"It is good," agreed the young man. "Do they have storytellers?"

"Of course. Everyone does. How good, we will see."

"They use hand-signs?"

"Yes. I know some of their tongue, but you can use the signs. You may hear some new stories!"

No one was more pleased at the prospect of the evening's entertainment than Plum Leaf. She was so proud of her man's skill with the stories that she never tired of listening to him. It had been swift, their courtship and marriage. Sometimes she still could not believe that it had happened. But here she was, far from home, with a husband she adored, experiencing new places, new people. Owl had been very kind to her, teaching her the role of the wife of a storyteller and trader. Plum Leaf, realizing the importance of the hand-signs, had concentrated on learning their use as they traveled. Already she felt that she was more proficient than Owl Woman and nearing the skill of her husband or even Turtle, the master of many tongues.

It was indeed a good evening of stories, the weather pleasant, the listeners' interest apparent, and the two storytellers at their best. Turtle seemed inspired and used stories that even his apprentice had never heard.

In addition, there was an ancient storyteller among the Growers who, as he warmed to the occasion, seemed more skilled than any they had seen. Sensing that he had an appreciative audience, the old man seemed to begin with Creation and follow through the generations toward the present. He had traveled much as a young man, he said.

"Do you know how we got corn?" he asked.

Without even waiting, he launched into the story. It was long, drawn-out, and began once more with Creation. The storytellers were fascinated. Even Turtle had never heard this tale. Owl left to retire. Plum Leaf tried to stay but found herself dozing. Finally she too gave up and made her way to their temporary camp.

Owl Woman and Lark were sleeping soundly as Plum Leaf snuggled down in her sleeping robes. She wished that her husband could soon join her. For a while she managed to stay awake but at last fell asleep, dreaming a confused tale. Her own new experiences on the great prairie became entangled with the stories. She was watching when, at Creation, the gods quarreled. The evil god, whose name she could not remember, was struck down before her eyes. His adversary, a benevolent figure, pried out the dead god's teeth and planted them like seeds in the rich loam of the prairie. In the inconsistency of the dream state, she watched the seeds sprout into cornstalks. By the time Storyteller joined her in their sleeping robes, humans had harvested their first corn crop.

She seemed to realize that she was dreaming, even as she did so. *I must remember this dream-story,* she told herself. *I must tell it to my storyteller.*

13

Storyteller did not know what he expected in the villages of the nomadic buffalo hunters. He had seen skin tents elsewhere, mostly a makeshift shelter of hides thrown in a haphazard manner over a frame of sticks. Somehow it had not occurred to him that people whose entire life consists of hunting buffalo would have a highly developed portable dwelling. Even Turtle's description, and the statement that such a lodge was often two or three times the height of a man, had not prepared him for this.

The lodges were scattered along the stream for some distance. Now that the camp was in sight, the travelers paused to dismount on the ridge above and allow their horses to blow.

"Someone comes!" pointed Owl Woman.

Two riders swept across the little valley, their horses at a dead run. They were well-armed warriors and appeared to be capable in their duties.

"Dog Soldiers," Turtle said, half to himself.

"What?" asked Owl Woman.

"Dog Soldiers . . . that is a warrior society of the Cut-Fingers. These will be their Wolves."

"Wolves?"

"Yes . . . oh, I forget. You have never been here. The tribes have warriors who circle the camp, or circle the main party when they travel. They are called Wolves after the wolves who circle the buffalo herds."

"And these are not your people?"

"No, but they are allies. Now their Wolves come out to meet us, to see that there is no trickery."

"Ah-koh!" he called out in greeting as the riders swept up the slope and slid their mounts to a stop. "Who is your chief, Dog Soldiers?"

"Who asks?" responded one suspiciously. "How is it that you know our tongue?"

"Ah, yes," said Turtle pleasantly. "I am Turtle, the storyteller and trader. My people are your friends, the People-Who-Trade."

"That much is true. And, you are called Turtle?"

"Yes. I have not been home for several winters. Now I seek my own tribe. You have seen them, no?"

"Maybe. Who are these others?"

"My wife, our son and his wife, our small daughter."

"How is your son called?"

"He is called Storyteller."

"Ah! He trades too?"

"Of course. We have much to trade, my friend."

Finally, the warriors seemed to relax. "It is good," said one. "Come, we will take you in."

The entire party mounted, and turned toward the camp.

"Are you at war?" Turtle asked. "Why such a challenge? And, where are my people camped?"

"Ah, my friend, we were only being careful. You and your party do wear a strange mixture of garments and customs, you know. Your people . . . about a day west of here."

This was more like what Turtle had expected from friends. But he had to admit that his was a strange caravan. He could see how they might arouse suspicion. And these were conscientious young warriors, taking their turn at Wolf.

"It is good!" he said. "Now, who is your chief? I must pay my visit."

"Of course. He is Five Elk."

"Ah, I remember him, from when I was your age," Turtle said. "A great leader . . . a credit to the Cut-Fingers."

"Yes. This is a proud people," one stated.

"And justly so," Turtle said. "We are proud to bring you stories and trade."

They were among the lodges now, and the newcomers, except for Turtle, were absorbed in looking at the dwellings, so unfamiliar in design. Each was made of many buffalo skins, squared and sewn together, maybe twenty or thirty skins in the larger ones it seemed. The doorways faced east to greet the rising sun, as Turtle had said.

A most remarkable thing about the lodges, to Storyteller, was their height. Some of the big lodges were five or six paces across. Since it seemed to be a general rule that the height was about the same as the width, the poles that supported the structure must be at least as long, plus another pace to allow for the protruding portion above. Even in the forests of his childhood, he had never seen so many long, slender poles. He could see them well. The weather was hot, and the people of the village had rolled up the bottom edges of the lodge skins, like lifted skirts, to let the breeze cool the interior. People sitting in the shady lodges watched the riders curiously. Some waved and smiled. There was much to learn about these lodges, the young man realized. He still did not see how they could be made habitable in a hard winter.

The party stopped before one of the largest of the lodges. It was brightly decorated with geometric designs and somehow radiated an aura of affluence. On a post in front hung a decorated shield, a lance, and a stone ax or club with a long handle. They had noticed such displays in front of most of the lodges.

"That shows who lives here," Turtle had explained.

Knowing this, it was possible to see that there was a design that could be an elk, both on the lodge cover and on the shield by the doorway. This, then, was the home of the chief, Five Elk. A dignified man who could be no one else was sitting comfortably in the shade of the big lodge, leaning against a willow backrest.

The Wolves spoke to the chief briefly in their own tongue and turned their horses away. The travelers dismounted.

"*Ah-koh,* my chief," Turtle greeted, using both words and hand-signs. "We are honored to stop in your village."

"It is good," grunted Five Elk. "Tell me, trader, you use our tongue well. Why do you also sign?"

"Ah, I grew up using the tongue of the Cut-Fingers as well as my own," Turtle explained. "I have been in your village many times when I walked in a younger man's moccasins."

"Ah, yes," said the chief thoughtfully. "Do I remember you? You were called . . ."

"Turtle, my chief. Yes, you might remember me, but I have been away many years."

"But why the hand-signs?"

"These others—my wife, my son, and his wife—they come from tribes far away. They do not know your tongue, so I used signs also."

"It is good. Welcome again."

Chuckling, Five Elk also used the hand-signs. It was a very polite thing to do for his guests.

"Now, you wish to trade?" he asked.

"Yes, briefly, my chief, if you wish. It is said that my people, the People-Who-Trade, are only one sleep away."

"That is true."

"I have been away from them for many winters. Now I return with my family."

"It is good. Family is important."

"Yes. May we trade tomorrow, then move on?"

"Of course. Our Wolves said you are also storytellers?"

"Yes. That goes well with the trading."

"True. I will look forward to it."

"It is good!" said Turtle. "Now we will make camp, before dark."

"Yes . . . there should be good places upstream a little way. You can turn your horses out with the herd. Our young men will take care of them."

"Thank you, my chief!"

They found the camping place and settled into their temporary camp, unsaddling and unpacking the horses.

"Shall we picket the horses, Father?" asked Storyteller.

"No, turn them out with the herd. They will find better grass."

The young man swung to the back of one of the animals to drive the others to the grassy meadow where the herd grazed.

"*Ah-koh!*" someone called. A boy trotted toward him, smiling.

"You are the Storyteller?" the herdsman signed. "I was told you might bring horses."

"Yes. We have ridden far, and they need to rest and find grass."

"I will see that they get the best. You will have a story-fire tonight?"

"Of course! I will look for you!"

He thought of himself a few seasons ago and his own eagerness at the coming of the storyteller. He swung a leg over and jumped to the ground, untying the rawhide war bridle to free his mount.

"I will be there!" called the youngster after him as he turned away.

Probably, in all his storytelling and story-listening experience, that evening was the most remarkable. Not only did the Cut-Fingers have an excellent storyteller, but Storyteller began to have a better understanding of the stories of Turtle. Some of the tales he had heard many times now took on new meaning. The great bowl of the sky, sprinkled with as many stars as there are grains of sand, it seemed, was a fitting background to dramatize some of the stories. In addition, he could feel the vastness of the great buffalo herds that reached from one horizon to the other. Before, he could only imagine; now he had *seen*.

"Once there was a season," Turtle was saying, "when hunting was very poor. This was in the old, old, long-ago times, not long after Creation. Seldom could the hunters find even a deer, and the people were starving."

Storyteller loved this tale, the coming of the buffalo.

"But there was one hunter who always hunted alone. His family remained fat, and the children happy. One day when all of his family had gone to the river to bathe, three of the other hunters crept into his lodge."

There was the usual expression of dismay. Such a thing was not done.

317

"They were starving, you see," Turtle went on apologetically. The crowd nodded understandingly.

Ah, thought Storyteller, *he really has caught them tonight. It is good.*

"Inside the lodge, they found a big flat rock," Turtle went on, with appropriate gestures. "It took two of them to lift it. Now, underneath was a large hole, and a buffalo ran out! The hunters quickly ran after it, so intent on the hunt that they did not replace the stone. When they looked back, more buffalo were coming out, one after another, more and more, until the whole prairie was covered with them."

The crowd gasped in pleasure, and for the first time Storyteller fully appreciated the description of the prairie and the great herds. A person bred to the woodland simply could not understand the numbers or the distances involved unless he had seen them.

"The hunter whose lodge had been violated," Turtle continued, "was a great medicine man, of course. A god, maybe. But he saw the great herds and realized that something was wrong. He hurried to the lodge and slammed the rock back over the hole.

"It was nearly too late. The whole plain was covered. The herds trampled the grass and fouled the water, and there were too many. But it was good too. Ever since, people have had buffalo to eat. And, when the great herds come through, trampling and fouling until the river runs dung, we remember how it happened."

There was applause and much laughter about rivers of dung, and finally the Cut-Fingers' storyteller rose.

"That is very good," he said approvingly. "Now, my story, too, is about the hunting of buffalo. Did you ever wonder why some horses, when chasing buffalo, always approach from the left, while others do so from the *right* side of the animal?"

The general murmur from the listeners told that there were some who knew and appreciated the story. Others did not know why. Still others did not care, probably.

And Storyteller had thought until now that he had heard nearly every story in the world. This was an eye-opener. Not only was it a new story, but he had not even realized until now that some horses *do* approach the buffalo from the left and some from the right. He felt like a child, just beginning to learn.

At the time of Creation, the storyteller related, it was seen that Man could not catch many Buffalo on foot. The People asked Sun Boy to give them a way to run faster than their quarry. Their wish was granted, but deferred for many lifetimes, until they were well established. Then, they would be given the Horse, to ride upon like the wind, faster than a Buffalo.

"But it must pass on the right," insisted a hunter, "so we may use the bow. One cannot sit astride and shoot to his own right."

"No, the *left*," argued another, who wished to use a spear, held in the right hand.

The council dissolved in angry shouts, and Sun Boy stopped them.

"Let the decision be with the Horse," he decided, "your Elk-dog who runs like the wind. Some will run to the right, some left, so each horse will pick his own hunter."

The storyteller spread his hands as if in explanation. "And so it has been ever since. Some right, some left."

Most of the listeners enjoyed the story, and laughed long about horses choosing their riders. Storyteller laughed too, though he did not fully understand. Full insight came a few days later, after they reached the camp of Turtle's people.

14

He soon had friends among Turtle's people. He was, by nature, an outgoing and friendly young man, and in addition, carried a degree of prestige as Storyteller. He was invited to join some of these new friends in an upcoming hunt. Only then did the humor and the full meaning of the Cut-Fingers' story become clear to him.

From the way everyone in the camp spoke and acted, it was apparent that this would be an exciting time. The weather had broken, with a change in the wind and a refreshing coolness to the breeze. Through the Moon of Thunder and the Red Moon, the prevailing wind had been from the south, cooling only a little at night. Rain-Maker occasionally charged across the prairie, throwing his spears of real-fire and thumping ponderously on his drums to give the Moon of Thunder its name. Between storms, the weather was hot, muggy, and oppressive. So it was with great relief that the people of the camp saw a change in the wind late in the Red Moon. They awoke one morning to find the grasses stirring with a breeze from the northwest, a slight chill in the air. Immediately, people began to talk of two coming events, the impending move to winter quarters and the great fall hunt.

"Which will come first?" Storyteller asked.

"Who knows?" Turtle shrugged. "It depends much on the buffalo. But it is time to decide now whether we winter here. We will need to prepare."

Thus far, they had camped in a temporary arbor, retreating to the lodges of friends or relatives only in the event of heavy storms.

"Where else would we winter?" asked Owl Woman.

"We could go many places," said Turtle. "We have before. But this is good." It was obvious that it would please him to stay with his people. "We must have a lodge," Turtle explained. "Five of us . . . we cannot move in with relatives."

So plans were begun. They would not need a pretentious lodge but must begin to assemble and prepare skins. Turtle's mother, aged and wrinkled but bright-eyed, was considered an expert in cutting lodge covers. She would advise, as well as assist in collecting skins. It was common for people to give her a skin or two in return for her expertise. Lodge-Cutter the old woman was called appropriately. She dragged out several skins.

"We will begin to sew these," she told Owl and Plum Leaf. "You will need more, maybe ten, but the fall hunt is coming."

Storyteller was beginning to see how the entire being of these people revolved around the migrations of the buffalo. They spoke of the fall hunt with a reverence that was almost a religion. Almost anything to be deferred was mentioned in terms of "before the fall hunt" or "after the hunt."

"It *is* a thing of the spirit," Turtle explained in answer to Storyteller's question. "I have told you of the Sun Dance in early summer, which the plains people celebrate. It honors the return of Sun, which causes grass to grow, which brings back the buffalo. The world starts over . . . a new Creation almost. Maybe next year we will be here for that."

Gray Otter, one of the young men of the village, had befriended Storyteller almost from the day of their arrival. He seemed intrigued by the stories and the young man who practiced the art.

"You will join us for the hunt?"

"Yes, it is good," Storyteller answered.

He was rapidly learning the tongue of Turtle's people. There is no better way than to spend time with a friend who speaks the tongue you wish to learn. Sometimes they would reach an impasse and were forced to augment the conversation with hand-signs, but these times were becoming less frequent.

"Will you use the bow or the lance?" Gray Otter asked.

Storyteller was unsure. He had never hunted buffalo. "Which would be best?"

"*Aiee*! I forget . . . wait! Have you hunted with a lance?"

"Well . . . no."

"Ah, then you use the bow? Does your horse run that way?"

"Otter," his friend blurted, "I have never hunted from a horse."

Gray Otter's mouth dropped open. "But you *have* horses!"

"Yes, to travel, but . . ."

"No matter, my friend. We will supply a horse. Now, you are familiar with a bow . . . that is good. I will find you a horse that runs to the right."

"I do not understand, Otter. Turtle also spoke of this. Why is that important?"

"Think about it," urged Otter. "You are sitting on a horse with a bow in your left hand. How could you shoot to your right?"

Of course. Once it was explained, the point was obvious. The hunter *must* shoot to the left side of his mount because he cannot turn far enough to the right. "What of the lance, then?" he asked.

"The same. A lance is braced under the right arm. The horse must approach from the *left,* because you cannot reach across the horse with the lance, no?"

Storyteller began to understand the story he had heard back in the camp of the Cut-Fingers.

"Otter," he asked, "how do you make a horse run right or left?"

Otter laughed. "Ah, you begin to see! You guide the horse with the reins, but in the hunt, both hands are busy. The horse must know what to do."

"Yes . . . I do not see . . ."

"Well, partly with the knees, but a good buffalo-horse does much of it himself. He enjoys the chase."

"Then the *horse* chooses which side?"

"Yes, mostly, but . . . when his training begins, we look to see which way he likes best. Then he may be traded to someone who hunts that way. Now . . . let us go and talk to my uncle. He has many good buffalo-horses. One that runs to the right . . ."

Otter's uncle did have many horses. He seemed pleased to be asked for help. "You use the bow?" he asked.

"Yes . . . I have little knowledge of the horse."

The horseman nodded. "Otter, bring the blue gelding!" he called. "Now, this horse is steady . . . he runs well, but is careful. Try him!"

Inexperienced as he was, Storyteller found that he rapidly gained confidence with the horse. It was a lanky, rawboned animal, sleepy in disposition. Under the tutelage of Otter, Storyteller simply sat on the horse at first, shooting arrows at an old buffalo skin stuffed with grass. The gelding stood quietly, eyes half closed, lazily switching flies with his sparse tail.

The next step involved becoming confident on the running animal. Gray Otter brought his own horse, and the two rode quietly into the open prairie. The gray shuffled along, disinterested. It was a comfortable rocking motion, and Storyteller began to relax. Suddenly, Otter kicked heels into his mare's flanks, and she leaped forward to a run. In a heartbeat, the gelding was transformed from a lazy, shuffling creature to an efficient hunter. He leaped forward like a cat, almost unseating his rider. Storyteller clutched at the saddle, trying to regain balance, while his mount pounded after Otter's mare.

Then, somehow, the young man realized that he was adjusting to the rhythm of the horse's gait. He began to relax, swaying with the smooth swinging flow of the animal's long stride. He had never ridden such a horse, or at such a speed. It was like flying! He drew abreast of Otter's horse, passing on the right side, and the significance of that approach flashed through his mind. Yes, if the running mare were a fleeing buffalo . . . He was not quite ready to release the reins to let the animal run, but he could see that it would work. Yes, he could draw the arrow to its head and release it as they swept past!

Now Otter drew his horse to a slower pace as they reached the top of the low ridge. The gray gelding protested, still wanting to race, but responded to the pressure on the rawhide. Both horses slowed to an easy lope, then a trot, and finally a walk.

"*Aiee!*" Storyteller shouted with delight. "It is like flying!"

Otter laughed, his eyes dancing with pleasure. "You did well, my friend! We will run a few more times, and then get the bow."

In another day or two, with gaining confidence, Storyteller could sweep past at a dead run and plant arrows in the target skin more often than not.

"It is good!" called his instructor. "You are almost ready."

The only exercise that remained was the pretended shot at the flank of Otter's mare. With confidence growing, he could now drop the looped rein across the gelding's neck, freeing both hands to use the bow.

Beyond that, there was only the waiting for the herds to come.

In the Moon of Hunting, called by the Growers the Moon of Ripening, all of the creatures of the prairie seemed to become aware of the coming autumn. The prairie flowers told of the change. Storyteller had noticed them when they first came into the grasslands. The roses had been blooming, toward the end of their season, and he had been impressed with the variety of colors. There were roses nearly white but also deep pinks and reds, with all the subtle shades between. The other flowers too showed a remarkable range of color, from white to blue to pink. One plant he especially admired showed clusters of bright orange blossoms. It seemed greatly favored by insects. Bees worked busily at the bright flowers, and butterflies hovered. He had asked Turtle its name.

"Butterfly plant, my people call it," Turtle answered.

All the spring and summer flowers were gone now, to be replaced by others. These were of different hues. There seemed to be two main colors, golden yellow and bright purple. At least six entirely different plants of different heights and shapes produced blossoms of precisely the same color. It was much the same with the purple flowers, though without such wide variation.

Most unusual of all were the grasses. At the Moon of Ripening, all of the prairie grasses suddenly began to thrust seed-stalks upward. To young Storyteller, in the woodlands of his childhood, grass had merely been grass.

He had done little to try to distinguish between different types. Now it became apparent that grasses that had looked much the same through the summer behaved much differently. He could distinguish at least six or seven. There seemed to be two "big" grasses. One was called real-grass, which suggested that it would be the largest. In fact, when the seed-heads formed, they were taller than a man. In occasional areas favorable to this growth, it was very difficult to find one's way on foot. It was necessary to mount a horse to see the way. Almost as tall was the feathery seed-head that Otter called feather-grass or plume-grass. Large and fluffy, these stalks were spectacular as they nodded and bobbed in the breeze. But again, one could become lost among the tall stems if one was on foot.

Otter laughed at Storyteller's amazement. "This is why these are called the Tallgrass Hills!"

The growth seemed more spectacular each day. At the same time, though days were warm, the nights brought an uncomfortable chill to the air. Squirrels were busy in the timbered areas along the streams. Turkeys and deer grew fat and sleek, and the first long lines of geese began to trumpet their way southward.

Then came the awaited news. A Wolf came loping into the village, to pull his horse to a sliding stop before the lodge of the chief who would organize the hunt.

"The buffalo are coming!" he announced.

15

Storyteller sat astride the blue roan gelding, waiting. He was excited. His heart was pounding so loudly in his ears that he feared it would disturb the herd. At very least, he thought, the other hunters must hear the thumping. He looked to his left and met the glance of Gray Otter a few paces away. Otter smiled reassuringly. A deer-fly bit his ankle, a sharp stab, and he flinched, swatting at the creature as it escaped his reach.

The hunters had been concealed in the tall grass of a little swale, waiting for the herd to move into position. He could see very little beyond a few paces in front of the horse. This was partly a result of the uneven lay of the land, but mostly his vision was obscured by the heavy seed-heads of the tall grasses—mostly real-grass, he noted. Directly in front of him, a large clump of real-grass had sent up perhaps ten or more stalks. Each was tipped with a three-fingered seed-head, just at eye level, and several similar growths along the stalk. Turkey-foot, Otter had called it.

"I thought it was real-grass," protested Storyteller.

"Yes, but sometimes this too," Otter explained. "See, the seed-head is shaped like the foot of a bird."

That had been a bit earlier in the season. Now it was more obvious, this local name for the plant. Yes, he thought absently, each stalk does end in a turkey-foot.

His horse was dozing in the sun, knowing from experience that it was not yet time to get excited. The animal shifted its weight from one hip to the other with a deep breath, much like a human sigh. Absently, it nibbled at a grass stem near its nose.

The young man felt a tickle against his right knee, and glanced down to see if the deer-fly had returned. It was one of the fluffy yellow heads of feather-grass, heavy and ripening, nodding gently in the breeze to tap ever so lightly at his bare leg. It was a beautiful day, clear and cool, but warm where the sun's rays struck.

Somewhere out of sight, one of the Wolves returned to report that all was ready. The herd was in position. The chief of the hunt gave a silent hand-signal that was passed along to the other hunters, and the long line of riders began to move slowly forward. Instantly, the roan gelding became alert. Head up, ears pricked forward, he knew what this activity meant. Storyteller had to restrain him slightly, but the animal responded to the tug on the rein, giving only a slight impatient toss of his head as he walked through the tall growth.

Now Storyteller could see ahead to greater advantage. The line of hunters was topping a low rise, and in the more level plain beyond he could see thousands of shaggy dark forms, grazing or standing calmly. Nervously, he looked toward Otter, who smiled and nodded reassuringly.

The hunters kept their horses at a walk, and the advance of the line did not seem to alarm the grazing buffalo in the least. The slight breeze, little more than a stirring of the air, was from the buffalo toward the advancing hunters.

"Their eyesight is poor," Otter had explained, "but their nose is keen."

They were almost within bowshot of the nearest animals before there was any reaction in the herd. It may have been a slight shift of the breeze, a chance scent. Possibly it was only that the hunters came within the limited range of the buffalo's vision.

The first indication was the reaction of a wary old cow. She raised her head suddenly, sniffing the air, not even chewing the wisp of grass already in her mouth. She took a step forward, started to lower her muzzle again, and then swung her massive head to face the hunters. A low warning rumbled from her throat, and other animals too turned inquisitively. The hunters were moving at an easy trot now.

Everything seemed to happen at once. The first buffalo wheeled and broke into a run. Then they were all running. Storyteller felt the roan leap forward under him, almost unseating him as they joined the pursuit. He did not remember consciously dropping the rein, but he found himself using both hands to fit an arrow to the bowstring.

He had wondered how to choose which animal to pursue but found that he had no choice in the matter. The horse had already chosen his quarry and was rapidly closing in for the kill. It was a fat yearling, and they swept into position so quickly that he was almost caught unprepared. He managed to loose the arrow and saw his feathered shaft disappear into the soft flank.

The running animal jerked convulsively and seemed to stumble. It was falling as the roan swept on past, already pressing toward the next victim.

Storyteller saw other animals falling, heard the shouts of the other hunters, and found himself yelling too. It was wild, exciting, like no other experience. He managed to fit another arrow, and in the tumult of exuberance, missed his target completely. He could have sworn that the horse tossed his head in disgust as he selected another animal. The one that had escaped was already lost in the dusty melee.

His next arrow struck poorly, perhaps glancing off a rib. He knew when he loosed the shaft that it was too far forward; he had waited a heartbeat too long. The stricken animal was running wildly, and he tried to fit another arrow. Otter closed in from the left and thrust home with his lance. The cow fell. Otter waved and quickly moved on, lost to sight in the swirl of dust, horses, horns, and shaggy hides.

A large bull loomed out of the dust, and the roan gelding shied away. Experience told him that this was something to avoid whenever possible. Storyteller, as an inexperienced horseman, did not anticipate the catlike sideways leap. He felt himself lose balance, but there seemed no time between the moment he left the saddle and the sensation of slamming into the ground.

He rolled and kicked, knowing that it was better to lie still but unable to do so. He was unable even to catch his breath and wondered if he was dying. There was thunder in his ears, the thunder of a thousand hooves. Dark forms swept past him right and left, and one young cow jumped directly over him. He could clearly see the animal's udder above him as she passed, immature nipples plainly outlined only a handspan or two before his eyes.

Then they were gone, the thunder and the shouts receding. He lay still, wondering if he dared move. There was little pain, only a feeling of being battered from head to foot. Oddly, the sensation he would remember was the rough texture of the grass against his skin.

Gingerly, as his breathing reverted to normal, he began to move a little. His hands, cautiously at first. It was gratifying to find that the fingers moved. The right wrist was painful to move, but it did move. Now he tried the arms; then feet and legs. It took great courage to try to sit up. He took a deep breath and rolled over. There was a sharp pain in his chest, and he felt for an injured rib—he could not tell. He was stiff and sore all over but felt that he must do something. He sat up carefully, holding the sore rib with his left hand.

Now he could hear the hunters returning, laughing and joking. Soon he could see them through the haze of dust. He could also see dark forms lying scattered across the prairie, some partly obscured among the grasses.

He crawled to the nearest of these and pulled himself up to a sitting position. Dust was settling now, and he was breathing much more easily—unless he took too deep a breath. That produced an unpleasant jab in the ribs.

A couple of hunters rode up.

"Aiee!" exclaimed one, "are you hurt?"

"Only a little, I think."

"It is better to hunt on a horse," the other man said seriously.

Storyteller started to explain but quickly realized that they were teasing him. There were dangers to the hunt, risks that these men considered a part of life. That someone might fall from his horse was expected and mildly amusing, though potentially serious.

"I will try that sometime," he said, and the others laughed.

"Can we help you?" one asked sympathetically.

"Maybe not. I will rest here a little while . . . my horse?"

"Yes, we saw it. Otter was catching it. That is how we knew."

Storyteller felt considerably better. There had been a moment when he felt that these men were unfeeling, uncaring, but now he understood. The hunting party had been quite aware of the beginner in their midst. Someone might have seen him fall, or they may have recognized the loose horse. These two had come back to see about him and the extent of his injuries, and to reassure him about the horse.

"You did well for a first hunt," one said conversationally. "One clean kill. Another with Otter's help."

He had been watched closely all along.

"It was a good hunt," the other added. "Many kills."

"It is good!" Storyteller managed to say. He was beginning to hurt now.

"Wait here," one of the men said. "Someone will be here to help you."

It was not long before Otter returned, leading the roan. "Can you mount?" he asked.

"I do not want to try," Storyteller admitted. "My rib, maybe. It hurts some."

Otter nodded, understanding. "We will bring a pole-drag to take you to camp," he suggested. He started to turn away, but turned back. *"Aiee,* your first kill was a good one!"

Storyteller did not particularly care. It had been a strange morning. The thrill of the hunt, the excitement, the wild abandon—then the fall, the injury. At this point, it did not seem a very good trade.

The butchering parties were moving out from camp now, looking for the kills of various hunters. They would be identified by the arrows, painted with the owner's individual colors, or by the lance wounds. He would have to tell them, Storyteller recalled, that his first arrow might have gone completely inside, or even clear through.

For now, though, he hurt in every fiber of his body. He would be glad to see Plum Leaf. She could always make him feel better. Maybe, even, about this.

16

There were times that winter when Storyteller thought he could be completely happy with Turtle's people forever. He would never have imagined that a lodge of skins could be so comfortable in winter. And the winter was fierce. Cold Maker's thrust was much more severe in the open plains.

They had finished a modest lodge before snow fell and equipped it with a lodge lining hanging straight down all around from about waist-high. The angular space between the lodge cover and its lining was used for storage and insulation against the cold. Unused space was stuffed with dried grasses, effectively stopping Cold Maker's blasts.

It would have been better, of course, if they had had their own lodge. There was little chance for privacy. Actually, there had not been since their marriage. This was accepted as the way of things, and the two couples and young Lark, now eight and growing rapidly, settled in for the winter.

There were long winter evenings of visiting, gambling, smoking, and telling stories. Since the people had no central meeting place comparable to the longhouse, these sessions were held in one or another of the private lodges, usually, of course, the larger dwellings.

Someone would step outside the door of his lodge as Sun Boy neared the edge and shout into the crisp winter air. *"Ah-koh,* my friends, come and smoke!" People would straggle toward that lodge, and the socializing would begin.

Both Turtle and Storyteller were always in demand because of their skills. Storyteller was held in high regard, especially by people his own age. Everyone knew of his adventure in the fall hunt. It had made a great impression that one of such a calling, a storyteller, would take the time and effort to learn the skills required to participate in the hunt. In addition, it was widely told, his first kill was worthy of an experienced hunter. The fact that the hunt had ended in an accident for Storyteller did not detract in the least. In fact, his willingness to take the risks, to share the dangers with the rest, made him more popular.

He felt the pleasure of approval, that he and his family were accepted, partly, of course, because Turtle was one of them, but there was personal acceptance too. There is approval that goes only to an outsider who tries to understand and respect customs not his own.

His ribs healed slowly. The second and third days were the worst, every bone and muscle aching. To have the unexpected jab of pain when he moved just so—that was the final indignity. Gradually he could get up or lie down without stopping to plan every motion for the least pain.

He came to appreciate the usefulness of the plains people's willow backrest. It was made of slender willow branches as thick as a man's finger laced across a frame of heavier wood. The flexible sticks bent slightly when a person leaned back, conforming to his weight, while the entire device was held steady by the part on which he sat. There was nothing more comfortable to his tender ribs than to loosen every muscle and sink back upon the rest.

The Moon of Snows was aptly named that winter. One attack after another Cold Maker threw across the prairie, but the People had chosen well the site for winter camp. It was a sheltered canyon with enough trees to break the force of the wind. The drifts became deep, but at times even that was an advantage. Many families banked snow around their lodges for added warmth.

The Moon of Hunger, once a dreaded time for these people, was now little more than a joke in good season. Since the coming of the horse a few generations ago, living had become much easier. There were jokes that the Moon of Hunger needed a new name, for there was seldom any hunger. The old expression, "Moon of Starvation," was practically forgotten. True, some of the elders and some of the more thoughtful realized that if ever the fall hunt failed completely, as it could—well, the results would be tragic.

But this winter there was no concern. The fall hunt had been good, better than average, and every lodge was well supplied. They had paused for a few days as they traveled south to winter camp, to trade with a village of Growers. Now, in addition to their supplies of dried meat and pemmican, most lodges had vegetables. Extra meat and buffalo robes had been bartered for corn, beans, squash, and pumpkins. Nearly every lodge had strings of corn and dried pumpkin hanging from the lodgepoles.

But even in a winter with plenty, the time of immobility is hard, especially hard, perhaps, on the people of the prairie whose world is wider from one horizon to the other. This wideness makes human companionship more important in the smallness of man in the vastness of the universe. Yet it also gives the dweller of the plains a sense of entrapment, a closed-in uneasiness when he is deprived of his far horizons. Under these conditions, he becomes irritable and quarrelsome.

In the closeness of the shared lodge, it became increasingly difficult to maintain good humor. Even with the knowledge of its cause, it was difficult. Turtle, the only one whose heritage was the prairie, was first to show the malady. He was short-tempered and gruff, sometimes going all day without a word. Owl Woman did her best to distract him, but in a lodge full of other people—*aiee!* And the sour spirit seemed to jump quickly from one to another.

It was with a great sense of relief that they welcomed the return of warm breezes. The petty squabbles of yesterday seemed absurd in the warming sunlight of the Moon of Awakening. A different sort of restlessness began to make itself felt. One evening, as a flock of geese honked overhead, heading north, Turtle voiced his new restlessness. "Where shall we go this season?"

Apparently no one but Turtle had given the decision much thought. Perhaps he had not either. There was a rather meandering conversation, largely based on reminiscences of past seasons, with little direction.

"Well, we must think of it," Turtle observed as they prepared for sleep.

Next morning, Storyteller arose to tend the horses. After the custom of their hosts, he had learned to provide food for the animals during snow time by chopping cottonwoods and feeding the smaller twigs and the bark. Horses could subsist, even when the scant winter forage of dried grasses was covered by the drifts.

"I will go with you," Plum Leaf said, jumping to her feet.

He started to say that she was not needed but paused. It would be good, he thought, to have her with him in the brightness of the sunny day, snow still covering the ground. There was no wind, and it was comfortably warm in the sun. The bright reflection of sun on snow was painful to the eyes after a little while. It was best, he had found, to avoid looking at the great expanse of white. There were, in fact, warnings of people who had been stricken snow-blind. It was a temporary condition, but painful and to be avoided if possible.

The two young people reached the sheltered area where the horses were wintering and began to cut cottonwoods. The animals came crowding forward, reaching eagerly for the strips of bark from larger branches. It would be good when they could graze again.

"It is good to be together," said Plum Leaf.

He knew that there was much more to this statement than appeared. It was filled with all the frustration of the winter—the sameness of close quarters in the lodge with no possibility of escape, the being together yet not together because of the absence of privacy. He had felt it too. Perhaps most frustrating of all was that it had been impossible even to speak of it. He knew it could not have been helped, but it was like, well, like the resignation to hunger when one knows there is no food.

"What are we going to do, my husband?" the girl asked.

"What do you mean?" He wanted her to express *her* frustration first, knowing even as he spoke that it was unfair. He attempted to modify his approach. "We will finish this and go back to the lodge," he said, feeling like an idiot.

"No, no, after that. This summer. After that."

Ah, now it was out in the open.

"We must talk of this," he said. "What would you wish?"

"I . . . do not take it wrong, Woodpecker. You know we both love your parents and little Lark, but . . ."

She paused, unsure of herself. He had felt much the same at times. He had noticed on their travels last season that sometimes there was very little trade. They would come to a village or camp, have a wonderful evening of stories, but there would be practically no activity the next day. As a youth, he had not even noticed. When they were three, living was easier, and he was reveling in the joy and prestige of being a storyteller.

Now they were five. It took more to supply their needs. The fall hunt had helped, but still they had benefited greatly from the generosity of friends and relatives. What now? It was apparent that they needed a lodge of their own. But where? It was equally apparent that neither he nor Plum Leaf wished to return to the political turmoil of his people. Hers, in a few years maybe.

Meanwhile, Turtle was already showing signs of restlessness to be on the trail, the life of the trader. In reality, Storyteller too felt the urge. But maybe he and Plum Leaf could stay a season with this new tribe, the people of Turtle. They had friends, yet Storyteller had grave doubts. Did he actually have the skill as a hunter to support a lodge and a family? He had been lucky at his first buffalo hunt, but suppose he had been killed, leaving Plum Leaf a widow among strangers? This was not his gift. His was the telling of stories, the use of words, learning other tongues and customs, trading.

It must finally come down to the thing that Plum Leaf had suggested but not said openly. They must separate from his parents, take different trails.

"It is as you say," he told her. "We must go our own way. But how shall we tell them?"

She smiled. The sparkle was back in her eye, the look of mischief that he loved. "That is your problem," she teased. "They are your parents!"

* * *

As it happened, it was not as great a problem as they feared. It was not many days before Turtle took him aside and self-consciously began a serious conversation. "My son, it is nearly time to go on the trail."

"Yes?"

He knew Turtle was serious when he used the term "my son." What could this be?

"Did you notice, last season, a village or two . . . Growers who had very little to trade?"

"Yes . . . we moved on quickly."

"True . . . because there was no trading to be done."

Storyteller did not see where this conversation was going. "Father—" he began, but Turtle waved him to silence.

"Let me go on. You are experienced in trading . . . enough to see that it is harder to support two families."

That was it, the point that he had not quite been able to grasp. They were *two* families now. They must take two paths.

"Now," Turtle continued, "it would seem wise if you and Plum Leaf would trade in one area, your mother and I in another."

"She knows of this?"

"Of course. She suggested it."

The thought flashed through Storyteller's mind that the two women may have planned the entire scheme.

"Suppose," Turtle continued, "that you go south and east. There are good tribes for trading, from here to the Big River. Or, across it, even. Owl and I will stay farther north. The Miss-ouri, O-hio, Illi-noy. Then we can winter here sometimes. Maybe each two or three years?"

It was a plan of such magnitude, yet so beautifully simple. Yes, it would work perfectly. They could divide . . .

"We can divide the goods we have now," Turtle was saying, "and start as soon as the weather opens up for travel."

17

"**B**ut she is such a beautiful child!" Storyteller protested.

"Yes," Plum Leaf agreed sadly.

The child appeared well formed in every respect—legs long and strong, chest full and robust, features well placed. But the infant had never taken her first breath. The woman who had assisted Plum Leaf in her labor—it had even been an easy delivery—had breathed her own breath into the tiny lungs and massaged the chest, but there had been no response.

Plum Leaf cradled the baby to her breast, crying quietly. Storyteller wondered—if they had been somewhere else, among his own people, maybe, or on the plains with Turtle's tribe? Would there have been those with medicine powerful enough to bring the tiny spirit into the world of the living? Well, it was no matter now.

The old woman lifted a keening wail, the Song of Mourning of her people, for the dead child. The parents would mourn too with ceremonial purging of the grief through songs and chants, each in the custom of home, of their own people.

It had been Plum Leaf's first pregnancy, a time of great joy for the couple. It was now nearly two years since their marriage. For most of the first year, they had been traveling or living in close quarters with Storyteller's parents. When the couples decided to separate, it became an especially happy time. There was no need for some of the concerns that had been a necessary part of their first year. Not that there had been friction between them, for there had not—at least, less than average, they had all agreed.

But there had been the concern for traveling with a small child. At each stop, each village where they had traded, they had had to seek shelter and food for five people. Transportation too when they traveled by water. There was much difference in the size of the vessels required to carry one couple and baggage, and to carry five people and baggage.

In addition, decisions concerning where to go and how long to stay were simpler. It now concerned only the two of them, and they were a couple in love. They wandered where they chose, sometimes aimlessly, sometimes on a whim. They made good trades and poor ones, camped in good places and bad. They made love, and that was good. And when they discovered that Plum Leaf was pregnant, it was all that their world had lacked. They began to talk of two seasons hence, when they had agreed to meet Turtle and Owl Woman at the winter camp of Turtle's people.

"Ah, they will be so pleased!" Plum Leaf giggled. "But think, Woodpecker! This child who now kicks me will be in his second summer when they see him!"

And now it was over.

"You are young—you can try again," said the woman who had helped.

The young people nodded, but both knew. It would never be the same with another. This was their first, the child that had been welcomed as the fruit of their happy union and for some unknown reason had never taken breath. There might be others but never *this one*.

Plum Leaf recovered her strength slowly, partly because of her grief perhaps. They stayed for half a moon at the village where the labor had taken place and then moved on.

They experienced new sights, sounds, tastes, and smells, and it was a happy time but with a sober overtone. They were more mature, more aware that the world was filled with troubles. There were times when in the warmth of the sleeping robes they shared, they talked of the possibility of another pregnancy.

"Do you wish a child?" she asked him.

"Of course, if you do."

"Oh, yes . . . but, Woodpecker, what if . . . maybe it too would be dead."

Both were a little fearful but agreed that it would be good, even with the risk of another such loss. Several times that next season, Plum Leaf believed that she was pregnant. But each time it proved untrue. They moved on, still enjoying the life of the trader.

They wintered, the second winter of their marriage, with Plum Leaf's people. Her mother, though she had not been ready to become a grandmother, was visibly saddened by the loss and mourned the dead child. Then she recovered and gave the same advice they had heard before.

"You are young . . . you can try again."

Plum Leaf took the remark rather badly, though she said nothing until later when she spoke to Storyteller. "Should it hurt less because we are young?"

"No, no," he crooned gently. "They only try to help."

They wintered there, and Plum Leaf thought that surely in these familiar surroundings, their medicine would be good, and she would conceive. But it did not happen. They even made love, one early morning in the Moon of Falling Leaves, in their enchanted clearing, certain of its powers. It was an inspiring interlude and startled a pair of rabbits bent on similar activities, but no pregnancy resulted, at least for Plum Leaf.

When spring came, they moved on to new areas. By previous agreement, they would seek out Turtle's people this fall for a reunion with Turtle and Owl, and to spend the winter.

"Just ask the Growers," Turtle had suggested as a means to find the camp of his people.

With some difficulty, they did so and at length encountered one of the Wolves, who proved to be none other than Gray Otter.

"*Aiee!*" he greeted warmly. "It has been too long, my friend! Will you go on the fall hunt with us?"

"We will see," said Storyteller, placing a hand on his chest. "I have none too many ribs left!"

"Come," urged the excited Otter. "The others will be glad to see you!"

"Are my parents here?"

"No, not yet. They are coming too?"

"Yes. I think so. We agreed to meet with you this year."

"Well, the season is still early. They will be along. But come, tell us of your travels! You have new stories, things to trade?"

"Of course!"

Turtle and Owl Woman arrived two suns later, and there was a happy reunion.

"Ah, how Lark has grown!" Plum Leaf exclaimed.

Most heartbreaking, however, was a new babe at Owl Woman's breast. It was a boy of seven moons, with a thoughtful gaze and large dark eyes. The tears came as Plum Leaf cradled the infant and rocked him in her arms. She had almost forgotten her grief but found it just below the surface, ready to bubble up again.

"That must have been difficult," Owl Woman said sympathetically after hearing their sad tale.

Plum Leaf was grateful that Owl did not repeat the now offensive remark about their youth and trying again.

"At my age, I did not really need this one," Owl Woman said, "but ah, he has been a joy. May you have such a one, Plum Leaf."

"I hope so, Mother. Thank you!"

The two embraced, feeling closer now than when they last parted.

"We have much talking to do this winter," said Owl. "You must tell me all the places you have been."

"Yes, you also!"

Storyteller found that he was reluctant to throw himself wholeheartedly into the hunt. It was not fear, exactly, but caution. He was not ready for the risks involved in such dangerous activity. There was a sense of responsibility, a slight shift from the carefree time of youth with its wild escapades. His was the responsibility of a husband now.

He noticed the same change in Otter and in others of their age. These men now had their own lodges, wives, and children. He felt a pang of regret over that as he saw the little ones at play and heard their laughter. He knew that it must be worse for Plum Leaf.

He did enjoy the hunt, the sense of flying that he remembered from his first wild ride on the buffalo-horse of Otter's uncle. But he was more cautious, as well as more experienced. He did make two kills and assisted with a third.

Gray Otter's new wife, Heron, seemed to relate quickly and well to Plum Leaf. It was not long before the young women became best friends. Heron approached her husband with a suggestion. Could Storyteller and Plum Leaf share their lodge for the winter?

So they wintered together, a more satisfactory arrangement than living with Storyteller's parents and their small children. However, it was a bittersweet season. Toward autumn, Heron realized that she was pregnant. Once more, there was the hurt for Plum Leaf, who was not. She managed to be happy for her friend through the early moons of the pregnancy, rejoicing with Heron at the quickening.

But when the Moon of Awakening came, both Plum Leaf and her husband realized the increasing stress that their friends' happiness was placing on them. It was a great relief when they were able to assemble their packs and take to the trail of the trader again.

PART II

THE TRADER

18

The Traveler moved along the trail, his heavy pack balanced high on his shoulders. He paused a moment to shift the load and readjust the rawhide straps that cut into the muscles across his chest and shoulders. Ah well, another day would soon be gone, and they would camp at a place they knew, up ahead. Good water—a spring that bubbled up from the rocks.

He licked dry lips and turned to look back at the woman who followed him. She carried a smaller pack, one that would have seemed massive to one unaccustomed to such travel. She never complained. Plum Leaf was still beautiful, he thought, after all the years. It seemed only a short while ago that they had married. But his bones and joints reminded him, after a long day's travel or on a cold morning as they rolled sleepily from the robes.

His wife drew closer, lifted her face, and smiled at him. Sweat beaded her brow. This type of travel was not his favorite, or hers, he knew, but there was no alternative just now. They had decided to winter among her people this season, the Forest People, and her village was accessible only by foot trails.

Plum Leaf's favorite mode of travel was by canoe after she overcame the initial fear of water that is common to the landsman. Her face would reflect the pleasure, and her eyes would sparkle as their craft slid smoothly along one of the great rivers, taking them to new places to trade.

His own preference was to travel by horse. Though his own background was not that of the prairie, he had come to love it. It was the land of his stepfather, Turtle, who had taught him the skills of the trader. There was something about the vastness of the far horizons that always drew him back, no matter where else they had traveled and traded. He still remembered with a thrill the wild abandon of his first buffalo hunt—his broken ribs. *Aiee,* he would hate to take such a fall at this stage of life!

It was a good life though. They both enjoyed the life of the traveling trader. There was only the one thing, the sadness never quite out of mind. They no longer talked of it, but he could tell. He had seen the tears that welled up in her eyes when she watched children at play. In all the years, Plum Leaf had never succeeded in carrying another child. They had wondered if the very active life they led had affected her childbearing, but it seemed not. A season or two, when they had believed her to be pregnant, they had ceased travel, just to be sure. But it seemed to make no difference.

So, they had ceased talking of it. They had thrown themselves wholeheartedly into the life they had chosen. Looking back, he thought perhaps their personal loss had pushed them on. The years had passed so swiftly. It must be fourteen, maybe fifteen winters now since their tiny beautiful girl-child had failed to take breath. His own tears welled up.

They had returned once or twice to that place of sorrow but had hurried on. He knew that their tendency to travel on, to be always on the move, had affected his reputation as a trader. Not unfavorably, for he was known to be honest and fair. But, their far-ranging ways had added a name to those he used. To some, he was still the Storyteller. To most, he was the Trader. But as one with whom they bartered had once asked, was there anyone who had ever traveled so much? He had become known not only as the Trader but the Traveler.

He took a certain pride in this reputation because it was linked to a reputation as one who carried and traded exotic items. Their far-ranging travel and trade gave access to items not usually seen. The red medicine-stone, of course, for which there was only one source, to the far west of his own home country. He often carried the red stone, or medicine-pipes made of it, because its medicine was strong. But it was heavy.

There were other things, easier to pack and lighter in weight. Chokolatl was quite popular among some of the southern tribes, its value increasing as they moved north. There was a variety of vegetable that tasted like fire— "chile." Some of the Caddos with whom they traded used it occasionally, but it was not destined to be a popular item farther north.

More useful, and easy to carry, were the seeds of various types of corn. They had found at least five or six varieties in use in various places along the River of Swans and the River of the Kenzas. Growers in other areas were eager to try new types—some for grinding, for eating fresh, or for popping.

They had wintered with several tribes through the years. Some had emerged as favorites, those whose winter social customs were those they enjoyed. The stories, of course, continued to be a rewarding part of winter activities and replenished his supply for the coming season.

Twice, they had wintered with the people of Plum Leaf's village and intended to do so again. They had not returned to the region of Storyteller's home. Plum Leaf had never seen it. He was not sure he wanted her to, certainly not if the political instability was still there. He had not inquired, and he finally realized that he preferred to avoid it. He could not forget the sightless eyes staring at the sun, the freshly-skinned heads. Maybe next season they could go in that direction and inquire at least.

He stopped at a little rise and waited for Plum Leaf to join him. He knew she was tired, for he was. She took the last few steps and paused beside him.

"Shall we rest a little?" he suggested.

"No, let us go on, Woodpecker. It is only a little way to the camping place."

"No one calls me Woodpecker anymore except you."

She smiled. Most of the people they contacted knew her husband as the Traveler now, though many still called him Trader. Occasionally, one would remember the seasons when, traveling with his stepfather, he was the Storyteller. But, she loved to call him by his childhood name, the one his mother had preferred, Woodpecker. Many men, she had noticed, were still called by their childhood names where their mothers were concerned.

"You are still the charming boy I met as a child," she explained simply. "Shall we move on? We should be able to camp well before dark."

The camping place they sought was located at the crossing of two trails. It had been a place of reference for many generations. It was easy to describe: "I will meet you where the trails cross." People traveling in the area would necessarily pass this spot.

Its other feature was the unfailing water supply. Even in a dry year, the water seemed always plentiful, sweet, and good. Sometime long ago, some traveler had begun to improve the spring by cleaning out debris and removing stones to make the pool a little deeper. Through the generations, others had continued the upkeep. At the present time, or at least on their last trip, the pool itself, though no larger than a pace across, was deep and crystal clear. It was surrounded by ferns and grasses, worn away only at the side next to the trail where thirsty travelers approached. It was good to think of the cool water and the comfort of a fire in the coming evening chill. The couple moved on.

Idly, he wondered whether they would share their camp with other travelers. He rather hoped so. He enjoyed the companionship, the conversation, and news of other places. Plum Leaf had always said that he could always talk with anyone, even though they did not know each other's tongues. It was true, he had to admit. Such a problem was merely an obstacle to be overcome.

On the other hand, if they were alone at the spring, that was good too. They had never ceased to enjoy being alone together—to talk, laugh, and make the little personal jokes that a devoted couple shares alone. Tonight, either way would be good. They would camp early and enjoy the long twilight of the Moon of Falling Leaves, alone or with others.

It was now only a little farther, and they made a brief stop to rest. A slight south breeze stirred the leaves in a lazy fashion, though it could hardly be felt here. The timbered hills, though shady to travel on a warm autumn day, allowed little breeze.

This thought was interrupted by a slight but unmistakable smell carried on the stirring air. Smoke. There was no village in this area, and the only good campsite was the one they intended to use. Therefore . . .

"We will have company tonight." Plum Leaf voiced his thought.

They moved on, more cautiously now. It would not do to blunder into an unknown situation. It was still some time before they came within hailing distance. Storyteller remembered a landmark now, a large gray boulder on the west side of the trail. Through the trees ahead, a thin layer of smoke drifted. Good. Anyone who wished to conceal his presence or motives would not be so obvious about it.

Still, it was wise to be cautious. And it was only polite to announce one's approach. Travelers had been killed through misunderstanding, by approaching silently. To people who feared attack, such an approach was a threat.

He selected one of the tongues that was probably used in this area. "Ho, the camp!" he shouted through cupped hands.

There was a flurry of activity ahead, and he thought he detected sounds of people slipping into the woods. There was a long pause before an answering shout came. This told him much. It was a party large enough to be confident but still cautious enough not to be caught off guard.

"We are coming in," he called.

He had found that a bold, confident approach was always best. But there was something here that was not quite right. There seemed no danger but . . . something. Plum Leaf seemed to feel it too. The party ahead was cautious, almost too careful. Were they afraid of something? Could it be that the political situation here was uneasy? Carefully, they approached the camp, making certain that none of their moves could be taken as aggressive.

With a practiced eye, he looked around the clearing where the trails crossed: Several men, judging from the robes and supplies strewn around. A hunting party, it seemed, but—ah, there was the cause of their uneasiness! Three children, who appeared to be prisoners. They must not pay too much attention to that.

"Greetings, my brothers," he announced broadly in his wife's tongue, at the same time using hand-signs.

The others nodded, but said nothing.

Storyteller strode boldly toward the spring, Plum Leaf at his side. He flopped to his belly to drink, trying to show a lack of the fear that gnawed at his stomach. He rose and wiped his mouth.

"Ah, that is good," he signed. "It is very dry to the north."

Men were coming out of the woods, back into the clearing. Seven in all, he counted, unless there were some still hiding.

"Who is your chief?" he asked in hand-signs, hoping to establish better communication.

Several of the party looked toward a burly man who now stepped forward.

"I am White Bear, chief of the People," he signed. "How are you called?"

Storyteller was accustomed to the sign for *human* or *people*. It was used by all to indicate their own tribe. Well, he could inquire about that later.

"I have been called many things," he signed, with what he hoped would be taken as a friendly smile. "Just now, I am called Traveler."

There was a slight rippling chuckle of humor, and the group began to relax a bit. Traveler rummaged for a bag of tobacco and signed to White Bear again.

"Join me in a smoke?" he invited.

The captive children watched, wide-eyed. Traveler tried not to look at them. This situation promised to be difficult for Plum Leaf.

19

The hunting party, it became apparent as the "smoke" progressed, was closely allied to the tribe of Plum Leaf's people but spoke a different tongue. Traveler had found that in such a case, it was prudent to continue hand-signs, even if some conversation was possible. He explained their presence here, their intention to winter in Plum Leaf's village, and their trading customs.

"You have things to trade?" inquired White Bear, looking curiously at the packs of the newcomers.

"In the morning," assured Traveler. "The light will be better."

It was true that shadows were lengthening, and the chief of the party nodded in understanding. Yet it was sometime later before the subject of the captive children came up. White Bear was almost casual about it. "Yes, they are from one of the tribes from the west. Plains people. They came into our region, and we have watched them. It was a dry season for them, I suppose. Usually they do not come this far."

"But the children?"

"Oh, yes . . . we caught them in the woods."

"What will you do with them?"

"Who knows? Sell them, maybe."

Traveler was still fishing for information. Every fiber of his being cried out in sympathy for the captives, and he knew it must be worse for Plum Leaf. The oldest of the girls was about the age that her child would have been. He tried to seem nonchalant. "They look strong," he said. "A little thin, perhaps."

"You wish them?"

"No, my chief! I have no wish for burdens of this sort."

He watched the children closely for the rest of the evening. The youngest, a boy of perhaps six, was not handling his captivity well at all. He alternately cried and smiled. The man who seemed to be his captor teased and played with him, and the boy would respond a little, only to cry again when let alone.

One of the girls was sullen and despondent, but the eldest was defiant. She kept calling out words of encouragement to the others. She was a proud, mature young woman. She could not be more than fifteen, just beginning to fill her buckskins with the soft curves of womanhood. And although she was a captive, she was undaunted. In her eyes was the expression that he had heard called the "look of eagles." It was that of a captive bird of prey, ready to slip from its fetters and escape at any opportunity.

During the course of the evening, he noticed that the older girl talked quietly to the others a great deal. Something was brewing there. Their captors seemed not to notice, but Traveler gained the strong impression that an escape of some sort was in the making. He hoped not. The children had very little chance of success and might be killed or maimed just for trying. At best, their captors seemed quite unsympathetic. He had seen White Bear cuff the older girl, whom he appeared to claim, merely for talking too much. It was possible that such a man could kill a prisoner in a rage if she displeased him.

Even if an escape was successful, the children would have little hope of returning to their own people. They would be in strange and unfamiliar country, and any people they might encounter were more likely to recapture than help them.

He tried repeatedly to think of some way that he might help the children. Through the years he had seen many captives. It was not unusual. Most of them were treated fairly well and eventually adopted into the tribe of their captors. He was not certain why this situation bothered him so much. Maybe middle age was affecting his emotions. Or maybe it was merely the age of these captives. He kept thinking of the proud older girl in terms of their lost child. If she had lived, this was how he would have wished her to be.

And what would the future hold for this one? Some tribes made a point of stealing young women for wives or to barter to someone else. This girl was certainly pretty enough to attract attention.

He did not speak of any of this to Plum Leaf, but he was certain that her heart was heavy too. They prepared for sleep, and he made certain that he had a clear view of White Bear and his captive as they all settled in for the night. White Bear tied a rawhide thong around the girl's ankle and his own.

Any movement beyond the length of the fetter would rouse him from sleep. This gave the girl an arm's length of motion but no more. The other children were similarly tied.

Traveler had intended to stay awake and watch, but he was tired and drifted off. It was much later that he awoke, dimly aware of quiet activity near by. The girl seemed to be picking at the thong around her ankle. White Bear, flat on his back, snored regularly. Traveler could see quite well by the light of the three-quarter moon that had now risen, and continued to watch. The girl had freed her ankle and paused to rub it for only a moment. She now produced another thong from somewhere in her dress and appeared to tie it to the one on the chief's ankle. What could she have in mind?

He almost chuckled aloud when he realized what she was doing. Very cautiously, she unwound the new thong and extended it to a small sapling a short distance away. The chief was certainly in for a surprise when he jumped up to pursue the escaping prisoners.

Now what to do? He hated to interfere, but these children were about to cause themselves more trouble. His head said that he must help prevent the escape. According to the customs of this tribe, the children were the property of their captors. It would be a breach of his hosts' customs to interfere. Still, his heart refuted the whole situation. He glanced at Plum Leaf, who appeared to be sleeping soundly.

There was a flicker of motion to his left, and he glanced that way. A large owl silently glided across the open patch of sky on fixed silent wings, rising to land on the stub of a dead tree at the edge of the clearing. It was a wondrous thing, *Kookooskoos,* the creature of the night, a silent and efficient hunter. He was distracted for a moment, watching the bird as it looked down into the camp. What did it see? Were there scraps of fur or feather among the belongings of the sleeping party that resembled a mouse or a bird, something for the hunter to strike?

Suddenly the owl stretched its neck and gave its hunting cry, a hollow rendition of its name. "Kookooskoos!"

The cry seemed very loud at this close proximity. There was a stirring in the clearing as sleepers awoke, and then everything happened at once.

All three of the captive children jumped to their feet and ran toward the woods, in different directions. Men sprinted in pursuit. White Bear took one long step, and was jerked from his feet by the thong that tied him to the tree. He landed heavily, partly in the coals of the dying fire. The impact forced a grunt of pain from the big man, followed immediately by a roar of rage. He rolled frantically away from the hot coals, brushing at his smoking buckskins and still roaring.

Afterward, Traveler thought that he might have done well to let the girl escape, but there was no time to think. She dashed toward him and tripped over some irregularity of the ground as she passed. Almost by reflex, he grabbed her, trying to pinion her arms. She was a fighter—she bit, clawed, and scratched, tried to trip him, even butted his face with her head.

Finally she relaxed into submission. He waited a moment to make sure that it was not merely a ploy and then began to relax. White Bear came over, still cursing, and jerked her hands roughly behind her to tie them. Then he shoved the bound prisoner to the ground near his sleeping robes. The cut end of a rawhide thong still trailed behind his left foot.

Traveler could hardly keep from laughing after the excitement. Though it was a serious situation, it was incredible that this slip of a girl had nearly done it, nearly accomplished an escape. And it had been such an amusing sight, the burly chief rolling in the fire, roaring in pain and rage.

White Bear turned and grudgingly gave the *thank* sign. Men were building up the other fires, and light now flooded the clearing. Others were returning to the firelight, dragging the other captives. Nearly everyone considered the entire episode uproariously funny. There were many jokes at the expense of White Bear, who did not seem amused.

"What is it?" asked Plum Leaf, rousing sleepily.

"The children tried to escape," he told her.

"Did they get away?"

"No."

She did not answer but lay back on the robes, staring at the sky. There would be no more sleep tonight. Still, they did not talk.

Traveler was pondering the situation, trying to make a decision. Normally, he would discuss the problem with Plum Leaf, but on this, he could not. Of one thing he was sure. He could not go on down the trail wondering what was to become of these children, especially the proud one.

If he had his choice in the matter, he would have bought all three captives to protect and care for them. That was impossible. At most, he might be able to trade for one. The defiant older girl, of course. He could not say why, but his heart reached out to her. And he did not know how Plum Leaf would react. He believed that she would approve. But if he was unsuccessful in trading, would she be angry or sad? It was a situation that gave him no guarantee of success either way. And any outcome might trouble Plum Leaf. Well, he must try.

At first light, he approached the chief. "This one gives you trouble," he signed. "Trade her to me and be rid of her."

"Why do you want her?" White Bear asked suspiciously. "I have no wish to trade."

"She is not worth much," Traveler agreed, "but I like her spirit. I might find some small thing to trade."

"She *is* worth much," signed the chief indignantly. "You have nothing that I want, but what would you offer?"

"I have some things in my pack."

"I will look. You want all three?"

"No, only the scrawny one. I could not afford the better ones," Traveler joked.

It was part of the preparatory manuevering, a preliminary to serious trade. Both knew it and enjoyed the sparring. At least Traveler did. The prospective buyer tried to emphasize any faults, while the seller just as strenously emphasized quality.

"She is strong," White Bear was saying in hand-signs. "Here, feel her." He squeezed her arms and legs, and invited Traveler to do so. "She can work hard. Besides, she is nearly a woman. She is pretty. She will make a man's bed warm in the winter. Maybe I will keep her."

"This is only a child," protested Traveler.

The girl's facial expression indicated pure revulsion. In keeping with the spirit of the trade, Traveler ran his hands over her body, arms, legs, buttocks, and the small budding breasts. "No," he signed, "there is not enough meat here to warm a bed. But I will offer some small things anyway."

White Bear nodded. "Well, let us look."

Now the trading began in earnest. The trader placed a variety of small items on a skin spread between the two seated men. A stone knife, some arrowpoints. White Bear dismissed the objects with an indignant wave of his hand. That was the expected reaction. If the chief had not ridiculed the first offer, something would have been wrong.

Traveler cleared the skin and tried again. He placed a knife of some quality on the skin. It was a desirable item of black volcanic glass from the far western mountains. "This stone is made in fires below the earth," Traveler stated importantly.

White Bear picked up the knife, tested its edge, and grunted. "I have a knife. You have nothing else?"

There was a murmur around the watching circle. White Bear had turned down a very good offer. The black obsidian blade, with its superb workmanship, was a great prize. Bear was driving a hard bargain.

Traveler was not surprised, but he spread his hands as if in consternation. "I have a medicine-pipe," he offered.

"Let me see it."

This was the trade that Traveler had intended. He drew out the pipe case with its ornate quillwork and buckskin fringes. There was a low mutter at its beauty as he handed it to the chief. "The red stone comes from only one quarry, my chief," Traveler boasted. "A sacred place, far to the north."

"Of course. Do you think I have never seen a medicine-pipe?" White Bear signed indignantly.

He handled the pipe a bit longer, then placed it on the skin. "No," he signed, starting to rise.

Now the onlookers gasped. Why would anyone turn down such a trade?

Traveler was taken completely off guard. This should have completed the trading, and White Bear should have felt that he had a bargain. "Wait, my chief! I have nothing else. What could you wish?"

White Bear turned, a determined look on his face. "Your knife!" He pointed to Traveler's waist.

"My knife? I could not give it up!"

It was the medicine-knife, the precious metal blade that he had obtained from the French long ago. He had thought never to part with it. It was his proudest possession.

White Bear was turning away. "So be it!" he signed.

Traveler drew the knife from its sheath, allowing the sunlight to flash in dazzling beauty from its polished blade. "Wait," he called again, holding the knife aloft. "This—for all three." He pointed at the other children.

"Of course not! This is the one you want!"

Traveler, the experienced trader, now realized that he had been out-traded. "It is good," he signed, handing the knife to White Bear.

At this point Plum Leaf, who had watched glumly without comment, began a tirade. "What are you doing?" she shouted at him. "Your *knife,* which you had before we were married? Your finest possession? Wood-pecker, you have gone mad!"

He turned and gestured her to silence. They would speak of it later.

He turned to the girl. "Come on, girl," he signed to her. "I hope you are worth it!"

20

Traveler motioned the girl to him. They must establish some things from the first, and the defiant look said that he might have bought more than he bargained for. He was still smarting a little, angry over having been bested in a trade. White Bear, as the two parties prepared to take their separate ways, had taken every opportunity to show off his new acquisition, the medicine-knife. Once he drew it merely to cut a strip of dried meat, which he could have easily bitten or broken in two. Traveler knew that such blatant show was for his benefit, to remind him of the trade and his loss.

"Come here, girl," he motioned. He tied one end of a thong to the girl's wrist.

"What is this?" she signed in mock surprise. "You have not tied me before!"

"Be still!" He tied the other end of the thong around his own waist. Plum Leaf glowered and said nothing. He turned to White Bear. "Here we part, my chief," he signed. "My wife's people live that way."

He pointed south. Plum Leaf had already shouldered her pack and entered the trail, a tunnel of leafy green through the woods. He marveled, as he often had, how a woman can express anger by the swing of her shoulders and hips as she walks. A trifle angry with himself, he gave a tug on the girl's fetter and pointed down the trail.

The girl turned, calling to the other children, a tirade of rapid speech that he did not understand. It seemed likely that she realized they would never see each other again and was shouting her good-byes. The others were crying.

This was no time to become sentimental, he told himself angrily. The situation was already bad enough, and worsening rapidly. Plum Leaf had not spoken to him since the trade.

He shoved the girl forward, and she stumbled a step or two, then turned to face him. "Do not push me," she signed. "I can walk without help." There was a dangerous glint in the proud eyes.

"Then do it!" he signed.

She turned and hurried down the trail after Plum Leaf. He had wondered if the girl might slow their travel, but it quickly proved otherwise. Her long legs, he noticed, could match his own stride for stride. In fact, the long fetter became a hindrance a time or two over rough parts of the trail when he was slowed by the heavy packs. The thong would tighten and throw them both off balance.

Late in the morning, they paused for a brief rest. The girl pointed to the thong on her wrist. "I can travel better without this," she signed.

Plum Leaf broke her silence for the first time with a resumption of her tirade. "You are mad, Woodpecker! The girl is not worth the effort. She will run away. You are like a rutting bull elk!"

Ah, so that was it! Plum Leaf was jealous of this child just blossoming into womanhood. "We will speak of this later," he said firmly.

He turned back to the girl. "You will promise not to run away?" he asked in hand-signs.

There was a long pause before she answered, as she considered the option. Finally she began to sign. "I cannot promise that, my chief. I am of the People. I will escape when I can."

Traveler threw up his hands in dismay. "Listen, little one! You are in strange country. Winter is coming. Give your promise for now."

She thought for a moment. "I can change it, later?"

"It is good. You will let me know when?"

She nodded and held out her wrist, and Traveler cut the thong. The girl sat, rubbing the wrist.

Plum Leaf resumed her tirade, but he spoke quickly. "Look, we have made a bargain. She will not run."

"She will! She is not to be trusted!"

He turned back to the girl to verify the terms of the bargain. "You will not run unless you first tell me that the agreement is finished. Agreed?"

The girl nodded. Plum Leaf sat glowering, and another idea occurred to Traveler. He might as well take advantage of the situation. "One more thing!" he signed. "If you break your bargain, Plum Leaf says she will kill you!"

He knew that Plum Leaf would do no such thing, but maybe the thought would serve as a deterrent. But, to his surprise, the captive turned to Plum Leaf and began to sign. "If I am dead, I am of no use to you. I could not even be sold. Still, a woman of my tribe keeps her promises. I agree to the bargain."

Plum Leaf sat speechless, and the whole thing struck Traveler as humorous. He turned to the girl. "It is good!" he signed. "Girl, I like your spirit. How are you called?"

"I am Pale Star."

"We will call you so. Yet I am made to believe that this star is not a pale one! But come, let us go on. Cold Maker comes soon."

As it happened, Cold Maker came the next day, much sooner than he had guessed. They were traveling well, still a few sleeps from Plum Leaf's village, when the sky began to darken. There was a crisp chill in the air. The captive girl became quite anxious, glancing at the darkening sky.

He was amused. Among her people, this could be quite a dangerous situation. A storm on the prairie at this season—well, it was time to make winter camp and stuff the lodge lining. Pale Star became more anxious, and by the time he called a halt, she seemed nearly frantic. He selected a flat place against an abrupt slope that faced south, and they dropped their packs. Here, he signed to her, they would build a lodge.

"Of what?"

"Brush of course!"

She still seemed puzzled, and he was reminded again that brush shelters among the plains people were only for summer use and had no sides.

"You gather firewood," he signed. "We will build the lodge."

He and Plum Leaf had barely lashed the horizontal pole to two saplings to form the front edge of the roof when the girl came slipping quietly back. Her hands were empty, and Plum Leaf gave a grunt of disgust, but it quickly became apparent that something was urgent.

Pale Star motioned them to quiet and quickly signed her news. "There are deer in the woods!"

He nodded and picked up his bow. "Show me!"

He admired the graceful way she moved ahead of him, threading between the trees and thickets. This was a young woman of some skill. Finally she motioned again for silence, and pointed. "Just ahead! In the oaks."

The two peered carefully through the brush and small trees.

"There are three . . . one lying down."

"I see them."

He drew the arrow to its head, and the string twanged as it sped on its way. All three animals fled, and Pale Star looked at him in disappointment. But he had seen the arrow strike. It had been one of those rare shots that the bowman knows will strike true, predetermined when the missile leaves the string. He had felt it, even before he saw the shaft strike between the ribs of the fat doe.

"We have fresh meat tonight," he signed.

He waited awhile, then crossed the clearing and began tracking—a few drops of blood on a fallen oak leave, a bloody smear. They had gone less than a long bow shot when they came to the fallen doe. The animal was quite dead, the feathered end of his arrow protruding like a strange growth from the chest wall.

"Go and bring Plum Leaf," he signed as he drew his knife to begin butchering.

It was that evening that Plum Leaf first began to accept the girl. Without being told, Pale Star plunged into the work of butchering when she returned with the other woman. It was merely an act of self-preservation, of course. If food is plentiful, no one goes hungry. This girl, he supposed, had helped butcher buffalo all her life.

But the effect on Plum Leaf was apparent. They had not yet talked of the acquisition of the girl, and he was not looking forward to the ordeal. He finished the ceremony of apology to the deer and turned to help carry the first load of meat to the camp. The captive was just lifting a bundle of meat when Plum Leaf spoke. "She may be useful, after all," she conceded.

Traveler's heart leaped for joy. Now maybe things could get back to normal.

The lean-to was finished none too soon. Fat fluffy flakes of snow were falling silently through the trees or hissing softly into the dry oak foliage. The fire was crackling, strips of meat broiling before it on sticks. They all ate their fill, propped more strips of meat to dry and smoke-cure, and Plum Leaf spread their sleeping robes in the shelter.

At first, Pale Star seemed reluctant to share their bed. The previous night she had rolled in a robe they had given her, a little apart from her captors. But tonight—on a snowy night, body warmth is a precious commodity not to be wasted. It was snowing harder now. It was apparent that, reluctant or not, there would be a real need to share the shelter and the robes.

Traveler was concerned. He and Plum Leaf had still not discussed the captive. He could not comfortably suggest that he take the middle position. His wife had already questioned his motives for buying the girl. And surely Plum Leaf would not want her between them. As for suggesting that Plum Leaf take the middle, and the girl her other side—ah, how could he have created such a dilemma? He avoided the mention of the subject as long as he could.

Finally, just when he was ready to speak, Plum Leaf saved him from the embarrassment. "Here, girl," she signed. "You will be warmer between us."

She could not resist, however, a glance of contempt and warning at her husband. Then her face softened for a moment. "She has little body fat," Plum Leaf explained apologetically. "She would be chilled easily."

Traveler nodded agreeably. He was in no position to argue anything with Plum Leaf.

It was a long time before he fell asleep. Cold Maker howled and drifted the snow against and around the little shelter. Once he felt a cold breath of wind persistently whistling through a hole in the brush wall of the lean-to. He rose, went outside, and kicked the drifting snow deeper against the shelter. There—that would be warmer. He replenished the fire before he crawled back into the robes and stood looking at the two sleeping forms for a moment.

He would have loved to snuggle up to Plum Leaf, as he always had, but it was impossible. He considered attempting to go back to bed on the other side. No, there was not enough room, and she might be angry. Finally he crept back under the robe in the place he had just vacated. It was still warm. Not like snuggling next to Plum Leaf, but at least the blast of Cold Maker's breath no longer came through the wall.

"Mother, I would learn your tongue," Pale Star signed.

They were lacing strips of the meat on green sticks and propping them over the fire. This produced a combination of drying, cooking, and smoking that was not unfamiliar to Star's people, it seemed. It had been decided to stay in this camp for another day while the wet snow disappeared and travel became easier. Meanwhile, they would salvage as much as possible of the venison in this manner.

Plum Leaf was startled though pleased by the request. "My tongue, or his?" She pointed to her husband.

The girl shrugged. "Both, maybe. Which do you use together?"

"Both. Mine with my people, his for his. When we are alone, both, sometimes."

Pale Star worked with the venison strips for a little while, and then signed a question. "We go to your people now?"

"Yes. Three, four sleeps. We winter there."

Traveler happened to observe this interchange. He was pleased that the two were conversing but was also puzzled. The girl had asked if their goal was the village of Plum Leaf's people, as if she already knew it. *How* did she know?

He thought for some time and finally realized. On the night before he traded for her, Traveler had told White Bear that they were headed for his wife's people. And he had used *hand-signs*. The girl had seen and remembered. What a quick mind! It was also apparent that she was a good worker. The time that it would have taken to prepare and smoke-dry the meat strips was virtually cut in half.

Sometime later, the girl asked a question of Plum Leaf as they worked. "Have you had children?"

Ah, too bad, he thought. But the girl had no way to know.

He watched the tears well up in his wife's eyes as they always did when the subject arose.

"One," she signed. "She is dead."

It was fortunate that at that moment Sun Boy overcame his foe. The rays of his heavenly torch burst through the clouds, and its warmth could be felt.

Plum Leaf's expression relaxed somewhat, and she smiled. "Cold Maker's first war party is always a short one," she signed.

21

It was remarkable to Traveler how rapidly the two women became close. As it happened, the thing that he had feared never occurred—the discussion with Plum Leaf about his motives for the trade. It was no longer necessary. Plum Leaf first accepted the fact that another pair of hands made the tasks lighter. Accepting the girl would take longer.

Still, he was pleased to see them communicating. As he had suspected, Pale Star was extremely intelligent. In addition, she seemed to have the facility of learning languages. In a short while, she was speaking the tongue of Plum Leaf's people well enough to chatter conversationally. Moreover, she seemed to have virtually no accent. Well, he told himself, some have the gift of tongues; some do not.

Plum Leaf was still rather reserved until early in the Moon of Long Nights. It was then that the menstrual flow signaled the arrival of womanhood for the captive girl. The attitude of Plum Leaf seemed to change suddenly. The sisterhood of women everywhere came to the fore, and instantly Plum Leaf was solicitous and helpful. She explained the customs of the menstrual lodge. The menstruating woman would spend a few days each month with others in similar circumstances, in a special lodge at the edge of the village.

"Aiee!" exclaimed the girl. "She is sent away?"

"Of course!" Plum Leaf retorted. "It is not so with your people?"

"That she is dangerous, yes. It is known that a bow touched by a menstruating woman will never shoot straight again. But our women are careful not to endanger anyone! She is not banished from her lodge!"

Ah, that streak of pride again, thought Traveler, shaking his head.

If he had known the rest of the story, there might have been much more shaking of his head. For Plum Leaf took the girl aside in private conversation. "You do not understand," she confided. "This is a good custom."

"To be pushed out of one's home?" Star was still indignant.

"No, look, child . . . this removes one from the duties of the lodge too. You will see the same women each month, who become your friends. And who understands but another woman?"

It was in this way, then, that the two became almost conspirators. Almost without realizing it, Plum Leaf came to regard the welfare of the captive quite personally, and during the long dark days and nights of that winter, the relationship grew and prospered. The girl in many ways came to fill the place of the lost daughter. Plum Leaf felt her frustrated maternal instinct become calm and serene, and her heart reached out to the girl. She was strict, as one is with a first child. Perhaps the response of Pale Star was as astonishing. The captive *responded* like a daughter. She was solicitous of her foster mother, finding little helpful things to make tasks lighter, in the best tradition of a loving child.

Traveler was astonished. He felt excluded from the relationship that he saw forming almost before his eyes. He was not entirely excluded, however. Pale Star showed great interest in his language skills. No sooner was she becoming fluent in the tongue of Plum Leaf's people than she began to inquire into his. He had his doubts about her ability to absorb so much so rapidly, but she did well.

She also showed a great interest in his stories. When during some of the long winter evenings he would be entertaining a group around the story-fires, Pale Star would always be there, listening with rapt attention. He had first noticed this quite early, even before they reached Plum Leaf's village. They had camped at a small town to participate in storytelling and trading. He was using hand-signs as well as oral narration because he knew that there were several in the audience of varied backgrounds. He was certain that the captive girl had little knowledge of any of the languages represented there. Yet when his eyes happened to fall on her, Pale Star sat watching and listening, an expression of absolute delight on her face. It must be that she was following the hand-signs.

Then there came a time, late in the winter, when she seemed to have a complete change in attitude. Suddenly there was no interest in learning more language. She seemed to forget what she already knew. Frequently she asked for a repeat of some comment or question. He wondered if she was losing her hearing. He had almost decided that it must be. It was known to happen, even in the young, in the rigors of winter. She did not appear ill, however. She remained cheerful and helpful . . . *aiee,* it was puzzling!

Then he noticed, at a story-fire late in the Moon of Hunger, a further puzzle. Pale Star hung eagerly on every word, eyes shining with anticipation, completely involved in the narrative. How curious, he thought. He experimented a little, dropping his voice to a whisper. The girl's facial expression and half-smile of pleasure still indicated complete understanding. So it was not a hearing loss. He stopped the hand-signs that accompanied his story, and it seemed to make no difference. She still understood, quite well.

What, then? He pondered a long time as he lay in his sleeping robes that night. There had been no chance to talk to Plum Leaf of his suspicions. Star or other people were always present. That was one of the things about the close social contact of a winter season. There was little opportunity for private conversation.

Then it suddenly struck him, the answer he sought. The girl must be pretending. But why? Ah, yes, of course! He had almost forgotten their bargain—her need to escape and her temporary promise. There had been little reason to think of it through the winter, but soon it would be possible to travel. The time would come when Pale Star would announce that her vow was at an end. He was certain that she would do so, would live up to the agreement. He could not think that she would do otherwise.

But meanwhile it would be to her advantage to appear as ignorant as possible. He chuckled silently to himself, his heart holding a confused mixture of emotions. He found himself feeling pride at her cleverness. At the same time, the threat of her loss was alarming. After all, he had paid dearly —no, that was not it. He was almost ashamed of that thought. It was—how strange—it was the way a parent must feel when a grown daughter prepares to leave the lodge. A sadness . . .

There was no way, he realized, that Pale Star could be prevented from escaping. She was far too resourceful. It would be only a matter of time, it seemed, until she would announce her intention to revoke her vow. Well, when the time came, they would let her go. He could not find it in his heart to consider tying her, as they might have done before she became a part of them.

This status was reinforced one afternoon by a strange incident. An old man approached Traveler with an offer to buy the girl. Traveler flew into a rage, and called the man a number of uncomplimentary things. "Son of a snake!" he shouted. "Get away from my family!"

Bewildered, the old lecher protested. "I only tried to do you a favor," he snapped. "I have offered a good bargain, and—"

"Go!" Traveler cried. "You have nothing I want."

Shaking his head, the man retreated, puzzled at this reaction.

Pale Star had seen the entire event and seemed mildly amused by it. Traveler wanted badly to explain. Surely, there was a difference, he thought, between his own acquisition of the girl and the proposal set forth by this—this rutting animal.

Then he remembered that his wife had called *him* something of the sort. But that was different, he told himself, and besides, it was before she became like a daughter. His original motives—could he have actually thought of Pale Star as?—no, of course not. He was irritated at himself over the very thought.

As spring approached and the Moon of Awakening brought long lines of geese to the sky, Traveler began his usual restlessness. The winged travelers honked their way north to distant breeding grounds, and the frustrated migration urge that remains in all of us began to rise in his breast. He longed to be on the trail. This year, they had decided, would be the season to work their way north and try to learn of the political situation in his home country.

He wandered restlessly out of the village, wishing to be alone to think. There was a hilltop a couple of bow shots away where one could see a long distance, and he found himself turning in that direction. It troubled him that Pale Star would tell him soon that their agreement was at an end. He needed to be alone to think. Maybe he could spend a little while alone on the hill.

He emerged from the trees and looked up the grassy slope. To his disappointment, someone was already there. He started to turn back but recognized Pale Star. The girl was standing at the highest point of the hill's crest, her face uplifted to the sky. Her hair streamed out in the wind as she watched the geese. In that moment, he felt a kinship for her that he had never felt before. He understood the restlessness that had brought her here. It was much like his own.

One thing struck him as odd. He would have expected her yearning to be for home—the wide skies and far horizons of the prairie. But she should have been facing west, or northwest. Instead, she faced north, her gaze following the migration of the great birds that trumpeted their way overhead. So, he thought, it was not one urge, but *two*. Pale Star longed for home, but also to move on, to see new things. Her urges were much like his own! Except, of course, that his urges would lead him in the same direction, north.

He climbed the slope to stand beside her. She nodded to him, but neither spoke for a little while.

"Little one," he said finally, "it is almost time to go home." It was an experiment, a trial statement to see what her reaction would be.

She turned thoughtfully to look at him for a moment. "Yes," she said slowly, "time to go home."

He was not at all certain that they were talking about the same thing.

22

↔

ometimes he felt as if he had spent all his life on the trail, bent
beneath a heavy pack. Usually he enjoyed the travel, the new sights,
even this woodland travel overland on a forest trail. But then there
were days like this—warm, muggy, not a breath of air stirring in the closeness of the dense woods. Sweat streamed down his face, stinging his eyes,
salty on his lips.

He knew that the two women behind him were equally uncomfortable.
Star, especially, whose own prairie country was wide and open, felt closed in
and trapped by this forest. He remembered that Turtle, his stepfather, had
occasionally mentioned such a feeling. Turtle was native to the prairie land
of far horizons too.

Plum Leaf, who had grown up in the woods, had no such problems of the
spirit. But she too suffered physically from such a day. If tomorrow was not
better, maybe they should camp for a day or two, or until there was a break
in the weather.

Their season had started well. Actually, it was still going well, except that
for a few days, here in the Moon of Growing, it had become oppressively hot
and hard to travel. They were headed generally northward, stopping to trade
at the villages they encountered. They had fallen into a pattern of travel, with
Traveler in the lead, Pale Star next, and Plum Leaf bringing up the rear.

It should be only a few more sleeps now until they reached the village of a good friend, Hunts-in-the-Rain. There they could barter for a canoe, and travel would be easier. Maybe tomorrow they would strike the river and follow it upstream. No more than a day or two, as nearly as he could recall. It had been a few years since they traded this area. He wiped the sweat from his forehead, shifted the pack, and moved on after a glance at the women. Star looked up and smiled. Plum Leaf, farther behind, did not notice the pause.

Pale Star—what a difference the girl had made in their lives since last season. She had been quite useful, helping with the packs and the carrying. It would be difficult now without her. And that time, he was sure, would be soon. She had matured so rapidly. Last season, he had thought he was buying a child, but the person who now followed him on the trail was a woman. She had grown taller, a little—she was already tall when he first saw her. But she had been in that leggy, slightly awkward stage, like a fawn . . . no, more like a colt, just a trifle clumsy, not yet accustomed to the skills of using such long legs.

And in that year, the girl had become a woman. Maybe it was not that she had grown taller but merely appeared taller because of her maturity. Her body had filled out, and she was a woman of great beauty now, in face and form. He had seen the young men look at her and resented their glances. But all this would soon be over, he was afraid. She had said nothing more since the day on the hilltop. Actually, she had said nothing then, beyond the vague remark about going home. Even that had been only a repeat of his own statement.

Still, he felt that there was much understood that day that was unspoken. It had been as if their spirits touched. It was a strange thing. There had been times when they had felt close, as father and daughter, but this was something else, something that was not like family closeness. It was more. Yet not like man and woman . . . no, he did not think of her in that way. It was a communion of the two spirits; there was no other way to understand it. He *felt* her need to go home to the prairie. He was sure, too, that part of the sadness he felt at the prospect was *her* sadness. He was a little surprised that she had not yet spoken of this, voiced her intention to end their bargain.

Traveler was experienced in evaluating their location, direction, and distance. He was aware, as they traveled north, that there would soon be a time for decision. It was time to turn westward if one's goal was the prairie home of the Elk-dog People, Star's people. He was certain that she knew this because he had watched her skill in orientation. He doubted that Pale Star could be "lost," anywhere. So she was aware that the time was at hand to revoke her promise. Why had she not done it? Of this he was unsure. It would have been to her advantage to do so.

Maybe he would never understand that part, but he was certain of one thing. Star knew that the time of parting was at hand, knew it, probably, better than he. Yes, within the next few days, before they reached the river, probably, she would announce the end of their agreement. And, he thought, he would do nothing to stop her. How could he? A few moons ago he would have. But now, what could he do? One cannot prevent the departure of a loved one, or a friend.

He rubbed his right eye, to relieve the sting of a rivulet of sweat, or maybe a swelling of tears. Nonsense, he told himself. This was ridiculous. He and Plum Leaf had enjoyed many years of this life, just the two of them. How could this stranger have become such a part of it in only a few moons?

He wondered whether Plum Leaf felt as he did. Probably not in quite the same way. That was odd too. Plum Leaf, with whom he had always shared his innermost thoughts—they had never really talked about the girl. Maybe because of her suspicions at first . . . She had apparently realized that these fears were groundless long ago. But it is hard to discuss a mistake, even with a loved one. *Especially* with a loved one, maybe.

There was a good stopping place ahead, and a rest would do them good. They could pause a little while by the stream there and go on more comfortably. He shrugged the pack straps from his shoulders and set the burden beside a tree. He looked back down the trail. Pale Star was approaching, an expression of great relief on her face. Maybe they should have stopped earlier.

The girl shed her pack beside his. She straightened, stretched her arms and shoulders, smiling to herself with the ecstasy of relief for tired muscles.

"Where is Plum Leaf?" he asked conversationally.

"Right behind—" Star began, then paused to look down the trail.

The two looked at each other, puzzled for a moment, and then Star was running down the path. Traveler followed a bit more slowly, his body no longer equal to a hard sprint, even in a potential emergency.

Plum Leaf was seated with her back against the bole of a large tree several hundred paces back the trail. She had dropped her pack directly in the trail. Her eyes were closed, her face ashen.

"Mother!" Pale Star cried, dropping to her knees to encircle the woman with her arms.

"I am all right," protested Plum Leaf. "I only stopped to rest a moment." But her skin was clammy, and her breath came in hoarse, rasping gasps.

Traveler came running up. "I am sorry!" he blurted, dropping to his knees beside her. "I did not know . . ."

"It is nothing, Woodpecker. I will rest a little . . . it will be better."

He and Star looked at each other across the limp form. "It is good," he said, his voice tight. "We will camp near here. We all need rest."

He picked her up and carried her to the place they had left the packs. Pale Star picked up the bundle the sick woman had just dropped and followed. They made her as comfortable as possible on a thick sleeping robe and drew aside.

"She is very sick, Traveler," Star whispered.

"I know. What can we do?"

He felt lost, helpless, like a child. He could not think. There had been no time in his life so devastating. Even when their child was stillborn, he and

Plum Leaf had had each other. Now he was without support. The threat was overwhelming. He was dimly aware that Star was speaking.

"Oh . . . what?" he mumbled.

"I said, do you know any plants that could be used?"

"I . . . no, I do not know."

Star seemed quite concerned. "Traveler, this is not my country . . . I do not know what grows here. *Aiee,* if only we had my uncle, Looks Far. He is a great holy man."

"It is too far," he said sadly. "Do you know what he might have done?"

"Aiee, I am not a holy person!"

She was silent for a little while, lost in thought. "I can make her something," she murmured, half to herself. "There were dried rose fruits near the trail." She turned to him. "Can you find some fresh meat?"

"I will try."

"It is good. I will start the fire and look for some other things."

Traveler picked up his bow and headed aimlessly into the woods. He did not even realize that he was letting Pale Star take charge.

It was perhaps sheer chance that led the yearling buck into the clearing ahead of him—that, or providence. The creature stood there staring at him, frozen still as stone. It took his confused brain a few moments to realize what he was supposed to do. Then he slowly raised the weapon and drew the arrow to its head. The string twanged, and the animal gave three convulsive jumps and fell, kicking its last.

Now, with something to do, he was functioning better. He cut the throat to let the animal bleed and slit the belly to begin the butchering. He wondered if Star needed any special parts. He knew that the plains people sometimes used raw liver as a tonic. He gutted the creature, made a hasty formal apology, and then began to drag it back toward the camp.

The fire was burning, and Pale Star had dug a little pit near it, in the custom of the plains people. She was preparing to cut one of the packs apart to use the rawhide in the cooking pit. Several stones were already heating in the fire.

"Ah, you have a deer!" Star exclaimed. "It is good! A fresh skin is more nourishing."

She took the deer skin and spread it as a lining in the hollow, fleshside up. Traveler carried water to fill the pit, and Star began to take the heated stones, as big as her fist, and drop them into the cooking pit with willow tongs. Each produced a sharp hiss and a burst of steam. Soon the water was bubbling.

"Use stones from the hillside," Plum Leaf called weakly. "Those from near the spring contain water spirits."

"Yes, Mother," Star answered. "I know."

Of course she would know, Traveler thought to himself. A woman of the prairie would learn quite early that a stone from the stream placed in a fire explodes violently as the spirits escape.

Star was busily adding ingredients to her stew—strips of meat, a handful of onions that she had found growing near the spring. The smells of cooking began to waft around the clearing.

Plum Leaf, who had been dozing, awoke and began to show some interest. Star took a wooden noggin and dipped a cupful of the simmering broth. She allowed it to cool a little, then carried it to Plum Leaf. Carefully she lifted the sick woman, an arm around her shoulders, and fed her sips of the broth.

"It is good, Star," Plum Leaf said.

"It will make you strong, Mother."

Plum Leaf soon tired and fell asleep as soon as they eased her down. But her color was better, her breathing regular.

Her fever rose that evening, and she seemed unresponsive. Pale Star stayed up all night, cooling the fevered face with water and stroking the hands, talking softly.

For three days, the ordeal continued. Star concocted a mixture of cooked liver and pounded roseberries, held together with melted fat. "Buffalo fat would be much better," the girl observed, "but this may do."

She also fed the sick woman bites of fresh raw liver. It was a custom of her people, she explained to Traveler. "The sun makes the grass to grow, and the buffalo eat it. In this way, the spirit of the sun is captured and stored in the buffalo's liver. My people crave it in springtime after a winter of dry meat."

"Do you think it is the same with deer liver?" asked Traveler anxiously.

"I do not know, Uncle. Maybe so."

The third night, Traveler insisted that Star get some rest. She had hardly closed her eyes through the long vigil. Reluctantly, the girl consented. "Maybe a little while . . ."

But day was breaking when Traveler woke her gently. "Wake up, little one," he said, smiling. "Your medicine has worked. The fever is gone, and she is better."

23

True, Plum Leaf seemed to have passed the threatening narrow point in the trail of her illness, but she was still very weak. It was three more days before she began to gain enough strength to consider traveling.

Traveler was encouraged by her improvement, perhaps too much so, because he began to make plans to go on. Pale Star warned of the weakness of the recovering Plum Leaf, but he brushed her objections aside. "She is strong. She will do better in the north country."

It was a day or two before Traveler realized what was happening. The roles of the two women had reversed, and their traveling positions as well. Plum Leaf had taken the middle position on the trail, and Pale Star brought up the rear. It was now Star who called ahead to him that the older woman must rest. Star chose the campsite, the most comfortable spot for Plum Leaf, hovering, comforting, bringing water.

And Traveler allowed Star to assume this role. Probably it was part of his denial of the reality. He was unable to admit that the patient was not really gaining much. Any progress was quite slow. Once, Star announced with finality that Plum Leaf would be unable to travel. Traveler accepted this without question, and they spent a day of rest. It was a great relief to have someone else making the decisions about a situation that he found so unacceptable.

He had completely forgotten his fears about Star's leaving. He had absolute confidence that she would not do such a thing. Plum Leaf needed her, and without a second thought, Traveler knew that Star would be there when she was needed.

His main concern was for Plum Leaf's recovery, and he found that he had no real judgment about that, so the help and support of Star was doubly comforting. He knew that it would be easier traveling when they reached the river, which should be only a day or two. His friend Hunts-in-the-Rain would help them find a canoe.

When they rounded the last turn of the trail and the river stretched before them, it was with a great sense of accomplishment. He stopped and gazed across the expanse of water at the fringe of willows on the far side. The women came up beside him.

"*Aiee!*" exclaimed Star. "How do we cross?"

Traveler laughed. "We do not, little one! This *is* the trail."

"The *trail*? But Uncle, I . . ."

"Yes, the Big River, the Missi-ssippi. We follow it north. We will trade for a canoe."

Now came the problem that occurred occasionally. Star was unfamiliar with the word *canoe*. He tried several tongues without success and finally resorted to handsigns.

"*Boat?*" the girl asked incredulously.

"Of course!" Then he laughed again, realizing the reason for her consternation. To this girl from the prairie, a "boat" was the round unmaneuverable "bull boat" of the Mandans, also used by a few others, primarily for crossing streams or small bodies of water.

"This is a different sort of boat," he explained. "Long and narrow . . . made of bark . . . you will see."

"Where do we get this boat?"

He could see that she only half believed him, and reluctantly at that. He saw the dread in her eyes as she watched the swift muddy current sweep past. It reminded him of the reaction of Plum Leaf when she had been introduced to the river.

"We will travel upstream to the village we spoke of," he explained. "It is maybe two or three sleeps."

They rested, then moved on, following a well-used trail along the river. Pale Star continued to watch the stream at every opportunity. She seemed fascinated, yet repulsed. He could imagine the dread that the water's depths must hold for her. Her people were good swimmers, but their streams were clear and sparkling for the most part, certainly nothing like this. She probably imagined it peopled with monsters.

Star was amazed to see two men in a canoe well out in the stream. He called her attention to the men, who appeared to be fishing but waved to them. This was good. The village must be less than a day's travel away.

As he had expected, they were welcomed warmly. This was one of the villages that he especially enjoyed. They had been here many times, and both the stories and the trading were always profitable. People recognized him as they entered the town, calling out greetings or making hand-signs.

"Will there be stories tonight?" a man signed.

"Of course! Bring your friends!"

A young man ushered them to a longhouse and invited them to stay there. "My father sends his welcome," he explained.

"Your father is Hunts-in-the-Rain? Ah, you have grown up since I saw you! Tell him I will visit his lodge in a little while."

He must make the mandatory courtesy visit as soon as Plum Leaf was settled. She looked tired, but now she could rest. It was easy, in this friendly place, to forget what he suspected, that Plum Leaf was much sicker than she pretended.

The story-fires burned bright, and the crowd gathered that night to hear this most favorite of storytellers. He was appreciated here, and nothing inspires a teller of stories like a good audience. He warmed to the occasion. He used hand-signs as well as the tongue of their hosts for the benefit of any outsiders.

He first told of things that would interest the children, ending that portion with the perennial favorite, how Bobcat lost his tail. It was originally long, he related, and dragged on the ground. In that way, it was frozen in the ice of a stream when Cat paused to drink and there was a sudden change in the weather. Cat tried long and hard, but finally elected to sacrifice his tail to free himself.

The crowd rocked with laughter. Then their chief rose. "It is good, Traveler," said Hunts-in-the-Rain, chuckling, wiping tears of laughter from his eyes. "Here is our story."

The chief then related how Spotted Cat was instructed at Creation to be a night hunter and never, ever, to show himself by day. He did so but one night stayed too late and failed to reach his den before the sun rose. An eagle, wakening for the day's hunt, mistook the long tail for a small furry creature and swooped down, snatching the tail off short. Bobcat is still a night hunter, careful to avoid being seen in daylight.

The crowd responded with approval. Traveler was interested to note that Pale Star seemed quite absorbed in the stories.

As the crowd quieted, Hunts-in-the-Rain spoke to Traveler. "Is the Bobcat story of the girl here the same as yours?"

Traveler turned to Pale Star. "The chief wishes to know if your story of Bobcat is the same as mine."

"No. Tell him it is different."

Traveler relayed the message and turned back to the girl. "He wishes to hear your story."

"But I do not speak his tongue!"

"Use sign-talk."

The listeners were becoming restless as the girl rose to face their host.

"My chief," she began in hand-signs, "I speak none of your tongue, but I will try."

The chief nodded and relaxed to listen.

"In long-ago times, as has been said," she began, "Spotted Cat had a long tail."

The crowd nodded.

"In my country, among my people, there is a legend of the Old Man of the Shadows. He is a trickster, who can help or hurt. You have such a trickster?" she asked the chief.

"Not quite. We have heard of him."

"Yes. Well, Old Man had changed himself into a hollow tree, and Spotted Cat hid inside. But, Old Man played a trick. He made a knothole behind, and Cat's tail hung out."

She made a ring, like a knothole, with the thumb and forefinger of her left hand. Then she waggled her right forefinger through the hole to represent the tail. The crowd was chuckling, but her face remained quite serious.

Ah, this child is good with a story! thought Traveler in surprise. The crowd hung on her every hand-sign.

"A hunter passed by, and saw the fine fur of the tail," she continued. "He chopped it off to decorate his bow case."

She paused for effect—*just the right pause,* Traveler thought—and then continued quite seriously. "You can see that this story is true. Even now, there is still fur on bow cases."

The girl sat down, still somewhat embarrassed, while the listeners rocked with laughter.

How clever, thought Traveler. *A double twist . . . Bobcat's short tail and the bow case.* And she had managed it all with only sign-talk!

"Who is this girl?" Hunts-in-the-Rain whispered. "You did not have her before!"

"No, we bought her, last season."

"She is good with the stories. May we have more?"

"I will see."

He turned to the girl. "Stand up," he motioned. "The chief wishes to talk to you."

Hunts-in-the-Rain smiled and nodded. "Where are your people?" he questioned.

"Far to the west, my chief, in the Sacred Hills."

"How are they called?"

"We call ourselves the People, as most do. Some call us Elk-dog People."

Hunts-in-the-Rain nodded.

Now a new idea struck Traveler. Here was something quite useful that he had only begun to suspect. "Star," he suggested, "would you tell us of your people's beginnings?"

He did not know her Creation story and had no idea what she might tell, but he recognized a natural storyteller. She had already captivated her audience. And in sign-talk!

Star shrugged, still embarrassed by all the attention. "This story too tells of Old Man," she began. "He brought my people from inside the earth. It was soon after Creation . . ."

She went on, describing the cold, the darkness, and the hunger in the depths of the cavernous nether world. Her audience was completely absorbed.

"Then Old Man sat on a hollow cottonwood log and tapped it with a stick. First Man and First Woman crawled through to the outside." She paused and seemed to be waiting for something.

The crowd sat quietly, and finally a young man rose. "Are they still coming through?" he asked.

Ah, Traveler understood now. This was part of the game. The listeners try to catch the storyteller in a contradiction. Why is not the whole world filled with Star's people? This must be a trap, to let the storyteller catch the listener.

He watched as the girl turned an indignant frown on the innocent questioner. "Of course not," she signed. "The third person was a fat woman. She got stuck in the log, and no one has been through since!"

The listeners were delighted. They laughed and hooted at the young man who had been the innocent victim of the joke. He was embarrassed, but it was part of the evening's entertainment. Star thanked him with a smile, which seemed to help his embarrassment considerably.

The stories went on far into the night. Traveler was seeing Star in an entirely different light. She could be very valuable in the trading as well. In one evening, she had completely charmed this village. She was bright, attractive, and intelligent, and could help with the bartering. Yes, he would teach her. She could learn quickly—a sympathetic smile, a friendly glance, a suggestion perhaps of a more lenient trade. Judging from this evening, he felt that she would enjoy it.

He watched her—laughing, excited, eyes dancing, she was enjoying the attention, the laughter at her jokes. Well, enough for now; keep them a little hungry. Besides, he wished to go and see how Plum Leaf was doing. She had chosen to rest rather than attend the stories. Ah, she would be pleased with Pale Star's success.

He stood to speak to the crowd. "Now we must rest, my friends," he called jovially. "We have traveled far. Tomorrow we trade. I have many fine things—knives, arrow points, tobacco. And we will need a canoe!"

The crowd was beginning to break up.

"Ah, my friend"—Hunts-in-the-Rain was chuckling—"that one, how is she called, Pale Star? She is good, Traveler! A good addition to your trading."

"Yes, that is true," Traveler admitted. He was not quite ready to admit that until tonight, he had not fully realized her potential.

"Is she your wife, a second wife?"

Anger rose, and Traveler fought it down. It was a logical and reasonable question, and he was not quite certain why it bothered him so much. It was much like the feeling he had had when the lecherous old man had tried to buy her.

"No, my chief," he managed to say quite calmly, "she is more like a daughter. She is the child that Plum Leaf and I have never had."

The chief nodded. "I see. You bought her for this purpose?"

Traveler realized that his friend was merely making conversation. How could the man understand the change that had come into their lives since this proud girl had joined them? Traveler was not sure himself. Sometimes . . .

"Sometimes, my chief, there does not seem to be a purpose. Things just happen, and the purpose becomes clear later."

Hunts-in-the-Rain nodded. "It is so. But this has certainly happened well for you!"

24

Traveler watched the young man suspiciously as the trading progressed. That one had first caught his attention as the storytelling broke up.

There had been a number of young men casting admiring glances at Pale
Star. Well, that much was as it should be. But this was different, a dark
predatory gaze. It was like that of a hunting wolf as it creeps upon a sleeping
buffalo calf. Or a snake, yes a snake, approaching a nest of hatchling birds.
There was something even worse, maybe, a malevolence that reached out to
disturb the easygoing quietude of the pleasant evening.

And here was the same man this morning, hanging around, watching the
trading. Star was bothered by the man's presence, he knew. His bold stare
was making her quite uneasy.

The trading had actually gone quite well. Traveler had explained to Pale
Star how she might be of help, and she responded almost eagerly, taking
over many of the functions of Plum Leaf, who was still quite weak. They
could converse a little in the tongue of Plum Leaf's people, not understood
by those who came to bargain. Then, if it seemed good, hand-signs were
added.

"Smile at this one. Wait until we bargain a bit, then start to sign," Traveler suggested.

"Sign what, Uncle?"

"Ah! When I nod, you sign something like 'oh, let him have it, Uncle.' Or suggest something else he might want."

The girl understood immediately and gave every indication of becoming quite skillful. She was quite adept at communication, and people related to her with trust. She would be quite useful.

And then came the arrogant staring young man whose presence was becoming so disruptive. Star virtually ceased to function, so threatening was the man's presence. Traveler could not fault her for that because he felt much the same. It was disrupting the trade to have the aggressive intruder hanging over the bartering. He would have sent the man on his way except that it was poor custom to send potential trade away. In truth, Traveler too felt a little fear of the intruder.

The man and his companion seemed to be outsiders, probably visitors from another tribe. In fact, yes—the pattern of their moccasins, the cut of their garments, marked the two as men from the northeast. Unless Traveler was mistaken, they were of a tribe that was an enemy of his own, at least when he was last home . . . ah, how many years?

Maybe it would be best simply to send the men away. They were not only making Star quite uneasy but driving away trade. It appeared that the two were unpopular visitors. An interesting situation. If one is not welcome, why would he stay? He studied the men, trying not to be too obvious. One was large and heavyset, with a broad face and massive jaws. He appeared glum and irritable, probably not too intelligent.

The other man, whose arrogant stare was so unnerving, appeared to be the leader, the bearlike one the follower. The slender one moved with a sinuous gliding motion, like a hunting cat, alert to fly in any direction if the occasion arose. This man, though the smaller of the two, was certainly the more dangerous.

The crowd had thinned out now, and no one was waiting to trade, largely, Traveler thought irritably, because of the interference of the intruders, who were still loitering nearby, ogling Pale Star and making remarks to each other in their own tongue. Then the smaller, the evil-looking one, approached the trader.

Hunts-in-the-Rain, who happened to be nearby, watched closely. *He feels it too,* thought Traveler. *Something is wrong!*

"I am Three Owls," the newcomer began, using hand-signs.

"What is your nation?" Traveler inquired. "You are not of these people."

"No. I am a visitor here." He paused, shifting his weight from one foot to the other. "I would trade," he continued, ignoring the inquiry about his tribe. "You want a canoe. I have one."

Traveler was still suspicious. "What is your tribe?"

"It does not matter. Do you wish to trade?"

Traveler thought for only a moment. That was his purpose, after all. He swept a hand over the goods spread on a robe before him. "What do you want for your canoe?"

Three Owls smiled thinly, a smile that was humorless, oily, more like a leer. "A small thing . . . the girl, there."

Traveler managed to control his anger. He even managed a smile. "No, she is not for sale."

"Everything has a price . . . she is not your wife?"

"She is my daughter."

The exchange was getting out of hand. Traveler was tense and angry, as a trader must never be.

"No," insisted Three Owls. "She is of another nation. I know that. You bought her, so there is no reason you could not sell her."

"But I will not!"

His anger was rising, and Three Owls pushed on. "I only want to help you. We have a canoe and offer a good trade. This girl can tell us stories and warm our beds."

Traveler sprang to his feet, reaching for his knife. Three Owls dropped to a fighting crouch, knife ready, and smiled at the approach of the older man. People scattered.

"Stop!" came the ringing voice of Hunts-in-the-Rain. He stepped between the two and continued in sign-talk, slowly and deliberately. "You should both be ashamed. You dishonor me by fighting when you are guests in my village!"

The combatants relaxed the fighting stance a little.

"Put away your weapons!"

They did so, still cautiously.

"Traveler, your tribes are enemies, back in your north country?"

Traveler nodded, still not taking his eye off Three Owls.

"I am sorry, Traveler," the chief continued, now using his own tongue. "I suspected, last night. They have been here nearly a moon. Troublemakers. I knew they were from your country, but . . ."

"It is nothing," Traveler signed. "I will not dishonor your hospitality, my chief. But I will trade nothing to him."

"Of course."

Hunts-in-the-Rain then turned to Three Owls. "It is best," he signed, "if you and your friend leave. You have insulted the family of my guest."

For a moment, Traveler was not certain that Three Owls would go. After a long pause, the man sneered contemptuously at the chief, made an obscene gesture at Traveler, and stalked away. He turned for a moment to cast a covetous leer at Pale Star.

Traveler had an uncomfortable feeling that they had not seen the last of this man. He turned to the chief. "Who are they? He is very strange."

"Ah, my friend, they are nothing but trouble. Three Owls, the small one is called. The other, Winter Bear. They are relatives, it is said. I am glad to be rid of them. But you must be careful!"

Traveler nodded. "May we stay a few days, to let Star learn to use the canoe? That will put them farther ahead of us."

"A good plan! Of course, be welcome."

They watched as the angry Three Owls threw his possessions into a canoe moored at the river's edge. He and Winter Bear *(What an appropriate name,* thought Traveler. *Big, grumpy, and dangerous)* climbed into their canoe and pushed off, moving rapidly upstream. Traveler devoutly hoped that they had seen the last of these two.

"What was the nature of their troublemaking?" he asked thoughtfully.

"The one, Three Owls, is a bully," Hunts-in-the-Rain explained. "The other mostly follows along, maybe. They try to start fights. No one here has had courage to fight them. It is said that they nearly killed a man downriver before they came here. They tried to take his wife. . . ."

Traveler shook his head, and then changed the conversation. "Now, my friend," he said more jovially, "about the canoe. Do you know of someone? . . ."

"Maybe so. Let me ask, while you continue trading. I assume you did not wish to trade the girl there?"

Traveler smiled ruefully. How different, a joke by a friend. "I think not today."

Hunts-in-the-Rain walked off, chuckling.

"I have found your canoe!" the chief announced. He was smiling broadly. "Small Fox has one. I know this canoe . . . a good one!"

It was late in the day, and the trading had tapered off. Plum Leaf, feeling a little better after her rest, was sitting outside now and had been taking an interest in the bartering. "Go ahead," she said. "Star and I will handle this. For anything big, we will ask them to wait for you."

Traveler hesitated only a moment. "It is good," he decided. "I will not be long."

The two men walked to the edge of the village, and Hunts-in-the-Rain pointed to a canoe that rested upside down on a rack of poles. "There!" he said proudly. "One of the best!"

"Ah, you sound as if *you* own it!" accused Traveler.

Both men laughed.

"No, no, Traveler, but I do know the craft."

"Why does Fox want to sell it?"

"Oh, he married a widow who owned one. They have no use for two."

Traveler nodded, thinking to himself that this would make trading more favorable for him. He looked at the canoe. It was nearly four paces long, slightly upturned at the ends. Good craftsmanship. Its lacing was tight, and the seam well pitched. A trifle wide, yet that might be an advantage. It would be slower, but there was no need for a fast craft. The wide flat bottom would make it more stable, a good quality for a trader's craft, especially for a trader with an inexperienced paddler. Plum Leaf was an expert with the canoe, but he wanted Star to assume much of the responsibility until his wife was better.

And now he must teach the girl in a very short time. No matter, she was quick to learn, strong and well coordinated. But she had never been in a canoe. The width—yes, this one would be much harder to upset than most. And the narrower type, though better in white water, would not be practical for the amount of baggage they must carry.

He thumped the canoe near the prow, noting that the ring was true. The craft was solid, the birchbark sound and in good condition. "A bit shoddy," he mumbled as if to himself. "How many seasons old?"

Hunts-in-the-Rain laughed. "You are not trading with me, Traveler," he said. "Save it for Fox."

"Yes, of course! Where do I find this fortunate man who has a new wife and two canoes?" Traveler chuckled.

The chief turned, looking toward the village. "Ah, here he comes now!"

25

↔

The flimsy-looking birchbark shell trembled on the surface, wobbling dangerously. Star, in near panic, tensed every muscle and tried to balance her weight.

"The middle! Stay in the middle!" cried Traveler.

There were times when he doubted that the girl would be able to learn the use of the canoe at all. It seemed foreign to her culture.

"Keep your weight low!"

The girl crouched, gripping the sides of the craft. Gradually, the trembling subsided.

"You have really never seen a canoe before?" he asked, knowing the answer. "Your people do not use them?"

"Of course not!" she snapped. "What use would we have for such a thing?"

It was true, he realized. Star's people traveled with horses. A stream was only an obstacle to be crossed, and for that, a canoe was not needed. The girl simply could not conceive of the stream itself as a trail, a means of travel. Well, she would learn. She was quick, mentally and physically.

The quivering of the canoe, which seemed to give it a life of its own, was quieting now. Strange, he thought, how a canoe knows when a beginner

378

steps into it. A canoe does have a spirit of its own, he reflected. The spirit of this one was good, though a trifle mischievous. He had never seen such a delicate trembling as when the girl first stepped in. It was as if the craft recognized a stranger, one from another culture who knew nothing of canoes.

He had tried the canoe himself before consummating the trade, and found it to be well balanced, stable, and quick to respond. There would be much difference, however, with a loaded canoe. The weight of the baggage would place the balance farther forward, another paddler in the prow. But this canoe would be good for their purpose.

After the custom of his people, he had painted eyes on the prow.

"Why is this, Uncle?" the girl had asked.

"So it can see its way . . . avoid danger to us."

Star had shrugged noncommittally. There were many things of each other's customs that she would never fully understand, but she dealt with it well, he thought. She had the ability to accept, even without understanding. This quality was invaluable to one who would trade in different areas among those whose customs are different.

"Now move to the front and sit down . . . in the *middle*," he told the girl.

Star looked forward and sighed. "That looks so far," she protested. "Could I not sit in the back until I learn?"

"No, no, little one," he laughed. "The experienced paddler sits in the back. It is he who guides the canoe. Now go ahead."

She took a step, still holding tightly to the sides. The canoe rocked alarmingly but then steadied.

"Good!" he encouraged. "Now another step."

Cautiously, the girl moved forward, a step at a time. By the time she had taken the few cautious steps, she was gaining confidence. Each quivering of the craft was shorter than the previous one. Traveler was pleased, though not surprised. The girl adjusted quickly to all things. Very soon, her spirit would be one with that of the unfamiliar craft.

He pushed off from the shore, stepping over the end into the canoe. They slid smoothly over the surface, still moving from the force of his push. Yes, this would be a good canoe, he thought. He lifted his paddle and took a stroke or two. The craft was quick and responsive. Good.

"Now," he called, "take your paddle and try it. You must sit up straight. Use your arms, not your back."

At the first try, the canoe tipped sharply. Before he could speak, however, the girl had made the necessary adjustment, and the craft became steady again. They maneuvered back and forth, upstream, down, and across the current. He taught her how she could assist in the steering by bracing her paddle motionlessly against the canoe.

"Uncle, I have seen one man handling a canoe alone," Star said. "How is this done? How can he steer without changing sides?"

"Ah, that will come later, little one, when you have more skill," he assured her. Yes, she was learning quickly.

Even so, it was several days before they had practiced enough to challenge the river. They had placed objects in the canoe; stones at first, to give a low center of weight. Later, their packs were substituted, and it remained only to add the slight weight of Plum Leaf. She would ride in the middle, with Pale Star in the front and him behind.

He was startled when he assisted Plum Leaf into the canoe on the morning of their departure. Her body seemed so frail. He practically lifted her into the canoe where she sank back against the packs, breathing heavily from even that slight exertion. Star arranged the packs around her, attempting to make her comfortable. The girl had learned much about the canoe in the past few days!

Plum Leaf seemed to enjoy the smooth travel on the river. She slept often and woke to spend much time watching the trees slide quietly past.

They stopped well before dark, and she managed to stroll along the sandy bar for a little while. It was not long before she tired, however. Pale Star had prepared the sleeping robes and now helped Plum Leaf to lie down. Traveler was shocked by her weakness. *Well, she will be stronger tomorrow,* he told himself.

But she was not. Day by day, he could see her failing. It was a situation totally unacceptable to him, and he refused to think of it. Instead, he focused on another worry. They had progressed far enough north now that it would be time for Pale Star to take back her vow. The girl had given no indication that she knew, but he was certain that she did. They were past the nearest route to her home country, but she had said nothing. Surely, soon she would do as he feared and announce that the bargain was at an end.

Star had become skilled at helping Plum Leaf and looking after her needs. Besides, the girl was becoming an excellent help with the canoe and the stories and trading. With the present condition of Plum Leaf, Traveler did not know how he could manage without Star. If Star made her break, he did not see a way . . .

Traveler found occasion to talk with her about it. "Little one, I would speak with you." His voice was tight with emotion.

"Yes?"

"Long ago," he began, trying not to let his voice quaver, "you gave me a promise that you would not try to escape."

She nodded, and waited a moment for him to continue. "Yes, Uncle?" she prompted.

"But . . . you have never—taken back that promise," he said haltingly. "Why?"

"Well, I—"

"Do you wish to do so now?" He pushed on, afraid of the answer. "I said nothing when we were passing the place where your trail pointed west. I wondered if you knew."

"Yes," she said softly, "I knew. But Plum Leaf was sick and needed me."

"But she is better now," he insisted. "If you wished, you could take back your pledge and escape."

Now he really feared her answer. Star took a deep breath, and began, speaking very slowly. "Uncle . . . someday I will return to my people. When I am ready, I will tell you."

The answer pleased him, and he knew he could trust her once more. He chuckled. "Fair warning?"

"Of course, Uncle."

"It is good."

She went on, as if she needed to explain. "I have not yet learned enough about the use of the canoe. You must teach me more."

It was a deception, he suspected, to conceal her real reason for staying. He appreciated it and chuckled. "I will teach you, little one. You will tell me when you have learned enough?"

Star laughed, the strong laugh that he and Plum Leaf had come to love. "You will know! But yes, Uncle, I will tell you before I leave."

In the dim twilight, Traveler felt a tear of relief creep out of the corner of his eye and trickle down his cheek. He brushed it aside, hoping that the girl had not seen. She had told him what he desperately needed to know, even without saying so in words. She would not leave as long as Plum Leaf needed her.

He started to speak but found his throat dry and husky. He swallowed hard and spoke again, firmly. At least, he tried to sound firm, but his tight voice seemed only gruff as he spoke. "We must sleep. Tomorrow will be hard work."

He was glad for the deepening darkness, which concealed the emotion that he was sure would show on his face otherwise.

The next day, Plum Leaf seemed to enjoy the journey somewhat more. They glided smoothly, making good time. She watched the scenery and the occasional creatures along the river.

Once they rounded a curve of the river to see a doe drinking daintily at the water's edge. Star, in the prow, saw it first as the animal lifted her head to stare, her large ears spread wide. The girl pointed silently with her paddle. Traveler too stopped paddling and watched. The canoe drifted forward under its own momentum. The doe stared, completely motionless. The paddlers also were frozen in the beauty of the moment.

Then there was a movement behind the animal, and a tiny fawn tottered out into the open, then another.

"Twins!" said Plum Leaf softly. "It is good. In a year when the deer suckle two, there is food in plenty."

Traveler had thought that she was asleep, but he was glad that she had been awake to relish the scene. With her gentle and sensitive nature, she had always enjoyed such things.

"Yes," he agreed. "Maybe this is a good sign."

Plum Leaf did not answer, but her silence spoke powerfully. Traveler wished that he had not spoken of good signs. He was afraid that Plum Leaf was concealing the severity of her illness and was suffering more than she would admit. It was not good.

He saw very little that day that was good. Here they were, many sleeps from any of their own people, alone and friendless. Their closest contact, other than slight acquaintances, was the village of White Squirrel, and that was still many days' travel upriver. Plum Leaf was sick and helpless. For perhaps the first time since he was a child, he felt alone and helpless. He longed for simpler times when small hurts could be comforted by his mother, softly crooning as she rocked him in her arms.

Tears came, and he quickly brushed them away again, hoping that Pale Star did not see. Pale Star. What a strange thing, how important she had become. A short few moons ago, she had been a defiant prisoner, tied to prevent escape, and possibly dangerous. He had not doubted her ability to cut someone's throat in his sleep if necessary to make her escape.

Now, of course, she was no danger to him or Plum Leaf. She had become a daughter, and not merely a daughter, but a special daughter on whom they could rely. Pale Star was perhaps the only solid and trustworthy factor in the world that seemed to be crumbling beneath him. In this strange world of contradictions, his greatest help was this girl who had openly vowed to escape and was now held only by a temporary promise. It was a promise, however, that he knew was as reliable as the rising of Sun Boy's torch tomorrow.

26

t was perhaps ten sleeps later that it happened. In truth, Traveler had
nearly forgotten their clash with the two strangers at the village of Hunts-
in-the-Rain. His mind had been preoccupied with the ailing Plum Leaf,
who seemed no better, perhaps a little weaker.

They had stopped early because the day was hot and the work of paddling was hard. A wide stretch of sandy beach lay before them, inviting a
weary traveler to stop and rest. Star, in the prow, pointed with her paddle,
and Traveler, with little more than a grunt of agreement, turned the canoe
ashore. They were within a stone's throw when Star suddenly gave a shout
of warning and backpaddled frantically. The canoe swung from its course
and pivoted sharply, but the momentum carried it forward. He barely caught
a glimpse of the dead snag in the water as the canoe slid gently alongside with a slight scraping noise. Then it was behind them. He turned the
canoe back toward deeper water. Where there was one such limb lurking
beneath the surface there might be another. It was one of the dangers of
river travel. Some great oak, a fallen giant, might lie beneath the river's
surface for a generation or more before the shifting sands of floodtime freed
it to continue downstream. This had been a very dangerous obstacle. It
pointed its broken tip nearly downstream, like a giant spear just below the

surface, ready to pierce the belly of any canoe that chanced on it. Star had done well.

"Good, little one," he called to her.

It had been a skillful maneuver, one worthy of an experienced paddler, and she had saved them from destruction.

"Another place, ahead there," he called. "Does it look safe?"

"Maybe so, Uncle. Let us go slow."

They beached the canoe, perhaps two bow shots below their original choice. Star leaped out and pulled the prow on shore, then stepped back to help with the packs. Traveler assisted Plum Leaf to a comfortable resting place and tossed a few sticks toward the place where their fire would be.

"I go to bathe," Star announced. "I will bring more wood." She slipped into the trees and made her way back downstream.

"Be careful!" he called.

She was probably going back to that smooth sandy beach where they had nearly impaled the canoe. He smiled in appreciation of her quick thinking and skill, then turned to start the fire—a handful of dry bark from a dead cottonwood, a tiny cone of small twigs, then some sticks as thick as his finger.

He was taking out his fire-sticks, wondering whether he should learn to use the metal fire-striker . . . Maybe while at his own home village he could trade for one. The French supplied many of them for trade, he had heard. It was an object to be used with a stone of flint. Would the fire be the same, he wondered, as a fire made with the sticks? Probably, he thought. Fire is fire, is it not?

His pondering was interrupted by Pale Star's scream from downriver. "Traveler!" she yelled, her cry sharp and urgent, "load the canoe! Hurry! We must leave!"

Without a moment's hesitation, he began to throw things into the canoe. It would be foolish to do otherwise, and he must trust the girl.

"Traveler!" she screamed again. "Can you hear me?"

"Yes, yes," he called without pausing in his hurried tasks. "Come on!"

"Load the canoe! There is trouble!" came her answer.

He lifted Plum Leaf and placed her tenderly in the canoe, then turned to see Star, panting from exertion, slipping into her buckskin dress.

"Get the packs," he called.

Only two remained, and she grabbed them as she ran past. She dropped the packs into the canoe and scrambled to her position. Traveler pushed off and leaped into the stern.

Neither spoke until they were well into the current. Finally he rested his paddle. "Little sister," he asked in bewilderment, "will you tell me what is happening?"

She poured forth her story. "Those men . . . Three Owls, the one you quarreled with . . . they tried to catch me!"

That could certainly be, he thought. "Where are they?"

"I am trying to tell you! Their canoe . . . they came toward me where I was swimming . . . you know that tree? I got it between them and me—" she paused for breath, "and it speared their canoe!"

"It *did*? The log speared their canoe?" He laughed aloud.

"Yes, Uncle. But I am afraid they will repair it and come after us."

Traveler sobered. "Yes, they will. But it will take several days, and we will be traveling those days."

"What does it mean, Uncle? They left first. They should have been ahead of us."

"Yes, little one. It is not good. These men mean us harm. They have waited for us to pass and then followed us. But it is good that now we know."

"But what will we do?"

"Nothing, except watch and be prepared to protect ourselves. We will travel well, of course." He wished that he had as much confidence as he had tried to suggest. He knew that this was indeed a desperate situation.

"You know these men, Uncle?" the girl asked.

"No, but I know their tribe. They are enemies of my people."

"But that is far away!"

"Yes," he agreed, "it should not be so. Even enemies should be friends in strange country."

"I do not understand."

"Nor do I." He had thoughts that he could not share with her. *But I do understand. They hate me, but not because I am the enemy. It is because they want you, little one.* "They are very dangerous," he said. "We must take great care."

They paddled awhile, and it was Pale Star who finally broke the silence. "What will we do now, Uncle? It will soon be dark."

"Yes. I think we cannot stop now. At least, not on this side of the river."

"There will soon be a moon," Plum Leaf said. "We could travel."

Her voice sounded weak and old, and Traveler's heart was heavy. "But you are tired!"

"Yes, but afraid too," she answered. "We must move. I will be all right." She lay back and curled up in the center of the canoe like a little child.

There was little choice. The tired paddlers resumed their task while the sky darkened and stars began to appear. Nightbirds called in the darkening timber along the shore, and a coyote on a distant hill gave his eerie chuckle, answered by his mate.

It was nearly dark when the moon rose, red and full, over the trees along the far shore. They were traveling nearly northwest, and in some stretches of the stream, a long stripe of golden light would be reflected for a few moments. He heard Pale Star in the prow exclaim softly at the beauty of the scene. He wished to share it with Plum Leaf, but she seemed to be sleeping soundly.

The moonlight was a great help in their travel, and they moved on. The excitement of their escape had overcome the tiredness of their bodies. But now the quiet of the night gradually calmed their anxieties, and the dead weight of exhaustion began to affect tired muscles again. They had placed a considerable distance between them and their pursuers. Maybe when an opportunity presented, they could stop.

He looked down at Plum Leaf. A bright shaft of moonlight fell across her face. Her eyes were closed, and she was smiling. It was a calm, comfortable smile, free from worry and pain, an expression he had not seen for many days now. Tears came to his eyes, but they were tears for himself, for he was happy for her.

He continued to paddle, but now he was tired, his muscles protesting each stroke. He saw a sandbar ahead with a fringe of willows.

"We will stop there," he told Star, pointing.

The girl nodded without speaking, and the canoe turned toward the bar. Star jumped out as the prow grounded, pulled the prow farther ashore, and turned to carry some small items ashore. Traveler gathered the frail form in his arms and was just stepping to the sand when the girl returned.

"Is she all right, Uncle?" Star asked with concern.

"Yes," he murmured. His voice sounded hollow and wooden, even to himself. "She has crossed over," he explained. "She is dead."

He stood there, numbly, holding her in his arms, not knowing quite what to do. He was dimly aware that the canoe was swinging behind him in the current and that Star stepped past him to retrieve it and drag it ashore. Then she approached him again.

"I am sorry, Uncle. You knew?" Her voice was husky.

He nodded. "Yes," he said. "I have known all along."

"I too," Star almost whispered. "Here, Uncle, let me help you. Bring her here." She led the way to a level spot and spread a robe. "There. Now, put her there. We will care for her."

They built a little fire, and together they wrapped the frail remains in the robe, tying it securely.

"In the morning," said Star, "we will take her up that hill."

Traveler hardly noticed that the girl was making the decisions. He did not care. His mind was numb, his world undergoing changes that he could not fully accept.

"Would it be all right if I sing my people's Mourning Song?" Star asked.

Tears filled his eyes. "She would like that."

The clear keening wail of the Song of Mourning floated across the river, and sadness echoed from the brushy hillside behind them. Traveler knew that it was good, that Plum Leaf would understand the affection of this young woman from far away, mourning her loss.

When morning came, they carried Plum Leaf to a rocky glen on the hillside and scooped out a pocket beneath the ledge. Gently, they tucked the slight form away. They carried stones to cover the grave and then sat down for a few moments, looking at the peaceful scene.

"This looks much like the woodlands of her home, Uncle."

"Yes, I saw that too," he said.

27

They loaded the canoe and pushed off. Traveler looked downstream for any signs of pursuit while Star waited. He pointed upstream and dipped his paddle. The girl looked at him for a moment and seemed to shrug, but he did not notice. They moved out into the stream. He paddled slowly, reluctant to leave somehow. He felt incomplete, as if he had left a part of him behind in the rocky glen on the hill. It had been a long time, many winters, since he and Plum Leaf had started life together. Now he was alone.

He had not stopped to think about what he would do now or why they continued upstream. They had been going in that direction, so they continued. But he was thinking of her and the manner of her crossing over. "It is good," he said to himself.

"What?" asked Pale Star.

He must have spoken aloud without realizing it. He was embarrassed but went on to explain. "It is good, that she crossed over on the river. She loved to travel on the river. Did I tell you how good Plum Leaf was with the paddle?"

"No, Uncle. I never saw her use the canoe, you know."

"That is true."

He had forgotten that. He was so used to thinking of Plum Leaf as she had always been. And Pale Star had become so adept with the canoe, he had not had to think of it. Now it was coming back, the first time Plum Leaf had tried the canoe. She had been off balance, and the canoe had upset, throwing them both into the river. They had laughed together, laboriously emptied the swamped canoe, and tried again. They were young then, and everything they did was wonderful as long as they were together. Plum Leaf had tried hard and learned rapidly. She had become one of the best, so skilled with the handling of a canoe that it seemed she must have done it all her life. Now her supple limbs were stilled in death.

Star was speaking.

"What?" he said, returning to the present. "What did you say?"

"I said, what will we do now?"

"Oh."

"Traveler, we must plan. Where are we going? You have not told me. . . ."

He was tired and did not want to think, but he could see that the girl was irritated at his indecision. "You wish to return to your people now?"

"Of course!" she snapped, but then her face softened. "I am sorry, Uncle," she said sympathetically, "but we must plan. We cannot just keep traveling on the river. I do not know where we are going, or why. Please tell me your plans."

She was right, of course. He really had no plans, and she was forcing him to face reality. That was probably good. He was still floundering aimlessly, not knowing or really caring what his next move would be. Maybe talking with the girl about it . . .

"Of course, little one." He tried to sound more confident than he was. He had agreed to tell her his plans, but he had none. "Look," he continued, "let us stop on the sandbar ahead. We will talk."

The canoe slid gently to rest, and they disembarked, dragging it to a safer spot. Both turned to gather small sticks for a fire. No council of any importance could be held without the ritual fire, and both recognized this as an important discussion. They started the tinder, and as the flames began to embrace the larger sticks, both sat down on the sand, facing each other across the fire.

"Now," Traveler began, "what must we do?"

Astonishment showed in the face of the girl. He realized numbly that she had never seen him in such a role—tired, old, indecisive. She paused a little and seemed to gather her words carefully. "Uncle, you have been good to me, but you know that I would wish to return to my people."

He nodded, only half listening.

"Would you come with me, to the country of my people?" she went on quickly. "You have never been there. You could trade. My father would be proud to thank the man who has helped me."

Traveler had not even considered such an idea. Of course she would want to go home, but—a glimmer of interest penetrated his numb thinking. Maybe this . . . new country, trade, away from the familiar trails that he and Plum Leaf had traveled. "I am made to think that this is good," he said, still half lost in thought. "But there are many problems. It is far, and the season is passing."

"But we would go faster, traveling downstream, with the current."

"That is true. But we would have to slip past our enemies and then wonder if they followed us. Their canoe may be repaired soon."

He realized that it was still foreign to her thinking to consider the river as a trail. One could not easily take a shortcut or go around a danger. The trail led only upstream or down. But a plan was developing in his mind. Yes, it would work! "Look, little sister," he went on, "here is a plan: Let us go to my people. We can winter there and then, in the spring, travel to your country."

Star thought for a moment. "How far to your tribe?" she asked a little suspiciously.

"Nearly a moon, but closer than yours. We can get supplies, goods to trade . . . pipestone, arrowpoints, tobacco, and have better trading with your people next season."

He did not even notice that he had been using the term "we" in talking of next season's trade. If Star noticed, she said nothing about it.

"It is good!" she agreed.

"Good. Then we go."

"Tell me first, Uncle, about our journey. You said we go overland?"

"Yes. Then we come to the lakes, the Big Waters where my people live."

"You mean, *this* is not the Big Water?"

There followed a discussion confused by language differences and Pale Star's unfamiliarity with any body of water too big to see across. Ah well, she would understand when she saw the Big Water.

"But I promise you now, little one, I will take you home to your people," he concluded.

"It is good!" she cried as they rose. "How long now until we leave the river to go overland?"

"Not far . . . three, four sleeps."

They scattered the fire, tossing the larger sticks into the water. Both felt much better as they launched the canoe and moved on.

As they made camp that evening on an especially beautiful stretch of the river, Star stood for a moment in appreciation of the bright evening sky.

Traveler too watched the changing hues of red, yellow, pink, and purple, shifting, ever changing. How many sunsets he and Plum Leaf had enjoyed together! He had almost turned, just now, to call her attention to it before realizing that she was not here. He must remember to tell her—no, he could not do that, either.

"She would have loved it," he said to himself, not realizing that he had spoken aloud.

Star turned to face him. "Uncle," she said gently, "I am made to think that she still does."

They moved on upriver, and Traveler began to recover. It was not easy, and some days were worse than others, but at least he now had plans, goals, something to look forward to. Star had proved herself a capable canoeist, storyteller, and trader. Yes, they would make a good team. He looked forward to their arrival at the village of White Squirrel. There they would leave the canoe and travel eastward, overland. Squirrel was one of his best friends, and trading was always good there. Star could try her stories on a new audience, and he could bask in the pride of such a daughter.

He began to plan, to look ahead. Only a few more sleeps, and they would be at White Squirrel's. There they would trade, but first the stories. Yes, he would ask Star to tell her Creation story, with its joke, and her people's version of Bobcat's tail and the bow case. He thought of the stories he would tell, the gestures he would use for effect. This could be the best trading day ever, after the evening of stories he was planning. They would be a fine team, he and Star. He must tell Plum Leaf, but no! His pleasant thoughts dissolved again, like fog blown from the surface of the river when the wind quickens. She was gone, and he could tell her nothing.

Tears came again, as they had frequently the past days. There had been no chance for the customary three days of mourning. He and Star had pushed on to stay ahead of their pursuers. Plum Leaf would understand, he knew, but he was not sure he did. Would it hurt less, he wondered, if there had been time to spend in mourning? Would that have prevented these times of sorrow that kept striking him now? And how long would it go on?

"What is it, Uncle?" Star asked him.

"What?"

"I said, what is it? You stopped paddling."

"Oh . . . it is nothing. . . ."

He lifted the paddle and dipped it into the water. The canoe moved forward again, its course straightening. Star resumed her own stroke.

Well, someday, he thought, *someday, when the mourning is finished, it will not hurt so much, maybe. If that time ever comes.*

Until then, maybe he could spend some time in private mourning and still manage to do the necessary things, like guiding the canoe. He smiled to himself. Plum Leaf would have laughed at him, the way he was behaving.

Now what had he been thinking of before? It had made him excited and pleased, and—oh, yes, the stories, the trading. He would think about that. And then, when he was alone, he would think of her and mourn, a little at a time, until his mourning was finished.

If that time ever came.

28

↔

White Squirrel welcomed them to his village. "Come, you will stay with us!"

He looked behind them, toward the canoe moored below, its eyespots looking up the slope. "Where is Plum Leaf?"

Traveler swallowed hard. "She is dead," he said simply.

"Dead? That was a strong one, a great woman, my friend. I am sorry to hear this."

Behind him, his wives began to wail a song of mourning. Plum Leaf had been well liked here.

"Yes, it was hard to let her go," Traveler agreed. He tried hard not to show the tears that still came easily.

"Is this your new wife? asked White Squirrel, indicating Pale Star.

Traveler felt the flash of indignant anger but tried to throttle it. "No!" he snapped irritably. "This is my daughter."

"Oh," said Squirrel, pretending to understand.

Traveler was not quite certain why this reaction came so quickly. The very thought that Star could be anything but a daughter to him was offensive. He was twice her age.

There was an uncomfortable moment. Pale Star stood watching, not understanding this moment of friction between old friends. She did not know the language of this village, and no one was using hand-signs, so she had no idea what was causing the conflict. She knew it must concern her because their host and his two wives were all looking at her. However, their looks were of friendly curiosity, nothing else.

White Squirrel was caught completely off guard. He had asked a legitimate friendly question of his old friend and received a hostile answer. This was hard to grasp. In the many years he had known Traveler and Plum Leaf, he had been certain that they had no children. Yet here, after the news of the death of Plum Leaf, Traveler had introduced this remarkably beautiful young woman as his daughter. Squirrel had been ready to congratulate him for his good taste and good fortune in wives, but—well, it was no concern of theirs, whatever arrangement the two might have. Traveler had always been a strange one.

White Squirrel beckoned them inside and assisted with their packs. "My lodge is yours," he said. "You have much for trade?"

"Of course. Many things. And we have no use now for the canoe. I will trade it or leave it here until next season if you will allow."

"As you wish." White Squirrel nodded.

"We will see how the trading goes," Traveler suggested. "Maybe we will keep it . . . store it here."

There was a gasp from Star, and Traveler turned. A young woman was strolling past, wearing a bright-colored blanket of the sort used in trade by the Yen-glees. These had only begun to come in during his last trip to the area. He had considered their value for trade, but they were bulky to carry.

But Star, he realized now, would never have seen a wool blanket. He was amused at her reaction to the flaming colors, bright reds and yellows. The woman paused to speak to one of Squirrel's wives, and Star studied the fabric. "How is this?" she asked. "The paint is on the *fur* side of the robe? Not on the skin side?"

Traveler laughed and interpreted for the others. Pale Star was embarrassed at their amusement, and Traveler hastened to explain. "There is no skin side, little one. They use only the fur."

He asked the woman with the blanket to show the girl. She was pleased to do so, turning a corner over and back to demonstrate how it was made.

"*Aiee!*" exclaimed Star. "Fur on *both* sides? What sort of animal grows fur on both sides of its skin?"

He saw that the girl partially understood and was now amused at her own error. She would probably make a story of this.

"Star," he explained, "you remember some tribes who weave plant fibers into mats or cloaks? This is much the same, with the fur of animals."

"But, the colors . . ."

"Yes . . . I have been told that the animal whose fur is used is white. They color the fur before they weave it."

Star felt the soft wool of the blanket between her thumb and forefinger, relishing its luxury. "Why do you not have one, Uncle?"

"I had one, but I traded it. They are much prized."

"There are many blankets now," White Squirrel said to Traveler. "The Yen-glees like them for trade."

Traveler turned to Star. "He says there are more now. Someday we will get one for you."

"Really? What sort of people are these Yen-glees, Uncle?"

"They come from far away, across the Big Water . . . no, how can I . . ." There was the problem again—words not in the girl's culture. ". . . the Big Salty Water," he finished. "They have many things of strong medicine."

"They are hair-faced?"

Traveler remembered that Star had once mentioned a legend among her people, a story of a hair-faced outsider. The stranger had joined her people and become a prominent man. A sub-chief of some sort, it seemed. Was it not . . . yes, Star herself claimed to be a descendant of the man. This would account for her question, though he could see no connection. Star's people were much too far west.

"Some of them are," he answered. "Mostly, they cut their face hair with knives instead of plucking it."

"Medicine-knives?"

"What?"

"Medicine-knives, like the one you traded for me?"

He was constantly amazed at Pale Star's powers of observation. So long ago, when she was a prisoner, and she still remembered that trade.

"What? No, no! That was a knife for eating or skinning, even fighting. They use a special knife for face hair. It is used for nothing else."

She thought a moment. "Is the knife for cutting face hair made of the same shiny rock?"

"Iron? Yes, they make many things of iron."

"Where does it come from?"

"They dig it from the ground, I am told. How do I know, little one? You ask too many questions."

White Squirrel interrupted. "My friend, how long will you stay with us?"

Traveler shrugged. "Three, four sleeps. Until the trading is finished."

"You go to your people?"

"Yes."

"It is good! I will take a party that way soon. You can travel with us for safety."

It was not until later that the significance of that remark sank home. The stories were over for the night, and he and Star had spread their robes for sleep. They were outside, at their own fire. When the weather was good, most people slept outside.

He thought that Star was asleep. She had been magnificent in the story-telling, and had completely charmed her audience. It was good to have such a companion to help with the stories and the trading. But she must be tired now. It had been a long hard day. He was surprised, then, when she spoke.

"Uncle, what is the danger?"

"What danger?"

"White Squirrel has said we would travel with them for safety. If we must seek safety, there must be danger. From what? The Yen-glees?"

He lay quiet. How could he tell her of the strange situation, where men skin the heads of other men for a few items of trade?

"Uncle?" she asked. "Are you asleep?"

"No, no, I was thinking, little one. It is a very confusing story. We do not want to start it tonight. Now sleep! There is much trading tomorrow."

"Will many know the hand-signs?"

"Some. Not all. The stories went well. It will be the same."

She had used hand-signs, and Traveler had interpreted. But they were nearing the region where hand-signs were less frequently used. It was fortunate that Star learned languages well. But no matter, he thought. He would be with her, and in the spring they would move back west where hand-signs were commonly used.

It gave him a good feeling too, somehow, to think that Star would be going home and that he would be of assistance in her homecoming. He thought back to the first time he had seen her—a captive child, miserable but proud. It was a good thing he had done, to buy her. At the time, he had not done so as a generous act. He could not have said why he had done it.

But the presence of the girl had been a big change in their lives, his and Plum Leaf's. Star had grown to a woman, a very beautiful woman, though he still thought of her as a child. He did not know what the future held for her, did not want to think beyond a season or two when she would be helping with the trading. She was a help in many ways. He thought of the last days of Plum Leaf and realized that without Star's help—he did not know how he could have survived. The tears that came so easily welled up in his eyes again. But he thought that it was becoming easier.

He shifted his thinking back to next season's trading on the prairie. He enjoyed the open skies and far horizons of the region, the country of his stepfather's people. Star's country must be much like that. He wondered if they hunted buffalo in the same way, with lance or bow. His memory drifted back to his first buffalo hunt with Gray Otter. The thrill returned—the excitement of the chase, the thunder of hooves in pursuit through tall-grass prairie, the rush of the wind past his ears, and the smells of autumn. It would be good to be there again, to renew the sights and sounds of his youth.

And he looked forward to meeting Star's people, the holy man, Looks Far, of whom she spoke so highly. He was a relative of some sort, a wise man from whom one could learn much perhaps. Running Eagle, grandmother of Star, who had been a warrior, Star said, and was still an important person in their nation. It would be good to meet them.

Sleep was long in coming, but eventually Traveler dozed off. He slept well, better than for many nights recently. His sleep was untroubled now because his concern for Plum Leaf was behind him, and he was among friends.

He did dream, but the dreams were pleasant. He was young again, riding a fine buffalo-horse across open prairie with the wind in his ears while his beautiful young wife, Plum Leaf, watched with pride from the hilltop.

29

The trading was excellent; the renewal of acquaintances and friendships rewarding. Traveler elected to keep the canoe. It was stored on a rack of poles, and White Squirrel promised to look after it. They would need it for the trip downriver next season.

"Use it if you wish," Traveler urged. "Its spirit appreciates the contact."

"Yes, that is true. A canoe becomes lonely."

"Or, if a good trade comes along . . ."

White Squirrel laughed. "Traveler, I would not presume to enter your area of skill!"

Traveler laughed too. "It is good, my friend. Do as it seems best to you."

Squirrel nodded. "Now," he went on, "about this journey. Can you and the girl be ready?"

"When do you leave?"

"Two days. We are to meet at a council of one of our allies."

"We will be ready . . . two mornings from now?"

"Yes." White Squirrel paused, then added an apparently unconnected thought. "It has become dangerous to travel alone, or with a small party, Traveler."

Traveler shook his head. "More than the last time I saw you?"

"Oh, yes. Much worse!"

"How many men will you take?"

"Maybe ten . . ."

Traveler was startled. "That many? Fewer would be unsafe?"

"Maybe not, but . . . times change, my friend. It is not like the old days. And in strength there is safety."

Traveler was astonished, and depressed. Time was when he and Plum Leaf had traveled without fear almost anywhere. The only time he had been really afraid was the experience as a youngster, with Turtle, when he had seen the sightless eyes of the dead man staring at the sun while the skin was ripped from his head. That was bad. But that was long ago, ah, maybe twenty seasons. That too seemed impossible, but . . .

"Squirrel, is this sickness, the killing of men to skin their heads . . . is it spreading westward?"

White Squirrel thought a moment. "Yes, maybe so. The Yen-glees and the Fran-cois, you know. Each wants to go west before the other."

"But why?"

The other shrugged. "Who knows what goes on in the minds of these people? But one thing I know: If they will pay for the fur of men, other men will skin it!"

He must explain this situation to Star, Traveler knew. But it was so complicated. Where to begin? Well, there would be time. He would tell her later.

There were nine in the party besides Traveler and Star. At first, some of the other men had seemed concerned that an old man and a young woman could not keep up, carrying their heavy trade packs. It was amusing to see their increasing respect as the days of travel fell behind them. Such travel, of course, was a way of life for the Trader and his companion.

Their course was basically an eastward one, following an age-old trail that wandered along the grassland and into more heavily timbered country. The warriors of White Squirrel had become more alert and attentive after only a day or two of travel. The main body stayed closer together, with scouts in front and on the flanks.

It was enough to attract Star's attention. "What is it, Uncle? Is there danger?"

He tried to smile reassuringly. "Maybe, maybe not. But keep your bow ready."

The girl was carrying a bow that they had obtained in trade at Squirrel's village. It seemed to give her confidence, and he had learned that she had great skill with it. Among her people, she had explained, both boys and girls were taught the use of weapons in their learning process—the Rabbit Society, she called it.

"Some of our women have been great warriors," she boasted. "My grandmother, Running Eagle, killed over fifty of the enemy."

Even allowing for the usual exaggeration, Traveler thought, this grandmother of Star's must have been quite a woman. "Somehow, this does not surprise me, little one," he teased.

During a halt on the second afternoon, one of the scouts returned to report suspicious activity ahead. It might be nothing, but it would be well to remain alert.

"What is it, Traveler? I do not understand. What did the Wolf say?"

"There is sign of the enemy," he told her. "We must be ready."

The warriors around them were checking weapons, touching the knives at their waists, fitting arrows to bowstrings.

"Will there be a fight?" Star asked.

"Maybe. We must be ready. Have you killed, little one?"

"Of course!" she snapped, but then softened. "Only small game, and one deer, Uncle. Not men."

They remained alert, but nothing happened that day or the next. But there came a morning when the calm of the dawning day was shattered by a yell of alarm. Traveler leaped from his robe and looked to Star's position. The girl was already up, shuffling into her moccasins, her bow ready beside her.

Around the clearing, men were running, dodging, and there was a buzz of arrows searching through the gray light of dawn like angry hornets. An attacker charged into the clearing, heading toward Star. It was like a dream as Traveler moved to help her. One moves so slowly and ineffectively in such a dream.

The girl dropped calmly to one knee and fitted an arrow to her bowstring, but before she could loose it, the warrior fell heavily. One of White Squirrel's men stooped to retrieve his ax.

In a few heartbeats, it was over. Two of the attackers were dead, and two of Squirrel's party had been wounded. One sustained a long knife slash, the other an arrow through the fleshy part of his upper arm. There was much excitement, laughter, and the retelling of individual experiences.

The man who had retrieved his ax now drew his knife. He squatted, circled the crown of the dead man's head with one deft slash, and jerked the scalp free. There was a gasp from Pale Star.

"What is it?" he asked. "Are you all right?"

"What? Oh, yes, Uncle. And you?"

"Of course."

The girl was pointing. The bone of the dead man's skull gleamed white in the growing light. "He skinned the hair."

"Yes. He took the scalp of the man he killed."

"But why?"

"Ah yes," he said sympathetically. "Your people do not take scalps."

"Of course not. Why would we do such a thing?"

"Ah, little one, you have much to learn."

All the pent-up emotion seemed to boil to the surface, and she turned on him, furious. "How am I to learn," she yelled at him, "when you tell me nothing? And stop calling me 'little one'!"

He stared at her a moment, started to laugh, and then became serious. "You are right," he admitted. He had almost called her little one again, but caught himself. "Come, sit," he continued. "You are right. You are a grown woman, and there are things here that you need to know, for your own protection."

During the next few days, as they stopped for water, rest, or the night's camp, he attempted to explain the complicated politics of the region. She already knew of the hair-faced outsiders but had trouble understanding that there were two tribes of them.

"The Yen-glees and Fran-cois," he explained, "are enemies in their own land. They come here and are still enemies. There are not enough to kill each other well, so they ask our tribes to help."

"But why?"

"Each tribe has its own enemies. Is it not so in your country?"

"Yes, but—"

He waved her to silence again. "So, our people kill each other as they always have, but are given gifts by one side or the other, Yen-glees or Fran-cois."

"Gifts?"

"Yes . . . knives of iron, blankets, other things."

"But I still do not understand. What has that to do with this morning?"

"Oh, yes, the scalps. Well, if someone is to be rewarded for killing enemies, he must have proof, yes? The scalp is proof of a dead enemy."

He could see the revulsion in the girl's eyes. "They are rewarded by the number of scalps they bring? That is no proof. They could be anyone's hair!"

He was not surprised that a woman as intelligent as Star would see the heart of the problem immediately. "Yes," he agreed, "some sell scalps to both sides."

"Which side started this, Uncle?"

"No one knows now. People take scalps more to show their manhood now, anyway."

"Which side are your friends?"

"I would like to trade with both," Traveler said earnestly. "There is more trade that way. So I try to stay friends with both by killing neither. Sometimes it is hard."

"Which side do White Squirrel's people fight for?" she asked.

"I am not sure. Neither Fran-cois nor Yen-glees have come this far west yet. They probably have not decided."

"But, Uncle, they take scalps!"

"Yes, but that is something else, now. It does not matter which side, to many. Scalps are a thing of value, like furs, or to prove manhood. Some who take scalps here do not even know how it started."

He could see that she did not understand at all. In truth, he did not himself. How could he explain a region gone completely mad, skinning each other's heads for money or glory? Both groups of outsiders pushing west; the Fran-cois to the north, the Yen-glees on the south, each trying to push faster than the other. And *why*? No one was certain. At least, no one he had encountered knew why it was so important to push to the west. The customs of the hair-faces were very strange, and he doubted that he would ever understand their ways of thinking.

How much more confusing it must be for Pale Star. He had grown up with the knowledge of the outsiders and their strange ways, and he did not understand. What chance that this child of the prairie people could grasp the meaning of the whole confused conflict? He felt more sympathy for her than ever before. It would be good to forget the danger and horror of what this region had become. Next spring, when he and Star went west—he almost wished now that he had agreed to Star's request and tried it this autumn; the weather was holding well. No, that had not been a reasonable choice then and was not now.

They would soon reach his people and would winter there. Then, as soon as the spring began to awaken, they would travel. This region had become so threatening, so dreadful, that he could hardly wait to shake its dust from his moccasins. They would start west. There would be risks, but new sights and sounds, new tongues to learn, new stories to tell. He would do as he had promised Pale Star—return her to her people.

30

I t was good to travel in the safety of numbers, but it was a mixed blessing. The very presence of Squirrel's warriors seemed to remind them of the madness that had overtaken the land. But those same warriors had gradually become more relaxed in the ensuing days.

Star did not understand. Traveler did not, either, and was at a loss when she asked him, "Is the danger over?"

"What? How do you mean?"

"The warriors are not so watchful as they were. Is there no danger here?"

Traveler pondered a moment. He had not noticed, but now that the girl had called his attention to it, the change was apparent. Was there something different about the region where they now traveled? "I do not know, lit— Star. But it is as you say. Come, we will ask Squirrel."

The young chief was quite matter-of-fact in his answer. "Yes, we are nearer the town of the Fran-cois."

Traveler was puzzled. "And they protect . . ."

"No, my friend, not exactly." White Squirrel chuckled. "But those who scalp anyone for the value of their hair are more reluctant to do so here."

Traveler was still not certain how this worked as he tried to translate for Pale Star. "Maybe," he ventured, "those whose hearts are bad do not show their bad intent too close to those whose hearts are good."

The girl nodded. "Maybe." She seemed thoughtful and finally spoke again. "Uncle, there is a story among my people. It was a bad season for hunting, and the council decided that if the buffalo came, no one would hunt for himself, only in the planned hunt. That way, there would be more meat for all."

"What has that to do with this?"

"Let me finish, Uncle! One man went out to hunt by himself and made a kill, far from camp. He was found out when *his* family had meat and others were hungry."

"But, what—"

"I am trying to tell you! He could not have hunted near the camp because he was breaking the order of the council."

"But he was found out anyway," argued the puzzled Traveler.

"Yes," Star agreed impatiently, "or there would be no story. But he was *less* likely to be found if he was far from the camp.

"Maybe . . ." Traveler was still not quite certain what she was implying.

"Never mind, Uncle."

"No, wait, I see your thought. It is as I said. Those whose hearts are bad . . ." He turned to Squirrel. "Do the Fran-cois, or the Yen-glees, know about the trade in scalps?"

"Of course! They pay—"

"No, no. That there are some who buy and sell scalps like beaver pelts?"

"Oh. No, probably not. They suspect, maybe. But one person's hair looks much like another's when it is off the head. Some may suspect, but who is to say? A scalp could be from an enemy or from a stranger. They were killed far away, maybe. We try to prevent our young men from this."

Traveler nodded. It was much as he and Star had surmised. He turned back to the girl. "Yes," he translated, "that is it. There would be more danger to those whose hearts are bad nearer to the town of the Fran-cois."

"So, this removes the danger to us?"

"Sometimes. It is like when we were with Hunts-in-the-Rain. Enemies who are guests in another's territory do not fight. There is a truce."

Pale Star nodded, half lost in thought. He could sympathize with her confusion, for he was confused himself. And in the back of his mind was also the vague idea that even such a truce does not protect against someone who is without reason. Ah, well, each day starts anew. An unfinished thought came to mind. "What happened to him?" he asked.

"Who?"

"The man in your story. The hunter who broke the order of the council."

"Oh. They sent him away."

"Banished him? Put him out of your tribe?"

"Yes. And his family. His wife was quite angry with him. There were those who wanted to let her stay, and she could have, maybe. But she chose to go with him."

"What happened to them?"

She shrugged. "I am not sure. Maybe they joined the Head Splitters."

"Ah, I have heard of the Head Splitters. They are your enemies?"

"No. They once were, it is said. We are allies now."

"What made the change?" he asked curiously.

"A greater danger . . . an invader, from the north. It is before I was born. You have heard me speak of Looks Far, the holy man?"

Traveler nodded. "Yes. He is your kinsman?"

"That is the one . . . he helped to bring the two tribes together. He and another holy man, of the Head Splitters."

Traveler remembered vaguely having heard the story of this war and how the invasion had been stopped. Yes, Turtle's people had known of it—a buffalo stampede, created by the two holy men, by combining their medicines. Could one of these men still be alive?

"Star," he asked, "you mentioned Looks Far before . . . He is still living?"

"Of course! At least, when I was stolen, he was. You will meet him, next season, when we join my people."

Several times the party encountered travelers who were apparently friendly. They paused to visit with White Squirrel, usually in vaguely familiar tongues, sometimes with hand-signs. The conversations were about the weather, the trail, and scarcity of game. On a more cautious note, they spoke of the power struggle between the two groups of outsiders.

"Things are quiet now," one party told them. "The value of scalps is low this season. Maybe it will be better next year."

Traveler was revulsed. How could they calmly discuss the price of such a commodity as men's scalps?

Then came the evening when, as they camped, White Squirrel approached. "Tomorrow we part." Squirrel used hand-signs so that Star could understand.

Traveler nodded. "We thank you for your kindness. It has been good to be with your people, my friend."

"You are welcome in my lodge," Squirrel said, smiling. "Your canoe will be safe until you return."

"We will come in the spring."

White Squirrel then turned to Pale Star, smiling. "It is good to know you, also, little sister. Take good care of my friend Traveler."

Since their first day with Squirrel, he had not questioned, or even mentioned, the relationship between Traveler and the girl. If there was a question in his mind now, White Squirrel kept it to himself.

The next morning, where the trail divided, White Squirrel led his party on the fork that led northeast. Traveler and Star watched as the last man turned to wave and was quickly swallowed up in the forest. They lifted their packs and moved onto the other path, nearly due east.

It was a relief, actually, to be separated from the main party. They could talk more freely, could set their own pace, and had a freedom of decision that did not depend on someone else's whims. Traveler had to admit the presence of the warriors had bothered him. It served as a reminder of danger and bad times. Yes, this was better. And in a few sleeps, they would be in his home village. The excitement of homecoming was beginning to mount.

Apparently Star noticed it too. "How far to your people?" she asked during a rest stop.

He smiled. "Three, four sleeps." He felt confident, relaxed. He was going home. This was his country. He had not expected to feel like this. Maybe the day would come when he would not mourn in his heart quite so continuously. Maybe.

"You will find it good to see your people," Star suggested. "You have parents?"

"No. They are dead. A sister . . . We will stay with her."

"She has a husband and children?"

"Yes . . . you will like her family."

"Tell me more about your people."

"There is not much that you do not know. You know enough of our tongue to speak to them."

"How did you begin to travel and trade, Uncle?"

He smiled. That seemed so long ago. He lighted his pipe with a stick from the fire and settled back against a tree trunk to relax and tell his story. Star listened, attentively.

"When I was little more than a child, younger than you, Star, there came to our village a traveling trader. He was very good to me. My father had been killed, and my mother married the trader." He paused and chuckled. "He courted her with a courting flute. Do your people use the flute?"

"No, but we know of them." Star smiled. "That would be very romantic."

"Yes . . . I courted Plum Leaf with the flute. Turtle . . . my stepfather taught me."

Suddenly he realized something. He had talked of Plum Leaf with no tears. In fact, there had been pleasure in the remembering. Those glorious days with the world ahead of them . . . "It was wonderful, Star," he said simply.

She smiled, understanding. "Plum Leaf was a special woman, Traveler. She helped me, more than she knew."

"I am made to think she knew, little one," he said with a smile.

The girl smiled back, and he realized that she had not even complained at his calling her little one. And it was good.

31

It was a pleasant place, where they camped that evening. They had decided to stop early. The fine weather was holding, and there was no urgency.

After the parting with White Squirrel, the two had begun to talk. They found great pleasure in sharing this companionable activity. Perhaps it was that both were now alone and that the companionship was needed. Of course, there was the fact that Traveler, in his bereavement, was purging his grief. He had passed the initial period of mourning that had been so difficult for him. He had survived his loss. Now his stories of Plum Leaf were of the happy times. Pale Star, in the flower of young womanhood, was an avid listener to his tales of romance. She shared her memories of Plum Leaf.

"She hated me at first, Uncle," Star recalled.

Traveler laughed. "She was angry at *me* because of you!" he admitted.

"How can this be?" the girl asked in wonder.

"Well, I . . . Plum Leaf thought I had made a bad trade. My best metal knife . . . my *only* metal knife! It *was* a bad trade."

"*Aiee!* That does not speak well of me! Am I no use to you?"

Both were teasing, and both knew it. Then Traveler became serious. "I do not know why I bought you. I felt sorrow for you, but for the others too. It was meant to be, maybe." There was a slightly uncomfortable moment, and he continued. "Some have thought that I wanted you for a wife."

"I know . . ."

Now he was embarrassed. "That was not in my thinking, Star."

"I know. You would not have kept calling me little one."

He smiled ruefully. "I thought at first that was the reason for Plum Leaf's anger. She thought I wanted you."

"Oh," Star said thoughtfully. "I did not think that."

"I came to think not," Traveler went on. "I never spoke of it with her. Very soon, she came to think of you as a daughter . . . as I did."

"Tell me of your daughter, Traveler. You have mentioned her. . . . She is dead?"

"Born dead," he said sadly. "Her spirit was unable to enter her body. A beautiful child. We were never able to conceive, after that. It was not meant to be." He paused and chuckled. "Plum Leaf once asked if I wanted another wife, to have children."

"She did?"

"Yes . . . I did not want another. Any child would not have been hers . . . Plum Leaf's and mine."

"Then if she once offered to take another woman, Traveler, that was *not* why she disliked me at first."

He nodded, smiling. "I thought of that. No, Plum Leaf just saw it as a bad trade. But she came to love you, Star."

Now it was time for Star's eyes to fill with tears. "Yes, I know. And she was like a mother to me. Traveler, I will be pleased for you to meet my parents. We will be your family."

Traveler smiled. "The trail is my family, Star. I have friends everywhere. But *you* are my daughter."

"It is good," she signed, as if to avoid speaking. She rose to add some sticks to the fire.

They would have to gather more before dark, Traveler thought. This was a place he had camped before, a pretty glade with a good spring. It was one of those campsites that had been used for many generations because of availability of water and the favorable lay of the land. This generation favored the spot for the same reasons the previous generation had, and the ones before that and before, all the way back to Creation, maybe.

There was, however, one major disadvantage. Frequent visitors meant frequent fires. Blackened spots and unburned fragments of charcoal could be seen all over the clearing. They too might go all the way back to Creation, at least back to the time the red fox stole fire from Sun Boy and gave it to Man. But fires need wood. In such a campsite, all dead wood is quickly gathered by travelers and used for their fires. This makes it necessary to search farther from camp for enough fuel to last the night.

"I will get some wood," he said, rising to his feet.

"It is good. Be careful."

An odd remark, he thought. But maybe not. He knew that Star was still concerned about the scalping and unrest, though they had seen no other travelers since leaving White Squirrel.

He was also aware that Pale Star disliked the woodlands intensely. A child of the prairie, she always spoke of a trapped feeling when she could not see very far. He could understand that. There was a feeling to the wide horizons of the prairie that was awe-inspiring. One could see the smoke of a campfire a day's travel away. There was such a feeling of bigness, of sky and earth. It made a person feel big yet at the same time small, tiny even, as part of the prairie. He had spent enough time there to understand what Star meant when she talked of a need to "stretch her eyes."

He found a dead cottonwood and was busily breaking limbs from it, tossing the sticks in a pile. Maybe he would come back for another load. It was a giant of a tree, its base rooted far below the rim of the bluff on which he stood, overlooking the river. Below its top was a tangle of smaller trees and brush. The uppermost branches of the dying giant projected conveniently for him to break from his position above. It was odd that other travelers had not yet discovered this source of fuel. But it appeared to have been dead for only a season and was some distance from the campsite. He had had difficulty finding any dry sticks nearer at hand.

As he turned to toss a stick aside, he caught a glimpse of motion and turned quickly. A man stood among the trees, watching him, only a few steps away. There was something familiar about the heavyset bearlike figure. That was it—bear . . . *Winter Bear,* companion of the irrational Three Owls. This could not lead to any good. Traveler tossed his sticks aside and stood to face the danger. He glanced quickly around for the man's companion but did not see him.

Winter Bear smiled thinly, but with his mouth only, not with his eyes. It was not a friendly smile but a cruel one, a leering mockery that saw humor in this situation, desperate for his opponent.

Traveler licked his dry lips, realizing just how hopeless his predicament was. He was virtually unarmed, only the small knife at his waist. He was confronted by a much younger man, perhaps half his age, twice his size. Horrified, he watched the big man reach methodically for the ax at his waist. There was nowhere to run with the cliff behind him.

Then, as he drew his knife for a last effort at defense, an even more horrible thought occurred to him. Three Owls was not here, but he must be somewhere nearby. Pale Star was alone at the fire . . . "Star!" he shouted at the top of his lungs.

His voice was drowned in the bearlike roar of his assailant as he rushed. Traveler dodged aside, still more agile than the heavyset Bear. He hoped for an instant that the rush would carry the big man over the edge, but it did not.

There was a halfhearted swing of the ax, but it missed, and Traveler circled warily. He longed to run, but it was several steps to the trees, and he dared not turn his back. He had seen men use the small throwing axes, and the way this one held his ax, high and balanced. . .

Traveler backed away, ready to dodge a blow. He circled back toward the edge. Maybe that was worth another try if he could entice Bear into another rush.

But stupid though he might appear, there was a certain cunning in the big man. He smiled the cruel smile again, and readied his ax. It seemed to move slowly, so slowly—back over Winter Bear's shoulder, and then forward . . .

Traveler watched the weapon, the handle rotating around the heavier blade. One revolution, two . . .

He was starting to turn when the blow struck. Then everything accelerated to a frantic rush, and in only a couple of heartbeats, it was over. It was a slanting blow because his head was turning, and it struck just above his right eye with a sickening thud. But Traveler did not hear. By pure reflex, his right hand jerked upward, wrenching the ax free.

Then the pain struck—searing, blinding pain, causing him to cover his face with both hands while blood gushed into his eyes. He staggered backward, off balance, toppling over the edge, consciousness fading fast.

Long before his limp form struck the rocks below, Traveler's world had plunged into complete blackness.

Winter Bear lumbered to the edge and peered over at the crumpled body below. He grunted, stooped to pick up his ax, and wiped it clean on the grass before tucking it back in the thong around his waist. He looked over the edge again and seemed to think a little while. Then he turned away with another bearish grunt of disgust. The scalp below was not worth the tough climb to the river and back.

Besides, he wanted to see how his cousin was doing with the girl. Maybe Three Owls would share his good fortune. Winter Bear moved toward the campsite by the spring at a lumbering trot.

PART III

THE WATCHER

32

The old woman shuffled along the narrow path at the edge of the water, carrying her fish. It was a good fish, one that would last her for several days. Or maybe she could dry some of it for the coming winter. She had few supplies. Maybe she could kill a deer before Cold Maker swooped in from the north. It was hard, the life she had. Sometimes she wondered how she had managed to live all these winters. How many now? She had lost track. No matter, it was too many.

More to the point, *why* had she struggled to survive? Many times she had been near death. She had been condemned to death once, by her own people. It had been in her foolish youth, and her actions had indeed been stupid. She had had a good husband, her own lodge, but no children yet— the whole world before her, and she had thrown it away. A young man from the neighboring tribe, one of their allies, had encountered her at the stream as she bathed. Her husband was gone on a hunt, and the man was friendly. Strange, she had forgotten his name now. He had stayed near the camp of her people, and the romance developed quickly.

Short Horse had returned to find his wife in the robes with a stranger. The man was blameless. She had not told him she was married. Her husband could have killed her outright but instead took her before the council.

Judgment was swift. As she had thrown away her marriage, so she was to be thrown away—"left on the prairie." It was a death sentence, to be carried out by the Warrior Society. Very seldom used, it had been a generation since such a sentence was pronounced. There was no harsher punishment for a woman of the northern plains, and it was usually reserved for such crimes as treason against her people. Or infidelity.

She remembered little of that day. She had been taken on foot some distance into the prairie, accompanied by about thirty men of the Warrior Society. She remembered the first six or eight who assaulted her before it became painful. Then the whole sequence became a tortured memory, half forgotten in the agony. Sometime after a dozen, fifteen, or twenty had performed the rape, she had lost consciousness, and perhaps that saved her.

She awoke. It was night, a full moon shining. She was alone. She had been wakened by a pair of coyotes, apparently attracted by the scent of blood. Her feeble movements frightened the animals away.

Surely she was dead. She had never heard of one who had survived the throwing-away ceremony. But if she was dead, why did it hurt so much? It was the next day before she was able to drag herself to the stream to drink, another two before she could half crawl back to the camp.

It was deserted. The band had moved on. Of course—They would have moved away from the site of the throwing away, the area taboo now. With something like panic, she had realized that she too would be taboo. No man would lie with her, for in the way of her people, she was dead. She could not marry. No one would help her.

She had stayed there for several days, scavenging the refuse left behind. If she was to survive, it must be on her own. Her pitiful plunder was not much—a worn-out robe, a pair of discarded moccasins. She had lost her own footwear. She covered the holes in these moccasins with scrap leather from another cast-off garment. Her most important find was a knife, a real prize. It was not a discard, but an implement someone had lost. Slender, sharp, a fine gray-blue stone blade. She still had it, after all these years.

Her most urgent need had been for food. She found some sand plums and was fortunate enough to kill a rabbit with a throwing stick but was soon hungry again. She found her way to a village of Growers who had traded with her people. They had heard. They were amazed that she was alive and seemed afraid of her. Out of kindness, they gave her a pouch of corn and a few strips of dried meat. It was plain, however, that she was unwelcome. They considered her dead.

Somehow, she had survived that first winter, living in a tiny cave in a cutbank of shale and clay. She had grown thin, near the edge of starvation, but each time she was about to give up, something would prevent her demise. Once an aging buffalo bull was pulled down by wolves within sight of her cave. After they had gorged themselves on the carcass, she approached boldly, drove the animals off with a club, and quickly stripped as much meat as she could carry. That supply, dried and hoarded carefully, lasted her a long time.

Another time, she startled a hawk as it made a rabbit kill. The bird attempted to lift its still-warm prey as it rose to avoid the rush of the half-starved woman. At the last moment, the hawk released its burden to facilitate its own escape. It circled above, screaming in indignation while she rushed forward to pick up her prize.

By that first springtime, however, she had become so filled with self-pity that she wanted to die. In the Moon of Greening she sought out one of the other clans of her people. Not her own—she did not wish to see them, ever again. She demanded of the band chief that she be allowed to die.

"I am already dead," she had told him. "Someone must kill me, so that my spirit may cross over."

The matter was discussed that evening by the council. Her story was already known throughout the tribe. But she found no comfort in their decision.

"Since you are already dead," the band chief announced solemnly, "we cannot help you."

They gave her a little food but made it plain that she could not stay. Furious, she left the camp.

After that, years of wandering. When she found herself far enough from her tribe's region, the people she encountered were not aware of her sordid past. Still she was received strangely. It was many years before she realized why. She was a trifle mad. Her disheveled appearance, her garments a mixture of castoffs from all the tribes she had encountered, her actions a trifle irrational, originally from hunger, then from habit.

The madness itself had become some degree of protection. Any tribe, anywhere, is reluctant to kill a person afflicted with madness. The release of a deranged spirit might be dangerous to anyone in the immediate area.

She had not realized this. She wandered from one people to another, unwelcome anywhere. But she began to notice their ways and to adopt the use of new food plants by watching local customs. She stole from crop-fields of the Growers and collected scraps and leavings after the hunters. When she found herself in the area where men trapped beaver for their pelts, she followed the trappers, salvaging the discarded carcasses for food.

Gradually she migrated to the east. In that area, she had learned that men skinned the hair of other men for its value. She still wanted to die— occasionally, anyway, though less often through the years. Her scalp would have had some value at that time, though it was old and ratty now. But an impossible dilemma had developed. If she requested that anyone honor her wish for death, that in itself was proof of her madness. She had become known as mad and thus protected from scalphunters by their fear for their own safety. A spirit this deranged? Ah, it should not be released!

Her hate for all humans had grown through the years while her pattern of living had stabilized, that of a recluse. She had found a cave near the foot of this bluff overlooking the stream. It was sheltered, had access to water, and was near enough to the trails of trade that she could take advantage of any chance she might have. Travelers on the trail seldom noticed her cave because its entrance was hidden, and the river was too small and meandering at this point to support canoe travel.

She fished in summer. She had learned the technique, and how to make the barbed hook of thorns, from a tribe she stayed with for a while. In winter, she followed the beaver trappers. At any time, she might scavenge after travelers on the trail above who camped for the night at the spring. She had occasionally stolen small items—not too often because she did not wish to attract attention.

She had given up the idea of dying now. There had been many chances, and she was still alive, for what purpose she had no idea, but she had come to accept that her time had not come.

She had fished all night at the deep hole where the river swirled under an overhanging willow. It was an ideal spot, productive from season to season. This night, however, there had been no action until near dawn. Then she had felt the tug on the line, tied loosely around her wrist in case she fell asleep. She knew it was large by the way it had struggled, but she managed to keep her rawhide line taut and draw the fish to shore.

It was good. She whacked the creature's head a time or two with the club she always carried and sat down to catch her breath after the struggle. There was a great sense of satisfaction. She watched the yellow light of the false dawn brighten into sunrise and finally rose to make her way back to the cave.

She stopped to rest occasionally because the fish was heavy. The stick that she had inserted through the gills to carry it was slippery, and her grasp grew tired. But now, as the sun was rising, she neared her cave. But something did not look right ahead, something lying in front of the opening. Could there have been an intruder?

The old woman hurried forward, still clutching her fish. There, lying practically in the doorway of her lodge, lay a crumpled body. There was a pool of blood under the head, and a gaping wound above the right eye, splinters of bone showing white against the black of dried blood. She cursed under her breath. Someone had killed a traveler for his scalp on the trail above and tossed the body over the edge. It had happened before but not right in her doorway. Well, she could dump it in the river, let it float downstream so that it would not attract flies.

First, however, she would salvage anything of value. She removed the moccasins and shirt, and considered the leggings . . . no, she could not use them. Then she noticed a thing that was puzzling. The man had not been scalped! A sense of alarm ran through her mind. Why not? There was something odd here. She looked the body over again very carefully. There was no other wound, only the ax cleft above the eye. A single blow. If the enemy had struck him once, knocking him over the edge—ah, that was it! The scalp was not worth the climb. Or perhaps the killer was frightened away by the man's companions. No matter . . . there was no use wasting a good scalp.

She drew her gray flint knife and grasped the man's hair. A single slash, and she gasped in surprise. The knife wound was bleeding! He must still be alive! She looked again in the brightening daylight. Yes, it was true. Not the dark sluggish blood of a corpse, but bright red blood, the fluid of *life*.

She thought about it for a little while. It would be simple enough to wait until life ceased, but inconvenient. She would have to step over the bloody form, maybe for most of a day. It would be easy to cut the throat and have it done. Or, go ahead and remove the scalp now. The man had not moved when she made her first slash. He was as good as dead anyway. She lifted the knife, but paused, and the situation struck her as humorous. Here was one person, already dead, preparing to scalp another already dead, but both still lived.

She threw back her head and laughed long and loud. Well, no matter, she decided. She could watch him for a while until he crossed over. She had nothing better to do.

33

Without understanding why she did so, the old woman straightened the broken limbs and prepared the body as if for the burial scaffold. She really had no intention of carrying out the ceremony. As soon as he was dead, she would take the scalp and roll the corpse into the river, and that would be the end of it.

It did bother her, though, the way the flies were gathering as they became active with the warming of the day. The wound that her knife had made had now stopped oozing, and she thought maybe—but no, there was a pulse. It was weak and thready, but she could feel it, there in his neck. She shooed the flies from his wounds and from the clotted blood in his eyes. Finally she covered the head with a scrap of blanket to keep the flies off and, she finally admitted to herself, because she did not like to look at his face.

She studied his unconscious form as he lay there. He was a man of middle age, she judged, lean and wiry. His garments were a mixture. The breechclout and leggings were of the plains, the shirt of the woodlands. His moccasins, which she had already removed, were hard-soled with rawhide, much like those of her own people. This was completely different from the soft puckered-toe style that was almost universal here.

His hairstyle—it was hard to tell, it was so filled with dried blood. The head was not shaved, however, and there was no elaborate plaiting, merely a simple braid on either side. There may have been a headband or a cap, now lost. It was no matter now.

She cleaned her fish, filleted it in strips, and built a small fire just under the overhang of the bluff to start the smoke-drying process. She tossed the entrails into the stream and paused to watch a few moments. It was important to see what sort of scavengers came to the feeding. She had been baiting this section of the stream for years, and it had been very productive at times.

She returned to the fire, ate a chunk of fish, and checked the pulse of the dying man again. No, still alive. She shrugged, mumbling to herself. Was this inconvenience worth the price of the scalp? Maybe she should just forget the scalp and roll him into the river. He would never know. No one would ever know, or care. Well, she would wait a little longer.

By midday, the sky was becoming overcast. A gray cloudbank moved in from the west. She had been here long enough to know what sort of change to expect. Not a hard rain, probably, at this time of year, but a cold drizzle. And colder tonight. She moved up and down the path for a while, bringing a store of firewood that she piled just inside the cave.

The still form in front of the entrance showed no sign of life, and she felt the neck again. No, still pulsing. She could just tighten her fingers there for a little while . . . no, it was better to wait.

The first tiny drops of rain began to spatter down, spotting the gray of the rocks to a mottled appearance for a few moments. Then everything became wet and shiny as the rain increased. She retreated inside. Through the door of the cave she could see droplets of rain dancing on the naked chest of the man outside or plopping soddenly on the scrap of blanket over his face. There was a chill in the air now. That would probably push his spirit on over, she thought.

Then, for the first time in years, a spark of something glowed for a moment amid the bitterness of her life. No one, she thought, should cross over this way, in a cold rain with no one to care. There had been a time in her life when she was virtually dying, and there had been no one. What if someone, anyone, had been there to comfort her, to show concern? Would it have changed her life? She wiped a tear from her leathery old cheek, the first time in years she had felt any self-pity. For a while she sat and watched the rain patter on the still form outside.

Finally she rose, cursing to herself, and shuffled out into the drizzle. It would do no harm to drag him inside. Let him die there, in shelter and relative comfort, and with a companion. She could drag the corpse back out later, after he crossed over.

He was heavier than he looked. She took his feet under her arms and backed toward the entrance. When she got the body moving, it was easier, sliding it on the muddy path. She pulled him inside and stopped, panting a little from the exertion. Then she rolled him over to spread a blanket, rolling him back onto it. Well, nothing now but to wait. She cursed to herself at the inconvenience. She often cursed to herself, a long-standing habit.

She smoked her pipe, using only a little tobacco, for her supply was scant. She had extended it some with shavings of red willow twigs toasted brown over the fire. She needed to find more. This man had none on his person, but maybe in his possessions. No, his killer would have plundered the possessions of the victim. Well, she would go up, after the rain stopped. Maybe something would be left. But not in the rain.

She drew the blanket around her against the chill. If the dying man were awake, she noted, he too would be cold. That thought bothered her. She sat there, finally cursed again, and threw a tattered scrap of an old robe over him.

Through the afternoon she sat there, rising to tend her fire or turn the fillets of fish occasionally. The unconscious man in the cave remained unchanged, but when she felt his throat toward evening, the pulse seemed stronger. She cursed again. Surely, he could not last much longer—the ax wound, the splintered bone. . . .

It was nearing dark, and the cold drizzle was falling steadily when she was startled by a groan. She turned quickly. The man's left hand was twitching convulsively. As she watched, the odd jerking motion spread, involving the arm, the leg, the entire left side of the body. It was severe; the pull of the muscles was enough to distort the left leg above the knee where it had appeared to be broken. The whole effect was frightening, and she watched, fascinated, holding her breath while the jerking movements continued. Then they became quieter and subsided.

The old woman exhaled audibly. She realized that she had been holding her breath through the entire episode. What did it mean? There was something more here than she had thought at first, and she was a little frightened. This man must have a powerful spirit, a spirit of a different kind. For a moment, she thought that it might have been better to roll him off the path into the river as she had thought at first. Then she recoiled from the thought. No, she must not think this way. Maybe the frightening demonstration she had just witnessed was a threat, a reminder, maybe, that the spirit lived and had no intention of crossing over. She might even be considered responsible for his well-being. Maybe this was some sort of holy man whose medicine was so powerful that he could not be killed, even by the blow of an ax to the head.

It was an awesome responsibility that had been thrust on her. Had she known, perhaps she might have evaded it, but it was too late now. The man was here, in her cave. If she thrust him back out, his spirit might seek revenge when he died. Of course, if he died *in* the cave, the bizarre spirit that had caused the convulsion would be released *right here,* with her.

She could see only one course of action open to her now. It was too late to avoid whatever consequences there might be. She must give this man the best care possible to gain favor with his spirit when, and if, it crossed over.

She was beginning to doubt that now. What strange and powerful medicine had kept the man alive this long?

Darkness was falling. She built up the little fire for light and rummaged in the cave for anything that might be of help. First, his head. Very gently, she removed the rag that she had thrown over his face so that she would not have to watch him. She laid it aside, brought water, and cleaned the clotted blood away. The head wound itself she did not touch. Not yet.

In the back of the cave was an assortment of small packets, things she had saved—herbs, seeds, plant medicines. She had been in contact with many tribes and had learned from them all. She assembled her various items and began her tasks.

One plant she burned in a little pile beside the fire. Its ashes were scraped together and carefully placed in a bowl. Meanwhile, she ground the dried leaves from another packet with some dark dried berrylike fruit from yet another. A root from still another, pounded and ground—she could not remember exactly the source or uses of some of these things. There was surely a song or chant connected with the use of each, but most of these she did not know or had forgotten. She formulated her own song as she formulated the salve in her bowl, mixing the medicinal powders with carefully hoarded buffalo fat from a gourd.

"Oh, Unknown Spirits," she sang, "look with kindness on these efforts; let this holy man be cleansed and helped. . . ."

Very gently, she spread the salve over the edges of the wound. A splinter or two of bone she picked out as she did so, consigning these to the fire. "Let no bad spirits enter this door," she sang, "the door of this man's life, or even the door of this lodge."

She finished covering the open wound with her salve and brought out a scrap of white linen. It had once been part of a French soldier's shirt and was one of her prized possessions. It now became a bandage.

"I close this door," she announced in song, covering the wound. "The holy man's spirit will not come out through this cleft, nor will evil enter in. . . ."

She finished her task and sank back, exhausted. She was tired, from the physical effort of the grinding and pounding but also from the tremendous energy required of the spirit. It seemed as if she had been wrestling with spirits all night.

For a little while she slept, then woke to replenish the fire. The unconscious man seemed unchanged as she felt his pulse and laid her hand on his cheek, looking for fever. He was warm but not hot. There was only a little bright red blood on her bandage, and that was good—clean blood from where she had started to lift his scalp. Ah, how stupid that had been!

He groaned, and she remembered the broken leg. She should fix that. She split the legging to remove it and carefully felt the thigh. Fortunately, there was no protrusion of bone through the skin. The limb was relatively straight, but she remembered its sharp angulation before she had rearranged him. Then she had dragged him by the legs. Well, it appeared in a good enough position, but she would need splints. And it was dark and raining outside. The splints would have to wait until morning.

She settled down with her back against the cave's wall, drawing her blanket around her against the chill. "I will take care of you," she said to the quiet form.

Outside, the drizzle fell steadily.

34

When daylight came, the woman tried to evaluate how the wounded man looked. There was not much change. His pulse was steady, his color still pale, but he was deeply unresponsive. At least, he did look better with the bandage covering his gaping head wound.

Twice during the night he had convulsed again. Each time, it had started with that writhing, grasping tremor in his left hand. It had been frightening to watch. At least, she told herself, these had been no worse than the first.

The storm had passed, and she stepped outside to greet the sun. The world, still sodden from the drizzling rain, now dripped from every rock, bush, and tree. There was the smell of warm leaf-mold, the earthy smell that was unfamiliar to her people of the prairie.

She chopped three splints for the broken leg, laid them inside the cave, and took a large bottle-gourd to bring water. The river itself appeared roiled and muddy, but she knew a place. Some fifty steps upstream, a wet-weather spring trickled clean clear water from the shale of the bluff. It flowed across a rocky shelf that formed that portion of her path and fell gently to the river an arm's length below. She held the gourd under the trickle at the point where it emerged from the bluff, waiting until it was full. She drank, sucking noisily, directly from the same trickle, then made her way back to the cave.

The woman had created a problem for herself. She had elected to take care of the unconscious man but was not certain how to do it. Well, she could at least splint the leg. While she cut strips of buckskin from his leggings and padding from the scraps of an old robe, she thought about it. She estimated that he had been wounded just before dark the night before last, the night she was fishing. Then it would be two days ago tonight, two days since he had eaten, probably. That was no problem yet. It was possible to fast for many days. But not without water. Three or four days, at most, was as much as one could live without water. His lips already looked dry, his cheeks hollow. She wet the tips of her fingers from the water-gourd, and gently moistened his lips. There was no response. She tried another dip of water. Maybe she could spoon a little water into his mouth. She would try that later, if she found courage. She must be certain that he could swallow. If not, the water would run down the wrong tube, and she could drown him with a single mouthful.

She turned her attention to the leg, which still seemed relatively straight despite the seizures. The pad that she had made from the buffalo robe fit nicely around the thigh, tied loosely with thongs. She propped the foot upright with a couple of large stones; the toe continually wanted to sag and point outward. She could hear and feel the grating of the broken bone, and the man moaned softly. It was good that he was unconscious, she thought.

When she had the foot adjusted appropriately, the splints were positioned. One with a fork, a broad open fork, was placed in his groin, well padded and tied at several places, ending below the knee. The other splints completed the procedure. There. She was proud of the result. It should hold the leg until healing began. It would be a long time, she knew, before that leg would bear any weight, however.

"But you cannot use it now, while you sleep, anyway," she told the still form. "Now we have to try some water."

She talked cheerfully, as if he could hear her. It was not for him but for herself. She dreaded this next step. If he had no way to cough, how could she tell if he was drowning? Just a little at first. She must be sure that he was swallowing the water, not letting it trickle into his lungs. Her hand trembled as she poured a bit of water from the gourd into the horn spoon. Very carefully, she brought the spoon close to his lips. Her shaking hand spilled a little, and she cursed softly to herself as she paused to steady her hand. Only a little at first. The water trickled between his lips and across his teeth to disappear somewhere. He showed no reaction.

She had a moment of panic. Was he drowning? She could see no motions of breathing. What could she do? "Come on, *breathe*!" she muttered irritably. "Swallow!"

Desperately, she massaged his throat, then paused and waited. There was no reaction, no sign of life. But wait—though she could see no deep breathing, his color was still good, well, *fairly* good. She realized that the previous day his breathing had often not been perceptible for a time. She watched his chest. *Yes!* He was breathing! She wondered, then—the water? Her ear to his chest, she listened, and there was no gurgling sound. Just then, came the best sign of all. The lump on the front of his neck, that curious hard knot that men have but women do not *moved.* Slowly and deliberately, it bobbed upward toward his jawbone, then downward.

The old woman gave a little squeal of joy. "You swallowed!" She chortled. "It is good! Let us try another sip. . . ."

This time, her hand was steadier, and she did not spill quite so much. Even better, the swallowing sequence seemed to come more easily. She found that if she lifted his head and shoulders, it seemed to help the swallowing. In this way, she managed to feed him several spoonfuls of water.

"There!" she declared triumphantly. "We will try again, later. It is good!"

It seemed not to matter to her that it had taken most of the day to fix the leg and experiment with the water. There was a thrill of accomplishment, a pride and a spark of interest that she had not had for a long time. *Aiee,* she had forgotten to eat! She laughed at herself, and ate a few bites of her fish.

"Now," she told the silent form, as if he could hear, "if you can take water, you can take soup. I will make some!"

She still liked to boil soup in a cooking pit, after the custom of her people. The pit was already there, just outside the cave's entrance. She kindled the fire, placed several of her cooking stones to heat, and turned to prepare the pit. Some of her precious supply of dried meat went into the skin-lined pit with some chunks of the half-smoked fish, dried beans, water from the gourd, and a tiny lump of buffalo fat. She would add some fresh onions maybe, later, but they grew some distance downstream. She lifted the heated stones with her willow tongs and began to drop them into the cooking pit.

"There!" she said finally. "We will let it stew for a while."

She looked at the unresponsive form in the cave and smiled. She did not smile often. She did not talk often, either, beyond mumbling to herself. Sometimes she even answered. But there was seldom anyone to talk to, really talk. Her usual habit was a mumbling word or two combined with idle thoughts. This was new, rather enjoyable, to have an uncomplaining listener.

She did not know how much he could hear. It was much like the time she had found a fledgling crow that had fallen from the nest, except of course that it had squawked, pecked her fingers, and eaten ravenously. She had originally intended to eat the bird after it grew a little. But she had come to enjoy its company and had kept it. It would ride on her shoulder and was a great amusement to her. Then, one day, it flew away with some other crows and never returned. One thing about this man—he would not leave, for he *could* not, at least not for a long while.

Now she found herself talking to him, and it was good to think that maybe he could hear a part of it. "I do not know who you are, traveler," she told the quiet form, "or why you traveled this trail. How are you called?" She paused as if she expected an answer, but then continued. "Well, since I have no name for you, I will call you the Traveler. What is your tongue, Traveler? You are not likely to understand mine, but I do not know if you understand anything anyway. But we will talk."

She was only dimly aware that she was saying "we" as she spoke to him. He was rapidly becoming a part of her life, though he had done virtually nothing to reciprocate beyond a moan or two. But he was alive, at least so far. Through all the years, there had never been another person who had consented to be with her like this.

The days passed, and she fell into a pattern of daily activity. She cooked, fed him the broth, ate the solids herself, gave him water, and cleaned him when his bladder leaked. His bowel, of course, was empty since he had taken no solid food.

She talked to him often, almost continuously now. "This is a fine day, Traveler, is it not? The good weather holds. I have brought us onions today. You should enjoy these. Here, have some soup. Come on, swallow."

"It looks stormy today, Traveler. Do not worry. I have kept warm for many winters. I will take care of us."

"I have to leave you a little while now. I have to hunt. A rabbit maybe? We need a deer before Cold Maker comes. I will take the bow."

The woman was hoarse at first from the unaccustomed talking, but that soon subsided. She still knew nothing about the unconscious man. She had climbed to the top of the bluff during his first few days with her, trying to learn something about him. There was a trail up the face of the rock, which she hated to use. It was a difficult climb, but she felt a driving curiosity about this man that drove her to investigate.

Her effort brought little reward. The rain had washed away most of the sign. At the top, where the big dead cottonwood outside her cave overhung the rim, someone had been breaking away branches. Strangely, he had not carried the fuel away. *Ah,* she thought, *it was probably my traveler.* Yes, there was a pile of sticks, ready to carry, but he had been interrupted by the attacker with the ax. She could find no tracks, but then the rain would have destroyed them.

She tossed the pile of firewood over the edge to the path below. She seldom wasted anything. Then she made her way very cautiously to the campsite by the spring. The last part of the distance she covered very quietly, peering around the trees as she advanced. She did not know why she needed to use caution, but after all, someone had had cause to murder here, and quite recently.

The glade was abandoned. She poked around but found very little. There was sign that two or three people might have camped here recently, probably on the night that the stranger was struck down. They had departed before the rain, however. No one had used the trail since.

"Well, Traveler," she said aloud, "I have found nothing. You will have to tell me when you wake up."

But that had been many days ago. There were times now when she wondered if he would ever change. What would happen if he never wakened but still lived?

There had been a time in her life when it would have been easy for her to avoid this responsibility. She would simply have rolled him into the river. Her hate for the world and everything in it, especially humans, would have driven her to it. But the past days had changed her. True, the days were alike, following one after another like beads on a string. But she had a certain purpose to her existance now. Since her throwing away, no one had depended on her for anything—no one or no thing, except the crow, ungrateful wretch that he was.

"Ah, Traveler, will you leave me when you are able?" she asked him. "Will you be like the crow?"

It was not a serious question, she was only talking. But she could not remember anything that had given her more pleasure than simply being needed. Without her, the man would die. Therefore, she was responsible for his life. It felt good when she half lifted him to feed him, cradling him against her as she crooned words of comfort. Somehow, she felt that he knew, though his only response so far was to swallow, moan occasionally, and wet himself. She moved his limbs, except for the broken leg, feeling that he might begin such movement on his own if she initiated it. Her maternal instincts were awakening after sleeping a long time. She had never had a child, and this helpless creature was filling the empty spot in her heart. She would rock him gently in her arms after feeding him, crooning fragments of a half-forgotten lullaby from her childhood.

It was after one of those episodes that she saw the first signs that he might really hear some of what she said. She had fed him as usual, talked of the weather as she did so, and then held him cradled in her arms, rocking him gently while she sang. Finally she eased him back onto the pallet, gently arranging his limbs into what appeared to be a comfortable position.

"You stay here," she instructed, though it was plain he could not do otherwise. "I will be back soon."

She was halfway out the door of the cave when she heard a rattling sound in his throat. She turned anxiously. Could he be choking? She knelt at his side, watching his blank facial expression change to a frown. The eyes remained closed, but the lips quivered and finally parted. Fascinated, she watched, holding her breath.

"M-m . . . Mama!" he whispered.

Then he sank back, exhausted from the effort.

35

He drifted in and out of consciousness in a dreamlike state. At first as his senses returned, he was aware of nothing but the blinding pain in his head. There was no sense of time, place, or identity. Gradually, he realized that it was sometimes dark but sometimes light. He would awaken, though not completely, realize that it was dark, then waken again to find it light. There was no sense of time, but a dreamy drift that had no beginning or end.

He could not see. The light and the dark were as much as he could distinguish. It hurt to try to see, and he would close his eyes again.

There was another person . . . yes, his mother. She was not always there, for sometimes he would rouse and find himself alone. He would feel a moment of panic, then drift off again, exhausted. But she always came back. The panic that he had felt at first eventually gave way to sadness, loneliness. He did not like to waken without his mother. No child should have to do that. When *he* was grown, with a child to care for . . . he drifted off again.

It was good when his mother cradled him in her arms and spooned soup into his mouth. He felt warm and protected. Sometimes he felt that he was about to choke, and she would gently rub his throat to help him swallow.

He could not talk. It was too much of an effort. Even the strength to *think* related thoughts was beyond him. The light hurt his eyes, so he opened them mostly by dark. That seemed to prevent the blistering throb in his head to some extent. Of course, he did not reason it out. That was beyond his ability. He simply learned by experience that light hurt his eyes and made his head pound, so he kept them closed.

He could not move either. That seemed a goal beyond reach, an unattainable thing. Well, that was to be expected. An infant does not walk at first. In some strange way, he had become an infant, unable to do the things that even children do. He must rely on his mother. She fed him, cleaned him, cradled and crooned to him, and it was good. She talked to him too, and he wondered how long it would be before he would understand the babble of syllables that made no sense.

All of this was quite gradual. Some days were better than others. There came a day when he made a startling discovery. There were two kinds of light. One was bright and glaring, and came in through the place where his mother came and went. When that light was there, he kept his eyes tightly closed. The other was soft and yellow and flickering, and gave a good feeling that was warm and safe. Sometimes, after the flickering light, Mama would feed him and rock him, and it was good.

Very slowly, his thoughts began to take form. He could consider simple ideas for more than the space of a few heartbeats. He wondered whether his mother knew this. It was a great achievement when he managed to make a sound. He tried again and again, making only gurgling noises. Even then, he was able to accomplish it only in his mother's absence at first. When finally he was able to mumble to her, she was as pleased as he.

She had fed him, rocked him, and talked to him in the strange syllables that meant nothing to him. Maybe that was supposed to come later. She prepared to leave again. He did not want her to do so, and he rallied all his strength to call out to her.

"M-m . . . Mama!"

She turned in astonishment and hurried back, taking him in her arms again, talking rapidly in sounds completely unfamiliar. He wanted to respond but did not know how. With great effort, he managed to speak again.

"Mama . . ."

She hugged him and rocked him, and warm tears ran down her face and splashed upon his. He was unable to speak again but succeeded in blinking his eyes a few times before the glare forced him to keep them closed.

"It is good!" She chortled. "You are growing stronger, my little one. Soon you can tell me who you are."

He understood not one word, but he knew that his mother was happy with his accomplishment. He would try again to please her. But not now. He was tired, so tired.

When he awoke again, it was dark except for the light of the flickering fire. Yes, *fire.* That was the name of the flickering yellow! Other things must have names too. He would have to learn them. *Learn.* Yes, he would come to know, to understand. He could not say the words that now came crowding into his memory, but he must keep trying. There was something urgent. What was it? A dreadful danger. But how could an infant know? . . .

The stress and excitement of returning knowledge was too great. He watched with fascination as his left hand began to twitch, then undulate. He had no control, and it was a horrible thing to watch. Something alive, a part of him, yet not. The tremor spread, involving his entire arm and leg on that side, and he cried out in terror. His mother was at his side in an instant, but he was barely aware of her approach before the full force of the seizure descended upon him, forcing him back into black oblivion.

He awoke to find her holding and rocking him, crooning soft words of comfort. He was completely exhausted and wanted to sleep. As soon as she realized that he was awake, the rhythm of her song changed. Her lullaby quieted him. She eased him back onto the pallet, and he slept.

He was spending an increasing time awake now. He was discovering things about his body. His left side remained useless. His mother moved the left arm and leg through their range of motion at least once every day and rubbed the wasted muscles. He could, with great effort, move the right arm, but the leg was tied, somehow, with sticks. It hurt to move it. She indicated that he was to wiggle his toes as much as he could.

He was beginning to understand more each day. The leg had been injured and would heal. The pain in his head too was from some sort of injury. There had been a bandage on it at first, but now it was open to the air. He managed to feel the area over his right eye with his fingers—an irregular crust, in the process of healing. That was odd. How does an infant become injured?

He also found that when his eyes were open, he saw two of everything. The doorway to their lodge, the fire, even his hand before his face appeared twice. With great effort, he could induce the muscles to coordinate and bring the two images together. When he was tired or drowsy, it was impossible.

There were many puzzling things too. He studied the lodge where they lived, a strange lodge. But why did he think, how could he know it was strange unless he had seen other lodges? For that matter, how had he known about light and dark, and how to close his eyes? And why could he not understand his mother when she talked to him? He was beginning to recognize some of her words by repetition and their use: *food, eat, sleep* . . .

These were not the same words he knew. And this raised the great question. How did he know *other* words for these things? He could not *say* them yet, but he knew that his mother's words were different from his, and how could this be? How could he have learned different words? And how, after all, could he know that different words *existed*? He had never seen anyone since his birth except his mother. Then how did he know that there *were* other people and different tongues?

This hit him with a tremendous impact. There must have been other things that had happened to him—before . . . before *what*? Before his birth? No, no, something . . . the injury? He did not know what had happened to him, but if this incident was not his birth, then *what was it*? And his mother . . . He tried to remember.

His mother was young and beautiful, and when she crooned lullabies, he had understood the words, at least part of them. Now he did not. His mother had grown old too, while he . . . how had he remained an infant? But wait —his mother . . . his mother was dead! He clearly remembered mourning for her. And how had he . . . He held his hand before him and stared at it, confused. This was clearly not the hand of an infant but of a man of middle age. How . . . how did he even *know* that? He was not an infant, and this woman . . . This was not his mother!

He longed to talk to her, to ask. But he could not speak beyond a few mumbling syllables, and he could not understand her tongue. Who was she, and how did he happen to be in her care?

And who was *he*? At first, it had not seemed important. He was himself, and it had not been necessary even to ponder his own existence. But now it had begun to be important, this thing of his identity.

There was very little about this world that was familiar. Had he crossed over? Was this some sort of transition into the world of the spirit? Was the old woman a guide to show the way? Surely not. This was a world with food and water and pain, heat and cold, but who is to say that the spirit-world does not have these things? If he were able to talk, he would ask the woman. If of course he knew her tongue.

In addition to these troubling questions, there were the dreams. He dreamed of traveling, by canoe, on foot, or horseback. There was someone with him . . . a woman? His mother perhaps. No, his wife. Had he had a wife? Yes, he thought so. Was this old woman his wife? No, no. Sometimes there were two women in his dreams. Stories . . . They told stories!

Then, unexpectedly, would come the terror of the dream. Repeatedly, he would see a threatening figure—a man, a big man, with an ax. The ax flew through the air toward him, and he would try to escape, but in vain.

He would awake, terrified, in a cold sweat, and the woman would come to hold him and comfort him. He would cling to her, his one link with reality, and she would croon to him again the strange words whose tone he understood without understanding their meaning.

There was something else too, the gnawing question that had begun to bother him since he had awakened. It was a sense of something not completed, a necessity or responsibility. And it was urgent. There was great danger to someone. Someone close to him, a woman? This woman, in the cave? Cave, yes, that was this strange lodge! But the woman? No, someone else. The woman in his dream? There were more than one. Who were they?

The entire puzzle bothered him more and more as the days passed. He must find a way to ask. He did not know how to identify the people in his dreams, but maybe this old woman would know. If he could only understand her. But how could he ask? He could not ask because he could not speak and did not even know who he might be.

The woman continued to talk to him, cheerful and encouraging, seemingly not bothered by his lack of understanding.

When the breakthrough came, both were amazed that this mode of communication had not occurred to them before. The woman had been gone for some time. When she returned with a pair of fat rabbits, he was beginning to be concerned. The day was warm, and he was thirsty. The thought had occurred to him that if she was unable to return, he would die here, alone, with no food or water. That of course made him thirstier, and by the time she returned, he had become quite anxious.

She dropped the rabbits just outside the entrance to the cave and stepped in to speak to him. She talked as she always did, as if he could understand, and it irritated him slightly. He must find a way . . .

"Mama . . . ," he said. It was the only sound with any meaning that they shared.

"Yes, Mama is here," she crooned in her own tongue. "I have brought rabbits, and we will eat. Let me fix them."

He understood not one word, and his frustration overcame him. Without realizing what he did, "I want water!" he signed with his one good hand, giving the flowing-water ripple of the fingers.

The woman stared at him. *"Aiee!"* she cried. "You know hand-signs?"

He stared, confused. Slowly and carefully, she repeated, using the signs only. "You have hand-signs? You asked for water!"

It was his turn to stare. "Yes!" he gestured excitedly. "Yes, we can *talk* with the signs!"

36

E ven so, their communication was slow and halting. He did not have
the use of his left hand, and many signs require both. In addition, he
tired easily, and there was still the possibility of the seizures.

"How are you called?" he asked.

The woman smiled and shrugged. "I was called Pretty Flower," she
signed. "That was long ago. Now, no one calls me anything."

"I have called you Mother."

"That is true. To most, I am a crazy old woman. How are you called?"

"I do not know. How is it I am here?"

She shrugged again. "Who knows? Someone tried to kill you, and you
fell at my door."

"My leg is broken?"

"Yes. It has been two moons now. It is partly healed."

"My head?" He touched the wound, now well healed.

"An ax maybe. You have enemies?"

"I do not know. An ax?"

"Yes."

He was thinking. The dream . . . an ax, whirling, spinning. It was a
frightening thought. "But who am I? How am I called?"

"I call you the Traveler," she stated.

"Traveler? I have been called that. How did you know?"

"I did not know. You were traveling on the trail above when someone tried to kill you."

"But I have been called so. I have been called other names too. I cannot remember." He pondered a moment, then continued. "It is strange, Mother, that you chose my name to call me by. Am I dead?"

The old woman threw back her head and cackled with laughter. "Maybe so. *I* am dead! We make a good pair, then."

"Was anyone with me?" he persisted.

"Before? I do not know. Two, maybe three people camped above the night you died. I could tell little . . . the rain . . ."

He nodded absently. This was gleaning little information. "What moon is it?" he asked.

"The Moon of Madness," she signed, and laughed again. "Is that not right?"

"I have been here two moons?"

"Yes, almost. It is almost winter."

He tried to think. There had been plans for the winter. Where had they been going? Where had *who* been going? He did not even know who had been with him. Why had they not stayed to help him?

He tried another question.

"What is your people, Mother?"

She touched the back of her left hand with her right fingertips to indicate *tribe* and made another sign that was familiar to him. It was that of a tribe from far to the west, the northern plains. Strange, that he knew such things but not his own name.

"What is yours?" Pretty Flower was asking.

"I do not know, Mother. I seem to know more than one . . . Could that be?"

"Maybe. Your mother's, your father's people—are they different?"

"Yes . . . maybe so. Traders . . ." He looked at her in amazement. "I am a trader!"

"Your people?"

"No, myself. *I* am a trader, but that was not my tribe. It was the tribe of my almost-father, my mother's husband."

The confusion revolved around the fact that the tribe of his stepfather had two signs in common use. They were designated both as the Traders and as the Mother-Tribe. Both understood this, but the conversation in hand-signs became confusing.

"So, who are your mother's people?" Flower asked.

"I cannot remember. One of the forest-peoples, maybe."

"Traveler, you are tiring. . . . It is best that you rest now. Sleep. I will wake you to eat."

He thought that he would be unable to rest, but he fell asleep, exhausted.

When he awoke, there was a thrill of excitement. They could talk more, and maybe he could remember.

But it was slow, so slow. He could not sign and eat at the same time, and either was difficult with one hand. This provided some incentive to recover the use of his left hand. Already it was possible to move his fingers a little.

"Try your toes too, your leg," the woman advised as she moved the flaccid limbs for him. "Come on, you help too. You are no deader than I!"

She goaded him into motion, making him angry sometimes. At other times, she was very gentle.

"You have had children, Mother?" he asked.

"No. What would I do with children? You are enough nuisance to me! Have *you*?"

"No . . . no, I think not. But I cannot remember. . . ."

There it was, that urgent threatening thing that seemed to hang over him. Something he could not remember, could not quite grasp. Other things were coming back—his childhood, his travels . . .

"I was married!" he remembered suddenly. "Plum Leaf! Yes. She is of one of the southern forest people."

"She was with you?"

"Maybe. Someone . . . no, Plum Leaf . . ."

Again the questions came sweeping back over him. Why had his companions, whoever they might have been, abandoned him? Even if they thought him dead, they should have cared for his body. Unless of course they had been the ones who tried to kill him. There was something missing here.

But his memory was returning, little by little, usually his earlier memories first. He awoke one morning to an insistent drumming on the trunk of the dead cottonwood. *Woodpecker!* he thought.

He looked over to Pretty Flower, stirring sleepily. "Woodpecker!" he said in his own tongue, thickly and with great effort.

"What?" she signed.

"Woodpecker," he answered with the sign.

"Of course. The dead tree is full of bugs."

"No . . . yes, that is true, but that is my name!"

"Woodpecker?"

"Yes . . . my child-name. My mother was Owl Woman!"

"It is good, Woodpecker! You remember more and more."

Physically, it was very discouraging. They were now well into the Moon of Long Nights. Pretty Flower had spent long days carrying firewood and piling it near the cave. She had also killed a deer, and they should have ample supplies for winter. But the recovery of Traveler's physical abilities was hindered in many ways. By this time, it should be possible for him to stand and use his healing leg for partial weight bearing. This was not possible because of the paralysis. His unbroken left leg still had severe muscle loss. It would not stiffen in the extended position to hold his weight. The left hand and arm too were weak. And he dared not place his full weight on the newly healed right leg.

Worse, perhaps, were the problems with his eyes. When he was tired, he was still troubled with double vision. Even when his eyes were functioning well, the glare of daylight was still torture. The woman humored him, trying to adjust their waking hours to avoid the brightest part of the day.

Gradually, the double vision improved, but the sensitivity remained. Like Kookooskoos, the great owl, he had become a creature of the night.

There were other discouragements. He had been aware that his lips did not work quite properly. Especially on the right side, his mouth refused to close properly. He drooled constantly, oblivious to the draining saliva. When Pretty Flower was around, she would wipe his face, but when he was alone, he would forget. Spittle would drain from the corner of his mouth, soaking the front of his shirt. He had seen people with such an affliction and had pitied them. Now it was an embarrassment to him. There had never been much that he could not control until now.

There was one other shock before the river froze and Cold Maker settled in to stay for the winter. He had dragged himself out to the water's edge just before dusk, hoping to bathe without the help of the woman. The air was still, and in the calm back-eddy of the pool below the cave, he looked over and saw his reflection in the surface of the water.

He recoiled in shock. If he had been asked before that experience about his appearance, he could not have answered, for he did not know what he looked like. But whatever he imagined, it was not this. There was a livid scar from his hairline to his right brow, a crimson slash that glared against the normal color of his skin. The right side of his face drooped as if it were melting and running off. The skin of his cheek, his mouth, the corner of his eye—all sagged downward, lending a grotesque appearance to his facial expression.

At first, he did not even recognize the face but then looked more closely. He was still staring in consternation when he saw the form of Pretty Flower standing over him, looking at his reflection with him, over his shoulder.

"What is it?" she asked.

He did not answer for a moment. "My . . . my hair!" he blurted. "It is white!"

It was true. Somehow, he had expected it to be as black as a crow's wing. Was it not like that when last he had seen it? Or was it white then? As white as driven snow.

"Come," Flower signed, "I will help you back to the cave."

Numb from the experience, he half crawled back, assisted by the woman. He was quiet and thoughtful that evening, and awake, listening to Pretty Flower's soft snores through the night. He was older than he thought, much older. When day began to lighten the eastern sky, he had new memories to share.

"Mother, I remember, now. My wife, Plum Leaf . . ."

"Yes?"

"She is dead. We mourned her, on the river."

"Ah, I am sorry, Traveler. And you had no children?"

"No. Only Star."

"Star?"

"Yes, my daughter, Pale Star."

"But you said . . ."

They stared at each other for a moment, the woman puzzled, Traveler horrified. The color drained from his face. Pale Star . . . the men who had followed them . . . the man with the ax—Winter Bear! That was the reason for the dream, the threatening danger that he had been unable to remember. The danger was not to himself but to the girl, who had become closer than kin.

"I must go to Star!" he signed frantically.

"Lie down!" Flower signed. "You cannot go anywhere. You will only bring on another seizure. Now, tell me about this Pale Star."

The story poured out, with tears and anguish. There were a few things that he could not recall, but his memory of the threat to the girl was strong. With it came the anguish, the guilt and remorse. He had failed her. After buying her from her captors, he had betrayed her, allowed her to be caught by the sadistic Three Owls and his companion. At least, it was probable. It was possible that Star had escaped capture, but it seemed unlikely. And that had been three moons ago! Waves of guilt struck him again. By now, she could be dead! No, he could not accept that.

Pretty Flower absorbed the story and nodded thoughtfully. "Yes, but you cannot blame yourself, Traveler. You nearly died, defending Star."

"But I failed! Now I must find her!"

"Be sensible," she signed impatiently. "You cannot travel from here to the stream's edge there. I will have to go."

"But, Mother, it is too dangerous."

"Nonsense!" She flipped at her hair carelessly. "This old scalp is worth nothing. Everyone here knows me—a crazy old woman, harmless. I can find out more than you anyway."

He argued some more but had to admit that it was the best plan—the only plan unless he could speed his recovery. There was really no choice.

37

Pretty Flower started that very day. She gathered a few supplies and left plenty within his reach.

"I do not like to leave you," she told him, "but you will do well. Move your leg!"

He nodded impatiently. "Remember," he signed, "two men, a tall girl, very beautiful."

"Yes, yes, I remember."

She shouldered her pack. "I will be back . . . three, four sleeps. Maybe more. You wait"—she paused and laughed, "you can do nothing else!"

She turned away, then back for one last bit of advice. "No one will come here," she stated, "but if they do, you act a little crazy. No one harms a person with a crazy spirit."

And then she was gone. The next few days were the most difficult of his life. He had never been alone for any length of time. True, he had enjoyed periods of solitude, alone with his own private thoughts. But that was by choice. Now his private thoughts were not pleasant. They were confused, often threatening, and he had no choice. He could do nothing but wait.

Since his entire life had been spent in active communication with a wide variety of people, he was now doubly at a loss. Not only was he unable to speak, beyond slurred monosyllables, but there was no one to speak to. It was two days before he settled down to a resigned waiting. He tried constantly to talk, speaking to himself aloud, answering himself, working hard to improve the sounds that spilled from his distorted lips. He became hoarse from using neglected vocal structures, waited a day, and tried again.

His frustration was actually beneficial. It forced him to move, to drag himself around the cave and to the water's edge. His strength was growing, day by day. He did not dare yet to place his full weight on his injured leg. He was able, however, to draw himself to a standing position, leaning against the rock of the cliff. It took all his willpower and most of his strength to do so. When he stood, half sitting on a protrusion of the stony surface, it was a magnificent accomplishment. The night breeze ruffled his hair, and though he shivered from its chill, it was good. Yes, he *would* walk again. He would somehow find a way to help Pale Star. He had promised, had assured her that he would take her home to her people on the plains. This memory was becoming a singleness of purpose, a driving force that was all-important.

Most of his activity was at night because the light still hurt his eyes. He was beginning to see himself as a night creature, brother to the owl and the bobcat. He could understand their preference for the night. It was pleasant, the concealing darkness. It was also pleasant to curl up in the warm robes during the painfully bright time of the day. Again, the thought of the bobcat in its lodge in a cleft of the rock, or Kookooskoos in his hollow tree. Yes, he was like them, by day and by night, in his own cleft of the rock.

His thoughts became more strange as his solitude extended day by day. It was easy to believe sometimes that he was the only human on earth. Or, more likely, that he was for some reason or other suspended between worlds, between Earth and the spirit-world. Surely, he had not crossed over yet. No, of course not. He still ate and drank. And yes, there had been the old woman. Unless she too was caught between.

He thought more about that. Since his injury, he had seen or heard no one. It was a frightening thought. If true, though, why was he not allowed to cross over? He must be dead from the ax wound but kept here for some purpose. What purpose could it be? He pondered that at length before the answer came to him. Of course! He must help Pale Star. That was his reason for being. And the crazy old woman, who was also dead, was kept between with him to help him!

He felt better having come to that solution. He was still restless and impatient but felt that he understood. It made the waiting a little easier.

On the third evening—or maybe the fourth, he was not sure—he awoke to find a new chill in the air. It was overcast and growing dark earlier than usual. The odd blue-gray color of the low-hanging clouds appeared ominous and told of coming snow. He built up his fire. It was good that it had not gone out entirely. He wondered if he could rekindle a fire, his left hand virtually useless.

By dark, plump flakes of snow were falling from the blackness of the sky.

Traveler was concerned, both for himself and for the old woman. Would she be able to find shelter? And did it matter if, as she had said, she was already dead anyway?

That brought him back to the puzzle of his own status. But he was beginning to have more confidence, a sense of purpose. There *was* a purpose to all this. He was still alive, or perhaps caught in between worlds, for a reason. His purpose for being was to save Star. He had promised, and he had failed her. Now he must redeem that failure by helping her. That was the reason for his continued existence.

Idly, he wondered . . . if he and the old woman were dead and caught between worlds, could they be seen by ordinary mortals? They could of course see each other, but would they be invisible to others? Maybe they had the power to *become* invisible, like the Old Man of the Shadows in Pale Star's stories. He tried it, concentrating as hard as he could to achieve invisibility, but nothing happened except that it made his head ache. But, he wondered, if one is invisible, can he see himself? He held up his good hand and studied it. No, there was no suggestion of transparency. Well, he might already be invisible to mortals but seen by himself and Pretty Flower. They seemed to have a similar existence. He would not know for sure until he encountered other persons and was able to watch their reactions.

He watched the snow fall, the flakes illuminated briefly for an instant as they sifted past the doorway and the light from the fire. Then they fell soundlessly, to add to the growing depth on the path outside. Well, that would make the cave easier to warm.

Another thought occurred to him. The old woman had instructed him how to behave if anyone came. Ah, he *could* be seen, then, at least part of the time. It would be interesting. . . .

His thoughts returned to Star and her stories. She was good, maybe the best storyteller he had ever known. He knew that he was good, taught by his almost-father, Turtle. Would he be able to tell stories again, he wondered? If he could regain his ability to speak, what tales he could tell. And if in addition he could make himself invisible—ah, what a show that would be! He would do it only after dark. That would lend to the mystery. Maybe . . . was that why the Old Man had forbidden stories of himself until after dark? He slipped off into fantasy again.

After a while he decided to try to tell stories. It was a long time until daylight when it would be time to roll in the robes and sleep again, so he would try it. He tried to ignore the strange gurgling noises that came from his lips, saliva dribbling. He could see little progress but recalled that two moons ago he could make no sounds at all.

He became tired of speaking and turned to exercising his flaccid arm and leg. He had neglected that since the woman had gone. She had pushed him to move the lifeless limbs, to keep them moving, and he had not continued to do so. Well, he would now. Maybe she would not scold him too much if he did well until she returned.

When dawn came, the snow had stopped. The brilliance of the sun on the sparkling world of snow and ice was torture to his eyes. The thin film of ice along the banks of the stream reflected Sun's rays. He retreated into the cave and covered his head against the brilliance.

He did not know how long he slept before he was awakened by the sound. It was a familiar sound, a squeak of footsteps in new snow. Anxiously, he watched the cave opening, his eyes slitted against the glare. The opening darkened, and he sighed with relief to see that the figure stooping to enter was Pretty Flower.

The old woman dropped her pack, nodded to him, and tossed sticks on the fire to warm her hands. Neither of them spoke or signed for a moment. He was anxiously awaiting her story, but beyond a grunt and a nod, she barely acknowledged his presence.

Finally, he could stand it no longer. *"Ah-koh!"* he said aloud, accompanying the exclamation with the hand-sign for question, *"what?"*

She roused herself from the fire and turned to him. "I have talked to some who have seen a young woman," Flower signed. "Tall, pretty . . . she was with two men, as you say. One big, like a bear . . ."

"Go on, go on," he urged impatiently. "She was all right?"

Pretty Flower shook her head sadly. "The woman was alive then . . . it was three moons ago, Traveler . . . much can happen."

"I know. But she *is* alive!"

"Yes. It was said this woman seemed to be a slave-wife to one of the men, maybe both. But she carried herself with pride."

"Ah, yes. That is Pale Star."

"But, Traveler, there is more. These men are known here . . . bad men. The one, Three Owls, is a crazy . . . not crazy like you and me, but dangerous. He would kill for a scalp, but worse! Just for the fun."

Traveler's heart sank. "I must go to her."

She gestured derisively. "You cannot go anywhere! Besides, winter comes. But look, there is more. The other man, Bear, is his kinsman. He is stupid, but safer to be with."

She paused, and then broke into a cackling laugh. "Bear is safer, but he is the one who killed you! Anyway, I learned more. They were going to *Mishi-ghan*. There is a town of the Fran-cois there, a new town, with warriors. It is maybe six sleeps from here."

"I have heard of it." He nodded. "Why do they go there?"

She shrugged. "Who knows? There is trade in scalps . . . many people to steal from. Maybe he will sell the woman there. There are many men . . ."

Traveler's heart cried out against the thought, denying what he must admit was quite likely. "Mother," he signed, "I will do as you say. I must stay for the winter. But then I will go to her."

She laughed contemptuously. "How? You cannot walk!"

"I *will* walk," he signed positively. "When spring comes, I go to Mishi-ghan!"

38

Sometimes it seemed that the winter would never end. Each time the sky would clear, it was briefly and in vain. The weak and watery yellow of Sun's torch would barely begin to warm the frozen world before Cold Maker came roaring back, howling in rage, to attack again. In the course of the battle, Sun had been pushed far to the south.

They moved around very little during the Moon of Snows and the Moon of Hunger. There was no reason to be outside when Cold Maker was abroad. Their food supply was in the cave. The Moon of Hunger, even, was not much of a threat. Pretty Flower, through many winters, had reached a conclusion. The Moon of Hunger was named so for people who did not plan for it. She had come close enough to death from starvation that she had become cautious and thrifty. It was not that she planned to eat well but that she planned for survival. A woman alone with less insight and less tenacity would have starved long ago.

Traveler still avoided the brightness of day. The glare of light on a world of snow was still a torment to his senses. It was uncomfortable to his eyes and caused his head to ache long afterward. Consequently, he had completely adopted the nocturnal habits of the night creatures.

He could feel his strength returning. During every waking moment, he was constantly flexing his muscles, moving fingers and toes. With his right hand he would lift the limp left arm, placing it in positions that would force him to attempt its use. There was little sensation in the hand but some motion, very slight at first. The left leg also was slow to obey his commands. It was discouraging. When he discovered how to use the weight of his crippled left leg to swing it into a locked position of extension, it was his greatest triumph. He could walk! It was a strange gait, of course. A step forward on his right leg, the bone newly healed and still weak, then swing the left leg by a toss of the hip, let the heel strike the ground to straighten the knee to a locked position, and stand on that leg to step forward again.

He fell often at first. The flaccid left leg did not want to become completely straight, and he could not always tell if it was solidly braced to bear his weight. Impatiently he would thrust the knee into alignment with his one good hand and shift his weight to it. The cave was so small that such exercise was difficult too, a step or two, turn and back. The old woman complained, at both his antics and his nocturnal habits.

"You will fall into the fire while I am gone!" she predicted. "You will lie there and burn!"

He laughed at her. "No, Mother, I could roll out of the fire. You are not gone much anyway."

"I have to get away from you sometimes," she fretted. "Moving around all night, grunting and making those noises. Why not sleep at night?"

"The light hurts my eyes. Maybe you should sleep by day!"

She threw up her hands in resignation. A sort of truce evolved in which there was compromise. Each refrained as much as possible from disturbing the other's sleeptime. Pretty Flower spent part of the day in sleep to adjust to his nocturnal ways, but not without complaint.

"You want me to become a bat or an owl!"

"Why not? *I* have!"

Her other complaint, about his "noises," was a worry for him too. He was trying to learn to speak again. It was very difficult. He would attempt a simple word, but what came out of his mouth was entirely different. The most frustrating thing about it was that the woman could be of no help. To her, nearly all of his sounds were gibberish. It would be necessary for him to learn her tongue so that she could tell if he spoke it correctly.

This led to long sessions in the cave during long winter nights when the snow fell softly outside. Very slowly, he began to have an understanding of Pretty Flower's language. It was quite helpful, though exhausting. He would struggle to make a sound, and she would smile at his success or sometimes laugh at his failure. But prior to that, he had had almost no way to tell whether the idea that came out of his mouth with the word was as he intended.

He began to tell stories to her, using hand-signs as well as spoken words. That was helpful too as the strength of his vocal cords returned and the sounds became more normal. The old woman was delighted with the stories. It had been most of a lifetime since she had heard stories. She cackled with laughter over the Creation story of Star's people and the fat woman who became stuck in the log. He told her of Bobcat and the many theories about his missing tail.

Sometimes he would have a bad night. "Your words make no sense, Traveler. Rest now, and you can tell me tomorrow."

That was always a frustration, but it too was helpful. He found that when he was tired or did not feel well, he made more mistakes. Rest and well-being improved his skills. That was good to know.

Eventually, Sun started a new thrust, a war party into Cold Maker's hunting ground. The days became longer, the breezes warmer. There came a day that marked a change. Traveler awoke as shadows lengthened to welcome the night to find a soft noise along the cliff face and in the woods above. It was the drip of melting snow and ice, falling gently from trees, bushes, and rocks to plop into the layers of snow on the ground. The buds on the maples were already swelling, and the twigs of the willows were becoming yellowish in the sunlight. It was the Moon of Awakening.

With the Moon of Awakening came the restlessness that he had always felt at this season. He watched the geese on their northward trek, envying their apparent ease of motion. This season, the urgency was infinitely stronger. He must go to help Pale Star. The snow had barely started to melt when he began to push for departure.

"You could not even climb the path to the top of the cliff!" Pretty Flower reminded him.

"I *could*!" he insisted. "Look, I stand and walk!" He took a step or two on the level strip in front of the cave. "See?"

"No, no, Traveler. Not only you. *I* would not attempt that climb. The path is slippery with melting snow. I have been here for many Awakenings, and I know. You have never climbed it before."

It was true, and when he thought about it, he had to admit it. But that seemed only to make the frustration worse. He fretted and brooded, and became intolerable to be with.

"Traveler, go out and walk up and down the path along the river," Flower said one night when he had become particularly unpleasant. "It is moonlight, so you can see a little. It will help your strength to walk."

Angrily, he lurched out into the night, dragging the left leg. For some time he walked up and down the snowy trail, perhaps a stone's throw in either direction. Once, he slipped and fell on an icy spot.

By the time the eastern sky began to pale with the gray of the false dawn, he was exhausted. He would sleep well that day as he sought his burrow with the other night creatures. It had been hard work, but it had allowed him to see what he could do. He began to see his infirmities more realistically. The old woman was right. It would be a slow, hard journey. Some six sleeps, Flower had said. But with the handicap that he faced, it would be at least twice that, maybe fifteen sleeps, half a moon or more.

For the first time, he began to wonder what he would do when he arrived at this Mishi-ghan. Always before, there had been no question. Once he had reached his destination, he could handle nearly any eventuality. But now, even as he drifted into an exhausted sleep, his muscles were twitching and crying out over the abuse they had suffered. He still had a long way to go toward recovery. At least, he told himself, the use of his voice was coming along well.

He awoke that evening, stiff and sore. It was sheer torture, but he knew that he must spend more time exercising on the trail along the stream. It was warmer tonight.

"I go to walk," he told the woman.

She nodded, noncommittally. "But eat first," she ordered.

Impatiently, he wolfed down the stew she had prepared and lurched out the doorway. Dusk had just descended, and the great hunting owl sounded his hollow cry from downriver.

"Good hunting to you, Kookooskoos," Traveler said aloud as he began his painful march up and down the trail.

In three or four nights, he could begin to see a more rapid change. His muscles no longer cried out in agony. If he pushed himself too hard, it still made his head throb, but he was learning his limits. Flower had been clever to goad him into anger and force him to be realistic. He smiled to himself at the realization. Someday, maybe, he would tell her that he knew.

In another few days, his strength was gaining rapidly. He still had a severe limitation of the left leg. It refused to lift properly, and the foot dragged at each step, but he no longer had to lock the knee consciously. It still required special effort, but it happened without the need to stop and think about it. It had become a normal pattern, though it would appear strange to those fortunate enough to walk normally.

This lopsided gait, swinging and dragging, would still be far slower than his old mode of travel, perhaps half the speed, but it would get him there, given time.

That was his concern now. Did Pale Star have time? He refused even to consider the possibility that she might not be alive. What had happened to her since he last saw her might be worse, however. It had been six moons now, nearly seven. Pretty Flower's information that the girl had been seen in the company of the two renegades and seemed to be a slave-wife—*aiee,* the hurt. He must go to her. He was certain that he could and *would* kill her tormentors with his one good hand if he must. Grimly, he struggled on, dragging himself along the dark stony trail.

There came a night, however, when he climbed to the top of the bluff. He had planned it for several days. The moon was past full but would be rising in time to give him some light—not the glare of sunlight, which would have made his head ache, but the soft light that would let him see. He knew where the path began. It followed a rift in the rock. He sat and rested a little while, then began the climb. Pretty Flower would be sleeping by now.

It was harder than he had thought. He must make every move with the right leg and drag the left to a secure position before tightening the knee to attempt the next step. Halfway up, he became exhausted and frightened, and paused to wait until he was calmer.

When he reached the top, he was disoriented at first but managed to find the campsite by the spring. The smell of smoke as he approached told him that someone camped there. He skirted around the area, uncertain why. Several heavily bundled figures lay on the ground near the smoldering fire. There was a man on watch, leaning against a tree. Traveler observed him a little while and melted into the forest again.

He was back at the cave before the sun rose. Pretty Flower was stirring sleepily.

"I am ready," he told her.

"Ready for what?" she grumbled.

"To go to Mishi-ghan. I have been to the top and back."

She looked at him in astonishment. "Up the cliff?"

"Yes."

"It is good. When shall we go?"

"You?"

"Of course!" she scolded. "Someone will have to look after you! You are not able to take care of yourself!"

39

They traveled at night and holed up in the brush during the day. Pretty Flower complained, but that had become her way. She complained about the trail, the weather, the slowness of their progress, and night travel.

It was slow, of course. Traveler, with his lifetime of experience on the trail, was constantly frustrated by their rate of travel. Dawn would come, and they had covered so little distance that he would fret.

"Then you must do better tomorrow," the old woman would say sarcastically.

It was some time before he realized that she was still goading him to keep him moving, to keep his anger and frustration working for him. It was doubtful that she fully realized it herself. They were developing a strange relationship, supportive to both, by constant complaint and criticism.

When they neared the French fort, she began to make plans. "You will stay behind," she said, "while I go to find out, to learn about your Star."

"No! I will go!" he insisted.

"Traveler, you must think about this. One does not crawl into a bear's den without knowing whether the bear is at home."

It was true. He had worried that his sudden appearance might become a danger to Pale Star. In addition, he had been constantly concerned about his appearance. It had been such a shock when he looked over the bank into the water. His distorted face, sagging left arm, the snow-white hair—he would never have recognized himself. He was quite self-conscious about it and dreaded the reactions of others. He may have been unaware that this was part of his reason for becoming a creature of the night. His eyes might adjust to the daylight in time, but time would not change his grotesque appearance. Time would make that only worse. He was increasingly reluctant to let anyone see him, and the protection of darkness helped to remove that threat. As for Star, there was no way, he decided, that she could be allowed to recognize him. His pride would not permit that this young woman who had been closer than a daughter would see him like this.

No, he had decided as they neared the region of the fort, he would remain unseen. Invisible, as it were. He had begun to think of himself as nearly immortal now, an avenging spirit. Yes, an invisible creature of the night, unseen but seeing all. When he had learned what was needed, with the help of Pretty Flower, he would wait until the proper moment and then strike down the renegades to free Pale Star.

An ax—yes, the silent flight of a thrown ax, whirling out of the darkness to complete the vengeance that was due. It was appropriate that the weapon that had been used to strike him down would be the instrument of revenge. One at a time, out of the darkness . . . He relived the scene in his mind many times and relished it.

After that—well, he did not know. A plan would develop, later. First, Star must be freed. He did want to carry out his promise to take her to her people, but he would not think about that yet. The thing of primary importance was the destruction of Star's tormentors. He was reluctant to approach the matter of how he could keep his promise, restore her to her home, and at the same time remain invisible. Later, he would plan.

Pretty Flower left him there, hidden in a brushy cleft in the rocks, and continued on toward the fort. He managed to sleep some during that day but mostly in short spells separated by periods of anxiety and worry.

When evening came and the other night creatures began to stir, he became even more restless. He did not know when to expect the woman's return. What if something had happened to her and she *never* returned? Alarmed at the thought, he fed the little fire they had built after daylight, carefully choosing only dry sticks that would not produce much smoke. That was one good thing about the woodlands—a fire, or a person, could not be seen from very far. He thought again of Flower's advice in case of discovery. He could pretend to be crazy easily enough.

But if she never returned, what then? He had only a sketchy idea of the direction of the French emplacement. If he was forced to find it himself, would he be able to learn what he must? His speech was continuing to improve, and surely he could use the tongues of this region, near his own nation. He wondered whether Pretty Flower would have difficulty communicating here. Of course, she had rarely talked to anyone until he dropped into her life from the cliff. He now realized that this may have been part of their problem initially—Flower's long-disused speech skills. She was doing much better now. She must have used many tongues to survive alone all the way from the western plain.

Idly, he wondered about her story. She had been quite vague about it, mentioning only that she had lived alone since leaving her people many seasons before. In his own confused condition, it had not occurred to him until now to wonder why it had been so. Some people became reclusive by choice, some were outcasts. . . .

The night passed and most of the next day before he heard someone's approach. He quickly concealed himself in the bushes, watching the path that they had entered by, a path scarcely worthy of the name. The bushes parted, and he was relieved to see the familiar form of Pretty Flower. Nothing had changed about her, although she looked tired. He rose to greet her by the fire.

"How is it?" he asked, half fearful of the answer.

She dropped her pack, and turned to him. "It is good," she stated. "The woman is alive. She is married."

"But that is *not* good! We heard that she was a slave-wife of—"

"No, no, Traveler," she said wearily. "Star is not with them."

"Then who . . . what . . . ?" he demanded impatiently.

"I am trying to tell you. Let me do so. Then I must rest. I have had little sleep."

"I am sorry, Mother. Go on." It was all he could do to remain calm and listen.

"I came near the Fran-cois town and began to ask," she began. "Everyone knew the name of Pale Star. She came, with the one man—"

"*One* man?" he interrupted.

"Yes. Let me tell. It is said that he killed his kinsman."

"But which—"

She held up a hand for silence. "Three Owls killed the other, before they arrived here. Scalped him. His own kinsman!"

She shook her head and clucked her tongue disapprovingly while Traveler waited impatiently.

"How is this known?" he blurted finally.

"She told it, after . . . Oh, *she* killed the other one!" Flower chuckled with delight. "The man, Three Owls, fought with another man who tried to help Star. A scout for the Fran-cois . . . half-breed, called Hunting Hawk."

"Wait, Mother, who was killed?"

"Three Owls, the man you seek. He was winning the fight, and Pale Star came up behind and killed him."

"But what of this other . . . Hunting Hawk?"

"Oh, she married him."

Traveler was having difficulty absorbing all of this. "But, so soon? . . ."

"It is not soon, Traveler," Flower said irritably. "This all happened last autumn . . . six, seven moons ago."

"But I . . ." He could not realize that Star would ignore him in her plans, in her life. He was sure that she too felt much like a daughter to him, as he felt like a father to her. And he had promised to take her home. She should not have . . .

"She heard of your death, Traveler," Flower was saying gently.

"You *talked* to her?" he asked anxiously.

"No, no, but I saw her. A beautiful woman, with the look of the eagle about her. Now, let me get some rest, and then we will go to see her. She will be pleased that you are alive."

"No!" he cried in alarm. "I am not . . . I cannot . . ."

"What? We come all this way, and you do not want to see her?" she almost shouted at him.

Pretty Flower was exhausted, and this was beyond her comprehension. "Why did you come?" she yelled in anger.

"I . . . I am sorry, Mother. I had to know, but I . . . She must not see me, like this."

"Good. Then let me rest, and we start home." She turned to seek her sleeping robe.

"But I want to see her," he protested.

Flower had started to lie down but almost bounded up to stand, furious, hands on hips. There was fury in her face. "You said—" she began.

"No! I want to see her. I do not want her to see me."

"*Aiee!*" she shouted. "You *are* crazy! I should have taken your scalp and pushed you into the river when I found you!"

She turned her back to him, wrapped herself in her robe, and lay down near the fire, her face away from him. He stood, saying nothing. He realized that he was on thin ice and did not wish to exacerbate the situation further.

Then she rolled to her back and spoke again, more quietly. "Let me sleep now. We will talk, later."

"It is good," he answered eagerly. "Mother, one thing . . . Do you know how Star killed Three Owls?"

"I *told* you," she snapped irritably.

"No, I mean . . . what weapon?" He could not have told why that was important, but it was an answer that he needed.

"Oh," she said, chuckling. "I did not say? With an ax!" She turned away again.

Traveler smiled to himself. It was a lopsided smile, but he did not have much to smile about anyway. But now he understood why it had been important for him to know. An ax. He had spent all these moons planning how he would wreak vengeance for Pale Star. Now, in a strange and illogical way, *she* had carried out vengeance for *him*.

He wondered whether she knew.

40

Than spring and summer, there came to be tales of a half-human creature who inhabited the area around the French fort of Mishi-ghan. It was an ethereal thing, standing on two legs, but moving with an odd gait, like no other creature anyone knew of. Some tried to track it but soon lost the trail. It seemed to drag something behind it, which some said was a deliberate attempt to brush out its tracks even as it lurched along. This seemed unlikely, though the half-breed scout Brulé, known to the natives as Hunting Hawk, had strong opinions about it.

Hawk had probably seen it more than anyone, for reasons even he did not understand. His wife had seen it too. They agreed that it appeared much like the figure of a man. Star had watched it in the moonlight once as it crossed a clearing. A lurch forward, like a long step, and then a dragging motion with the other foot or leg or whatever—a tail perhaps. Hawk, one of the finest trackers in the territory, was sure it was human, or nearly so. He had tracked it far enough on two occasions to convince himself that it wore moccasins, even though the moccasin tracks were always nearly obliterated by the dragging appendage.

It had never been seen except at night. Usually it was around the perimeter of a camp or a lodge, or near the fort itself. It would stand in the shadows and always appeared to be watching. It had loose flowing white hair and either a polyglot assortment of ill-fitting garments or a very unusual shape with fluttering projections and swinging appendages.

It appeared harmless, though several people had been quite frightened when they encountered it unexpectedly in the woods. It seemed uninterested in *doing* anything, beyond watching. It became known as the Watcher. No one ever tried to interfere with its movements because it seemed to have such strange medicine. Some said it was a ghost, but Hunting Hawk, who had tracked it, was inclined to think that most ghosts do not leave tracks. At first, since it seemed attracted to Hawk and his wife, there were those who thought that it might be the ghost of Three Owls, the man killed by Pale Star to save her husband. This helped to convince people to let it alone, for the evil in *that* ghost might be considerable.

In time, Hawk and Pale Star refrained from telling others that they still saw the Watcher frequently, and the stories quieted somewhat. But they both knew it was still there. It was attracted to them, but since it was not aggressive and seemed harmless, why not let it be? Pale Star was sure that her uncle back on the plains would have treated it in this way. And this uncle, Looks Far, was a famous holy man of her people, wise beyond all.

Consequently, though many had seen the Watcher and many more had heard the tales of its appearance, no one interfered with it. It was accepted in the area as something that defied explanation, but is that not true of many things?

There had been one odd encounter, which Pale Star often pondered in later days. She had been going to the shore for water. It was well after dark, but she wished to set some dried corn to soak. It was not really necessary, but she always felt that soaking made the grains more plump and tender, and improved the flavor of the stew.

The moon lacked a few nights before it would be full, but there was enough light to find her way. The path was familiar, and it was only a little way, less than a bow shot.

It was not that she *saw* anything at first but *felt* a presence. That in itself was odd because there were many people in the area. The lodge that she and Hawk shared was one of a hundred or more scattered between the walls of the fort and the lake shore. She knew most of these people. Since the death of Three Owls, there was no one she really feared. Everyone knew her, of course, after the spectacular fight in which she had been able to kill her tormentor and save the life of Hunting Hawk. He had since become her husband, and the community had approved. Everyone had been, and still was, friendly toward her.

But tonight there was a strange feeling, a sense that someone was out there in the darkness, someone, or some thing, whose spirit reached out to her. It was not a threatening spirit, and she felt no fear. This had been about the time of the first rumors of the night-creature who watched. It had not even been called the Watcher yet.

Star felt confident that there was no threat there on the familiar path to the lake shore. She moved ahead, rounding a giant old tree at a turn of the path when she saw it. It was hardly an arm's length away, face-to-face. She was unsure of the creature's nature, then or later, though she realized afterward that it must have been what others were calling the Watcher. She was startled but felt little fear, only curiosity. She was looking directly into the creature's eyes and felt that it was more alarmed than she. The thing was very nearly human in shape, although somewhat stooped and twisted. The eyes too were twisted somehow, one distorted in shape by the overhanging bulge of the brow. Most unsettling, however, was the haunting quality of the eyes, dark and deepset in the distorted half-human face. Their gaze reached out to her in a searching, yearning way. She could feel the spirit reaching out to her, but the feeling was mingled with alarm—and regret, regret at having disturbed her.

Then a shifting of the scattered clouds in the spring sky hid the moon for a moment, and the thing was gone. She continued on her way and later discussed the occurrence with her husband.

"And you were not afraid?" he asked.

"No," Star answered, a bit puzzled. "There seemed no need for fear. It means us no harm."

Hawk shrugged. "Maybe you imagined it. The moonlight and shadows—"

"No!" she snapped. "I know what I saw."

"Yes . . . I meant only . . . Star, you are different. You see things that are not there. No, that is not it. Things that are not seen by others. Maybe this is a thing of the spirit, like the Old Man of your people in the stories you tell."

Her anger calmed. "Maybe," she agreed. "But I *did* see it, and I knew how it felt."

Traveler and Pretty Flower had argued over what should be done next after they arrived at the fort. With the somewhat bizarre sense of responsibility that he still felt toward the girl, he insisted on remaining in the area. Flower would have been happy to go home to her cave, but a new dimension had been added to her life. It was more than twenty years since anyone had relied on her, since she had felt useful and needed. The crow had needed her for a while, but when it learned to fly, she had felt abandoned, useless.

The coming of the desperately injured man had changed her life. Someone needed her, could not have survived without her. It was easy for her to assume, then, that this was meant to be, that for this purpose she had been spared from death on the prairie. It gave her a warm feeling, this mothering role. She had never been a mother, did not know how it might feel, but her maternal instincts had come to the fore, and she had been pleased to help the helpless one who had been thrust so rudely into her life.

So when Traveler had stated his intention to stay in the area and look after the well-being of Pale Star, she reacted appropriately.

"I must stay here," he said. "I must know that her husband treats her well and that she is happy."

Pretty Flower threw up her hands in mock consternation. "Ah, that I should be reduced to this," she complained. "Looking after a helpless madman who wants to look after someone else, but who must not know of it."

Traveler bristled. "I am not helpless, Mother. I came all this way. Go back to your cave! It is no matter to me."

"And let you die? You deserve it, and are probably dead already but too stupid to fall down. No, I will not be blamed for that!"

He continued to protest, she to complain, even while they made arrangements to stay. Pretty Flower found a hidden cleft in a rocky glen off the beaten paths that crisscrossed the area near the fort. By moving a few stones and piling poles and brush for a roof and one side, she created a rude shelter. A strategically located skin or two to shed the weather, and it would furnish shelter from the elements.

"It is a poor thing, compared to my cave," she complained.

"Then go on back to your cave," he retorted.

"And who would look after you?"

Gradually, the two misfits established a sort of routine. By day, Traveler slept while the old woman shuffled around the fort, listening and watching. She sometimes helped with someone's butchering or tanning, and would be given some meat, corn, or dried pumpkin in return. Sometimes someone would give her food or a castoff robe or garment, out of pity. She had long since lost the pride it would take to refuse. And she listened. People would gossip in the presence of a mumbling half-crazy old woman, saying things that they would ordinarily not share before a stranger. She was a nonperson, invisible almost.

She saw Pale Star often and once even helped the young woman dress an elk skin. Flower was uneasy about that and pretended to understand less than she actually did. Star was kind to her and gave her some elk meat and pemmican.

"Do you have a good man?" Flower ventured to ask in hand-signs so that she might answer Traveler's questions when she returned to the hut.

Star laughed, her voice like silvery water in a prairie stream. "Of course, Mother, but I will not share him!"

Both women laughed, and Flower shrugged in dejection as if that had been her intent. "It does no harm to try!" she signed.

She could have carried on a conversation aloud but had decided to avoid it. She might hear more if people thought she could not understand.

"I like your Star," she told Traveler that evening.

He would rise before dark, they would talk a little, and Flower would tell him anything she had learned. Then Traveler would go and prowl with the night-creatures while she slept. At dawn he would return.

In his identity as the Watcher, he was able to learn much. His hearing had always been acute, and it seemed not to have suffered from his dreadful injury. Or maybe he *was* supernatural, immortal, and possessed of acute senses. No matter. He learned to stand perfectly still for long periods of time, watching, listening. He found that if he remained motionless, as a rabbit freezes, he was seldom noticed. This strengthened his suspicion that he had the gift of invisibility.

Sometimes he saw Star but was careful not to approach too closely. There was the occasion, of course, when he had encountered her on the trail, face-to-face. They were quite close, and for a moment he thought Star had recognized him. Then a shifting cloud allowed him to melt into the darkness of the trees. He was more careful after that.

He loved to roam around the outskirts of the story-fires because he missed that world, now a part of his past. There were good storytellers here, and sometimes he was able to listen to Star's stories. He would shed tears in the darkness as she skillfully brought forth the stories he knew so well—her Creation story, Bobcat and his tail, why Fox is red. He remembered them all.

Once he saw her match wits with a medicine man of the Fran-cois. The man was a good storyteller, he had to admit. Traveler had begun to understand some of the French tongue, which was in common use by the natives also. He was able to follow the story fairly well. It was a Creation story about a beautiful place with First Man and First Woman when the animals still talked. At least, the real-snake did. The snake told the woman to eat something, Traveler was unsure what. But she did it and gave some to the man. This made a great father-spirit very angry. The man blamed the woman, and she blamed the real-snake, so the father-spirit drove them all out into the world. It was very good, and the audience loved it.

Then Pale Star rose. She used both the previous storyteller's tongue (ah, she had learned that already) and hand-signs as he had taught her.

"It is good, Uncle," she began respectfully. "I especially liked the part about the real-snake."

The holy man smiled, pleased.

"I am glad, my child. You are blessed."

"Now, here is the story of my people," Star began. "In long-ago times, they lived inside the earth where everything was dark and cold. Then Old Man sat astride a hollow cottonwood log and tapped on it with a drumstick. First Man and First Woman crawled through, and then some others, and—"

The holy man sat staring at her in open-mouthed astonishment. "Stop! This is blasphemy! Heresy!"

He jumped around, so excited that the silver chain with its dangling emblem sparkled and reflected the firelight.

Traveler was puzzled. He did not know what these words meant. It was apparent that the Fran-cois storyteller was quite angry at Pale Star. But why? He had finished his turn at the stories. Now it was time for Star to tell hers. To interrupt was very impolite.

Pale Star drew herself proudly to her full height, made taller by her queenly confidence. The dark eyes blazed, but her voice was strong and calm. "You are very rude," she said. "We have listened to your story, and now you refuse to listen to mine. I am going home."

She swept her blanket-robe around her in a sweeping gesture and turned on her heel. There was a murmur in the crowd, and people began to rise and follow her.

"Wait! Wait!" called the Fran-cois medicine man. "Come back! I will tell you more."

But the audience was leaving. From his place in the darkness of the trees, Traveler chuckled with pride. Pale Star had beaten the man at his own game. And in his own tongue.

41

Pretty Flower was first to encounter the information that something was about to happen. There were rumors about an exploration to the west. Each time the rumor was repeated, the direction, destination, and goals of the venture were different. A trek to the northwest, to explore more of the chain of giant lakes, like the one on which the fort was located. No, straight west, across the Missi-sippi, to see what lay beyond. Ridiculous, said another, it is a war party, to strike at the Yen-glees to the south.

There was even more disagreement among the rumormongers about the size of the upcoming mission. It would be full platoon strength. No, bigger. Troops were coming to join the garrison and move on together. No, only a handful of men. Maybe a scout or two.

When Hunting Hawk, called Brulé by the French, began to assemble supplies, it became apparent that the party was a small one, only a few people. By the next day, the identities of the entire party were known.

The leader would be Lieutenant André Du Pres, whom the natives called Sky-Eyes because of the strange light color of his eyes. It had been quite a surprise to find that Sky-Eyes could actually see quite well. Such light eyes had been seen before only in the blind. He was somewhat new to the area but appeared eager to learn and was well thought of by the natives.

The other Fran-cois was Sergeant Jean Cartier, a more experienced woodsman. He had long been known by the descriptive name of Woodchuck because of his full jowls and slightly protruding front teeth. The party would be guided by the scout Hunting Hawk.

An element of surprise was that the wife of Hunting Hawk would also accompany the expedition. But why? There were rumors about that too, some quite ribald and obscene. None of these were taken seriously. The respect that the community held for the proud and dignified woman from the plains simply did not permit it. The theories then boiled down to two. It might be that on a journey that was expected to be long, Hunting Hawk had simply requested permission to take his wife. On the other hand, maybe Pale Star's skill with languages and hand-signs might be needed. Either way, everything pointed to a long journey.

And how many warriors would go? Pretty Flower cautiously ventured to ask. *None.* None at all? Only the four people? It was unthinkable, but it seemed to be true. That set off another flurry of rumors, none of which seemed to have any basis in fact.

Traveler was devastated. Three years ago, he and Flower had come here. It did not seem so, but three winters had come and gone. He had gradually regained much of his strength, except that his left foot still dragged awkwardly and the left arm was still all but useless. But he had learned to use the abilities he still had. His balance was better. His speech had improved so that there was hardly any slurring. He had talked to no one except Pretty Flower, but this had given him the practice that he needed.

He had become even more of a recluse, however. After the novelty of his first appearances as the Watcher, people had a tendency to forget. True, there was a strange someone or something out there in the darkness, but its presence was uneventful. Soon, even the tales of the Watcher were used mainly to frighten recalcitrant children into proper behavior.

He continued to be concerned about the welfare of Pale Star. Her husband was well respected, a skilled tracker who seemed to act as a Wolf for the French. Hunting Hawk treated her well, but there was a slight doubt on the part of the Watcher. The spirit of the couple as they related to each other was good but not as he would have wished for Star. He could tell, as he observed them and felt the quality of their combined spirit, that their marriage was lacking something. There was commitment, yes, and loyalty. What was lacking, maybe, was the excitement that he and Plum Leaf had experienced so long ago as they started their life together. That had been a single-ness of purpose that had been undeniable. He shed a tear at the memory. But even as he did so, he realized that few marriages are as meaningful as his and Plum Leaf's had been. Maybe he was expecting too much for Star. If she was happy . . .

But no! There was a quiet attitude that he felt, a communication with the girl's spirit that occurred when she was alone. He could almost read her thoughts. Sometimes the feeling was so strong that he would quietly leave, afraid that she would feel his presence. The thing that he could read in her thoughts was something unfinished, unfulfilled. That she and Hawk had no children yet? No, something else. Through the many nights that he kept watch over her, he tried to solve the riddle.

When the answer came to him, it was so obvious and such a part of *him,* he was amazed that he had not seen it before. It revolved around his own unfulfilled promise—to take her home.

He sensed the change in her spirit immediately when the rumors about an expedition began. Flower told him what she had heard, and that very night he sensed the change in Pale Star's spirit as soon as he drew near in the darkness. There was an excitement. At first he mistook it for the natural excitement of one who is about to begin a journey. Then it became more apparent—a sense of relief, of the accomplishment of something long awaited. He did not understand. Why was it so important to her, this journey to an unknown destination? Her spirit felt a different, more intense excitement than the others of the party. What was the difference? An unknown. But wait, he thought. Does Pale Star know something unknown to the others? *Yes,* that must be it! He thought some more and began to reason it out.

This appeared to be a journey of exploration into unknown country. No one in the party had been to the west, beyond the Big River, probably, *except Pale Star.* The Watcher almost laughed aloud when he realized what was happening. Regardless of the reasons for the journey, only one of the party knew the country to the west. She would be able to lead the others, overtly or in any number of subtle ways. The end result was inescapable. *Star was going home!*

He told Pretty Flower of his conclusion at dawn as she grumpily rolled out of the robes to begin her day. The old woman was always like a bear aroused from winter sleep when she awoke each morning. "It is many years since I woke with anyone," she had once told him apologetically.

He still did not know why and did not venture to ask. If one chooses the life of a recluse, what is that to anyone else?

On this occasion, she was growling, hawking, and spitting, as she did each morning to clear her nose and throat. Between the sickening noises, he explained his discovery.

"Good!" she croaked. "Now maybe we can go home too."

"Home?"

"To the cave! There is no need to stay here."

He thought about that for a time. He had promised . . . "No," he said finally. "I will go with them."

This loosed a tirade like none he had heard before. "You are mad!" she yelled at him. "Completely mad! I thought you were crazy to stay here to watch over your Pale Star, but *aiee!* You are crazier than I am, even. You cannot go with them!"

"Not *with* them, but I can follow, to see that it is well with her."

"Traveler, this is too much. You are strong now, but this—"

"I promised," he interrupted.

They argued until the sun was high, but she could not dissuade him. "Go, then," she finally snapped. "I can do no more for you, now that you have become completely mad. I will see if I can learn when they will leave." Angrily, she shuffled out of the shelter.

She was calmer when she returned, late in the day. "They leave at daylight tomorrow," she reported. "I will fix a pack for you."

She busied herself with packing dried meat, pemmican, and an extra pair of moccasins into a rawhide bag, stuffing each item almost angrily. "You will need a weapon," she told him. "You can take the small ax. I do not know what else you could use with one arm."

"You . . . you are not coming?"

For a moment, he thought that she would begin to shout again, but she calmed quickly. "Traveler," she said quietly, "I could not stand the journey. My bones ache with the changing weather. You are younger—" she paused, and a little bit of remaining pride came to the surface as she continued, "not *much*, but younger. But you are strong, except for your arm and leg. Your spirit is willing, and you can follow them, maybe. I will go back to my cave— if a bear or somebody hasn't taken it over."

He was quiet.

"After you take Star home," she went on a trifle sarcastically, "you can come back if you are still alive. If you want, of course."

He was quiet for a moment before he spoke, his voice a little husky. "Thank you, Mother."

It had not seemed to occur to him that there might come a time when he would be alone. He had slipped easily into the routine of living with old Pretty Flower. An odd routine, to be sure, but an interpersonal exchange anyway. And he still had never experienced a period of aloneness such as that he now faced.

"Here!" Pretty Flower said, tossing the rawhide pack in his direction. "I will probably be asleep when you leave."

She was not, of course. As the gray light of morning began to pale, he gathered the few items that he possessed and prepared to leave. He hesitated, unable to express the things that he felt. This reclusive old outcast, whose full story he would never know, had brought him back from the very edge of death. He had spoken to no other living being since that time. He still had the feeling sometimes that he might actually be dead, crossing back and forth from the spirit world each night. How would one know? Could he not easily be a spirit, as some who had seen him around the fort insisted?

"Go on, now," Pretty Flower fussed at him. "They will start without you, and you will never catch up."

"Yes," he said flatly.

There was so much that he wanted to say. She had fed and changed him like a baby, had, in effect, raised him a second time. She had left her own lodge to help him in his resolve. He picked up the pack and swung it to his shoulders. It was clumsy and difficult because of his useless left arm. She made no effort to help him but busied herself with meaningless little tasks in the hut.

He tossed his robe across his back, looked at her for a moment, and blinked back a tear. Tears seemed to come so easily now. Was this a thing that spirits do easily? He cleared his throat.

"Goodbye, Mother. I thank you."

He waited, but she did not answer, and he turned away.

Pretty Flower straightened outside the hut and watched him vanish into the morning mist like—well, like a spirit. Now her eyes filled with tears. "Goodbye, my little one," she whispered. "May your trail be easier than I think it will."

She turned to gather her possessions, planning her own journey back to the cave that had been her home.

42

I t was not easy, the task of following the party. The pace was being set by Hunting Hawk, who was young and agile.

After the first day, in which he fell far behind, Traveler decided on a different approach. He had overtaken the party long after dark when he was more comfortable anyway. The light had bothered his eyes considerably during the day. Twice he had been obliged to leave the trail to avoid being seen by other travelers. He must do something differently. Why not travel at night, *ahead* of the others? This would let him locate possible dangers and intervene as he was able. He could probably estimate where they would make camp and conceal himself to wait there. There were few branches to this well-traveled trail. If a questionable fork was encountered, he would wait there until the others passed and then follow.

This proved quite practical. Well into the night, he left the area where the little party had camped. He was familiar with this area and knew that there were few main crossings or divisions to the trail. He even estimated the place where they would camp and was delighted to find that he was correct.

He remained hidden, of course, and was able to watch while Pale Star began to instruct the two soldiers in hand-signs. That was good. He could respect men who wished to learn the ways of the people they would encounter. He had been pleased, too, that the two Fran-cois had abandoned their impractical blue and white uniforms for the buckskins of the natives. That was Hunting Hawk's suggestion, most likely.

He was disturbed by one attitude that he saw on the part of the lieutenant, Sky-Eyes. Actually, it was nothing more than a sense of how the man *felt*. Traveler, since he had become the Watcher, had developed this ability to see into the thoughts of others. It was part of the sense of immortality he sometimes felt. It was as if his spirit could reach out and commune with those of others, without their knowledge. It had been uncomfortable at times to sense an evil scheme, half formed, in someone that he watched. Gradually, he had learned to deal with it.

But this was different, different in one respect—it concerned Star. He had felt the lust and envy on the part of men as they stared at her beauty. Sometimes it angered him. He had finally resolved his uneasy thoughts with the realization that Star or Hawk, or both, could handle the unwelcome attentions of any man with evil on his mind. That had made him feel more confident.

The thoughts of the lieutenant were slightly different. Not lust, but honest admiration. There was a difference, of course. Any man with normal feelings and needs would be attracted to such a woman. But appreciation of her beauty, with recognition that she was unavailable, was quite different from the scheming thoughts of how it might be possible to bed with her. The lieutenant actually seemed embarrassed by his thoughts, which were above reproach. The Watcher sensed respect for both Star and her husband, and for their union. It was plain, however, that if circumstances were different, Sky-Eyes would immediately have a romantic interest.

The Watcher was pleased with the way the lieutenant chose to deal with his feelings. He avoided contact with Pale Star—as much as he could in a party of four. It was good.

It was somewhat disconcerting to him, then, to sense a similar feeling on the part of Star. She seemed attracted to Sky-Eyes but chose the same method to put aside her feelings—avoidance. The Watcher had the strong impression that neither was aware of the other's feelings. Hunting Hawk too seemed completely oblivious to this interaction.

The Watcher wondered whether Hawk's mixed blood was a factor in his lack of recognition. The light-skinned outsiders certainly seemed less concerned with things of the spirit. Maybe they did not have the usual ability to see and feel such things. But no, it was probably not that, he decided. More likely, he, as the Watcher, had developed more sensitivity than most. Whatever, everyone concerned seemed to be handling the situation well, but it would bear watching.

An incident on the trail a few days later gave him more confidence in the abilities of this group to meet emergencies. In his travel that night, he came upon the camp of a party of seven heavily armed men. He spent some time scouting the camp. This was a dangerous area, with numerous scalphunters.

He decided to stay near these men to see that they did no harm to the party of Star and the others. He found a hiding place where he could observe unseen.

It was past midday when he noted increased activity. One of their Wolves apparently reported the approach of another party. Two of the warriors ignited smoldering matches on their thunder-stick muskets. Then they all scattered to conceal themselves, except for the leader. That one stood casually in the clearing, waiting, a throwing-ax held casually in his left hand. That was worth noting. Was it so that he could give the peace sign with his right? Or because he was left-handed and the ax was ready in his throwing hand? Or *both*? The Watcher slipped his own ax from his belted waist and made ready. He would prefer not to show himself but would intervene if he must.

Hunting Hawk entered the clearing and paused to greet the waiting warrior. The others of his party spread out beside him, weapons ready. The Watcher stared, fascinated. He could not hear the conversation but gathered that the leader of the war party was delaying communication to give his allies time to get into position. He could smell the acrid smoke from the matches of the muskets. Hunting Hawk and the others must smell it too.

Hawk was speaking, apparently to the other leader, when the hidden warriors began to show themselves. Hawk had apparently demanded that they come out of concealment.

Then everything happened at once. The left-handed ax-thrower let fly at Sky-Eyes, and the Watcher was concerned that he would not be ready. He nearly broke from concealment to help, but the lieutenant was equal to the threat. He pointed a little hand-held thunderstick that must have been a special kind. It seemed to have no burning match but exploded anyway. The enemy leader was thrown backward, to land heavily on his back, apparently stone dead. His ax flew harmlessly.

There was another shot from one of the attackers, screams of pain, and the remaining enemies were gone. The Watcher noted with pride that Star herself had used the throwing-ax to good advantage. Her opponent lay dead, the ax jutting from his forehead. Still another warrior was transfixed by Woodchuck's arrow. One more of the fleeing scalphunters seemed badly wounded, swaying as he ran, an arm dangling helplessly.

The Watcher was pleased. This fighting team to which Pale Star belonged was certainly able to defend well. Star's skill with the ax was a pleasant surprise and gave him a feeling of confidence.

Hunting Hawk was methodically harvesting the scalps. It was pleasing to note that although Star had had no qualms over killing an attacker when necessary, she did not participate in the scalping. The Watcher was proud.

The party moved on. They did not camp at the spring where Star had been abducted. His impression was that she had asked Hunting Hawk not to do so. They moved on, heading toward the village of White Squirrel.

Now they passed places where he and Star had camped, and he felt the tug of nostalgia, the mourning for Plum Leaf. He could tell that Star too was remembering better times. She was quiet and morose, withdrawn from conversation around the campfire each night. He longed to talk to her, to comfort her and assure her that he would still see her safely back to her people on the prairie.

At the village of White Squirrel, the party was welcomed. They would buy canoes here. This presented the Watcher a new dilemma. How could he follow the party on a river trip? Maybe his travels were at an end. He sat in the dark, tears coursing down his cheeks—why did tears come so easily now? Well, maybe it was over. He had done all he could. They would buy canoes and move on. He remembered the selection of the canoe in which he and Star had come upriver, the canoe in which his beloved Plum Leaf had crossed over. It had been a good one, the best craft they had ever owned.

He almost leaped to his feet as the thought struck him. That canoe had been left *here*! He had told White Squirrel to use it or sell it. Could it still be here? Usable?

He searched for some time before he found it, the small trees and bushes had grown so much in the intervening years. He ran his right hand over the craft, trying to evaluate in the darkness what could not be seen. Was it still sound? The bark was dry and peeling in some areas but was firm to the touch. The tiny cracks would quickly swell shut when placed in the water.

Before daylight, he concealed himself nearby and was able to watch as Star and White Squirrel came to evaluate the canoe. Star ran her fingers over the painted eyes on the prow, lost in thought. Finally they turned away. He could tell that Star had rejected this canoe. He was glad, for two reasons. They should select a new canoe for their purpose. But also, that would leave this one for his use, if he was able to launch it. And if so, could he handle it? He thought so. It would not be as difficult as traveling upstream. It was necessary only to drift with the current, guiding occasionally.

After dark that evening, he made his way back to the pole rack where his canoe rested. He would launch it, drift downriver for some distance, and conceal himself and the canoe until the explorers passed, so that he could follow. He placed his shoulder under the prow and heaved gently. It moved easily, and he eased it back onto the rack. Now, he could not lift, balance, and carry with one good arm. He looked at the gentle slope, uniformly stretching down toward the river. If he could lift the canoe down from the rack, he could slide it quietly to the water. But paddles. He thought for a moment, then reached up under the inverted canoe. Yes, they were still there, tucked behind the cross members.

He lifted the prow again and shifted sideways, straining to clear a young tree that limited the swing of the prow. That was accomplished, but now the stern was entrapped by the brush. He set the prow on the ground and stepped to the rear. Now the hard work would begin. He tugged at the stern of the canoe, cursing the handicap of his limp left arm. The canoe moved a little. Maybe he could use a pole to pry it over a little for a straighter pull. He searched for a suitable pole but could find nothing.

Maybe he could concentrate on the prow. He had moved that more easily. He moved there, lifted and pulled. The canoe slid forward a hand-span. Now he had a new problem. If the stern dropped from the rack unsupported, it would crash to the ground and very likely shatter the fragile shell.

Anxiously, he cast an eye to the east where the sky was graying. The village would soon be stirring. He hurried to the stern again and tried to lift the canoe with his one good arm and shoulder, straining every muscle. Sweat poured from his body despite the chill of the night. At first there was only firm resistance, but suddenly the craft moved, smoothly and easily.

He looked up and was alarmed to see a man handling the prow, expertly lifting and drawing it forward. Without a word, the helper moved toward the river, moving slowly to give the other a chance to get under the stern and achieve balance on his shoulders. They reached the shore, inverted the canoe, and set the prow into the water. It was not until then that he recognized White Squirrel.

The two men straightened.

"Good day to you, Uncle," said White Squirrel conversationally. "May you have a successful journey."

The Watcher did not speak. How long had his old friend been watching? He was certain that he had not been recognized. He decided to pretend that he could not speak. In truth, he probably could not without breaking down in emotion.

"It is good," he stated in hand-signs in the growing light of dawn. He must hurry now. "Thank you for your help."

He lifted his pack from where he had placed it near the river and set it in the canoe. He stepped in, and White Squirrel gave the canoe a shove. In the space of a few heartbeats, the canoe and its ghostly occupant were swallowed in the morning fog of the river.

White Squirrel stood looking after it for a moment.

"Good-bye, old friend," he said softly.

43

He rode downstream, letting the current carry him, using an occasional stroke of the paddle to direct the canoe across the river. There was an urgency, a need to be out of sight before the fog lifted. He should be far enough downstream that when he concealed himself, there would be no chance of a stray fisherman accidentally discovering his hiding place.

It was good to be on the river, traveling with little effort. He did not think of the fact that he would not be able to travel back upriver. That would be hard work, paddling against the current, even for two canoeists. For a single one-armed man, return would be impossible.

His hiding place was behind a screen of overhanging willows on the west bank. The canoe slid comfortably into the shelter, and he tied the prow to a sturdy limb. He was certain that the exploring party was not prepared to start the journey today. They had not yet selected canoes. Such a journey would always begin on a morning, so he would merely watch for a while after daylight each day. From this vantage point, he would see them pass, would wait a reasonable time, and then follow them. Until then . . . he wrapped himself in his robe, stretched full length in the bottom of the canoe, and fell asleep, the lapping of water lulling him with its rocking motion.

It was two more days before the party passed, in two canoes. He could plainly see them, out near the middle where the current was strong. Hunting Hawk guided one canoe, Sky-Eyes in the prow, while Pale Star was paired with the sergeant. That one, in the prow of Star's canoe, seemed to have handled a canoe before. The lieutenant was inexpert but trying hard. Yes, he would improve.

The Watcher observed them as they passed, then on down the river until they were out of sight. It took some courage to push the canoe out from under the willows into the open. Nervously, he chewed some dried meat while he waited a little longer, just to be sure. Finally, he eased out into the current. He kept close to shore, for quicker concealment in case it was needed and because the current was slower there. In that way, he would never quite overtake the other canoes in the main current unless they stopped. They would stop at night. He would pass them in the darkness, perhaps stopping to observe them if it seemed prudent. Then he would hide again as dawn approached and wait until they passed again.

He was pleased that his eyes seemed to be tolerating the daylight well. He wondered if Pretty Flower had been right, that he only wished to be active in darkness to avoid being seen. Well, no matter now. That had been as good a reason as any, anyway.

The day slipped past as smoothly as the water that carried the canoe. When shadows began to lengthen, he steered to shore. He did not yet know how early the others might want to make camp, and he certainly did not want to encounter them unexpectedly. He sat, listening to the murmur of the water, the soft sigh of the breeze in the trees above him, and the slap of a beaver's tail across the water. A loon called, and its mate answered.

He waited until it was nearly dark, then pushed away from shore. It was some time before he saw their fire, a tiny point of light in the darkness of the wooded shoreline. He steered into the quieter water next to shore and drifted as close as he dared.

The two canoes were pulled well up on the bank, the fire on a flat area a few paces beyond. He could hear their voices as they discussed the day's travel and continued the hand-sign lessons. He had gathered through his previous observations that the mission of this party was to find a waterway of some sort, to the southwest. This puzzled him because it was well known that the Big River, the Missi-sippi, ran straight south. Some said it emptied into a huge salty Big Lake, a long, long way below. He had never been that far, but the stories of the southern tribes with whom he had traded seemed true enough.

And Pale Star should know this. She would not wish to explore the lower Big River since her people were far to the west. He was already certain that she meant this trip to take her home. If he was correct, the party would leave the Big River to head west, overland, when the time was right.

One other possibility occurred to him, though it seemed unlikely. Star and her husband might leave the others to head overland. But no, that did not fit. Hunting Hawk was known to be loyal and dependable. He would not abandon those for whom he scouted. But Pale Star had no such loyalties!

He thought back to the time, years ago, when Star had been his prisoner. She had agreed to the pact. She would not attempt to escape and return home without giving him warning that the bargain was at an end. Could it be that Star had such a bargain with her husband? It had been a marriage of convenience in the beginning. . . .

The more he thought about it, the more he was convinced that there was something of the sort. He must learn more. He drifted downstream a few hundred paces and beached his canoe. Then he made his way back toward the camp, to watch and listen. His skill as the night-dwelling Watcher came into its own as he approached quietly, searching for a spot where he might conceal himself.

He settled in, outside the circle of the firelight, and tried to attune himself to the spirits of those around the fire. Star's spirit was familiar to him, of course. He could feel the proud courage of her, but something else too. A sadness, maybe. It was a feeling that something was almost over, a thing that was nearly past. He pondered that a little while. She was surely preparing to go home. But this should give her a light and pleasant spirit. There was a hint of that, but of some sorrow too. Yes, she might regret a separation from her husband yet still carry it out.

He wondered whether Hunting Hawk knew. He had no definite feel for the spirit of the man and turned his attention back to Star. He saw her glance at the tall lieutenant and was startled to see a flash of genuine affection. But wait—surely Star would not be guilty of infidelity. *No,* he decided, *she is attracted to Sky-Eyes but will not be unfaithful.* Yes, that would fit what he knew of the girl. She might leave her husband to go home but would never be unfaithful to him. She would control her attraction.

He watched the lieutenant for a little while, reaching out to feel that spirit. *No,* he thought, *Sky-Eyes does not know how Star feels, and that is good.*

Just as he reached that conclusion, the lieutenant glanced up at Star. She was looking the other way at the moment, and the Watcher was startled again. Sky-Eyes had a strong attraction to Star. *And she does not know that, either,* he thought. It was somewhat overwhelming to watch these two, each with the burden of a forbidden emotion, unknown to the other.

He watched until the fire burned low and the party retired for the night. He became more strongly convinced as the evening wore on that he was right. These two, Pale Star and Sky-Eyes, were strongly attracted to each other, but neither knew of the other's feelings. The reaction to these disturbing feelings was quite similar for both. They avoided each other, avoided eye contact, any closeness at all, and did not even speak to the other unless it was necessary. To a casual observer, it might appear that these two carried an extreme *dislike* for each other.

He recalled that they were in different canoes for the journey and wondered who had initiated the pairing. Maybe it was merely coincidence. The two most experienced with the paddles should, after all, be the two steersmen. That would be Hawk and Pale Star, of course. One of the soldiers would be placed in the front of each canoe. Maybe the fact that Sky-Eyes was assigned to Hawk's canoe had been merely an accident. But maybe not. Was it Hawk's choice, because he suspected his wife's feelings for the lieutenant?

He watched Hunting Hawk carefully. The man was relaxed, quiet but cheerful, and spoke easily to any of the others. There seemed no suspicion on the scout's part. Well, time would tell, the Watcher supposed. He backed away carefully, avoiding the sergeant who was standing watch, and moved back to his canoe to start downriver.

The pattern worked well, though sometimes it was difficult for him to match the pace set by the others. With the help of the current, his experience, and skill as a night creature, he managed to observe their camping place each night. Sometimes it was well located for him to watch and listen. On other nights, he was forced to forego that activity because of unfavorable terrain and lack of suitable cover.

Each night that he did watch, his impression of Star's attraction to the lieutenant was strengthened, but also the feeling that she would never do anything overtly to express it. For her, there was not only her strict upbringing but a stronger goal: *home.* There was still no indication how she expected to accomplish that. The party was far enough south now that it would soon be time to move westward into the plains and hills of the tallgrass prairie. Pale Star must know that, but as far as the Watcher could tell, she had made no move to alter the daily journey on the river.

He began to wonder now not *whether* Star would make the break, or even *when,* but *how.* Would she announce her intention to leave? That would be like Star. But then the others might prevent it. She must have lost much of her trust in others by this time. He tried to decide whether Hunting Hawk knew of the impending event.

He studied Hawk at great length, trying to decide whether Star would have told him any of her goals and plans. It was difficult to grasp a feel for the man's spirit. It was a bit morose, impenetrable. The Watcher perceived a little doubt and mistrust—no, not mistrust exactly, more like a knowledge, a resignation. Hawk knew that someday he would lose his wife, not to another man but to the freedom of the prairie. The Watcher knew that feeling well. Ever since he had become well acquainted with the girl-child he had bought, he had known that someday he would lose her.

One does not keep an eagle captive and expect it to remain when escape is possible. A fettered eagle will allow itself to be fed to keep its strength and fitness. But no matter how many years it may be, when the chance comes, the comfort of the padded perch and the sureness of the meat provided is forgotten. The eagle will spread her wings and soar, back into her own element, into freedom.

44

The weather change made river travel miserable, sometimes impossible. There were days of mist and rain, and occasional visits from Rain Maker himself, with the boom of his celestial drum and his spears of real-fire crashing down on Earth with a vengeance. The Watcher could do nothing but take cover and wait. At least he knew that the other party was subject to the same limitations. They could not travel either but would be seeking shelter as he was.

The overturned canoe was ideal protection. He dragged it up the bank a little way and lay beneath it while the rain drummed on the shell. He slept for a while and wakened to find it still raining. He was sure that the others were upstream and that they would wait until the downpour was over. The rain continued as darkness fell, and he knew that he need not watch. He slept, then woke, chewed a little of his dried meat, and drank from a rivulet of water that trickled from the overturned shell. Then he slept again.

Dawn was marked not by the rising of the sun but merely by the fading of the blackness to dull gray. The driving rain had stopped, but a slight mist continued to wet the earth. It formed in fat drops on the trees and bushes, and dripped to the sodden turf. He propped up the canoe so that he could sit under it and watch the river. There would be no travel today.

Pale Star was the only one of the party with experience on this part of the Big River, and she knew the treachery of the incoming streams after a rain. Any storm system sweeping across the plains could drop great amounts of water into the tributaries upstream. Those smaller streams could be quite dangerous, rushing down in a torrent to catch a traveler unexpectedly in an area that had been relatively free of rain.

Along the Big River, the problem was slightly different. Other large streams emptied into the main river at intervals. These rivers might be swollen, carrying flotsam that could become dangerous. An unwary canoeist passing by the mouth of such a river at flood stage could be threatened by an attack of floating logs, trees, and brush driven at a considerable speed, easily damaging a canoe—this, of course, in addition to the danger of being overturned by the sudden onslaught of an unexpected sideways current.

Star would know such things. She had gained much experience from their travels on the river. Besides, the girl had an intuition, a feel for such things. Yes, he had not realized it so much at the time, but it seemed quite likely that Pale Star possessed a gift, the gift of the spirit. She had spoken of her kinsman—what was his name? Looks-Ahead, or some such. *Looks Far,* that was it! A great holy man of her people. Yes, in the blood of Pale Star there must be much of this gift, this ability to relate to things of the spirit.

He shifted his position a little, settled comfortably, then shifted again to avoid a troublesome drip of water on his left elbow. He wondered when Star would make her break westward. She could go by canoe, up one of the tributaries they would pass, but he thought not. That would take her northwest, too far north to find her people. No, she would leave the river and go overland. It would remain to be seen whether she would take the others with her or abandon the party altogether.

He was staring dreamily at the river, wondering when the fog would lift, when he saw the canoe. He gasped in astonishment.

The craft held two people. It was quite near the shore, or he would never have seen it through the mist. In the space of a heartbeat, it was gone, swallowed in the gray fog of the morning. It had been within calling distance. If the paddlers had looked up, they could have seen him. Unless he was mistaken, the steersman had been Hunting Hawk, and the lieutenant, Sky-Eyes, had been in the prow. He peered through the fog and saw the other canoe slip past like a silent ghost. There were two people in it also, though he could not identify them.

This meant, then, that Star had not yet left the party. She was still guiding them, and she must have made the decision to travel. But *why?* She knew better, understood the dangers involved. It must be that this was part of her plan, this madness of traveling in a dangerous situation where one cannot see.

Another possibility struck him even as he struggled to drag his own canoe into the water—more chilling, more dangerous, than his other theory. Could it be that in her preoccupation with escape from the expedition, her judgment was clouded? That she was overlooking the danger because she was thinking of other things?

He stepped into the canoe, tossing his pack ahead of him. Fear gripped him. He had been nearly helpless before, having only his right arm to use the paddle and to steer. Now he felt completely at the mercy of the river. Before, it had been a calm friendly spirit. He had only to let the current carry him, with a stroke of the paddle occasionally to maintain direction. Now it was completely different. In his anxiety for Pale Star and her party, he had lost the kinship with the river. He was fighting it, unable to control his progress. The same current that had carried him gently now fought back, turning and twisting the canoe as it moved.

With great difficulty, he controlled his panic and spoke softly, trying to reestablish his contact with whatever spirits lay in the depths of the dark water. "I would travel on your surface, Mother," he whispered. "I will harm nothing, will leave no tracks, but I cannot do this alone."

There may have been an imperceptible change in the motion of the craft. He was not certain. "There are those who need me," he pleaded.

The canoe rode through a back-eddy, turning completely around once. As the craft emerged from the other side of the whirl, he gave a skillful stroke of the paddle, and the prow headed downstream. He began to relax now, riding with the flow instead of fighting it.

He stayed near the shore, not wishing to come too close to the others in the fog. Everything was still, the sounds of the creatures who made their homes here muffled by the fog, but he heard the croak of the small green heron. It could have been a bow shot away or just out of sight, concealed by the fog.

There was no warning when the crisis came. One moment, he was riding the current complacently, comfortable in spirit if not in his wet buckskins. Within a few heartbeats, he felt the tug of the river from the right and saw a tangle of floating sticks and brush bearing down on him. He managed to avoid the hazard, but as he did so, was aware of being shoved forward by a new current. He must be passing the mouth of another river, a large river, judging by its force. The other realization came quick on the heels of that. Floating debris would gather along the banks as the river receded, but the flotsam was apparently directly in the middle of the stream's mouth. This river was *rising*, was at flood stage.

The bloated carcass of a buffalo floated into his vision, bobbing gently in the swell where the two currents met. Beyond that was a cottonwood, torn loose by the roots in the powerful flood. He tried to steer around these obstacles and reach the west shore. He was now far more concerned with survival than with the other party. Even at the time this seemed ludicrous. If he was concerned about his own survival, he must *not* be dead, after all!

Somewhere ahead of him in the fog he heard excited shouts and a yell of alarm. His canoe was completely out of control now, being swept helplessly along on the torrent. The curtain of fog lifted, and tragedy loomed ahead of him. Rolling along in the current was an old giant of a tree, probably an oak from its shape. It may have spent decades in the river, its trunk so water-logged, it barely floated. Now, pulled loose from its resting place by the flood, it was carried along. Jagged snags of broken branches caught at the muddy bottom and lifted again as it rolled. The dead giant seemed to live again. Great limbs rose, grasping like huge claws at anything that came within their grasp, disappearing beneath the water again as others reared to take their place.

To his horror, he saw the crushed and broken shell of a canoe caught in a back-eddy, circling slowly. He thought he saw a body in the water but could not be sure.

He was being carried by the current directly into the grasping horror of the rolling tree and could do nothing to avoid it. There was a grating sound as a massive limb rose under his canoe, raising the prow. The craft slid away and bobbed on.

Then, right beside him, scarcely an arm's length away, another branch rose above the surface, thrusting upward like a groping arm. Impaled upon it was a canoe, the other of the French expedition. In a moment, it was gone again, pulled under by the inexorable roll of the sodden monster. Both canoes, then, had been destroyed.

A cry of anguish escaped the Watcher. He dropped the paddle and raised his face to the sky. Why? Why had he been saved from death by the ax long ago, to come to this? And to be unable to help Pale Star in her final time of need—ah, this was worst of all.

He had no control over his canoe and did not care. He had failed completely, after all, to help Star in any way. Even his pitiful attempt to follow the expedition, to assure himself that Star was with her people, that was a failure too. Surely no one had survived the destruction wrought by the trees. He sat waiting for his time to die. Surely the next thrust of the clawing arms would drag him too to his death. He clung to the sides of the canoe, eyes tightly closed, braced against the coming impact. He found himself mouthing the Death Song of one of the nations he knew. He could not remember which one.

The earth and the sky go on forever,
But today is a good day to die.

And then the water was calmer, and the clawing tree was behind him. Hesitantly, he opened his eyes and found that the river around him, though still swift, no longer seemed angry. Maybe . . . could he ride the current to safety?

It was not until then that he noticed the water rising *in* the canoe. It was pouring in through several cracks in the rotting old shell. The canoe was breaking up under him.

There will be no one left to tell the tale, he thought.

45

"Wake up, Uncle!"
The voice was distant, and he had difficulty understanding at first.

"You must wake up now!"

He was tired, so very tired. He had not realized that it would be so exhausting to cross over. He remembered drowning, trying to cling to the pieces of the canoe as he went down. A strange sensation, looking up through the water at the dull gray light of day. He could not remember what had happened next.

The voice that kept calling to him was that of a woman. His mother? No, that had been after the ax wound. But it must be someone who had already crossed over, someone who had been waiting.

"Plum Leaf?" he managed to gasp.

The woman chuckled. "Ah, he *does* awake," she said to someone else.

Confused, he tried to think what tongue she spoke. It had never occurred to him to wonder what tongues were spoken on the Other Side. He understood the words, but it was not his own tongue. One of many he had used, maybe. But it was not the tongue of Plum Leaf's people either. And not that of Pale Star, or of old Pretty Flower. Something was wrong. . . . He opened his eyes.

A young woman was bending over him, speaking to him and trying to rouse him. He had never seen her before. Behind her was a capable-looking young man. This must be some sort of welcome for new arrivals. He would be expected to make an acknowledgement, he supposed. He adjusted easily, through years of practice as a trader, and addressed them in the tongue they had spoken. "Good day to you," he said huskily, "I am pleased to be here on the Other Side."

The woman laughed. "Ah, you nearly were, Uncle. We thought you were dead when we dragged you from the water."

"It is nothing," he said. "I have been dead before."

The two chuckled again, a little nervously. He thought about that for a moment. Could he be still alive? "Who are you?" he asked. "Where is this place?"

He tried to sit up, but they persuaded him to lie back. It did feel better to lie back and rest. Slowly, the story came out. These two, who appeared to be young lovers, had found his body, as they thought, washed up on a sandbar amid pieces of a wrecked canoe. He moaned, and they dragged him ashore and tried to resuscitate him. They had a small fire going, which was helping to drive away the damp and fog. Its warmth was welcome after his chilling experience.

Then he remembered. *Aiee,* what of the others? "You saw no one else?" he asked.

"No, Uncle, only you. Was there someone with you?"

"No, no. Not *with* me. Another party—two canoes."

"They were chasing you?"

"No . . . friends of mine. I was following them."

"We saw no one, Uncle. Maybe they went on downstream."

No, he had clearly seen two wrecked canoes and at least one body in the water. He should sing the Song of Mourning for Star, as she had done for Plum Leaf, but he was not certain. If by chance she had survived, it would not be good to have mourned. It would invite trouble.

"You rest a little by the fire here," the woman was saying. "Then we will help you to our village."

"Could . . . will someone look for my friends?" he pleaded. "Their canoes were broken. It was near the junction of the two rivers."

"Ah! That is far *upstream!* Uncle, you must have floated a long way before your canoe went down!"

He did not remember. He had seen the water leaking into the canoe, and dimly remembered trying to reach a floating log, but—well, no matter now.

It was several days before there was any word. Yellow Birch, as the young woman was called, came to him, gently and seriously. "We have learned of your people, Uncle!" she announced. "Three of them—"

"But there were *four!*"

"Four? No, they found only three."

Fear clutched at his chest. *Which ones?* He tried to remain calm. He dreaded the answer that he sought, but he must know. Maybe the one who had escaped was Star. "Tell me of it," he asked sadly. "Where were the bodies found?"

"Bodies? No, no, Uncle. Three were *living*. The next village upstream found them. But then, one is dead?"

"Maybe so," he agreed, his mouth dry as ashes. "Tell me of the ones who were found."

"Of course. A woman . . . very beautiful, they said . . . her husband, and another man."

He heaved a deep sigh of relief. Star was alive! Tears of gladness streamed down his face.

"Is her husband blind?" Yellow Birch asked curiously.

"Blind? No, why do you ask that?"

"Oh—" the girl seemed puzzled, "they said his eyes were light-colored. Like the sky, someone told us. But he can see, you say?"

His brain whirled in confusion. The man they were describing as Star's husband was not Hunting Hawk but Sky-Eyes, the French lieutenant! He had observed their affinity for each other, though the two seemed not to know it. But now they did? And what of Hunting Hawk?

There was only one possibility, as far as he could reason. The man who was lost must have been the husband, and Star and the lieutenant . . .

"The one man wandered into the village, half dead," Birch was saying. "He told of the others, and some men went to look for them . . . or their bodies, of course. They found the woman and her husband . . . maybe three sleeps later. His head was hurt."

"He is badly hurt?"

"No, they said he is better now. The woman had cared for him. Their supplies were gone, but she had done well for them."

Yes, he thought, *she would do well.* The two must have discovered their feeling for each other during the time they were striving for survival. But to be accepted as man and wife? *Aiee!*

"I must go to them," he said.

Yellow Birch laughed. "No, Uncle. You are not strong enough to travel. Besides, they are gone!"

"Gone? How is this?"

"They bought some supplies and went on!"

"Down the river?"

"No, I think not. West, someone said."

Of course! Nothing could deter Pale Star from her goal for very long. She was headed home.

"Both men went with her?" he asked.

"Yes, I suppose so."

"When?"

"I do not know, Uncle! I will try to find out."

"It is good. I must follow them."

Yellow Birch sighed in exasperation. "You must be stronger first. You rest and eat, and we will learn all we can about your people and where they went. Spotted Bird will go and ask at the other village."

He knew that it was true. At this time, he would not have had the strength to travel very far. Impatiently, he settled into a routine of resting, eating, and walking to gain strength.

These were friendly, pleasant people who had taken him in, and he enjoyed the life in their village. It was much like that of his early childhood. As days passed, he wondered how he could repay them for their kindness. They seemed not only to pity him but to respect him for his age and wisdom. He thought himself not as old as he looked but was grateful that the people seemed to accept him easily, despite his distorted scarred face and paralyzed arm. Maybe he would not have had to fear returning to the life of normal people.

Some things he could not do, however. He could never be a trader. It would be impossible for him to lift and carry. He could not travel well. He now realized that it would take everything he could muster just to follow Star to her people. But he *must* do that. He had promised. He still could not bear to think of having her see him like this, but he felt that he had to make certain she was home.

It was on a cool quiet evening that he began to realize that there was one skill that remained to him. He was seated near a small fire that someone had lighted for warmth and for its spirit. Several children were playing near the edge of the circle of light when they suddenly stopped to listen. In the distance, there came the laughing, chuckling cry of a coyote. From another quarter came the answering call of another.

"Do you know why he laughs?" asked the old man.

They looked at him curiously. "Why, Uncle?"

"Well, it was in the long-ago times, when the world was young. All the animals could talk, and people too. All tribes spoke the same tongue, you know." The children gathered around him. It had been a long time, but the skill of the storyteller is never forgotten. He began to warm to a receptive audience.

"People had no fire yet, and they wished to cook their meat. But where could they get some fire? Real-fire was too dangerous. When Rain Maker throws his spears, who would be brave enough to catch them? Or who could hold them, or use them to cook with? They had to catch the fire from somewhere else."

"With a flint!" suggested a bright youngster.

"No, no," smiled the storyteller. "They had no metal to make the spark. No one had thought of rubbing-sticks yet, so they decided to steal it from Sun Boy."

There was a murmur around the circle.

"They could not decide how to do it," he continued. "They argued for a long time. Finally Coyote came and offered a bargain. He would steal the fire and bring it. 'I can run faster than you,' Coyote said, 'so I will not be burned.' The people thought about that. 'But what will you ask in return?' they wanted to know. Coyote chuckled. 'Only the leavings from your kills.' Ever since, the scraps and unused parts of every kill belong to Coyote. That is why he laughs. He made a good bargain."

"But, Uncle! How did Coyote get the fire?" a child asked, wide-eyed.

"Oh, yes! Coyote waited until Sun Boy slid beyond Earth's rim. Then he ran quickly, reached over, and grabbed a brand from Sun Boy's torch. He ran quickly, to keep from being burned. But the torch was cool and red, of course, because it was evening."

The listeners nodded.

"Now, Coyote forgot one thing. He ran so fast that the wind of his passing fanned the firebrand in his mouth. It became hotter, and flames swept back along his sides, scorching his fur."

"Really?" asked a fascinated listener.

"Of course! Next time you see a coyote, look at his fur. Since that time, all coyotes have a scorched stripe down each side, where the fire almost burned him!"

"Tell us another story, Uncle!"

He lay staring at the sky a long time that night before sleep came. He was beginning to understand something. A part of his struggle after the ax nearly killed him was that he had lost his identity. He could no longer be the Trader or the Traveler because he no longer had the ability to do so. He had denied that fact and had become depressed and bitter, shunning human contact. He had become the Watcher because in that way he could, partly at least, fulfill his promise to look after Pale Star.

He must still do that. He could never rest until he saw her safely home. But meanwhile, he had rediscovered something.

He still had an identity that he had almost forgotten. In fact, he had come full circle. He was the Storyteller again.

46

He still considered himself supernatural, of course. How else had he survived death, not once but twice? Once by the ax, another by drowning. There was no question in his mind. He might be a little crazy too. Pretty Flower almost certainly was. He could account for his own madness by the head wound, but she had never told him how she had arrived in her present condition, and he had never asked. But he was grateful to her.

The purpose for his survival? It was obvious to him: to see Pale Star back to her people, he had always known that. But now that he had reestablished himself as the Storyteller, all the pieces seemed to fall into place. He felt good about himself now, felt that he was useful. It had been a thrill to watch the faces of his listeners as he retold the favorite stories he had gathered in his travels. Bobcat's tail, in all its versions. The story of why Woodpecker's head is red, and of Kookooskoos, who hunts at night.

The people of this river village were charmed by the Storyteller, especially the children. They could not do enough for him, and as he prepared to depart, they plied him with gifts of supplies, new buckskins, and robes. Finally he asked that he not be given any more.

When the time was set, he chose a buffalo robe, new leggings and shirt, and new moccasins. A rawhide pack was stuffed with jerked meat and pemmican, as much as he could carry, and he gave away everything else to those who had helped him.

"We would like to have you stay," Yellow Birch told him, "but we understand. You must look for your people."

It had been half a moon since the accident, and there was little chance that he could overtake them, even without his handicaps. He would merely head west, asking as he went. He knew that news travels fast on the prairie. And the Growers, who traded with everyone, would keep abreast of the happenings in all directions.

It was not difficult to follow the trail of the three.

"Oh, yes, we heard of them . . . a very beautiful woman and two men."

"Yes, they stopped with us. She is a teller of stories. . . ."

"Her husband has blind eyes, yet he sees. . . . We wondered at that."

"No, they did not come this way, but my nephew talked to a man who had seen them. Farther south . . ."

He traveled as fast as he could, hoarding his supplies carefully. He could stop for a day or two and tell stories in return for more, but he hoped to keep moving. He had a general idea of the area where Star's Elk-dog People might live, but it was unfamiliar to him. She had once mentioned the River of Swans, but no one he encountered had heard of such a place. He struggled on, westward.

He became aware that he was losing weight. The increased activity, the hard work of travel, was requiring more effort and therefore more food than he had used for a long time. He could not continue on the scant rations he was allowing himself. He began to use a little more food but saw his supplies dwindling and resumed his more meager fare. Somehow, though, he grew more tired, and traveled shorter distances. He had to stop for a little while at some camp or village to regain his strength. That, or find fresh meat. *Aiee,* how good that would be! His mouth watered at the thought of browning hump-ribs over a fire of buffalo dung. But how could he kill any game, even if the opportunity arose? Frustrated and becoming depressed again, he pushed on, growing weaker.

It was perhaps the night of the driving rain that finally broke him. He was unable to start a fire because of an unexpected damp and gusty wind. He tried again and again, but sparks from his French fire-striker failed to live on the damp tinder. He spent the night wrapped in a robe, shivering against the rain that flapped the robe's edges and chilled him to the bone.

When the storm broke and blue sky appeared the next morning, reason told him that he could not go on. Yet his heart told him that he must.

He staggered on, defying the gnawing suspicion that he had already failed. There was gnawing of another sort too. Hunger pangs plagued him throughout the day, for his food was gone. Logically, he could have stopped to look for food, but he was beyond reason now. He struggled on. He somehow convinced himself that fasting would bring him closer to the purity of spirit that he sought. Of course! Why had he not seen that before? He had only to stop eating to become more supernatural than he already was! In time, he would become pure spirit, immortal. That would free him of the pains of hunger, the cramping muscles in his legs, and the throbbing in his head that had now returned.

He managed to build a fire that night and was a little more rational for a while. He thought of Star and that the man with whom she traveled was now assumed to be her husband. That had happened quickly! But he had known already of the feelings of the two for each other, though they had not. If Hunting Hawk had been lost in the river, they would have been drawn together, depending more on each other for survival. This would have allowed them to discover their inner thoughts.

There was no doubt that Star would have appropriately mourned her husband. The young woman had a strong sense of tradition. In the custom of her people, the three days of mourning would be followed by a return to the ways of the living. It was the way of things. And after those three days, well, one must look ahead. Star had taught *him* that when they lost Plum Leaf.

He slept fitfully and awoke toward morning with a fever. Intermittently, he woke and slept, confused and disoriented. He did not travel at all that day but lay in his robes, delirious at times. He was forced to rest by the demands of his sick body, against his will.

When the sun rose the next morning, his thoughts were bright and clear, his understanding keen. Colors were more intense, the most puzzling things simple. *Aiee,* he should have thought of fasting before! It was exhilarating, wonderful! He could do anything.

He had never undertaken a vision quest, as some do. His coming into manhood had been distracted by travels and trade. Now he wished that he had tried it before, the fasting and spiritual growth. What a wonderful feeling, to understand all the world and be able to do *anything*! He could go on now and follow—whom was he supposed to follow? Oh, yes, Pale Star. He must help her! No matter, he would fly. That would be easier than walking. He should have thought of it before. Now that he could do anything, and do it instantly, there was no hurry, of course. He could fly on later. He fell asleep, still enjoying the prospect.

This was an extremely dangerous situation. The delirium brought on by fever was hopelessly mixed with the uplifting clarity of spirit produced by his fast. To undertake the fast of the vision quest, one must be in top physical and mental condition. He had been in neither and in addition had suffered the stress of a wet night in the cold rain. The unfortunate combination gave him delusions that were potentially destructive. What if, for instance, he had been camped near the edge of a precipice, convinced as he was that he could fly?

But this was flat, rolling land, the beginning of the great grassland. And he did not have the strength to attempt flight, though he would not have believed it. In his delirium, he was invincible, immortal. He would accomplish whatever he wished when he got around to it.

Then, as the fever raged, he began to hallucinate. Plum Leaf walked into his camp—not thin and pale, as she had been in the last days on the river, but strong, healthy, and young again. That was good, for with his achievement of immortality . . .

She smiled at him and came close but would not let him touch her. There was a sweet-sad, sympathetic expression on her dear face, and then she faded and was gone, though he called after her.

Much later, he realized that there must have been a time when he hovered once more on the edge, about to cross over to the Other Side. His hallucinations peopled the air with disembodied spirits and strange half-real, half-spirit beings. He watched, rather enjoying the experience.

Then another figure walked out of the mists of his delirium to accost him. "Uncle, you must do something! You cannot just stay here. Where are you going?"

The voice and the content of the words were both familiar. Had this happened before?

"Star?" he asked. "Is it you?"

"You must decide, Uncle. I cannot plan for you. Get up now!" she scolded.

He struggled to his feet. The day was just dawning. Now, what . . . yes, he was supposed to go west. . . . He turned so that the warm rays of the rising sun struck him across the shoulders and shuffled forward.

Pale Star sat up in the robes with a gasp of surprise. It was near dawn. "What is it, Star?" her husband asked sleepily.

"It is nothing," she said. "A dream."

"You jumped," he observed. "Are you all right?"

"Yes . . . yes, I think so. A strange dream, Sky-Eyes. I was with Traveler again."

Sky-Eyes was fully awake now. "The dream of the bad one, Three Owls?" he asked sympathetically.

"No, no." She smiled at him in the dim light. "I do not have that dream often now. This one I have not felt before."

She paused, puzzled. "I have told you of Plum Leaf, who became like a mother? When she died, on the river, Traveler gave up. He could not decide what to do. This dream was about that . . . no, not that. *Aiee,* I am confused, Sky-Eyes. I was talking to him, but not on the river. It was on the prairie!"

"But what . . . I do not understand, Star. A dream of the river, the prairie . . . What difference does it make?"

She thought for a moment. "I do not understand either. But in the dream, he needed me, as he did on the river!"

"But what difference?"

"Sky-Eyes, I do not know, but this dream, on the prairie. Traveler did not . . . *I was never with them on the prairie!* How could I dream of it?"

"One may dream of anything," her husband said thoughtfully. "Who knows?"

She nodded, still thoughtful. "Maybe I will ask Looks Far about it."

She snuggled back into the robes beside him and drew him close. "It is early," she whispered. "Let us stay here a little while."

47

The Growers found him when they reached the cornfield to begin the day's work. He was lying between the rows of growing plants where he had fallen. Fortunately, his fall had not damaged many of the tender young stalks.

At first they thought he was dead, but he moaned when they touched him. They carried him out of the field and placed him in the shade of a sycamore a few paces away. A couple of the young women stayed to minister to him, and the others went back to work. It had been assumed that the old man was dying. With his snowy hair, he appeared to be very old. He was very thin and weak, and had a high fever. However, the girls decided that this was a challenge. They cooled his brow, brought sips of water and broth in a gourd dipper, and he began to show more signs of life.

The village was astounded at the old man's will to live. He grew rapidly stronger. He was from a tribe far to the east, he told them, using hand-signs. That in itself was a bit remarkable. It was well known that the eastern people did not readily use hand-signs.

They asked him questions as he gained strength. His memory improved as his lungs cleared and a more healthy color began to return to his cheeks. He had been dead twice before this, he told them, once from an ax wound to the head, once from drowning. He did not know why it seemed impossible for him to cross over.

There was much discussion whether the old man was lying. Those who believed him had the weight of evidence on their side, in the livid ax wound over his right eye, that and their own observations on the day they found him. Surely he had been as near to death as one comes without crossing over.

He, in turn, began to ask questions. He was following, he said, a party of three people—a man and wife, and another man. "Have you seen them? The woman's husband has blind eyes, yet he sees."

Such a description was hard to put into hand-signs, so he was pleasantly surprised when they were able to answer. "Yes, they were here. The man's eyes *are* strange. He is called Sky-Eyes."

"Yes, that is the one. It goes well with them? Where did they go?"

"They said they were searching for her people, the Elk-dog People."

"You know the Elk-dog People?"

"Of course! They camped here for the winter."

"Ah! You speak their tongue?"

"Yes, Uncle. They trade with us, for many generations."

Now the stranger became quite excited. Haltingly at first, he tried some words in the tongue of the Elk-dog People.

"How is it," someone asked, "that you speak in this tongue?"

"I was taught by the woman, Pale Star," he answered eagerly.

"Ah, yes . . . she is a storyteller. How do you know her?"

"She is my almost-daughter."

"It is good! You are a storyteller too?"

"Yes. I will—"

"Wait, Uncle," interrupted an older woman. "You rest now, and eat, and when you are stronger, you can tell us your stories."

"Yes, but . . . where did they go? I must follow them!"

"Not now, Uncle. Later. The Elk-dog people who camped here are their Eastern band. They go to their Sun Dance. You can find them."

"But how?"

"Start southwest . . . ask Growers."

"Of course."

"But now, Uncle, wait until you are stronger."

It was an impatient time for the Storyteller. He wanted to be traveling but knew that he was too weak. He did have the gratification of telling his stories once more, to people who were interested and appreciative.

In his own thoughts, however, he was becoming unsure of his mission. He had been certain that he had been denied the opportunity to cross over, had been spared from death twice—no, three times now. He had also been certain of the *reason:* to help Pale Star return to her people. Now it appeared that she had already done so, and without him. He must make certain, of course, that Star had actually made the contact, but beyond that, what was he to do? The driving urge to do right by the child he had purchased had dominated his existence for so long. What now? In his preoccupation, he had never thought beyond that point.

His time of recovery with the Growers gave him time to consider. Star was now a woman, restored to her people, and with a husband who appeared devoted to her. What now would be his own role? It was quite puzzling to him that he would be spared from crossing over, repeatedly, driven by the mission of helping Star, only to find that he was not needed at all. Ah, well, some things are not meant to be understood.

As soon as he was strong enough, he insisted on leaving. The Growers were quite helpful, telling him as much as they knew about the area where the Elk-dog People were holding their Sun Dance this season. It would be somewhere in their Sacred Hills, he was told, west of the River of Swans.

"Come and stay with us again, Uncle! We would hear more of your stories!" they urged.

"Maybe so . . . ," he agreed tentatively.

He was still unsure. He would be unable to trade or travel as he once had. Yet he could see a pattern developing. Twice he had been taken in, almost dead, by people who seemed willing to have him around merely to hear his stories. Maybe he could travel a little. He had no desire to go back to the region of his childhood, now so unsettled and dangerous. The part that had been good was gone.

So he traveled more slowly now than he had when he wore a younger man's moccasins. He found that he was feeling a thrill, an exhilaration over the tallgrass country, the Sacred Hills of Star's people. There was a special spirit here. It was rather like that of the country of his stepfather, Turtle, and the Trader-people. Yet it was different. He could not say how, but it was like nothing he had ever felt before. It was a spirit that was exciting and at the same time calming. He felt that he could understand the spirit of Earth, of all Creation, better than he had, ever before.

The sunrises and sunsets were glorious, spectacular beyond belief, seen above far horizons. He began to realize how important it had been to Star to return home, and *why*. He was a child of the woodlands, yet he was feeling a closeness, an understanding, a oneness with the land, that was more awe-inspiring than anything he had ever felt. It was, somehow, as if he had come home, though it was an area he had never seen before.

He found too that the urgency was gone from his mission. He must still find Star and assure himself that all was well with her, but the worry and concern were no longer there.

It was ten sleeps, maybe more, before he encountered two Wolves on horseback. He assumed that they were outriders from a traveling band. He stopped and held up his open right hand in the hand-sign of nonaggression.

"*Ah-koh*, Uncle," one of the warriors greeted him, using both hand-signs and speech. "How are you called?"

It took a moment for him to realize that the man was speaking the tongue of Star's Elk-dog People. He must be careful now. There was a moment of panic. He still did not want Star to see him in his present condition. He had not stopped to consider. How could he find Star's people without the risk of revealing himself to her? Well, it was too late now. Maybe she would not recognize him. She had not, that time in Mishi-ghan, face-to-face, so long ago.

"I am called Storyteller," he said in voice and handsign. "Your tribe is Elk-dog?"

"It is, Uncle. You speak our tongue?"

"Only a little. I speak many tongues."

The other nodded. "What is your tribe?"

"Ah, I have no tribe. I travel and tell stories."

He could see the expressions change a little on their faces. They thought him a little crazy. Well, maybe they were right. "Who is your chief?" he asked. "I would pay my respects."

"Red Feather," answered one of the Wolves. "Come, the band is just over the ridge there."

"Is it not time for your Sun Dance?"

"*Aiee,* Uncle, the Sun Dance is over! We are moving to summer camp."

He thought about that for a moment. These people must be moving northeast. That would mean that they were the Eastern band of their nation. He tried to remember. Had not Star spoken of hers as the Southern band?

The two men turned their horses now, and he walked between them, back toward the ridge. Maybe he could seek information.

"Yours is the Northern band?" he asked innocently.

"No, no, the Eastern, Uncle."

"Ah, yes . . . How many bands in your nation?"

"Five."

"Named for four winds, and . . . what?"

"No, no . . . there is no Western band. On the west, there are two, the Mountain and Red Rocks. Then the Northern, our own, and the Southern band. Why do you ask, Uncle?"

"I only wondered. I once knew someone of the Elk-dog People."

"Ah! How was he called?"

"I . . . it was long ago . . . *Aiee,* I cannot remember."

The other nodded sympathetically.

"I am made to think," said Storyteller carefully, "that he said his was the Elk-dog band. Could that be true?"

"Maybe. Our Southern band is sometimes called that, as well as the nation."

"Where will the other bands summer?" he asked, still fishing for information.

"Who knows? The Red Rocks have their own place. The Mountain band northwest. It is no matter. We will meet next year for the Sun Dance."

The Storyteller was somewhat familiar with the Sun Dance, the most holy of religious celebrations for the nations of the plains. "Was your Sun Dance a good one this year?" he asked.

"Yes. Very good. One of our women who was stolen as a child was returned to us!"

"Returned?"

"Yes! She made her way back to us. Brought two men. One, she married, here in our band."

"She was of your band?"

"No, no. The Southern band. But the other man—Woodchuck, he is called—he married one of our women, Pink Cloud, the daughter of our band chief, Red Feather."

"Then they are here? With your band?"

"No, Uncle. After the Sun Dance, they went on west, with the Red Rocks, to see the mountains. The one man, the one with strange eyes—he makes pictures in a stack of thin skins, like—"

"Yes, I have seen such a thing," Storyteller mused. "Some people call them talking leaves."

It had happened well, he thought. He had wondered how he could find out about Star without asking, and now it had just happened. And he did not have to worry about Star recognizing him. Not yet, anyway.

48

The Storyteller had been quickly welcomed by the people of the Eastern band. He had found a place and was quickly accepted. Storytelling was an art that was greatly honored here, and his old skills quickly found approval. His language skills improved, and as he became more at home, he began to pay more attention to detail—the effect of light and shadow, the flickering patterns of firelight on a lodgeskin, the background the observers would see *behind* him in the darkness.

The People loved it and responded to it. The wandering Traveler, now the Storyteller, had found a home. They had welcomed him. He had been taken into their lodges and into their hearts. The Eastern band of the Elk-dogs had never enjoyed the prestige of the others, he was told. The Real-chief, elected over the whole nation, was usually from the Northern band. The Southern band had been the first to acquire horses, several generations ago. The greatest of holy men in the nation was Looks Far, of the Southern band. And so it went. True, the new chief of the Eastern band, Red Feather, had distinguished himself as a young man in the war with the Blue Paints. That was why he had been elected chief upon the death of Small Ears.

But overall the Eastern band had had little to make them proud. The other bands scoffed and made jokes about their foolish ways. Red Feather had given them pride, but there was much resentment, even now.

The alliance was a natural one. The Eastern band welcomed the Story-teller at first merely because they liked his stories. Through the long moons of winter, however, he had become more greatly honored and more greatly appreciated. The People began to realize that they now had something special to share and boast of when the Sun Dance brought all the bands together. No other band had such a skilled storyteller. There had been none, in fact, since the death of the legendary Eagle, of the Southern band, generations ago.

But this man . . . *aiee,* he knew the stories of *all* nations. His strange appearance, the odd manner of his behavior, and the vagueness with which he spoke of his past all combined to create an aura of mystery. He had simply walked in out of the prairie, where no one should have been. He had been alone and on foot, and had calmly greeted the Wolves who discovered him. Some said he was crazy, of course, but it was no matter. There were also those who were convinced that he was some supernatural being. Maybe the Old Man of the Shadows himself!

The Storyteller himself was unaware of most of this, realizing only that he was respected and honored. This was reassuring and gave him confidence, and it was good.

So the winter passed quickly for the Eastern band, and it was almost a surprise when the Moon of Awakening arrived and the buds began to swell on the trees. The People looked forward to the Sun Dance and the opportunity to boast a little to the other bands of the tribe, to show off their Story-teller.

The Storyteller was somewhat concerned over this. He had never envisioned such acceptance that these people would want to boast about it. He wanted to see Pale Star—yes, of course. But he was still reluctant to let her see *him.*

It was in the Moon of Growing that they prepared to move to the area where the Sun Dance would be held. The French sergeant, now known as Woodchuck, came to the Eastern band with tragic news. His wife, the daughter of the band chief, had been killed in an accident during the spring hunt, far to the west. A wounded bull—the bereaved husband broke down in tears as he told the story. She had left an infant son, who was now in the lodge of Pale Star and Sky-Eyes. They would bring him to the Sun Dance, to be given to his grandparents to raise if they wished.

Red Feather's lodge, relatives, and friends of the dead woman began the ritual of mourning, which would last three days. Then, as they resumed the ways of the living, Woodchuck prepared to leave the band, to return to his own people in a far place called Mishi-ghan. It was apparent that he was not mourning well, holding in his grief, and it was hurting him badly.

Storyteller felt sorry for the young man and felt an unusual closeness to him. He knew how it felt to lose a beloved wife. He would have liked to talk to Woodchuck, not only to comfort him but to ask him about Star. He did not dare to do so. However, the two men did come into close proximity a number of times, and Woodchuck showed no sign of recognition.

With Star, it would be different. Though it had been several years, they had been very close. Could he trust that she would not recognize him? In a moon or two, he would see her at the Sun Dance. He considered asking Woodchuck if he could travel with him, back to Mishi-ghan or to rejoin Pretty Flower. But no, he would stay with the Eastern band. He had found a place here among the people of Pale Star, even though it was a different band of Elk-dog People.

Woodchuck moved on, headed eastward, still appearing depressed and morose. It was as if the People should have mourned for *him,* so pitiful he seemed over his loss. He had been very popular with the People, having a gift for carving wood. Several people in the band possessed fetishes that had been carved by the Woodchuck. They would take pride in his work for generations. But now it seemed that they could not help him.

"Someday, maybe he will return," said Red Feather.

But now they must turn their attention to their own journey. They would meet the rest of the tribe at Turkey Creek for the Sun Dance. The day of departure was selected, and the People began to stow their belongings in rawhide pack bags for travel. Young horses, not yet accustomed to pulling baggage on pole-drags, were quickly taught their function. Heavy logs or pack-carriers filled with stones were lashed to the drag, and the animal was led or driven around the meadow to accustom it to the load.

It was shortly after dawn on the day of departure that the first of the big lodges came down, and by noon, the winter camp of the Eastern band was empty. Only a few worn-out garments and discarded belongings marked the site of the village. A dog or two hung behind to forage through the refuse as the caravan headed southwest across the rolling prairie.

The Storyteller had been living with a middle-aged couple, relatives of Red Feather. He rode at the side of Lizard while She-Elk rode the horse that pulled the pole-drag. This had been a good relationship. Their lodge had had no children, and the company of one such as the Storyteller was both interesting and a matter of prestige.

Storyteller was enjoying the sense of belonging, of being part of a family again. He had found that he also enjoyed the travel of a horse under the vastness of a prairie sky. He remembered the thrill of the buffalo hunts long ago with Turtle's people and his friend Gray Otter. He could not have participated in such a hunt now. He was stiff and sore, even after a day's slow travel. But the thrill was still there.

He was apprehensive about the Sun Dance meeting. There was no question but that he would see Pale Star. His doubts had faded somewhat now. He had a measure of self-respect, which had been missing for years. He had reestablished himself as an honored storyteller. Despite his handicaps, he had done well at that. His garments, sewn and decorated by She-Elk or some of the other women, were new and of good quality. His hair, once wild, dirty, and unkempt, was now clean, well-groomed, and plaited in the style of the People. If he must meet Star now, it would be with a degree of pride and dignity. It would not be with helplessness, crippled and unable to talk, drooling from distorted lips. True, there was still considerable disability, but it was well controlled. And many things, though not controllable, are made less through pride and confidence. He filled his lungs with clean prairie air. It was almost like being young again.

A disturbing thought struck him. Suppose Pale Star would not *want* to recognize him? After all, their contact, which began when she was little more than a child—she had been traded like a horse. Tears filled his eyes, and he brushed them away with his good hand as he rode. The entire part of her life that related to him had been one long and varied tragedy.

No, he decided, he would wait. If she recognized him, so be it. He would try to explain. If not, he would say nothing. But either way, he decided, he had found his place with the People. The Traveler had come home to stay.

49

The Sun Dance was a glorious annual event for the People, partly religious, partly recreation, and partly social with the renewing of friendships and greeting of relatives. Parents who had exchanged their children with relatives of another band joyfully reclaimed their own. Everyone remarked about how each had grown in the intervening year and how much maturity each child now exhibited. The children reveled in the opportunity to display new skills and relate their experiences while with the lodge of a favorite aunt and uncle.

There were horse races, foot races, shooting contests, and gambling— something for everyone. Meanwhile, the preparations for the ceremonial Sun Dance went on.

There was the usual news of each band, accompanied by political rumor and gossip. The tragic story of the death of Pink Cloud, daughter of the Eastern band's chieftain, was one of the major items of discussion. The two outsiders, brought back by the returning Pale Star last season, had been popular and well liked. Both marriages had seemed good, and to have one end in tragedy . . . *aiee!* But that is the way of the world.

Pale Star, now large with child, handed Cloud's child to his grandparents. "He will always be mine, a little bit," she admitted.

"Of course," Red Feather agreed. "We will always think it so."

One story of some interest to Pale Star was of a new storyteller, an old man who had wandered in out of the prairie, said to be living with the Eastern band. He seemed to have no tribe but had adapted well to the ways of the People and was greatly respected. Some in the Eastern band declared without reservation that he was a reincarnation of the Old Man himself.

"But you know how *they* are," someone was always sure to say.

"Do not say that," Pale Star retorted. "They have done well under Red Feather."

"Of course," the other apologized, "but Star, you know . . ."

Yes, of course. It was tradition to make jokes about the Eastern band. An inept person, or one who suffered an illogical bit of bad luck, was chided with remarks like "Well, his grandmother was of the Eastern band."

But now this band had something to boast about—the finest storyteller seen for generations. It was almost enough to make up for the loss of one of their favorite daughters.

"Sky-Eyes, we must go and see this storyteller," Star told her husband. "Tonight, we will see. . . ."

The Storyteller had chosen a location that offered the dark background of rocky bluff and trees behind him for the stories. He had planned well, Star noted. The stark snowy whiteness of his hair stood out against the darkness across the stream as he began to talk.

"In long-ago times," he began, "when Earth was young and all the animals could talk, Bobcat had a long tail. . . ."

Star listened intently as the Storyteller wove the storylines skillfully, intertwining them, relating one to another.

"That is odd," she whispered to her husband. "I have never heard anyone tell that story but Traveler."

"The man who bought you?"

"Yes. But he was much younger."

"So were you!" Sky-Eyes chuckled.

He received an elbow in the ribs. "No, really, Sky-Eyes. This man is very skillful. I have always wondered. Could Traveler be alive?"

"But you said he was killed by Three Owls!"

"No, Winter Bear. I said I was *told* that. Let me—"

Just then, the Storyteller finished his tale. There was a murmur of approval.

Pale Star jumped to her feet, and strode forward. "It is good, Uncle," she began very formally, with no hint of recognition. "As these others know, I have traveled much. There is another Bobcat story which I have heard, from far east of here. Bobcat, as you have said, had a long tail . . ."

If the People had happened to look at that moment, they would have seen just a hint of a tear in the eye of the old man. But they would also have seen that he was smiling.

It was a strange lopsided smile, but a smile. A smile of . . . well, of something like *pride*!

WORLD

$\longleftrightarrow$

OF

$\longleftrightarrow$

SILENCE

PART I

↔

Speaks-Not

1

As a child, Possum never doubted that he was loved. It is strange, perhaps, even to question the amount or intensity of such a nebulous thing as love. It is a thing that cannot be weighed or measured, only felt. It is a thing of the spirit, as real as the spirit of a budding tree, or new grass in the Moon of Greening. Or a sunset, a distant storm over the plain, or the laughter of clear water over white gravel shoals in a prairie river. All of these are things of the spirit, like . . . like love. Not only seen or heard or tasted or touched, but *felt,* in the fullness of spirit that is known to those who love and are loved.

Though one cannot measure the extent of love, it was apparent that there had never been a child among the People whose parents loved him more. This was an idyllic union, admired, sometimes envied by others of the Eastern band. Possum's mother, Otter Woman, had been a Warrior Sister, sworn to chastity until she chose to resign her high position to marry.

She could have continued for several more years if she chose. The honor of this office was great, and she performed it well. The dance steps, the ceremonies, the elaborate costuming, all seemed designed with this young woman in mind. Her tall form and graceful movements were greatly admired by all, both members of the warrior society and the spectators. There had never been a Warrior Sister so skilled, so well suited to the position. Or so beautiful, it was said.

Any one of many young warriors would have gladly died for her, both those in the Elk-dog Society and in the other warrior societies, the Bowstrings and the Bloods. It was no great surprise, however, when she chose Walking Horse, a young man of the Elk-dogs. He came from a prominent family, that of Red Feather, an important chief of the band back in the days of the Blue Paints War. Horse was surely destined for greatness, but remained as humble and friendly as if he did not even know about it.

These two young people had been friends since their childhood together in the Rabbit Society. They learned to swim, run, wrestle, to use weapons, and to ride with skill. When, at puberty, they graduated into the diverse worlds of men and women, these two remained good friends. Others of their age paired off and established their own lodges, but these two seemed in no hurry. Such a friendship needs no proof, but stands by itself.

This one had lasted so long, however, that the entire band was relieved when it came to fruition. Otter Woman resigned her position as Warrior Sister to marry Walking Horse, and the People rejoiced with them and for them. A union based solidly on a friendship that already exists is a good one, the old women told each other. And it seemed true. The love between these two handsome young people shone in their eyes and in their actions. The People laughed and made jokes, but they were pleased, and sometimes envious of this happy couple.

A child of such love will also be loved, and it was so with Possum, who was born the following season. It was not that he was such a beautiful child, for he was not. But he was born with the wide-eyed, knowing stare that some infants have, already old and wise, yet inquisitive about new surroundings. Beyond that, his face was narrow and long, and carried a droll expression of underlying amusement at the strangeness of all things. The first thing that anyone noticed about the child, however, was his hair. Many infants are bald, some have hair that lies close to the head like a fur cap. This hair, nearly three finger-breadths long, stood erect, bristling in all directions. In addition, it was not quite the jet-black color that was familiar to the People. An occasional infant was born with hair of a lighter shade from the influx of blood from outsiders. There had been intermittent contact with Spanish, French, and with other tribes through the generations. Usually the baby hair gave way to a color that was uniformly dark. At least, not noticeably different. It would undoubtedly occur in this case, and the color was no detriment. Many of the People, in fact, proudly traced their family back to Heads-Off, an outsider who brought the First Elk-dog to the Southern band, and became a subchief.

The child would probably be a handsome man, too. Both parents were quite attractive. But that was in the future. Just now his appearance was amusing. Nearly everyone who saw the infant was made to smile. The wide-eyed, solemn, yet amused expression, the bristling hair that stood erect like . . .

"His hair is like that of a porcupine," chuckled Walking Horse.

"No, no," said Otter Woman in mock rebuke. "It does not bristle with quills! It is soft fur, like that of a possum."

So, the child became Possum. It was a baby name, one that would be discarded soon anyway. But it was bestowed with love, which was apparent to all, and especially to Possum.

Such a child, loved by his parents and amusing to all, responds well to the actions of others. Possum smiled early. As others smiled, chuckled, or laughed, he began to do so in response. He regarded everyone as his friend, and related to all with delight. He grew chubby and happy, nourished not only by the breasts of his mother but by the extra nutrition of the spirit . . . the love of all who knew him. He returned that affection with a love of his own, a love for everyone he met. That in itself was ironic, in light of later events in his life.

It was in the Moon of Awakening that he became ill. That, too, was ironic. A small infant, one might suppose, would be most subject to illness in the dark moons of winter. Possum, of course, was sheltered and protected and well cared for, and prospered through that period, even the Moon of Hunger.

It had grown quite warm on several sunny days before the end of the Moon of Awakening. But Cold Maker, saving one last sally for the end, swept down once more, coating the prairie with ice and blowing his chilling breath. It was a chill that seemed to penetrate through and through, clear to the bone. The People hovered over their lodge-fires and waited for Sun Boy to return and drive Cold Maker back to the Northern Mountains and his caves of ice.

And it happened, of course. It has always been so. But the People were weary of winter's cold, and their spirits were vulnerable. The changes, from cold to warm, then cold and warm yet again was too much for mere human flesh to bear. A sickness raced through the camp, striking down old and young alike. A sudden cough, a rapid warming of the skin, and increasing difficulty in breathing. There were those who insisted that two different spirits were involved. One attacked the elders, filling their lungs and choking their ability to move air in and out. The other was limited to the young. It was a particularly severe form of an illness that sometimes struck the children. It, too, was accompanied by a cough, fever, and difficulty in breathing. Some died from this, too, their skins reddened and blotchy, hot to the touch in their last days.

The holy men did not attempt to explain the differences, but only assisted as best they could. Dances, prayers, and chants of supplication. Plant powders in the lodge-fires to produce pungent smoke. Sweat-lodge ceremonies, which seemed to help some with the lung congestion. There were also potions and teas to help the cough and reduce fever.

Despite all these efforts, the Song of Mourning was heard almost constantly. The very old and the very young were hard hit, of course.

One old warrior, half blind and infirm, challenged the spirits that had claimed his grandson. He arrayed himself for battle, painted his face, and walked out into the chill of the night, singing. It was not the Mourning Song that floated back to the ears of the distant listeners, but the Death Song:

The Grass and the Sun go on forever,
But today is a good day to die.

It was a statement of intention, a declaration that he intended to die fighting this thing that was killing the People. Perhaps his death would appease whatever spirits were claiming the old and the young.

Finally he was heard no more. His body was found later, where he had fallen facedown, apparently in midstride, fighting for breath as his own lungs failed.

Who is to say what turned the course of the battle? The chants and potions of the holy men, or the Death Song of old Red Snake? Maybe the combined prayers of all the families whose old and young had fallen ill. At any rate, the battle had turned. There were fewer new cases. With the warming days, those still ailing were brought out into the sunlight, and this, too, seemed to hasten their recovery.

But it was too late for Possum. One of the last to be struck down, the infant hovered between life and death. Otter Woman slept little, and then only fitfully and for short periods. Mostly she held the baby, rocking and crooning to him, and praying.

The holy man performed his rituals and prescribed a syrup of plant teas and honey, but he was not encouraging. He said very little, but it was apparent that he was exhausted. It must have been many days since he had been able to rest. Otter Woman felt sorry for him as he finished the ceremonies and shuffled away. But she feared that he had said little because he held little hope for the infant Possum.

The child lay near death for four days and nights, while his mother hovered, rocked, fanned, crooned, and bathed the fevered face. The blotchy roughness of hot dry skin persisted, and it was difficult not to despair. Possum no longer took the nipple well, and her breasts became engorged and tender. She knew that when he began to improve, he must have nourishment, so her breasts must continue to produce. To keep the flow coming, she milked it out with her fingers, catching the flow in a small gourd. She managed to feed a little to the sick infant from the gourd each time, sacrificing the rest to the fire. Maybe that would appease the hungry spirits that were devouring the children. Anyway, it could do no harm.

Of most concern to her was the look on the infant Possum's face. Where he had always worn a look of amused understanding, now his facial expression was one of worry. Of *terror,* almost. He no longer smiled. Day after day, his fever and labored breathing were accompanied by the pained, anxious expression. It was as if the child *knew* of his desperate battle for life, and was uncertain whether anyone could help him. Otter Woman sometimes had the strange feeling that *he* knew what to do but was unable to communicate it to her.

"Tell me, my child," she whispered when they were alone. *"What must I do?"*

The infant would stare into her face with burning dark eyes and whimper softly, nothing more. Then she would fall into an exhausted sleep, and wake again with no answers.

At last came a morning when she awoke, frantic that she had slept too long. There was no sound from the child. His eyes were closed. *He is dead!* she thought, reaching to touch the tiny face. But it was not cold. Cool, yes. The fever had broken. The big dark eyes opened now, and the infant looked straight into her face. There was a new look. The frantic, terror-filled stare that was so frightening had changed. The old look, of amusement and understanding, flickered there. Weakly, but it was there.

Then, that most beautiful of all sights . . . the infant smiled. He had not done so for days. Weeping, she gathered him into her arms and cradled him, rocking gently. Eagerly, he turned toward her and she opened the front of her mothering-shirt to put him to breast. He sucked hungrily, draining the life-giving fluid. Her body responded, and she smiled when the other breast began to leak in unison.

"Your time will come," she whispered softly as she wiped the spill from her shirt. "Our man-child eats again now!"

Walking Horse entered the lodge, and she called to him excitedly.

"Look! The fever is gone . . . he feeds!"

Horse dropped to his knees beside her, and the two clung to each other, their tears of joy mingling while the tiny Possum continued to feed noisily.

"We must give thanks," she murmured.

"Yes. At the Sun Dance . . . we will make a good sacrifice."

"What?"

"I do not know. We must consider. A horse, maybe?"

Otter Woman smiled. "I do not know. We will speak of it later. For now, our joy is enough."

And it was good.

2

The Sun Dance was especially meaningful that year. The family of the Real-chief had procured a magnificent bull for the ceremonial effigy. Its fur was dark and thick, especially fine for this late in the season. The head had been propped facing the east, and the effigy of logs and brush, with the skin stretched over it, was so lifelike that there was much comment.

That was good, for this must be a special Sun Dance. Everyone had been affected by the illness that had swept through the winter camps of the People, three moons before. The Eastern band had been hardest hit, with nearly every family either in mourning or rejoicing that they had been spared. There were many bittersweet reunions with relatives from other bands, people clinging together and weeping in the sharing of their grief.

Those whose loved ones had been spared, like Otter Woman and Walking Horse, offered gifts and prayers of thanksgiving. Three fine furs they had chosen to sacrifice in appreciation for the survival of their son. An otter, dark and shiny, a thick soft beaver, and a beautifully colored foxskin were offered. Ceremonially, the couple walked to the west end of the brush-roofed medicine lodge where the buffalo effigy stood. Slowly, with great emotion, Walking Horse tied each skin in turn to the poles of the open-sided lodge. As Otter Woman handed each symbol of their gratitude to her husband, there was a hushed murmur among the onlookers. The People were impressed by the value and the beauty of the gifts. These sacrifices were of the best, befitting the status of this couple, as well as the depth of their gratitude.

Many other sacrifices were made that season. There were beautifully carved and decorated prayer sticks, garments, footwear, a blanket. One warrior gave up his favorite bow to fulfill a vow. He had promised this to atone for the survival of his beloved young wife. Another promised a horse, to be left behind at the end of the last day of ceremonies. Surely the prayers that accompanied such lavish sacrifices reached appropriate deities. It was a time of thanksgiving.

There were, of course, prayers of entreaty also, and vows of penitence if only this would be a better year than the one just past. And above all, there was the basic theme of the Sun Dance: joyous celebration for the return of the Sun, the grass, and in turn, the buffalo.

This was Possum's first Sun Dance, of course. Not yet a full year old, much of his understanding had yet to come. Still, the toddler was impressed by the whole scene. He had never seen so many people before. And, since this was a child who had always loved people and the communication with other human beings, the youngster was in his glory. He wore a broad smile during the entire five days of the celebration.

Of course, he received much attention, as a pleasant child does. His friendly smile, his droll expressions, all attracted more attention. In addition, the story of his having been spared from near death by the fever was well known. Friends and relatives from other bands came to offer congratulations and after-fact sympathy for the dreadful experience. Each of these spent time laughing and playing with the child. Many times, Otter Woman answered the same question.

"Why is he called Possum?"

Patiently, she explained. The reason was not so evident now. His hair had grown darker and longer. It was long enough, in fact, that it was possible to begin to plait the locks after the manner of the People. Slender strips of otter skin were braided into the plait, to lengthen and fill out the total effect. The otter strips would be worn until his own hair was long enough to complete the effect. This made Possum look even more like a wise old man. It also, however, completely destroyed the reason for his baby name. For a while, Otter Woman explained it to each questioner. Finally, she decided it was useless. One who had not seen the infant's appearance simply could not understand.

"It is only a name," she would reply now, and that seemed to suffice. For her, he would always be Possum, her baby, anyway. Besides, at his First Dance at the age of two years, he would receive a new name.

Meanwhile, she would continue to rejoice in the fact that he was *alive*. What a blessing, to have come so close to losing him. *Aiee!* She shuddered at the thought, and held him close again, as if she would never let go.

He was beginning to walk some now, which was worrisome. All the confusion and excitement of the Sun Dance, the hundreds of people milling around day and night, the horses and dogs. . . . Otter Woman was anxious lest the toddler wander off and be stepped on in the excitement. She need not have worried . . . all of the People looked after all children, their own and others'. She knew this, but this child was *hers*. People smiled at her maternal protectiveness, and understood. She had nearly lost this child.

Walking Horse was pleased at the child's reactions to the entire Sun Dance celebration. Possum seemed interested in watching, and not in the least alarmed by all the noise and confusion. There was always a great deal of yelling and shouting, especially around the area where impromptu horse races were always taking place. Many infants were frightened by this noisy pastime, but not Possum. He watched the proceedings with the same delight that was evident in everything he observed.

At last, the Sun Dance was over, and the bands went their separate ways. It was necessary to do so. The People had prospered in recent generations, and had grown. It had been a time of relative peace, since they had become allies with the Head Splitters, their former enemies. That was long ago, now. The two nations had joined against a greater foe, the Blue Paints from the north.

With no enemies, both nations had prospered. With no casualties in battle, population had increased, and larger seasonal hunts were possible. The Head Splitters were frequent visitors, often taking part in the Sun Dance of the People, since they had none of their own. But the increase in numbers at the Sun Dance led to other problems. The grass needed for the hundreds of horses that gathered each season became scarce very quickly. Likewise, there was a limit to availability of food and water. Hundreds of people require a great quantity of food, and game soon became scarce.

Once, it was said, the gathering for the Sun Dance lasted nearly a full moon. Now, it was necessary to split up and move apart to avoid a shortage of food and grass for the horses. The first of the big lodges came down the day after the final ceremonies were completed. The Mountain band was the first to go. Theirs was the longest journey. By evening, however, the Red Rocks had headed west in their long, ragged column, their baggage piled on pole-drags. The visiting Head Splitters accompanied them, since their territories more closely approximated each other.

The Southern band was in no hurry to go, since the gathering was in their own range this season. They began to pack in a leisurely fashion.

The Eastern band, too, had a shorter distance to travel, but they began preparations. They had been, for many generations, the butt of ethnic jokes. Those of the Eastern band were regarded as foolish people, bad luck people. No one knew how it had started . . . possibly because of their slightly different terrain and proximity to the woodlands. Anyone who found himself in a ridiculous situation was sure to be teased, even in the other bands. A man who had been bested in a horse trade, for instance, might overhear a conversation: "Well, you know, his grandfather was of the Eastern band."

There were ribald jokes and stories about the Eastern band. The first horses they obtained, for instance, they led around for a long time before they learned that they were to be ridden. In the other bands even now, a common remark concerning a lame, blind, or otherwise useless horse might be: "Maybe you can sell it to the Eastern band."

There had been a concerted effort on the part of Red Feather, their great leader, to live down this reputation for foolishness. He had met with some degree of success, and gained respect, but it was not complete. The band still worked hard to avoid the jibes that were so quick to come. It was good not to be the last to arrive for the Sun Dance: ("They just found their way here.") Or the last to leave: ("Are they *still* not organized?")

So, by common understanding and generations of slighting remarks, it had become custom. The Eastern band would strike their lodges not first or last, but somewhere between. They were ready to depart shortly after Sun Boy reached the top of his run.

"Where do we camp tonight?" asked Otter Woman. She lifted young Possum to the back of one of the dependable old pack mares and tied him in place.

"Medicine River," Horse answered. "So they say, anyway. It is good. There should be water and grass."

"Not at the Rock?"

"No, no."

"Good. That place bothers me."

Walking Horse laughed.

"It bothers many people. That is why people avoid it."

Medicine Rock had a big part in the tradition of the People. It was there, it was said, that Eagle, the great storyteller of long ago, had spent a winter with Old Man himself, while his broken leg had healed. Many did not believe it. The place had always had a reputation for supernatural happenings, however, even before that. There was no doubt that its spirit was strange. It had been of benefit to some, accounting for Eagle's survival in the old legend.

Then again Medicine Rock had been the site of the final defeat of the invading Blue Paints. By the combined strength of the medicines of two young holy men, one of the People and the other from the Head Splitters . . . It was unclear how it had happened, but those two caused a mighty herd of buffalo to push the enemies over the cliff to their deaths.

Since that time the People had avoided the area. The brooding appearance of the gray stone, already noted for strange spirits, added to the knowledge that many enemy spirits had departed from human bodies in that place. There were some who professed to be unafraid. But when the time came to exhibit courage, even they were hesitant. Why take chances? one asked offhandedly. There were better places to camp or to hunt.

The traveling band passed the cliff on the other side of the river, perhaps hurrying the horses a little to be far away by the time darkness fell. Three young men, goaded by the bravado of their inexperience, left the column to ride nearer the river and observe the face of the Medicine Rock cliff more closely.

They soon returned. No special reason, they insisted. A cliff is simply not very interesting. They raced forward to join the head of the column. Older and wiser people smiled at the folly of youth. They knew quite well that without the forbidding spirit of that rocky wall, those three youths would have spent all day exploring it.

They camped that night some distance to the east of the Medicine Rock. It was a beautiful camping place, downstream far enough to be free of the oppressive thoughts that clung to this stretch of Medicine River. Maybe it only seemed that the People stayed closer to the camp fires that evening, huddling near the warmth that was not really needed on this warm summer night.

Next morning they moved on toward the River of Swans, where they would camp for the summer. Otter Woman was glad to be moving away from the place. She felt somehow that its mysteries were linked to the future of her child, swaying happily on the back of the roan mare.

3

t was autumn before they began to suspect that something was wrong. The Eastern band had experienced an uneventful summer, and were in the process of deciding on a site for winter camp.

There was always a variety of opinion, and various people were quite vocal about their preferences. Some liked the edge of the woodlands to the east. Timber served to break the wind and give shelter from the full force of Cold Maker's chilling breath. Lodges erected on the south, or downwind side, of even a small area of brush and trees gained much in shelter.

The major disadvantage to the wooded area east of the River of Swans was the risk of attack by the Shaved-Heads. These were a nation of fierce and warlike people, partly grower and partly hunter. The shaved heads of the men provided the descriptive hand-sign that expressed their name. A single roach of hair was left standing from front to back, with the sides shaved. These people bitterly resented any intrusion into their woodlands. Traditionally, it had presented little trouble for the People, who were oriented to a nomadic existence on the plains anyway. But the proximity of the Eastern band, and their tendency to make foolish moves . . . *aiee,* one must not think so! This was part of the argument, especially for those opposed to such a winter site.

The location that was gaining favor in the band was to the south of their usual range. There, great areas of scrub oak bordered on open tallgrass prairie. The oaks were especially desirable as a windbreak, it was argued, because they kept their dead leaves on the twigs for most of the winter, providing better protection from the north winds. In addition, the more southern location would provide a milder winter.

"The birds know that!" declared one old woman indignantly, pointing to the long lines of migrating geese, all pointing southward.

Perhaps the best argument for some, however, was that there was less risk of attack by any who might live there. The People were not especially fearful by nature. Since the coming of the horse and their resulting expertise with its medicine, they had held their own with any nation on the plains. Discretion, however, is the better part of valor. *One does not seek trouble,* an old saying of the People observes, *for enough will seek him.*

Ultimately, a southern site among the scrub oaks was selected. It would look out on grassland, the heritage of the People, yet still furnish shelter from the wrath of Cold Maker. Otter Woman was preparing their belongings for travel, packing and arranging, while she glanced from time to time at the play of the children.

There were several of them, ranging in age from a mere toddler or two, to a spirited girl, perhaps four summers old. The girl was mothering the others, directing their play. Otter Woman smiled. It was good to see happy children, learning by their play. In a few years, this child would have a lodge and children of her own. Already she was acting out her role as the woman of her own home.

"Come on, Speaks-Not," the little girl called with a sweeping gesture of her hand.

It took a moment for Otter Woman to realize that the girl was speaking to *her* child, Possum. *How odd,* she thought.

"Why do you call him that, little sister?" she asked, puzzled.

The girl shrugged. "He never speaks," she explained as the children continued play.

"But he is only a baby," Otter Woman explained.

"True," agreed the girl cheerfully. She ran to rejoin the others.

Otter Woman was thinking rapidly. Much as she wished she could keep him a baby, he was not. But what *should* he be doing at this age? She must think about it. . . . The child had been conceived in the Moon of Falling Leaves. She smiled at the memory, a warm sunny day with the cottonwoods their brilliant yellow and the tall prairie grasses sending up their bright seed-heads. . . . But no matter. Possum had been born during the Moon of Thunder. A cooling rainstorm had swept across the prairie. It was good, because the weather had been hot and muggy for days. The storm had cooled the night and made her labor more comfortable. *Thank you, Rain Maker,* she had whispered.

Possum had been eight or nine moons old, then, when they nearly lost him with the fever. *Aiee,* how frightening! But now, he was some four moons past his first year. *Should* he be speaking? She tried to remember other children whom she had observed. When had they begun to speak? Her younger brother . . . but she had been only a child herself then, and could not remember.

She mentioned the question that was in her mind to Walking Horse, but he seemed unconcerned.

"Some speak sooner than others, I suppose. Does he not make sounds?"

"Yes, of course."

The child had made sounds before his illness, and still did, to some extent. It was difficult to remember. Many of the sounds of Possum's vocabulary were limited to grunts when he wanted something—a drink of water, another bite of food.

"Why should he speak?" Horse asked jokingly. "He has everything he could want!"

"It is not funny, Horse," scolded Otter Woman. "I am made to think that something is wrong."

"But what? He is fat and happy, and growing well!"

"Yes, but . . . *aiee,* let us watch him closely. We must talk to him often, try to teach him words."

They tried, but their efforts were disappointing. Most attempts resulted in more gutteral grunts, quite similar to all his other noises.

"Never mind," advised Otter Woman's mother. "He will talk when he is ready."

Otter Woman remained unconvinced. *Something is wrong,* she told herself as she watched him at play with the others. *I must find it.*

It was after the move to winter camp that she began to see the problem in its true light. She had become aware that a child or two in the group where Possum played were younger, but speaking more. Still, not everyone grows alike. It was puzzling to her that sometimes Possum was responsive to the others at play, sometimes not. *What is it that makes the difference?* she asked herself. *Why* does he respond only a part of the time? And why only with the grunting sounds that were becoming so worrisome to her?

Finally there came a day when she began to realize the extent of the trouble. Possum had paused in his play to look over at his mother. Otter Woman smiled and he smiled back. Just as he did so, Far Dove, the mothering-girl, called to him. The girl was quite close, but he showed no reaction at all. She spoke again, but as she did so, touched his shoulder. Instantly he nodded eagerly, and turned to join the others in some new game. What . . . how was it different when he was *touched*?

Otter Woman puzzled over this for a long time. Why should the touching make a difference? She continued to watch. When Possum was *looking* at the one who spoke, it seemed to make a difference, too. By that evening, she thought that she understood. But she must be sure. This was a very serious discovery.

She selected a choice bite of one of Possum's favorite delicacies, a confection made of pounded hackberries and dried meat, held together with tallow.

"Come, little one," she called, "here is a treat for you!"

Intentionally, she did so while he looked elsewhere. The child showed no response whatever. Again she called, now more loudly.

"Here, Possum! Come and get your favorite bite!"

Again, there was nothing. She waited now until he turned and looked at her. Without speaking, she extended the tidbit, and the child ran to her, grunting eagerly as he reached for it.

Otter Woman did not know whether to be happy or sad. She had solved the riddle of Speaks-Not, but the answer was not good.

Walking Horse returned to the lodge to find her crying.

"I have learned why Possum does not speak," she told him.

"Why?"

"He speaks not because he hears not."

"But he makes sounds!"

"Yes. But he does not hear the words of others."

They experimented at great length, speaking or even shouting, both near and far, with Possum watching them or not. To Possum this was an amusing game. Each try, however, verified the finding of Otter Woman. The child could hear nothing at all.

"Maybe it will come back," suggested Walking Horse.

"No," she said slowly, "I think not."

"But why?"

"It is a trade, a bargain," she told him.

"I do not understand."

"Nor do I. But think when he was so sick with the fever, and almost died? We prayed for him to live."

"True, and our prayers were answered," said Walking Horse.

"For his life, yes. But his hearing was taken in exchange. The spirit that wanted his life was persuaded to take only his ears."

"*Aiee!*" said Walking Horse softly. "Is that it?"

"I am made to think so."

"Can it be cured?"

They consulted the holy man, he who had treated the fever. The holy man examined young Possum at length and finally shook his head.

"There is nothing I can do."

"But your gift is one of great power, Uncle. You saved his life!" protested Walking Horse.

"That is true," admitted the old man, "but there is something that you must understand, my son."

He paused a moment, and then spoke to the couple very slowly and gently.

"Part of my gift, my medicine," he said, "is the knowing of when not to use it."

"And that is now?" asked Otter Woman, a little sharply. "You will not even try? You tried before, when he was dying!"

The holy man nodded, a little sadly. "Yes. Then, there was a slight chance. Now, there is none. I have seen this before, with this sickness of the children."

"But—" began Walking Horse, but the holy man waved him to silence.

"One time *never* to use my gift," he said flatly, "is when I know it will not work. I am sorry." He turned away, then paused to turn back for a moment. "Yet, as you have said, he *is* alive."

4

Speaks-Not. The name stuck. It was not intended as ridicule, or even unkindness. It was simply a way to designate an individual from others. It was soon known to all that Speaks-Not did not speak because he did not hear.

"We must use hand-signs as we talk," his mother insisted. And so it was.

In many cultures, in most, perhaps, and at any time in history, a loss of hearing would have been a great handicap. Speaks-Not was fortunate, then, to have been born at the time and place that he was. Any of the many nations that peopled the Great Plains could communicate with any other, through the universal hand-sign language. It had been a necessity for trade. Simple and effective in use, the hand-signs were understood by groups using dozens of tongues and dialects, who did not and would never understand each other's spoken words. Speaks-Not, then, had arrived in a world where communication could be carried out even if *no one* ever spoke. Everyone had the ability to speak with the signs. It remained only to encourage it.

He learned quickly. Otter Woman had been quite correct in her assumption that this was a child of high intelligence. Other children, too, learned hand-signs more quickly because they were being used. It was like a game, and none of the children in the Rabbit Society were even aware what was happening. They were becoming fluent in the use of hand-sign talk. In later years it was noted that a whole generation of the Eastern band had become exceptionally skilled at hand-signing. Many of these became traders, story-tellers, and leaders in diplomacy because of this extra advantage.

For now, however, no one was thinking of such far-reaching effects. It was only that one of their number, Speaks-Not, used hand-signs exclusively. To talk with him, it was necessary to use the signs. No one thought much about it. It was merely a fact of life, like coming inside the lodge if it rained.

The adults, too, found it interesting, amusing, even, to talk with a small child in hand-signs. In the learning system of the People, all adults felt a responsibility to any child, and to his need to learn. For this child, it was no different. When the time came for the Rabbit Society to learn the dance, some wondered if Speaks-Not could hear the rhythm. This proved no problem.

"I am made to think he feels the beat of the drum," his mother observed.

It seemed to be true. The rhythm and cadence of this child's steps were as true as those of any child in the band. He seemed to sense the vibrations of the drum by means other than his ears. Through his skin, perhaps, the tingle of the vibrating, throbbing drum entered his senses. In this way, Speaks-Not was able to participate as fully as the others in the ceremonies. He, too, could feel the primeval heartbeat of the world, the pounding of the sea, the boom of the thunder, through the rhythmic beat of the ceremonial drums.

When it came to instruction in weapons, Speaks-Not was at no disadvantage at all. He became adept at the throwing-club, hunting rabbits with the best. When they graduated to the bow, he proved skillful at that, also.

Without realizing it, the youngster began to depend more on observing color and motion than the others. Since he did not hear, he did not realize that the others were depending on the sounds of birdcalls, rustling leaves, or the snort of a suspicious deer, still unseen in a thicket.

There was one who did realize, an old man, well past his prime. He had held a reputation as an expert tracker in his day. His name told his story: Tracks-Well. He watched the youngster as he grew and learned. It had been many years since the tracker had helped with instruction in the Rabbit Society. His stiffening joints and aching bones made it difficult to keep up with the lively children.

But this was a special case. It was not that time yet, but some day, he knew, there would come a time when these youngsters would take part in organized hunts. It would be necessary to communicate, with shouts occasionally, but surely with birdcalls and animal sounds. No one else seemed to notice that problem ahead. This bright and capable boy would be at his biggest disadvantage yet when that time came. To face the situation in its worst light, it must be admitted that Speaks-Not would never be a reliable hunter in an organized group hunt. He would be unable to follow the signals of the others.

With this in mind, the old man resolved to help the boy compensate. He would help him develop the powers of observation that make a keen tracker. Tracks-Well had a theory that his own gift, the expertise for which he was admired and envied, was not merely a gift. Certainly not a gift like that of the holy man, a gift of the spirit. No, the gift of the tracker was that of the ability to observe and interpret. Tracks-Well had a hunch that anyone could do it, if he would pay attention. It was something that could be developed, encouraged. Maybe all "gifts" could, he sometimes thought, even those of the spirit. But no matter . . .

He approached the instruction of young Speaks-Not very carefully. He did not want to make the boy feel different from the others. Unless, of course, he could be made to feel superior. That was not out of the question, if the youngster was as bright as he suspected.

Tracks-Well started by recruiting several of the children for a tracking lesson. At this age, both boys and girls learned the same skills. The entire session was carried out within a bow shot of the camp. He called attention to small things . . . a red-winged blackbird on a nest that he had noticed. She flew off in alarm, while her brightly colored mate loudly scolded and threatened. He was able to show them the eggs.

"There are two kinds of eggs," observed one girl.

"Yes"—Tracks-Well was careful to use both words and signs—"the white one with brown spots belongs to the redwing. The bluish egg is another."

"*Aiee!* They share a lodge, Uncle?"

"No. The other bird sneaks in to leave the egg for the redwing to hatch."

"She leaves her child for another to raise?"

"Yes, it is so."

"What bird does this, Uncle?"

"The little brown bird that follows the horses and the buffalo."

It was a matter of great wonder. The children were interested, but one boy was impatient.

"What has this to do with tracking?" he demanded.

"Ah, yes." The old man nodded. "It has everything to do. Tracking is to notice and learn."

Some were alert and impressed, but the questioner was not.

"Suppose," the tracker continued, "you come upon such a nest. The mother still sits on the eggs. You know that nothing has passed by to disturb her lodge. And see her warrior husband? He puts on a great show . . . much flying around and fluttering. That would show that an intruder is near."

"The one who leaves her young?"

"No, no. That one is stealthy. She would not disturb the owners of the lodge. I was thinking of a larger intruder. A deer, a bear, a man, maybe."

The lesson continued, with turtles on a log in the stream. The little group crept close enough to see without disturbing the creatures. There were six, of varying sizes, sunning themselves in the warm afternoon.

"See, some are dry, one is wet. What does that tell us?"

"The one has just joined them?" asked a boy.

"Yes! What more?"

"The others have been there longer. Long enough to dry!"

"And?"

"And they have not been disturbed," signed Speaks-Not, "for a long time."

"It is good!" replied the tracker.

He was delighted. As he had suspected, the boy was a keen observer, and if he continued to take instruction well, could be helped much.

At length the group began to lose interest. It was enough for the day, and they headed back toward the lodges. Some of the children hurried ahead. Speaks-Not paused by the side of the path, looking at the ground.

"What is it?" asked Tracks-Well as he approached.

"The ants. They hurry to repair their lodge where someone stepped."

It was true. An anthill, scattered by a hurrying moccasin, lay in disarray. There was a frantic scurry of excitement, with workers beginning to rebuild already. A light was dawning in the eyes of Speaks-Not, shining with excitement. He pointed and signed again.

"We can tell that someone just passed here!"

The old tracker nodded, pleased. This was going well.

"When?" he asked.

The boy looked puzzled for a moment. Only a moment, though, before he smiled.

"Just now." There was interest, almost mischief in his eyes. "If it were longer, they would have their lodge repaired."

"Right! It is good."

Now, he must encourage, but not push too hard. He continued, cautiously.

"There are some," he signed, "who look but do not see. You are one who sees. It is good!"

The boy smiled and ran off ahead among the lodges. Tracks-Well was quite pleased with the afternoon's progress. He would continue. It had been some time since he had felt so much satisfaction over anything. Even his stiff old bones felt better about the world.

There was no reason why this boy, Speaks-Not, could not become a very skilled hunter and tracker. Already, he was observant. Yes, to be sure, Tracks-Well reflected, there are many different kinds of gifts. From this one, something had been taken away, but maybe something had been given, too. The boy certainly had the gift of observation. While he did not speak or hear, he could *see*!

5

The skills of young Speaks-Not expanded rapidly. There were others, too, who took an interest. Stone Breaker, the weapons maker, taught him to work the flint. He learned to choose the best slab of blue-gray flint, how to strike flakes from the edge with a hammer-stone. Then, to press fragments from the edges with a tool made of a tine from a deer's antler, to shape and sharpen.

The boy managed to produce some quite adequate scrapers and knives, even a spear point that impressed his tutor. But his heart was not in it. He wanted to be out in active pursuits with the others. He did not yet realize that he was receiving special instruction. Various of the People, seeing that this boy would face problems not shared by the others, were attempting to help prepare him. Since he did not remember a time when he had the ability to hear, however, Speaks-Not did not miss it. He did not think of himself as being deficient in any way. And, while this was a healthy attitude, it raised another problem for him.

Like all youngsters, Speaks-Not was quite attentive to that which interested him, and bored with that which did not. He saw himself as a skilled hunter and warrior in a few years. Consequently he was eager for the instruction imparted by Tracks-Well. The sedentary vocation of Stone

Breaker, though perhaps more suited to his limitations, did not hold his attention. The weapons maker understood this, but was determined to give him at least a working knowledge of his craft. There might come a time when Speaks-Not would welcome that bit of experience.

There were others, too, who took a special interest in this boy. It was not from any sense of pity, but only that this is how things are, and they must be dealt with. And it was in this spirit that Speaks-Not accepted the extra help, not even realizing that it was out of the ordinary.

There was one, however, whose company he appreciated. Far Dove, the little girl who had mothered the others at play, seemed attached to him from the first. Though she was a season or two older, they were practically insepa-rable. With an uncanny instinct, she was able to foresee circumstances that would bring about potential problems. Thus she would quietly forestall them. Some children have this ability quite early, and it is apparent that they will become people who are loving and caring. Others, unfortunately, will never learn it, and remain children emotionally.

This relationship, however, was one that seemed a gift of the spirit. These two understood each other, as a couple will who have been together for many winters. Dove was not obvious about it, but quite matter-of-fact, never patronizing or belittling. She seemed to accept their relationship as a duty, but a pleasant duty that pleased her and brought a rewarding sense of accomplishment.

The People watched this relationship develop with pleased amusement. Long before the children came of age, it was assumed that they would estab-lish their lodge together some day. For now, it was amusing to see them playing together, mimicking the occupations of adults as they prepared for adulthood.

Otter Woman, though she remained concerned for her firstborn, gradu-ally came to be more comfortable with his hearing loss. Walking Horse teased her about her little bit of jealousy over Far Dove, and that helped to put it in proper perspective. She was able to laugh about it and enjoy watch-ing the young pair.

Then, she became pregnant again and a small girl-child was added to their lodge. There was less time, now, to be concerned with the special problems of Speaks-Not . . . he would always be "Possum" to her. The baby girl needed her more now than Speaks-Not did. It was actually good, she told herself, that she could rely on young Far Dove. Even so, there was a twinge of maternal guilt that she could do no more for him. Maybe it was supposed to be so, she reflected.

In due time, the children of the Rabbit Society grew old enough to learn new hunting skills. Speaks-Not was perhaps twelve summers old when those who had been instructing them decided to organize a hunt. The band had hunted well, and there was no real need that fall. This hunt would be primar-ily for the instruction of the young. Their quarry would be elk. A scant half-day's travel from the camp was an area frequented by a band of elk.

Their migration patterns were more predictable than those of buffalo. The great buffalo herds moved over far-flung distances, following the seasons. South in winter, then starting back to the north in the spring with the greening of the grasses. No one really knew how far these migrations might take them. It was enough that they were available to hunt each spring and fall as they passed in thousands through the grasslands of the People.

Elk, however, moved in a pattern of only a few days' travel. If not hunted intensively, they could be found in the same area again. Their movements, in fact, were much like those of the People—a few days' travel to the south for the winter, back to the north each spring.

This season the scouts, or "wolves," of the Eastern band had watched the elk herd carefully. There were a number of young hunters who were ready for the experience of an organized hunt. A good winter's supply of buffalo meat was already drying on the racks or stored in the lodges. If the elk hunt was successful, it was good. There would be extra meat and robes to trade to the growers for corn, beans, and pumpkins. If not, it was no great loss, and the experience would be valuable. It would involve perhaps a dozen or fifteen youngsters, mostly boys, but a few girls. Many of the girls had become women, their child-bodies blooming into softly rounded curves in all the right places.

Women of the People were traditionally beautiful . . . tall, long-legged, and well formed. With these changes, many of them left the shooting and hunting skills behind, concentrating on the skills of the homemaker. There was no pressure to do so. It was a matter of choice. A woman could become a warrior if she wished. Most did *not* wish, because they were now drawing the attention of young men a few seasons older. It was exciting, flattering, and they began to pair off within a few more seasons.

In the case of Far Dove and Speaks-Not, she had begun her spurt of growth. It was apparent that she would be an attractive woman. Her young male companion, however, would not mature for another few seasons. This is the way of things. She was nearly a head taller, and much shapelier, and they made an odd-looking couple. They were amusing to watch, and some of the People wondered whether their friendship could survive this.

They need not have worried. Far Dove had long possessed the maturity to handle such situations. The two actually found amusement themselves in little personal jokes between them about the different rates of their physical changes. Meanwhile, the girl managed to fend off any serious suitors, though their efforts to impress her were sometimes quite flattering.

She continued her practice with the bow. She had no ambition to become a warrior-woman like the legendary Running Eagle. It was merely the consequence of her ongoing relationship with Speaks-Not. For now, they would hunt together.

Therefore, as plans for the hunt developed, she was one of the girls who elected to take part. There was one other, a burly young woman whose mannishness had long been noted. No one was surprised that she chose the role of the hunter.

There was much excitement among the young hunters, much preparation of weapons, much boasting by some. Older members of the band watched all this with amusement.

"This will separate the men from the boys," observed one old man.

"Yes," agreed his friend, taking a slow puff at his pipe. "But look—there are boasters and there are doers. This will separate them, also."

The hunting party set out well before daylight. There was a special ceremony, and the holy man sang the Wolf Song, a prayer for success in the hunt.

Young Speaks-Not was fairly trembling as they left the lodges and started along the trail. The morning was chilly, but his trembling was mostly from excitement and anticipation. Very soon, however, he found that the trembling had stopped. The leaders of the hunt were setting a punishing pace, and it took all his effort to keep up. In the dim starlight, he kept his eyes on the shoulders of the youth in front of him, and struggled on.

They had traveled a great distance by the time Sun Boy thrust his torch over Earth's rim. The leaders called a rest stop, and the exhausted youngsters dropped to sitting or squatting positions.

"*Aiee*," signed Far Dove, "they travel fast!"

She dropped to sit beside him.

"They only do it to teach," Speaks-Not answered.

"Yes, but we already know that it is possible to travel fast."

They laughed together, and began to relax as they caught their breath. It was all too soon that the signal came back down the line. The party was moving on.

The sun was well up when they paused again. The leader gathered them around him.

"We will wait here," he said. "Our wolves will join us."

It was only a little while until one of the wolves who had been following the elk came down the ridge and approached. Everyone rose eagerly.

"Sit down," he gestured. "I will tell you of this."

They did so, and he went on to explain the hunt. Far Dove signed in turn to her companion.

"The elk are in the meadow over the ridge there," the scout explained. "Maybe thirty—"

His explanation was interrupted by a ringing call, the bugling sound of a bull elk searching for a mate.

"Ah, that is what I was about to say." The instructor smiled. "It is the rutting season, and the bulls may be dangerous, so be careful. Now, we will go around the shoulder of this hill, and spread out across the mouth of the valley. The other wolves will drive them toward us. Come."

He turned to lead the way around the hill, then paused for a moment.

"No talking, from here on," he reminded. "Now, you also see that we are moving *into* the wind? That is so the wind carries their scent to us, not ours to them."

They moved carefully into position behind rocks and clumps of brush, taking places a few paces apart. The animals would run between them.

"Try not to shoot each other," the teacher admonished in signs as they settled in.

The young hunters smiled to themselves, knowing quite well not to laugh aloud. Now came a distant shout and the sound of hoofs.

Speaks-Not glanced over at Dove, a few paces away, and she smiled.

"They have started," she signed. "The hunt begins!"

6

Speaks-Not was already beginning to realize that there were problems here. Apparently Far Dove and the others had heard distant sounds. He had not, of course, but no matter. He would watch Far Dove for signs, and he certainly could shoot at any animal that came close enough.

He looked across the little valley, its lush grass dotted with bushes here and there. There was some motion . . . yes! A yearling calf trotted into view, head high, and then retreated the other way, disappearing into the tall real-grass. He glanced over at Far Dove, but she was watching up the meadow and did not see him.

That, he realized, was to be the problem. They could not constantly maintain eye contact. Both must watch elsewhere, too. But now he was distracted . . . there was a tremor, a sensation, which he felt rising from the earth through his feet and ankles. He was kneeling, and his left knee, where it rested on the ground, also transmitted the feel of buzzing or distant rumbling. It was a vibrating sensation, like the feel of horses running. Then the truth struck him. These running animals were the quarry, the elk herd in the meadow in front of them. The wolves had started the drive, pushing the animals toward the young hunters who waited. He gripped his bow and tried to look everywhere at once. On his left, Lame Bear squatted, waiting. To his right, Far Dove glanced over and their eyes met. She smiled briefly in nervous excitement, and both turned their attention to the front again.

Dove was quite concerned over this situation. She heard the rumble of activity as the animals began to move. She also knew that her friend Speaks-Not could not hear it. How much he could feel through the earth's vibration, she was unsure. It was much like the situation of the dance, she supposed. He had told her that the throb of the drum was exciting, so he must feel it. Could he also feel the rumble of drumming hooves? They must talk of it later.

Her attention was distracted as a yearling cow dashed past. She lifted her bow, but too late. The creature was gone. Another crashed through a fringe of brush, and she loosed an arrow, but knew that she had missed. She could see other elk running, leaping aside as they chanced to encounter one of the hidden hunters. There were shouts now. Her heart beat wildly with the excitement. A cow with a calf at her side loped between Lame Bear and Speaks-Not, closely followed by a young bull. Probably, Dove thought, the cow's last year's offspring. The yearling was closer to Lame Bear, and the youth skillfully sank an arrow just behind the rib cage. For an instant, it appeared that Speaks-Not too would shoot, but he held back. Now Far Dove saw the reason for the half-joking admonition about trying not to shoot each other. The yearling had been between the two young men. The path of each arrow would have been almost directly toward the other hunter. She felt a glow of pride at the way both had handled the moment. Lame Bear had apparently been sure of his target and had successfully downed his quarry. Speaks-Not had held his shot to avoid risk.

The young bull made three spasmodic leaps and fell kicking in the grass. Lame Bear jumped up and ran to finish it off if necessary. Speaks-Not turned to watch, distracted for a moment. It was then that Far Dove saw the bull elk emerge from the tall grass in a low place behind a screen of willow. It was a magnificent animal, as large as a horse, it seemed. The great antlers must have been as wide as the span of a man's outstretched arms as he lifted his head and swung it threateningly. He was excited, disturbed, but certainly did not appear to feel threatened. It was more as if the animal were looking for an adversary, expecting a fight with all the confidence of past victories.

Far Dove saw the exact moment when the animal's searching glance fell on Speaks-Not. The bull paused only a moment to paw the sod with one front hoof as he lowered his head and charged. Dove saw the gleaming tines of polished antlers pointing like so many lance points toward Speaks-Not's unprotected back.

"Look out!" she screamed at the top of her lungs. It was pure reflex, because if she had taken time to think she would have realized: It was of no use to cry out, because her friend could not hear her anyway.

"Look out!" she screamed again. She was on her feet now, fumbling as she fitted an arrow to her bow, unsure whether to shoot or to run forward, and doing neither very well.

There were little things about the scene that were developing before her eyes that she would remember always. The shiny white tips on the tines of the bull's antlers. Many of them, for it was a big bull, with many mating seasons behind him. There was one strip of skin hanging from an antler. It was a narrow shred, a remnant of the soft fuzzy coat that had adorned the budding new antlers through spring and summer. Now the bull's antlers were hardened and mature, as hard as bone. Harder, maybe. The animal had polished his rack of weapons by rubbing off the soft skin against trees and brush. It might have been, even, that he had already been engaged in battle for the favors of some of the cows in the band. At any rate, somehow that narrow strip of unshed skin was more horrible in her memory than any other part of the scene before her. She saw the bull's eyes home in on the kneeling youth's unprotected back as he rushed. The leathery strip swung, bent backward by the wind of the bull's forward motion.

She was running forward now, still yelling her warning, knowing that it would do no good. Lame Bear was standing near his fallen quarry, about to shoot another arrow into the still-kicking body. The shouts of Far Dove finally attracted his attention, and he raised his head. Only then was he aware of the danger. Speaks-Not, in turn, saw the look of alarm in the face of Lame Bear as he looked past at something beyond. There was no time to turn, but Speaks-Not seemed to sense the rush of something behind him. The boy rolled aside, and the bull's momentum carried him past the place where Speaks-Not had knelt. There was only a slashing blow aimed at the rolling figure as the bull faced his next enemy, Lame Bear. Bear's arrow was already fitted to the string, and he raised the bow and released the arrow directly at the charging bull elk.

It was a futile gesture. No part of the forward rush of the animal's charge would be vulnerable to an arrow. The thick skull plate of the lowered head, the massive antlers, the bony shoulders and hard muscles of the forequarters—it might be that a lucky shot with an arrow would stop such a charge, but it would seem unlikely. As it happened, no one ever knew what had become of Lame Bear's arrow. It may have missed cleanly and been lost in the tall grass. . . . Or, maybe it lodged in some part of the bull's muscular frame, to remain there.

Far Dove saw and heard the tremendous impact as the great bull struck Lame Bear. He had no time even to start to run. His body was skewered, lifted, and tossed high, to descend limply back to the grass. Dove had one fleeting impression of the mighty bull, front legs braced, every hair on his back raised in anger like the hair on a dog about to fight. The massive head swung once more in a gesture of disdain, and the bull lunged forward and disappeared into the open prairie.

Dove and Speaks-Not rushed forward. Lame Bear's eyes were open, and he blinked in confusion, trying to focus as his sight dimmed. Blood trickled from several wounds in his chest and abdomen. "I . . . I . . ." He tried to speak, but the eyes were glazing and they could see that his spirit was slipping away.

"Bear, I am sorry," Speaks-Not signed.

The dying youth showed no sign of understanding. There was a rattle of the last breath in his throat, and then no more breath at all. The two friends looked at each other and back to the dead youth.

"He is dead!" signed Speaks-Not.

Far Dove nodded. It was a frightening thing, to see the lifeless form of a companion who had been with them all their lives. A short while ago he had been laughing and talking, excited over the hunt. Now he lay here, as dead as the elk that lay beside him. His first elk kill . . . and his last.

The sounds of the hunt were fading now, the rumble of hooves receding out onto the plain. There were cries of success, and people ran to look at each other's kills. Speaks-Not and Dove sat silent, taking slight comfort from their nearness.

"*Aiee!* He is dead?" said a surprised voice behind them. It was the leader of the hunt.

Far Dove lifted her eyes and turned to face him.

"Yes, Uncle. He made this kill, but another bull came. . . ."

"I see. . . ."

"It was my fault!" gestured Speaks-Not excitedly. "I should have been watching."

Dove shook her head. "No, Uncle. That is not true. The bull ran at Speaks-Not here, he rolled aside and it ran at Lame Bear, who was standing."

"You saw it all, then?"

"Of course."

The older man drew Speaks-Not aside.

"Look," he signed, "when we hunt, sometimes we are hurt. Bear knew that. He would not blame you."

"But I should have seen, and warned him, Uncle!"

"No, no. Do not think so, Speaks-Not."

But it was apparent that he would. The heart of Speaks-Not was very heavy.

7

From that time, the day of the elk hunt, there was a noticeable change in Speaks-Not. He had always been different from the others because of his hearing loss. But, he was so active and capable that no one had seemed to notice the difference. Possibly it was because he never considered *himself* different. He did not know a world of sound because he had never experienced it, beyond a few brief moons as an infant. Therefore, he did not miss it. There were few limitations on his activity as he grew up.

Now, he had encountered a real problem, and it had not come out well. The family of Lame Bear was in mourning, and the young hunters, Bear's contemporaries since their earliest days in the Rabbit Society, were numb with disbelief. The hunt had been successful, and they should have been celebrating, talking excitedly of possible invitations to apprentice themselves to the warrior societies. This hunt had been on foot, organized by men of the Bowstring Society. This was the old, conservative group who favored tradition and had a tendency to resist new ways. Many of the young men were attracted to such tradition.

Others, however, were budding horsemen, candidates for the Elk-dog Society, in whose custody rested the mystique of the horse. The elk-dog medicine itself, the silver bit worn by the First Elk-dog, was kept in the custody of a holy man of the Southern band. It was used in tribal ceremonies, of course, but more importantly, it was considered that its custodian must be a member of the Elk-dog Society.

The Blood Society, fiery young radicals by political standards, had had a large part in the history of the People. They had been, at various times, responsible for the near destruction of the Southern band, and for its salvation. There had been a time, it was said, when the Bloods were banished from the tribe for a few seasons. But that was long ago. The Bloods, though they still had a reputation as radicals, had mellowed through the years. In some respects, they were now almost as traditional as the Bowstrings themselves.

Young hunters always looked forward to their coming of age, and the invitations of the societies. This would have been the time, but a dark shadow hung over the camp, due to the tragedy of the elk hunt. It was not that such an accident was uncommon. It was a way of life. A hard, dangerous life by many standards, but not considered so by the People. It was merely the way of things. That a hunter would be gored by his quarry was one of the dangers of being a hunter. Yet this was different, somehow.

The funeral-wrapped body of Lame Bear was lifted to a tree scaffold, along with his favorite weapons and some food to see him safely to the Other Side. The mourning continued. This was very impressive to his young friends, but no less so to the older members of the band. This was a very unsettling thing, the loss of an apprentice hunter on his first hunt. An omen? And for whom? Did this signify bad luck for all the participants of that fateful hunt? The young people denied it to themselves and in their private conversations, but doubts remained. No initiation hunt could be considered a complete success that resulted in a death.

Significantly, though there was no openly stated policy, there were also no invitations to join warrior societies. It was a time of indecision. It was generally thought by the young hunters that there must be another hunt to neutralize the misfortune of the first. But there was no announcement. No one seemed willing to make a decision.

Speaks-Not was deeply depressed, still feeling the responsibility for the tragedy. He and Far Dove talked much of it, sometimes in vigorous argument.

"It was not your fault!" she signed angrily at him.

"But I could have done something!" he protested. "I was not looking where I should have been. I could have warned him, I could have shot at the bull."

Dove calmed somewhat. It would do no good to shout at him, as she had been doing, because he could not hear her. She must be gentle and logical. She smiled at him.

"Speaks-Not," she signed, "you know that these things happen. You could not know that the bull would come up behind you. No one could. It happened. That is all."

"But because I did not see the elk, Lame Bear is dead. *You* saw it. Bear saw it. No, it is my fault. I did not see."

"You cannot see everything," she protested. "Nor can I. It happened."

"No, Dove, you do not understand. I did not know the bull was coming because I could not *hear*. You heard it, saw it. You called out to me, maybe."

Far Dove said nothing, but was remembering her frantic screams, unable to get his attention. It had been a terrible moment, and she had feared for him.

"I am made to think," Speaks-Not went on, "that I am a danger to others."

"No, no," she protested, but he waved her to silence.

"Yes, I am, Dove. I could not hear your call, I could not hear the rush of the bull, could not feel it until too late. If I had, even, I do not know if I could have warned Bear."

Far Dove was silent, for much of what he said in sign-talk was true. She hated for him to see it. She hated to admit it, herself, because she had always admired his spirit, and believed that Speaks-Not could do anything he chose. Now, it seemed that she was wrong.

"I will never hunt again," Speaks-Not signed.

He rose and left her sitting on the cottonwood log, where they often met to talk together. She started to go after him, but held back. She had no argument to offer. Maybe he would overcome this some day, but for now, there was nothing she could do. Her heart was very heavy.

But wait . . . there were those who could help, maybe. Of course! Tracks-Well, who had taken an interest in the boy. Only now was she beginning to understand the significance of that. The old tracker was feeble now, but it was not his tracking skills that she sought, but his advice. Tracks-Well could talk to Speaks-Not, show him that there is more than one way to hunt elk.

Pleased, she slid from the log and hurried to find Tracks-Well. She stopped before his home, identified by the trail of hoofprints painted across the lodge cover, and tapped on the taut skin.

"Uncle," she called, "it is Far Dove. I would speak with you. May I come in?"

There was the sound of motion inside, and a woman lifted the doorskin and beckoned inside.

Tracks-Well was seated, leaning on his willow backrest and smoking. He nodded a greeting.

"*Ah-koh,* Uncle," she said formally.

"*Ah-koh.* What is it, daughter?" he asked.

She did not know quite how to begin.

"I . . . well, you know of the hunt?"

He nodded. "Yes . . . too bad. You were there?"

"Yes, Uncle. I saw it."

He puffed his pipe a moment, and finally spoke. "What is it you wish to speak?"

"You remember a young man who is called Speaks-Not?"

"Yes, he is a son of Otter Woman and Walking Horse? Is he your friend?"

"Yes, Uncle. Since we were small."

The old tracker smiled. "I thought so. But what? . . ."

"His heart is heavy, Uncle. He thinks this was his fault. The hunt . . . Lame Bear."

Tracks-Well came straight to the point: "Was it?"

"No . . . I . . . I think not. The bull was coming . . ."

Rapidly, she blurted out her story, pouring her troubles before him. ". . . and he said he will never hunt again," she finished.

The tracker puffed two long puffs on his pipe and blew a cloud of bluish smoke that drifted lazily upward to flow out through the smoke hole of the lodge.

"So," he said at last, "maybe it *was* partly his fault?"

"No! I mean—"

She stopped short. She had been denying it, protecting Speaks-Not, but was it not true? Maybe his guilt was justified. Not intentionally, of course, but if he had heard the charge of the bull, or heard her screams of warning, it might have made a difference.

"Maybe," she agreed.

It was a hard thing to accept. How much harder, then, for Speaks-Not.

"Do you remember, when you were smaller," the tracker asked, "and I came to show your friend about the tracking?"

"Yes, Uncle. But what? . . ."

"For this day, little one. As you have learned, Speaks-Not cannot hunt with others. He cannot hear signals, or shouts of warning. But this could not be told to him. He must try it to see why. This, he did."

"But Lame Bear?"

"Yes, that is too bad. My heart, too, is heavy for his family. But, would it really have made any difference? If someone with hearing had been where Speaks-Not was, would it not have happened the same?"

"Maybe," Dove admitted. "But how can one tell?"

"We cannot," Tracks-Well chuckled, "unless we do it again, and that cannot be. But think now . . . would it have been different if *you* had been standing in the place where Speaks-Not was?"

"I cannot tell. Maybe, maybe not."

"Yes. We can never tell."

"But, Uncle, he says he will never hunt again."

"So I have heard. But it seems unlikely. No, he will hunt again. Maybe not in a hunting party. Would he come to see me?"

"I can ask him, Uncle. May I say you wish to see him?"

"Of course, if that is needed. Do you think he would *not* come?"

"I do not know, Uncle. His heart is very heavy. I will try."

"It is good. If he does not come, we will wait. There is no need for hurry."

She started to turn away, but paused.

"I am made to think," she said slowly, "that he needs this visit soon." Then she smiled. "Or, maybe *I* do. My heart is heavy *for* him, Uncle."

The old tracker watched her go, and admired the swing of her lithe young body. *A fortunate boy, that Speaks-Not,* he thought to himself, *to have such a woman. Aiee,* any man should be proud to have the heart of Far Dove heavy for him. Tracks-Well felt good about it, though. It was too bad about the boy who had been gored. But to teach this one, Speaks-Not, what he must know had taken only one lesson. A hard lesson, yet one that was necessary to the young man. Now, Speaks-Not could settle down to learning the special skills he would require.

8

"It is true. I will never hunt again!"

The boy was defiant.

"Then it is good," agreed Tracks-Well easily. "It will be as you say." He paused for a moment, as if in thought. "You will become a maker of weapons, then?"

Speaks-Not looked at the old tracker sharply. It was apparent that his thinking had not progressed this far. Tracks-Well waited, amused. He had noted that although the boy had shown talent in the working of flints, his heart was not in it. The tracker had seen the glow in the child's eyes long ago, when he watched the red-winged blackbirds or the ants beside the trail. Tracks-Well had known even then that this youth's keen powers of observation had marked him as a special person. He did not know yet precisely what form the skills would take, but they were there.

"I do not know," signed Speaks-Not. "Maybe so."

At least, he was indecisive now, Tracks-Well noted. Until now, there had been little indication that the boy was willing to think past his stubborn declaration to refrain from hunting.

"Yes," signed the tracker thoughtfully. "It is good to do something, so that one may eat."

"I can hunt for myself!" Speaks-Not gestured impatiently.

Ah, yes, thought the old man. *That is what I wanted to hear!*

"Why, of course!" he signed as if surprised. "It is good that you have thought of this! You are already better than most at watching."

"How do you mean, Uncle?"

"Ah, I remember you as a child, Speaks-Not. We watched the ants together, remember?"

The boy smiled at the memory, and it was good to see the smile.

"I must eat ants, or hunt like they do?" he asked, mischief in his eyes.

Tracks-Well chuckled. "The bear eats ants, so we could, too. But meat is better. So, there are better things to hunt. Deer . . . buffalo."

"Buffalo? That takes many hunters, and horses!"

"Sometimes. But there are many ways to do some things."

Now the boy seemed eager.

"I do not understand, Uncle. Will you tell me of these?"

The tracker seemed to consider for a little while, frowning in indecision.

"I do not know," he signed slowly. "I am old . . . my legs are stiff and slow."

"But you can teach me, Uncle."

There was more apparent indecision, and finally Tracks-Well nodded.

"Well, maybe. We will try."

"Ah, look! Horse tracks!" the old man gestured.

The two had come down to the stream at the suggestion of Tracks-Well, to begin the lessons in earnest.

"Why to the stream?" Speaks-Not had asked.

"There are more tracks. Besides, it is near. We do not have to walk very far."

"But I would learn—" Speaks-Not began. The tracker waved him down.

"Later," he signed. "First, we start here." He pointed to horse tracks in the soft earth along the stream.

"That is easy," observed Speaks-Not. "A horse came to water."

"Of course. But tell me all you can of the horse."

"Uncle, a horse is a horse. I will not be hunting horses, anyway."

"You might. But for now, look and think. What can you tell me of this animal?"

The boy studied a little while, then began to sign.

"One horse . . . alone . . . not in a hurry."

"Good! How do you know these things?"

"Only one set of tracks . . . walking . . . dung, there . . . it stopped for that, so it was not alarmed. It stopped to crop grass there, at the water's edge."

"It is good," agreed the tracker. "Now, what did it look like?"

"Uncle, I did not *see* it—only its tracks!"

"Of course, but we can tell much." He watched while the boy studied the tracks again.

"A big horse," Speaks-Not finally indicated.

"Tall, or fat?"

"Tall."

"How do you know?"

"His feet do not sink too deeply in the mud . . . he has a long step. The feet are not very big. So, tall and thin."

"Is he fast?"

"*Aiee,* Uncle, I do not know. . . ."

"Look, then . . . the track of the hind foot, there, is on top of that of the front foot. Sometimes ahead, even. A long step, a *fast* horse. Is he sure-footed?"

Speaks-Not sighed deeply and started to sign, but then knelt to study the tracks again.

"Yes," he indicated finally. "The right front foot toes out a little, and he tosses it, but it should not bother him."

Good, thought the tracker. He had seen the slight blur of sand at the outer heel of each right front track. The horse was "paddling" with that foot, but his pupil's evaluation was accurate. It would probably be no handicap.

"Now, *when* did he drink?"

Speaks-Not studied the tracks again.

"Early this morning. The sand is drying around the sharp corners of the tracks." He leaned against the trunk of a big cottonwood and smiled mischievously. "The horse was sorrel in color, with a white spot between his eyes. His left ear had a notch in the tip."

Tracks-Well stared in astonishment. The boy was either picking up information that he himself had overlooked, or was behaving in a completely foolish manner. Slightly ruffled, he became stern.

"And can you tell its owner?"

"Of course. It is the gelding of Black Squirrel."

"You are only guessing!"

"No, no, Uncle! Some, yes, but look!" Speaks-Not turned to the bole of the cottonwood and plucked three long hairs from the bark. "See? They are red . . . almost no horse has a red tail except a sorrel. How many tall, thin red horses are there? And Squirrel's gelding has a white spot on his face."

Tracks-Well was pleased, even though mildly irritated that he had not seen it himself. It was largely as his pupil said. Only the last point was a guess, that this particular tall thin red horse was that of the warrior Black Squirrel. Even that was a good guess. Most sorrel-colored horses of the People were shorter and heavyset. Only a few were tall and thin, and this narrowed the guess considerably. But maybe . . .

"How do you know," he asked, "that these red hairs came from the horse that made the tracks? They could have been left on the tree's bark long ago."

"That is true," signed Speaks-Not, "but I am made to think not. No other horse has walked here since the rain, a few suns ago." He paused to touch a leaf of the cottonwood, now yellowing with the season. "See, it is dusty now. But the horsehairs were not." He drew the hairs between thumb and forefinger, and held the hand out toward the tracker. "I did that before I picked the hairs from the tree bark. This is probably the same horse."

Tracks-Well nodded, still a bit disgruntled that the young man was noticing things that he had overlooked. But it was good, he kept reminding himself. That, after all, was the purpose of this teaching. Speaks-Not would need all the powers of observation available to him, since he lacked one, that of hearing.

"It is good," signed the tracker. "Now come, we will talk of other things. Let us sit on the hill, there." He pointed to a grassy knoll where they could overlook the valley and the river.

"It is good," he repeated some time later, when they had made their way to that point and seated themselves on a rocky outcrop. "You look well, notice things not seen by others. You did that as a child, and you must continue to do so."

Tracks-Well paused a little while. He was still a bit out of breath from climbing the knoll, and his left knee was protesting the unaccustomed activity.

"Now, watch a little while, and then we will talk of what you have seen."

That would allow him to catch his breath. There could be no conversation while they watched the valley, because to talk with the signs they must watch each other. He heard the distant cawing of a crow, and caught a flash of motion along the river, far downstream. He glanced at Speaks-Not and saw that he, too, was watching the crows. Good. The young man had spotted them without the advantage of having heard their cries. Three of them, chasing an owl and calling loudly for assistance. Even now, more birds were answering the call, sweeping upstream to help repel the threat.

He touched Speaks-Not to divert his attention.

"Tell me what you are watching."

"The crows."

"Yes. What of them?"

"Three of them . . . they found the owl, and now they chase him. Others come to help."

"It is good. Now, what can we tell from all this?"

Speaks-Not pondered a moment and then brightened. "Nothing else is happening there. No people, no hunting cat or wolf."

"Good! Now let us look at far distances. . . . The open place beyond. There are animals grazing there. What are they? Horses? Buffalo?"

Speaks-Not gave him a quick look, as if to say, *are you serious?* It was a difficult test, because the distance was great. The dark objects against the golden hues of the autumn grass were so far away that their color was lost. Not quite melting together into the blue of distant hills, but far enough to make it impossible to see color. That loss begins only a few bowshots away, when horses of red, brown, bay, or roan, even spotted animals are indistinguishable. Size becomes more important than color. An elk, grazing with the horse herd, might be overlooked, while a deer or antelope would be smaller. A buffalo larger, of course, but their spirits do not mix well with those of horses, and they stay away.

"I cannot tell, Uncle," Speaks-Not signed now. "Is there a way to tell?"

"Maybe. Look, at great distance; if you can shut out all but what you wish to see . . ."

The tracker drew out of his shirt a scrap of rawhide, as big as two handspans square. It was partly tanned, and stiff to handle, but Tracks-Well rolled it into a tube and tied it with a buckskin thong. The hole through the device was large enough to insert a finger.

"Now, look through this at some of your creatures, there."

Speaks-Not peered through the tube for a moment, and then looked back excitedly.

"How is this, Uncle? They are horses. They look bigger and closer!"

Tracks-Well smiled. "I do not know *how,* only that it is so. But now, you can see that one cannot always carry such a thing, no?"

"That is true," the boy agreed. "One *could,* but not easily."

"Yes," agreed Tracks-Well. "So, what could be done?"

Speaks-Not pondered, but could not answer.

"What do you always have with you?" asked the tracker. "Your *hands.*"

He lifted his hands with fingers spread, and then curled them, nearly closed, into a replica of the tube, one in front of the other. Speaks-Not quickly copied the act, then gestured excitedly.

"It is the same!"

"Not quite," admitted the tracker, "but much handier. Now, try it on the creatures to the left, across the river."

Speaks-Not swung his glance, and studied the far grassland for some time. Finally he turned.

"I cannot tell, Uncle. They are farther away."

"Yes. Do they move?"

"I . . . maybe. But looking through the hands . . . I can see only one thing at a time."

"Good. That is the way with that trick. It takes away something. Now how can we tell if one of those animals moves?"

Speaks-Not pondered a while. "We must see it next to something else," he signed. "A tree, maybe."

"Ah, but there are no trees there!"

The boy nodded, puzzled.

"Then we should plant one!" signed the tracker. He had been toying with a stem of sumac that he had broken from beside him. Now he ceremonially stuck it upright in the sod in front of him. "Really, we need two," he went on, "so here is another." He took a second stick, and placed it a pace closer, sighting carefully across the two toward the dark figures on the distant plain. "Now, look. They point at the animal to the left of the others."

"I see. Then we watch?"

"Or wait, and look again. Maybe we should place another stick . . . there! This one points to the two on the right."

The tracker lay back, relaxing in the autumn sunlight while his pupil sighted across the three sticks. When the young man turned back, Tracks-Well went on with his signing.

"Now, while we wait . . . about the hunt . . ."

"I do not wish to talk of it, Uncle!"

"No, no, not *that* hunt. Just . . . you said you would hunt for yourself?"

"Yes. I can do that."

His manner was defiant.

"Of course," agreed the tracker patiently. "You asked of different ways."

"Yes. Forgive me, Uncle."

Tracks-Well pushed on.

"Now, you can hunt with a horse, but usually the hunters do that with others. The problems would be as you found before. So, you hunt alone, as we are doing now."

"But we are not hunting."

"No, but we could be. If we see game, and the direction it is moving, we could go there and be waiting. It is as we have said. Look, and see, and then see yet more!"

"What if we see no game?"

"Ah, yes! Then we set traps. Snares, deadfalls."

"I have been told of these, Uncle. They are used by others, but not much by the People."

"That is true. Long ago, before the coming of the horse, our people used them. Now we hunt mostly buffalo and elk. But it is good to know the old ways. They might be important. We will talk of such things later. Now, look at your sticks."

Speaks-Not sighted across the two lines of sticks, and looked back, pleased.

"Uncle, the one at the left has not moved. It is a bush or a rock. The others are not where they were. They are animals."

The tracker smiled. "That is true."

"Did you know that already?" the boy asked.

"The bush, yes. I found it yesterday. The others, no. That was just a thing of good luck."

9

Speaks-Not lay perfectly still. If one does not move, he had learned, he is not seen. The rabbit knows this, and hides from the hawk or from the hunting owl by freezing, motionless until danger passes. Sometimes, of course, he is seen and becomes food for the hawk's young, but this is the way of things. Most of the time, rabbit's people survive by freezing. Much more often, anyway, than if they moved. Usually the rabbit who is caught is one who, in panic, tries to run.

Tracks-Well had urged him not only to learn this, but to practice the skill for future use whenever the need arose.

"See how long you can remain frozen without moving, like the rabbit," the tracker suggested. "It saves his life sometimes. It might save yours."

The main purpose of remaining invisible, however, was that of hunting.

"You can sometimes crawl, in stalking game," the tracker reminded, "but sometimes not. You will not be able to tell whether you are making noise. Dead leaves do much talking."

"They *do*?" It was hard for Speaks-Not to understand this concept. Not until he had lost his chance at a shot several times did he understand the problem. Not only must he avoid warning the quarry with scent by placing himself *down*wind, but also with sound. *Whatever that may be,* he thought to himself. Tracks-Well had certainly been right. It was more difficult for him to stalk game than for others.

This had led to the tracker's suggestion. "Let the game come to you!" he advised. "It needs only this skill, to remain frozen like the rabbit. It can be learned."

This was a warm spring day, and Speaks-Not lay in a secluded thicket, watching through an opening into a little meadow beyond. He had already, through long days of practice, mastered control of his muscles. Hardly ever now, did he have the uncontrollable twitches and spasms that had bothered him at first. It had been difficult in the beginning to ignore the sudden muscle cramps that would seize his calf or thigh. His natural reaction would be to grasp the offending muscle and massage the cramp out of it. It had been difficult for him to concentrate, to think beyond, to realize that in a little while the hard knots would soften and relax and the pain would go. It required the utmost of concentration. Eventually, he had learned, and the process of dissociating his thoughts from the pain came almost naturally.

Even so, it had been even harder for him to tolerate the minor annoyances that came to one who was absolutely motionless. At first it was amusing to watch birds and other small creatures, who appeared not to see him at all. A tiny bird, no bigger than his thumb, lighted on a twig within an arm's reach and sang loudly to establish its nesting site. He could not hear the song, of course, but knew by the rippling of the tiny throat. He smiled to himself.

Once, he almost lost his resolve in panic when a real-snake came crawling directly toward him. He could have gotten up, but after all, that would defeat the purpose of the exercise. With great difficulty, he managed to hold to his frozen position. The snake came closer, then paused as if confused. Speaks-Not was sprawled full-length on his belly, and the creature seemed to look directly into his eyes, only a pace or two away. The flickering tongue searched the air, questioning, trying to interpret the unfamiliar situation. This snake was large, as thick as his arm and as long. An old man of a snake, perhaps, one of many summers. He could count the dozen or so rattles at the end of its tail. They were quiet, the quiver of warning not present. The snake was merely wary, not threatened.

For a time, it seemed that they were playing the same game. The snake was utterly motionless except for the flickering black tongue. *How like a tiny flame,* thought Speaks-Not, *except for the color.* He could plainly see the forked tip of the tongue, playing in and out of the mouth, almost more quickly than the eye could see. He could almost follow the thoughts of the creature as it cautiously considered the confrontation.

Finally the snake seemed to reach a conclusion. It began to move again, sliding smoothly in a fluid motion that seemed like no motion at all. Its course was not away from him, or quite toward, but a sort of diversion from its previous course. Through the stems of dogwood in front of him, past a clump of dry last-season's grass, past his face at only an arm's length.

Speaks-Not rolled his eyes to the left as far as he could to watch the snake as it passed. He dared not move, other than that. The portion of the snake's body that he could still see grew smaller, narrower, and finally the patterned colors of the creature's body were followed by the rings of the rattle, the color of untanned rawhide. Then it was gone.

Now what? he thought. How would he know when it would be safe to move? Well, he had intended to spend much more time here anyway. He would simply continue his motionless vigil, and let the real-snake continue with whatever it is that may occupy a real-snake's afternoon.

He almost jumped in spite of himself when he felt the body of the snake gliding smoothly past his leg. Was it possible that the creature would try to crawl *under* him, as it would a rock?

He had barely time to note that distressing thought when he felt the weight of the snake's body as it lifted to crawl over his left ankle. It was all he could do to hold still. He closed his eyes and waited while the fluid-smooth path of the snake slid across the ankle, then touched the other and across it also. Though it was a warm day, his sweat was cold. *Think, now,* he reminded himself. *While it is moving like this, it is not preparing to bite.* He wondered, if he were bitten, what it would feel like. No, he must not think such thoughts.

The bulk of the snake was heavy, much heavier than he had thought it would be. It was with a great sense of relief, then, that he felt its weight lessen, first on his left ankle, then on the right. Then, it was gone. *Thank you, Uncle,* he thought silently. *A good day to you, and good hunting.*

After such an experience, almost anything became easy. He related the event to his teacher, and Tracks-Well laughed loud and long.

"*Aiee!* It is good!" he signed.

Speaks-Not was disgruntled at first by the tracker's lack of sympathy.

"It was not good at the time!"

"No, but you handled it well, and *that* is good! Your real-snake has done a good thing for you."

"Yes, he did not bite me!"

The tracker collapsed into another fit of laughter, then sobered.

"That is true," he agreed, "but more important, he has *taught* you. For this, you should be grateful."

"And I am, Uncle." He could smile about it now. "At that time, though, I was grateful only to be unbitten."

Both laughed now.

In the long run, an even greater annoyance was from lesser creatures as he practiced his motionless ordeal. Mosquitos, gnats, flies. It required great willpower not to jump when the sharp stab of the deerfly's bite stung into a bare ankle like a hot coal. He considered using longer leggings, taller moccasins, or wrapping his ankles with a protective piece of buckskin. That proved the most effective protection.

But he was learning. He finally realized that though a motionless position on his belly was easiest, it was not quite practical. When his intended quarry did make its way down the game trail, he must be ready to shoot. He could not rise and prepare his stiffened muscles to shoot before the quarry was long gone. No, he must freeze in a position that would allow him to be ready at any moment.

He tried sitting and kneeling, but it was not practical. The bow seemed clumsy, getting in the way of a clear shot. Finally he decided that his best position was standing. He could lean against a tree and by locking his knees in the fully extended position he found that he could relax and allow his muscles to loosen.

"You are much like a horse that sleeps while standing," Tracks-Well teased him. "Still, it is good."

It was more difficult to decide how to hold his weapon. He could not hold it extended in a position to shoot, but it must be ready. He must be able to draw the arrow with a minimum of motion. He tried various positions for the bow, and finally decided that it would be most practical to fit an arrow to the string and hold the bow in his left hand as he would in shooting. His left forefinger would hold the arrow in position, and the tips of his right fingers would rest on the string, ready to draw. This would permit either a quick shot or a slow and deliberate one, depending on the circumstances.

It was some time before he had the opportunity to test his theories. When it did happen, it was totally unexpected. It was near dusk, and a chill was gathering. Speaks-Not was leaning against a sycamore and beginning to think of going back to the camp, when a sudden motion caught his eye. There, only a few paces away, stood three deer. All were bucks, for it was nearly time for the birthing of the fawns. The does would be together elsewhere.

There was one wary old buck, his fuzz-covered antlers just beginning to sprout well. His two smaller companions, probably yearlings, were showing their first spikes of antlers. They would be shed in the winter, and next season's growth would be more impressive.

The three were apparently unaware of his presence. They were browsing quietly. Now would come the proof of his skill. He selected one of the yearlings, the one that appeared fattest. The old buck was larger and in good condition, but his flesh would be tough and stringy.

Very slowly, Speaks-Not began to lift his weapon, beginning to draw the string as he did so. Once the old buck lifted his head to look around, and the young man stopped and froze for a moment. It was a great strain on his muscles, but just as he thought he could stand it no longer, the buck resumed his browsing. At the last moment the animals seemed to sense danger, but the arrow sprang forward and flew true to its mark. The yearling sprang forward in bucking jumps, the feathered shaft jutting from the rib cage. The others leaped away and disappeared, as Speaks-Not stepped out to watch his stricken quarry. It ran perhaps a hundred paces before collapsing in death.

It was with great feeling that Speaks-Not stopped before the still figure to perform his apology in sign-talk.

"I am sorry to kill you, my brother," he gestured, "but on your flesh our lives depend. May your people prosper and become many."

10

⬌

"Speaks-Not, are you angry with me?" Far Dove demanded. The girl appeared half angry herself, half sad, and quite puzzled.

"No. Why would you ask this?" he signed.

"I have not seen you. Were you avoiding me?"

"No. I have been learning from Tracks-Well."

"But I could help you. It has always been so between us."

"That is true, Dove. But this is different. This I must do alone."

The girl was quiet for a moment, and a tear glistened at the corner of her eye.

"You do not need me anymore," she accused.

"No, it is not that! This thing . . . the things I have been learning . . ." How could he explain?

Now Far Dove hurried on, hurt and anger in her every gesture.

"At first I thought that I did not see you because of the season," she ranted. "It was turning cold, and no one was outside much. But I did not even see you during the days of sitting and smoking and games in the winter. I thought you were with the young men, gambling with the plum stones. But then someone said no, you had avoided them, too. By that time the Moon of Awakening had come, and they told me you were out of the camp somewhere."

She paused, and the tears welled up again.

"There was a time," she went on, "that when you were out of the camp it was with me."

"This is different. I have been learning from Tracks-Well, and it is done alone."

"But I could help you. We have always hunted together."

He shook his head. This was not going well at all. He had been so preoccupied with all his new skills and methods, that he *had* neglected their friendship. Now Far Dove was angry, and seemed unlikely to consider any explanation.

"It is not that way," he insisted. "This is something that I must do."

He did not know that the start of his instruction from the tracker had actually been suggested by Far Dove. She, too, had apparently forgotten. That which had saved him from despair had been of her doing, and now both were unaware of it.

"It is good," she signed sarcastically. "You would rather be alone than with me. Then let it be so."

"No!" he signed. This situation was deteriorating rapidly.

He wished for her to share his success. The kill that he had made two days ago, the fat yearling, had made him confident and proud. This he had wished to share with Dove, but when he encountered her, she had been cold. Cold, but never more beautiful.

The past few moons had seen changes in Speaks-Not. He had begun to grow taller. His body had begun to sprout hair in new places. There was even a fringe of fine hair along his upper lip. By tradition, this was said to trace back to Heads-Off, the hair-faced outsider who had brought the First Horse to the People. This facial hair was a mixed blessing. There was a certain honor involved in carrying the blood of a legendary leader. Heads-Off, though an outsider, had actually become a subchief in the Southern band, it was said. On the other hand, a heavy growth of facial hair presented problems. It was much more difficult to maintain one's appearance. Much more uncomfortable, too. The plucking of each hair from the skin to produce a smooth face was not only tedious, but painful. Sometimes his fingers ached from holding the clamshell tweezers.

Along with these changes in his body had come new feelings toward the women he encountered. He wanted to be near them, to notice the attractive shapes of legs, the swing of their hips as they walked, the bulge of soft curves under soft buckskin. All women were good to look at, he decided. But the one that attracted him most was Far Dove. How had he failed to notice the excitement that the changes in her body now evoked in him? Now he had begun to dream of her, to imagine the feel of her soft yet supple body against his.

He had been a little embarrassed about his fantasies, but had finally accepted these feelings for what they were. He was becoming a man. This was something that he longed to share with Dove, but he was not quite ready. First, he must prove himself as a hunter.

This he had done, and it was time to resume the friendship that had always been so important to him. It would still be a few seasons before they could marry and establish a lodge together, but they could begin to plan, to dream ahead. . . .

And now, he felt it slipping away. Far Dove turned on her heel and strode off. He followed, trying to gain her attention. Then she stopped and turned.

"You do not want me," she accused, "but there are those who do! Gray Fox has wanted to court me. Maybe I will marry him."

The weight of despair crashed down on the world of Speaks-Not. Gray Fox was older, more than twenty summers, probably. He had lost his wife to a sudden illness the past season. Since that time Fox had shown much attention to the younger women. Most wanted nothing to do with him. He was known as a poor provider, and as a gambler. He was inept at that, too.

"Gray Fox?" he signed in astonishment. "Dove, do not talk so. You cannot do that."

Now fire flashed in her eyes. "And you cannot tell me what to do!" she gestured angrily. "You wish to be alone, be so!"

She whirled and strode away. Later, he decided that he should have run after her, but he did not. He was hurt, confused, and angry himself. He watched her go, and his world coming to pieces around him, and his heart was very heavy.

He did not think that she would actually accept the advances of Gray Fox. Surely she could see the error in that. And she had always, since she became a woman, fended off all suitors. It had been an unspoken thing, but one that was there, an understanding. She would wait for him, for Speaks-Not, her friend. He was not sure how this had just happened, how that understanding had been lost, but he knew that it was gone. Maybe she *would* look to Gray Fox. The thought was intolerable to him.

He spent a sleepless night, tossing and turning in his robes, imagining Far Dove in the embrace of the ineffective gambler. The thought sickened him. By morning he was in the depths of despair.

"What is it, my son?" Otter Woman asked.

He had no answer. "It is nothing," he signed as he lifted the door-flap and went out of the lodge.

"What is the matter with him?" asked his father.

Otter Woman shrugged. "I do not know. He was happy yesterday, over his kill."

"Yes. And that is good," said Walking Horse. "But something must have happened before evening."

"I am made to think," said Otter Woman thoughtfully, "that this is a thing of love. He is becoming a man, you know."

Walking Horse smiled. "Yes, I have seen this. But, Otter, I thought that he and Far Dove? . . ."

"That is true," agreed Otter Woman. "I do not know. They have not seen each other very much this winter. Maybe they grow apart. She is older, but that has been good, for them. *Aiee,* I hope nothing is really wrong between them."

"I, too," agreed Walking Horse. "That is a special young woman."

"Yes, I have thought so, too. We will see. It may be that something else bothers him."

Speaks-Not wandered aimlessly, uncertain in his despair. Many times that day he determined to go to Far Dove to try to set things right. But uncertainty, anger, and pride interfered. Finally he sought the comfort of Tracks-Well, who had been instrumental in helping him overcome despair after the tragedy of the elk hunt.

The tracker, skilled though he might be at his own craft, was of little help. His young pupil had been exposed to that most feared of all human experiences, the fury of a woman scorned. It had come at such an inopportune time, too. The boy had only barely regained his self-esteem by making his successful deer kill two days ago. Tracks-Well had rejoiced for that. It was exactly what the boy had needed.

And now, this. It was doubly unfortunate that it had happened to Speaks-Not at such a young age. He did not yet have the maturity to understand. Most young men, when maturing and learning the ways of women, were courting girls perhaps two or three seasons *younger* than they. In this case, the reverse was true. The girl was older, and this lent a whole new dimension not only to the relationship but to the problem at hand. A disappointment in love should happen to no one this early, Tracks-Well thought. Speaks-Not was dealing with enough problems already, more than most boys of this age.

"Surely, Speaks-Not," he suggested, "she will feel differently today. Go and see her, talk of these things. I will talk to her if you wish."

"No, Uncle, I could not ask that. And I could not go to her. I am made to think that her mind is made up."

Tracks-Well worried about the situation for the rest of the day. He wished that he had more expertise in the ways of women. He and his own wife, Fawn, had always been close. Maybe he could ask her. He did not know whether that would help. They had never had occasion to speak of such things.

Many times, later, he wished that he had gone directly to Far Dove and talked with her. Things might have gone differently. When it did occur to him to do so, it was too late.

He had slept restlessly, half-waking and uncomfortable, and it was near morning when he woke suddenly with the idea. Dove had come to *him* when Speaks-Not needed help. It would be no different for him to approach the girl for the same purpose. Good! He would approach her and explain the circumstances under which Speaks-Not had spent the time alone. She was a highly intelligent young woman, who should be interested in the welfare of her friend.

He waited until midmorning, then made his way across the encampment to the lodge of Dove's parents. The girl herself greeted him, looking up from her work. She had been fleshing a fresh hide with a scraper.

"*Ah-koh,* Uncle," she greeted. "You wish to see my father?"

Her manner was stiff and formal.

"No, it is you I come to see," he told her. "It is about our friend, Speaks-Not."

She stiffened, but said nothing.

"He is at a difficult time," the old tracker began.

"What is that to me?" the girl snapped angrily.

Tracks-Well drew back in astonishment. *Aiee,* this was worse than he thought!

"Well, I . . ." he stammered, "I thought that you and he . . . I mean . . . I only wish to help him."

The girl glared. "I, too, once. But he does not need me now, or want me."

The tracker had the strong impression that she was blaming *him* for this misunderstanding.

"No," he said gently, "I am made to think that he—"

"It is nothing to me!" she interrupted. "I am to marry Gray Fox."

11

For Speaks-Not, it was a crushing blow. Worse, perhaps than any of his life. Worse than the disappointment of the elk hunt, with guilt over having been responsible for another hunter's death. He could scarcely remember when Far Dove was not a part of his world. His earliest memories included her, at play with other children, and always ready to help.

Their quarrel alone had been a terrible thing. He wished now that he could have simply said he was sorry. Sorry that, in his preoccupation with learning the lonely skills of the tracker, he had neglected her. Probably, he realized, he had thought in the back of his mind that he *would* apologize. After both had had time to cool off and see things more rationally, he would have gone to her. Now, it was too late.

Surely he had never expected that Dove would carry through on her threat to marry Gray Fox. He had thought that she was half joking. A cruel joke, to punish him, but surely not serious . . . *aiee,* how could he have suspected?

He had learned the awful rumor from an unlikely source, his mother.

"Possum, I am told that Dove is soon to marry Gray Fox. Have you quarreled?"

He sat, numb with disbelief, unable to answer for a little while.

"Yes," he finally nodded. "I did not know . . . she did not . . ." he paused, unable to continue.

"Did she mention this plan to marry?"

"Yes . . . I thought she only said it to make me angry."

Otter Woman saw that this was no time to continue the subject, so she busied herself with the quillwork that she was embroidering on a shirt. Her son rose and left the lodge. She wanted to ask where he was going, but did not wish to intrude.

Speaks-Not wandered aimlessly. When he rose to go, he had intended to go to the lodge of Dove's parents, to confront her, apologize, and beg forgiveness. Then surely all would be well. She would laugh and tell him that she was only teasing him to get his attention after his many moons of neglect.

However, before he arrived at her lodge, he had begun to recover from the blow of his mother's news. This was simply more of Dove's subtle way, he decided. She was trying to shock him back to reality. He knew that she would never go through with such a marriage. She only wanted him to come crawling, to be able to control him at her whim and watch him suffer. The thought angered him. He realized that he must think of this at greater length before approaching her. He diverted his course and climbed to the top of the nearby hill where he and Tracks-Well had gone before.

A long time he spent there, trying to puzzle out the workings of Dove's thinking. Why would she announce such a thing? To embarrass him? Maybe. To force his attention? Almost surely. Then, when he came to apologize on his knees, she would laugh at him and reveal that she had not been serious in her threat to marry Gray Fox.

This angered him. Where at first he had been crushed, his heart heavy with grief, now he began to feel resentment. How could she treat him so? He had done nothing to deserve such torture! Finally he came to a conclusion. He would not go along with her little scheme. Even though Dove was willing to play petty games to annoy him, he would not allow her to do so. He would not apologize. Let *her* worry about him. At the last moment, he knew, she would realize that her little tricks were unsuccessful; she would announce their coming marriage, and Gray Fox would grieve.

Yes, that was the solution. He could maintain his dignity, and show her that she could not treat him so. It would be hard, but in that way he could maintain his independence. *It is good,* he thought to himself.

Now, how should he occupy his time for the next few days? Maybe he should avoid all contact with Far Dove. Yes, that would be good. Let her suffer alone, wondering about him. Suffer, as she had expected *him* to suffer. This idea began to seem better and better. He would go on a hunt, for a moon or two, to test his newly polished skills of observation. Yes, it was good. It would be like a vision-quest, though he would not seek a vision this time. There were other things that would divert his attention. He must plan just how he would ask her to establish a lodge with him, when the time came.

He watched the western sky until Sun Boy splashed it with color and neared Earth's rim with his torch. Then he hurried down the hill to the encampment. He felt much better now that he had reasoned everything out and had a plan.

"Ah, we wondered about you!" Walking Horse greeted in hand-signs.

"I was thinking, alone," he answered. "Father, I would go on a quest, alone."

"A vision-quest?"

"No . . . I need to try some of the things I have learned from Tracks-Well."

His father nodded. "How long?" he asked.

Speaks-Not shrugged. "Maybe a moon, maybe more."

Walking Horse looked very serious. He was quiet for a few moments.

"Is this about Far Dove?" he finally asked.

"No . . . well, a little, maybe. She is trying to tease me with her threat to marry Gray Fox."

"You knew of this?" Walking Horse appeared very concerned.

"Yes . . . she threatened me with Gray Fox."

"And you quarreled?"

"Yes. She is trying to force me to apologize. So, I will leave for a little while, and let *her* worry."

His father nodded, but still seemed uneasy. "My son, is it wise to go at this time? Maybe you should go to her first—"

"No!" interrupted Speaks-Not. "This is probably what she expects. I will not play her games."

Tracks-Well, too, had doubts.

"Why now, Speaks-Not?"

"Because, Uncle, she only wishes to torment me with this. To make me come crawling to her, to beg like a whipped puppy."

"I do not know, my son. She seems serious."

"Because she is angry! She knows that my heart is heavy, and it *is*. I *have* neglected her, as I spent much time alone these past few moons. Now, I will go out alone to see if I have learned. When I return, I will go to her and she will understand, and we will form our own lodge, Far Dove and I."

Tracks-Well had talked to her, though he did not want to reveal that fact, and had grave doubts. The girl was angry, yes, but he had seen no indication of repentance or forgiveness.

"Maybe you should talk of this to her before you go."

"My father said the same. I told him no, too. I will not play her games."

"Speaks-Not," the tracker began cautiously, "I am made to think that no man has understood women, ever. You and I are not likely to be the first.

But this bothers me . . . ah, well, so be it. You know her better than I. Now, where will you go?"

"I have not decided, Uncle. Upstream on the River of Swans, maybe."

"That is good. Pretty country. What will you do?"

"Travel a little. Try some traps and deadfalls, maybe. Hunt as you have taught me."

"Yes. Remember, furs will not be good. They will be past prime."

"That is true. I was thinking more of snares, for rabbits, maybe. I can watch those who wear fur, think how I would set traps this winter."

"Yes. That is good. And you can snare rabbits for food."

"Unless I make a good kill or two. I can do that, you know."

"And that is good."

The tracker wished that he saw a little more maturity in his pupil. The boy had done so well . . . *aiee,* too bad that this conflict with the girl had happened just now. He knew that in spite of his confident attitude, the heart of Speaks-Not must be very heavy. Maybe it was a good idea for the boy to get away, to regain his perspective.

Ah, life seemed so complicated sometimes! Tracks-Well was glad that such worries as lovers' quarrels were far behind him. He and his wife had been together many winters now. Their children were grown and in lodges of their own. It had been good to have the company of Speaks-Not. It was like having one of their own around again, and it was good. Mostly good, anyway. There was, of course, this same worrisome thing, the uncertainty whether the young people would make the right decisions.

He watched Speaks-Not go, threading his way among the lodges. Fawn came up behind him and put an arm around his waist.

"It is like having one of our own around again," she observed.

"Yes, I was thinking of that," he agreed. "Both good and bad."

His wife chuckled, the low, throaty laugh that he still loved. "Yes . . . will he be safe?"

"Yes, I think so. He is good . . . maybe better than I was at his age."

"*That* good?" she teased, but Tracks-Well did not smile. "You are concerned about the girl?" she asked.

"Yes. I am made to think she is serious. He thinks she is just teasing him."

"Maybe both are true," Fawn observed. "But look, my husband, they must have their chance to make their mistakes, just as we did!"

"Did *you* make a mistake?" he asked, now teasing her.

"Maybe," she said flirtatiously. "Did you?"

He hugged her around the waist. "I am made to think not, woman."

12

$\longleftrightarrow$

Speaks-Not left the encampment with a certain amount of confidence. He was somewhat bitter at his childhood sweetheart, even a little vindictive. There was, however, a certain sense of satisfaction. She would worry about him, but that was as it should be. After the way she had treated him, she should be made to suffer a little. The thought of such revenge was sweet to him. He was glad that he had seen through her little games.

Of course, there was some degree of loneliness. One night in particular, with a full moon silvering the prairie, and the cool south breezes stirring the new grasses . . . *aiee,* it was beautiful! He stayed awake most of the night, sitting up and wrapped in his sleeping-robe. There was a feeling of excitement and expectation, a thought that if he closed his eyes he might miss something thrilling and important.

Only one thing was missing . . . he would have wished to share the excitement and enchantment of such a night with the one person most important to him in all the world. How perfect such a night would be, if Dove were by his side, wrapped with him in his sleeping-robe, sharing the warmth of their bodies against the night's chill. At one point, with the moon high overhead, he actually rose and began to prepare his few belongings for travel. He would go back to her, starting now. . . .

After some deliberation, he came to his senses. One does not start a journey in the middle of the night. Besides, his return now would tell Dove that she had won her childish game. No, that would never do. He spread his robe again and lay down on it, to watch the majestic trail of the Seven Hunters as they wheeled around the Real-star. It *would* be perfect, though, if she were lying here beside him.

A great hunting owl swept overhead, darkening a handful of stars in its passing. He felt a chill, an omen that he did not like. He had wondered about the owl, the hunter of the night. People told of its hollow hunting call, a sound that was eerie in the darkness, like a disembodied spirit who had lost its way. He tried to imagine what it would be like to hear such a sound. He could not remember having heard sounds of any sort.

Well, sometimes in the dim recesses of memory . . . his mother . . . He *could* remember her holding and rocking him gently as a small child. Her lips had moved comfortingly, and he could feel a humming vibration on his skin as she caressed his face with hers. She must have been singing, he now realized.

Such were his flights of fancy as he stared dreamily into the night sky. He wondered how it would feel to be held and caressed and kissed by Far Dove. He could imagine *her* lips, humming against his skin. The thought was marvelously exciting. Ah, well, that time would come.

He traveled, enjoying the freedom of his young manhood. He followed the River of Swans westward, stopping to visit villages of Growers along the way. Sometimes he made a good kill near such a village, and traded meat and the skin for supplies. Fresh corn, potatoes, once a new pair of moccasins. They fit poorly, not being of the same design as that of the People.

Far upriver, a Grower told him that the People's Northern band was in summer camp a day's travel to the west. He decided to visit them. At least, he could obtain a pair of moccasins of more familiar fit.

He stayed with the Northern band for several days, renewing acquaintances and friendships.

"Stay with us," a distant cousin urged. "We will be starting for the Sun Dance in half a moon. You can meet your people there."

He considered this possibility, but decided against it.

"No," he finally indicated, "this is a sort of quest. I hunt alone. But I will see you again at the Sun Dance."

Yes, that would be good. He would have more time to practice his skills; he would *not* return to his own Eastern band, but meet them, also, at the Sun Dance.

"How is it that you do not ride a horse, Speaks-Not?" his relative asked.

That was a complicated thing, one he had considered himself. It was hard to explain. A horse was fine for traveling long distances. It was good for hunting buffalo with either a lance or a bow. But Speaks-Not had decided that it would not work well with his style of hunting, the silent wait. There would be long times while he stood motionless, watching and waiting. What would his horse be doing? He must either tie it, which would not be very practical—the creature must eat—or turn it loose to graze, when it might easily wander away. Besides, if he ever found himself in a situation of danger from potential enemies, the horse would be a liability. His enemies could hear the call of a horse, but he could not. He would expose himself to much less danger by remaining alone.

All of this, reasoned out over a period of time, was difficult to explain to his questioner.

"It does not work well," he signed, "for one who hunts alone. For travel, maybe."

"I will lend you a horse for travel," his cousin suggested. "You can give him back at the Sun Dance next moon."

It was very tempting. It was a long way back to his own band, and his feet were sore. He could start there on horseback and travel more rapidly and comfortably. Or he could start across country, and arrive at the Sun Dance site before the others. It would give him a chance to see more country, to explore. . . . He was actually enjoying his time alone a great deal.

"It is good!" he signed. "The Dance is on Sand River, no?"

"Yes. Come, let us pick a horse for you."

They looked at several animals and finally selected a well-built roan gelding of quiet disposition. Its gaits were smooth, and it appeared to be an easy keeper. Speaks-Not rode with his cousin until he was familiar with the horse, comfortable with its spirit.

"He is not a buffalo hunter," the owner cautioned.

"That is fine," Speaks-Not answered, "for that is not my way of hunting anyway."

Even in the short time that they had been riding together, Speaks-Not had noticed one thing, however. Communication was very difficult. Most hand-signs required the use of both hands. On a horse, one hand was required much of the time to guide the animal, except at a walk. If a hand were required to hold a weapon too, conversation would be quite difficult. Yes, he concluded, for one with his style of hunting and tracking, a horse was good for travel and for little else.

He left the Northern band and made his way southwest, in no particular hurry. He stopped from time to time, hunting a bit, trying snares for a rabbit sometimes. He was never hungry, and all in all it was a thoroughly enjoyable interlude. Only one thought marred the journey sometimes. He missed Far Dove. He would see something beautiful, or interesting, and wish that she had been there to share the pleasure.

He watched a game involving a crow one afternoon. It was the crow's behavior that attracted his attention. From some distance away he saw the bird jump from the ground into the air, nearly the height of a man, then settle back. He paused to watch. There was some sort of motion on the ground, but he could not distinguish it. A snake, perhaps?

He tied the roan to a sumac stem and circled up a little draw to come closer. It took a little while, for he crawled the last few paces. When finally he parted the grass and peered over the rise, he was astonished. There, not a stone's throw away, the crow was busily engaged in a game or contest. Its playmate was a rabbit! The rabbit stood a few paces away, and the two watched each other warily. Suddenly the rabbit *charged* directly at the crow. This in itself was curious, because rabbits do not charge. Buffalo, buck deer or bull elk in season, bears, wolves—all may be dangerous because of their tendency to rush at an intruder. But a *rabbit*?

The crow stood perfectly still until the rabbit was hardly a hand's span away, then leaped into the air as it had done before. The rabbit shot past beneath the bird, went on a few paces, stopped, and turned to face the bird again. The crow, meanwhile, settled back to earth, facing the rabbit's new position.

Puzzled, Speaks-Not tried to think what this might mean. Was the rabbit trying to defend a nest of newborn young from the crow's predatory approach? He watched the repetition of the charge and the leap into the air. . . . Why did the crow not merely fly away? The strange performance continued, the crow alighting in precisely the same spot each time. Then there was a shadow overhead, and a red-tailed hawk sailed effortlessly past, hunting. The rabbit froze for only an instant, then made a dash for the safety of a jumble of nearby rocks. The crow rose and flapped away, cawing indignantly at the intrusion. Speaks-Not could tell that by the open beak and rhythmic pulsations of the throat as it passed over him. The hawk sailed on, either not hungry, or realizing the futility of a hunt in the rocky domain of this particular rabbit.

Speaks-Not hurried forward. He had marked the spot where the crow had settled back each time, and wished to know . . . he half expected to find a rabbit's nest, possibly with tiny hairless newborns, the prey of the crow. To his surprise, there was nothing. A flat, bare patch of earth . . . not even grass. He spent some time searching in an ever-increasing circle, thinking that he would find a nest, or at least something to explain the peculiar behavior of bird and beast. Still there was nothing. Still puzzled, he went back to his horse. His only conclusion was that it had been a game of some sort. Both creatures knew that it was a game. Neither was threatened by it. Until, of course, the hawk entered the scene. *Aiee*, how strange and amusing . . . he must tell Far Dove. He wished that she could have seen it with him . . . the retelling could never be as good. Well, they would be together soon.

There was one other incident that would prove significant later . . . much later. He came to a gray cliff, facing the south. It extended along a clear swift river, stretching to the west as far as perhaps half a day's journey. He did not realize its presence until after he had crossed the river and glanced to his right. He had approached from the north, and on that side the cliff could not be seen. Level plain extended right to the edge of the bluff's face. Curious, he turned to his right and rode along the river, looking up at the rocky face. Then it occurred to him—this was Medicine Rock. He had seen it once before, at a distance, as the band passed by. He had been no more than nine or ten summers old.

The story of Medicine Rock had been told that night at the story fires. More than one story of the Rock, actually . . . what was it? Yes, a young hunter of the Southern band, was it not? Lost and injured, he had spent a winter here. Its medicine was strong. Something about the Old Man of the Shadows himself . . . but that was probably just a story.

The other, only a few generations ago . . . an invader from the north had been defeated here. The combined skills of two young medicine men, one a Head Splitter . . . Was that not when the People and the Head Splitters became allies? He thought so. There was also something about buffalo . . . yes! A stampede, caused by the combined medicines, had almost totally wiped out the enemy by pushing them over the bluff. This very bluff, he now realized. He could see the rim far above, through the tall sycamores that grew along the river. It was easy to see how it could have happened. *Aiee, what a fall!*

He paused to water his horse. Something white caught his eye on the other shore, and he waded across the riffle to investigate. It was a buffalo skull, bleached white by the sun and wind and water. There were other bones, too, moldering in the sod of the narrow strip along the bank. He could see others, too, lodged in crevices in the broken face of the cliff.

He looked up, nearly straight up the cliff's face. Dark, forbidding gray stone, pocked with crevices and holes and small caves. Its spirit could be felt. He felt drawn, however, like bees to flowers in spring. He longed to climb that rocky face, to commune with whatever spirits might dwell here.

But wait . . . was there not something else to the story? Why had the People passed at a distance instead of along the river? Thinking back, he could remember his mother's dread of the place. *I do not like its spirit,* she had said.

Apparently there were many others who shared this apprehension. He recalled, now, there had been a saying that his father had told him. *We pass this way often,* Walking Horse had said, *but at a distance.*

Standing there on the grassy bank and looking up, Speaks-Not could feel the power of the place's spirit, but little of the dread. Of the legends about this place, were not all favorable to the People? Maybe it was all in one's attitude, how one related to such spirits.

Anyway, he told himself, someday he would return and climb that forbidding rock face. He could see footholds and places to grasp, even from here. There was a great cleft, like a giant ax wound, just to the right of where he stood. The jumble of gray stone tumbling from the cleft would provide good footing. Well, not today. But someday, he would return and explore this Medicine Rock.

13

It was sometime before the Sun Dance that Far Dove realized she had made a mistake. The greatest of her life, probably. She had been furious at Speaks-Not. It had been hurtful for him to ignore her while Tracks-Well instructed him, but she understood that. She had intended only to tease him, hurt *him* a little. But then, when their confrontation came, everything seemed to fall apart.

She was still bewildered. How had that happened? She tried to recall the conversation of that fateful day when her life had been turned upside down. There was nothing really significant, no one remark or turning point. It was just that . . . *aiee!* How *had* it happened? She had suddenly found herself angry at him, and had taunted him with Gray Fox. That should have been a joke between them. Instead, Speaks-Not had become angry in turn, and had *forbidden* her. . . . He should not have done that. It still angered her to think of it. But of course, *she* had then overreacted.

After her anger cooled, she had considered going to him. But that, of course, would be to admit that he was right in forbidding her to see Gray Fox. Not that she *wanted* to, but that she would *not* be told what she must or must not do. She kept hoping, expecting that Speaks-Not would come to his senses and approach her with an apology. Nothing happened.

She saw an opportunity when Tracks-Well approached her in behalf of his apprentice. She did not know whether Speaks-Not knew of this overture or not, but it seemed an opportunity to force the reconciliation. Now she realized that it had been a mistake to say that she was about to marry. *Aiee,* what a mistake!

The story had spread through the band like real-fire. Or, she thought glumly, more like a prairie fire in a high wind. Real-fire strikes once, in a crash of thunder, and is gone. The dry grassland, though, from one tiny spark, burns like tinder, devouring everything as far as the eye can see. Sometimes, devouring the person who dropped the spark. She shuddered at the significance of that thought.

The rumor had come to Speaks-Not as she planned, but he had not come running to her to restore their friendship, as she had hoped. She had guessed wrong. Instead, he had left the band. No one seemed to know where he was going or for how long. She had been rejected once more, and her anger flared to hatred, almost.

An even more unexpected result of the fire she had thoughtlessly kindled came when word reached Gray Fox. He, of course, took the rumor for fact, and assumed that here was an invitation to come courting. She had always rebuffed him before, avoiding his advances. Now he was encouraged and pushed his courtship to a staggering intensity.

It became a great joke in the encampment. There were wagers as to its outcome.

"She will never marry him."

"But he needs a woman."

"He has needed one for a season, but he is not a good provider."

"True. And this woman is too clever to overlook that. Besides, she belongs to Speaks-Not, no?"

"They quarreled, and he is gone."

The arguments raged on, an amusing diversion for most, but a blow to the heart and soul of Far Dove. She was spared the worst of the ribald jokes by sheer sympathy, but the pressure began to wear on her. And, Gray Fox seemed to be everywhere. She could do nothing without his following her, dogging at her heels. Her resistance began to wear thin.

"Marry him," advised an old woman, only half joking. "That will get him away from you!"

In the end, that was the sort of unreasoning logic that led to her decision. She turned on Gray Fox as he followed her on her morning chores. She was gathering firewood, and his presence was overwhelming, his person close.

"If I agree to marry you," she demanded, "will you let me alone?"

"Of course! Anything you wish is yours. You will see!" he cried, delighted.

Once the decision was made, she found herself in near panic. She wanted badly to talk with Speaks-Not. Maybe he could help her find her way out of this. Yet, he was part of the problem, not part of the answer. Her anger at him rose again, for allowing this situation to happen, though she knew that she was responsible. At least, partly.

She arrived at a compromise in her thinking. She would set a time for marriage, to stop the suffocating nearness of her suitor. A time far in the future. That would give her control of the situation. Then, when Speaks-Not returned, she would approach him, distasteful as it was to admit her mistake. That would make everything right, and she could tell Gray Fox that she had changed her mind.

"I will marry you," she told Fox, "just before we start to the Sun Dance."

She had calculated carefully. Speaks-Not, it was said by his parents and by Tracks-Well, would be gone "a moon, maybe more." The Sun Dance was fully three moons away, and he would return long before her final decision was necessary.

Her move was quite successful, at first. Gray Fox stopped dogging her steps, allowing her welcome room to breathe. The respite was good for her, and there was a certain sense of gratitude toward Gray Fox for keeping his part of the agreement. She tried to push aside the thought that she did not intend to keep her part. Actually, when she did think of it, she began to feel a strange emotion . . . pity for the inept, not-too-bright man, a compulsive gambler and somewhat inadequate hunter. She began to feel responsible for his troubles. Not for the loss of his wife, of course, though that, too, was to be pitied.

The couple had had no children, which was good. A woman marrying Gray Fox would not have another woman's children to raise. *What am I thinking?* she asked herself in panic. *I have no such intention.*

But, her maternal instincts continued to surface. Ironically, it was the same sympathetic understanding that had led her as a child to befriend a younger child who could not hear. She developed a sympathy and understanding for Gray Fox and his problems. She began to dread the time when she must tell him the truth. How would he respond?

At the end of a moon, she began to expect the return of Speaks-Not. There was no particular reason, except the vague "a moon, maybe more." She had fastened on that hope, and in her mind it had become fact. She saw his parents occasionally but was hesitant to ask if they had any word. Otter Woman was still kind and friendly. . . . If they had word of Speaks-Not, she would surely share it. For years Far Dove had been almost family.

There was, however, a change in Otter Woman's attitude at about this time. Her quiet cheerfulness gave way to a certain sadness. Dove assumed that Otter missed her son. This should have brought the two women closer, but seemed to drive them apart. Dove finally realized that the older woman resented the talk of Gray Fox that whispered through the camp. She wished that she could share her troubles with this kind woman who would someday share her son . . . *aiee,* there it was again! Otter Woman was part of the problem, not the answer. Dove could never share her resentment of Speaks-Not with his mother. And Otter Woman would surely resent the deception involving Gray Fox, if she knew. They drifted apart, and there was sadness on both sides.

It was the Moon of Growing Grass, nearly time for the Moon of Roses, when a traveling trader stopped with the Eastern band of the People. He was interesting. He told many stories, and had a variety of commodities to trade. Black obsidian arrow points, red pipestone from the north, a bitter brown cake he called *chocolatl,* from which could be made a stimulating drink with hot water.

But he carried news. His own tribe, whose hand-sign indicated the "nation of traders," lived along the eastern slope of the mountains, he said. They had frequent contact with the Mountain band of the People.

"But your Northern band, too," he added. "I have just been with them a little while. Oh, yes, I nearly forgot! A message . . . one of your young men is there. Speaks-Not, he is called."

Quickly, someone summoned Walking Horse and Otter Woman.

"You have seen our son?" Otter Woman asked excitedly.

"Yes, yes, a fine young man," said the trader expansively, for he was adept at his vocation. "He sends you a message! He will travel to the Sun Dance, instead of back here. He will meet you there."

"It is good," said Walking Horse proudly.

And it was, to know that their son was alive and well. Both parents were quite relieved, and treated the visitor with great respect and honor, giving him small gifts.

It was not so with Far Dove. She was present when the trader told his news, and her heart leaped with joy for a moment. But wait . . . this was wrong! She had been depending on his return to help her escape the dilemma into which she had become entrapped. Now, though the thought of his well-being made her glad, the cold truth began to grip her heart. Speaks-Not would not return to assist her. A flash of anger came over her. How dare he be so inconsiderate! He did not really care at all that he had destroyed her world. Tears filled her eyes, and she turned away to be alone.

She ran, once she was out of the crowd among the lodges, along the stream past giant old cottonwoods and sycamores to a pleasant place that she had found, where no one would see her. There, she spent a long time crying silently. It was as if she mourned for a husband that had never been. Yet, Speaks-Not *had* been a part of her life, for most of it. She could hardly remember when he had not been a major part of her waking thoughts.

Now he was gone, and she felt that she was in mourning. No one else would understand, she knew, and there was no one with whom she could share her grief.

Finally, her tears exhausted, grief began to turn to anger. When someone died or was killed, it could not be helped. It was the way of things. Death comes as part of the circle, and is expected, sometimes. One has little control over such a loss. But *this* . . . Speaks-Not had *chosen* this. He had deliberately shunned her once again, had abandoned her in her time of greatest need. The more she thought on it, the more furious she became. He probably thought that she would come crawling back to him. She would show him!

Dove rose from the soft grass where she had lain crying and composed herself. She washed her face at the stream, replaited her hair, and adjusted her dress. Then, calm outwardly but burning with anger inside, she made her way back among the lodges to look for Gray Fox.

It was not difficult to find him, because he still seemed to be everywhere, though at a greater distance. He was respecting their odd bargain. She strode directly to him, stopped, and planted her feet with determination. Her heart was beating wildly, like the struggles of a trapped bird in the hand.

"Fox," she said, "I will marry you tomorrow."

14

The People began to gather on Sand River, late in the Moon of Roses, for the annual Sun Dance. It was the greatest event of the year, a mixture of joyous celebration, reunion with friends and relatives, and of course the fervor of religious ritual. It was a time of great excitement, races and contests, gambling, feasting, but also prayers of thanks for the return of the sun, the grass, and the buffalo, on which the life of the People would depend. Solemn ceremony mixed readily with the more earthly pursuits, for is it not all one, the world and the spirit?

Speaks-Not arrived in the designated area to find the Southern band already present, and their camp established. The site this year was in their customary range, so they had a shorter distance to travel. He paid his respects to their chief, according to custom.

"Ah-koh, my chief," he signed, "I am Speaks-Not, of the Eastern band."

The old chief nodded.

"It is good. Your people are near?"

"I do not know, Uncle. I have been traveling. I will meet them here. The Northern band is a few sleeps behind me," he signed.

"Ah! You have been with them?"

"A short while. I hunt alone."

"You are the son of Otter Woman and . . . White Horse, is it?"

"Walking Horse, Uncle."

"Ah, yes. Fine people. Your mother is a distant relative. We go back to Heads-Off, you know."

Speaks-Not nodded, thinking of the tweezers and the plucking of the facial hairs from his upper lip. He should take care of such things before the arrival of the Eastern band. He wished to appear well-groomed and confident when he met Far Dove. She would have come to her senses now, and they could resume their friendship and their lives together.

He left the lodge of the band chief and wandered around the camp area. It was a good site, with plenty of grass and the clear stream for water. He mentally noted where each band would camp. The Mountain and Red Rocks bands to the west, his own to the northeast. Due east, of course, was open, to greet the rising of Sun Boy with his torch. In the same way, the lodge doorways would all face the east, and for the same reason. In addition, there was a more practical reason. Prevailing winds would be from the south, and the smoke flaps on the lodges must be quartering downwind to draw properly.

To the southeast, there would be an open space in the camp circle of the bands. It was also left open in the corresponding circle of the Big Council. The chiefs and subchiefs of each band would take their assigned places, with the space to honor the rising sun. But there would also be an open space to the southeast. It had been so for many generations, it was said. There had once been another band, according to legend. They had been killed by enemies long ago, it was believed, when the People lived much farther to the north. It was one of the reasons for the migration southward to the Sacred Hills. There the People had found the spirits in tune with their own. Even that was so long ago that no one knew how long. Still, the extinct band was honored in memory by the empty place in the circle. It had become known as the Lost Band. There was always the possibility that some descendant of a survivor might appear, to claim his seat in the Big Council. Sometimes he wondered about the fate of the Lost Ones.

He wandered on, enjoying the sights and smells. Even though only the first band was present, there was a sense of excitement in the air, an anticipation of the festival.

It was that very evening that a young man loped into camp from the west on a horse that had been ridden too hard. He carried news. The Red Rocks were only a day away, and a delegation of Head Splitters was with them. Head Splitters, having no Sun Dance of their own, often attended that of the People. It was good to share the stories and ceremonies of others. The Red Rocks had also been in contact with the Mountain band, and they would arrive a day or two later. It was good, and excitement mounted.

Speaks-Not could hardly wait for his own Eastern band to arrive. He had never been away for this long, and found that he was missing his parents. Tracks-Well, too, of course, who had become like a grandfather to him.

Mostly, he had to concede, he was anxious to begin his reconciliation with Far Dove. He thought of her constantly, and could visualize every mannerism, every motion of her body. The little crinkles at the corners of her eyes when she laughed . . . her smile. Ah, it was good.

Impatient, he rode out with a few other young men to see if the Eastern band might be approaching. He knew these youths only as acquaintances and soon tired of their company. They were interested only in racing around, showing off, and generally behaving foolishly. He parted from them and struck off on his own.

There was a high, flat hill some distance to the north. He had noticed it, coming in. From there he should see much. He loped his horse in that direction, an easy gait to let the animal release pent-up energy. The roan had become quite excited when the other horses were racing, and it would be good to tire him a little. An easy lope should do that. The roan was quite comfortable to ride, and Speaks-Not found himself enjoying the day immensely. He had no special responsibilities, the excitement of the Sun Dance was at hand, he would see his parents and young sister. . . . Best of all, he would see Dove. They could enjoy the fun of the festival together, and begin to make plans.

He drew the gelding to a stop on the flat hilltop and began to search the prairie to the east with his gaze. He had learned to sweep back and forth with his eyes constantly to compensate for his absent hearing. Then, every little while he would glance to his rear. This technique had been suggested by Tracks-Well. He had used it himself many times, the tracker said, when he had had a need for extra-careful observation.

Immediately, Speaks-Not saw a long column in the distance, easily seen by the fuzzy plume of dust that lay alongside like a rolled robe of yellow fur. His heart beat faster as he tried to calculate how long . . . They would have to stop for the night, he realized. Well, he would join them! It was well past midday, but he could reach them as they made camp, without even pushing the roan. He remounted and started east. He did not know whether his erstwhile companions had even seen the approaching travelers. Probably not, unless they had become considerably more serious since they parted. He was inclined to doubt such a possibility. No matter . . .

Shadows were growing long already when he loped into the camp of the Eastern band. They had apparently just stopped, because everything was utter confusion. No one would erect the big lodges for a one-night stay, and there was a scurry to select family campsites and erect such brush shelters as each considered appropriate. Here and there a campfire began to blossom.

A young man waved a greeting to him and Speaks-Not pulled his horse to a stop.

"My parents?" he signed.

"Yes! Over there." The young man pointed toward the thin strip of timber along the stream.

Speaks-Not turned his horse aside, moving through the crowd at a walk. His mother rose from her fire-making, saw him, and raced forward with arms spread wide. He slid from the horse to her embrace, and it was good.

"You have grown," she signed, laughing. "Look at your shoulders!" She felt his muscled arm appreciatively. "You are a man!"

"Of course he is a man!" Walking Horse signed as he approached.

For a little while everyone signed at once, and they laughed together.

"Did you have a good trip?" Speaks-Not inquired.

"Yes, good weather, no trouble. But what of you?" asked his mother.

"Good. I spent some time with the Northern band."

"They are here?"

"No. I came ahead. The Sun Dance is a day that way," he pointed. "I came to meet you."

"It is good," signed his father, touching his shoulder. "You will camp with us tonight?"

"Yes. Do you have a sleeping-robe? I did not plan to find you, and left mine behind."

"We will find something," his mother signed, laughing. "Now, sit, I will fix something to eat."

"Good. But now, I must find the camp of Dove's family. Have you seen them?"

There were blank looks on the faces of his parents.

"You do not know?" he signed. "It is nothing. I will find them."

He turned and started away.

"Wait!" called Otter Woman instinctively, though she knew he would not hear. Frantically, she turned to Walking Horse. "Go after him. It is better that we tell him."

Horse nodded and trotted after their son. He came alongside and caught at the arm of Speaks-Not.

"It is all right, Father," the young man signed. "I will find them."

"No, no, Possum. You do not understand. She is not with her parents."

A feeling of panic washed over the young man, and he felt a cold sweat.

"Something has happened to her?"

"No. Well, yes. When you left, she was very sad."

"Go on!" Speaks-Not signed angrily. *"Where is she?"*

"She is with her husband, maybe."

"Husband?"

"Yes. When you did not return, she married Gray Fox. She said she had told you."

Speaks-Not stood, staring at his father, trying to keep from bursting into tears.

"No . . ." he signed. "Yes, she said this, but she was angry. I thought she meant only to torment me."

"I fear it is more, my son. She lives in his lodge."

All of his worst dreams and fears had now come to reality. Always before, he had awakened and been relieved that it was not true. This time he could not waken. Far Dove was lost to him forever. His life, his world, was falling to pieces around him, and his heart was very heavy.

"Come, my son," his father signed, taking him gently by the arm to lead him back to Otter Woman's fire.

"No," Speaks-Not pulled away, equally as gently. "I must pay my respects to Tracks-Well, tell him how it went on the trail. I will be back."

He would, of course, go and seek out the lodge of the old tracker. That part was true. He would also return to the camp of his parents. But mostly, he had to get away, to be alone in his grief. He would return after dark.

15

They did not meet at the Sun Dance. Both were occupied with other things, but in truth, neither one wanted it. Speaks-Not spent the time with his parents for a day or two and then became restless.

"I will leave tomorrow," he told them.

"But you have just come back to us," protested Otter Woman.

She knew his problem, or at least she thought she did. He was not ready to face the daily risk of encountering Far Dove, now the wife of another. What a waste . . . they had made such a happy couple as children. Well, no matter now.

"Could you not wait until after the Sun Dance is over?" she asked.

She knew the answer. He could not, because he would surely encounter Dove. The heart of Otter Woman was heavy.

"I must go, Mother."

She nodded. "Where will you go, my son?"

"I do not know. I hunt alone."

"Yes."

It was a clumsy moment.

"You will go to see Tracks-Well?" she asked.

"Of course."

"It is good."

The interview with the old tracker was far from satisfactory. Of course, at this point in his life, Speaks-Not was made to feel that nothing in his world was satisfactory.

"*Ah-koh*, Uncle."

"*Ah-koh*." Tracks-Well returned the signed greeting. "I have not seen you." There was a slight accusation in the remark.

"That is true, Uncle. Forgive me. But, I . . ."

The tracker waved aside the apology. "I know," he signed. "Here, sit with me."

Speaks-Not sat, and there was no talk for a little while. He studied the old face, watching while the tracker took a stick from the fire to light his pipe. The pungent smoke circled the old man's head in a bluish cloud. Odd, thought Speaks-Not, that he had never noticed how old Tracks-Well had become. But that is the way of things. . . . The tracker puffed until the pipe was going well, and then offered it to the sky before he handed it to Speaks-Not.

This was a social smoke, rather than a ceremony, but is there not ceremony in all we do? Speaks-Not lifted the pipe again, then took three leisurely puffs before handing it back.

"I am leaving, Uncle," he signed.

The old man nodded. "This does not surprise me. . . . The girl?"

"No! Well, yes, maybe. But I am made to think that I should be alone."

The tracker chose to sidestep that comment. "Where will you go?" he asked.

"My mother asked that, too. I do not know. It does not matter, if I am alone anyway."

"Some places are dangerous."

"All places may be," Speaks-Not signed curtly.

The tracker saw that his heart was heavy, and did not pursue that theme, but left it with one final admonition.

"You will be careful?" It was not really a question.

"Of course."

"It is good. Now, tell me of your quest just past."

"Not really a quest, Uncle. I hunted, traded with Growers. It was good."

The tracker nodded approval. "You will do the same elsewhere now?"

"Yes . . . maybe I will see the mountains."

"It is good. You will enjoy that. They have a powerful spirit. Different, but . . . well, you will see."

Speaks-Not nodded. "Oh, yes, Uncle, I tried the snares."

The old man smiled. "Good. You caught rabbits?"

"Yes . . . I tried only rabbits."

Both were still for a little while, and finally Speaks-Not resumed, on a different subject.

"Uncle, what do you know of Medicine Rock?"

"You have been there?"

"Yes, I passed there on the way here. It is a place of powerful spirits, no?"

The old man nodded. "Our People avoid it. You know the stories."

"Yes, Uncle." He was not quite certain why he had mentioned this.

"Looks-Far, the holy man, might tell you more."

"No . . . I was only curious."

Tracks-Well nodded. It was odd, he thought, that the young man would ask about the Rock. Well, maybe not. It was a very impressive place. Speaks-Not was going through a very difficult time, and was vulnerable. His spirit was searching. . . .

"Are you going back there?" he asked.

"Medicine Rock? No. Someday, maybe."

"It is good," signed the tracker. "But be careful."

At least, the young man did not feel an urge to return there now, and Tracks-Well was glad. Things were too unsettled in the life of Speaks-Not to encounter the powerful spirits who lived there. No one was absolutely sure as to the nature of those spirits . . . good, bad, or both?

"When do you leave?" he asked, changing the subject.

"Tomorrow . . . dawn."

So, the young man was leaving without taking part in the Sun Dance. He must be deeply troubled. *Aiee,* too bad that things had happened so. Both Dove and Speaks-Not so headstrong, unable to yield. They had been so good for each other! Well, there must be some explanation, though he could not see it now. Things happen as they must. But *aiee,* how hurtful, to watch the young make their mistakes!

Now, Speaks-Not rose.

"I must go, Uncle."

"I know. You must get ready to travel."

"Yes. I will not forget your help, Uncle. You have taught me much."

"It was nothing . . . try the deadfall trap this winter!"

"I will! I will see you again, maybe next season."

But you will not, thought the old man. Then he answered in signs. "Yes. May your trails be easy!" *But they will be hard, my son,* he thought privately. *I wish that I could help you.*

He watched Speaks-Not as he walked away. Fawn came and stood by his side, resting her hand on his shoulder.

"His heart is heavy," she observed.

"Yes. And mine for him," said the tracker sadly.

"You have done what you could," she said comfortingly.

"It was not enough. We should have talked to the girl, Fawn."

"She would not have listened. But, it is too bad."

* * *

Far Dove watched him go from a distance as he left the camp at dawn the next morning. She understood, and her heart was heavy in the knowing. She longed to run to him, to try to explain. She would have, but she belonged to another.

Her husband still slept in the little brush shelter. She had built it herself, because from the time they arrived, Gray Fox had been involved in the races, gaming, and gambling. That was all right . . . many husbands helped, but many did not. At least, when he was gambling, he was not around to bother her.

She had located their temporary lodge as far as possible from that of Otter Woman, because she did not want to see Speaks-Not. Actually, she now realized, she did want to see him, but *she* wished to remain unseen.

Gray Fox had been absent until near morning, wagering on the plum-stones with his friends, she supposed. He owned few horses, and she hoped that he was not losing too many more. When he came in, she pretended sleep, elbowed away his approach, and lay as still as possible until his snores told of sound sleep. Then she rose and made her way out of the camp. She noticed the graying of the eastern sky, preparing for the coming of Sun Boy, and stopped to watch the colors change.

There was some slight activity behind her, and she slipped into the bushes, not willing to be seen. Someone had caught a horse . . . his own, probably, since he was quite open about it. Any outsider lurking around to steal horses would be more furtive. Then she recognized a mannerism . . . Speaks-Not . . . what was he doing? She almost stood and stepped forward to greet him, but realized that she must not.

It was growing lighter now. Speaks-Not finished knotting the bridle in the horse's mouth and swung to the animal's back. She watched him ride back toward his parents' camp and tried to understand what he was doing. The only reason that she could think of to bring in a horse at this time of day was in preparation for travel. But where would he go? No one would normally leave the Sun Dance. She trotted around the encampment to approach Otter Woman's lodge from the other side. She was quite anxious not to be seen.

She peered through a screen of willows and saw that she was right. There was Speaks-Not, tying a bundle of supplies to his saddle while his parents watched. He was starting a journey. But why? . . . Then it came to her, and tears filled her eyes. She had avoided him because of the heaviness of her heart, and he must be doing the same.

He swung to the saddle and reined the horse around. In the growing light he looked larger . . . he had filled out, his shoulders seemed broader, his arms more muscular. She longed to be near him, to talk to him. He waved to his parents as he rode away toward the west. The first yellow rays of the rising sun struck his shoulders as he nudged the horse into an easy trot.

She watched his back until his figure began to grow smaller in the distance. *Good-bye,* she whispered. Then she rose, circled the camp once more to come in from the other side, and gathered an armful of buffalo chips for the fire. That would explain her absence.

Gray Fox was still asleep, but the camp was coming awake now. It would be a day of excitement. The Sun Dance itself had not begun, but the preliminary rituals were in progress. In the distance she heard the singsong chant of the priest on his circuit of the encampment, calling the announcement. This ritual would be repeated each morning until the appointed day.

Always before, Far Dove had looked forward to the excitement of the occasion, the joy in celebration, the games and races, dances, prayers of thanks and of entreaty. The buffalo effigy at the west side of the Sun Dance lodge, an open-sided brush arbor, was being erected even now, under the direction of one of the holy men.

Today, the usual joy was not there for Far Dove. All of the excitement and pleasure that she saw in others was wasted on her, for it was like ashes in her mouth. She had watched joy leave her life, riding out of the encampment on the back of a spotted horse. Her heart was very heavy.

It was to be even heavier, however, in the moon following the Sun Dance, when she realized that she was pregnant.

16

Far Dove dropped the armful of sticks and buffalo chips near the fire and swung the cradle board from her back. She propped it against a tree and began to prepare the fire. She had not seen her husband since they arrived. Fox had quickly joined his friends, and she would probably not see him very much for days now. She could not believe that it had been a year since the last Sun Dance. In other ways, it seemed a lifetime.

The infant, who had wakened at the sudden cease of motion, opened large dark eyes and made infant sounds.

"Ah, you are awake, Little Man," his mother called. "Be patient, and I will feed you!"

There were satisfactions to motherhood, she reflected. Almost enough to make up for the heartache of the past year. She had watched Speaks-Not go with much hurt in her heart. Her anger was beginning to leave in the realization that much of her present situation could have been avoided. Why, *why* had she not simply gone to him? Her foolish pride had resulted in a poor marriage and the loss of much that her life held dear.

She had resolved to *make* a marriage of it, especially after she discovered her pregnancy. Gray Fox had seemed delighted at that prospect. At first, that is. Then, as she became larger and clumsier, he seemed to resent the loss of her efficiency. It was no great problem, since he was seldom at home anyway. That, in a way, was the *good* part.

She had had to make do with the scant essentials provided by a poor provider. She tried to maintain their garments and the dilapidated lodge cover as best she could. But patches do show, on a dress or on a lodge cover. Usually there was enough to eat, though she occasionally resorted to a rabbit hunt herself. Gray Fox seemed not to notice.

She had been furious with him when he lost his new moccasins in a silly wagering game, on a toss of the plum-stones. She had spent many days in decorating those shoes with intricate designs in quillwork. She resolved not to do so again.

Perhaps worst of all that year had been the pitying looks of her family and friends. That hurt her pride. She was determined not to accept any help offered out of pity, but finally realized that her own pride was hurting her again.

It was in the late stages of her pregnancy that she encountered Otter Woman one morning. Both had gone to fetch water at the stream, and there was no one else around. The meeting was clumsy for a moment. They nodded a greeting, then busied themselves with filling waterskins. It was Otter Woman who finally broke the silence.

"How is it with you?" she asked.

"Fine . . . it is good," answered Dove quickly. She knew that this was more, a deeper question than a mere greeting.

"I mean, really," Otter Woman pushed.

Both women stopped at their tasks and straightened to look at each other.

"My heart is still good for you, my almost-daughter," blurted Otter Woman.

Tears welled into the eyes of Far Dove. They did that often now. It was the unsteady emotions of her pregnancy, she supposed.

"And mine for you," she answered.

Both laughed, and they embraced for a moment. Now the torrent was loosed, and they began to talk. Of woman things, of the coming child. Far Dove felt far better than she had for many moons. It was good, and they talked long.

As they prepared to part, Dove managed to ask a thing that she had been longing to know.

"Have you heard from your son?" Dove inquired, trying to be quite casual.

Otter Woman looked at her keenly for a moment, but then answered smoothly, as if it were of small importance to Far Dove.

"Why, yes," she said. "A traveler, not long ago. He spent some time with the Head Splitters, the man said, then wintered at Red Rocks."

"He is well?" asked Dove unashamedly.

"Yes. It is said that he is greatly respected as a tracker now."

Dove nodded. "He was always good at that."

"He has changed his name, too," Otter Woman went on. "We did not know that until now."

"How is he called?"

"Hunts-Alone."

Far Dove thought a moment, then smiled and nodded. "That is good!"

"Yes," agreed his mother, "but he will always be 'Possum' to me!"

"Of course," Dove laughed.

"He is coming to the Sun Dance, they said."

"Ah, that is good." Inwardly, she was not sure. "I must go, almost-Mother. It is good to talk to you again!"

"Yes," agreed Otter Woman. "Let us not be strangers, Dove."

Again, the tears came easily.

"Yes," said Dove, "let us not be."

They parted, and it was good.

The infant arrived in the last days of the Moon of Hunger. Snow and sleet pelted down on the ragged lodge cover as Cold Maker pushed one of his final forays of the season before retreating to the northern mountains. But it was good. A brief labor, common to the long-waisted women of the People, and then the indignant squall of the new man-child.

The women allowed Gray Fox back into the lodge to see his wife and son, and he was pleased. That was probably the high point of the marriage, but it was quite brief. Soon Fox was as uncaring as ever, and even more absent. And again, for Dove, that was good. She settled into a new life as a mother, and found a happiness that surprised her.

Until now, that is. Now, it was a matter of great concern that Speaks-Not, now Hunts-Alone, was expected at the celebration. She viewed the expected meeting with mixed emotion. She wished to share with him the joy of her son, yet at the same time there was still a part of her that wanted to taunt him. *This could have been yours!* She wanted to show him. And over all was the fact that it would not be considered proper for her to do more than greet him in passing. It would be a worrisome time.

She had not seen him yet. The Eastern band had been here for two days now. Dove had waved to Otter Woman as they went about the routine of the camp, but had not talked since their arrival. She was certain that Hunts-Alone was not yet staying at his parents' lodge. It was not readily apparent whether he would do so. He had been staying with the Red Rocks band and might continue to stay there. Or with the Head Splitters.

But both the Red Rocks and any Head Splitters who still might choose to attend were late. There was no concern—they had much farther to travel. He would arrive, with one group or the other, and stay either with them or his parents, she supposed. Maybe, even, he had a lodge of his own . . . *he might have a woman,* she thought, and then tried to convince herself that it was of no concern to her.

The baby was crying now, and she unwrapped it from the cradle board to lift it to her breast. She was still nursing, crooning softly to the infant, when she heard the welcome shout. Then there was thunderous greeting as the young men rushed out to meet an incoming column. The mock charge, with the horsemen of both groups voicing the deep, full-throated war cry of the People . . . *aiee,* it was exciting! She wished that she had been able to see it. To ride in the charge, even. She had always thought it would be good to do that, once, before she settled down with children. But now . . .

The riders now circled the camp, still howling the war cry, raising a dust that would soon have women shouting threats at them. She smiled and shifted the baby to the other breast.

She still wondered about Hunts-Alone and began to watch for him. The newcomers were obviously the Red Rocks, for they were the only band yet to arrive.

Then she saw him. *Aiee,* a fine-looking figure of a man! He had grown even more and had become more handsome. She was having feelings now that no wife should have. Especially, she told herself, with her husband's baby at her breast. She ducked her head to avoid recognition. She saw him inquire, presumably about his parents' camp. Then he dismounted and turned away, toward that direction. Her heart was beating wildly. Someone spoke to her, and she turned, startled.

"What?"

"I said, where is my food?" asked Gray Fox.

"Yes, in a moment," she said brightly. "Your son still needs his!"

Fox mumbled something and sat down while she busied herself, preparing meat. She handed him a bowl and a horn spoon, and he began to eat. When he finished, he belched loudly, rose, and scratched his belly.

She started to ask where he was going as he walked away, but decided against it. It did not matter much. There were new arrivals, many of them gamblers. It was like a sickness with Gray Fox, and she knew that he would have sought out other gamblers by sundown. She did not understand quite how men could spend all day or all night watching a handful of plum-stones painted red on one side skitter and bounce on a spread skin. A horse race, maybe. At least that was exciting! She hoped that he would not lose too much. She had given up hoping that he would win. He never won. . . .

The moon was high when they came looking for her. She had been asleep for a while after dark, but had been roused by the baby. She had fed him and returned to her sleeping-robe, lying there in the darkness beside her dying fire, listening to the night sounds. Sounds of nature and sounds of the encampment, she noted. There was no time, it seemed, when all was quiet and everyone slept. At any time, day or night, during the time that the entire nation was gathered for the Sun Dance, someone was awake and making noise of some sort. There were songs and dances, the rhythmic beat of distant drums. Of course, there were people who were awake merely to visit quietly, to exchange news and stories with friends and relatives they had not seen since last year's Sun Dance.

Gray Fox had not returned. She had not really expected him, of course, and did not care. She was tired anyway, and if he came home she would have two mouths to feed instead of one. She smiled to herself at the thought . . . two children to care for . . . not far wrong.

The three people approached, two men and a woman, and stood before her, tense and formal.

"Far Dove?" inquired one of the men.

"Yes. What is it?"

Now she recognized the woman . . . one of the Warrior Sisters, a priestess of the Blood Society. Something must be wrong! Dove sat up, alarmed. Why should they be here, looking for her? Their faces were tense and serious, even in the moonlight. Thoughts raced through her mind . . . something had happened to Hunts-Alone! No, of course not. She was embarrassed to have had such a thought. Her parents? . . . No . . . *what*?

"Your husband is dead," said the Warrior Princess.

"But how? . . ." Dove stammered. It was unreal, like a dream from which one cannot wake.

One of the men spoke.

"Our hearts are heavy for you. He was gambling with us and some of the Head Splitters. He was losing and accused one of the visitors of cheating, a man called Wolf's Tail."

Far Dove sat, listening to words that seemed to have no meaning for her. The man's voice droned on.

"Fox tried to kill him with a belt-ax, but Wolf's Tail drew a knife and stabbed him in the belly. It is as I have said it."

Her thoughts were still numb, detached. She understood the delegation and their approach. There must be no mistake, no blame of anyone. If the council was asked to judge this event, these would be the witnesses. They had seen the fight, and there was no room for doubt. This had been explained.

"Wolf's Tail was only defending himself," the man finished.

"Yes, I understand," Dove said huskily. She had so many things to think of. . . .

The delegation started to turn away, but she called them back.

"Wait. Please tell me . . . was the man, this Wolf's Tail . . . *was* he cheating?"

The spokesman waited a long time before answering. "No," he said firmly. He waited again and finally blurted, "Far Dove, your husband was cheating. I am sorry."

So, she thought. She was not really surprised, only numb, unbelieving that it had actually occurred. *I must mourn,* she thought.

"Thank you," she half whispered.

They moved on, and she lifted her voice in the Song of Mourning.

It was three days later when she looked up to see Hunts-Alone approaching. He strode straight to where she sat holding the baby. She was embarrassed that her appearance was not good. The ashes that she had placed on her head had sifted down over her neck and shoulders. Hunts-Alone should have known better than to come here at this time, anyway. Her anger rose at his lack of consideration. After all, she was in mourning.

Then she saw his face, and her anger melted. There was so much grief and hurt and sympathy. . . .

"My heart is heavy for you," he signed, "but this is enough, Dove. It is time for us to heal the hurt in our hearts. When your mourning is over, I will come for you."

She wanted to jump up, to fly into his arms, but she managed to remain outwardly calm.

"It is good," she signed.

PART II

HUNTS-ALONE

17

Hunts-Alone rose and stretched and walked around a little to work the night's stiffness from his joints. He had begun to realize the meaning of the old men's talk. There was no question any more. The weather was directly connected to stiffness in one's bones.

Dove was feeding the morning fire. Around them, the other families of the Eastern band were coming alive to begin the day. It had all the makings of a glorious day in early spring.

He left the cluster of lodges and went a little way outside the camp to empty his bladder, nodding greetings to other men who were occupied in the same way. Then he paused a moment to greet Sun Boy as the first rays of the torch slanted across the prairie . . . a short prayer of thanks for the day.

Life was good, he reflected. He and Far Dove had been together many winters now. *Aiee,* what heaviness of heart there had been, before they finally joined. But it was good, then. They had learned a difficult lesson, and profited by it. They laughed sometimes at the childish pride that had prevented their coming together for so long.

Now, their children were grown, and except for the youngest, Young Crow, were in their own lodges. And Crow, he thought, was showing much interest in Feeds-His-Horse, a young man of the Elk-dog Society. They would probably marry soon. Dove thought so, too. They had watched the young people together not long ago.

"Those two make a good-looking couple," Far Dove had signed.

"Yes. Our lodge will soon be empty."

She took his hand. "Is that bad?" she teased.

They had never, in all their years together, had their lodge just to themselves. Dove's son by her unfortunate marriage to Gray Fox had known no other father than Hunts-Alone. Called Bull's Horn, he was now grown, a respected hunter, and with children of his own. Then had come another son, only a year younger, Many Birds. The two had become inseparable. It was several seasons, then, before Young Crow joined their lodge. She had been a joy to her father, but was now ready to make her own way in the world. And their lodge, always blessed with children, would seem empty.

"What if we find that we do not even like each other?" Dove teased, in mock alarm.

"It is a risk we must take," he smiled. He put an arm around her. "Maybe it will be better, no?"

Now, he returned to the lodge, to find Crow chattering with her mother as she assisted in the preparation of food. The girl rose from her kneeling position by the fire to greet him.

"Good day to you, Father," she signed.

He nodded, smiling. It was good to see the face of this one, always happy, always eager to greet the joys of the world. Everyone loved Crow.

Hunts-Alone and Dove were doubly blessed. Neither of their own children had inherited the loss of hearing. Bull's Horn, though now their own, had of course been sired by another, so could not inherit the weakness of Hunts-Alone. It was his alone. He had never missed something he did not remember, though it had affected his life profoundly. His name, even, had reflected the necessity that his hearing loss had caused.

It had made him a better tracker, to be sure. Hunts-Alone had always been in demand when an extra-keen eye was needed. Many times he had given thanks for the firm yet gentle guidance of Tracks-Well. The old tracker was long gone now, but Hunts-Alone thought of him each time there was an especially demanding need for a tracker's services.

The years were passing now, and his eyes were not quite as keen. A younger man or two showed great promise, and he had helped to teach them, as his mentor had taught him. There was a slight disappointment that neither of his sons were particularly interested in his skills, but it is often so. They had grown into fine hunters, and respected men.

They were still virtually inseparable, as they had been since childhood. Bull's Horn, a year older, was usually the leader, though it was an easygoing good-natured leadership. They anticipated each other's thoughts, and were regarded as a team in the organization of the group hunts. Both had picked up more of their father's powers of observation than they realized, he thought. After all, does not any hunt depend partly on the hunter's skills in observing the world around him? He was proud of them both.

With Crow, however, he had a special relationship. This was a child born old and knowing. It could be seen in the wide-eyed look of wonder with which she greeted the new world into which she had arrived. She was the pride and joy of her father, and spent much time with him as she grew. Her childish joy and her smile of delight in all things made his heart good. He spent more time with her than he had with the boys when they were small. It was not intentional, but more time was available to him now. There were fewer demands on him as his lodge had fewer mouths to feed.

Hunts-Alone and his small daughter shared little jokes and dreams and heartaches. She was the child of her mother, too, which made her even more endearing to him. He loved to watch the two working together, the child learning woman-skills and woman's ways. And he was proud, his heart good.

He always knew, of course, that she would marry some day. He wished a good husband for her, and young Feeds-His-Horse certainly seemed to fit the requirements. He was handsome, intelligent, a good hunter, and well respected by his peers. He appeared to be a natural leader, and would surely be a man whose voice was respected in council. There was no reason to think that he would not become band chief some day. There were few serious candidates.

Young Crow and Far Dove were certain of it, and even talked of his election to the office of Real-chief, the most important position in the nation. True, it was usually held by a leader from the Northern band, but that was not a requirement.

"Maybe it is time for the Eastern band to come into its own," insisted Far Dove. "Why not? We have had great leaders, but have always been scorned."

"True," agreed Hunts-Alone. "But it is partly our fault. The Eastern band sometimes deserves the foolish reputation."

"So does every band, sometimes," Dove signed. "But, the jokes are about us, not the others."

"Some of our people like it," offered Young Crow. "They think others will expect less of them because they are of the Eastern band. They are lazy!"

"That may be," her father agreed. "But we have had respected leaders. Red Feather could have been Real-chief, but his age was wrong. The position was not open during his best years. Maybe you are right, and it *is* time. Feeds-His-Horse may be the one."

He was half teasing, the women knew it, and Crow blushed becomingly.

"Oh, Father . . ." she signed.

He shrugged as if bewildered.

"You women brought it up. What does a mere man know?"

Such teasing became increasingly common, and it was no great surprise when Crow indicated to her parents that spring that she and Feeds-His-Horse wished to wed.

"It is good," agreed Hunts-Alone. "Can he support you?"

It was almost a ritual question, which would be relayed to the young suitor. Horse, already expecting such an inquiry, would have decided what gifts he would bring to the parents. The purpose of such gifts was twofold: to impress them with his affluence, and to partially compensate them for the loss of a beloved daughter.

The choices were good ones. A beautiful robe for Dove, with a unique blue-gray color found very seldom in the buffalo herds that migrated through the Sacred Hills. It was an expensive present, and he must have given several horses for it.

For Hunts-Alone, the choice was probably harder. It would normally have been a gift of horses, a fine buffalo hunter or two, perhaps. But it was well-known that Hunts-Alone had different needs. His need for a horse was only for travel. Or, of course, for its own intrinsic value.

The young man led a mare to the lodge of his prospective father-in-law and paused before the door. Hunts-Alone stepped outside, soberly looking the animal over, as Horse untied the blue-gray robe from the mare's back and handed it to Far Dove. This was a ceremony, to be cherished and remembered. Dove was delighted.

The young man then untied a lavishly decorated bow case and handed it to Hunts-Alone.

"I know you have little use for horses, Uncle," he signed, "but maybe you can use this poor gift. It is a small thing to help your grief at the loss of such a daughter from your lodge."

Hunts-Alone nodded stiffly. The gift and the speech had been well-done. The bow was of excellent quality. But Feeds-His-Horse was not finished.

"Now, this mare," he went on, "you may find use for."

Hunts-Alone walked around the animal, admiring her beauty. A fine head; wide-set, alert eyes; ears pricked forward. Her back was long and strong, her legs straight. She was of the gray roan color admired since the People saw the First Elk-dog. At her side, a small foal nursed.

"She is young," Horse was signing. "This is her first foal. It carries both the blood of First Horse and of the Dream Horse of our ancestor, Horse-Seeker. The mare is back in foal to the same stallion. May she bring you many more fine horses, Uncle."

Again, it was a fine gift and a fine speech. The value in this mare was not in her usefulness to her new owner, but in her potential for producing horses of great value. Hunts-Alone was touched.

"It is good," he signed. "Welcome to our lodge."

It was sometimes custom for a new husband to live with the bride's parents until their own lodge was ready. This was the invitation.

"Yes, welcome," offered Far Dove in both speech and sign.

"Thank you both." Feeds-His-Horse answered. "But I . . . Crow and I . . . our lodge will be ready soon. We will wed after the Sun Dance, if that pleases you?"

"Of course. It is good."

It was later that evening when the importance of this event began to make itself felt on Hunts-Alone and Far Dove. The fire had burned low, and they were preparing to retire to the sleeping-robes by its flickering light. Young Crow was out with her intended husband, radiantly happy with the courtship and with the plans for their lodge together.

"Our lodge will seem empty," he signed. "It is as we said before."

"Yes," agreed Dove, "but it is good. This is a fine young chief, a fitting man for our daughter, my husband."

"That is true. But I will miss her."

"I, too. But here, come to bed." She lifted the edge of the robe invitingly. "Maybe I can show you that there are good things about an empty lodge, too."

18

It was little more than a year later that the lodge of Crow and Feeds-His-Horse was blessed with a small girl-child. She was so like her mother from the beginning that her grandfather was completely charmed. This was the child of their youngest, and she held special meaning for Dove and Hunts-Alone. She was called South Wind, after the fresh breezes that cross the prairie to relieve summer heat.

In addition, Young Crow had always selected a site for her lodge that was near that of her parents. Thus, they had extra opportunity to see the child develop. At any time that the situation offered, Hunts-Alone could be found amusing his tiny granddaughter.

"It is too bad that he cannot hear the sounds that she makes," said Crow to her mother as they watched the two together.

"That is true," Dove agreed, "but he has never heard. He uses her smiles, her eyes, the way she looks at him."

"I know, Mother. It was so with me when I was a child. But look at them . . . was ever a grandfather so devoted?"

The two women laughed together and turned to other things. There was some concern that summer that the weather was hot and dry. This made the hunting poor, and there was beginning to be talk that unless the fall hunt was good, it would be a difficult winter.

The council of the Eastern band considered at great length and argued about the best course of action.

"We should go out farther into the prairie for the fall hunt," insisted one. "There are more buffalo there."

"Usually, yes," came the answer. "But this season, the grassland has had drought, too. Worse than we have here. There may *be* no buffalo!"

The argument raged on. The Eastern band had always been split by argument, it seemed. They, of all the People, had been located for generations at the juncture of the grassland and the forest, the eastern border of the People's range. They had gradually adopted some of the customs of the forest people. None of the other bands of the nation was as dependent on deer as a staple food, preferring to hunt buffalo in open country.

Possibly even the leaders of the Eastern band did not understand why every council session produced argument, but it was so. They were in a state of change, in the process of shaping their culture. The Southern band had, many lifetimes ago, begun to winter among the scrub oaks in the southern part of their range. The Red Rocks and the Mountain bands had established winter sites in their western habitat, and the Northern band in the timbered bottoms along the River of the Kenzas or on the Platte. All bands hunted and camped for the summer in the grassland, but the Eastern band marginally so. They seemed indecisive, and this led to the strengthening of their reputation as foolish people. The more they were ridiculed, the more they were angered. And of course, when one is angry for whatever reason, he does not speak well in council.

For all of these reasons, not clearly understood by anyone, there was always wrangling, division, and indecision in the councils of the band. They had now lost any cohesion and political pride that had been established a generation or two ago by their statesman and leader, Red Feather. They seemed doomed to argument.

"This happens too often!" shouted one man. "We should plan ahead, *plan* to winter in the forest to the east, not just when we are starving!"

"Of course!" another answered sarcastically. "In the country of the Shaved-Heads! They will welcome us into their lodges and feed us."

"Not that far," retorted the other. "Only a little way into the forest. Establish our own territory."

"They will welcome that!" snapped his opponent.

The argument raged on. Hunts-Alone was bored with it. He had never enjoyed councils, anyway. Not only was he a loner by nature, but the arguments were difficult for him to follow. Some, but not all, of the speakers used hand-signs, and there was a disconnected result that he could follow only with difficulty. Sometimes Far Dove sat with him and translated, but their interest had lagged through the years. Participation seemed futile anyway. Let the younger generation take over, make the decisions.

Crow's husband did seem interested, and his voice was respected in council as a voice mature beyond his years.

"He will be a leader," Dove told her husband. "It is as I have said. Not yet, maybe, but someday! Look, they listen to him!"

Bull's Horn and Many Birds, too, seemed to respect the voice of their sister's husband. Often, the three were to be found on the same side in the discussion. They argued against some of the hotheaded young men who wanted to invade the domain of the Shaved-Heads.

"The People do not need another Lost Band," observed Feeds-His-Horse. "One empty spot in the circle is enough."

There was much nodding in agreement, but in the end, those who favored wintering in the woodlands won out.

"Our band is large," the predominant argument insisted. "We will go in openly, but peaceably, not aggressive. Our size will protect us."

Hunts-Alone, when he heard of it, was astonished and quite concerned. "This is very foolish," he told Dove. "The Shaved-Heads will see only a big band of intruders. This is dangerous!"

That very night, his sons and Feeds-His-Horse approached him.

"Father," began Bull's Horn, the eldest, "our hearts are heavy for the council's decision."

"And mine!" Hunts-Alone signed. "This is a bad thing."

"So we think. We wish to part from the band . . . stay near the edge of the forest, stay together."

"Who?"

"We three families. You and Mother, if you will join us. Anyone else who wishes."

"Yes, of course! It is good!"

"To split the band?" asked Dove. "Is that not dangerous?"

"Which is more dangerous, Mother?" asked Crow. "To stay where it is safer or go into the forest where the Shaved-Heads hunt?"

"*Aiee,* I do not know."

The family discussion continued intermittently for several days. It was a calm discussion, however, with none of the bitterness and anger of the band's council. Gradually they came to a meeting of the minds. When the time came for the band to move, they would stay behind. They would move later to a selected spot where the band had wintered before. It was nearer anyway, had proved safe, and game was in fairly good supply. Many Birds and Feeds-His-Horse made a quick journey to verify these impressions.

"It is good," they reported.

So it was decided. They announced the family decision to a few friends. One young man and his wife, relatives of Feeds-His-Horse, elected to join them. There was a great deal of ridicule as the story spread, but in the end, when the Eastern band broke camp to move into winter camp deep in the woods, five lodges stayed behind. Let the others risk the wrath of the forest people, the Shaved-Heads. They would plan sensibly and cautiously, alert to the needs of their families, ready to avoid danger rather than face it. It was good.

A few days later the little group struck their lodges also and moved a few days to the south. It was a good site, to which Many Birds pointed. A clear running stream that would not freeze, a steep hillside covered with brush and trees which rose to the north, a view of open country to the southwest. The lodges would be sheltered from the howling winds of Cold Maker, and the snow would not drift badly in this isolated meadow. There would be enough grass for the horses. These young families did not yet possess large herds.

They helped each other set up the lodges, a few paces apart. A tripod of three poles tied loosely at the proper distance from the ends, spaced carefully by pacing. Then the other poles, leaned into the tripod in turn, the bases resting in a circle that would mark the size of the lodge.

All doorways faced east, for a number of reasons reaching all the way back to Creation. Does not Sun Boy approach over Earth's eastern rim? He must be welcomed by the People on his daily run. In a more practical sense, the position of the doorway also determined that of the smoke hole. Winter winds come from the north, summer breezes from south and southwest. Rarely does an east wind affect the region of the People. Since smoke flaps must be quartering downwind to draw properly, this allows proper adjustment of the flaps with the slender smoke poles.

The heaviest work in erecting the lodges was the hoisting of the lodge skin into place with the last pole, the one to the west of the circle. The men shoved the pole upright while women drew the heavy cover around the other poles and pinned the edges above the doorway.

By the time the shadows grew long and Sun Boy painted the western sky with his fall colors, the winter camp was established. There would be more work—winterizing the lodge linings with dry grass, building snow fences of brush—but that could be done later. For now, the fires were lighted, signifying their presence.

That was almost ritual, a concession to whatever spirits might inhabit a place, an announcement of the newcomers' presence. By the fire, a statement is made: *here we intend to camp.* A pinch of tobacco was offered, tossed in each fire that evening, to indicate goodwill.

With this gesture, hoping that the spirits might be appeased and feel only goodwill toward the little band, they began to prepare for their first night in this new winter home.

In his silent evening prayer to the setting sun, Hunts-Alone asked protection and peace, both for his family and for the foolish people of the main band who had invaded the country of a dangerous enemy.

19

↔

They had made a good choice, Hunts-Alone reflected as he sat before his lodge and smoked in the warm sunshine of late autumn. This was a pleasant place, with none of the hustle and bustle of the larger camp. Hunting had been good. Even now, racks of drying venison were loaded with fresh meat. The young men hunted well together, and had harvested several deer. He would have preferred buffalo, the taste so much milder and sweeter, but no matter. All meat is good, some just better.

He watched the children at play, enjoying their enthusiasm. He glanced over at the baby, South Wind, propped near him in her cradle board. She was developing rapidly, it seemed. A very mature child. He was not surprised, of course. Her spirit was an old one, wise from the experiences of many lifetimes, perhaps.

At the rate the child was growing, she should be walking by the time they left this camp for the Sun Dance next spring. That would be good. He would feel much better when the entire Eastern band was united again. There was something about the division of a people who should be one that bothered him immensely. He could not forget the Lost Band and the empty place in the circle of the Big Council. And that chance remark by someone in the council, a few moons ago. *We do not want another Lost Band*. It *had* been a foolish thing, to weaken the band by dividing it.

Yet, he agreed with the young men of his family. The foolish ones were those who took the Eastern band into unknown territory, probably claimed by fierce Shaved-Heads. And in weakened condition, from the loss of five warriors, when the young men of his own family refused to go. Well, four, anyway. Hunts-Alone realized that his own reflexes were slowing, his strength ebbing, as the winters took their toll. But his eyes were still good, his tracking skills still sharp. At least, so he told himself.

His pipe was dead, and he decided to renew it. The afternoon was young, the sun pleasant through his buckskin shirt. In his pouch was the special mixture that he had decided was good for himself. Tobacco, of course, but a generous portion of sumac, a touch of cedar, and a bit of catnip. Sometimes when tobacco was scarce, he extended it with shavings of red willow bark. That was not necessary today, for tobacco was in good supply.

They had been visited recently by a traveler, a trader who seemed surprised to find them there. He was a jovial sort, as one must be who trades with everyone and has no enemies. His stories were good, and his visit had been welcome.

Hunts-Alone knocked the ashes from his pipe and repacked it with a pinch of the mix from his pouch. He beckoned to one of the children and signed that he needed fire. The boy jumped eagerly at the chance to assist his grandfather and brought a glowing stick from the cooking fire in front of one of the lodges. Hunts-Alone thanked him and patted the boy's head approvingly.

He settled back comfortably again, but there was still the uneasiness that he had felt earlier when he thought of the Eastern band's division. He wished again that the leaders had not quarreled, dividing the band. But it was done now. The main portion of the band, some forty lodges, were strong enough to defend themselves. This little family group was in a safe area. Both should winter well, if the larger group had found good hunting too.

Yet his mind wandered. What if the main part of the Eastern band was forced to fight the entire nation of the Shaved-Heads? It would be a bloody war . . . one that could have been avoided by common sense. But, in such an event, if many of the main Eastern band were killed, this family band— these children of his and Far Dove's—would become a powerful political force among the People. He himself had not been interested in politics because of his limitations in speaking, but he recognized the importance of leadership. Surely, this winter would be good either way. Leadership qualities in his sons would be recognized. In Feeds-His-Horse, too. He was constantly more impressed with that young man.

Ah, well, these were daydreams. Even though things looked good in all ways, he would feel better when the Eastern band was reunited. He was uncomfortable with the idea of a divided group. He tried to tell himself that it was no concern of his, that the Eastern band could take care of itself, even if there were five men absent. Well, four, anyway.

Two days' travel to the southeast, a trader stopped at a winter camp of lodges that were obviously of the prairie type. He was startled at first . . . there must be forty lodges! Then he remembered . . . yes, the family group. The Elk-dog People. This must be their parent band. Their Eastern band, was it not? Ah, yes. Good. That gave him a subject of common interest to talk about. He could bring news of relatives and friends, and would be welcomed.

He strode in, leading his two pack horses, and followed by his wife.

"Ah-koh!" he called in the People's own tongue, accompanied with the hand-sign for peaceful greeting. He had found it quite useful to use several tongues in addition to hand-signs. His people, traders by tradition, used many tongues. Their home territory on the eastern slope of the mountains brought them in contact with many other nations, and they traded with all.

These people, who had strangely split their band and moved into new territory at the same time . . . ah, that appeared foolish! But had he not heard? . . . Yes, the Mountain band of this same nation was a neighbor of his own people. They made jokes about the foolishness of their Eastern band, did they not? He chuckled to himself. Yes, it was all coming back to him now. There were many jokes and stories that were told in more than one nation. The same jokes, told about some foolish group. The tribe across the river, an imaginary tribe somewhere, or as in this case, the Elk-dog People joking and teasing one of their own bands, the Eastern band. He must be careful about foolish people jokes. Ah, well, he could still tell such stories, but make someone else the butt of the jokes. An imaginary tribe, maybe. Yes, that would do.

He was welcomed warmly. These were usually friendly people, he recalled. Proud, capable, sometimes a little haughty, even. But generous and open. A quick glance around the camp showed him all that he needed to know about how they fared this season. Few new lodge covers, some meat drying on the racks, but not an abundance. They had fared not quite as well as their own splinter group at the prairie's edge. Well, he would trade here for a day or two and then move on. The commodities that this band would have for trading would be few.

"A day or two," he remarked to his wife. "Then we will move on."

"Yes. They will have little to trade. Why did they come here?"

"Times were poor . . . drought, so the other group said."

"A dangerous move. Is this not the land of the Shaved-Heads?"

"Yes. And yes, it does seem foolish. But maybe they will be safe. They are many . . . see? Maybe forty lodges!"

She nodded, unconvinced. "We go on to the Shaved-Heads next? I wonder if they know of this camp?"

The trader shrugged. "Maybe. That is not our worry."

"That is true."

A trader must remain neutral. He can have no enemies, because he is vulnerable, traveling alone, and carrying valuable goods. His only real protection is his friendship with all those he meets.

They paid their respects to the band chieftain, an aging leader who seemed to have no real sense of direction. It was easy to see how one faction or another could influence a vote in this band.

There was small talk and a small gift of thanks for the band's hospitality.

"How long will you stay?" asked the chief.

"Only a day or two. We must be planning where we will winter."

"I understand. Where will that be?"

"We have not decided. South of here, someplace. Our bones do not like cold winters."

The old chief chuckled. "Nor do mine! But we will stay warm here. There is much fuel, shelter from the wind . . ."

And danger from your neighbors, thought the trader. Aloud, he said, "Oh, yes! We stopped with some of your people, two sleeps past. Five lodges . . ."

"Ah! Yes, some of our young men. Very foolish, to leave the main band, are they not?"

It was a ticklish moment. The trader knew that he must not take sides in an internal political squabble. There was no way of knowing what dissension might still smoulder here. He did have an opinion—that the foolish ones were the main band, who had penetrated deeply into the hunting lands of a very fierce adversary. He could not say this, so he only smiled and shrugged, to indicate that it was of no concern to him.

"They are well?" asked the chief.

"Yes, they too are drying venison," he said casually, "preparing for winter."

There were a few other inquiries during their brief stay. Specific inquiries about this lodge or that, and they were able to answer most of them.

"They appeared to be doing well," he told the questioners ambiguously, "as you of the main band are." *Better,* he said to himself. *They are practically in their own territory.*

They spent a pleasant two days and traded tales around the story fire. More stories were exchanged than goods, for times were hard for these Elk-dog People, and they had little to trade. The trader's wife mentioned this on the trail later.

"That was not a profitable stop."

"True. Except for goodwill. Maybe next season will be better for them, and they will have many robes, much meat, furs to trade."

"Maybe," the woman agreed. "If we come this way again."

"We will, someday. But I was thinking of finding them next season in their own country, on the plains."

"Yes," she agreed. "But I am made to wonder if we will ever see them again. Or, if *anyone* will."

20

A day's travel from that place, but in a different direction, a meeting took place that night. Light from the council fire glistened on heads that were shaved along both sides to leave a strip of hair standing erect down the center. Some men wore ceremonial paint, for important decisions were to come from this council.

The circle quieted and the council officially came to order, the elderly leader of this village presiding. There was ceremony and ritual first, befitting the serious nature of the occasion. A young man drew the symbolic pipe from its case, filled it, and handed it to the old chieftain. He in turn lifted it to the sky, lighted its fragrant contents, and puffed a cloud of bluish smoke. Then he handed the pipe to the man on his left. There was a silence of reverent meditation as this ceremony proceeded around the circle.

The pipe returned to the leader, who again offered it to the heavens, then to the four winds, and handed it to his pipe bearer.

"Now," he began, "we are gathered, my brothers, to consider matters of great importance to us and to our people."

There were nods around the circle. This was part of the ritual. The old chief recounted briefly the history of the nation, its triumphs and problems, since long-ago times. It had been heard many times by all those present, but how can one look at a problem without looking again at how it all began?

"It has been many generations," the chief droned on, "since our people came here to these woodlands. Here we have found it good. There are deer and turkey and bear, and our corn and potatoes and beans grow well."

More nods around the circle.

"But now, there is a threat to our people. Outsiders from the plains are pushing in."

There was a mutter of discontent.

"Two winter camps of the skin-tent people are known, within a sleep or two of here. There may be others."

The murmur rose, its tone more excited. Not everyone had been aware of *two* incursions. The speaker waited for the council to quiet, then continued.

"These are thought to be of the nation called Elk-dog People."

This, of course, was well-known.

"My chief," interceded an old warrior, in a formal request to be heard.

"Yes, Black Bear, speak to us in your wisdom."

Bear cleared his throat and began. "My chief, have not these Elk-dog People camped near the edge of our forest for many winters? When summer comes, they move back onto the prairie."

"That is true," agreed the chief. "But here, Mouse Track, tell us what you have seen."

Mouse Track, a much younger man, was respected for his scouting ability. His were the eyes and ears of this village. The circle gave him undivided attention.

"It is true," he stated. "There are two camps. These are an eastern band of the Elk-dogs, who often camp for the winter along a river to the west of us. The River of Swans, their name for it. Sometimes, in a dry year, they camp in the edge of our forest. It has been no problem. They have good horses we can steal, and their women are long-legged and very beautiful."

There was general laughter. It was well-known that the prairie women made good wives. Little girls were valuable for resale or trade, though this was mostly an opportunistic effort, not a customary thing. The loss of an occasional child angered the Elk-dog People, but not enough to precipitate outright warfare.

"They give up their horses more easily, I think," Mouse Track went on, producing another round of laughter. He waited for quiet.

"Now, this present situation is different," he went on more seriously.

The laughter and joking stopped abruptly. He glanced around the circle, letting the weight of his words sink in.

"Their main camp, what we believe to be the Elk-dogs' farthest eastern band, have come much deeper into our territory than ever before. They are a day's distance south of here."

"*South?*" asked someone incredulously.

"Yes. My brothers, this may become a serious matter, if these wanderers decide to settle down and stay."

There was an intense but short-lived mutter, and Mouse Track continued.

"The other camp, only a handful of lodges, is at the forest's edge, where they have camped before, the whole camp."

"What happened that time?" someone asked.

The old chief answered. "Nothing. We let them alone. Took a few horses, a girl or two. They went back to their treeless prairie in spring."

There was a chuckle.

"Will they not do the same thing again?" a man called. "It has been a dry year. Their hunting was probably poor. When the rains come, they will go home."

"It is not that small band that worries me," said Mouse Track. "It is the others, the main camp."

"Then let us kill them," someone shouted. "Take *all* the horses and women."

General laughter quieted under the serious stare of the chief, who held up his hand for silence.

"How many warriors are there, Mouse Track?" he asked.

"In the main camp, forty or fifty lodges. Probably that many warriors."

To some, the seriousness of this situation had not been apparent until now. The murmur that now went round the council circle was a sober one. The thoughts of most of those present were probably the same: They could attack such a camp and probably win, but there would be much bloodshed, much mourning.

"Maybe we could kill a lone man sometimes, keep bothering them, make them feel that it is dangerous here," an old warrior suggested. "Steal their horses . . . by spring they will be glad to go, and there is little risk."

There were derisive sneers from some of the younger warriors, not as experienced in the ways of war as the old men.

"Maybe we can attack the small camp instead," joked one. A roll of laughter relieved the growing tension for a moment.

"Wait!" cried a warrior. "Let us think on this! Maybe it is good. We can kill those at the small camp, to show the rest a lesson."

"But how would they know?" demanded another.

"We could go and tell them," suggested the jokester.

"No, be serious. Traders pass through. There is one in the area now with his wife. They carry news. Everyone will soon know."

"But winter is coming," Mouse Track pointed out. "Traders will not be moving around. This one is following the geese south, even now."

There was a moment of hesitation. Then a man spoke who had not yet been heard. He was middle-aged, quiet, known to his people as a skilled hunter and merciless in war. Respected and possibly feared even by his own people, Chops-His-Enemy had earned the name at the age of seventeen in his first taste of battle.

There are those who dread battle, those who fear it, those who glory in the songs and dances of celebration after a victory. Some love brave deeds, and the counting of honors on the fallen foe. Occasionally, though, there is one who enjoys the battle itself, for its own sake. Such a man is feared by his own people, because they do not quite understand his joy in the killing. But in time of war, he is *useful* to his people, as a leader and example. Such a man was Chops-His-Enemy.

"Let us do as someone has said," he began. "Take them a message. A head or two of their brothers from the smaller camp, as a warning. Leave them on a pole outside their camp for them to find."

There was a long pause, a moment of silence that dragged on. The time had come to stop the jokes and laughter. This was real, the decision to be made today.

The man who finally broke the silence was not one with the wisdom of years, but a young man, without experience but eager to "blood" himself and gain honor in combat.

"It is good!" he cried.

There may have been those who would have preferred a more peaceable approach. A warning, perhaps, a trading session and a demand that the outsiders move on. Their voices, if any, were not heard, or not noticed in the enthusiasm for war that now mounted. Theirs was a tradition of maintaining their rights by force, swiftly and violently. This plan would satisfy the innate lust for blood, drive out the intruders, and let some of the young men taste combat. A ground swell of enthusiasm began to rise, shouts and songs, and a few jumped to their feet to dance a step or two in their exuberance.

The old chief finally quieted the crowd long enough to resume the talk of the council.

"Chops-His-Enemy, will you lead the war party?"

The warrior's eyes glittered with pleasure. Something like a smile played over his face, and he licked his lips as if in anticipation.

"I will be honored to do so, my chief."

"It is good. When? How many?"

Chops-His-Enemy glanced at the sky as if to question the weather. The late autumn had been uncommonly warm and pleasant, but it could end at any time. The season was late, and the time of change was unpredictable.

"Tomorrow," he said. "All who wish may go. We will count many honors, steal many horses."

"And women!" shouted a young warrior.

"No!" said the war chief firmly. "That is a nuisance, and the others might come to steal them back. We kill them all. Anyone who goes will do as I say!"

This brought a moment of silence, broken by the old chief's remark of approval.

"It is good. It shall be as our brother says."

21

↔

Hunts-Alone sat on the knoll behind the lodges, and looked across the open country to the southwest. He had discovered this place soon after they had established their little camp. It offered a view of the grassland that was his home, a place of far horizons. It was only two or three bowshots away, but it was secluded and remote from the everyday activity of the camp.

He had always felt comfortable when he was alone. It gave him a chance to relax, to meditate, to watch the creatures of the world around him. Probably his methods of hunting, from which he took his name, encouraged this habit. Far Dove understood it.

The autumn had been beautiful here in the edge of the woodlands. They had watched the colors change in the foliage of the trees. Bright crimson of sumac gave way to the gold of the cottonwoods . . . very brief, that stage. Then came the rich mixture of reds, yellows, and golden tints among the oaks and maples. Trees that were unknown on the prairie turned startling colors, contrasting with the cedars' green. There were colorful shrubs, too, largely unfamiliar to the People.

He missed the more muted hues of the tall grasses of home. They were more subtle, but as great a variety as the colors of the woodlands. There to the southwest, where he could see open vistas from his knoll, he could imagine . . . yes, surely that large patch on a distant slope would be real-grass. He could distinguish its dark reddish color as it ripened. It would be taller than a man's head now. Closer, a meadow in which heavy yellow heads of plume grass nodded above the pinkish clumps of shorter types. It was good, the sights and smells of the season mingling in the still golden sunlight.

Days were shorter now. It must be near the end of the Moon of Falling Leaves, and approaching the Moon of Madness. Days were growing perceptibly shorter. All of the leaves had not yet fallen, because the weather had been uncommonly fine. The long, still-sunny period before Cold Maker's return had been a good one. Second Summer, the People sometimes called it. It did not occur every year, but when it did, *aiee,* it was wonderful. Hunting was good, the days were warm and the nights cool . . . good for snuggling in the sleeping-robes with a warm bedfellow.

It had also given time to winterize the lodges, and this had been accomplished. Everyone, even the children, had helped cut and carry the curing grasses that were stuffed into the space behind the lodge linings for insulation. Natural brush shelter belts had been augmented with brush cut and piled in strategic rows. The dried meat was stored, in good supply. Skins were being dressed and tanned, but there was little urgency in any of the activity now. The little winter camp was ready.

And still, the Second Summer held. Warm, lazy days, sitting, visiting, smoking, playing games with the children . . .

"I am afraid we will pay for it later," observed Far Dove. "Cold Maker is watching from his ice cave and laughing at us!"

There was no argument. Everyone knew that winter would soon sweep down upon them. Yet it is hard to take such things seriously when the sky is so blue, the autumn sights and smells so pleasant. With the warm rays of Sun Boy's torch soaking through one's buckskin shirt, who can think of Cold Maker?

This long pause in the season also gave Hunts-Alone the opportunity to *be* alone. He would climb the knoll, recline at his ease, and meditate, giving thanks for all that was his. A fine family, a good life, grandchildren, a world that was good. He was ready to slow down, to let the young men take the lead, make the decisions. He did not mind the chance to sit in the sun, smoke, and meditate on past accomplishments. He lay back and watched a hawk high above him making circles in a cloudless sky. The red-tail . . . not hunting, just soaring . . . too high to hunt. It, too, was enjoying the day, the weather. A good day for soaring, if one were a hawk. *Good day to you, Grandfather,* he thought at the bird. He was certain that it dipped a wing in greeting.

Such things were things that he had come to notice from his long habit of hunting alone. The actions of other creatures had taken on more meaning than they had for others. He considered this a good trade.

Today, however, he was not alone. He had carried the baby with him. The child was fussy and irritable, unusual for her usual happy disposition.

"I think her teeth bother her," Far Dove had said.

"But she has no teeth," Hunts-Alone signed.

"They are trying to come through—ah, you are teasing!" She struck at him playfully.

"Here, Father, give her this to chew," Young Crow suggested, handing him a strip of dried meat. "I have work to do."

He cradled the child in his arms and offered her the teething strip. She fought it for a moment, and then as the hard texture began to soften, she sucked at it eagerly.

"It is good!" signed Far Dove.

Hunts-Alone shifted the baby to his left arm and signed with his right. "I will take her with me to the hill."

The women nodded and returned to their tasks, and he placed South Wind in her cradle board and proceeded to his special post.

The infant had fallen asleep on the way up the hill, lulled by the swaying motion of his walking. He set the cradle board down, shading her face carefully, and now lay enjoying the day as she rested comfortably. He looked at her frequently, because he could not hear her if she chanced to awake and cry. This was not a conscious action on the part of Hunts-Alone. It was merely the way he did all things.

He glanced at her again, then rolled on his side and propped himself on an elbow to overlook the camp below. It was growing late. Still some time until sunset, and the babe still slept . . . well, he could stay a bit longer. He hated to disturb her sleep. How pretty she looked, relaxed in sleep. Long, dark lashes on rosy cheeks, so like her mother as a child.

He lay back again, looking at the sky. The hawk had circled lower now, and had been joined by another. The pair swept toward the Earth in dizzying spirals, and finally both landed on a dead snag some distance away. It was on a hillock similar to his own, beyond the camp. They were probably choosing a spot to roost for the night, he thought.

He looked at the baby again. Should he wake her? *No,* he thought, *she is comfortable now. I will wait . . . no hurry.*

It was sometime later that he realized he must have dozed. He was not certain what roused him, for the baby still slept. His experienced glance swept the area before him. The hawks . . . still there . . . he must have drowsed off for only a short while. The sun was a distance from Earth's rim yet.

Then a flash of motion caught his eye. The hawks on the distant stub suddenly rose together and flapped to gain altitude. Odd . . . one should have risen first, *then* the other. For both to fly at the same moment, they must have been disturbed. *By what?* Still he was only mildly interested, not alarmed. He knew that the men were probably out and around the camp, the women gathering wood for the fires.

Yes, he saw now, there was one of . . . yes, Feeds-His-Horse was walk-ing toward the camp. Hunts-Alone relaxed. The young man's appearance must have alarmed the birds, caused them to fly. He glanced at the still-sleeping baby for an instant, and back at the approaching figure. Feeds-His-Horse was coming from the area of the hawks' perch. The birds were still wheeling and circling over him. Not *directly* over him, actually . . . a chill of fear swept over Hunts-Alone. Something was not right! Something *else* had alarmed the hawks on the dead tree.

That thought was not even quite complete when Feeds-His-Horse seemed to stumble in midstride. The leg that was swinging forward never reached its next step, and the young man fell heavily on his face. A feathered shaft jutted from between his shoulder blades.

A painted warrior suddenly leaped from the bushy slope and dashed past his victim, pausing only to count honors by touching the still form. Other warriors were flitting among the trees. He could see their shaved heads and roached hair . . . dozens of them.

Hunts-Alone had snatched up the cradle board and was running down the slope. He did not have the ability to shout a warning. Then he paused a moment. *What am I doing?* he thought. The attackers were nearer the camp than he. He could not warn the others. But here he was, running unarmed into a fight against stronger attackers, and carrying a baby! Had he gone mad?

He set the cradle board down and prepared to run on. But no, he could not leave the child. They would all be killed, leaving the infant to die in the woods . . . he must take her . . . no . . . The baby was awake now, catching the feel of his fear and anguish. From the open mouth and twisted face, he knew that she was screaming. She would be heard!

Instinctively he clapped a hand over the tiny mouth to stifle her cries. She struggled, frustrated, and wriggled against the cradle's restraints, her large dark eyes alternately squinting and open wide, brimming with tears.

He looked toward the camp, unable to help as the attackers moved at will among the lodges. He could see several bodies on the ground. The lodge of Bull's Horn was blazing, black smoke from the burning lodge skins and the stored provisions rising in a greasy column into the clear blue. A warrior thrust a torch into the dry grass in another lodge lining. There was a puff or two of cottony white smoke as the grass ignited, then a change to dirty black when the lodge and the supplies began to burn.

He could see no one alive except the attackers. Surely the children . . . no, there was a small corpse against a burning lodge. Roach-maned warriors were hacking, mutilating . . .

It was good that the unused vocal cords of Hunts-Alone could not pro-duce much sound, for he would have screamed in his agony. He sat, holding his hand over the mouth of the baby and watching everything that mattered in his world go up in greasy smoke. Everything except this tiny child.

He thought of an old story of a woman in such a situation. She had choked her own baby to keep it from crying out and revealing the where-abouts of her people to the enemy. She had saved her people by this sacri-fice. He had never really believed that a woman could do so. He was certain of it, now. Especially since this small wriggling bundle was all that he had left of everything that he lived for. He must protect her, at all costs.

From his anguished throat came a croaking, gurgling cry, one that could not be heard at any distance. It was the only sound that he could muster in mourning for his loss. Tears streaming down his face, he wriggled his way into a dense clump of bushes, the cradle board held tightly to his breast.

In the western sky, the setting sun slowly changed the blue to blood-red.

Below, warriors went on with the looting until it was too dark.

"There should be one more man," someone called. "Five lodges, only four warriors."

"Let him go," answered Chops-His-Enemy. "Maybe it is good. He can tell the others what happens to invaders into the land of our people. We have what we need."

22

↔

All night Hunts-Alone lay huddled in the bushes, shivering with the night's chill, sheltering the baby with his own body warmth. He knew that she cried sometimes, because he could feel the resonance of the tiny voice through his hands, arms, and skin. He tried to prevent it some of the time, but at other times he hardly cared. What was the use? And he cried, himself. Great, heartrending sobs, choking sounds from a little-used voice box, sounds that would have been unintelligible to any listener.

He did not know when the Shaved-Heads left, because he could not hear their shouts and cries as they methodically burned, sacked, and mutilated. Sometime before dark, probably. He ventured a look at dusk and saw no activity, but could not bring himself to go down and view the carnage yet. He knew there would be no survivors. He had watched the methodical slaughter. The very thought wrenched another great sob from his throat, and he held the baby close.

He drowsed occasionally in the night, and then would come awake in alarm, roused by the stiffness in his limbs or by the stirring of the child's body. He would recoil in horror from the thoughts that recurred with returning awareness. For a long time he could see the flickering light of the horrible greasy fires that were still devouring all that had been dear to him. He was torn between the desire to go and look and the need to protect the infant in his arms.

During that painful time, his mind went through the whole range of human emotion. Fear, frustration, grief, anger, hate, the desire for revenge, resentment . . . yes, resentment over the plans for winter camp set forth by the young men. Resentment at them, and resentment that he had listened and agreed. Resentment at the Eastern band for their decisions. *They deserve their foolish reputation,* he thought bitterly. They became responsible, in his tortured mind, for the loss of his family.

The hate and bitterness began to grow, like an evil destructive thing. He hated the Shaved-Heads for their part in his loss. But not them alone. His own people . . . the Eastern band, his sons, for their foolish decision. He had forgotten that only that afternoon he had been pleased and proud over the same choice. Everyone . . . no person in the world escaped his hate. Except Far Dove, of course, and she was dead. He was sure of that, for he had seen her fall.

The thought brought another sob. How could he go on? He was alone, horribly, completely alone, except for this helpless bundle in his arms. If it had not been for the baby, of course, he would have run down the hill, to be slaughtered with the rest. He *must* go on, for her. She had no one else, no protection. They were alone, the two of them, against the whole world. There was no one, anywhere, who could be trusted.

This very sense of isolation, this alone-ness, may have saved his sanity. There would be those, years later, who would argue that his sanity had *not* been spared. But at any rate, his alone-ness made him begin to think, to plan. Was he not called Hunts-Alone? His were the skills called upon for such a situation. The protection of this infant, he decided, had been thrust upon him, because only he could have done it. His confidence began to revive, at least a little bit.

He must wait until daylight. One major limitation was his inability to function in darkness, and he was well aware of this. The loss of a single sense is a major deficit for most people. Hunts-Alone did not miss it, but when darkness robbed him of a second mode of contact with the world, it became devastating. Those who are active in the time of darkness must depend heavily on a sense of hearing, because vision is diminished. And Hunts-Alone had no hearing. He would wait.

By morning, of course, the baby was hungry and crying. He had all but given up trying to quiet her. It was of great concern to him how her needs for food could be met. Under normal circumstances, one would look for a nursing mother who could share her milk, but this did not even occur to him. The whole world was now his enemy, and he could trust no one. He and this child would live or die together, asking no help. But he must find food. Not for himself, but for the baby. He could fast, but a child cannot.

As soon as it was light enough to see, he started down the slope, carrying the cradle board. The baby quieted somewhat, comforted by the rocking motion. He was cautious, pausing to look long and hard every few steps. He was still not certain that the Shaved-Heads had really gone. At any moment they might burst from hiding, their insatiable bloodlust ready to finish the carnage.

Nearing the shattered camp, he placed the cradle board against a tree and began to survey the destruction. With a sense of unreality he looked from one still form to another, his mind unable to really comprehend. How could he care for them? The task seemed insurmountable. The formal scaffold burial ceremony was out of the question. He could not build so many scaffolds. He suffered, wept, and finally decided on a mass grave. He found a crevice in the rocky hillside . . . yes, that would serve his purpose.

First, though, something to feed the child. He could hardly have believed, a day earlier, that today would find him stepping past the bodies of his loved ones to rummage in the ruined camp for provisions. Most of the lodges lay in ashes, but a portion of one lodge skin was intact. He pulled it back. Ah! This would help! In the space behind the lodge lining here, there had been supplies and possessions stored. That, perhaps, had been the means by which this part had not burned. There was no dried-grass insulation to ignite here, on the south side of the lodge, and for some reason the supplies had not been plundered. Maybe the fire had been too hot to approach at the time. For whatever reason, here he found a quantity of dried meat stored in a rawhide pack. The pack was scorched, but the meat was intact. That would help. There was also a small quantity of a food that was a favorite of the People. Dried meat, pounded fine and mixed with melted tallow, nuts, and dried berries, also pounded. This was considered a proper food for children or recovering invalids. Good! He thought that this might be useful for the baby. He set the pack aside.

Perhaps a more important find was a folded buffalo robe. Apparently it had not been needed and was merely stored for future use. It appeared brand-new. The fur was badly damaged on one side, but that would not affect its warmth to any extent. He laid it beside the rawhide pack, then took some of the food and returned to the baby.

She was ravenously hungry, but was having a difficult time satisfying her needs by gnawing the hard strip with no teeth. In distress, he tried to think . . . water! Yes, she must have water. He cut a scrap of leather from the unburned lodge cover and rolled it into a cone to carry water from the stream. Patiently, little by little, he dribbled the precious fluid into her mouth. She sucked at it eagerly.

Meanwhile, he was chewing some of the meat and tallow mixture himself. He had seen women do this to provide easier food for a child. When it was soft, he transferred the contents of his own mouth to the baby's. Her eyes widened in surprise for a moment, but then she gulped at it, seeming to reach for more. He was pleased and repeated the process. Finally, the child appeared satiated and fell asleep. He spread the buffalo robe and tenderly placed her on it.

There was need to see what else he could find, but now he must return to the tragic task of taking care of the dead. One by one, he dragged or carried the mutilated bodies to the cleft and tucked them inside. He sat and cried a long time over Far Dove. He had done his best to carry out the formal funeral preparation for her, though he could not for the others. Using the unburned lodge cover, he gently wrapped and tied the precious bundle and carried her to her final resting place. He was glad that she had not been mutilated like some of the others, and that her death had been quick . . . an ax. . . . He collapsed into tears again and lay beside her a little while.

Then he prayed for the spirits of all of them, and began to carry stones to cover the cairn. It was a long and difficult task, and he paused once to feed the baby again.

The tasks of burial complete, he turned again to present needs, rummaging through the refuse to salvage what he could. Weapons would be important. Unfortunately, the attackers, too, would have considered them important.

He had been wearing a flint belt-knife, and that was good. His bow, which had been hanging at the lodge door, was ruined, one limb burned in two. He did find three arrows. One virtually intact, one broken, and one salvageable, the feathers partly burned. This gave him an idea, however. He scratched through the ashes of all the lodges again, and found several usable arrow points, some metal and some of stone.

An important discovery in this activity was a small ax head with the handle burned off. He recognized it as the weapon of Feeds-His-Horse. It was iron, one of those acquired in trade from the Spanish in Santa Fe. A valuable find! He could replace the handle at any later time when he had an opportunity.

For now, one more important find was a waterskin, overlooked, maybe. It was hanging on a small tree near one of the burned lodges, as if nothing had happened. It was important, because now he could carry water as they traveled. That brought another thought. Where would he go? He had not considered that. The burning hate for all people, which had troubled him during the night, now swept over him again.

Vengeance . . . if he could manage to kill a few of the Shaved-Heads, to avenge his loss . . . He could strike a lone warrior here and there, disappear into the forest, to return and strike somewhere else.

But he realized that he could not do that. He had the child to think of. If it were not for her, he would have become a vengeful, ghostlike figure to strike terror into the hearts of the Shaved-Heads.

No, he realized. He could not have done so. If it were not for the baby who lay here now, sleeping on the damaged robe, he would be dead. He would have rushed down the slope to join the fight, and he would have been killed with the others. Maybe his would have been one of the heads that by now must adorn poles somewhere in the country of the Shaved-Heads.

He must leave, now. It was growing late, and he could not stand another night near this place of horror. He gathered and packed his meager possessions and prepared to leave. Feed the infant again . . . one more good-bye at the grave that held all that had mattered to him. More tears . . .

He turned back to place the baby in her cradle board. He would wear this cradle on his back, freeing his hands to carry the other bundles as he traveled. Where? He had not decided. Only that it must be away from here. Back into country where he felt more comfortable. Tall-grass country, to the west. But for now, he set his goal on a thin strip of trees that he could see from the knoll. It was isolated, a little island in the distant grassland. Not too far away . . . Yes, they could reach it by dark.

He swung the cradle to his back, picked up his packs, and turned his face toward the setting sun.

23

It was another terrible night in the timbered strip. He dared not light a fire, so he wrapped himself and the baby in the fire-damaged buffalo robe for warmth. His fitful sleep was interrupted frequently by the restlessness of the child. He knew that she must be hungry and uncomfortable, but there was little that he could do to help her, except to warm her body with his own and provide a little food and water from their meager supply. *It will be better, later,* he thought at her, hoping that she would somehow grasp such an idea. Actually, he did not quite believe it himself. There were times when it seemed useless to try to go on. But he must survive, for the sake of this baby. . . .

During the times when he did manage to doze a little, he would wake in terror, tortured by the dreams. In these he relived the horror he had experienced on the knoll, watching helplessly while his family was slaughtered below. He would find himself running to help, but so slowly that he could not do so. Or, trying to strike at the attackers, unable to land a blow. Then in a panic, he would recall the baby and turn to save her, to find the cradle board nowhere . . . the slope and the knoll at its crest devoid of life. He would waken at different points in this confused dream sequence, damp with a cold sweat. He would have screamed if he had been able.

There was another dream, perhaps even more troubling, in which he seemed to hover like a hawk over the scene of the butchery. He was strangely detached, watching the horrifying events below but seeing them as of lesser importance. With some interest he watched a man carrying a child in a cradle board, and realized that it was himself. *Odd,* he thought . . . *how can one watch himself?*

He wakened from this dream, greatly concerned. He could understand the horror and grief and fear that he was experiencing, but this . . . could he be dead? He *and* the baby he had tried to save?

He shifted his position, and the stiffness and pain in his left shoulder told him he was still alive. That shoulder had never been quite the same since an encounter with a bear, long ago. It always gave him notice of a change in the weather. And the dead, as far as he knew, would not have the aches and pains of age and old injuries.

There was also the matter of hunger, the gnawing in his belly, and the way it rolled and gurgled. Yes, both he and the baby had already felt the need for food and water, so they must be alive.

By the time the gray of the dawn faded to yellow, he was certain of that fact. They *were* alive, through some miracle. As soon as the sun's rays made it possible to see the surrounding prairie, he was on his feet, searching with his skilled sense of distant vision. There was nothing important that he could see. A distant heron, graceful in flight, making his way to some distant pool . . . *The season is late, Uncle,* he thought. *You would do well to move south to whatever winter camp your people make.*

Winter camp . . . tears came to his eyes again. There *was* no winter camp for those he loved. Their bones would winter in the crevice for all time, now. He realized that his pain and grief were for himself and not for those he had lost. They would return to Earth, from which all life comes. His head told him this, but his heart was not yet ready to accept it. The anguish of his loss was too fresh.

And now, he must plan. They had escaped the danger from the Shaved-Heads, at least for now. He must continue to be watchful, but he thought that there was little chance of the war party's return. There would be no purpose in it.

But what now? Where could he go? With winter coming, he and the baby must have shelter, food, protection from the cold. . . . It seemed an insurmountable problem. He thought it unwise to even consider trying to contact the main band. They were somewhere deeper into the Shaved-Heads' territory anyway. It was quite likely that they, too, had been destroyed. The anger flared again. He should have done more to resist such foolish decisions as theirs. It had been sheer idiocy to challenge the might of the Shaved-Heads. He began to hate the leaders who had been responsible. If they were dead, they deserved it. If not, they probably would be before winter was over.

He wondered about the possibility of joining one of the other bands. The

Northern band would probably be the nearest, but he did not know where they intended to winter. He felt a certain resentment toward them, anyway. They had always been so smug, so superior, in their attitude toward the Eastern band. The jokes . . .

What of the Southern band? He knew even less of their winter plans. The scrub oak country somewhere . . . He would not even know where to look. The Mountain and Red Rocks bands, of course, were far away, too far to consider.

Who would be of any help, then? Their only close allies were the Head Splitters, far away to the southwest. Farther, even, than the other bands of the People.

The Growers? There were several villages that he knew. The Growers always traded with everyone, to stay on good terms and guard against the ever-present risk of raids by more warlike hunting tribes. But he had nothing to trade. No Growers, or anyone else, would welcome the approach of an old man and a baby with winter coming on. They would be two more mouths to feed, and nothing whatever to offer in exchange.

His resentment was beginning to grow. A strange thing, resentment for people he had never met. It may have started with his hate of those who had perpetrated the wanton killing. But mixed with this was the resentment toward his own people, who must accept part of the blame. If it had not been for their decisions . . . Once more his thoughts came full circle, with yet another cycle of pain, resentment, frustration, and hate. Added to that, his lifelong tendency to alone-ness now resulted in a destructive transformation. Little by little, he was reaching the point where he felt that he could ask no one for help, could trust no one. At the same time his feelings continued to resolve themselves, and gradually focus in one direction . . . *hate*. It was no longer limited to one person, one group, but spread to include the entire world . . . every other human being except the two of them: himself and this tiny child.

But he *would* survive, he vowed. Survive to raise this baby girl, to teach her the devious ways of all people, teach her, too, to trust no one, to hate the customs that had brought them so near to death. And to survive, only for this cruel twist of fate. The tears flowed again—now not only tears of grief, but of frustration and hate.

He was a little mad, of course, though one afflicted with madness usually does not realize it. If he had, at this stage, encountered any other people, they surely would have recognized his madness. It would have furnished protection, because to all the various cultures in the area, it would be dangerous to harm a madman. To do so would release a dangerous spirit, seeking a new abode. Probably even the Shaved-Heads, perceiving him mad, would have treated him with respect. They would not have harmed him.

Ironically, then, as his mind continued to retreat from the reality of the things he had witnessed, it pushed him farther from human contact. He was determined that he would make contact with no one. Not a single human being, friend or foe, must know of their survival. In making this decision, he wiped out all possibility of help. And this, when anyone they encountered, even an enemy, would have felt obliged to help them.

By the time the sun was well started up the eastern sky, Hunts-Alone was moving. He did not know where he was going yet, but he wanted to distance them from the scene of tragedy. Away, out onto the prairie, away from the dark foreboding forest that had been their doom. The far horizons somehow promised new life beyond.

He considered trying to steal a horse from one of the villages that dotted the streams like well-spaced beads on a string. His thoughts were clear and cunning, despite the madness. They could travel faster. . . . But what use to travel more rapidly, he reasoned, when one knows not where he is going anyway? He laughed to himself at such a joke. Then, too, he reasoned, it would be much harder to hide if they had a horse. On the open plain, a horse could be seen for nearly a half-day's travel. No, they must remain inconspicuous, let no one know they existed.

Hunts-Alone refilled their waterskin at a clear stream when Sun Boy paused overhead in his run. They rested a little. He took the baby out of the cradle board and allowed her to play on the spread robe for a little while. She seemed to respond well to the freedom from being tightly wrapped. She smiled, crawled on all fours, and sat looking around her.

"I will take care of you, little one," he signed to her, knowing that she would not understand. The signed message was for himself, not for her. She smiled.

He fed her a little, as he had before, and she gulped eagerly at the paste of chewed food, and at the water that he dribbled into her mouth. She was tired, then, and snuggled comfortably back into the cradle board when he was ready to start on.

Once he sighted some riders in the distance and hurried to hide. He did not even try to identify the riders. There was no reason to do so. He wanted to see no one, and did not want to be seen. He positioned himself and the cradled infant near the top of a rocky ridge, and watched the distant riders carefully. They seemed to be following a dim trail that would bring them near, but not too near the hiding place. Good. He would stay here.

He turned to glance at South Wind. She was crying. This bothered him, because he had not known. He was not certain how far a baby's cry might be heard. He had not had occasion to wonder such things until now. But he must take no chances. Quickly, he covered her mouth with his palm as he had done before, during the massacre. He could feel the vibration beneath his hand, and the frustrated baby struggled against it. Finally she quieted, and her dark eyes stared at him in frustration. Cautiously, he removed the hand. The infant started to pucker her face for another cry, and he quickly replaced his palm.

It was not easy, but by the end of the day the pattern seemed established. He was certain that South Wind understood his hand sign for "quiet!" She did not like it, of course, but understood it.

The distant riders had not come close enough to worry about, and had passed on, out of sight. He watched the distant prairie from a prominent hilltop that evening as the sun sank, but could see no sign of other human life in any direction. He waited until after dark and continued to watch for the glint of distant fires. Still, he saw nothing. That was good, though a bit unusual. There should be a town of Growers somewhere . . . ah, yes! As it became darker, he could see a ruddy glow in the far distance. That would be on the river he had seen to the north. It was reassuring to know where the town was located so that he might avoid it.

He now carried everything to a little ravine below the crest of the hill and ventured to build a small campfire. It was good, and helped him to return to the reality of the world for a little while. He offered a small piece of his dried meat, placing it in the fire, and prayed silently for a little while.

When the fire died, he rose and gathered all their possessions again. Just in case someone had seen their fire, they would sleep elsewhere. He moved, then, to a previously located spot and spread the robe.

He lay there a long time, pondering tomorrow. He still did not have any definite goal, except to avoid people. *Forever!* He would find a place where people never came. But was there such a place? He tried to think whether he had heard of such places. . . . The deserts to the southwest, of course, but that was far away. And the desert was uninhabited largely because no one could live there. There was no reliable water and no game. No, it must be a place that *was* livable, but not used. This seemed an unlikely combination, though. If it had water, grass, and game, it would be worthwhile for someone to live there. Except, of course, if there was some taboo or curse on it, to frighten people away. In that case, it would . . . *Wait!* His eyes widened in the realization that there *was* such a place, and that he had been there.

Of course! he thought to himself. *Medicine Rock! No one ever goes there!*

24

He must travel rapidly, he knew. The season was late, and at any day Cold Maker would come swooping down to catch the unwary. There were times when he feared that the whole thing was an intricate scheme on the part of Cold Maker. He and the baby were being lured out into the open prairie to die of exposure in the first cruel thrust of winter.

There was a slight temptation to stop and prepare for protection, but he resisted. *You cannot tempt me!* He silently indicated his defiance with an upraised fist toward the north. No, he must not stop. The only effect that such a temptation had was to reinforce the threat that he already felt. That, in turn, made him hurry even more.

He had a few days' supply of the salvaged provisions. Enough, he thought, to sustain him and the baby until they reached their goal. They would require very little. Fasting would sharpen his senses anyway, and stretch their supplies.

Day by day the conviction grew in him that once his goal was reached, they were safe. Had he paused to think rationally, the utter folly of the whole thing would have been apparent. His goal was a place completely unknown to him, except by the legends of the People, and those were always coupled with dire warnings. In the twisted mind of Hunts-Alone, however, the warnings were for others. For him and for the small bundle in the cradle board, such warnings and threats of evil were of benefit. Dread of whatever lurked in the dark rock of the cliff would keep others away.

That was good, because he wanted no contact with other people. The bitterness that had begun with his loss had continued to grow as they traveled. He had been betrayed by people, his twisted mind continually shouted at him. There had been only a few who were loved ones, and now they were dead. Tears still came each time these thoughts recurred. Then would come again the wave of hatred and frustration. Every hurt, every thing bad in his life, he told himself, was because of association with others. The tragedy of his first hunt . . . how much better when he learned to hunt alone.

Yes, anytime that he was completely on his own, he had been able to handle whatever came. It had always been better. He tried to review his life logically and to think of exceptions. Yes, a few. His parents, dead now. Then the kindly teaching of old Tracks-Well. That had prepared him well for what faced him now. But the tracker himself was gone, long ago. Few friends . . . the others hunted together and formed friendships on the basis of those relationships.

And Far Dove. She had been the most important person in his life. She and the children that they had shared. Now they were gone. Dead, every one, some struck down before his eyes. Their grandchildren, too, except for this one that he carried. When these thoughts recurred, he was always forced to stop a little while, because tears impaired his vision, and the great choking sobs racked his throat again. And he always came to the same conclusions: Of all the people in the world, only a few had ever been an influence for good in his life. Those were dead. He wanted no others. It would be good, he thought, if he and little South Wind never encountered another person, ever. He was not able to think of the future for her, only that the two of them had survived. He had, partially through accident, managed to save the child. Now, her continued survival was all that mattered. He plodded on.

He had a general idea of the location of Medicine Rock, and headed straight for it, within limitation of the terrain. He did try to avoid any areas that had a well-traveled appearance. Sometimes they traveled by night, when there was enough moonlight. He carefully skirted the village of Growers that they passed, to avoid all human contact. There would be few people traveling at this season, he knew. The hunting tribes would have established their winter camps. Traveling traders would have long since decided where they would winter. At home with their own people, or as guests of some other tribe for a season. Either way, it was likely that the decisions had been made long ago.

Yes, no one was likely to challenge the danger of Cold Maker's return. He would not do so himself, except for necessity. That recalled again the urgency of his journey and quickened his steps. He glanced to the north-west at the thickening sky. *Not yet,* he thought. . . .

He allowed them the luxury of a fire when he could, and that helped. The warmth revived his old bones, drew out the stiffness, and let him continue. Beside such a fire one night, he fitted a new handle to the salvaged ax head. That gave him new confidence. Until now, he had been virtually unarmed, but escape and distance had been more important than weapons.

Now, however, he was realizing that he could not hunt for food of any significance with a belt-knife and a small ax. He thought about it there by the fire, while he finished scraping the new handle on his ax and hefted it for balance. He was starting virtually from nothing.

He recalled his childhood days in the Rabbit Society. All the children, both boys and girls, had learned to use the throwing-sticks. These were actually only a short, stout club, used very little in serious hunting. Still, the first kill of most children as they learned to hunt was that of a rabbit, and usually with the thrown club. He should be able to revert to such methods.

And snares . . . yes, that was a possibility. He could probably snare rabbits . . . he assumed there would be rabbits at or near Medicine Rock. But, even so, that would not see them safely through the winter. Snaring or clubbing small game would be only a day-to-day thing, which was a danger-ous way to approach winter. People entering the season on a hand-to-mouth basis would surely not survive the Moon of Hunger. No, he must, in some way, make a kill. A kill of a large animal. He would prefer a buffalo, but an elk, maybe. Even a deer would probably see them through the winter, if he wasted nothing. Surely, there would be deer in the timber along the river at the Rock.

And to make such a kill, he must have a weapon. A bow or a lance . . . he preferred the bow. Many men used a lance, but usually on horseback. It was a good weapon. A bow, however, could be used at greater distance. The lance could be thrown by a man on foot, but he must be very close to his quarry.

On the other hand, a crude spear would be easier to make. A bow would be quite complicated, and would take some time. Time that he did not have . . .

He must do something, however. It gave him some sense of security that he now had the ax. He would begin to gather materials now, limited by his ability to carry much more than he now had. Wood for arrow shafts, maybe. There was a dense growth of prairie dogwood where he had camped, scarcely an arm's length away. He cut a few stems for arrow shafts and trimmed them to length. He could fit points later, from those in his pack, and feathers at any time.

Wood for a bow? . . . It would need some time to cure, and would be too heavy to carry. But wait . . . there was a straight, smooth trunk of the thorny bow-wood tree. He had noticed it before dark. He could cut a staff, and use it as such while he allowed it to cure. It would serve as a crude defensive weapon, and he could shape it later.

He could not wait, but rose and walked to the thorny thicket, looking in the dim light for the tree he remembered. Yes, there it was! He could not see it clearly, but could cut it in the morning.

While he was thinking along these lines, he realized that for the arrows he would need feathers. There would be turkeys, and this, too, could be food, maybe. The People seldom ate turkeys, but there was no taboo against it, as there was for bear. It was a good possibility. This, in turn, made him wonder what other sources of food might be useful. Beaver? There should be beaver in the river below the Rock. He was becoming impatient to get there and see what there might be that could be of use. Well, first he must get there, and quickly. The night was frosty, and he shivered as he drew the robe around him and lay down next to the sleeping child.

Hunts-Alone paused at the top of the ridge to orient himself. He was following the river now, in a generally northwesterly direction. Surely, it could not be too many days' travel to the Rock. Each range of hills that he crossed brought him nearer. He had half expected to see the Rock from this ridge, but it was not so. The tallgrass prairie stretched before him, its winter colors showing pinks and yellows on the near hillsides. More distance added a violet, then a bluish haze to the ridges a day's travel away. In the far distance, the gray-blue of the most distant ridge faded into the gray-blue of the heavy sky. Or was that last ridge to the northwest actually a cloud bank? He shuddered at the thought, and turned away to follow the course of the river with his eyes.

In summer, it could have been traced by the darker green color of the trees against the green of the grasses. Now, most of the leaves had fallen. Stark white skeletons of sycamores stood out in contrast to the darker gray of the other trees. In some areas oaks still held their dead foliage, dull brown in color now.

He traced the river's course by the slender ribbon of timber, winding snakelike across the prairie. Surely, he should be nearing the Rock. Could it be possible? . . . A chill of fear gripped him, a chill that had nothing to do with the bite of the wind, which had shifted to the northwest this morning. Could it be that he was following the *wrong river*? If so, he thought, they were in deep trouble.

Hunts-Alone glanced at the dark line on the distant horizon. *Aiee,* it *was* looming larger. It *was* a storm front, a major thrust on the part of Cold Maker! They must not be caught in the open.

He had been following the river on the higher ground to the north side, because travel was easier. Now, he must seek shelter, and quickly. He scanned the river's course to the west, hoping against hope that he would see the stark cliffs of Medicine Rock. There was nothing. In fact, the general course of the river upstream seemed to have less timber than in this area. A half-day's travel away, its direction seemed to be almost directly east and west, and he could see even less of the gray ribbon that suggested trees along its course. His heart sank. He *must* be on the wrong river. He was traveling not toward shelter, but directly out into the treeless flatland, where death would be a certainty with no more protection than they had.

Well, he would fight to the end, for the child. First, they must seek immediate shelter from the approaching snowstorm. He turned down the slope toward the river, and the scant protection that the trees would provide. If possible, they should be on the other, the south side of the stream. He was following a faint game trail, and would go where it led. Deer, for instance, might have used it to reach the shelter of a thicket.

He emerged from a rocky hillside into a small meadow, and beyond that could see white gravel. Good . . . maybe a riffle, where the river could be crossed. It was true. . . . He clattered and splashed across, and turned to follow the stream on its south bank. Already, he felt relief from the icy breath of the northwest wind. Here below the trees it was almost calm.

The baby on his back was fidgeting uncomfortably. *A short while longer, little one,* he thought. There, ahead, a thicket more dense, more protection from the wind . . . dead wood for fuel . . .

He hurried into a little clearing and dropped the packs, swinging the cradle board from his back. The baby was crying, but he must first start a fire. He took out the firesticks and began the ceremonial task. The wind, which he had feared might make it more difficult, actually seemed to help. It fanned a spark that grew on the brown powder formed at the whirling spindle's tip. Gently, he wrapped it in his cedar-bark tinder and held it aloft while he breathed life into it from beneath. As it burst into flame, he thrust it into the little pyramid of dry sticks that he had gathered quickly. It was growing rapidly colder, and his fingers were numb as he began to add larger sticks.

It had been close . . . too close. The sky was dark now, though it was still midafternoon. Cold Maker howled in the trees overhead, in his frustration at the escape of his intended victims. Hunts-Alone smiled a grim smile and shook a fist at the howling wind. He had managed to beat Cold Maker, at least this time.

As he propped sticks across some bushes and hung the robe to reflect the fire's glow, he noticed that it had begun to snow.

25

The storm was brief, as those early in the season often are. Sun Boy made his countermove by midmorning the next day. The white blanket that had been cast over the world was actually quite thin, and already was beginning to disappear. Hunts-Alone decided to wait until the traveling was easier, and settled down by the fire, somewhat impatiently.

He could not see much beyond the thicket from their campfire. The baby was sleeping. He stepped out into the open to orient himself and plan the course of his travel, when the time would come. He was on the south side of the river now, and looked upstream to the west. Should he travel on this side now, in the lee of the timbered strip, in case Cold Maker sallied forth again? It would be better protection, but the traveling might be harder.

With these thoughts idly wandering through his mind, he looked across the little meadow at the rise a bowshot away. The smooth blanket of snow was unbroken except for the tracks of early-rising rabbits. Maybe he should . . . yes, it should be possible to obtain fresh meat while he waited. He noticed tracks of deer, too. The animal had come from the dogwood thicket, there, where it had probably spent the night. It had paused to drink at the riffle, then traveled westward, casually and unalarmed. It was a good sign.

A coyote appeared on the rise to the south and stood watching him. *Good day to you, Uncle,* thought Hunts-Alone. *And, good hunting!*
 This, too, was a good sign.

A flash of motion caught his eye, and he turned to watch a crow sail across the meadow to land in a dead cottonwood near the river. *Aiee, a third sign!* His spirit rose within him. He began to gain an optimism that he had not had since . . . since the tragedy that had destroyed his life. Quickly, he put that thought behind him.

No, he would see if he could find a rabbit, while the snow cover still helped him. It amused him that he might be able to use Cold Maker's weapon, the snow, to their own benefit. First, he must have a club or throwing-stick. He turned back toward the river . . . had he not seen? . . . Yes, there! A beaver had been working among the branches of a cottonwood it had felled, and sticks of various sizes were left behind. He chose one as thick as his wrist and a convenient length for throwing, and turned back to the network of tracks in the meadow. The coyote watched him closely.

I do not forget you, Uncle, he thought at the creature. *The bargain between your people and mine is still good. The leavings of my kill are yours.*

It had been so since Creation, when Coyote stole fire for Man. Coyote's request, the leavings of any kill, had been honored by the People ever since. As a reminder of the ancient covenant, each of Coyote's people still bears a scorched stripe down the side of his furry coat.

Now Hunts-Alone selected a fresh-looking set of tracks and followed it. He lost the trail once where it became tangled with others, then sorted it out again. The tracks separated from the others and headed toward some clumps of dry grass well out in the open meadow. Yes, a likely place. He moved cautiously, eyeing the trail, then paused motionless to study it.

The footprints were two long marks of the hind feet, with the smaller prints of Rabbit's front feet slightly behind, for that is how Rabbit's people travel. Hunts-Alone did not even think of this, it was so basic to his skills. His observation was that the trail led to the clumps of dry grass, *but did not come out the other side.* His quarry, therefore, must be still in hiding there.

Very cautiously, he approached the grass clumps, looking, looking, his throwing-stick ready in case the rabbit should panic and run. *Ah, there!* He saw a glimpse of a shiny black eye, betraying the presence of his quarry in the almost perfect camouflage of the grassy bower. Yes, now he could see the crouching form, the ears flattened against the back. . . .

Without breaking his stride, he swung the stick as a club, and the rabbit lay kicking in the snow. He picked it up, the appropriate apology going through his mind, then placed it on the ground again, propped in a lifelike position.

I am sorry to kill you, my brother, he signed, *but I need your flesh for the lives of myself and my little one. May your people prosper and be many.*

He picked it up again, held it aloft to show to the coyote on the slope, and waved to his fellow hunter, indicating success. All the signs were good. He would dress out the animal, leaving Coyote's share.

Now, if only he could determine where he was, and whether he had made a mistake . . . was this really Medicine River? He glanced upstream, for no particular reason, and stopped in amazement. There, only a few bow-shots away, the north bank of the river rose in a sheer cliff, dark-gray and foreboding. But how . . . why had he not seen this? His thoughts whirled in confusion. For a moment he considered the possibility that the power of Medicine Rock was so great that it was sometimes here, sometimes not.

Then he steadied, and began to think the situation through. He had been traveling on the grassy flat that formed the north bank of the river. The *higher* bank, so that he could see ahead with greater ease. The light had been poor as the storm came in, which had further limited visibility. He realized now that his view yesterday, which had appeared to show fewer trees along the river, was a trick of his own vision. The north bank had gradually risen, and he had been looking *across* the river's course. The impression of fewer trees was created when the bluff became so high that nothing but the tops of the tallest trees were visible. The heavier timber and the tangled thickets that snuggled and prospered in the warm shelter of the cliffs at Medicine Rock were invisible from the north.

Of course, he thought. The ancient legend of the way the People had defeated the invading Blue Paints from the north depended on this factor for surprise. The Rock was never well seen from the north side. He almost laughed at his own stupidity. He had been worried that he was lost, perhaps even on the wrong river. Now, he realized, he was not only right, but had already arrived! *This* was Medicine Rock.

The area that he sought, of course, would be some distance upstream, where the cliff was at its highest. No matter. It was a good day, and his heart was good as he finished skinning and cleaning the rabbit. He left the skin, head, and entrails where he had made the kill, and waved to the coyote again as he turned to hurry back to his camp and the helpless child.

She was awake, her bright dark eyes wide open, looking around the little clearing with curiosity. She smiled at him, and he smiled back.

Yes, many of their problems were behind them. But many more, of course, lay ahead. He began to build up the fire, choosing carefully the driest of sticks, and those from trees that would produce little smoke.

While the flames grew, he took a cottonwood stick and fashioned a spit on which to cook the rabbit. Fresh meat would provide a welcome change, and the moist juices would give strength for the days ahead.

He stood looking up at the rocky face across the river, still holding his packs and with the cradle board on his back. Time was swept away, and he remembered this experience as a young man. Yes, there, the riffle where he had crossed . . . the crevices, filled with the bones of long-dead buffalo. Once more he experienced the excitement of the place, the power of its spirit. There was, of course, the slight sense of foreboding, but that was good, Hunts-Alone told himself. It was that feeling that would keep others away.

He shifted the weight of the cradle board, and glanced at the sun, now bright in the clean blue of the autumn sky. A little past midday . . . He stepped into the icy water of the riffle, running a bit faster now from snow melt. The snow was almost gone, except for scattered patches on the shaded north side of trees and bushes.

His feet crunched in the white gravel of the riffle, sending a strange thrill of anticipation up through his ankles and lower legs. He was glad that the river was no wider, though. By the time he had reached the other shore his toes were numb, and his teeth chattering in protest.

Yes, there . . . the suggestion of a long-unused path that would enable one to climb the cliff's face. Most people, he thought, would overlook it, for the lower portion was quite poorly defined. In fact, he thought, it might require one or both hands to make the climb. This could lead to problems, for it would be necessary to carry food, water, and fuel up that path. But this, too, was good. It would discourage those who might consider trespass.

Now, how? . . . He wished to climb the rock, but hesitated to leave the child below. He considered several possibilities, and finally decided to leave everything except the cradle board at the foot of the cliff, and return for it later. It never occurred to him that he might *not* find a cave or cranny that would provide a satisfactory abode for him and the baby. Was this not the Medicine Rock that had sheltered Eagle, the legendary warrior and story-teller of the People?

He wrapped his provisions and the few small things that he carried into the robe, and tucked the bundle behind a clump of dogwood next to the cliff's base. Then he began to climb.

It was difficult going. Many times he was forced to unsling the cradle board and place it on a rocky outcrop above him while he climbed over fallen debris. Even so, he realized that the path could easily be improved for easier use. Not too easy . . . It must still appear too formidable for any merely curious passer-by to attempt. He could also contrive baffles and traps to confound the unwary intruder.

In one place, the path was blocked by a dead tree that leaned its top against the wall. It was necessary to squeeze past a sizeable branch that obstructed his progress. But this, too, was good. The fallen giant would provide much fuel, easily accessible to the path. It was as if it had been provided, and his heart was good. Best of all, the dry fuel was of sycamore, which would burn well with little smoke.

When he came to the cave, it was as if he expected it, or as if he had been there before. Some insight, perhaps, given to him in compensation for his hearing loss. Perhaps only some dim racial memory, handed down through the generations of the People. Regardless, he was certain that this was the place that he sought. The strange part was that he had sought only a hiding place, a place of shelter from the evils of the outside world. *Any* place, any at all that would fulfill their needs for survival.

This was more. When he saw it, there was a familiarity that he had not expected. He *knew* this place, though he did not know how. He had a strong feeling that it was the very hole in the Rock that had sheltered the injured Eagle long ago. He stepped inside and looked around in wonder. The afternoon sun, slanting warming rays into the cavity, also illuminated it.

The ledge outside, he realized, was wide enough so that the opening could not be seen from the ground. Good. There were also signs of habitation long ago. . . . Charred remains of a long-dead fire, the blackened sticks covered with a fine powder of dust that had drifted in through many generations. There were even the remains of a willow rack at the back of the cave, which had once held supplies or possessions of a previous inhabitant.

He propped the cradle board against the cave wall so that the infant could see, but decided to leave her confined until he made the necessary trips up and down the path before night. And, he must hurry. . . .

"Little one," he signed, "we are home now. This will be our lodge."

He turned back down the ledge to retrieve their few possessions.

26

Hunts-Alone worked frantically in the remaining daylight preparing for Cold Maker's next sortie. Fuel would be important, even more so than food, perhaps. The cave was sheltered against wintry blasts from the north, and it was warmed by its southern exposure to the sun. Yet, he knew that on many days there would be no sun, and that the wind would be searching out every nook and cranny in the cold rock.

So, he carried wood, trip after trip up the steep rocky path. In places the ledge was dangerously narrow, a real barrier to one with a burden. Even as he negotiated the hard places, he rejoiced in them. These were the features that would deter intruders from approaching. He could also make the path along the cliff's face *more* difficult by placing boulders in strategic places. He even noticed one spot that would lend itself well to a deadfall. He could devise a trap, a rock slide to be started by any intruder who tried to climb the Rock.

But he would think of that later. For now, survival must depend on preparation of necessities: food, water, and shelter, though not necessarily in that order. Because of the threat of bad weather, shelter and warmth were the first consideration. Next, water. He was concerned that at times the ledge might become impassible because of snow and ice. Of course, one could *eat* snow and ice for necessary moisture. But if there happened to be only enough to make the path slippery and dangerous . . . Well, one cannot foresee every hazard that life presents. He would deal with such things as they came.

Meanwhile, he would form habits that would be helpful. At each journey to the base of the cliff, he would drink all that he could hold, and carry a full waterskin back to the cave. He would need more waterskins . . . ah, well, that too, could come later. As soon as he had collected enough firewood for a few days, he must try for a kill. Already, he was observing the habits of a band of deer that seemed to frequent a thicket a little way downstream. The vantage point of the ledge gave ample opportunity to follow the patterns of their activity, and he began to take note for the day when he would stalk them for food.

Over all the frantic activity that thrust itself upon him was one over-whelming concern: the safety of the baby. He could not be with her every moment. It was impossible to carry her on his journeys up and down the path. Yet he must face the very real danger of a fall from the ledge. South Wind was crawling already. He had, so far, managed to prevent danger by confining her to the cradle board. A small child who is familiar with such restraints accepts them easily. But soon she would walk. By custom, this would mark the end of the cradle board. By that time, a child becomes too heavy to strap on one's back anyway. It can carry its own weight.

Yet he knew that a toddler is limited both in agility and in judgment. A stumble, too near the edge of the shelf . . . *aiee,* he did not want to think of it! He must devise some method for protection.

But for now, there were more urgent needs. Shadows were growing long, and he must start the fire. . . . Their first fire in the rocky cave, and a most important one.

The first fire in a new camp was always ceremonial, a formal ritual to announce one's presence to whatever spirits might live here. In effect, *I am here, here I will camp,* a solemn request for permission to inhabit this place. It was quite important to establish good relations with the spiritual powers in a new camp site. In this case, it was essential. In the strange and somewhat twisted mind of Hunts-Alone, the entire future would depend on such a relationship. There must be not only tolerance on the part of the powerful spirit or spirits of Medicine Rock, but *help,* in the form of protection and assistance. He had no qualms about asking for such help, because there seemed no other path.

Once more, as he prepared his tinder and small sticks, he thought of the events that had brought them here. Bitterness and hate welled up again, hate against those who had butchered his loved ones, and against all whose advice and poor judgment had led to it. Against *all people*—no human being escaped his tormented thoughts. No one, except for the tiny girl who lay there in the cradle board. She was innocent of all the guilt borne by the humans of the world. The bitterness, which was like the taste of ashes and gall in his mouth, mellowed when he looked at the baby. He propped the cradle so that she could watch, and so take part in the Song for Fire.

It was a strange "song," of course, one that was completely silent. He built his tiny lodge of sticks in the fire pit. . . . *How many generations since a fire was kindled here,* he wondered, *and by whom?*

The fire-bow twirled the spindle, and the dust ignited well . . . a good sign. He blew the spark into life and thrust it into the tinder as it blazed. Then he added larger sticks . . . not too many. They had no need for more than a small fire.

Then he backed away a step and knelt in reverent prayer. In hand-signs, he followed the age-old ritual. Thanksgiving for life, for fire, for this place in which to camp. Then the ritual of supplication, the request for permission, followed by that for protection and help. It would have been a moving thing to watch, had there been any eyes to see other than those of the baby. Even she seemed impressed by the solemn ceremony, staring at the growing fire, the little curls of flame that rose and took root on larger sticks, to grow some more.

Who is to say that the heartfelt efforts of Hunts-Alone went unnoticed by the spirits of the Rock? As the cave began to warm, he felt a warming in his heart. His mouth no longer tasted like ashes, and his confidence began to grow. He spread the robe on the cave's floor and released the restraints on the cradle board. The infant rolled happily in the firelight, making soft little sounds that her grandfather could not hear. But, he could see her happy smile, and it was good. He felt safe here.

He looked around the little cave, planning, and stepped to the ledge to glance at the setting sun. Yes, there was much to be done. Some sort of curtain to hang in the opening . . . It would prevent the glow of their fire from being seen by passers-by. It was unlikely that anyone would be traveling at night anyway, but sometime . . . Well, that was for the future. A deerskin door cover—yes, he would think on it.

Maybe a willow rack to hold supplies and possessions, there at the rear of the cave. . . . Someone had done so, long ago. He smiled grimly to himself. There was certainly no need for such a rack in the foreseeable future. They had no supplies, and few possessions.

He prepared some of their precious dried food, chewing the leathery strips for the baby. She accepted it eagerly. It distressed him to see that she had lost weight. "We will eat better, little one," he promised in hand-signs. With that idea in mind, he began that very evening to shape his bow, scraping and thinning the wood by firelight. It would take many days, he knew.

As he worked, he was still thinking of one major concern, the safety of the baby on the ledge. There could be no trial and error. South Wind must be taught the danger, for her first mistake would be her last. But how? . . .

He tried to remember some of the tricks that he had seen women use to protect small children. Children were the future of the People, and were cherished by all. Therefore, everyone looked after all children. *Everyone.*

But there is no one, he thought. And that, of course, was the problem. When he was otherwise occupied, there was absolutely no one to supervise and watch this child.

He thought of a custom on the plains. A baby would often be tied on the back of a dependable old mare, which would then be turned loose to graze. This was known to be useful, since the swaying motion developed a sense of balance. The People were excellent horsemen. Some children were able to ride well almost before they could walk, as a result of this custom.

Well, no matter, he thought. Even if he had such a mare, he did not see how it would help. He could not bring the animal up here, and if he must carry the baby down, he could simply let her play on the grass or on the white gravel of the riverbank. That did not answer the potential danger of falling.

Yet, the matter continued to nag at him. There must be something that could be done . . . keep from falling . . . *Wait!* A child was tied on the mare's back to keep it from falling to the ground. Was this not a similar thing? He had been using the cradle board for such a purpose, but could the child not simply be *tied*? A rope or stout thong around the waist, perhaps, tied firmly to the rock of the wall. Yes, that might do! He glanced at the cradle board. Its lashings might provide a fetter for the purpose. And was there not a spot, halfway down the trail, that would provide a place for the baby to play? Yes, he thought, a wide strip of ledge, a shallow cavelike overhang, a large boulder . . . Well, he would look in the morning.

For now, South Wind had eaten and drunk, and had fallen asleep on the robe by the fire. She was beautiful in sleep, long dark lashes lying on smooth cheeks. Cheeks that were not quite as full and shiny as they once were, but he would remedy that with better food. But her beauty, the beauty of innocence, was there, the only beauty left in his world that had fallen to pieces in that one horrible afternoon.

He covered her gently with a corner of the robe. Later, when he prepared to retire, he would tie her in the cradle board for safety. He must, at all costs, guard against any chance of South Wind's awakening to crawl around on her own. Until, of course, he had an opportunity to think through his idea for a fetter to prevent her falling.

He picked up the staff and resumed his scraping and shaping. Bright yellow shavings curled from the blade of his ax and fell to the floor beside the fire. He began to feel a little better. Once he was armed, in possession of a bow, he could do almost anything. His confidence was returning. Or, maybe it was the spirit of the Rock entering his life.

27

He sat on the ledge and looked across the river at the prairie beyond. The trees were budding, the pale green leaf buds swelling more each day. The gray-green upper branches of the cottonwoods were visibly alive with flowing juices, and willows were yellowing with the same life-bearing fluids.

It had been a long, terrible winter, but they had survived. Sun Boy, having renewed his torch, was once more becoming the victor in his annual war with Cold Maker. The rays felt warm and good as they bathed the south face of the rocky cliff. Hunts-Alone was as close to being happy as he had been since the evil days last autumn. He would never be happy again, he constantly told himself. He was doomed to bitterness and loneliness. But he wanted no companionship, except for that of tiny South Wind.

He turned his head to look at her, sleeping in the cave, and smiled in spite of himself. She was such a joy . . . growing and developing so rapidly. He did not remember that the process had been so rapid with his own children. His and Far Dove's . . . a tear trickled down his cheek. Every thought seemed to come back to the haunting memory of his loss.

He heaved a sigh and shifted his position to bask more luxuriously in the sun. Rising currents of warm air were wafting up the face of the cliff as the warming process continued. The scent of plum blossoms mingled sweetly with another. . . . He tried to identify the fragrance. Probably the purplish-lavender flowers of the redbuds along the creek, he decided. Maybe the hawthorns beyond. It was too early to be the grapevines which clung precariously to the bushes and small trees that grew in crevices of the wall. He would be able to identify those easily anyway. The honeyed odor of the almost unnoticed grape blossoms was sweetest of all.

A flight of geese caught his eye as they came sweeping across the sky from the south, beating their way majestically toward their summer home somewhere in the northland. *There must be hundreds of them,* he thought. He started to count, but gave it up. The first leading lines in their pointed formations were already sweeping past him, up and over the cliff beyond. It was always a thrill to see their migration and wonder about their summer camping places. *They are much like the People,* he thought, *moving north and south with the seasons, only farther because they travel more easily.* Then, at the thought of the People, the bitterness returned to spoil his mellow reminiscences.

At least, he thought, *we have survived.* In spite of enemies, foolish ones of his own people, and unwise decisions on the part of his own family, they had survived. He and South Wind, none other. It had not been easy. There had been times when he almost despaired. It may have been only stubborn anger that enabled him to go on. The bitterness alone may have driven him to greater effort. The Moon of Long Nights had caused him much concern. Sometimes he had almost been convinced that this time, Sun Boy's torch *would* actually go out, leaving the world to freeze in the darkness. Even so, he was not prepared for the Moon of Snows. He had never seen such snowfall. Cold Maker had whipped the blowing, drifting white across the prairie to drop it over the rim of Medicine Rock. To drop most of it, it seemed, directly on the ledge in front of the cave's mouth. It was frightening, the morning that he drew back the hanging doorskin to see only a wall of white.

Fortunately, by that time he had made two deer kills, and they had meat. They huddled inside, carefully hoarding their firewood supply and eating the wall of snow for water. He did not know how many days . . . he should have counted, maybe.

The Moon of Hunger, despite its name, was not so bad. They did have food. Fuel was a greater problem. On any day that the trail down the cliff was open, Hunts-Alone spent all the time that daylight allowed in trips up and down the path carrying wood. He could not believe how rapidly the fire devoured his hard-won fuel supply.

In spite of the hardships, South Wind had seemed to thrive. With great pride he watched her take her first steps, in the cave. He had long since solved the problem of a possible fall from the cliff. A stout rope, braided from strips of deerskin, was fastened to her waist and tied to a solid anchor whenever he was not giving her his total attention. It had taken a little while to determine the exact length that would be appropriate. He wanted her to approach the edge but not be able to slip over, even with the safety line.

There had been one time when he misjudged, and South Wind toppled over. She did not fall far, but dangled halfway in midair for a moment, frantically clawing to regain her position. It had frightened her badly, though probably no worse than her guilt-stricken grandfather. In the long run, the accident may have been a good thing, for now she was more cautious. Seldom did she even stretch the rawhide fetter to its full length. She avoided the ledge's rim, as a burned child avoids fire.

And now, she was walking and beginning to use hand-signs, and eating well. *That* was a major triumph. Hunts-Alone had been so thrilled with her first tooth that he felt like dancing. More had quickly followed, and it was a pleasure to see her gnaw at the strips of venison in her own right, without the necessity of having them prechewed.

There was a great sense of triumph in the fact that he had been able to *do* it. Single-handedly, he had enabled the two of them to survive when their world fell apart. They had weathered that first dreadful winter. And, they had survived winter in better circumstances than they had begun it. They had weapons, food, skins, a lodge in the cave. Best of all, they now approached an easier season.

He could do more exploring up and down the river. It was possible that they could have some sort of temporary brush shelter, as the People often did in summer. Yes, they could live outside in good weather, and retreat to the cave when Rain Maker threatened. He could devote more time to their comfort, not merely survival. *That* would be good! There had been days when the chill in his bones had caused his knees to cry out in protest at the agony of the path up the cliff. Now, he could already tell that the warmth of the sun was softening stiff joints, making his knees feel younger again.

He hoped that there would be an opportunity for a buffalo kill or two this season. He was hungry for the sweet meat of the great beasts. It had been long since he had experienced the luxury of well-browned hump-ribs, cooked over a fire of buffalo dung. And South Wind had never had that pleasure. Even fresh venison could not compare.

Then, too, a buffalo robe or two would be useful. They had only the one damaged robe. It had been possible to huddle for warmth, but he must plan ahead. The girl, as she grew, must have her own bed, her own sleeping-robes. It could be no other way.

He was still not thinking logically, of course. His mind still told him that he must raise the child in the ways of the People. At the same time, he was convinced that she should be raised to trust no one, and never allowed such human contact. At this point in his life, after the tragedy of last season, he was unable to see that if one of these premises is true, the other cannot be.

He watched a pair of beavers on the river below. Next winter, maybe he could contrive traps to procure beaver. They would provide warm garments, as well as the meat of the beaver, which was said to be quite acceptable food.

Then a different odor brought him fully alert. *Smoke!* Alarmed, he rose and scanned the horizon. *Yes, there!* A dirty yellow-gray smudge to the southwest. The breeze was blowing from that quarter, toward them. His initial reaction of alarm was that of the prairie-dweller. A grass fire in the winter or spring can be a highly dangerous situation. On a windy day, it becomes a wild thing, racing across the land from one horizon to the other, faster than a horse can run, scouring the earth from river to river. Sometimes, jumping across a stream, to race on.

For the grassland, there is purpose in this devastation. It cleans the prairie of brush and trees, and results in a more pure mixture of the nutritious grasses that provide graze for the ruminants and, consequently, meat for man. It has been so for thousands of years, the cycle on which not only the religion, but the life of the People depended.

Hunts-Alone was not thinking such deeply philosophical thoughts as he watched the smoke thicken and spread across the distant prairie. He was thinking of danger. He could begin to see the flicker of orange flame now, a writhing snake sprawling across the plain. The pungent odor of smoke was stronger.

Suddenly, he smiled. They need not worry, here on the cliff. He had been thinking in terms of skin lodges in open, grassy prairie. This concern did not apply. The river would stop the fire anyway. This location had been spared from the devastation of fire for many generations, as evidenced by the huge old sycamores and oaks along the stream.

He felt South Wind come up beside him.

"Look, little one," he signed. "Fire!"

"Fire?" she signed in answer, her eyes wide with wonder. She put her hand in his, a little afraid of the vastness of the spectacle.

"It cannot reach us here," he signed. "Come, sit, we will watch."

The fire swept closer. *It is good,* he told himself. When the grass is burned, the new growth is faster, and is lush and sweet. This attracts the grass-eaters. *Maybe there will be buffalo.* This was a device, a ritual, almost, to *bring* buffalo. The People often burned the grass for this purpose.

The line of fire swept closer, and the smoke thickened. Fragments of ash began to drift down like tiny black snowflakes and settle on the watchers. When flames crossed the ridge across the river, leaping like a thing alive, they could feel the heat. South Wind crept close to him in fear, and he placed a comforting arm around her.

The fire raced through a dead stand of plume-grass, leaping high from the impetus of heavier fuel. It threaded through a clump of sumac, igniting dead stems and killing live ones. On down the slope, through the thinning grass to the stream's bed, where dry grass gave way to white gravel, brush, and trees.

Then it was over. Here and there, a smoking sumac stem or buffalo chip, a remaining flicker of orange in a heavy clump of grass. Beyond, blackened earth, as far as eye could see. In a few days, Hunts-Alone knew, the blackened earth would be green. Greener, with more and better growth than areas not burned. Surely this would bring the buffalo. Was it not always so?

"This will bring buffalo," he signed to South Wind. "Meat, robes, it is good."

The little girl looked doubtful.

"You started the fire?" she asked.

"No, I . . ." He stopped in alarm, dismayed that he had not thought of this.

Who *had* started the prairie fire? Sometimes, it was true, they were started by real-fire, the spears of lightning thrown by Rain Maker. But there had been no storms for several days.

The likeliest occurrence, then, was that the fire had been started by *people*. It could have been an accident, a cooking fire or campfire out of control. Or, a fire started on purpose to bring the buffalo. Either way implied people.

But what people, and where? They could be several days' travel away, or just beyond the horizon. There was no way to tell. It was a matter of concern to him, because he wanted no people here. They must take great care, not to give any sign that would lead anyone to suspect that the Rock was inhabited.

28

↔

, t was much later before they actually saw any other people. Hunts-Alone never knew whether those who had started the prairie fire accomplished their purpose or not. It accomplished a good result for him, anyway.

A great herd of buffalo had arrived within a moon, eagerly following the spring growth of grasses in the burned area. They came from the south, and drifted toward the river to drink. Sometimes there were so many that they fouled the water for a little while. Then they would stand staring at the cliff, as if wondering how to pass such an obstacle. That was a matter of great wonder to him, since these herds must have been migrating on this prairie for many generations.

Finally some wise old cow would seem to remember. Possibly she had passed this way before, or maybe it was only an instinct or herd memory. She would wander up and down the river for a little while, then suddenly start downstream with a determined gait. Others would follow, and soon the entire herd was in motion, flowing like the current of the river itself.

He realized that they would cross the river and ascend the rise on the other side, through the cleft that he had used last fall. How did they know it was there? He was never certain, but he realized that their predictable pattern could be used to his advantage. During that spring migration he managed to kill two fat yearlings by concealing himself at the river and waiting with infinite patience.

Too late, he realized that he had made the first kill much too far from the cave. He spent many trips up and down the river, carrying meat to cook and to dry. The hide, too, was a problem. He could hardly lift the freshly skinned hide. Against his better judgment, he partially dressed it at the site of his kill, watching constantly for any approach of other people. There were none, however. When he had trimmed and scraped much of the flesh and fat from the skin, he was able to half carry, half drag it to a safer spot to continue the process. He had never realized how much the People depended on each other for this heavy work. He had participated, but there were always other hands to help. Now, there was no one.

A large part of that first kill was wasted. Rather, it was salvaged by the coyotes, who found it a great good fortune. Hunts-Alone was careful, when he made his next kill, that it would be nearer the cave. That made things much easier, and he was able to do a more efficient job with processing and storing the meat and skin.

He had many misgivings about this. In case any travelers chanced to pass by, it could attract attention to the fact that someone was living at the Rock. But, he decided, it was a risk that he must take, for now. Once he had managed to establish their existence here, it would be easier. The time of slim survival during that first winter was behind them. It was no longer a matter of mere survival, but of a more comfortable and worry-free life-style.

During that summer he tanned skins, using the methods of the People, with brains and mashed liver. Some of the women would have laughed at his efforts, but his skill was increasing. The second deerskin that he converted to buckskin was better than the first. Yes, he would be able to make garments for himself and for South Wind. It would be an easier winter.

The girl was growing rapidly now, and seemed to bear few scars from the events that had destroyed their lives. She was walking, using hand-signs fluently, and asking questions about everything she saw. Sometimes Hunts-Alone became so weary of her hand-sign for a question that he shook his head in despair.

"You will drive me to madness," he would sign.

In answer, he would receive yet another question, the upraised small hand, fingers spread, wrist motion rotating it slightly.

"Why?"

It was his misfortune that the same sign could also mean *where, how, when, what*—any question at all. He almost regretted that she had learned that sign. But it could not be helped, and if she questioned, he must answer. The results were good, he must admit. She learned quite rapidly. As he had expected, this was a highly intelligent child. It was a joy to watch her develop and learn.

He still took the precaution of tying the cord around her waist, anchored to a firm object, when he was not actually within arm's reach. He was concerned about this. He did not believe that the child understood the danger. Finally, with many misgivings, he intentionally tied the rope a little longer. Now it would be possible, at the farthest point of its reach, for the girl to topple over the ledge, but to be held by the rope. Then he concealed himself to watch from around the first bend in the path.

South Wind played for some time, with sticks and the pretty stones that were her toys. Finally she wandered near the edge, and it was all he could do not to rush forward. One of her toys slipped from her hand, she reached for it, toppled. . . . It was too much, and her grandfather rushed forward.

The child dangled, only partly over the rim, crying angrily, grasping at the ledge, and badly frightened. Not so badly, perhaps, as Hunts-Alone. It had been a terrible experience for him. He gathered her in his arms, crying himself, and hugged her tightly.

"You see," he signed, "you must not go near the edge."

It was a hard lesson for both, but it had been well learned. The restraint was used for several moons more, but it was now virtually unnecessary. South Wind was always cautious about the ledge and its obvious dangers.

One afternoon, on a trip down the path, Hunts-Alone paused to look curiously at some of the bleached bones in a crevice. This was mute evidence of the great stampede that had killed the invaders long ago. These were mostly of buffalo, but he saw a skull that he thought was that of a horse. He could not see it well, packed among other bones in the dim crevice. He wondered what might have happened to its rider. He climbed down, curious, to investigate further.

Yes, it was a horse, but he could see no remains that appeared human. Idly, he picked up a bone that had once been the thigh-bone of a buffalo. The rounded end was smooth and white, and looked much like the egg of a duck. It felt good to his palm as he stroked it.

A smile came to his face as an idea struck him. He would take it to South Wind as a plaything. He had brought her pretty stones, shells, oddly shaped bits of wood that he found. He felt sorry that she had few toys. Most little girls would have a doll. . . . He looked at the polished white bone and yet another idea emerged. He smiled more broadly.

For the next day or two, when he had the time and could do so unseen by South Wind, he worked at his creation. Some scraps of fur and buckskin, a little pigment from a nearby cutbank and charcoal from the fire, mixed with fat to hold it . . . He held up the finished doll to admire it, and was somewhat disappointed. The face on the rounded bone was not quite right. There was a quizzical expression that he had not quite foreseen. The hair, tied on with a buckskin headband, looked pretty good. He had not tried to make a dress for the doll, but had wrapped it in a "robe," tied with a sash around the waist. A short stick tied across the bone formed rudimentary arms.

It left much to be desired, he realized. From a purely objective view, it was not worth the effort. Yet, he wanted to do *something* for the little girl who had become his entire life. Maybe it would amuse her.

"I have brought you a friend," he told her as he handed the doll.

He could hardly believe the joy in her eyes as she hugged the doll to her. She could know nothing of babies and motherhood, yet she *did* understand, and her maternal instincts made this her most important possession. It was always in her hand or at her side, and she slept with it at night.

He could see that she made comforting little sounds to it as she rocked it. She also talked to the doll with hand-signs. "Little Bone," she called it, and spoke of it as a person. This bothered him some, but he remembered that little girls have names for their dolls. Then he was amused that he had, himself, thought of the doll as a person, an intruder. It did not fit with his idea of no contact with other humans, ever. But such amusement was harmless, he told himself. Let her talk to her doll, as little girls do.

The Ripening Moon was nearly past when they saw the people. Actually, South Wind saw them first, and touched his arm to get his attention.

"There," she motioned. "People."

It was a column in the distance, a band on the move. There were horses pulling pole-drags, dogs running alongside, warriors riding as scouts or "wolves."

Hunts-Alone drew the child back on the ledge out of sight, and glanced at their fire to see that it was making no smoke.

"We must be very quiet," he cautioned.

He used the sign that had become so familiar when it was essential that the baby's crying not be heard by the Shaved-Heads. A finger on the lips was a warning. If she cried anyway, the palm over the mouth . . . he had not had to use that for many moons. South Wind understood the need for quiet, if only to prevent the discomfort of the hand over her mouth. But this was a new experience, the hiding from people. She had no memory of their escape after the massacre.

"Why?" she signed.

"They must not know we are here."

"Why?"

"People are bad . . . evil. We do not want them here."

"They will hurt us?"

"Yes."

"*Eat* us?"

"No, no. But kill us, maybe. We must be still. Come, we will watch them."

At the rim of the ledge there was a bushy growth. The two lay prone and watched through the branches and leaves.

"We must not move," he cautioned. "Movement is easy to see."

"Lie still, Bone," the girl warned her doll. "You must not be seen."

The party, Hunts-Alone judged, was moving to winter camp. The distance was too great to identify them. Head Splitters, maybe. Possibly even the People, but he wanted none of *any* of them.

"Where do they go?" asked South Wind.

"To winter camp."

"Will we go to winter camp?" she asked.

"No. We have the cave. It is our summer *and* winter lodge."

"It is good."

"Yes."

A movement below caught his eye. A mounted warrior . . . one of the wolves of the travelers. The man was riding along the edge of the timbered strip, looking along the river and occasionally up at the cliff. Quickly, Hunts-Alone gave the girl the sign for quiet again.

The man was curious, but seemed a little nervous. He was aware of the powerful spirits of the Rock, it seemed. And the other travelers were giving the place a wide space. It was good. That was as it should be, he thought with satisfaction.

Now the man paused to water his horse, glancing nervously upward while the horse bent to drink. Hunts-Alone watched uneasily. Had they inadvertently left any sign? He could think of nothing, but he must be more careful. Yes, he would explore up and down the river to make certain there was nothing. He had become too careless.

The warrior remounted, and swung the animal's head around. A heel in the flank and the horse leaped forward at a canter. The man was eager to move on.

"He sits on an animal," South Wind signed in wonder. "An elk?"

Odd, thought Hunts-Alone. *She was too small to remember!*

"An elk? No," he answered. "But they are sometimes called elk-dogs. Those are Elk-dog People."

"They are bad?"

"All people are bad. That is why they must not find us."

South Wind nodded, satisfied for the present. Soon, the intruders had passed on out of sight.

29

I t seemed no time at all until South Wind was no longer a helpless toddler, but a growing child. One has small ones in his lodge for only a short while, Hunts-Alone reflected.

Her rapid development was a mixed blessing. She required less care, and that was good. The agility of the girl was remarkable. She could dart quickly among the rocks, and skillfully negotiate the treacherous path like a deer. *No,* he told himself, *compared to her, the deer is clumsy.* She found other paths on the cliff's face, ones that her grandfather dared not even try. There were other caves and crevices in the scarred face of the rock, too. "But none as good as ours," she assured him.

"You must be careful, Wind," he cautioned. "The rocks are dangerous."

"Of course, Grandfather," she told him, laughing. "I am always careful."

So, while it was good to see her become more independent, there was worry, too. He was afraid that as she grew to need him less, she would be exposed to unforeseen dangers, and that he could not protect her. Could not warn her, even.

Despite these worries, it was a good life. Both had adapted quickly to the strange, forced existence into which they had been thrust. South Wind knew no other, of course, and Hunts-Alone was in a position to shape and teach her to his own distorted way of thinking. They were very close, because neither had any other human contact. In addition, they spent much more time together than is possible for nearly any two people under normal circumstances.

There were lazy summer afternoons and long winter evenings that were good for storytelling. Hunts-Alone had never been a storyteller, because of his major impairment, but now he found that he enjoyed it. The eager brightness in the little girl's eyes was a thing of wonder for him as he tried to remember and retell the old tales from the story fires. He found that he had retained much more than he realized.

South Wind was intrigued by the legends of the old times when the animals talked. She did not exactly understand, however.

"But how could they talk, Grandfather? Did they once have hands?"

This was a problem to explain, because there was no other human, none with a voice. And Hunts-Alone could not adequately describe something that he had never experienced. At least, not that he could remember. Talking was done with hands, and animals had none.

"You know how it felt, when you were sleepy, and I held you, when you were small?"

Small was a relative term, of course. South Wind had no more than five or six summers now. He could not remember.

"Yes, Grandfather . . . like this!"

She placed her face against his shoulder and hummed softly.

"Yes, that is it. Animals make such sounds, too."

"I have heard them, Grandfather," she replied excitedly. "The coyote does this."

She threw her head back and though he could not hear it, he was certain that the resulting sound would be much like that of the coyote to any listener.

He nodded. "Yes, that is it."

"Then they can still talk," she signed in wonder, "with these noises?"

"Yes, to each other."

"Then what do they say?"

"I do not know, little one. They talk of weather and hunting, I suppose."

There came a time when he had to at least make a try at explanation.

"They make these sounds, which you feel but I do not," he explained. "I have no ears."

She laughed and reached to playfully flip at his left ear.

"You *do*!"

"But they are not like yours," he answered. "Mine are dead, they do nothing."

The big eyes widened with wonder. She stuck her fingers in her own ears.

"Like this?"

"Yes, like that."

"Because you are big and I am little?"

Her face was puzzled.

"No, no. Most people have ears, but I do not."

"Then how is it that I *do*?"

Hunts-Alone threw up his hands in frustration.

"Because it is that way!"

She asked other troublesome questions, too. If she could use her ears to "feel" what the animals said, could she not understand their talk?

"Maybe so. You should try," he suggested.

The result was a little frightening. She would tell him what she heard.

"The coyote sings to another, over there," she explained. " 'Come here,' he says, 'the grandfather has killed a deer, and has left our share!' "

He marveled at her understanding, and was pleased. It was good to see her quickness.

One thing he was completely unable to approach in his thinking: the future. In his mind, it would always be this way. His thoughts refused to accept her as anything but a child of five or six summers. Laughing with the happiness of a child, coming to him with her small hurts and scratches, falling asleep on his lap at the end of the day. It would always be so, he told himself, rejecting any other thought that tried to surface. There would be no others in their world. Any others were not only unneeded, but unwanted and dangerous.

South Wind loved the hiding game, which was used whenever it was discovered that there were people threatening their world. There were several places that she could go if people were discovered. The selection of *which* hiding place was dependent on where they happened to be. The cave was a good place, but in the unlikely event that anyone started to climb the trail, there were other places. One, the most inaccessible, Hunts-Alone had never even seen. She had only told him of it. All of her hiding places, however, must allow her to watch, unseen. She seemed to understand this well, and he felt confident that she could avoid any intruder.

The times when they saw people were rare, of course. Usually a passing band at a distance. Each time he was pleased to see that they gave the Rock a respectful distance. No more than two or three times a summer were people seen at all. Usually, a lone scout or two would come closer, looking up at the cliff in some degree of awe and wonder at the power of its spirit.

How astonished they would be if they could see the agile flesh-and-blood nymph who scampered over the rocks and crevices. It was quite likely, he thought, that if anyone did catch a glimpse of South Wind, they would be sure they were seeing one of the legendary Little People.

In addition to her agile ability on the rocky cliff, South Wind could soon swim like a fish. The People had always had an affinity for water, and it was important to their ways. Most camp sites were chosen at least partly for the stream or lake at hand. Except in the coldest weather, a daily plunge was almost ritual.

South Wind took to the water very quickly, and was a much better swimmer than her grandfather. She could swim underwater almost as well as the beavers that lived in the deep pools of the river below the cliff. Once she followed a large beaver to its lodge.

"I found the door to his lodge, Grandfather!" she related excitedly. "I could have gone in!"

Hunts-Alone was alarmed.

"You must not do that, child! Beavers have strong teeth. You see how they cut trees!"

"But they know that I mean no harm!"

He thought frantically. How to . . .

"Look!" he signed. "We would not want someone in our lodge uninvited, would we? It is the same."

She thought about that for a little while.

"I see . . . we must be invited?"

"Well . . . yes. As we would want no one to enter our cave unless we wished it."

She quickly learned the skills of childhood, including the use of the throwing-sticks. Hunts-Alone was pleased when she brought her first rabbit to contribute to their food supply. She began to practice new skills with a small bow that he contrived for her.

He was astonished sometimes at her ingenuity, though it was frequently alarming. She had her favorite places to play, or to hide. One was a small cave, not really big enough for serious use, but wonderful for pretending. It was off the main path along the ledge, an inaccessible place that she found in her explorations. She took her grandfather there once, but it was with great effort that he made the climb. It was difficult for stiffening knee joints.

"It is good," he signed, puffing for breath. "It will be a good hiding place for you."

"A good place for me and Little Bone to live," she answered proudly.

He smiled.

"But I would be lonely," he signed.

"That is true. We will stay with you. But this will be Bone's cave, sometimes."

"It is good."

Another place was a wide spot on the ledge, partway down the cliff. A large boulder lay there, good for sitting or playfully hiding behind. It was, in fact, one of the places that he had tied her for safety while he went on his necessary trips along the river for fuel or to hunt. She had spent many days there since those times as a toddler. It was almost as much a home as the cave itself.

During good weather, Hunts-Alone could nearly always expect her to be there to greet him when he returned from a hunt. It was good, when he rounded the shoulder of the bluff, to see her sitting there on the boulder, waiting with her doll. She always greeted him with a warm smile and helped him carry whatever burden he might be bringing.

On one especially hot summer afternoon, he labored his way up the path, sweating profusely, to find her waiting on the boulder. Not quite as usual, however. She had removed her buckskin dress and piled it on the boulder with her doll.

He was mildly amused. On such a day, it was usual for them to go swimming when he returned. He assumed that, because of the heat, she had prepared for such activity already. There was an understanding that one does not swim alone.

Now she jumped from the rock and waved her greeting as he approached.

"It is good, Grandfather! Let us swim!"

He nodded agreement. He was tired, and it had been a fruitless hunt. That was no problem. They had supplies, but fresh meat was always a welcome diversion. Today they had none.

"Yes," he signed, "we swim!"

Then, to his horror, South Wind stepped to the edge and dived from the cliff. Terrified, he rushed to look over, expecting to see her broken body on the rocks below. She was nowhere in sight. Then the waters of the deep pool parted and she came thrusting up, laughing and splashing. She waved at him happily, but he was already turning to hurry down the path to the river. He was grateful for her survival, but at the same time furious with her for such an escapade.

"Come and swim, Grandfather!" she signed.

He broke into a frantic flurry of hand-signs, scolding angrily and demanding that she come ashore. Her face fell in disappointment as she waded ashore.

"But you said we would swim," she protested.

"But nothing of risking your life!" he stormed. "Wind, how could you do such a thing? You might have been killed!"

Tears were flowing now.

"I was not, Grandfather. The pool is deep, there. I know where the rocks are."

Now Hunts-Alone was confused and frustrated. What the child said was true, of course. She knew the underwater shape of the pool quite well. Better than he, and he had to admit that she was a better swimmer. He wished to bring her up strong and independent, but was unwilling to let her be so. He had not yet accepted the fact that it could not be both ways, and he was terrified of losing her. This would require much more thought. For now . . .

"That is true," he admitted, "but Wind, you must be careful. My heart would be heavy if I lost you. You will not dive from the ledge again?"

She smiled, wiping tears from her eyes as she stood in the knee-deep water.

"No," she agreed. But then her eyes twinkled in mischief. "Not unless I ask you first."

"It is good," he agreed after a long pause.

It was not, of course, but it was the best he could do.

30

South Wind did not remember how old she might have been when she began to wonder about other people. There had been several winters that she remembered, and there must have been others before that. Her grandfather, the only other person in her life, never talked of such things as how many winters. She could count, of course, because it was necessary to communicate in hand-signs how many deer in the timber or how many trips up the steep path along the ledge. But counting was never applied to time, and it did not occur to the girl to wonder about her age. She was small, Grandfather was big. It had always been so, and would continue to be so. There was no point in discussion of such things.

There was a time, however, when she began to wonder. She had always been full of questions. Sometimes that seemed to irritate her grandfather. Sometimes, in fact, she did it purposely to tease him, as children do. She had determined the signs that would indicate when she had gone too far. She always tried to stop just short of that, for her grandfather's anger was not a pleasant thing.

Most of the time he was kind and gentle, good with stories, and comforting when she hurt. It was a happy existence, overall. Grandfather was always quick to point out the beauty of the seasons, the colors of a sunset, the pleasant feel of the cooling south breeze in summer.

Only when the conversation turned to other people did he become grim and completely unyielding. She learned not to bring up that subject, for his moodiness was quite unpleasant and lasted a long time. She became skillful in guiding the conversation away from that topic to avoid unpleasantness.

Somehow, she sensed quite early that on this one matter, Grandfather might not be completely objective. She did not reduce it to terms of logic, but in essence that is what she did. If people are bad, evil, as Grandfather always said, *what about us? We are people, too. Are we evil?* She dared not ask. Someday, maybe.

So she grew and developed, learning skills of observation from one who was a master at it. She learned to hunt, and without even realizing it, utilized the methods of Hunts-Alone, augmented by her own sense of hearing, which he did not possess.

She climbed the cliff and explored every crevice and cranny. She swam in the clear stream in warm weather, and would then lie on the soft grass to dry in the warm rays of the sun. In colder weather, she could wrap in a warm robe of buffalo or beaver . . . she liked the softness of beaver. The cave was comfortable on even the coldest nights, with a slow fire warming it against the chill outside.

Occasionally there were childhood fears, and sometimes disturbing dreams. A recurring theme was one in which she wished to cry out in terror at some vague fear, but could not. If she cried out, it would smother her, somehow. She finally realized that it was related to her grandfather's sign for complete silence, the finger on the lips. That was used in two circumstances: to avoid alarming their quarry if they were hunting, or to warn against the presence of people. Gradually, she came to connect the smothering sensation with other people, since it did not occur during the hunt. She did not understand why it was so and did not wish to ask. The sensation was offset by the excitement of the hiding game when there were people in the area. It was stimulating fun to take Little Bone and go to hide quietly until the intruders had departed. For several seasons the game was an end in itself, and South Wind did not bother to wonder about the other people at all.

There was another kind of night-vision that recurred periodically. It seemed connected somehow to a dark crevice at the back of the cave. The shadowy recess was behind the willow rack that Grandfather had made before she could remember. The rack itself, and its stored supplies, cast eerie shadows on the cave wall, dancing and flickering in the fire's light. But behind that was the crevice.

It was a vertical flaw in the stone itself, running from top to bottom of the cave's wall. It was part of the natural formation that made the smoke from their fire draw well, and that helped with ventilation in the heat of summer. Near the floor, however, it widened. At its greatest breadth, it would have been possible to thrust her arm into the crevice as far as her elbow. She shuddered at the thought, and did not understand why.

What is it, anyway, this inborn fear that repels humans from dark, cavernous places? Some primitive racial memory that instinctively warns us against unknown or unseen evil in darkness? There are obvious fears of injury from creatures that dwell in such places . . . spiders, snakes, scorpions . . . these are only normal risks in life, and we learn to avoid injury from them. But take away all such fears, there remains an ancient, ill-defined dread of something worse lurking there in the darkness, unseen. Something incredibly evil and threatening. Children know of it, and their first night-terrors relate to its unformed threat.

And it was so with South Wind. Her most fearsome dreams centered around dark evil things that might emerge from that crevice to harm her. She would awaken in terror and cling close to her grandfather, who could defend against anything. Grandfather would rock her in his arms and hum softly to her, and her security would return. Then in the light of day, the fears associated with the crevice seemed foolish.

"Those are only pictures in your head," Grandfather would explain. "They are nothing."

Sometimes she wondered why the pictures contained no real form. But, she did not question the wisdom of her grandfather, who must know all things.

There was a time, however, when she did begin to do some thinking on her own. It was late summer, and they had not yet made the large-animal kills that would provide supplies for winter. Grandfather had gone to hunt upstream, looking for rabbits or any small game that would furnish fresh meat. He had suggested that she might wish to do the same near the cave. It was a big responsibility, and she was proud.

Her hunt, however, was far from successful. She lost an arrow in a difficult shot at a rabbit and spent a long time looking for it. She never did find it, but marked in her mind the area involved so that she could return later.

Just now, she wanted badly to procure *something* to show her skill. She skirted along the stream, watching for any chance target. Another rabbit, maybe . . . a squirrel . . . even a young muskrat of this year's brood would provide a nourishing meal. There were few muskrats here, though. They must compete in this section of the river with the larger beavers.

She paused, standing perfectly still for a little while, rolling her eyes to see the semicircle in front of her. Then she caught a glistening reflection near the water's edge, the eye of some small creature, hidden among the grass and reeds. She studied it a little while, trying to define what it might be. She had been thinking in terms of some small *furry* creature. The outlines of this animal showed no fur at all. . . . Or was she looking at moss, mud, and water? Then she smiled to herself, amused at her error. It was a frog, a green monster half the size of a rabbit. Its smooth skin blended well with the grassy shadows. Yes, now that she could visualize it, the image quickly took form in her head. She could see the wide mouth, little forelegs, and giant muscular hind legs quite clearly. The frog sat, half in and half out of the water, waiting for its prey. *It is hunting, as I am,* she thought.

Then another idea began to form, perhaps suggested by the bulging muscles of the legs. Would not a frog be good to eat? Some things eat frogs . . . she had seen raccoons catch them. And are not raccoons much like small people, using their hands to wash and prepare their food? Maybe . . . even as she thought, she was fitting an arrow and drawing it to the head. The string twanged, and the frog was transfixed, pinned to the mud of the bank as it kicked its last.

She retrieved the arrow and her prize, looking at it curiously. It was easy to skin, she found, and the pale flesh of the legs looked firm and good. She hurried up the path and blew the coals of the dying fire back to life. When Grandfather returned, empty-handed, the meat was already broiling.

"A frog?" he signed.

"Yes!" she answered proudly.

"We do not eat frogs."

"Why?"

He studied a moment. "It is not done!"

"It is by the raccoon people, Grandfather. They hunt for frogs."

"Yes, but our people . . ."

There it was again. Grandfather occasionally seemed to be about to refer to customs of *his* people, "our" people. He had done it once more, but then, as always, changed the subject.

"Well, let us try it," he suggested. "Is it ready?"

The meat was good, though there was not much for two.

"Next time, I will find *two* frogs," she suggested.

It was in the autumn of that same year that she experienced one of the most terrifying encounters of her life.

It was totally unexpected. She had gradually begun to hunt a little farther from the cave, and on this day ventured into a stand of dense timber upstream. She knew that her grandfather often hunted here, especially in winter, when the deer congregated here for shelter. He had warned her to be careful, for it was nearing the Moon of Madness, the rutting season. The buck deer are searching for mates, he had told her. They are aggressive and dangerous now.

So, South Wind was being very cautious. At least, she thought so. She had stooped to look at what may have been the track of a large buck when she heard the rustle of fallen leaves, near at hand. Alarmed, she straightened, embarrassed that she could have been so unaware.

The creature stood only a few paces away, staring at her. It was not a deer at all, but something infinitely more dangerous. A *bear*! No . . . Not a bear, either, but a *man*! He looked as startled as she.

In the next few heartbeats, South Wind's keen sense of perception burned a picture into her mind. He was tall, taller than Grandfather, even. His hair was not gray, but jet-black, like her own. He was dressed in buckskins, and carried a bow. Astonishment shone in his eyes as he stared at her. Surprise, and then something else . . . *fear*! He turned and ran.

The girl barely noted that, because she, too, had turned to run. Her heart was pounding as she clattered across the riffle and nearly collided with her grandfather.

"We must hide!" he signed quickly. "There are people camping over there!" He pointed.

She nodded, trying to catch her breath.

"Yes! I saw one!"

"Yes, there are several," he answered.

"No, no, Grandfather! I saw him, as close as you!"

"*He* saw *you*, too?"

"Yes, of course."

"*Aiee*, this is bad! What did he do?"

"Well, he ran, as I did!"

"He *ran away*?"

"Yes . . . I think maybe so."

He paused for a moment, then began to sign again.

"You go and hide. I will see."

Quickly, he crossed the stream and hurried toward the woods, his bow ready.

The band was preparing to camp for the night, a respectful distance from the Rock. Women were selecting places for cooking fires and establishing camp sites for their families. They were enroute to winter camp and had paused here only for the night. No lodges would be erected, probably few brush shelters, even. The weather was warm, for it was in the days of the Second Summer.

In the midst of all the evening's preparation there came running one of the young men. He was breathless, pale, and shaken, and for a little while, could not talk. The others quickly gathered around him.

"What is it, White Bear? Tell us!"

"I . . ." he panted, still terror-stricken, "I have seen one of the Little People."

There was a murmur, a ripple of excitement.

"But that is a good omen!" said one.

"Is it?" demanded someone else. "How do you know?"

"Our Little People help us, if we respect them," retorted the other.

"*Ours*, yes! But was this one of ours?"

"What did he look like, Bear?"

"Small," panted White Bear, "about this big. He wore buckskins and carried a bow. Big eyes, mouth open . . ."

"*Aiee*," someone exclaimed with a shudder. "What did he do?"

"I do not know. I ran away."

"That is good," observed an old woman. "The Rock is a strange place, of strange spirits. Maybe this is one of someone else's Little People. Could that not be dangerous?"

There were nods of agreement.

"I do not want to stay here," stated one woman firmly.

"Nor I!" another rejoined.

In a little while, people were gathering possessions, scattering the few fires that had been started, and catching up horses that had been turned loose to graze.

I t was nearly dark when South Wind and her grandfather met again at the cave.

"They are gone," he announced, somewhat puzzled.

"Yes, I saw from my hiding place."

"I do not understand, Wind. You did not do anything to him?"

"No. I ran. He ran, too."

"Yes. Well, I do not know. They left in a hurry. But please, little one, you must be more careful!"

31

South Wind was more careful after that. Several times she saw people, but mostly at a distance. The terror of the moment when she had faced one of the evil ones would haunt her dreams for a long time. Her grandfather was quite willing to use that scare to reinforce his point, of course. When he thought she was becoming careless, he would remind her of that narrow escape.

It was true, also, that the experience was told by the other party to the accidental confrontation. Told and retold, around the story fires of his band. That story grew and changed and became bigger than life, spreading to the other bands of the People. White Bear, it was now understood, had had a close encounter with the Little People.

Among some nations, the Little People are a mere humorous whimsy. For some, they are mischievous elves, helping children and functioning as keepers of lost objects. In some tribes, one must never confess to having *seen* one of the Little People, or he will die. The Little People of some of the northern tribes are fierce and dangerous, helping them fight their enemies. Still others tell of frightful gnomes who live underground or underwater and come to the surface only occasionally. These are very dangerous to all humans.

The Little People were not a big factor in the culture of Hunts-Alone's nation. Their existence was acknowledged, and tales were told around the story fires. Traditionally, these stories were whimsical and humorous. Many tales told of their helping lost or unsupervised children, though many others relied on the role of mischief-makers for the Little People.

One incident such as the confrontation at the Rock, however, could serve to change the entire attitude. A popular young man, whose bravery was without question, returning to camp with a tale of Little People . . . *aiee,* who could question it? And it was obvious that White Bear had been badly frightened by whatever he had seen. A small person with disheveled hair and carrying weapons . . . clothed in ragged furs . . . wide-eyed and staring. White Bear did not sleep well for a long time, his wife related. He would come awake in terror, reliving his experience at Medicine Rock.

So, one more legend was added to the mystic legendry of the Rock. It had always been a place where spirits dwell. Before the time of Eagle and his strange encounters there, even. And then, generations later, the great stampede of buffalo that had killed so many of the invading Blue Paints. . . . What had been the effect of releasing so many spirits from dying warriors at the Rock? It seemed hardly worth the risk of investigating its strange foreboding spirit. It was there, a place of spirits, without question. Why tempt the wrath of such spirits by asking too many questions?

White Bear had done so, being a brave and curious young man. His experience had demonstrated the folly of too much curiosity. He had, however, discovered something that had not been known before. Possibly it had not existed before, but it was now accepted as fact. Medicine Rock was the home of the Little People.

The net result of this discovery by one of their young warriors was twofold. First, his reaction to the contact began a subtle change in the attitude of his nation toward the Little People. They were regarded more seriously, and with a certain amount of fear and dread. The second result was more discernible. The People took more care to avoid the place of so much doubt and mystery. There was a great deal of reluctance to challenge the ominous spirits of Medicine Rock. When they camped in the area at all, it was at a greater distance.

To the old man and the little girl who made their home at the Rock, however, there was no noticeable change at all. Both of them became more cautious and observant for a while. But the seasons passed, they slipped into a comfortable routine of hunting, preparing meat and skins, gathering supplies of wood for winter's use, and hiding when people were sighted, even at a distance.

Inevitably, the active curiosity of South Wind began to reach out. She observed things, and wondered. She still did not question her grandfather about people, because of his predictable anger. She did ask him many things, and shared with him some of the things she saw.

She was watching a coyote one day, a young adult from the litter that had grown up in a den not a bowshot from the riffle below the cave. The coyote was hunting, and was unaware of her presence. She was lying on the ledge, partway up the path, comfortably relaxing in the afternoon sun. She had watched a water snake hunting frogs, and heard the death cry of the victim as it was swallowed slowly, still kicking, by the relentless action of the snake's flexible jaws. She would have loved to watch more closely, but to move would disturb the process. Maybe some day . . . Yes, she would hide there, near the reeds where the snake made its lodge. She would be able to see better. Some day . . . just now it was too comfortable in the warm spring sunshine to think of anything else.

It was then that she noticed the coyote. She admired its hunting ability . . . the slow stalk, the stealthy observation of a clump of dead grass that *might* conceal a mouse, or a rabbit, even. She had laughed many times at the high jump, to enable the hunter to drop from straight above on his quarry. Very seldom did Coyote miss such a catch.

Just now, she noticed, the coyote was nearing an area where she had seen a nesting killdee. Such birds build no lodge, she had noticed, but place their eggs in the open, on sandy or stony ground. She had examined the eggs, speckled and nearly invisible against a background of the same appearance.

Now the coyote was very near and seemed to become aware of the sitting bird. That would be too bad, she thought. She had hoped to watch the fuzzy chicks when they hatched. They were always amusing, tottering along to follow their mother on spindly legs as long as hers, almost. The chicks could run almost as soon as they were dry. But just now, the eggs would be defenseless. Even if the mother bird escaped, the coyote would eat her eggs. But that is the way of things.

The animal turned and took a slow, cautious step toward the thin scent that he had caught on the breeze. In a moment . . . South Wind's heart beat faster. . . . Just then, the bird seemed to notice the approach of the coyote. She sprang up and fluttered away, dragging a wing. The coyote pounced and missed his catch as the pitiful bird dodged aside. Badly crippled, she dragged herself away, crying piteously and in vain. The coyote leaped again, but again the screaming bird evaded the snap of his jaws. Three times he tried, and each time missed by the barest of margins. Surely the next try would be the last for the crippled killdee.

The coyote sprang, with even more determination. By this time the contest had moved several paces from where the eggs lay on the gravelly slope. And this time the bird dodged away and soared effortlessly into the air, no longer crippled at all! The frustrated coyote made one useless jump, missed by a long distance, and sat down to ponder his failure. Overhead, the killdee circled and stunted and screamed her own name at her would-be nemesis.

South Wind laughed and clapped her hands. It had been a clever trick by the bird to save her eggs. Killdee must have been taught such things at Creation by Old Man. Only with such tricks could Killdee's people survive Coyote's cleverness.

Now Grandfather was climbing the path, carrying a fat rabbit. He stopped and sat down, noticing her good humor.

"What is it, little one?" he signed.

She pointed to the coyote, now retreating over the ridge in disappointment.

"Coyote," she laughed. "Killdee fooled him with her broken-wing trick."

The old man smiled. "She is very good with that one. She saved her eggs?"

"Yes. They are there on the slope."

"It is good. You have seen them?"

"Yes, Grandfather." She paused a moment. "The killdee played the same trick on me, but I went back to look for her eggs."

"It is good," he answered, justifiably proud. "You see things, Wind."

The girl smiled, pleased at his praise.

"Grandfather, are her eggs good to eat?"

"Maybe. They are small . . . duck eggs are better."

"Why are duck eggs round, and the killdee's pointed on one end?"

"Why do you think?" He had learned that this was a technique to handle the incessant questions.

"Well . . . maybe the pointed end holds long legs. . . ." She paused, a hint of mischief in her eyes. "Or maybe it is so they cannot roll down the slope."

"Yes." Hunts-Alone nodded seriously. "It could be either, maybe." He paused a moment, pleased at her observation. "You have tried to roll them down the slope?"

"Yes, Grandfather. They roll in a circle!" she signed, laughing.

"That is true. Now why do the duck's eggs not do that?"

She thought a moment. "Because they are round."

"Yes, but *why*?"

South Wind thought a little longer, and an idea began to dawn. "Ah! They cannot roll . . . they are held in her nest!"

"Yes! And the killdee has no nest."

She nodded in wonder. "It is good!"

"Many things are good, little one. Among them, the fresh meat of the rabbit! Come, let us eat."

He rose and started on up the path. He was puffing a little, and his knees were reminding him that they had just experienced one more winter. It was good to see South Wind's interest, and her bright, quick manner of thought and understanding. It would stand her in good stead.

He immediately tried to change his trail of thought. He had conditioned himself not to think of the future. But he found himself inadvertently coming back to it from another side. South Wind was growing so rapidly now. A sudden spurt of growth . . . how many winters had she? Eleven? *Aiee,* he could not remember. For a number of years, he had managed to tell himself that things would always be the same. The two of them, living here in seclusion, untouched by the evils of others.

Now he was beginning to see that things *do* change, no matter how much we wish it otherwise. He was being forced to admit changes both in himself and in the child. His body was reminding him with every step that he was growing old. How would he deal with preparing South Wind for the fact that he would not always be with her?

And the changes in her . . . *aiee,* she grew taller, no longer a child. He was depending more on *her* all the time. She was a good hunter, and it pleased him greatly to see her observations about the killdee and the eggs. That was good in any case.

It bothered him some that within a few seasons, this child would become a young woman, with all the changes that would happen to her body. Once more, however, he managed to suppress such thoughts. That was far off, in the future somewhere.

He moved on up the path, his right knee creaking just a little as he climbed.

PART III

SOUTH WIND

32

South Wind sat on her boulder at the wide place on the ledge, deep in thought. There were things happening that she did not understand.

She looked down at her shirt, and at the way that her swelling breasts now pressed against the confines of the buckskin. It was a strange sensation, not completely unpleasant, when her body movements caused sensitive skin to rub against the soft-tanned garment. She pulled the neck of her shirt away from her body with one hand and looked inside, down the front. The rounded shapes there were much different than a season ago.

Her legs, too, were changing in shape, the calves swelling to produce different curves. It was good, she thought. Heavier muscles there would make her stronger, make climbing and running easier. She was proud of their appearance, though it was not a thing of vanity. It was more like pride in strength and ability.

She had grown taller, too. Now, she was almost as tall as Grandfather, who had seemed so big when she was a child. Sometimes she felt that she was still a child, because there was so much that she did not understand. She had grown up watching the growing up of other creatures and the way that they became adults like their parents. The coyote pups, the eaglets in the nest at the top of the big sycamore . . . She could climb to the top of the cliff and look down directly into the nest, while the parent birds circled and screamed their protest.

"Do not worry," she signed to them. "I will not harm your children."

Some things became adults very quickly, in only a few moons. Others, like the eagles and the red-tailed hawks, seemed to require two seasons. She and Grandfather had talked of this, sometimes in great detail. All creatures require different times, he explained. Larger ones usually take longer, but not always. And trees . . . how many seasons for an acorn to become a tree like the giants just beyond the riffle?

It was several years before South Wind began to realize that she, too, was growing and changing. She inquired about it, without much success. Yes, her grandfather conceded, it is the same with people, too. They grow into adults.

"How many seasons, Grandfather?"

"Many."

She could tell by the expression on his face that the subject was closed. He was wearing the stern look of disapproval that she always found so uncomfortable. The best course of action at such times was to change the conversation to something else, or to abandon it altogether. It had become her custom to do so without really understanding why. There seemed to be one common subject that always brought disapproval, however. Critical looks and angry retorts always resulted from any inquiries about people. *People are bad, therefore we do not talk of them,* was the idea that was lifelong for her. She did not know why.

She also wondered at the fact that the animals she observed usually came in pairs, a male and a female. It was somewhat different with buffalo, but she understood how it was different. Buffalo were herd animals, rather than paired. Each small calf had only one mother, though, from which to feed. Other cows might protect, but only one was *the* mother.

Her maternal instincts told her much about this. It was like her relationship with Little Bone, in a way. She looked down at the doll, lying on the shelf beside the boulder. She had known from the first that Bone was not real, not alive. She had talked to the doll as if it were a real person, using hand-signs, of course. South Wind had no way of knowing that the sounds she could make were a way of communicating between people. But her conversations with Bone were only pretending, and she was quite aware of this. The doll's face had been repainted several times, and her garments renewed as they wore out from the rigors of play. Grandfather had been quite helpful the first time or two, but then South Wind had assumed more responsibility as she grew older. Was she not the mother of Little Bone? That relationship, that caring and protecting role, seemed fairly clear to her. It was much like that of her grandfather for her.

It was always at this point that her logic and reason began to break down. There was something missing here, information that she did not have. It was in the forbidden area that caused her grandfather to become tight-lipped and angry. She longed to know more. Once again, she tried to reason it out. . . .

Most creatures have a mother to care for them. Except, of course, for the little brown bird that sometimes leaves its egg in the nest of the redwing. The bird that comes from that egg is raised by the redwing. *Could my mother have done this?* she asked herself. *Left me for another to raise?* No, it seemed unlikely. For one thing, mothering was done by females, protection by males, in most cases. Coyote males, of course, helped with feeding. She had watched that, the regurgitating of partly digested food for the pups. Later, both coyote parents brought their kills to feed the growing family.

But buffalo . . . she could think of other species, too, in which the male was not present. At least, not to any extent. But everything, it seemed, must have a mother. *Why do I not have a mother?* The question came back at her again. Was she like the egg in the redwing's nest? Or like the eggs of turtles and some snakes, deposited in sand or leafy loam and left, the emerging young to fend for themselves? Surely not. People must have mothers who care for them and nurture them; *as I do for Little Bone,* she thought.

She had sometimes observed passers-by at a distance on the rare occasions when people came near the Rock. There were clearly men and women, and the women often carried their young tied in a cradle board on their backs. This seemed a caring thing. But she could remember when she was quite small, and there had been no female. The only mothering person in her life had been her grandfather, obviously an adult male. An aging male, in fact. She knew that this was not her father, because the hand-signs were different. The "grandfather" sign was one applied to wise or aging males among the creatures that they observed.

So, there was no evidence of either a father or a mother, in her case. There had been a time when she assumed that it was so with humans, who are somewhat different than other animals. Her observation of the humans who came close enough to watch seemed to contradict this theory. Gradually, she had begun to theorize that she must have had a mother, and probably a father, too. It seemed only logical. And once more her logic brought her back to the impossible question: *Who was my mother?* And always, close on the heels of that was another: *Why does Grandfather refuse to talk about this?*

There were times when Grandfather's thoughts seemed inconsistent. He could be interesting and fun and could explain and answer her every question. Then at other times he would become grim and moody and unresponsive. This mood was always connected somehow with the mystery of her life and of her parents. People . . . Humans. There must have been something, some event, that had caused her grandfather's bitterness. She tried to imagine, as she had many times before, but with equal lack of success.

Her thoughts were distracted by a distant movement on the plain. Something that was not there before. Buffalo? . . . No, she thought not. She changed her position to see better and cupped her hands to clarify her distant vision, as Grandfather had taught her. Spring sunlight warmed her shoulder and arm from the new angle, and it was good. But this distant motion, dark across the new green of the prairie grasses . . . What sort of intrusion?

It was not long until she could see that the moving specks were people and horses. A band on the move, heading toward whatever people might do for the summer season. Their present course would bring them quite close to the Rock. South Wind watched, fascinated. It was a larger band than they sometimes saw. She suspected that there might be different kinds of people, because her grandfather seemed to react differently to some than he did to others. Their appearance was sometimes different, too. Different in the way they fixed their hair and in the cut of their garments. Grandfather had urged her not to watch the intruders but merely to hide and wait. Her natural curiosity had caused her to deviate . . . well, just a little. She had watched them quietly from safe hiding.

She paused to think for a moment about Grandfather's whereabouts, and whether he might be aware of the approach of the strangers. He was in the cave, she thought, sleeping. Grandfather seemed to fall asleep more easily than he once had. More often, too. She would go and make certain that he was aware of the danger. In a little while, that is . . .

The people were coming closer now. They were traveling parallel to the river and would come quite close to the Rock. She could see individuals and family groups, which once more stirred her curiosity. It was like watching buffalo, somewhat. There, a woman with a small baby in a packboard, with her yearling walking beside her and her previous year's calf on the other side. No, *child,* not calf, though it seemed much the same. And not a yearling . . . Grandfather had verified for her that it took many seasons for human young to mature. Ah, so many questions.

The column came closer. The young woman with the baby seemed very full in the chest, her shirt sticking far out in front. With surprise, South Wind suddenly realized the connection, and stared at her own breasts again. *This is how the young are fed!* she thought. *The milk of humans is between the front legs!* Her thoughts were spinning. *Am I to have young?* She paused, thinking more rationally. No, it could not be, without a mating ritual of some sort. And there was no male. . . . She sat, staring in wonder, lost in the enormity of her discovery. She must know more. Something like anger stirred in her. Why had Grandfather not told her of these things?

Grandfather! She had forgotten that she must warn him. She rose quickly and hurried up the path, stooping low in the places where she might be visible to the intruders.

"Where have you been?" Grandfather signed tersely. "I was worried. There are people!"

"I know, Grandfather. I came to tell you."

"They are preparing to camp here," he warned. "We must be very careful."

* * *

It was much later that South Wind's curiosity overcame her. It was fully dark, and the moon, a little past full, had not yet risen. The campfires of the intruders dotted the meadow a little way downstream. What were they doing?

Grandfather was fast asleep, snoring softly. It occurred to her to worry about that a little bit. Not too much. It would be taken for one of the sounds of the night, she thought. It was, after all, much like the cry of the little green herons that nested in the marshy shrubbery by the stream. Frogs, too, were noisy tonight. A few snores would hardly be noticed.

But she wished to get closer, to verify some of her impressions. Maybe she could actually see the big-chested woman feed her young. She rose quietly and slipped out of the cave and down the path, pausing only long enough to see that there was no interruption in the regular cycle of Grandfather's snores. If he woke, he would only think that she had gone to empty her bladder.

The fire-red rim of the moon was just beginning to appear over the horizon as she splashed across the riffle. She must be careful, because in a little while its light would allow easier visibility. She could see better, but could also be seen. That must not happen. She shuddered at the memory of her close encounter several seasons ago.

She approached the camp warily, from downwind, as she would have if she were stalking game. She could hear the murmur of voices, much like the sound of a flock of migrating birds, talking in flight. But softer, mostly. There was a good sound, a happy sound to it. Could this be something that she *remembered*? It did seem familiar, somehow. There was a tinge of irritation at her grandfather. He could tell her, if he only would! She must *demand* it, her right to know her own story.

South Wind was so preoccupied with her thoughts and with the array of campfires spread before her that she became careless. She was totally unprepared for the voice that spoke behind her. It was a voice that held a hint of anxiety and fear. A woman's voice, she realized, since it was much like her own.

"What is that noise?" asked the young woman.

South Wind froze, like a rabbit. It was an instinctive reaction, and in stopping her motion she also stopped the rustle that had caught the attention of the other. South Wind did not understand the sounds that the woman had spoken, but only the necessity to avoid discovery. There was silence for a little while, and then another voice, deeper than the first.

"It is nothing. Only a night creature."

"Yes, but what kind? A bear?"

The man chuckled, and it was a pleasant sound. What few sounds her grandfather made were similar to this, and they indicated that he was happy.

"No, no. Probably a rabbit, one as frightened as you."

Now the young woman laughed, and it was good. *I sound like that when I am happy,* Wind thought. *These are happy people. They do not seem evil.*

She had still understood nothing of the conversation.

"Come," said the young man. "Let us forget the rabbit."

"No, wait. . . . I am afraid. It is said that this is a place of the spirits."

"Yes . . . yours and mine!" he said.

She giggled nervously.

South Wind began to turn, ever so slowly, to see these people. Soon she located them, half screened behind a clump of willow. They were absorbed with each other, and it was easy for her to move into a better position to observe, while hidden from their eyes. It was good that she had accomplished this when she did, for the moon was growing brighter. It was now flooding the timbered strip with a lacy silver light that made things quite easily seen.

The two people were putting their faces together now, and their arms around each other. *It must be a mating ritual,* she thought. Then, as the moon became brighter, a strange sensation came over South Wind. It was a little bit frightening. The young man was very good to look upon in the moonlight, and as he took the woman in his arms, South Wind found her breath coming quickly, and *her* body responding. Her skin was warm, her hands sweating. For an instant, she wished that she was the woman in the arms of the handsome young man.

She took a deep breath to clear her head. *What an odd sensation!* Quietly, she slipped away, but she had learned several things.

The sounds that people made appeared to be a language, much like hand-signs.

People were happy and loving, at least sometimes. She began to wonder if they were *always* evil.

Lastly, she made a decision as she made her way back to the cave. She would demand that her grandfather answer the flood of questions that had recently been thrust upon her.

33

By the time she came to him, Hunts-Alone realized that he had made a monumental error in judgment. It was frightening to realize it now, and when he was alone he shed many tears of regret over the injustice that he had done to the child.

For several seasons he had felt his body beginning to show the ravages of many hard winters. A new ache or pain, a twinge in some previously unaffected joint or muscle. He did not have the dexterity in his fingers that he once had, nor the strength in his arms and legs. He saw this with the regret that a man does when he realizes that it is happening. The time comes when he is no longer able to do all of the things that a younger man does. The process is slow and gradual, yet it seems, somehow, that it occurs suddenly. One day, he awakens to find that he is old.

Among the People, this was accepted gracefully and with honor. Old age is greatly honored, because of the wisdom that comes with experience. At the end, of course, is death, but is that not only a part of living?

So, it was not that which concerned Hunts-Alone. It was the knowledge that South Wind would be left to fend for herself. That was something that he had failed to foresee. In the throes of his grief and bitterness, he had withdrawn. He had saved the helpless infant by his isolation, but now began to realize that he had done her an injustice. How bitter now the remorse, the wish that he could go back and relive the past ten or fifteen seasons. Again, he tasted in his mouth the regret of his mistakes, like the taste of ashes. The knowledge that he had done nothing to prepare the girl to meet the outside world hung over him constantly. It clouded his judgment and gnawed at the pit of his stomach.

The realization was gradual, and he did not quite know what to do about it. It was far easier to think of other things. Maybe tomorrow he would find a way to talk to the girl. For many moons this went on, as he suppressed his realization of the need. As long as he did not think of it, it did not exist, so he need not worry about it. Sometimes he could even think for a short while that there were only two people in their world, he and the little girl.

But it was becoming harder. He could no longer ignore the budding womanhood of his granddaughter. Sometimes he was startled by her appearance, and by the remarkable likeness to her grandmother, Far Dove. The way she moved, her smile . . . Soon, he knew, she would be a woman. He must explain to her about that, the menstrual taboos and customs. He was at a loss how to bring up the subject, because it was one usually taught by the women among the People. So that, too, was postponed, because it was easier than facing such a crisis.

Maybe he could teach her about that, the power and the hazards of the menstrual occurrence, and yet not get into telling about interpersonal customs. She could remain isolated after he had crossed over, living the self-sufficient life as the two of them had done since before she could remember.

Even as he held such thoughts, his conscience nudged him quietly. What would become of her then? Would South Wind live here alone in the Rock for the many winters of her life? Until she became old and crippled, and starved because she could no longer hunt? Or to die, perhaps, from accident or injury, to die alone, unloved, forgotten? Tears came, and he brushed them away. He rose with determination. He must right the wrong that he had done her. He would begin today, as soon as they were certain that the intruders who camped downstream had departed. He had seen the great interest that South Wind had taken in those travelers and knew that this was the time.

"Wind, I would talk with you," he began uncomfortably.

They had eaten and were comfortable, watching the sunset from the ledge outside the cave. It was good to have the intruders gone so that they could relax their vigilance a little bit, build a fire, settle back to normal routine. *Though that will no longer be,* he thought.

"Yes, Grandfather, I, too!" she signed emphatically.

"It is good. Go ahead."

The girl seemed hesitant, as if she did not know where to start. Finally she began to sign excitedly, her hands flying in the gestures, while tears pooled in her eyes.

"Who am I, Grandfather? Who are we? I have no father and mother, as other animals have. You are near and dear to me, and I have needed no other, but why is it that we *have* no others? You must tell me of these things, of people and their ways, of men and women. There are things I must know and understand!"

The tears were rolling down her cheeks now, and he blinked back his own.

"Yes," he signed. "It is good."

"It *is?*"

"Yes, little one, it is time. Long past time. I fear that I have done you great harm."

"No, Grandfather, you have not! But I want to know more."

"It shall be so. We must start back, long before you were born. To Creation."

"When all the animals could speak? I love those stories, Grandfather, but now—"

He gestured her to silence.

"No, now pay attention. There are stories of people at Creation, too."

"People?" That had been one of her questions. He had told very few stories that involved people. "Where did they come from?"

"My people . . . *our* people, came from inside the earth. It was dark and cold, and they longed for sunlight. So, First Man and First Woman crawled out through a hollow cottonwood log."

"Ah! Were you there, Grandfather?"

"No, no, it was many lifetimes ago."

It was only very slowly that he was able to unfold the story of the People, their move from a vague somewhere-else to the area of the tallgrass prairie, the Sacred Hills. That, too, was long ago. It was many tales, even, before he told of the coming of the outsider with hair on his face, who brought the first horse, which the People called an "elk-dog."

"Why, Grandfather?"

"Before that, they had only dogs to carry packs. The new animal carried packs, so it must be a dog . . . a dog as big as an elk."

She nodded, and Hunts-Alone continued.

"More important, Heads-Off—that was the outsider's name—"

"Why? Why was he called that?"

"Aiee, child, you ask too much. It was said he could take off his head."

Her eyes were big. "Was it true?"

"I do not know. Maybe so. Some say it was only a shiny hat that he removed. But his medicine *was* very powerful. It let him control the elk-dog."

"What was it?"

"A metal ornament . . . it is still among the People. The holy man of the Southern band wears it sometimes."

"Wears it?"

"Yes . . . around his neck, on a thong."

"You have *seen* it?"

"Of course. It is said that it was once placed in the horse's mouth, but now it is an ornament, a ceremonial thing."

He continued, telling of the People, their history and their legends.

"They began to hunt buffalo with the elk-dogs, which was easier than on foot."

"Then why do *we* not have elk-dogs? We do not have the power, the medicine?"

"No, that is not it. We could not hide an elk-dog in the cave."

She laughed at the thought, but understood.

"Then," he went on, "the People found that there were other hair-faced outsiders. Different kinds. Some with blue eyes came from the northeast."

"Blue?"

"Yes. We have traded more with another hair-faced tribe in a place called *Senna-Fay,* to the southwest."

"Traded?"

"Yes, the People gave them furs and robes in trade for metal knives and arrow points."

"Like your knife?"

"Yes. Some knives are stone, like our arrow points."

The process of education was not as painful as he had expected, although slower. South Wind repeatedly stopped him with questions, for her curiosity was boundless. The girl wanted to know *everything,* and he tried to oblige. Day after day they talked of customs and taboos, rituals and human interrelations. She learned of the Rabbit Society, in which the young are taught. And of marriage.

It was at this point that their communication began to break down. He could not bring himself to tell much of the tragedy that had destroyed his entire family, his life, even. Eventually, he managed to tell her that her parents, friends, all their relatives, had been killed. This, he continued, was why people are to be hated, feared, and avoided.

"But Grandfather, are all people evil? My parents? Were they so?"

"No, no," he signed impatiently, brushing tears from his eyes. "But they are dead. We can trust no one."

"Grandfather, I have crept close to some of the intruders to watch them," she admitted. "They seemed happy and loving, and not evil at all."

He was quite disturbed by her confession and became angry.

"You must not do such a thing! I have *told* you!"

That ended the discussion for several days. Only gradually was he able to resume the instruction. One thing that bothered him was that he had no clear goal in all this. He had thought to prepare her for what she would do after his death. Yet he did not know what it was. What would she *want* to do? Probably, she should make contact with the People, but his bitterness refused to let him admit to such a possibility. He could not approach a conversation that would speak of it.

It was several moons before he thought of a way to bring such things into the open. South Wind was making more of their daily decisions now, he realized, as he made fewer. It was good to share the heavy load with someone young and active. He would simply ask her opinion.

"Wind," he signed, "what will you do after I am dead?"

She stared at him a moment, startled, and then laughed.

"You are not going to die!"

"Yes, all things must."

"Of course, but not now. Not for a long time."

She left the cave and refused to discuss it further. This, he realized, could become a problem in itself. Then another thought came to him. *She will know nothing of how to prepare a body for burial. She must let me teach her.*

34

I t became a stalemate. There were things that he was unable to approach, and those that the girl was refusing to admit. In addition to this seemingly hopeless confrontation, Hunts-Alone realized that something was happening to his thinking. He was becoming forgetful.

At first, he thought that it was related to the strenuous effort to teach South Wind the culture of the People. That had been hard for him. But he also found that he was repeating himself.

"You just told me that, Grandfather," South Wind would laugh.

"What? Oh, yes, so I did, Dove."

"Dove? Who is Dove?"

He tried to conceal his panic.

"Oh . . . she was your grandmother. You look much like her."

But this worried him. Some days were better than others. Sometimes he could remember vividly the names of all his playmates in the Rabbit Society, but not those of his own children, without pausing to think and reason. On other days, he felt fine. If there had been nothing urgent about their conversation, he felt confident that he could remember anything he chose.

But there was still the urgency, a desire to finish imparting the knowledge that would let him rid himself of guilt. Guilt that he now felt for the injustice of having deprived South Wind of any normal life.

In addition, he became increasingly concerned that the girl could not face *his* death when it came. She continued to refuse to discuss it, to deny what must eventually happen. He was beginning to feel that it would be sooner rather than later. He could see that his body, as well as his mind, was showing the wear of his many seasons. He had no idea how many . . . the years all seemed to blur together now. Of one thing he was certain. They were moving faster, flying past at an accelerated pace.

He was not concerned with dying. It mattered little what happened to his bones. He would, in some manner, return to the prairie sod that had nourished him and become part of the grassland. The grass had been replenished since Creation by the blood, flesh, and bones of his People. His would be no different.

Except for South Wind. His concern was that *she* would be distressed by not knowing, not understanding what to do with his body. In some way, he must force her to face the inevitable problem. But how, when she refused even to admit that it would ever happen?

"Wind, we must talk of this!" he would insist.

And the girl would toss her head, pretending to be casual.

"Of course, Grandfather. Later. That is a long time off. We will speak of it when the time comes. Now, I must go and hunt."

But the time is coming, he would think to himself. *"Later" may be too late.*

He did not worry so much on the days when his senses were dulled. Then, when he felt better, he would worry because he had *forgotten* to worry, and felt guilty for neglecting the problem. Still, he found no easy answer.

Day followed day, with little change except that he grew a little weaker and more forgetful. He realized that their positions were changing. He was constantly depending more and more on South Wind to provide for the two of them, to make their decisions. It was the girl who made trip after trip up the path carrying firewood as winter neared. It was she who supervised the slicing and drying of their meat supply and carried water to him when his knees were too stiff to negotiate the path because of impending weather. Their roles were reversing. South Wind was becoming the caregiver, and he the cared-for. He did not like it, but had to accept that this, too, is part of life. Each one takes his turn as caregiver on his path through life. He had taken his turn, and now South Wind was returning his efforts. Of course, she was far from the helpless infant that he had carried to the Rock so long ago. A tear came to his eye as he remembered. How bitter he had been! It seemed not to matter so much now. At least, his life had been spent well in one respect. He *had* saved the baby, and she had grown into a fine, handsome young woman. She must rejoin the People, somehow. He did not know exactly how, and it made his head tired to think of one more problem that seemed to have no answer. It was easier to set it aside.

As for South Wind, she felt much of the same urgency, but along different lines of concern. She wished to know of her people, her parents, and their customs. And, though the learning, the gathering of information, was important to her, it seemed irrelevant, somehow. She felt the pressing need to *know,* but no urgency to do anything about it, to plan ahead. The concept that she would some day lose her grandfather, the only other person in her world, was so unacceptable that she refused to consider it, much less discuss it. That, in turn, prevented consideration of any course of action beyond such a loss.

There came a time when they almost stopped communicating at all, except for routine and everyday matters. Their major concerns were too painful to discuss, and it was easier to let things go on as they had, postponing decisions and actions until some vague later time in the future. This approach was made easier by the general philosophy of all of the hunting cultures of the prairie: Let each day take care of itself . . . why worry about something that has not happened yet, and may not? Their discomfort, of course, resulted from the fact that both knew, on a deeper level, that certain things *would* happen . . . *must* happen.

They did manage to survive the onset of South Wind's puberty, though it was difficult for both. The girl resented the inconvenience of menstruation, which interfered with her active routine. Some moons she spent those few days in seclusion in her own smaller cave, where she had hidden from intruders as a child. But it was small and uncomfortable. During most menstrual episodes she was merely careful to stay on her own side of the cave. She would procure enough supplies in advance so that Grandfather could prepare his own food, and so that she would not have to touch any of her own weapons. For a bow touched by a menstruating woman will never again shoot straight.

It must have been in her sixteenth summer that the outsider came into their lives. South Wind was standing on the ledge to greet the morning sun when she heard an unfamiliar sound. The call of a horse, searching for a companion. She had observed, when outsiders camped near the Rock, that their elk-dogs behaved in this way. A single animal, separated from others, becomes concerned. It looks in all directions and gives a long, trumpeting cry that says, in effect, *Is anyone here? Where is everybody?*

It was such a cry, and South Wind was surprised because she had seen no travelers. She stepped quickly inside to sign to her grandfather, who was rolling sleepily out of his robes, yawning and stretching.

"Someone is near. I have heard a horse's cry!"

He nodded. "You have seen someone?"

"No, only heard the horse. I will go and look."

"Be careful," he cautioned.

She nodded, picked up her bow and a few arrows, and slipped out.

It would not do to hurry. It was much more important to take time to observe. She had no idea how great was the threat . . . how many, how close? Only the sound of the elk-dog's cry. There were several good observation points along the path down the Rock's face. Places where she had played as a child, peering through the fringe of bushes that clung precariously in some crevice in the rock. She had pretended often that she was hiding from the evil intruders as she peeked between the woody stems to search the meadow and the slope beyond. Now, she did so for real.

She knelt in one of her favorite places and swept the area with her eyes. There was nothing. A great blue heron, fishing in a back-eddy below the riffle . . . a noisy squirrel in the big sycamore . . . a crow making its way across the distant blue of the morning sky. All the world seemed quiet and in place. Had she imagined the horse's call? She prepared to move on, but no! There it was again! The searching cry of a lonely horse. It was closer now. Just beyond that clump of willows downstream, maybe.

The horse and rider came into view, but something was wrong. The rider sat, or rather slumped over the horse's withers, quite limply. He was doing nothing to guide or direct his mount, it seemed. The horse in turn was merely wandering, pausing to crop a few mouthfuls of grass and then moving on. It was strange . . . something must be wrong with the rider. She could not see his face, which was hidden by the horse's mane as he lay face down, his feet and arms hanging loosely.

The animal found an area of good grass and paused to graze there. It was near enough for her to begin to observe useful bits of information. The man carried no weapons as far as she could see. Maybe a knife at his waist, but it could be only an empty scabbard. But no bow or spear . . . *why?* He must have lost them. Was he starving, then, because he could not hunt? No, that seemed unlikely. He appeared in good physical condition. And he could have eaten the elk-dog if necessary. What, then?

The horse turned, and for the first time she caught a glimpse of the other side. The animal's shoulder and foreleg were covered with blood. . . . Some of it dried and blackened, but some bright red, shiny and fresh against the light gray of the horse's color. Quickly, she interpreted this new finding. The horse was apparently healthy, so the blood must be that of the man. He was seriously wounded, maybe near death. She watched, fascinated.

He could have been wounded a day or two ago, she thought, judging from the dried blood. The horse could have come a long way. Her rider may have been able to direct his flight well at first . . . to travel a great distance trying to escape whatever enemy had hurt him. She could not see his wound, but the bright crimson stain suggested that he was still alive, or quite recently deceased.

Now, the horse lifted its head and looked around, still searching. It gave its long *where-are-you?* cry again. It was startlingly loud, so close, and South Wind jumped involuntarily. Then the animal turned and walked to the stream, its hooves clattering on the white gravel. Now it bent to drink, and the girl saw the rider's limp form begin to slide forward. So slowly, it seemed, his body slipped over the high point of the animal's withers and across the neck, to splash heavily in the shallow water. There seemed to be no effort on the part of the man to avoid the fall. The sudden splash startled the horse, which shied away, dragging the limp form for a few steps. *He must have been tied to it, somehow,* she thought. The horse quieted, started to move on, and then stopped at the tug of its burden, now dragging from a saddle that had been pulled askew. The animal gave a long sigh and stood quietly, waiting.

South Wind stared, wide-eyed. What to do? This man might be pursued by others. He was probably dead now, but would the horse just *stand* there? How long? And how long until any pursuers would come? This whole thing was far beyond the realm of her experience.

Grandfather! Of course! He would know what to do. She rose and scampered back up the path to the cave.

35

Hunts-Alone was instantly alert.

"Where is he? Did you see any others?"

He practically leaped to his feet, more alert than she had seen him in many moons.

"Come. We must take care of this," he signed as he turned to start down the path.

Soon, however, the old man was forced to slow down. He was breathing hard and paused to rest a moment, leaning against the wall of rock. Even as he did so, his eyes were seeking the far horizon.

"Which way did he come?" he asked.

"From that way."

"And you saw no one else?"

"No, but somebody hurt him."

"Yes . . . what sort of wound?"

"I do not know, Grandfather. I was afraid."

"Yes, it is good. You should be. But, any riders in the distance?"

"I saw none."

"Good. But we must watch. He may be followed. And he is still alive, no?"

"Yes . . . I think so. Some of the blood is still red . . . but, nearly dead."

"Ah . . . we may have to help him cross over."

"*Kill* him?" South Wind was astonished at this suggestion from her gentle grandfather.

"Maybe not." He moderated his statement. "But if he lives, he could tell others that we are here."

She nodded, numb at the thought. They had never killed, except to eat. The thought flitted through her head that maybe Grandfather thought they should *eat* the hapless warrior. No, surely not.

They reached the bottom of the path, splashed across the riffle, and carefully approached the still form on the ground. He lay unconscious, still tied to his horse by one leg. The animal had quieted now, and stood, still peering nervously at its erstwhile rider. The animal was a bit frightening to South Wind, who had never seen a horse up close before. She jumped when the animal gave a curious snort at their approach.

"Will it bite?" she questioned.

"No. But we must cut it loose so it will not drag him again."

Very slowly and carefully, Grandfather approached the taut rawhide cord and severed it, nearer the body of the rider. Now free of the unaccustomed pull on the twisted saddle, the horse relaxed somewhat and began to graze. South Wind stared at it in amazement.

"Come," motioned Grandfather. "We will care for that later. Let us look at the man."

They rolled the man over onto his back. He was of an age somewhere between that of South Wind and that of her grandfather, rather younger than older. *In his prime,* thought Hunts-Alone, a little sadly. He cut away the buckskin hunting shirt to expose the wound. *Ah,* a stab wound between the ribs . . . A knife, or maybe an arrow . . . A feeble, pulsing hemmorhage came from the wound. *A strong man,* thought Hunts-Alone, *or he would be already dead.*

But what to do with him? Simplest, and probably safest, would be to smother him, or cut his throat, load him back on his horse, and drive it away. This, however, was not in the heart of Hunts-Alone. Even the years of bitterness could not destroy the basic kindness that had governed the lifetime of Hunts-Alone. He must try to help this stranger, even though it might put them at risk.

South Wind touched his arm.

"His wound . . ." she asked, "a knife?"

"Maybe. An arrow . . . there may be an arrow point inside."

"Then he will die." It was a statement, not a question.

"Yes. We will try to make him comfortable."

South Wind looked up at the path along the bluff to their cave. Could they possibly take him there?

"No, not there." Hunts-Alone anticipated her question. "We could not carry him. We will keep him here. Now, go to the top of the rise and see that no one comes."

She was off in an instant, trotting up the slope. The old man turned his attention to the wounded warrior. Carefully, he palpated the wound, finally inserting a finger. He could feel no foreign object, but it might be deeper. No matter . . . The exploration started a little fresh bleeding, and he cut a piece of the man's shirt to place over the wound. Then with more strips he tied the bandage tightly around the chest. At least it would look better. *I should have let South Wind help with this,* he thought. *She could have learned.* But his efforts would not result in much success anyway. Maybe it was as well this way.

During the procedure, the wounded man had shown no signs of life. There had not even been a response to the probing finger in the wound. Hunts-Alone lifted an eyelid and found the victim's pupil wide and dark. . . . *Not good,* he thought. He felt for a pulse in the throat. *Fast and fluttering,* very faint.

Wind returned from the slope to report no sign of anyone in pursuit.

"He may have traveled far, Grandfather."

"Yes, it is true."

"Who is he? Is he of your people?"

Hunts-Alone paused for a moment. How deeply did he want to delve into this with the girl? *Well,* he finally decided, *why not?* It could be a learning time for her. Patiently, he began to explain his thinking to her.

"He is not of the People," he began. "His hair is not right, and his moccasins. . . . The cut is a little different, the thong at the heel. . . . No, this is a Head Splitter."

"You have told me of them. Once our enemies?"

"Yes, that is the one. Now they are allies of the People. They are hunters, like us."

"Where are his weapons?" she asked.

He had not thought of that. . . . A knife at the waist, but no bow or lance.

"He must have lost them in the fight."

The horse whinnied and South Wind looked up.

"What of the elk-dog, Grandfather?"

He had forgotten that in giving his attention to the man.

"The horse cried out?" he asked.

"Yes. I will go and see if it calls to others." She trotted away.

It pleased him to see her making such observations. She soon returned.

"No. It only asks," she reported.

"Good. Now, help me drag this man over by the tree there. And we must take care of the horse."

"Do what with it?"

"We must take off the saddle and the thongs in its mouth."

Her eyes grew wide.

"Is it safe?"

"Of course. Now help me here, and then you can go and bring the horse."

"*I? . . .*"

"Yes!" He signed impatiently. "Now come here!"

They dragged the limp warrior to the grass beneath the tree, and Hunts-Alone sat down to rest. Ah, how frustrating to have no strength even for such simple things!

"Now," he signed when he was rested a little, "bring the horse."

"But, Grandfather, I . . . *how?* It is large!"

"You do not *carry* it, child! It will walk!"

Finally he realized that she had never seen a horse at close range before. He must be patient.

"Look," he began, "see the dragging thongs at its mouth?"

She nodded.

"Good. That is the elk-dog medicine. There is a circle of rawhide around its jaw, that gives us power over it. Now, walk slowly over to it and take one of the thongs. It will follow you then."

"Are you sure?"

"Of course! It *must.*"

Very cautiously, she approached the creature. It raised its head curiously, soft brown eyes looking into hers.

"I will not harm you," she signed.

The horse took a step or two, then stepped on one of the dangling reins and came to a stop. She gingerly reached for the rein, and to her surprise the horse turned to follow her. It was a little frightening to have a big creature so close, but she tried not to show her concern.

"Good!" Hunts-Alone greeted as she came near.

"Now what?" she asked.

"Now I can help you. We must first take off everything except the medicine-thong, then remove that and set the horse free."

"Where will it go?"

"Anywhere it wants. Find some other horses and join them, maybe. Here, help me with these knots."

They slid the saddle from the animal's back.

"What do we do with this?" the girl asked.

"Leave it here for now," he signed. "We will dispose of it later, after . . ." He did not finish.

"He is dying?" she asked.

"Yes," he assured her.

Then a thought came to him.

"Wait," he signed. "Do not remove the medicine-thong yet."

South Wind had not even considered such a thing, but now asked, "Why?"

"We may need to use it."

He did not take the conversation any further, but he was starting to plan ahead. When the man died, they would have the body to dispose of, preferably far away. The horse could be used for carrying it. . . . The two of them could certainly not carry such a burden for any distance. Yes . . . He was pleased with himself for having thought of this.

"Here," he showed her. "We will tie the reins up over its neck, like this. Now, let it graze."

36

The wounded warrior never really regained consciousness. Once
or twice he moaned, but even that was not certain. It may have
been only the sound of a slightly different pattern of breathing,
his hard-won breath fluttering past limp vocal cords. Once the man opened
his eyes for a moment. They were blank, unseeing, as if the spirit had already departed and the body was empty.

"There is no one inside," the girl signed to her grandfather.

"Yes, the spirit still lingers, but only just barely," he answered. "He is
dying."

They sat by the still form all night, keeping a little fire going for light and
warmth. Several times, Hunts-Alone sent the girl to watch for the possible
approach of this man's enemies, but there were none.

"Should we try to feed him?" asked South Wind.

"No, he cannot swallow. He would choke," her grandfather explained.

Along toward morning, the victim's breathing changed. There would be
a long pause, when it seemed that another breath would not come. Then a
tiny, shallow effort, increasing slowly with each short breath that passed his
lips, longer and deeper until one or two seemed almost normal. Then another stop, as suddenly as it had happened before, and no effort at all for a
time.

"This is not good," Hunts-Alone explained. "These are the breaths of one who is dying." He had seen this before and knew that the end was near.

Still, the sun was peeping over Earth's rim before the spirit left.

"It is good," Hunts-Alone explained. "For his people, it is bad to die in the darkness. The spirit cannot find its way and will wander forever."

"Is that really true, Grandfather?"

He shrugged. "For him, yes. Our people do not fear such a death."

"Then it is different for different tribes?"

"Yes, of course. That is their custom, that of the Head Splitters, but not ours. I am made to think that the spirit of this one waited until daylight to try to cross over. He was a strong man, and very brave."

"Now what do we do with him?"

"We prepare him for burial. The ceremony of his people is much like ours."

This will do well, thought Hunts-Alone. He had had the long night to think on it, and this circumstance seemed to him to be perfect for the teaching of South Wind. He could show her the necessary preparations, the ritual, and they could care for this unfortunate warrior's last needs. Then, when his own time came to cross over, South Wind would understand what to do. Yes, it was good.

"We must find a place for him," he told her.

"What sort of place?"

"A scaffold . . . like a rack with a platform."

"But people will see it!"

"Yes, that is why we will not put it here. Downriver, a long way."

"We will *carry* him?"

"Ah, that is why we have kept his horse! Now, first, we must position his arms and legs. He will stiffen soon."

He straightened the legs and crossed the hands over the chest. The dead man's mouth had fallen open, and he tied the jaw shut temporarily.

"Now, we need some poles for a drag. Then we will use more to make the platform. But first, let us wrap the body."

"Wrap it?"

"Yes, in a robe. Go and get a robe. . . . Wait! Was there not a robe tied to his saddle?"

"Yes."

"Good! We will use that. Then we go to cut poles."

The tasks of caring for the body of the unfortunate warrior occupied the entire day. They wrapped the corpse after washing the face and hands and cleaning the dried blood away.

It was a challenge for South Wind to utilize the advantage of the horse, because she still feared it. But, with her grandfather's encouragement, and the absence of malice in the soft brown eyes, she managed. Hunts-Alone questioned whether he had the strength to walk far enough downstream. He climbed on a rock and mounted the horse, while South Wind walked along-side. She had no desire to come into such close contact with the animal.

A long way they traveled, it seemed. It was midmorning when Hunts-Alone pulled the horse to a stop.

"Here," he signed, sliding stiffly from the horse.

It was an area where a giant old ash tree was breaking down, its limbs broken, some hollow, others fallen to the ground under their own weight. But for many paces in all directions there grew a myriad of the old tree's offspring, tall and straight and as thick as a man's arm.

"Our poles," he signed. "And our scaffold."

He shuffled around, selecting four of the saplings for uprights on which to build the platform. Finally he nodded, pleased.

"These will be our corners. Cut that tree and that one, and the three over there."

The platform took shape quickly. They had brought lashings to tie the poles to the uprights, and the construction was simple. The platform need be only long enough for the supine corpse, and no wider than his shoulders. South Wind did most of the heavy work, but Hunts-Alone was still adept with the lashings.

"This is a good place," he observed. "The trees will grow, and this grove will be thicker and darker. Maybe no one will ever find him."

"Is it always so, the platform?" Wind asked.

"Usually more in the open," he admitted. "It could be somewhere on the cliff. . . ." He was trying to plant an idea. Some day, South Wind would be forced to make such a decision, and he wished it easy for her.

They finished the burial scaffold, then fashioned a pole-drag to pull behind the horse.

"I will ride on it," he told her. "You lead the horse."

South Wind wanted to protest, but she could see that her grandfather was tiring rapidly. He rolled onto the small platform of the drag and heaved a deep sigh of exhaustion. They had been working hard all morning, and it was now past noon.

The old man slept part of the way, but was wide awake when they reached the burial-wrapped corpse. He slid from the drag and stood stiffly.

"Now, we must put *him* on the drag, and everything that is his. Saddle, the small saddle-robe, his medicine bag . . . everything."

"Will you? . . ." she started to ask.

"I will ride the horse."

It had been a long time since her grandfather had had so strenuous a day, and she worried for him. But, he seemed to keep going, drawing on hidden strengths. He showed her how to pull the stiffened corpse up to the platform with the aid of the horse and a rope over a limb of the big tree.

"Now," he signed to her, "straighten him on the platform. Put all his things on there with him . . . except the saddle. Leave it on the ground."

It was nearly dark, now, as she swung to the ground.

"Is there a ceremony?" she asked.

"Yes, a song of mourning. They sing it for three days. But we cannot do that." He stepped over to face the silent figure on the scaffold. *"Ah-koh,* my brother," he signed. "There are those who will miss you, and will mourn for you. We have done what we can. May your journey to the Other Side be an easy one! May those of your people who stay behind prosper."

He turned away, and his face was tired and drawn.

"Are you all right, Grandfather?"

"Yes. Let us go home."

"How? . . ."

He paused to consider a moment.

"We should leave the horse and walk home, but. . . ."

"You ride the pole-drag, Grandfather. I will bring the horse back here."

He seemed indecisive, but nodded weakly. "It is good," he signed.

He slept most of the way back, wakening only when they reached the stream near their cave. He rolled from the drag and lay there.

"I cannot climb the Rock tonight," he told her. "Bring me a robe?"

"Of course, Grandfather. What shall I do with the horse? Take it back?"

"Not tonight. Take the pole-drag off. We can use the poles for fires. In the morning, take the horse somewhere and take the thong out of its mouth. Let it run free."

No sooner had he finished signing than he was asleep. She covered him gently with a robe from the cave, then cared for the horse. Then she wrapped herself in her own robe and sat down beside him. She was tired, but it had been a day that required much thought. She must ponder its events for a while before she slept.

As it happened, it would be several seasons before a hunting party of Head Splitters chanced upon the rotting burial platform in the ash grove. One side had given way, and a few bones were scattered among scraps of the burial robe.

"Look," said one man, "this is much like our burials."

"Those of the Elk-dog People are much the same," answered another.

"But when we lost Calling Bull . . . look, is this not his knife under the platform?"

They examined the weapon, and most agreed.

"It would seem so. How did he get here?"

Their tracker, who had been examining the area, spoke.

"We will never know. This scaffold was built maybe five summers past . . . the trees have grown." That was when Calling Bull disappeared after the battle.

The rest nodded.

"This was done well," one observed. "Whoever cared for him did well for our brother. He crossed over with honor."

"Yes. It is good," said the tracker.

The leader of the party spoke.

"Well, let us bury his remaining bones and move on. I do not want to spend the night in this area. Is not Medicine Rock near?"

"Yes," answered an older man. "Let us move."

37

For South Wind, the coming of the wounded stranger had been a major event. His death, the events surrounding his burial on the platform in the ash grove had given her an insight into her own heritage in a way that she had not experienced before. She had actually had the opportunity to see another human being at close range, to *touch* him. She had been saddened when he died, and felt a loss.

It was like the loss of the pets that she had occasionally encountered during her childhood. A caterpillar, a baby rabbit, a frog. These usually died because there was something wrong from the first, which had enabled her to catch the wild creature. Sometimes, though, it was a temporary matter, and the wild thing recovered, or matured, and was gone. Like the young crow with an injured wing. A narrow escape, perhaps, from the great hunting owl, *Kookooskoos,* who relishes young crows snatched from their roosting place in the darkness. She had cared for the crippled bird, feeding it and nurturing it back to health. It would ride on her shoulder or perch near her as she sat on her boulder at the ledge. The crow was her companion for many days . . . several moons, even. Then one day it flew to join some other crows who were passing by, and was gone.

She had been heartbroken, feeling abandoned and alone.

"But she has only joined her own people," Grandfather explained.

That did not help very much. She had mourned the loss for many days. Now, the loss of this human who had come, at no threat, was a similar sadness. She would have liked to talk with him, to learn more of *his* world. He had not seemed dangerous at all as he lay helpless and dying. Surely he was not completely evil. She wished that they could have helped him somehow.

She did understand the danger that he presented to them, and the concern that her grandfather felt. If he had recovered, this man would know all about them and their secret lodge at Medicine Rock. So it was as well that he had not recovered. Still, she felt a loss.

One thing *had* pleased her about the incident. She had seen her grandfather change remarkably. For one day, there, he had become alert and efficient. He was weak and unsteady, but his mind seemed clear and effective. He was more like the strong and dominant figure that he had been during her childhood, and the feeling was good.

She wished that it could continue, but it was not to be. The effort required to accomplish what they had done for the dead man had taken a great toll on Hunts-Alone. He slept for most of the next day, replenishing his strength. He never quite came back, though, to the point where he had been before the incident. It had apparently taken much out of him. He moved slowly and stiffly. This was logical for a day or two after such unaccustomed physical activity. South Wind felt it, too, the soreness in the muscles of her back, arms, and legs. But her stiffness was better in a day, while her grandfather continued to move as if he were crippled. This was a matter of great concern to her. It was as if he had called on a last reserve of strength and had used it up. She waited for it to be renewed, but it seemed that it was not to be. True, his day of extra sleep did seem to allow him to return to more mental alertness, but that was all. He seemed to have no interest in becoming more active, but only sat, rocking gently, lost in his own thoughts.

Sometimes, on his good days, he was communicative. The old urgency was there, the need to tell her all he could of the ways of their people. She listened avidly, and asked many questions, and that was good. But in a completely unpredictable fashion, Grandfather might be quite irrational. Sometimes he thought he was a small boy again. This was frightening, because she knew nothing of small boys or how to deal with them. At such times he greeted her with the hand-sign for "mother." That was frightening. At first she thought that he was teasing her.

"I am not your mother!" she chided.

"What? Oh, yes . . . who? . . ."

It was with a great deal of dread that she finally realized the depth of his confusion. She was his caregiver, and at the times when he thought himself a child again, the caregiver would be his mother.

At other times he called her by names that she did not know. "Far Dove," who had been his wife. Others who may have been relatives, maybe daughters. Possibly one of these was her own mother. She tried to inquire, but was never certain whether the answers she received were accurate. She thought not, because they were not always the same. Sometimes he seemed to regard Far Dove as his mother-figure, but he also mentioned such names as Otter Woman and Crow.

"Was she my mother?" South Wind would ask.

"Oh, yes," her grandfather would sign.

When she realized that he did so only to please her, and that he answered yes to any such questions, she was very discouraged.

"Was my mother's name 'South Wind'?" she asked as a test.

"Yes! That is right!"

After that disappointment, South Wind stopped asking. Along with the realization that her grandfather's mind was slipping came the sense of responsibility. She must care for him, protect him. Her maternal instincts came to the fore, and she began to mother him. Little Bone was forgotten, gathering dust in the cave. Grandfather was her child.

She called him Possum sometimes. He had used that name for himself, and it seemed to be a pet name from his childhood. He was pleased when she used it, and smiled happily, and it was good.

The thing that was not so good was her increasing feeling of being alone. It was like it had been when she was a child and Grandfather would leave her to go and hunt. She would cling tightly to her bone doll and wait for his return. The thought had sometimes crossed her mind: *What if he does not come back?* But he always did, and it was a joy to see him, to feel protected and unafraid.

It was like that now, the loneliness part. Little Bone had been set aside, and her comfort, yet the one she must protect, was Grandfather himself. Her presence was both a comfort and a responsibility. But there was a difference. As a child, she could hand-sign to her doll and assure Little Bone that Grandfather would return to care for them. Now, what could she tell *him*? There was no end to her uncertainty, no point at which she could tell herself, *Yes, when that happens, we will all be happy again.* She was completely unable to consider that the end point of the present situation was the death of her grandfather. And there were times, she reassured herself, when he was fairly lucid. On a good day, he knew who *he* was, South Wind's name, and all about their home here in the Rock. Unfortunately, the good days were becoming fewer and farther between.

South Wind's insecurity was manifesting itself in more frequent dreams now. The gnawing fear was returning, the dread of the dark corner of the cave, where she had envisioned the evil thing that lived there.

Her childhood dread of being alone crept back, and she relived the waits for the return of her grandfather, her protector. Asleep or awake, there was the smouldering dread, the suspicion that there really *might* be something that lived in the crevice, a dreadful thing of darkness. And now, there was no one to reassure her that it was only the imaginings of a child. The dread of the dark crevice was growing stronger.

What is it, this fear of dark places, this primal instinct? Does this dread go back to the caves and dens of a million generations ago, before the use of fire drove the shadows back and furnished early man with some protection from the hunters of the night?

South Wind might have been astonished, had she known that her grandfather, too, was experiencing such fears. As he relived *his* childhood in the deterioration of his mind, there was coming back to him the dread of things that lurk in dark places. He was glad that he had his mother . . . Far Dove . . . Crow. No, not those, either. If he could pause and think carefully enough, he could reassure himself. Usually, that is. This was South Wind, the child that he had raised. His daughter . . . no, granddaughter. Sometimes he could not be sure. There had been the massacre, when everyone was killed. He cried when he thought of that. It seemed to upset South Wind when he cried, so he tried not to do it, not to think of that.

He knew that he had some days that were far better than others. He tried hard, on those days, to tell his granddaughter (yes, *that's* who this is!) all that he could think of about the People. Those things were easier to remember, anyway. Some days he rather enjoyed telling her about it. The annual Sun Dance, the warrior societies, the holy men and women of the tribe. There was the vision-quest, on which young people fast and pray for guidance. The Rabbit Society, for the teaching of children. That made him think of Far Dove again, the childhood friend who had become his wife. That in turn made the tears flow, and he would hurry on to another subject.

But he felt that he was doing some good. South Wind *was* absorbing much of the culture of the People.

On his bad days, he could remember virtually nothing. It did not disturb him greatly, because he did not remember enough to cause him concern. If he had something to eat, a little water, and was neither too hot nor too cold, what was the worry? He could retreat into the happiness of childlike simplicity, where others do the worrying and the caregiving.

Even there, however, there are fears. The fear of the things in the dark. He could recall the many times he had held South Wind in his arms and rocked her gently, and reassured her that there was nothing there to harm her. But on the days when he became a child again, the fears of childhood returned. In reliving his childhood, he forgot the times when *he* was the strong protector, giving comfort against doubts. The doubts returned to him, too, bringing fears that evil things lurked in dark places. More specifically, he began to fear the dark crevice at the back of the cave. He did not want to look at it, because he might see some evil thing that lurked there. It appeared in his dreams, too, a formless wisp of dirty brown fog with some sort of evil intent.

In his more rational moments, he remembered that South Wind had feared that corner as a child. Odd, now that their places were being reversed, it would become a thing of fear for him. He said nothing, but when his fear began to come forward in his more confused moments, he knew that it helped to be held in her arms and be comforted, as he had once done for her.

In this odd manner, both were becoming aware of their dread of whatever the crevice might hold. It may have been only Fear itself, brought on by the insecurity of the future and the threat of being alone.

Neither was able to share such doubts and fears with the other, for completely different reasons. And the dark thing that dwelt in the crevice continued to grow, as it did in their minds.

38

Sometimes it seemed that the short and emotionally exhausting episode of the dying stranger had been a major turning point for Hunts-Alone. South Wind noticed, looking back, that his attitude had changed. It was as if something had been lacking, had wanted completion, and now it had occurred.

Almost from the day of their hard work at preparing the funeral for the unfortunate man, her grandfather seemed different. It was something that she could not define, but it was there. It was as if he had finished that task, the preparation of the body for the scaffold, and thus finished all other tasks, too. He still talked to her, told her things of the People. But it became increasingly clear that he considered his duties finished. It was not in a spirit of failure, although there was a sense of sadness for past mistakes. At times she had the impression that the thing which had seemed incomplete was his life. Now that he had participated with her in the ceremony of death and crossing over, it was finished.

She did not quite understand the mourning that he mentioned, celebrated with songs of grief and loss. There were songs, he had told her, to celebrate many things . . . fire, the morning sun, the return of the grass in the spring. It was quite difficult to understand the concept of a "song," when explained by a person who could not hear the song, nor sing it.

"We do not need it," her grandfather always explained. Instead, he performed ceremonies such as he had done for the dead man. A short statement, a prayer of thanks or of apology to the kill, or a statement to the spirits of a place . . . he had told her of that. A new camp must be symbolized by a new fire, and the simple statement, "Here I will be, here I camp tonight." She had seen her grandfather do these things, make these signs, many times. She thought that she understood . . . these were what he did instead of the songs of the People. She was not quite certain about what the "songs" might be, but she understood their purpose.

Now, the information that he gave her was in bits and pieces, disconnected scraps. Sometimes it was very confusing. Especially now, when she asked a question. The likeliest answer was "yes, that is it." Sometimes she knew that it was *not* correct, and this worried her greatly. What of the times that she asked and received wrong answers that she would never discover?

Even with all of that confusion, her main concern was for her grandfather. He had always been so strong, so sure, but now he had become hesitant, uncertain, and insecure. Weak, almost helpless. She realized with some alarm one day that he had not even been down the path to the river since they had carried the body of the stranger away. That had been more than a moon ago. She was now assisting him to walk the few steps outside and along the ledge to take care of his body functions. As she realized this, it also became apparent to her that he was not only weaker, but thinner. He was losing weight.

With this in mind, she began to watch him more closely. He picked at his food, seeming not to relish it as he once had. He would take a bite, chew slowly, swallow, and then just sit there, staring blankly at nothing. His spirit seemed far away. She would speak to him, and he would rouse, sometimes appearing surprised to find food before him.

"Grandfather, you must eat!"

He would turn and look at her, mildly irritated at her concern.

"Of course!"

But he continued to show little interest, and he became thinner and more frail. He seemed to lose control of bowels and bladder, and sometimes soiled himself. South Wind patiently cleaned him. On his worst days this seemed to mean nothing to him. He was a child again, and she the mother. It was then that he called her Mother, or sometimes Otter Woman. *Was that his mother's name?* She wondered.

On better days, at times when he knew her name, he was apologetic.

"Wind, you should not have to do this for me," he signed sadly as she washed the loose bowel excrement from his legs.

She smiled. She had thought of the distasteful task as merely a duty.

"You have done so for me, many times, no?"

"Yes," he nodded, smiling weakly. "But I am a burden to you."

"The burden is light. I was a greater burden to you!"

Still, she could tell that he worried about being a problem to her. On his more lucid days, that is. On some, he worried about nothing, or was cross and irritable. She was not certain which was harder, to have him understand nothing and not know her or to watch his sadness and remorse over the care she must give him. Her heart was heavy for him.

She hated to leave him, because of his intermittent confusion. On one occasion, she left him while he slept, to replenish their waterskins. She was gone only a short while, but she returned to find him outside on the ledge, tottering precariously. She dropped the waterskins and raced forward, at the same time trying not to alarm him. He seemed unaware of the sheer drop to the rocks below. He looked up and saw her as she drew near.

"Grandfather," she signed, trying to hide her alarm, "let us go inside now. Will you tell me of the People?"

"What? Oh, yes, Crow, it is good."

She had come to ignore his mistakes when he called her by the name of another. There seemed to be no point in belaboring it. She helped him inside, where he quickly fell asleep again, exhausted from his exertion.

She considered some sort of tether to prevent his falling off the ledge. Had he not once told her that as she learned to walk he had used a plaited length of rawhide around her waist to protect her from falling? She hesitated to initiate such a thing. She was not sure how he would react. Maybe he would be better . . . and on some days, it would be true.

There came a time, however, when the question of the rawhide tether solved itself. Her grandfather simply became too weak to stand. It was a mixed blessing. She could go for water, or fuel, or to hunt, with some confidence that he would not try to leave the cave. But her heart was heavy over the reason.

Autumn was drawing near, and as the days grew shorter and she laid up supplies for the coming winter, she was faced each day with a thought that she could not escape: It was highly unlikely that her grandfather could survive the harsh Moon of Long Nights, followed by the Moon of Snows. It was frightening to consider. She had denied this eventuality for so long, and now she could no longer ignore it. She had come face to face with the fact that soon she would be alone.

There were two parts to this. One, of course, the concern for her grandfather. But in her world, the death of any creature is only a part of life. She had seen the stranger cross over, and it had been a quiet thing. Grandfather had not seemed to fear death, except for leaving her. Sometimes, too, she felt that the frail form in the cave was no longer the same anyway. She had already lost him, the strong, dominant parent and teacher who had nurtured and taught her. That one held little resemblance to the failing, sometimes mindless person who now needed her care. *Maybe,* she thought, *his spirit has already crossed over, and only the body is left behind.* They had not talked of this, and she did not know whether it could happen.

In any case, she could see that the body could not continue as it was, losing weight and strength each day. That brought her to her second concern, which was not for Grandfather, but for herself. When he had finished crossing over, she would be alone. He was the only other person in her world, and when he was gone, what then? He had explained to her that when the spirit crosses over, it is still here, but is merely on the Other Side. That was a comforting thing, but how could she talk to him then? Without hands, how can a spirit sign? The thought of being alone, once a childhood fear that she had outgrown, now came creeping back. With something like panic, she thought of it . . . no one to talk to, to laugh with, to share stories, to protect. . . .

What about the dark thing in the crevice? Grandfather had been able to hold and comfort her as a child, and to make the bad thing go away. Now, in his childish moments, he seemed to fear it, and she had been able to help him suppress it. Together, they had repulsed the danger that lurked there. But, after he was gone, what would happen? Could she, alone, keep it in its place, away from any harm? Sometimes she felt like a helpless child again as she thought of it.

As it happened, the end came rather sooner than later. It was not in the throes of Cold Maker's winter sorties from the northern mountains. It was in the warmth of Second Summer. The season was late. A delayed frost had turned the sumac its bright crimson, the cottonwoods golden yellow, and the prairie grasses their assorted hues of pink and gold and deep red. The seed-heads of the tall real-grass nodded higher than her head, and the warm smells of autumn filled the clear blue of the sky. But the nights were growing long. Soon Cold Maker would come.

This had always been a favorite time for Hunts-Alone, and he seemed to rally for the occasion.

"Wind," he signed, "will you help me outside? I would sit in the sun."

She was startled. It had been several days since he even knew her.

"Of course, Grandfather."

It was easier than it once would have been. The thin frame was so frail that she could have lifted him now. Carefully, she assisted him to the ledge and helped position him comfortably, seated on a robe in the sun. He breathed deeply and smiled.

"It is good!"

All afternoon he sat there, watching the eagles soar and a distant band of buffalo graze their way across the valley. A long line of geese honked their way south. He could not hear their song, but he loved to watch them on their way.

Shadows grew long, and South Wind, returning with firewood, asked if he wished to go inside.

"A little longer," he signed. "Sun Boy uses wonderful paints tonight."

It was true. On the tallgrass prairie, the sunsets are the world's finest at any time because of the vastness of the sky. But there are none finer than those of autumn. The haze of Second Summer, lying over hills a day's travel away, lets Sun Boy paint the world and the sky with golds and reds and purples, and it is good.

"Yes," South Wind agreed. "It is good."

He insisted on staying until the first stars began to show against the gray-purple of the sky and the breeze became chill.

"Now," he signed, "help me inside."

He ate well, of fresh buffalo that she had killed, then rolled in his robe and fell asleep.

Sometime during the night, his spirit crossed over, quietly and without trouble. South Wind discovered this at daylight. He appeared calm and comfortable, and there was a faint smile on his lips. His long and troubled journey was over.

South Wind knelt beside him, touching the cold skin, knowing that it was over for him, and that it was good. This made it no easier for her.

She rose, blinded now by the tears that came in a flood, and retreated to the ledge. There, she greeted the rising sun with a long, keening wail of sorrow, which echoed along the face of the Rock and across the valley. She did not even think that someone might hear. She did not care.

In her grief, she now understood the Song of Mourning.

39

S outh Wind, after her initial grief reaction, began to undertake the tasks that she knew must be done. The body of Hunts-Alone already lay in a position that appeared comfortable, supine at full length. She folded his arms across his chest, weeping openly as she did so. His eyes were closed as if in sleep, and she straightened his head to face forward.

"There," she signed to the still form. She would do for him as they had done together for the stranger.

She sat a little while and thought about that, trying to remember. She had been preoccupied with the experience of touching and being near another human being. But, she recalled how insistent her grandfather had been that she observe and learn. She had thought it strange at the time that Grandfather had actually seemed pleased at the opportunity to care for the body of the departed one. Now, it began to make more sense. At that time, she had been denying to herself the possibility that she would ever be faced with this duty. Grandfather had seemed immortal. Now, she had seen him fail, had suffered the heartbreak of watching his mind go and his strength weaken. He had been so strong, in spirit and in body. The tears flowed again.

But now she must plan . . . where would his resting place be? In her mind, she thought of the scaffold in the ash grove. It seemed appropriate, the place of the only funeral she had ever seen. She was strong enough to take him there; frail as he had now become, she could carry him. The other man had been heavy, and it had been good that they had the horse to assist. Yet, she wondered whether it would be appropriate for Grandfather to rest with a stranger. She worried about this, even as she cleaned the body and wrapped the robe around him and secured it.

She covered his face last, pausing to shed more tears and once more to release her grief in a long wail.

"I will miss you, Grandfather. . . . I am already lonely for you," she signed. Then she tied the flap of the robe firmly around his thin shoulders and tucked in the edges.

She still had not decided where to put him. Not in the ash grove. There seemed no purpose in that, except that there was a corpse already there. The corpse of a stranger. Grandfather had chosen that place, but . . . yes, he had mentioned that it was a hidden place, one that would not lead passers-by to find their home in the Rock. But he had also told her something else. . . . It should be a high place . . . the cliff! Yes, had he not said something of that? It could be on a high ledge. . . . Not too near the cave.

She spent the rest of the day scrambling around the face of the Rock, searching for the right spot. One place was ideal, up near the nest of the hawks. The nest was abandoned now, but she knew that the birds would return to rebuild it and use it again next season. Grandfather would have liked that, high on the cliff, overlooking the tallgrass prairie, and near the soaring feathered creatures that he loved to watch.

But wait . . . the short and narrow ledge was ideal, but how could she bring him here? She had climbed here many times over the years. Not until now had it become plain to her that it could not be done without the use of both hands. She had never made the climb with a burden of any sort. Even her weapons and yes, her doll, had been laid aside when she came here. No, it was impossible. There was no way that she could bring him here. She sat there heavy of heart, listening to the murmur of the wind through bare cottonwood branches. Well, she must find another place.

She climbed down to sit on the boulder in her favorite play spot. It had always been a place of comfort, halfway between the river and the cave above. It was near the point where the dim path on up the cliff branched away. Her eyes misted again as she thought of the many days when she and Grandfather had sat together on this boulder, and he had held her, rocked her to sleep, or told her stories. She would miss his company here. . . .

Her eyes widened. Yes, why not? Why not *here*? She stood, took a step or two along the ledge, and looked back. Yes, there was a space, partly behind the boulder, a space of the right size and shape for a robe-wrapped body. The overhang would hide it against observation from above, and the ledge from beneath. In addition, he would be near, and would be in a place where she could visit him each time she passed up or down the path. She hurried back to the cave.

"Grandfather," she signed, "I have found your resting place! The boulder where we sit."

She felt that he knew and understood, and her heart was good.

It was a long and arduous task to bring him there. At some places where the ledge was narrow and the overhang steep, she could not carry the clumsy burden. She must place it on the ledge and drag it forward as she carefully backed along the path. The task was too great to begin now. Shadows were already lengthening. She would wait until morning.

Through the long night she sat and watched over the body, keeping the fire burning. From time to time she cried and tried to think of the good times, the way her grandfather's eyes crinkled at the corners when he was pleased. Though he had been a bitter old man, there were rare times when he had seemed happy and his heart filled with laughter. She had treasured those times, and would still do so.

She thought further of the things that she would leave with him. His bow and arrows, his knife. She was not sure what one would need on the Other Side, but they had sent the weapons of the stranger with him. Food, maybe . . . she spent a little while preparing small bundles of dried meat and some of his favorite mixture of pounded meat, dried plums, and melted tallow. These things she wrapped and tied and laid aside with his weapons.

Water? She thought not. Her impression was that the Other Side had plentiful streams of clear water, and that game would be plentiful. Had they not sent with the stranger only enough food for a day or two? Grandfather would surely make a kill soon after his arrival. A fat buffalo, probably, she thought. That was his favorite. Preferably a yearling cow, fat and tender. She smiled, remembering his delight at such a kill.

Daylight came at last, and she began her task. It took longer than it would have under usual conditions. She wished to handle her burden of sorrow gently and with great care. Frequently she stopped to rest, and when she did, she talked to him in signs.

"A little farther, Grandfather. We must rest a little while. Wait until you see the place I have for you. It is good, the place by the boulder, where we have sat for stories and to watch the valley. . . . Well, let us move on."

It was quite tricky to maneuver around some of the rocky twists in the trail. She had never realized before what a difference the shape of a burden can make. One as tall as a man, even though not heavy . . . even more so because this burden must be handled gently and with love.

It was past noon before Grandfather was settled into his final resting place. She positioned him so that she was facing the bundle when she sat sideways on her boulder. Also, she was pleased that from his position, the spirit of her grandfather could look out over the rolling prairie.

"See, Grandfather, is it not as I said?"

She did not know whether or how long the spirit might stay around. He had once said something about three days, but beyond that? . . . Maybe the spirit would come back sometimes to visit her. Yes, that must be it. Spirits must travel with great speed, so her grandfather would probably come back anytime that she wished to visit him.

Another trip up the path to the cave, and she placed his weapons and supplies at his side. She cried again, then stood to address the still shape in a formal manner.

"I will miss and mourn you, Grandfather. May your journey to the Other Side be easy. I have brought your favorite pemmican to nourish you on the journey."

She paused, uncertain.

"Will you come back to help me sometimes?" she pleaded. "I am alone, now, you know."

She stopped again and took a deep breath. Was such a request proper? She was unsure.

"But I will be fine," she assured him. "Have I not been taught well?"

She sat on the boulder, lost in thought, until it began to grow dark. When the night became chilled, she rose and went to the cave to bring her robe. She could not bear to stay in the cave tonight, alone. She built a small fire. She knew that it was not a good idea, but it did not seem to matter. It would help her to watch over Grandfather, and she somehow felt that responsibility. Anyway, she told herself defensively, there had been no sign of trespassers for some time. The People, he had told her, were somewhere else at this season, preparing their winter camps.

She, too, must do that now. There was much work, carrying firewood and drying meat to store against the onslaught of Cold Maker.

40

It was a bad winter. Not weatherwise, especially, but a time of deep emotional loss for South Wind. Her moods fluctuated, from confidence to loneliness to sadness and yes, to *anger* at her grandfather for leaving her.

With her lack of experience in the world of other humans, she had nothing for comparison. Her anger, therefore, was not over the injustice forced on her by Grandfather's strange hatreds. It was merely that he would leave her alone and unprotected. Of course, if she paused to think about it, she knew that he had had no choice. His time had come, and he died, not unpleasantly. His last day had been good, and she was glad for that. And for the fact that his troubles were over for this world. He was safely on the Other Side.

However, she saw all this with mixed feelings. Her own world had become infinitely more complex now. She had thought at first that it might be simpler. She would be able to come and go, to hunt without worrying whether Grandfather was safe. Whether he might have tried to get up and had fallen from the ledge, or gotten into some other danger.

Then such thoughts would bring guilt. She should not feel *good* that he was no longer here. She would think of the times when she was irritated with him or impatient over his inability to move and think and function in their little world. Many times she wished that she had been kinder and gentler to him in his last days. Almost forgotten was the fact that most of the time she *had* been kind and gentle. The things she now remembered with remorse were the exceptions.

She would also think of things she meant to ask him, and would realize that now it was too late. Or she would see something new. . . . A beaver lodge downstream that had not been there before. A doe with twin fawns, who had joined the herd that always wintered in the timber above the riffle. This animal was of a very strange color, more gray than reddish. There was always a variety of color in the deer herd, from red to gray to yellow, but this was unique and striking. She would enjoy sharing the information with Grandfather when she returned to the cave.

But then the truth would come to her. Grandfather would not be at the cave, waiting for her. He lay on the ledge, ritually wrapped in the custom of his people. At least, his body was there. His spirit had crossed over. She believed so, because that was what he had taught her. Then the loneliness would descend, and her heart was heavy.

Maybe this was one of the things that caused her to begin to talk to her grandfather. She passed the still form on the ledge many times a day as she tried to lay in a supply of firewood. One afternoon, already tired from a day that had been busy and hard, she paused at the boulder to rest. The armful of wood was somewhat heavier than usual, and she set it down for a moment, breathing heavily.

Despite the coolness of the late fall day, she could feel the dampness of perspiration inside her tunic. A rivulet tickled its way down her back between the shoulder blades, and her arms were sticky with sweat. Exhausted, she sat on the boulder and looked across the river at the distant grassland. Then she turned to look at the still form beside her. How many such trips up and down the Rock he had made through the years! And he had been old, his joints creaking in protest. Here she was, in the prime of her youth, exhausted and panting from the effort. She smiled wryly.

"Grandfather," she signed to the still figure, "you were quite a man!"

She wondered whether he would approve of her efforts to prepare for the winter. She knew how much fuel would be required through the long Moon of Snows. Actually, she had done much of the planning and providing for the past two winters. But it was different now. Last season she had been able to ask advice: "Is this right, Grandfather?" And he had nodded approval. Probably, she now realized, there were times when he had not even understood the question. He only nodded to end the annoyance of further conversation.

Now her breathing was easier. She rose.

"I must go, Grandfather," she signed. "The night will be cold. Cold Maker comes tonight, maybe."

It seemed logical, easy, to slip into the habit of conversation with him. He did not answer, but there had been many times that he had not when he was alive. There was little difference. Some would have thought her a little crazy, perhaps, but she had nothing with which to compare. It was comforting to her to talk with him. And was his spirit not here, only unseen because it had crossed to the Other Side?

It became perfectly logical to pause each time she passed the boulder. She would boast of her success in the hunt or tell him of her failure. A sudden shift in the breeze, bringing a warning to her quarry, a misstep that spoiled her silent stalk. She would laugh as she related the antics of a pair of coyote pups, hunting on their own now for the first time. She told him of the weather, the thickness of the ice on the pool below and the blossoms of frost crystals that adorned each grass blade and twig on some mornings. It was good.

Sometime later, she began to realize that she was spending time here instead of at the cave, and the reason puzzled her at first. Finally she admitted to herself that it was for companionship. Here, her grandfather dwelt. In the cave, there was no one.

Except, maybe, the dark thing in the crevice. And that, she knew, was something she must think about. During the first few days after her bereavement, it had been quiet. Now, it seemed to be coming to life again, more vigorously. She would have attempted without hesitation to fight a bear or a wolf, and would have felt confident in the outcome. But this . . . she had feared the imagined creature of darkness as early as she could remember. Grandfather had told her that it did not exist, and it gradually went away. Then, when *his* power began to fail, it grew again. Even *he* had seemed to fear it at the last.

She was confused. Of all the dangers that she might encounter in their world, Grandfather had given quite specific advice. How to avoid the bite of the real-snake, how to deal with a disturbed winter bear, roused by accident from her sleep. But in this one area she had no example to follow. She had received conflicting information: It is not there, it is nothing, yet it is something that must be feared. She wondered if it was something that had been held in check by the power of Grandfather's spirit. When he began to fail, the thing in the crevice became stronger. Now he was gone, and she felt a chill of fear. . . . Would it become stronger now? She tried to tell herself that *she* was strong and could control the fearful thing. Most of the time she was successful, but there were times when doubts overcame her. The dreams, when she was pursued by a vague and shapeless form and could not run. The times when she sat in the cave, alone, afraid to look at the dark corner because she might see something there.

She developed the theory that it feared the light. During the light of day she was never even concerned about the dark thing. She was stronger than anything that could lurk there in the crevice. Besides, was it not likely that Grandfather could help her, even from the Other Side? Was this not a thing of the spirit, and was not *he* a spirit now?

This worked quite well during the daytime, but with darkness came doubt. True, she had actually seen nothing, except in dreams, but fears came crowding in. For a few nights, she kept a fire burning brightly in the cave. Then she realized that this using too much of her fuel supply. It would not do.

A few nights were spent elsewhere when weather permitted. On the ledge outside . . . In a smaller cave where she had played as a child. That was not a good idea. The play-cave was smaller than she remembered, and she woke after a restless sleep, cramped and aching.

Finally another idea struck her. She would stay in the cave during daylight, sleeping when the creature in the crevice was inactive. Then she would go out at night. South Wind became one of the hunters of the night, a seminocturnal creature herself. This helped some, but there was also another problem, related indirectly to the first: What would she do now? Sometimes it seemed reasonable to merely go on as they had been doing, enjoying the fruits of the hunt and the solitude. But not *complete* solitude. There was the loneliness.

"What am I to do, Grandfather?" she asked.

There was no answer. At least not one that was apparent to her, and it was discouraging. Sometimes she considered leaving the Rock, but quickly rejected such thoughts. She would know nothing of what to do. So day followed day, and the winter nights likewise, and she went on. It came to be that her most comforting times were those spent with her grandfather. She would sit on the boulder, weather permitting, and tell him of all that she saw and did.

"The ice is breaking up on the river, Grandfather. It is almost the Moon of Awakening. The beavers were out today."

She even spoke to him of the thing in the crevice.

"I do not quite understand about that," she told him. "In the daylight, it seems powerless. At night, I am afraid, except if the fire gives light. So, I sleep mostly in the daytime. At night, I go out, and this is good. You know I like the outside night anyway. . . . The moon on the snow was beautiful last night."

She paused a little while.

"I wish you could tell me about the dark thing. I do not know how to fight it. Well, I will avoid it as I have told you. Only . . . sometimes I dream of it. It chases me and I cannot run."

She waited again, as if for an answer, but there was none.

"I wish that you could help me. You told me that there is nothing there, that it cannot hurt me. But I am made to think that it *is* there, and . . . I *am* afraid, Grandfather. I hope you can help me. I will go on as I have said."

She rose and started down the path toward the river. Then she paused and turned back.

"Grandfather, is it that it takes two of us to control the dark thing, to keep it in the crevice? Does one person have enough power to do it alone?"

She waited, still thinking about that idea. Grandfather had been virtually alone when he came there, with her as a tiny infant. And he had kept the evil thing in check. *So,* she told herself, *I can, too!*

"Yes, I can do it," she signed confidently as she turned away.

She wished that she *felt* that confident.

41

It was better when spring came. It was hard to be sad or morose when everything was bursting with new life. Even the Dark Thing seemed less ominous now.

Cold Maker withdrew to the north against the increasing power of Sun Boy's medicine. South Wind wondered if perhaps the Dark Thing and Cold Maker were allies. There were certainly longer nights during Cold Maker's season. Nights in which the thing in the crevice seemed more powerful. Or did she only imagine that? It was hard to take it seriously as she sat here in the warm sun and looked across the familiar landscape.

"It is good, Grandfather," she signed. "The geese are traveling north, many of them."

She wondered sometimes if her grandfather might be up there, traveling with them. She had seen him watch the long lines of geese until they were out of sight. There seemed to be a certain longing, a wish to go with them. Now, maybe he could do so. Except that she felt strongly that he was still here, still watching over her, somehow. She could not explain that, but she was certain of it.

She was a little more comfortable now with her loss and the loneliness that it brought. She had worried for a long time, had been bothered by the little things that she could not tell him. There were questions that she had always intended to ask but never did. And the guilt feelings . . . *did I treat him as well as I should have?*

Those doubts, fears, and annoyances had mostly been laid to rest by a strange experience. It had been in the Moon of Hunger, though she really had no hunger. The cave was well provisioned, thanks to the teachings of her grandfather. All her life he had insisted that they store adequate supplies, and it was now second nature to her. Starvation was not to be one of her worries. But she was restless and fearful for herself and for Grandfather. She was sleeping poorly, and found herself uncertain and indecisive.

Then came the dream . . . or vision, maybe. She was asleep, but is not a dream only a vision that takes place during sleep? She and Grandfather were seated on the boulder beside the path, watching the beavers in the pool below. Strange, she thought, is he not dead? She even looked beside the boulder to see the robe-wrapped form, but it was not there. Still, there was the strong feeling that this dream-vision was not of a time long ago. It was as if she recognized that it was all part of her dream.

She studied her grandfather's face. It looked younger, healthier. But she herself, her body and her dress, were plainly in the present. He saw her watching him and smiled.

"What is it?" he signed.

She was embarrassed and fumbled for an answer.

"I was only thinking," she answered clumsily. "You are looking well."

"Of course!" came his signed answer. "This being dead is no problem. Do not worry about it."

So she was right! He *was* dead, but was reassuring her. A feeling of calm, a warm comfortable feeling came over her, and she smiled. The worries, the unasked questions, the loneliness, all seemed unimportant now.

"It is good," she signed.

But there remained unanswered the question of the Thing in the cave. She hesitated, wondering if she should ask of it, or if that would be inappropriate. He seemed to sense her concern and smiled again.

"Do not worry," he signed. "Help will come."

She awoke, startled. But the sense of reassurance and calm was still with her. She was in the cave, and it was late afternoon. She rose and hurried down the trail to the boulder. The still funeral bundle was there, unchanged.

"Thank you, Grandfather," she signed.

From that day, she felt better, more cheerful. She did not know how it might occur, but only that somehow, all her questions and problems would be answered. Her worry was much less, her fears reduced. Even the dark crevice seemed less threatening. Maybe it was only that the nights were shorter now, but she thought not. Grandfather's reassurance had helped her immensely.

In turn, she was now talking to him more. Today, in the Moon of Greening, she sat and described in signs all the things before her.

"A redbird, Grandfather. He makes his nesting song."

She was not certain whether, in his present spirit-state, Grandfather could hear such things. That was something she had never fully understood anyway. When he was alive, she knew that he had not been able to hear the coyote's cry or the warning slap of the beaver's tail on the water. She knew that at least some of the people she had seen made sounds to each other. Did many people make such sounds, or were they the exception? It did not occur to her that her grandfather might be the exception. But maybe he could hear now.

Since she was not sure, she described to him the sounds as well as the sights and smells.

"I can smell the plum thicket from here, Grandfather. It is covered with bloom, and the smell rises up the Rock when the sun warms it. The grapevine on the cliff below the ledge is not blooming yet, but there are many buds. That will smell even better, no?"

She described the colors of the violets that were beginning to bloom, the sounds of the calling geese, and the hollow cry of the rain-bird, "though it does not look like rain . . . maybe he is mistaken. The night-singer is back, the gray and white bird who sings others' songs. I do not know if you can hear him."

And so it went. It was a great comfort to her, to have these one-sided conversations. Her comments were not answered, yet in a sense they were. Her answer came in the calm confidence that was now hers. Only a thing or two now troubled her: the question of what she would do in the future, seasons ahead. This was only a passing thought sometimes, when she was not feeling as confident as usual. There was no easy answer, and she was always able to repress the question. She could worry about that when the proper time came. A more worrisome thing was that of the fearful dark crevice in the cave. Despite the suggestion that it was weaker with the return of the sun, it *was* there.

On a dark and rainy day, when the only really comfortable place to be was the cave, she could *feel* its presence. On such days, she burned more firewood than she really should have and sat facing the dreaded corner, her back against the other wall in a defensive position. She would doze, and come awake with a start, almost certain that she had seen a Something move in the dusky corner. Or had she dreamed it?

This was disconcerting enough that she discussed it with Grandfather. At least, she told him of it, on more than one occasion. She received no concrete answer, but on each of these occasions she recalled her dream-vision. She had the assurance that Grandfather would be here and that help of some sort would be available when needed.

It was now late in the Moon of Roses. They had bloomed in all their glory, in reds and pinks and whites . . . even one clump that was pale yellow. The scent had been everywhere. The blooms were past their prime now, and the fruits beginning to swell on their thorny stems. She must gather some, but not yet. Later.

South Wind was watching the weather carefully. It would soon be the Moon of Thunder, with its towering cloudbanks reaching into the hot blue sky, growing until they gave birth to storms. Rain Maker was in his glory at this time, marching across the prairie, wrapped in his dark robes of driven rain, his drums rolling as he moved. He hurled spears of real-fire at random to strike lone trees or even people who were caught in the open. She had once seen him split a giant old cottonwood tree. The fiery spears of Rain Maker, Grandfather had told her, are drawn to this tree. That is why one should never take shelter under a cottonwood.

The river might rise if heavy rains came. It often did. But so far this year, the fine weather had continued. The clarity of the air was so accentuated that it was possible to see objects at great distances with greater clarity. Only in the warmth of the afternoon was there some distortion by the shimmering heat waves.

It was on one of these fine days that she first noticed the figure in the distance. At first she was not even certain that it was moving. Maybe it was a lone tree or bush, newly in leaf and grown larger than last season. She continued to look at it from time to time, and finally decided to use the sticks to determine whether it moved. She placed her twigs, sighted across them, waited, and then returned to look again. Yes, the distant object had moved. She was not particularly concerned, but curious. A lone buffalo, or perhaps a horse? She had seen scattered bands of both recently, but a lone individual . . . there was something different here. Carefully, she continued to observe the direction of movement by placing new twigs, until she could recognize the pattern of this progress. It appeared quite deliberate. The direction wavered with the terrain, the moving object sometimes even disappearing for a little while as it crossed some small watercourse or swale. But one thing was becoming certain: This was an intentional, deliberate course, and it was heading straight for Medicine Rock.

This was most unusual. South Wind was still not particularly concerned, though there was a hint of a distant warning in her mind. Why would a lone rider be approaching the Rock, usually avoided by people?

It was not long after this that she was able to distinguish that this was not a horseman, but a lone individual on foot. Much later, she determined that it was a man carrying a light pack. As he drew nearer, she continued to watch, gleaning new information bit by bit. The man carried a bow, but his demeanor did not seem aggressive.

Why would a man be traveling on foot, alone? Her grandfather had told her of the necessity for a horse on long journeys. Yet this man had none. Had his horse been lost or injured, killed, perhaps? No, there was none of the attitude of a defeated survivor in this man. He moved with confidence and purpose.

It was late in the day when he finally stood on the slope across the river, looking up at the cliff. He seemed to be studying the face of the Rock with interest and with purpose. He appeared young, not much older than she, maybe. He was not unpleasant to look upon, even though he represented a threat. Well, she could watch him. She was ready to play the hiding game if necessary, but felt compelled to watch.

The stranger shifted his pack and stepped toward the river. He paused to wash his face and fill a waterskin, and then, to her surprise, splashed across the riffle. He paused again to drain the water from his moccasins and looked up at the cliff.

He is coming up! She felt the grip of panic. What would she do? Such a thing had never happened before. She wished for the advice of Grandfather. Was she supposed to merely hide while the stranger climbed the path to invade the privacy of their lodge? Anger rose in her. Maybe she should kill him. But what then? Prepare *him* for burial, too? It seemed offensive to her, to share the Rock with the corpse of an invader.

Now he was starting to climb the path, with great determination, as if he had a purpose. She retreated upward, beyond the boulder and Grandfather's resting place, to an area from which she could see part of his ascent. There was a place where the path divided, one branch leading on upward, the other along the ledge to her boulder and on to the cave.

The young man climbed, pausing to study a crevice which she knew was filled with bones. That was a reasonable curiosity, but she still had no clue as to his purpose here. He moved on.

At the place where the path divided, he did not even pause, but climbed on, straight upward. South Wind breathed easier. She had hoped he would do that. The branch that led to the cave was not well seen from below, but this stranger was behaving so unpredictably. . . . He climbed on, out of sight, and she moved to a vantage point from which she could follow his progress. Why would he want to climb the Rock, for what purpose? Her anger rose, resentment against him for desecrating her world.

The stranger climbed all the way to the top, drew himself up and over the edge, and disappeared. She knew the place well, an open flat shelf of stone where the level prairie above came to an abrupt end at the rim of the cliff. It was near the hawk's nest.

But now what? Had he kept going? She thought for a moment. The day was late, and a traveler should be looking for a place to camp. This one obviously did not *fear* the Rock, but why did he climb to the top? The best camping place was below, on the south side of the river. There was more fuel, water was more convenient. He had filled his waterskin, so he must not intend to come back down.

South Wind slipped along the ledge and across a narrow place that she had discovered long ago. She had used it seldom. It was another path to the top of the cliff. She could go up there to locate the intruder and make certain that he had moved on.

She had not yet reached the top when a stray breeze brought a familiar scent to her nostrils. Smoke . . . the intruder had kindled a fire. Anger washed over her, making her face flush and her skin tingle. A *fire* . . . a declaration that he was camping here! The girl waited a moment, wrestling with her anger, and then continued climbing.

Before she reached the top, she heard the voice of the stranger, rising and falling in a sort of chant. This must be a "song." . . . There was an exciting quality about it, and even through her anger at the intrusion, she was curious. She would wait, for now. After dark, she would go up and look more closely at this stranger.

42

↔

Suth Wind squatted, watching the sleeping man. It was a risky thing, because the full moon was silvering the world and she could be easily seen if he awoke. However, this danger only added to her excitement. She felt a strange mixture of anger and curiosity. She must know more about him. He was young, as she had noted. He was also attractive, and she felt strangely drawn to him. There was an excitement stirring in her body that had nothing to do with the risk or the threat of an intruder. The risk did not bother her. She could kill him if she needed to. But this other feeling. . . . It felt, somehow, like she had felt that time when she watched the young couple with their arms around each other and putting their mouths together. It was a strange excitement.

But this young man . . . What was he doing here? She tried to puzzle it out. He had come carrying few supplies. She could see virtually none. His sleeping-robe, his waterskin, his bow and a few arrows seemed to comprise all of his possessions. He could not travel far so poorly equipped.

Yet again, it did not appear that he had been the victim of any misfortune. His attitude said plainly that his present activity was *planned* that way. For what purpose? It was very puzzling. A traveler, yet poorly equipped to travel. He had approached the Rock with confidence, though most feared it. His campfire was at a poorly selected place, away from water, but he had carried water with him as he climbed the bluff. And he had gathered a great quantity of firewood, though it was scarce at the top of the Rock.

She thought about it for a long time and finally came to a tentative conclusion. *This* was his goal. Here, at the cliff's rim. He had built his fire with deliberate ritual and had even chanted a song to mark the occasion. At least, that appeared to be its purpose. The fire was not needed for warmth, he had nothing to cook, and was not hunting. The fire was symbolic, then, the statement, "Here, I camp."

But for how long, and for what purpose? He could not last very long without food. . . . Wait! Her grandfather had mentioned such a thing! A young person would go out alone and fast for a period of time while he sought a vision. *The vision-quest!* Yes, that must be the explanation. And how long? *Three, four days, maybe more,* Grandfather had said.

South Wind had been fascinated by this idea, but it had been put aside for all the more important things of her grandfather's last few moons of life. Well, this might be a good opportunity to watch, unseen, while this stranger established his contact with the spirit world. She wondered if her presence would interfere. The vision-seeker was supposed to be alone. Well, she could not help that. This was *her* home, the stranger was the intruder. She would remain unseen, and if his quest proved unsuccessful, so be it. It was his fault, not hers.

It was threatening, though, to have the stranger present. She slept poorly, and her dreams involved danger and fear, and the unknown horror in the dark crevice. During her waking hours she was curious, and she tried to watch the intruder at every opportunity. She felt drawn to him in spite of the danger, as a moth is to the flame.

She discussed the situation with the still form on the ledge.

"There is a stranger here, Grandfather. I did not know what to do. I thought of killing him, but I think he means no harm."

She waited a little while, trying to decide how she might explain. She could not share with Grandfather the strange attraction that she felt toward the intruder.

"I am made to think," she went on, signing carefully, "that this is a young man on his vision-quest. So, he will finish his fast and then go away, no? No harm will have been done, if he does not see us."

She was not quite certain that her grandfather would approve of this interpretation, but she wanted badly for it to be right. She realized that in this case, silence did not necessarily mean assent, but chose to interpret it so because she wished it so.

"It is good," she signed, rising. "I will watch him closely and tell you all that he does."

As nearly as she could tell, the intruder had not eaten since he first climbed the cliff. She had eaten hardly anything, either. She could not build a fire without risking discovery, and she was unwilling to do that. It would be only a few days anyway, she reminded herself.

Probably not only the stranger on his vision-quest, but both of them, therefore, were feeling some of the effects of fasting. They were much closer in spirit than either realized. Of course the young man was not aware of South Wind's presence. Even had he known, it is likely that both would have been surprised at the similarity of their thoughts and feelings. The vision-seeker was feeling South Wind's dread of the threatening evil thing in the cliff, while she in turn was experiencing part of his vision-quest. Each was receiving part of the spirit-feeling of the other without realizing it.

As a result, the puzzled young man was experiencing the interference of the dark fear in South Wind's mind. She in turn felt *his* confusion. She also felt his vision-experience, the sensation of being inside the head of the animals he watched. She, too, knew the lift of the rising air currents against the wings of the red-tailed hawk, and the dull, sullen thoughts of the massive old herd bulls across the river. South Wind could not have told *how,* but she knew precisely when he found his animal spirit-guide, though she could not have told its identity.

Good! she thought. *Now his quest is over and he will go away.*

This did appear to be correct. She watched as he prepared to leave, extinguished his fire, and rolled his robe to carry. His waterskin was almost empty, she noted. No matter, he would fill it at the stream before he started to travel.

South Wind slipped away, down one of her own secret routes on the cliff's face. She would hide on the ledge around the shoulder of the rock from Grandfather's resting place. There was a bush there, and she could watch most of the young man's descent through its branches, unseen. She paused a moment at her boulder to sign to her grandfather's wrapped form.

"He is leaving now, Grandfather. I will watch him on his way. It is good."

She hurried on, to reach her place of concealment before the intruder's descent began. She had barely reached her selected observation point when she saw him, carefully picking his way down the cliff. He was doing well, she thought, for one unfamiliar with the rocky precipice. At one point or two, there would have been an easier foothold, but she knew that only from years of experience.

He arrived at the main path from the top. Good. It would be easier going now. She had not paused to think why his safety in this descent was important to her. If she had been asked, she would have answered that she wished him safely gone. If he fell, she would have to care for his body. Worse yet, if he were only injured in a fall, she would be faced with a decision. Should she help him or kill him?

Such tensions helped her to conceal even from herself the concern that she really felt for this stranger. She entirely overlooked the fact that in truth, she would miss the companionship of the spirit that she had felt for the past few days. For a moment, there even flickered through her mind the thought that she might follow him when he left, to learn of his ways.

Such thoughts vanished abruptly as he neared the place where the path branched. If a person ascended from the river, the path seemed to climb on and up. The branch that led to the cave was not well seen from below. But from above . . .

The young man paused and stared at the ledge for a moment while South Wind held her breath. He had noticed something. She, too, stared at that portion of the ledge. She had never before noticed how well-worn it looked. How could he *not* suspect something amiss? *Go on,* she wished silently, *there is nothing here for you.*

As if he had heard her unvoiced suggestion, the youth turned and started on down. South Wind was able to breathe again. But wait! He turned to look back up the path. He had only been testing his impression. Nodding in apparent satisfaction, he started back. Wind stared helplessly as he carefully studied the rocky path. She wondered if he was seeing footprints that she might have left there only moments ago. He seemed undecided.

She could tell when he made the decision. He seemed to nod to himself in satisfaction, and then to her horror, he stepped boldly onto the ledge that led to the cave. *I should have killed him!* she thought. She was unable to move as she watched him come toward her. Now he was approaching her boulder and the funeral-wrapped form behind it. She heard him gasp in surprise, and saw him jump back as he recoiled at the unexpected appearance of a corpse beside the path. He recovered quickly, then stepped back to examine his find more closely.

All the pent-up frustration and tension in South Wind's heart exploded in a wave of rage. She sprinted forward, her knife in her hand. The man turned to defend himself barely before she struck. He managed to deflect her knife thrust and grasped her wrist as the two fell heavily and rolled together on the ledge. He was strong, and South Wind felt that she was fighting for her life. But her anger at the desecration of her grandfather's resting place drove her to superhuman effort. Her opponent had not been able to draw his own weapon. She clawed at him with her free hand but was unable to reach his knife.

She *must* do something, and quickly! An idea came to her, a memory from her childhood . . . her grandfather had been very angry. . . . This same spot . . . With a sudden lunge, she rolled over, pulling her opponent with her and on top of her. She felt his weight, but at the same time her left shoulder reached past the rim of the ledge and out into empty space. The weight of the young man's body carried them on, their momentum toppling the pair over the edge.

He gasped and tried to kick free but she held tightly as they fell. He would have no way to know that below this point lay the deep pool, and he would be expecting death on the rocks below.

With a frantic cry he released her knife hand just before they struck the water. She slashed at him and missed. Both plunged deep, and she turned to see him swimming toward the surface. A stroke toward him, another knife thrust, just as they surfaced. She felt the flint blade rip into something, and the water began to turn red with his blood.

She was certain that the wound was not mortal. It had been a blind, slashing stroke. He was wearing buckskins, which would absorb much of the force of such a blow. He was still dangerous.

He dived again, and she hesitated. There had been time for him to draw his own knife, so she must be cautious now. She submerged and moved toward him. There . . . he was swimming underwater, heading deeper to escape her. The man was an expert swimmer. She lost sight of him for a moment, then saw a flash of motion off to her right. She turned to defend herself. No . . . a beaver! Then where? . . .

She surfaced, and looked quickly around to locate her opponent, but he was nowhere to be seen. Where had he gone? Surely if he had left the river she would see him.

A slight disturbance in the water at the other shore caught her attention and she focused on that. A giant sycamore grew there, and a tangle of its roots reached into the water like knobby knees. The splash had come from that tangle. There was a loud slap from the same area, the alarm signal . . . *beaver,* she thought.

Then where was the wounded man? She swam to shore on the cliff's side and explored up and down the narrow strip of land. There were no tracks or any sign that he had left the water here. She found one of his arrows, lost from above when he dropped his weapons at her attack. It floated, point down.

She crossed the riffle and searched the other shore. Nothing. *Strange,* she thought. Had he been wounded more seriously than she realized? Had he dived more deeply than he intended, and in his weakened condition lost consciousness and drowned? She was not certain.

She climbed the path and stopped at her boulder, exhausted. There on the ledge lay the stranger's bow and scattered arrows. It had been a narrow escape.

"Grandfather," she signed, still breathing heavily, "the man is gone. I tried to kill him. My heart is heavy that he disturbed you."

She rested a little more.

"He may be dead," she went on. "He was wounded. I cannot find where he left the water."

She was not certain that her grandfather would approve of the way she had handled this. She knew that he totally frowned on the escape of a wounded animal in the hunt. She wondered if the same thing applied to wounded enemies.

That had all happened so fast. She had been feeling kindly, even, toward the stranger, who after all, *had* been leaving. Then, his discovery and her subsequent rage. Her attack had been a mistake, probably. He might have been only curious, and would most likely have departed, out of respect for the dead. He may not even have suspected the presence of any living person there. Yes, that attack had probably been stupid.

"I am sorry, Grandfather."

She was also sorry, now that her anger had subsided, because the attack might have been unjust. She had rather enjoyed the presence of the vision-seeker. She had found him good to look upon, and she had watched him for long periods while he slept.

There was another curious thing, one which she could not share with Grandfather. She was not certain, even, that she wanted to think of it herself. There had been a brief moment, when she and the stranger rolled together in combat on the ledge. She had experienced a strange sensation, like no other that had been hers. As they had rolled, the closeness of his body, the pressure of his weight against her chest, just before they fell . . . It had been almost pleasant.

43

It was the next day that she found the place where he left the river. Partially screened by a clump of willows, the stranger had pulled himself up the bank and into the grass. She could follow his trail a little way, and it led directly away from the Rock.

She was a bit embarrassed that she had not seen him leave, and she tried to determine why. He had been an excellent swimmer. She had discovered that when they plunged into the river. Apparently he swam downstream underwater, emerging behind the screen of willows. But when? While she looked for him along the river? Or did he wait in hiding to emerge later?

And why did it matter? Only that it irritated her immensely to realize that it had been a situation over which she had lost control. She had a sense of failure, an anger at herself, that she found hard to forgive.

"He is gone, Grandfather. He has escaped, not dead as I thought, maybe. I have tracked him straight away from the Rock."

It was as if she asked approval from her grandfather for the way she had handled the matter. Approval was important, because she was unsure, herself. She did not totally approve of the way things had gone. There was no sign from the silent figure on the ledge, of course. She had expected none.

"I will watch closely," she went on. "If he comes back, I will be ready. He may die, though. He *was* wounded."

She was a little bit deceptive on that point. It was apparent that the man had been able to swim powerfully underwater. There was also no sign of blood where he left the river. His wound must have been slight.

South Wind was actually glad that he was alive. He had been good to look upon, and she did not like to think of his attractive body in some deep hole in the riverbed, food for fish and turtles. Even though he was an enemy, she told herself. But *was* he an enemy? She was quite confused. Alive, he presented a threat, because he knew that she lived here in the Rock. Yet she was glad that he was alive.

Looking back, she had to admit that she had enjoyed his presence here. It was exciting, challenging, and a diversion from the loneliness that she had felt since the passing of Grandfather. There was something else, too. The fearful dread of the Thing in the crevice had lessened during his stay here. She had not realized it until now. It had been a diversion to have him here, and she had not been so preoccupied with the Thing . . . no, it was more than that.

She recalled her feeling that she and Grandfather had been able, together, to control the evil, to keep it confined in its crevice. Then, when Grandfather's mind began to fail, the Thing became stronger, more threatening. She was sure that it had grown since his passing.

But during the last few days, while the vision-seeker had been here, it had not seemed so powerful. True, she had had a dream or two, unpleasant fears. . . . Not the dream of being pursued, though. Had the spirit of the stranger helped to control the evil? He probably did not even know about the dark Thing. Maybe he would not *need* to know. Maybe just the presence of his spirit . . . She was certain that it was a powerful thing, because she had felt his thoughts reaching out. He must have a gift of spirit, a holy man.

And she had tried to kill him. A sense of guilt and a certain fear swept over her. It must be a bad thing to kill a holy man. She was glad that she had failed, and she found herself wishing that he would come back.

What am I thinking? With a feeling almost like panic she rejected such an idea. She hurried to her boulder on the ledge.

"Grandfather, you must help me," she signed. "I am made to think that the man, the one I told you of, was a holy man. I have done great harm by trying to kill him. And now the Thing in the crevice grows stronger."

It was the first time that she had admitted her fears of the crevice to Grandfather. She had not wanted to worry him. *Do spirits worry* she thought to herself? Yes, surely there is concern for a loved one left behind. Did not Grandfather come to her in a dream, to reassure her? What had he said? *Help will come when you need it?* Something like that.

She felt better. It was a strange experience. It was almost as if her grandfather had reassured her, here in broad daylight, while she was fully awake.

"Thank you, Grandfather," she signed happily. So that was it. He could still supply help, support for her spirit when it was needed. And if the intruder returned, she could handle him, too. She would be more alert, more resourceful, less trusting. Yes, now she understood.

Why, then, in the next few days, did she become more fearful? Her dreams became more frightful, the chase more real before she awoke, the seeming reality of the dream longer after she was fully awake.

Once, when she took shelter in the cave against a sudden rain squall, she dozed off to dream that the Thing came out before her very eyes. Dark and dirty brown, a creeping, formless mist, it started like a wisp of smoke, curling from the crack to materialize in the cave. This time, the light of the fire did not seem to deter it. It grew larger, more threatening. There was an odor about it, a damp animal smell like the nest of a mouse, or maybe . . . yes, like a bear's winter den, heavy with body scent. And the Thing made a hissing noise as it oozed along the wall.

She awoke in a panic to find the cave empty. The hissing sound was now identified as the steady patter of the rain outside. She shrugged off her fears and got up to move to the cave door and watch the rain.

She could see the sheets of water move across the slope as a heavier shower passed. The river below seemed to be boiling as rain pelted its surface. She was cold, she realized, and at about the same time a few white pellets fell, mixed with rain, and bounced along the ledge. The sound changed, too, as larger hailstones began to crash through the treetops below her. Tattered leaves, torn from their branches, fluttered toward the earth.

Then suddenly the rain, hail, and wind stopped. A bird sounded its song, tentatively at first, and then in full volume as the sun began to strike through the overcast. The storm was passing.

South Wind turned to toss a stick on the fire, pleased that it was over. Sunlight could always be counted on to make a person feel better. She even smiled at the thought of her dream a little while ago. Boldly, she looked directly at the crevice, and there was nothing. *I do not fear you,* she thought silently.

It was unfortunate, perhaps, that at that moment a chance shift in the cave's air currents brought a smell to her nostrils. It was a damp animal smell, mixed with odors that were like rotting vegetation, a musty scent that she had smelled before. . . . *In her dream.* The hairs prickled on the back of her neck. *What an odd thought.* It was like a threat.

Startled, she stepped outside. The rain had stopped, and the day was brightening. The dream seemed far away. Well, she would go and visit Grandfather. That always made her feel better.

It was that night that the vision-seeker returned. South Wind became aware of his approach largely by chance as he crossed the slope in dim starlight. She was not even certain at first that it was a man. The form that cautiously descended to the fringe of sumac could have been an antelope . . . a coyote, even. The light was poor. By the time he had reached the sumac thicket, however, she had discerned that it was a man.

As skillfully as the other creatures of the night, she moved to a better vantage point. Yes, she identified him as the one who had been here before. Her anger rose, and she forgot that at one time she had actually wished for his return.

Before, he had come openly, honestly. Now, he came skulking in the night. Why would he do this, unless he meant her harm?

She spent the rest of the night watching, moving cautiously to try to ferret out his intentions. He had hidden himself in the sumac thicket and seemed to make it his intention to stay there. This was a new sort of hunt, in which she was the hunted. She tried to imagine what he, the hunter, would do.

He knew she was here, of course. His actions seemed to indicate that he wished to watch her, discover her daily routine. He had made no move to leave the thicket as day approached, so he must have chosen that as his watching place. It was a good place, giving a view of the cliff's face and the river. Well chosen . . .

What might be his purpose here? She did not think he intended to kill her, though that must be considered. At any rate, he first intended to observe. Now, what should *she* do? It would be easy to merely kill him and be done with it, of course. That was one option. But she still found him fascinating, and wished to know more. Regardless of his intention, she could watch his actions for a while. Watch him watching me! She smiled at the thought. She had a major advantage. She could watch him, unseen.

But wait. His purpose seemed to be to watch her, so to avoid suspicion, she must allow him to do so. At least, until she discovered his motives. Then she could kill him if need be, or could hide until he left. Another idea began to form. Maybe she could *capture* him! It would be dangerous, but it might be possible to question him, *ask* his motives.

First, she must avoid the appearance of suspicion. He must not know that she was aware of his presence. He wished to watch her, of course. As any good hunter would study the movements of his quarry, this one would probably spend the day observing her movements. So be it. But she must hurry, now. The gray smudge of the false dawn was already showing in the east.

She slipped across the river, avoiding the places where loose gravel would clatter, and started up the path. She must contrive a daily routine that would appear reasonable to the stranger, yet allow *her* to observe *him,* too.

She paused for a moment at Grandfather's resting place.

"He is back, the vision-seeker," she told him. "I cannot tell what he wants, but he is hiding to watch us. I will be ready for him!"

She hurried on, to gain a good vantage point before daylight. She rested a little, actually dozing for a moment or two before the sun crept over Earth's rim. Coming awake, her first task was to make certain that the man was still in the thicket.

Yes . . . a worried small bird with a nest in the sumac scolded indignantly. Soon she could make out a moccasin and part of a legging through the flickering shade of the sumacs. South Wind smiled. She knew how hot, damp, and mosquito-infested that thicket would be by afternoon. Well, he had chosen it.

Now she rose and moved around on the face of the cliff, trying to appear furtive yet to make certain that she was seen. Then she took her bow and descended to the river, pausing only a moment.

"He is there, Grandfather. I will let him watch me. And, I will be careful."

Boldly, she stripped and bathed in the deep pool, in plain sight of the watcher. He was out of bowshot, and there was no way that he could leave his mosquito-ridden concealment without showing himself.

She dressed, squeezed the water from her hair, and picked up her weapons. The watcher would probably expect her to hunt, so she would oblige. She was fortunate enough to shoot a fat rabbit very quickly, and then found a comfortable place where she could observe the discomfort of her adversary. All in all, this was rather enjoyable.

Finally she tired of the game and moved into the open with her rabbit, trying not to look at the sumac thicket. She crossed the riffle, clattering a little, and started up the path.

"He is there, Grandfather. It goes well," she signed as she passed.

She built a fire, using just enough damp fuel to make sure that the watcher saw a puff or two of smoke. She cooked and ate her rabbit in a leisurely way, one eye on the thicket. There was still no way to tell what the man might intend. Since he had not moved all day, she reasoned, he must make some sort of move tonight, probably after dark. She would be ready.

Now, where to conceal herself? Near the foot of the path grew a thicket of prairie dogwood. It dominated the narrow strip of land against the cliff's base, where the path started to climb. It was the ideal place for an ambush.

She timed her move at twilight, when vision is poor, and flitted down the path to settle in the dogwoods. Then she waited while the darkness deepened and the stars began to appear overhead.

Her timing was good, and she did not think she had been seen. It was only a short wait now, until a figure rose stiffly from the sumac across the river and came straight toward the riffle. Excitement rose in her. Her scheme was working. Now if the capture worked as well . . .

44

Ah, thought South Wind, *I was right!* He had waited until just after dark, and now would change his position, to ambush her as she passed. She had done well to hide here. It was amusing to see that he had actually selected the same thicket. . . . He crossed the riffle and approached the dogwood thicket, completely unsuspecting. She readied herself for the rush.

She had thought about it for a long time, of how she would attack. The easiest and safest way would be a single arrow, shot from concealment. Then it would be over. A knife thrust, almost as good. Or the ax . . . Her mind rejected all of these things. She had to admit, she did not wish to kill him outright. She *had* enjoyed his company for the few days of his vision-quest, and she had been pleased to see that he returned. It was a mixed emotion, of course, because there was danger. Maybe that in itself led to a thrill of excitement in his return. Then, too, there was a burning curiosity, a wish to know more about him. She *must* capture him, keep him alive at least long enough to learn something of the ways of people. He was the only human she had ever touched, except for her grandfather. And, of course, the wounded warrior who had come here already dying. He did not count.

Now, how to capture this young man with the least danger? She knew from the encounter on the ledge that he was strong. She did not want to become involved in a test of endurance. She must disable him temporarily somehow, handicap or confuse him until she could tie him.

This was a new problem. Any creature that she had ever wanted to capture, she had also wished to kill. Now, that was not the case. She thought of traps and deadfalls and snares. A snare seemed a likely possibility for a time, but she rejected it. It would be too easy to accidently strangle her quarry.

She finally decided. A simple blow to the head, not too hard. Then, during the next few moments, while he was weakened and confused, she would tie him. With this plan in mind, she had spent part of the day making preparations. Soft buckskin thongs, prepared with loops that could be slipped over a wrist and pulled tight. More, for his feet. She chose a stout throwing-stick with good balance for her initial blow. And, since she did not want to *break* his head, she decided to pad her club. She realized it was dangerous. If the first blow was not effective, it would only anger him and make him more dangerous. She could not account for her compassion toward this stranger. She simply did not relish the thought of the appearance that he would have if she killed him. She had, after all, watched him sleep, and had admired his fine features. It was not good, to envision this man dying with his head crushed, bleeding from the nose and mouth and perhaps his ears. . . .

She shook her head. She was having a hard time with this. Anyway, she told herself fiercely, if it should go wrong, she could revert to the knife.

So now she lay in wait, watching him approach her hiding place. Sweat moistened her palms, and her heart beat so strongly that she was afraid he would hear. He paused at the edge of the water, indistinct in the dim starlight, listening, cautious. Then he came quickly across the grassy strip to enter the thicket. *He does not even suspect,* she thought triumphantly. She readied her club, timed her steps, and swung. The young man was barely aware of the attack, she thought, before the *thunk* of the padded club. He dropped to the ground, and she was astride him in the space of a heartbeat, taking the thongs from her teeth and jerking the loops tight on his wrists and ankles. She bound his hands behind him.

During all of this, her victim did not move. He was completely limp. South Wind rose, trembling from emotion and from the sudden brief burst of activity. She was still breathing heavily.

Now what? she thought. She had not planned beyond this point. The man still did not stir, and anxiety rose in her. Had she killed him, after all? She knelt and felt the throb of the heartbeat in his throat. It was strong and regular, and his breathing, too, was good. She had seen two men die, and it was not like this.

Somewhat reassured, she dragged her prisoner into the open and stretched him out on the grass. She found the lump where her club had struck, behind his ear, and there was no blood. His left forearm was tightly wrapped. . . . That must be where her knife had struck before as they struggled in the water.

Now, what to do with him? The easiest thing was to leave him here until daylight, or until he recovered, whatever might be first. But she had doubts about that. What if someone came looking for him? No, she must hide him, and before daylight came. But where? She could drag him deeper into the thicket, but that would be cramped and uncomfortable at best. And, when the day warmed, it would be hot, damp, and mosquito-infested. She needed a concealed place where she need not worry about any passer-by seeing him, and where she could learn more about him. Some place as secure as the cave. *The cave!* She thought about it. Could she take him there? Why not? She had many times carried heavy burdens of firewood or meat or hides up that path. Her prisoner was heavier, but she need not carry, she could drag him.

Slowly, resting often, she began the task of transporting her prisoner. Before the waning moon rose, she had reached Grandfather's resting place. Here, she paused for a long rest. She checked the prisoner's pulse and breathing again.

"This is the man I told you of, Grandfather," she signed. "I will take him to the cave and learn more of him and his people."

She completed her task, settled him in the cave, and went back to bathe herself in the stream. She was hot and dirty from the night's activity. Returning to the cave, she found that she was exhausted. She was asleep almost before she stretched out on the robes.

She was up and out at dawn. Her prisoner was asleep, but showed signs of rousing. She would go and try to find something for food. Fresh meat would be better than dried strips from her supply. Besides, she wished to make certain that all traces of the man's presence here were eliminated, in case someone came searching.

Her hunt was not too successful, and she cut it short because she did not wish to leave her prisoner alone for very long. She had managed to catch one large frog . . . well, that would do for now. She hurried up the path, pausing hardly at all at her grandfather's resting place.

"Good day, Grandfather. I will be back later," she signed hastily.

The captive awoke, slowly and with much discomfort, as she built the fire and started to cook the frog. She thought that he had moved from his previous position, so he may have been awake before. She caught his eye and signed to him.

"You are awake!"

He answered with a series of sounds that had no meaning to her. She had heard others make such sounds, but not this close. These noises must be used to communicate. He tried again, different sounds, but she shook her head, not understanding. She tried a grunt or two, which seemed to mean nothing to him.

The meat was ready, and she signed to him. "Sit up. You eat, now."

He struggled to a sitting position, and she repeated, "Eat!"

Then she realized that he could not with his hands tied behind him. She released his ties and watched as he rubbed his numbed hands. She handed him the frog legs, and he began to eat, slowly.

"It is good," he signed. "How are you called?"

She was startled, but tried to recover her composure.

"No," she signed, "how are *you* called?"

"I am White Fox, of the Elk-dog People."

"What are you doing here?"

"I came on my vision-quest. I did not know anyone's lodge was here."

"But you came back."

"Yes. I came to help you."

She curled her lip to show disbelief.

"No!" she signed. "You lie! You hid and watched me!"

"But you tried to kill me, before!" he signed.

"Yes! You disturbed the bones of my grandfather!"

"I disturbed no one. I . . ."

Her anger flared, and he seemed to recognize that there was danger here.

"I did not know anyone was here," he signed more slowly and calmly. "I would not disturb anyone's burial. I was surprised, and stopped to see."

She pondered this, unsure.

"What is your tribe?" he asked.

"I have no tribe," she indicated.

"Is there no one?"

"Only my grandfather. He died in the Moon of Long Nights."

"I am sorry," he gestured. "No one else?"

"I need no one," she gestured defiantly.

He nodded.

"You and your grandfather," Fox signed. "Have you been here long?"

"We have been here always."

"You have never seen others? Other people?"

Cautiously, she answered.

"Sometimes they come here. We hide; they go away."

"Your grandfather," he asked, "talked with his mouth?"

"What do you mean?"

"People make sounds to talk."

He spoke the sentence as he signed it, and she was startled. Then she regained her composure.

"You spoke with sounds before," she signed. "I have heard others do this."

"But you?"

"Yes, but I do not need to."

She threw back her head and gave a little barking cry that sounded like a coyote calling to her pups. Then she shrugged as if to indicate that there was no purpose, and smiled, a little embarrassed.

"Your grandfather . . . did he make such sounds?"

"No, no," the girl signed. "He made no sound at all. He heard no sound."

"But you hear sounds. You could make sounds, too."

"Why?"

"It is easier. Look, I am called 'White Fox.' "

He used the words as well as the signs.

"Now, how are you called?" he asked.

She hesitated, then gave a shy smile.

"Grandfather called me South Wind," she gestured.

"It is good," Fox signed back. "South Wind."

He used the words as well as the hand-signs.

"White Fox," he said, pointing to his chest, "South Wind," pointing to her.

"South Wind," she said hesitantly, pointing to herself. She smiled again. "White Fox."

He nodded, pleased, and then reverted to hand-signs again.

"Did your grandfather tell you why he left his people?"

Her face darkened as the old suspicions rose.

"Because people are bad! There is danger!" she signed heatedly.

"But, your grandfather was not bad. You are not bad. I am not bad!"

South Wind hesitated for a moment of confusion. Then she came to a decision.

"It is time to tie you again," she signed.

She picked up a rawhide cord and stepped toward him. Fox was not pleased at the unpleasant prospect of being tied again.

"Wait! If my hands are tied, we cannot talk!" he gestured frantically.

The girl paused.

"No," she signed. "You are a danger to me!"

"No, no! I want to help you!"

"You came back. You hid and wanted to catch me," she accused.

"Yes, but only to talk to you. You would run if I came to you. And, you tried to kill me before."

She hesitated. She wanted to trust him, but was unsure. It was also tempting to share her fears of the Thing in the crevice. With him here, she was somehow more secure. How could she explain this?

"I thought you would disturb my grandfather," South Wind signed. "And, I was afraid you might be with the Evil One."

White Fox appeared startled. She knew somehow that he, too, had felt something. Perhaps only *her* fear. There had been a time when she felt the progress of his vision-quest, his spirit probing, contacting that of other creatures. And . . . and *her* spirit. Such thoughts brought back her insecurity. He had no right to invade her spirit! She became defensive.

"South Wind," he gestured and used words together, remembering that it had seemed to please her, "I am not with the Evil One. I learned of your fears, and that is why I came back. I wanted to help you."

It was too much, too fast-moving for her. She was not ready to trust.

"You lie!" she gestured angrily.

She seized his wrists and tied him expertly, despite his protests. Then she stood and faced him for a moment.

"Maybe you speak truth," she gestured, "but I do not know, so I must keep you tied. I go now."

She picked up her bow and left the cave.

45

Now, South Wind found herself with a problem she had not foreseen. She had managed to capture the young man . . . White
Fox, he called himself. Now, what? He lay tied in the cave while
she went to hunt.

It had not occurred to her to plan ahead beyond his capture. All her life
there had been very little planning, except for preparation and storage of
food supplies for winter. She must think of that soon, too. It struck her that
she was to hunt today for two, again. Not since the death of her grandfather
had it been so. Her hunting had been to supply her own needs only. It was
good, to have someone else. Her spirit lifted.

She recalled a time long ago when she had captured the coyote pup.
Grandfather had allowed her to keep it, and she had been pleased with the
responsibility. It was a living thing, dependent on her, not like her doll. Little
Bone . . . she smiled at the memory. Bone had been real to her, but did
not require care or food in the way her coyote pup did. The pup responded
to her, and they played together. It was also slightly dangerous. It could
inflict a painful bite, even in play.

She had had the pup for most of a season. When it matured, it ranged
farther away in its hunting, returning only occasionally. Then in the Moon of

Madness, when all animals (and people as well, Grandfather said) behave somewhat irrationally, it did not return at all. What is it about late autumn, she wondered? A final urge to migrate or to prepare for the coming of the Long Nights Moon ahead?

Strange that she should be thinking of this. It was several moons away. But she found that she was thinking of the similarities in her capture of the young man, White Fox. He was dangerous, like the coyote. Yet, like the pup, he was fascinating. She found herself hoping that, when the Moon of Madness came, he too would not leave her like the coyote.

Or the crow. It, too, had abandoned her. Grandfather had explained that it is so with wild things. They become wild again and leave. *Or die,* she thought. She had not realized until now that she had unconsciously resented the fact that Grandfather, too, had left her. Then came the twinge of guilt, again, that she would feel so. *I am sorry, Grandfather,* she thought.

She forcibly turned her thoughts back to her prisoner in the cave. She was fascinated by him. It had been an exciting experience to talk with him, to find that some sounds have meanings, as hand-signs do. *Names.* She smiled as she thought of the way he spoke . . . aloud, *and* with signs. "South Wind," she said to herself, quietly. *"I am South Wind."*

She could not make the sounds exactly like he did. She loved to hear his voice as he said her name. It was deep and full and resonant. She could hardly wait to learn more of the talk-sounds. It was as if she had been waiting all her life for White Fox to come. She thought of other things, too, like the odd feeling that she had when she remembered how it felt to wrestle with him on the ledge.

She was glad that he had returned. It was good to feel the presence of another person, another spirit. She regretted that she must tie him again when she left to hunt, but she could not trust him. Not yet. Not until she knew more about *why* he had returned. She must talk more to him about that. And about her other, her great fear that seemed to return in her sleep. The Thing in the dark, the Evil One. She had accused him of being allied with it, and he had denied it. He had, in fact, claimed that his return was to assist her in defending against it.

But *he knew of it.* That meant that she could no longer tell herself that it did not exist. It *must* be real, if this outsider knew. Again, she thought of her theory that *two* spirits were able to keep the Thing at bay, force it to remain in the crevice. One alone could accomplish this most of the time, but not entirely. This allowed it to grow and threaten. She must ask White Fox about this. If she was right, then the two of them could control it together. That was a nice thought, that they could do something together. She smiled.

She realized that she was already assuming that he spoke truth. She hated to do so without proof of some sort, but she was beginning to trust. The two of them . . . yes, her heart was good at the thought.

South Wind brought herself back to reality. Two of them meant that once more she was *hunting* for two. She must feed them both, at least until she and White Fox established what would happen next. How could she approach that subject? She had two fears if she released him from his fetters. One that he would become a danger to her . . . that fear was lessening rapidly. The other was that he would leave and that she would be alone again.

But she must stop the idle dreaming and concentrate on her hunting. It was good to hunt for two again. She must find something today, though. The frog had been primarily a symbolic thing, a sort of peace offering. She needed something more solid. The ideal kill would be a deer or a buffalo. That was unlikely, but a rabbit, maybe. She saw a movement in the clearing ahead and froze to identify it. A rabbit . . . yes, three of them, engaged in the mating dance of their kind. They would be preoccupied, and she should be able to secure one.

Carefully, she waited for the right target. *There, now!* She drew the arrow to its head and released smoothly. The feel was good, the knowledge before the arrow reaches its mark that its flight is true. She stepped forward to retrieve her quarry while the others scampered away.

She paused for a little while on the way back to the cave.

"I wish I could talk to you, Grandfather. I mean, that you could talk to me. There are many questions." She held up the rabbit. "I hunt to feed two, now. The man, White Fox, he is called . . . I have him tied in the cave. I learn much from him. Did you know, Grandfather, that people can talk with sound from their mouths? You probably knew. He knows of the Evil Thing, too. It is back. He says that he returned to help me with *it*! I do not know . . . I still have him tied. I will talk to him again."

She rose and held up her rabbit. "Now, I must go and cook this. I will come back later."

She hurried to the cave.

Her captive lay with a look of anguish on his face and motioned with his bound hands.

"What is it?" she signed anxiously as she untied him.

He motioned toward his hips and to his bound ankles and she finally understood. He had not had a chance to empty his bladder since last night.

"I am sorry," she signed. "But you will not run?"

He shook his head. As he stood, it was apparent that her question was unnecessary. He could hardly stand, on feet that were numb from lack of circulation.

"I am sorry," she signed again as he hobbled to the ledge outside. "I did not think!"

"It is nothing," he signed back, but she knew it was not true.

She turned to skinning and dressing the rabbit. He moved back into the cave and looked around. She saw his eyes light on his own pack and weapons by the supply racks. She touched his shoulder.

"If you try, I will tie you again."

He nodded agreement.

"I will cook meat," she signed.

In a short while the rabbit was sizzling over the fire, and she turned to him again.

"Now! Tell me more of the talk-sounds."

He began to teach her common sounds for everyday objects, and she reacted with delight.

"Did your grandfather ever mention your tribe . . . its name?" he asked in signs after she began to tire.

"No, I do not think so. Grandfather always said we had no tribe."

"But you were with other people. Some were killed, and the others ran away. You told it."

"Yes, that is true. I do not know."

"Let me show you signs for names of tribes," he suggested. "See if any look right."

He began to sign. . . . Growers? Forest People, Pawnee, Mandan, Head Splitters? She shook her head.

"Maybe the Forest People are the ones who killed us," she considered.

One last possibility occurred to him.

"This?" he asked, making the sign for a man on a horse.

The girl's eyes widened.

"Yes!" she signed eagerly. "Yes, that is the one!"

White Fox was astonished.

"Really? Elk-dog People?"

"Yes," she nodded. "Grandfather used the sign, a man on a horse."

"That is my own tribe!" Fox signed. "We call ourselves 'the People,' but others use the elk-dog sign, because the People used the horse long ago."

He paused, lost in thought.

"There was a story about an incident," he indicated, "a family or two of the Eastern band, camped apart from the rest. They were killed by Forest People."

"Then I am of *your* people?" South Wind was asking in hand-talk.

"Yes," he nodded. "I think so. My grandmother, who died long ago, was of your band, and her father was a chief."

The girl clapped her hands, delighted.

"It is good!"

White Fox smiled. He sat massaging his sore wrists and ankles. She saw the reddened and chafed stripes on his wrists.

"I am sorry," she signed.

"It is nothing," he answered again.

When the rabbit had finished cooking, South Wind divided it in half, and handed him a portion. Then she came and sat beside him. There was a new and strange closeness, a communication without words. It seemed that the discovery of who she was, where she had come from, was important to the girl. She was now more relaxed and cheerful. There seemed to be a trust not previously found here.

They finished eating, and she made no effort to retie him. Suddenly she jumped to her feet.

"Let us swim!" she signed, starting for the entrance.

White Fox rose to follow her. Even though she paused a moment to speak in signs to her grandfather, she reached the shore well ahead of him. Quickly, she stripped the shirtlike dress over her head and dived headfirst into the pool. Fox followed, quite self-consciously at first. They swam, splashed, and cavorted like otters in the clear water, laughing like delighted children, and it was good. White Fox's cares were cleansed away, like the sweat and accumulated grime from his skin. He completely forgot, for a little while, the ominous reason for his presence here, and he was a child again, enjoying the swim, the day, and a pleasant companion.

Even as they played, she was asking and learning. A small green heron croaked its raucous cry, and she lifted a right hand in the question sign.

"Heron," he answered aloud. "Little green heron."

"Green?" she asked.

"Yes. A color. Like trees, grass."

"Green!"

She laughed, and it was good to see his reaction. She waded from the stream to lie on the sandy strip of beach in the sun. Her companion followed, taking obvious care not to come too close. She realized that he was a bit afraid of her. Well, maybe that was good. After all, she had nearly killed him a few days ago, and he was still her prisoner.

The shadows were lengthening when she rose and picked up her tunic. Fox watched as she gracefully tossed it up and slipped it over her head, settling the garment over her shoulders and hips. She walked upstream a few steps to the riffle and knelt to drink, then started toward the path.

"Come," she gestured.

They returned to the cave, and she made no effort to retie him. There was a new bond between them, though they had not even begun to discuss why he was here. They prepared for sleep. South Wind indicated to him where to spread his robe on the opposite side of the chamber, and they settled for the night.

46

←→

When South Wind fell asleep that night, she was happier and more confident than at any time since her grandfather's passing. The sheer emotional strength of another person's presence was reassuring. It was like the protective feeling that she had felt when she was small and would take her tears to Grandfather for comfort. Now, it was not the tears of bumps and scrapes and minor disappointments. She had outgrown all that. No, she thought, this was more like the reassurance that Grandfather's presence had provided when her night-terrors had wakened her as a child. Or, maybe, her irrational fear of the dark crevice at the back of the cave.

In the clear light of day, she had always been able to reason that there was nothing there, and she was not afraid, even when she was small. It was only after dark, by the flickering light of the fire, that she would begin to wonder. She would cast quick glances at some half-seen movement in the shadows, and there would be nothing. But the uneasy suspicion would remain. Or she would dream, and waken in terror, to run to Grandfather's bed for safety and comfort. He would hold her and rock gently, and lay a few sticks on the fire. The blaze would bring light to the cave, and everything would be safe and happy again.

In time, she had outgrown the fears, and they had not returned until Grandfather's mind started to fail. Then it was as if the Dark Thing in the rock had been there all along, held at bay by the two spirits of South Wind and the old man. As Grandfather's spirit weakened, the Dark Thing seemed to grow stronger. Yes, that must be it. It required the force of two spirits to hold the Evil One at bay. The loss of Grandfather had so weakened her defense that it had become a danger. She had been able to avoid it by leaving the cave when the dark presence became too overpowering.

Tonight, though, there would be no need. She had a companion. She had enjoyed, even reveled in, the excitement of learning the word-sounds, and he had enjoyed it, too. She had seen that in the expression of his face, the light in his eyes. He was happy when he was with her.

She began to fantasize. They would stay here, sharing the cave together. They would be happy, and they would never need anyone else. White Fox would be her husband. She was not completely certain what that involved, but her grandfather's stories had implied that usually, a man and a woman live together. Her heart told her that would be good. Maybe White Fox would know more about it. She already had a feeling that it would feel good to be held in the arms of White Fox, as her grandfather used to hold her. No, it would be different. The feeling she perceived when she thought of White Fox was warm and tender and protective, and . . . well, it was *different*. Maybe she could ask him about it.

The fire was dying, and she lay there in the darkness, listening to the deep, regular breathing of the young man. She was too excited to sleep. She longed to waken him to talk some more, but felt it would be inappropriate. At least, she told herself with satisfaction, she would not need to leave the cave tonight to escape the influence of the Thing in the crevice. The combined strength of the two of them could deny it entry, could bar it from the cave.

There had been no thought of tying him tonight. After the day they had spent together, she could not find it in herself to distrust him. Besides, he had shown no sign that he would be dangerous. None, even, that he wished to leave. That helped with her fantasy about living here forever together. Maybe she should mention that tomorrow.

She regretted, now that she knew him better, that she had left him tied in the cave that first night. That had been a bad thing to do, to leave him helpless with the Thing while she went prowling. It could have been dangerous to him, and she was glad that he was safe. She would not do anything like that again. She only hoped that he would forgive her, and he seemed to have done so. At least, if he held resentment, he probably would not have been so pleasant to talk to.

She finally fell asleep, with a warm comfortable feeling that all was well. There was a companion only an arm's length away, who could be of help in an emergency. It was the most secure that she had felt for many moons. It felt almost as good as sleeptime had when she was a child.

It was perhaps not surprising, then, that after a period of deep sleep, she began to dream, and saw herself as a child. She and Grandfather walked along the stream, and he taught her to hunt and to shoot, and to swim like the beavers. Days were long and happy. She played again on the rocky ledges with her coyote pup, and felt the twinge of sadness when it ran away. She relived the long nights in the Moon of Snows when they stayed in the cave. They wrapped themselves warmly against the onslaught of Cold Maker, and huddled over the tiny fire that must not be allowed to go out. That was a time for Grandfather's stories, and she learned of other people.

She dreamed of the games they played when others came to the Rock, and how she must remain hidden and quiet until they left. All of these were happy dreams.

Then came the one with the old fear. She was still a child in this dream, but alone in the cave. Her grandfather would be back soon, but night was falling. Carefully, she placed a little stick on the coals of the fire, and it blazed up to throw a flickering light around the rough walls. The little girl looked apprehensively toward the dark crevice and shuddered. There had never been anything there when she looked, and there was not now. She looked away, resolved not to look again. But the flicker of the fire made little shadowy movements, which she saw out of the corner of her eye. She would look quickly, and the movement was gone. There was nothing there but the dark crevice.

She looked anxiously to the doorway, hoping to see the tall form of her grandfather against the dull smoke-gray of the twilight sky. There was no indication of his return. What if he *never* returned?

She whimpered softly in her sleep, like a child, and the dream continued. There came a time when her glance at the dark corner *almost* revealed something. A flickering, slithering Thing that moved briefly and was gone, a part of the rough rock of the crevice and the flicker of firelight.

Fascinated, she stared at the crack, like the bird who is stalked by the snake. Horrified, she watched a formless shadow vaporize, spewing from the crevice, like smoke or mist, but dark, dirty brown-black. There was an odor, too, of slime and decay, and a sense of evil that grew, threatening to fill the cave.

The little girl screamed out in terror and scrambled toward the entrance to escape. She ran headlong into the arms of Grandfather as he entered. He rocked and held her tenderly, and she felt secure again. Her sobs began to subside, and Grandfather reached to place a stick on the fire. Flames produced more light, and the cave brightened.

Then she was awake and no longer a child. The man who had placed the stick on the coals, into whose arms she had fled, was not Grandfather, but White Fox. He held her in his arms and rocked back and forth, crooning soft words of comfort. It did not seem to matter. She clung to him as her terror slowly subsided, holding her arms tightly around him, fearing to let go. She felt that if she did, he might disappear, and she would be defenseless again.

She could look over his shoulder and see the back of the cave in the flickering light of the fire. The crevice was once more only a crack in the rock, and there was no horribly evil brown mist from her dream of the past to threaten the little girl. It had been only a dream, as had her night-terrors of childhood. And, as her grandfather had dispelled her fears then, the man in her arms had done so now.

She released him from her embrace, and he did so, too, a little reluctantly it seemed.

"I am sorry," she signed. "A dream . . ."

He nodded sleepily.

"It is over now," he assured her.

Yes, she thought, it is over. Only a false vision in the night. A little embarrassed, she turned to pick up the robe she had flung aside, and spread it to return to sleep.

47

White Fox awoke next morning with such a mixture of emotions that he doubted he could grasp them all. He had come here on his vision-quest with no suspicion of all that he had now encountered.

Since the first time he saw Medicine Rock as a child and from a distance, he had been intrigued by the place and its legends. The tale of Eagle, who had spent a winter there while a broken leg healed after an accident. Eagle had been thought dead, but was discovered alive and well the following spring. The remarkable part of that story, to young Fox, was the change in Eagle's life. He had become a skilled storyteller and a seer of things of the spirit. It was said that no other could make quite so real the stories of Creation and of the Old Man of the Shadows. "It was as if Eagle had been there," it was always said.

Fox was also deeply impressed with the reputation of Medicine Rock as a place of the spirits. Everyone was a bit afraid of it, and the People took care not to camp too near. There was the additional impact of the incident in which the invading Blue Paints from the north were ambushed and killed in a buffalo stampede. That had taken powerful medicine. It was a cooperative effort by two holy men. One was Wolf's Head, of the Head Splitters, and the other a young man of the People. Looks-Far was his name. He was still alive, though many winters had whitened his hair and slowed his step. He was now the most respected of holy men.

White Fox had grown up in awe of this holy man, a distant relative. He had been a teacher to the youngster and had encouraged him to take his vision-quest to Medicine Rock when Fox inquired about it.

"It is a place of great spirit-power," the old man advised. "Some think it evil, but both good and evil are everywhere. It is how you approach such things. It is a good place to find your spirit-guide."

White Fox had already decided in his own mind, but had a few questions. "What of the spirits of the Blue Paints who died there, Uncle?"

Looks-Far nodded. "They crossed over. I am made to think that the problems we face here are often insignificant when we cross over. People once enemies may be allies, as we and the Head Splitters now are."

"Then you do not think the *place* is evil? The Rock?"

Looks-Far was silent for a moment, and finally spoke.

"My son, you are a deep thinker. Some day . . . but never mind. Now think on this: It is known that the Rock is a place of the spirit, a holy place, no?" He went on without pausing for agreement. "Now, look at the experiences of the People there. There may have been many, but those of which we have the best knowledge are two: that of Eagle, whose spirit was touched long ago, and the thing of the Blue Paints, in which I had a small part. But think on these. Both led to great *good* for the People, did they not?"

White Fox nodded.

"Now," continued the holy man, "what you have really asked is whether some places are evil and some good. This, I do not know. But I am made to think that what happens depends much on the spirits of those who approach such a place."

He paused, a puzzled look on his leathery old face, as if pondering how to explain.

"Some men and women," he said carefully, "are offered a gift of the spirit. Maybe you are one. Now, with this gift, you can do different things. You can refuse it, or merely not use it, which is really the same thing. That is no disgrace, but no blessing either. It is as if it was never offered. But if you accept it, use it, you accept a great responsibility. If you are offered the Gift, and use it for evil, it is very dangerous. If I misused the power of my medicine, it would kill me."

"*Aiee,*" murmured White Fox. "How will I know, Uncle?"

"I do not know how, my son. Many are offered the Gift much later than others. I am made to think that Eagle's spirit-gift came later, *after* his accident at the Rock. But, no matter . . . *you will know!*"

So White Fox had set forth in all his innocence to seek his vision. In retrospect, it had worked well. He had found his spirit-guide, though he had been aware of interference and the terror of evil dreams. He did not know yet whether, as Looks-Far seemed to suspect, he would be a recipient of the spirit-gift. He did feel that he had been given a powerful guide.

Some of the confusion of his vision had been accounted for when he discovered the presence of the girl. Now he realized that as his spirit had searched in its quest, it had encountered hers. That, of course, is why one seeks solitude for the quest, to avoid such chance contact. But he now understood, at least a little bit. The spirit he had encountered had been a troubled one, full of fears of evil, a lonely spirit.

At first, after the girl tried to kill him, he was happy to escape with his life, with the help of his guide. Unarmed and without supplies, he had hurried back to the summer camp of the Southern band, thankful for survival.

It was not until after he had broken his fast and talked with Looks-Far that he began to realize the situation. The young woman at the Rock might be in grave danger. In some strange way he felt a responsibility to her. There was no one at all to help her. The fear in her would grow, the terror of some unseen evil Thing. If it was not real, now, it would become real, for her.

But why should he risk his life to help her, he argued with himself. It should have been no concern of his. Yet it was. He had been greatly impressed, not only by the girl's beauty, but by her strength, her self-reliance, her skills of survival.

He went back to confer with the holy man again, telling him of his thoughts. Looks-Far had questioned him at length and finally nodded.

"What you are called to do, you must do," he agreed. "Listen to your guide, use all your skills, and be careful. Now, before you go, let me teach you some things that may be useful. Chants, some herbs that will help your spirit-contact, increase its power."

He had spent most of a day trying to cram that instruction into his brain, and had set off for the Rock again with many misgivings. He had no illusions. The girl might try to kill him again. . . .

Now, he had experienced an even more remarkable series of events. Instead of the way that he had planned things, he had been captured by the girl. There were times when he had feared for his life. But gradually, they had established communication. He was impressed with her abilities, with her quick mind, and her absorbing interest in learning all that he could tell her.

And, with her beauty. He had never seen a woman nearly so attractive. They were relating to each other so well. . . . It was no surprise, now, that their spirits had made the accidental contact. It was meant to be. His purpose, it now seemed, was to assist her in dealing with the evil Thing in her life. It had affected him profoundly to learn of her fears of the Evil One when she accused him of being associated with it. Not so much the accusation, but the realization that in his spirit-quest, he *had* encountered *her* terror.

Then, the incident in the night, when in the terror of her night-vision she had flown into his arms. She had mistaken him for her grandfather, who was apparently the only other person she had ever known. His heart went out to her. Without him, she would be helpless, he realized. There was no question in his mind that the evil Thing which she perceived to be in the dark crevice at the back of the cave could have grown stronger until it destroyed her. It could, and *would* have, without help. He was glad that he had been called to furnish that help.

There were some problems ahead, to be sure. South Wind had expressed the idea that one person alone could not keep the Evil One at bay in the crevice. It required the spirit-power of two to control it. Well, so be it. There are things impossible to explain. He kept thinking of the statement of Looks-Far. "It does not matter . . . if it is real to *her,* it is real, and dangerous."

He looked across the cave at the sleeping form of South Wind. She looked so innocent, so like a child, her long lashes lying on cheeks that were as smooth as the petals of the roses that still bloomed here and there on the prairie.

His heart went out to her, and he experienced a sense of gratitude that he could help her.

It would not be easy. There would be some danger. He already knew that, from the way he had been affected by his own contact with the terror in the crevice.

But he was confident. He would remain flexible. . . . "Nothing ever happens exactly like you thought it would," Looks-Far had said. Now, if he could remember all the other things that the holy man had taught him. And his biggest task, of course, would be to convince the girl that the two of them could handle anything, together. Only then would she be able to leave the Rock and return to the People.

48

$\longleftrightarrow$

S outh Wind sat looking across the valley, as she had done since childhood. Just downstream, the leaves of a giant old cottonwood whispered their soft song of the summer. She could see the deep pool straight below, where the beavers frolicked, and where she had so angered her grandfather long ago with her dive from the ledge.

That had been good, though. It had allowed her to use that same fall in her fight with the intruder. She smiled to herself, that she had once thought of White Fox as an intruder. She had actually tried to kill him!

"Grandfather," she signed to the still form beside her boulder, "there is much to tell you. I wish that you could answer, but . . . maybe you have. There is the young man I told you of, White Fox."

She paused, trying to think how she could explain. There was a tendency to lose her concentration when she thought of Fox. She wondered what he was doing now, back at the cave. He had remained there . . . he seemed to understand that she needed to be alone to talk to Grandfather. She would go back later, and maybe they would swim again, and he would teach her more of the talk-sounds. . . . She shook her head to clear it and returned to her monologue.

"Grandfather, you have taught me that people are bad, and I am sure that is true. But not *all* people. You and I . . . And, I am made to think that this man, White Fox, is not bad. He came here on a vision-quest, but came back to help me."

She paused again, pondering how to explain.

"Remember, Grandfather, when I was small, how I feared the dark, and the evil Thing in the crevice? You helped me hold it back, so I did not fear it? And then, when you were no longer able, it came back stronger, and it grew. But still we held it back, you and I."

She took a deep breath and continued.

"I hope you will understand how alone I was after you crossed over. The Thing grew, and is still growing, and I had no help to control its evil. Then White Fox came, and I was afraid of him at first. But he knew of my fears and of the evil Thing. I am made to think that he and I can control it. No, can *kill* it. You would like him, Grandfather."

Again she paused.

"I do not care any less for *you*, Grandfather. My heart was heavy when you left, and it is still heavy. I have mourned, but you were part of my life, the only person I ever knew. Now, I am made to feel that here is another who understands. You told me that help would come when I need it."

She was taking much longer with this than she intended, so she hurried on.

"My heart is good for this man, Grandfather, and I wish for yours to be, too. You need not worry for me, now. This is good."

She knew that she would not receive an answer, yet she felt that she may have, in the whisper of the cottonwoods and the call of the quail across the river. She rose, brushed aside a tear, and turned up the path to the cave. She was made to feel that, finally, Grandfather could rest in peace.

ABOUT THE AUTHOR

DON COLDSMITH was born in Iola, Kansas, in 1926. He served as a World War II combat medic in the South Pacific. After returning to his native state, he graduated from Baker University in 1949 and received his M.D. from the University of Kansas in 1958. Before entering medical school, he worked at several jobs, including YMCA group counselor, gunsmith, taxidermist, and, for a short time, Congregational preacher.

In addition to running his private medical practice, Dr. Coldsmith serves as a staff physician at Emporia State University's Health Center and teaches in the English Department. He also works as a free-lance writer, lecturer, and rancher. He and his wife, Edna, have raised five daughters.

Dr. Coldsmith produced the first ten novels in "The Spanish Bit Saga" in a five-year period. He writes and revises the stories first in his head, then in longhand. From this manuscript he reads aloud to his wife, whom he calls his "chief editor." Finally the finished version is skillfully typed by his longtime office receptionist.

Of his decision to create, or re-create, the world of the native Americans of the Plains in the 16th through 18th centuries, the author says, "There has been very little written about this time period. I wanted also to portray these native Americans as human beings, rather than as stereotyped 'Indians.' That word does not appear anywhere in the series—for a reason. As I have researched the time and place, the indigenous cultures, it's been a truly inspiring experience for me."